The Eddie Malloy Series

Richard Pitman & Joe McNally

We hope you enjoy this omnibus of the first three books in the Eddie Malloy series, which is growing all the time. For news of other titles, and more information, along with the chance to join our mailing list, please visit pitmacbooks.com.

Mailing list members get first notification of new Eddie Malloy titles, along with the opportunity to pre-order the next new title in eBook format at a huge discount.

Warned Off

Copyright © 2015 by Joe McNally and Richard Pitman
All rights reserved.

No part of this book may be reproduced in any form or by any electronic or mechanical means, including information storage and retrieval systems, without written permission from the author, except for the use of brief quotations in a book review.

Authors' note

This is a work of fiction. Names, characters, places and incidents are either a work of the imagination of the authors or are used fictitiously, and any resemblance to actual persons, living or dead, business establishments, events or locales is entirely coincidental.

Chapter 1

This was the earliest severe winter I could recall, albeit I was only twenty-seven. That put me about a third of the way through my life, I reckoned, and it was one of the things that made me decide to try to find my sister.

Of those twenty-seven years, a third had been miserable and the last five the worst. Whichever way I looked, I could see no improvement on the horizon, so I'd taken to booze to put some nice colour into my vision, and I was pleasantly drunk when I set off hitch-hiking to Newmarket.

It was good to walk away for a while from that old draughty caravan I'd lived in these past two years.

Christmas wasn't far off, and I longed for one evening by a warm hearth. My alcohol fuelled optimism had formed a rosy life for my sister, Marie. I pictured her in a thatched cottage in Newmarket with a big log fire. I hadn't seen her since I'd left school. She wasn't in the phone book. Address unknown, but Newmarket isn't that big. That's what I kept telling myself, when I hit the road, collar up, thumb out, plodding through grey slush: Newmarket isn't that big. Boy, would she be shocked to see me.

A truck thundered past, ignoring my silent plea for a lift and if the driver had looked in the mirror he'd have been surprised to see me smiling…it was at the thought of my return to the family fold.

Sheep came no blacker than me. Twice I'd shamed them. But fair play to their consistency. Even when I'd been right at the top, earning loads, my picture in the papers, the great boy wonder, they'd never come out of hiding.

I'd heard that my mother and father were somewhere in Newmarket, but, drunk or sober, I wouldn't have crossed the road to find them. Marie was different. She would probably have suffered as much as I did after they threw me out. I was sixteen then. Marie was eleven. Had I abandoned her? Is that the way she'd see it when she answered my knock on the door?

I never got to find out. When a van driver dropped me in Newmarket in the gathering dusk, my optimism was badly in need of a top up.

I stopped in the first pub I came across, and left at midnight with some old floozy who offered me a bed and the illusion of affection.

Come morning, a dull hangover and empty pockets stripped away my happy family yuletide ambitions. I left the sleeping beauty snoring and decided the solitary life of the caravan-by-the-dung-heap dweller was about as much as I deserved.

I quickened through the frosty air, trying to keep warm, heading south along the High Street away from the town. The cold worked on my bladder; I needed to pee. Fifty yards ahead I saw the entrance to the golf course, and I jogged along and hurried through the gate onto the deserted acres to duck into the bushes.

I sighed as I drew a yellow piss flower in the frosted grass, remembering, as I zipped up, forbidden childhood antics, happy rebellion…I smiled.

As I turned to walk back to the road, I saw a man's leg on the ground, sticking out from below a rhododendron bush, the rimed corduroy of his trousers clean above a bloodied brown shoe.

The body lay face down, left leg bent at the knee as though he'd been felled mid-run. The cold white layers on his clothes would have taken more than one night to thicken so much. I went to the far side of the bush and parted the foliage. His eyes were frozen shut. A crust of blood-tinted frost sealed a long deep wound on his throat. I recoiled, the stiff leaves closing with a rattle and a shower of tiny white particles.

I lurched forward onto my knees. The stale booze rose in my gullet and bubbled there, its foul taste making me scrabble for a handful of snow to eat to try to force it back down.

I hunkered for a while, frosty hands on my face, covering my eyes, trying to massage some sense into my head. This had to be something like the DTs or whatever they called them, hadn't it? I'd give up drinking now. Right here. No waiting for New Year resolutions.

Eventually I straightened until my hands were on my wet knees.

I couldn't make myself turn around to check again if it had been some crazy white mirage.

I bent my head and looked between my legs. The foot was still there.

A tiny sound escaped my throat, surprising me. It was like a child's cry. How could this happen? It was Christmas. I turned full circle, looking for something to cover him with, then I realized that it probably would not be a good idea. I noticed then the mess I'd made, finger scores and footprints and knee holes. The cops would not be pleased. I took one long last look at that bent and frozen leg, then headed wearily back into town.

Chapter 2

They put me in the back of a squad car with one constable. Another was in the front passenger seat. The sergeant drove us to the golf course.

Walking across the grass I harboured the strange hope that I had indeed been hallucinating and they would find nothing but my freezing piss flower and an undisturbed rhododendron bush.

But the sergeant saw the leg before I did, and he stopped, 'Right, get Soco on the radio. Start taping this off.' The constables hurried back to the car. The sergeant approached the corpse. I stayed where I was and watched the sergeant bend and part the bush. I wondered if it would make him sick. He turned and walked back toward me, pulling a handkerchief from his sleeve and blowing his nose.

He looked shocked and didn't try to hide it. 'As bad as you've seen?' I asked.

He turned on me, offended. 'What do you think?'

I shrugged. 'Apologies. Stupid question.'

'I know his wife well,' he said. 'Used to go out with her. They've got three kids.'

I felt useless, worn out and somehow guilty. 'I'm sorry,' I said. He left the young cops in place and took me back to the police station, gave me coffee and asked questions. Shifts changed. They fed me soup and chicken sandwiches and lemonade. It was late afternoon before they decided to let me go, by which time I'd learned the dead man was Danny Gordon and that he'd worked at the Horseracing Forensic Laboratory.

The sergeant double checked he had the right details for me, 'We'll be in touch,' he said and went and sat at his desk.

My feet were cold and wet. I was unshaven and dirty and still hungover. 'Any chance you can organize me a lift home?'

He didn't bother looking up. 'Nope.'

He hunted with one finger above his keyboard. I said, 'Remind me next time I get the urge to be a good citizen to walk on by.'

He ignored me. I said, 'In fact, come court day, count me out.'

'You'll be there,' he said quietly.

I headed for the door. 'Here,' he said. I looked round. He was offering me a banknote. 'That should get you home.'

Twenty quid. 'Thanks. Want me to sign something?'

'There's nothing to sign.'

'You're lending me this then?'

'No. Keep it. Happy Christmas.'

'I'll send you a cheque. What's your name?'

He concentrated on his keyboard, 'Santa Claus. Make a donation at midnight Mass.'

I pocketed the cash, 'Thanks. It's a sign of the staff shortages in the force when you have to play the bad cop and the good cop. See you sometime.'

'I'll look forward to it.'

Halfway to the door I turned and went back, 'Will you tell his wife I'm sorry for her troubles?'

He stopped trying to type and looked at me, 'I will. Now go home. It's been a long day.'

I went out into the deep dusk and the Christmas lights and the hurrying shoppers who exchanged greetings in this tight-knit little racing community. And I wondered how Danny Gordon's wife had felt when she'd opened the door to a couple of grim-faced cops with no tidings of comfort and joy.

I shook my head, shoved the banknote deep in my pocket and hit the road, hoping a dose of Christmas charity had seeped into some driver in a big warm Mercedes with a mini-bar in the back.

Chapter 3

Nine weeks after I'd found the body, McCarthy came calling. I didn't recognize him when I opened the caravan door; the only light was from a weak gas lamp hanging behind me, and though he looked up when he spoke he remained in shadow.

I stepped to one side. The lamp swung and flickered in the wind but lit his face enough for me to identify him as Peter McCarthy, Racecourse Security Services investigator.

'Hello, Eddie.'

The surprise at seeing him kept me silent.

'You remember me, don't you?'

I nodded. 'What do you want?'

'Just to talk.'

'The last time we talked it cost me my licence and eighteen months in jail.'

We stared at each other. The rain blew into his back and pattered in bursts on his Trilby. 'Give me fifteen minutes,' he said. 'If you're not interested in what I've got to say after that you can throw me out.' I moved aside.

'Hell of a night, eh?' he said.

I didn't reply. Wriggling his long coat off, he looked around.

'There's a hook behind the door,' I said. I slid a plastic chair from under the fixed table and left it for him, and went to sit on my bed in the corner. McCarthy fished in his jacket pocket and pulled out a handkerchief.

He held it up to the light. Smears and blotches stained it and he tried to find a clean patch. He noticed me watching. 'Nosebleeds,' he said. He'd got even fatter since I'd last seen him. About six feet two and forty pounds overweight, his face and dark untidy curly hair had a greasy sheen even after he'd wiped away the rain. Finally, he sat down, rested his arms on the table, clasped his hands and looked straight at me like I was a camera and he was about to start reading the news.

'Your ban expired yesterday,' he said.

'I know.'

'I wondered what your plans were.'

'Why?'

He shrugged, 'Maybe I can help you out.'

'What makes you think I need help?'

He looked around the caravan; damp, dirty, full of holes, which I'd plugged, though the winds coming off the fields still found their way in. God knows how many stablehands and labourers had used it before me.

'Not what champion jockeys are accustomed to,' McCarthy said.

'Ex-champion…I get by.'

'Come on, Eddie, how much longer do you want to be stuck in this box out in the wilds?'

'I'll move on when I'm ready, without any help from you.'

'You're bearing old grudges.'

'Damn right I am.' I got up to get a drink. I had a third of a bottle of whiskey in a cupboard under the sink. I filled a glass, feeling no more hospitable toward McCarthy than when I'd opened the door, but I offered him a drink.

'Coffee, if you've got some. Milk and two sugars.'

Lighting the single gas ring, I tried to figure McCarthy's angle. I had last met him when he'd been investigating my 'involvement' in a racehorse-doping ring. I'd had nothing to do with it, but they didn't believe me. They took away my jockey's licence for life and 'warned me off the turf' for five years.

The kettle bubbled and I sloshed some boiling water into a mug and left McCarthy to stir it.

I took the whiskey to my bunk. He looked at me and raised his mug slowly. 'Cheers,' he said.

He sipped coffee before taking up his newsreader's pose again. 'How close a touch have you kept with racing in the last five years?'

'None. I've no reason to.'

'Miss it?'

Racing had been my life. I'd been careful never to let them see that, "the authorities". The injustice hurt bad enough, I didn't want them knowing their "punishment" had ripped out my heart.

'Not anymore.' I drank and blinked as he stared me out.

'Liar.'

I glanced down, ready to check the time. Ashamed of my cheap plastic watch, I left my hand at rest below the table, 'Mac, I'm up early tomorrow. Tell me why you're here.'

McCarthy pulled out the dirty handkerchief dabbed at his nose then said, 'Toward the end of November we learned from a good source a new drug was being developed. Stimulant. Undetectable. The plan is to have it ready for the Flat season, which is now, what, about three weeks away? We got on to it fairly sharp and we were making reasonable progress till just before Christmas when things came to a dead-end with a man called Danny Gordon.'

It took a few seconds for the name to register, 'The guy I found with his throat cut?'

'The same. I think the man who had him killed is the man behind the drug. Gordon worked in the lab at the Horseracing Forensic Laboratory.'

'I know.'

'He was last seen leaving a Newmarket pub with two men about three days before you found him. Now, it turns out the same two men, or at least we're pretty sure it's the same two, were responsible for a couple of serious assaults about a week before Gordon's death.

'A crook called Walter Bergmark got a visit from two blokes. We can't find out what they wanted because Bergmark won't talk, but before they left, they pounded his ankles, feet and toes with a builder's hammer. He had to have his feet amputated.'

Involuntarily my toes wiggled.

'A week later the same two men, we think, called on Kristar Rask who's a bigger fish than Bergmark. He's been involved in syndicate fraud in England and bribing jockeys in Sweden.

'Again, Rask won't say what they wanted but they slit his eyelids with a scalpel, taped cotton-wool pads over his eyes and soaked them in weed killer…blind for life.'

I drank, 'Is that it?'

'Then they killed Danny Gordon.'

'You think I'm involved because I found Danny Gordon?'

'Nope.'

'So where do I come in?'

'We want you to find the killers.'

I looked at my watch. 'Your fifteen minutes are up, McCarthy, goodnight.'

'Hear me out, Eddie.'

'No thanks, I've heard enough.' I got up, finished my drink at the walk and rinsed the glass.

'Eddie, listen-'

'Look, Mac, you've won the bet or the contest or whatever it was you came here for. The let's take the piss out of Eddie Malloy trophy is yours. That makes you a dual winner. Now finish your drink and go away and amuse yourself somewhere else.'

'Take it easy for God's sake. I'm trying to help you!'

'Sure you are, like you helped me five years ago?'

'Oh, come on, Eddie, be fair!'

'Me be fair! What do you know about fairness? How much did I get from you and your people?'

'Listen, I never agreed with your conviction or your punishment. But I had to do the job. What would you have done in my place?'

'I'd have spoken up, that's what I would have done, said my piece before your bosses decided to take away my fucking livelihood!'

We spent the next five minutes arguing, going over all the old shit I'd buried years ago. McCarthy wasn't stupid. When I'd burned myself out he said, 'Remember Kruger?'

I nodded slowly. 'What's he got to do with it?'

'It was more what he had to do with your case. You were convinced it was Kruger who set you up, weren't you?'

'Kruger ran the doping ring, I know that. I wouldn't have said he set me up. It was nothing personal, he just didn't care who went down, as long as it wasn't him.'

'But you got him for it?'

'Oh, I got him all right. It cost me eighteen months in jail but it was worth it. If you guys had caught Kruger before you took my licence away, then we wouldn't be having this conversation.'

'We tried,' he said.

'Not too hard, though, did you? I managed to find him.'

He raised his open palms, apologetic. 'We didn't have enough grounds, Eddie, you know that, and we didn't have the time.'

'Well, you should have found the time, Mister McCarthy. You should have found the fucking time! If it had been someone important instead of just an upstart jockey you'd have found it, wouldn't you?'

He seemed ready to argue but stopped himself. 'Look, we're getting into another ranting match. It's pointless. We'll be here all night if we keep raking through it all.'

I glared at him.

He held his hands up, 'Okay. Okay. I'm sorry. I didn't come here to wind you up. Sit down for a minute, let me finish then I'll leave.'

I sat. He said, 'This case we're working on, the new drug. We got hold of some of it, not long before Danny Gordon died. It seems that a lot of the techniques used in the processing of these drugs can be very individual, peculiar to one man or one team, and sometimes this shows up in analysis. If you were right five years ago, and Kruger was running the doping ring then, it looks like he's at it again.'

My mind began to race, 'So if Kruger is behind this and he gets caught there's a chance you can pin the old one on him?'

'Probably.'

'Would that clear me?'

'The only chance of your name being cleared would be if Kruger admitted you had nothing to do with it.'

'And if he did?'

He shrugged, 'Who knows?'

I sat forward on the bed. 'Would I get my licence back?'

'We have to find him first.'

'Mac! Would they give me back my licence?'

He cradled the coffee mug and smiled, 'There'd be a hell of a stink if they didn't.'

Chapter 4

If emotions travel through your body like blood, then none had flowed through me for five years; the well had dried up. If they had trickled back, I'd have been able to handle it, but they gushed. I shook, felt panicky, got up and began pacing, almost marching. Glancing wildly in all directions I couldn't keep my eyes still. I covered them with my hands, rubbing hard, massaging my face.

McCarthy said, 'Eddie, go easy, you can't start tonight. You'll need to be fully briefed.'

I shoved my hands into my pockets and kept pacing. 'Tell me more about Kruger.' My voice sounded high-pitched, almost strangled.

'Later.'

'Now!'

'You're building your hopes too high. Be realistic. If you do catch him he's going to hate you enough to want to kill you. The last thing he'll want to do is clear your name.'

'I'll take my chances. I want everything you've got on him.'

'Slow down, man! Kruger is the main suspect but the evidence on the whole case is too scant to pin anything on anybody yet.'

'Just tell me, Mac!'

He got to his feet, 'Look, if you're taking this on let's do it right. We'll arrange a meeting and you can have the full file on the case.'

'Tomorrow, then.'

'For God's sake, Eddie, slow down!'

I stopped pacing and faced him, 'Tomorrow, Mac. I've taken it easy and slowed down for five years. I want this bastard Kruger and I want my licence back. Meet me tomorrow.' I felt as if my eyes were bulging.

McCarthy stared at me, 'Where?'

'Anywhere. Name it. I'll be there.'

His fingers went to his chin and he drummed on it, 'We need to be careful. Mustn't be seen together.'

'Mac, I'll meet you in a forest, or up a bloody mountain!'

'I've got to be in London in the afternoon, but we definitely do not want to meet there…what about the Red Ox, that little pub on the Wantage road?'

'Fine. Twelve thirty?'

'Have you got transport?'

'I can probably talk Melling into lending me his car for the day but I'm going to need one long-term.'

McCarthy hauled his coat on and pulled the brim of his hat low, 'We'll talk about it tomorrow.'

'Okay. Fine.'

He looked down at me and smiled, 'You'd agree to anything right now, wouldn't you?'

I sighed long and low and realized I'd been holding my breath, 'I suppose I would.'

He put a hand on my shoulder, 'Softly, softly.'

I managed to stop myself launching another attack. Softly, bloody softly. Easy for him with his cushy job and his fat pay cheque and his cottage on the hill. Like the majority of Jockey Club employees, McCarthy would have had an easy life, a public school education and his father's gang of city contacts to slide him quietly into a nice job.

I reached and slowly moved his hand from my shoulder. His smile faded. I said, 'I'll see you tomorrow.'

'Glad you gave me your time now, eh?'

'Good night.'

He tipped his hat sarcastically and left.

I sat on the bunk and put my head in my hands, and I covered my eyes as a brutal kaleidoscope of the past five years spun out the story that was branded in my soul.

Sorrow mixed with bitter resentment, and rage and hatred, and for five years it had just swirled around in there. Now a tap had been fixed to it with a little sign that said "relief". And I sat in that dirty old caravan, in that cold, muddy field, a castaway in a thousand acres of rural darkness, where nobody could hear me, and I wept like a child, the pain howling its way out of me and up and away into the night.

Chapter 5

My boss, Karl Melling had only four horses in and it didn't take long to feed them and muck out. I'd known him have up to ten. Some were out of training, ex-point-to-pointers, young unbroken ones, old rogues – they all had one thing in common, problems. Melling tried to sort out the physical ones and he expected me to deal with the mental ones.

I didn't tell him I'd be leaving for good. I asked to borrow his car for the day and it was grudgingly lent. The ten-year-old Saab started first time.

In Lambourn the pace of the rain beat the speed of the wipers, forcing me to slow as I drove through the valley. On the downland gallops, trainers would be working their second or third lots of the morning.

This, as the road sign said, was The Valley of the Racehorse. It had been my valley of fantasy as a teenager. Two thousand thoroughbreds were stabled here. The village and the rolling downland surrounding it held racing yards run by trainers, staffed with ambitious lightweight youngsters and more than a few old men whose dreams were long dead.

It was a valley of hope and optimism and envy so green it would have shamed the grassy gallops.

Up the slope to my right, a string of fifteen or more horses walked steadily along the ridge, their riders in all colours of plastic capes hunched against the downpour like Apaches coming from an all-night party.

On the roads, riders touched their caps as I drove past at walking pace. None looked at me, though I knew many of the faces. Mine would have been forgotten five weeks after I was banished, never mind five years.

I could have bypassed this place. A week ago I'd have crawled over broken glass to avoid it, with all its memories, its unfulfilled promises. And McCarthy wouldn't be pleased if he knew I'd travelled through here.

But what else would a man do on the morning his life began again?

THE RED OX was a white-walled pub by the river, its pebbled car park no bigger than a large front garden. I parked beside the only other car, a brown Volvo. The bar was small, warm and thickly carpeted. On the walls hung racing prints and a dartboard.

McCarthy was the only customer. He nodded as I approached.

'Am I late or are you early?' I asked.

'I'm early. I've got to be in London for two o'clock,' he looked at the barmaid, 'I've ordered sandwiches, will that do?'

I nodded, 'Sure.'

A briefcase lay on the floor beside his seat. He flicked it open and came up with a cardboard file thinner than a folded newspaper. Setting it on the table, he looked at me.

'What's that?' I asked.

'What we've got on the case so far.'

I pulled the folder toward me, 'Bulging with reports, eh?'

'I told you, our information dried up months ago. That's the result of only a few weeks' investigations.'

The barmaid brought the sandwiches and two glasses of beer.

I took a sandwich, bit into the pink ham and swallowed some beer. McCarthy's disappeared in a couple of bites, 'There's not really much else I can tell you. It's all in the file,' he said.

I nodded.

He said, 'Since I'm stuck for time would you mind if we didn't discuss it now? Could you take it away and read it, then phone me with any questions?'

'Sure,' I said and he smiled and relaxed. He picked up another sandwich.

'Can I ask you one question now?' I said.

He raised his eyebrows, chewed and nodded.

'How much are you paying?'

'For what?'
'For me.'
'As in?'
'As in wages, salary.'
'How does a grand a month plus expenses sound?'
'Mean.'
'It's a hard item to place on the budget, Eddie.'
'That's your problem. I've got to live.'
'How much is Melling paying you?'
'Melling asks me to break horses, you're asking me to catch murderers. And Melling throws in board and lodgings.'

He picked at his teeth with a fingernail, 'I'm arranging that for you, and a car.'

'Where will I be staying?'

'A friend of mine has a holiday cottage in the Cotswolds. I should have confirmation this afternoon that you can use it.'

'And the car?'

'A hire car will be delivered to you, just tell me where you want it and when.'

'Melling's place, tomorrow morning.'

'Okay.'

McCarthy continued working on his teeth and looking at me, 'We're agreed on a grand a month?' he said.

'And a ten grand bonus on Kruger's conviction.'

He shook his head quickly, 'You're kidding, Eddie, there's no way I can authorize that.'

'Ten grand is peanuts compared to what it'll cost if Kruger starts using this drug on the racecourse.'

'You've got Kruger hung out to dry and you haven't even opened the file,' he reached for another sandwich.

'It was you who said Kruger was the chief suspect.'

'Only on the evidence we've got. Anyway, he's supposed to be your big motivation, not the cash.'

'You said last night you had the budget for it.'

'Not that sort of money.'

'Listen, Mac, at the end of this, if I'm not dead or crippled I'm going to have to live on something till either my licence is returned or I find another job. Trainers will hardly be queuing up to sign me. Even with my licence it's going to be a long road back.'

'Can't do it, Eddie, not ten grand.'

I pushed the file toward him, 'Let's forget it.'

'What do you mean?'

'I mean forget it, I'm not doing it. I don't want the job. It doesn't pay enough.'

'We can't forget it! Where does that leave me?'

'Get your own guys to do it.'

'I can't.'

'Why not?'

He looked away. I rose and walked round the table and leaned over him, 'Why not, Mister McCarthy?'

'They're too busy.'

'Bull shit.'

He forced himself to look up at me.

'Tell me why, Mac, tell me why your boys won't do it?'

He looked away again.

'Then I'll tell you why – because they're scared. Isn't that right? Bergmark's crippled, Rask's blind, Danny Gordon's dead and your guys are shit-scared!'

He kept avoiding my gaze. I went on, 'Thinking this over as I drove here, the one thing bothering me was the reason your own team weren't dealing with it.' I straightened and walked slowly to the window. 'I can't believe I took in all the crap you gave me last night. Made a fool of myself in my hurry to take this on. You must have been pissing yourself laughing all the way home.'

'Don't be daft, man! I was there to try to do you a favour.'

'Bollocks. You were there to try and get me to take the chances your boys wouldn't because I'm a worthless has-been and it doesn't matter if I go the same way as the other three.'

I returned to the table and stood in front of him. 'Am I right, Mac?'

'I am having a bit of trouble with, er, morale on this one,' he mumbled.

We were silent for ten seconds then he spoke quietly, 'I'll pay the ten grand if you still want the job.'

I sat down. He pushed the file slowly toward me. I let him stew for a minute before picking it up.

'Good,' he said, smiling as he rose. He slung a business card across the table, 'Call me at that number around ten tonight and I'll give you details of the cottage.' I slid the card into my top pocket and drank some more beer.

'Must rush,' McCarthy said, 'I'll pay the bill on the way out.'

He walked toward the bar then stopped, turned and came slowly back, 'Eddie,' he said quietly. I looked up, smiling smugly, expecting an apology, 'You won't be wanting that last sandwich, will you?'

Chapter 6

It was mid-afternoon when I got home. Melling stood in the yard bawling at someone. His teenage son cowered in front of him, a broken halter trailing from his hand.

Melling was pushing him, thumping his chest with his open hand, shouting each word that synchronized with the blows. I decided to rescue the boy before he got bumped into the next county.

'Mister Melling, sorry to interrupt the family get together but can I have a word?'

Melling spun and faced me. He was an ugly sod with an uncommonly large head covered with more hair than a man his age should have.

'What is it?'

He was still shouting but concentrating on me now and not the boy, who took the opportunity and made a swift exit.

'Holidays,' I said. His scowl had been pretty bleak but he dug hard and came up with another wrinkle on his forehead, 'What?'

'Holidays, Mister Melling.'

'What about them?'

'I'd like some.'

'Don't be daft,' he turned, looking for the boy. 'Benny!' he yelled.

The only reply he got was a slight echo from an open box at the bottom of the yard, 'Benny! Do not you show your face back here without that filly!'

He grunted and started walking toward the house. I fell into step with him, 'About the holidays, Mister Melling…'

He didn't stop, 'I don't pay you to take holidays, son.'

'I need a month off.'

'I can't afford to give it to you and you can't afford to take it.'
'What does that mean?'
Stopping on the doorstep, he turned to look at me, 'It means, Malloy, that the first day you don't show in this yard for work, you pack up your troubles in your old kitbag and get your arse out of my caravan.'

He smiled and went into the house, slamming the door in my face.

Leaving in the morning would be a pleasure.

Reading the file didn't take up much of my evening. The evidence against Kruger was far from conclusive. It relied on my allegations of his connection with my case five years ago, a reported sighting of one of his henchmen speaking to Danny Gordon a month before he died, and a rumour Kruger had been in Austria for the past two years (his son, who worked for a large drug company, controlled a research lab in Vienna).

A report confirmed Kruger hadn't been seen in England for two years, that the henchman had disappeared since last seen talking to Danny Gordon, and that neither the crippled Bergmark nor the blinded Rask would answer 'relevant' questions. On the two suspected murderers, there was little information; brief physical descriptions, which, in essence, said, both big, fit, white and English. The only recent clue to their whereabouts was an unconfirmed report about them leaving Sandown races three weeks ago with a jockey named Alan Harle.

I knew Harle; he'd been a journeyman jockey when I'd been riding. Racecourse Security Services had not yet interviewed him, so he looked the most promising lead. The rest of the file consisted of reports on the assaults on Bergmark and Rask and the murder of Danny Gordon. There was a photograph of his body.

Staring at it reminded me of how I felt that day, and made me think a grand a month plus expenses was crazier than Russian roulette with five bullets.

At ten o'clock, I walked to the pub and phoned McCarthy.
'Eddie. Been through the file?'
'Yep.'
'Any questions?'
'Yes. Am I mad?'
'No, just desperate.'
He was right. 'If I end up dead, scatter my ashes at Cheltenham.'
'Don't be morbid.'

'Tell that to Danny Gordon.'

He tried to change the subject. 'The car'll be there in the morning.'

'What about the cottage?'

'I'll tell you about it…'

Chapter 7

McCarthy had said the place was isolated, and he wasn't kidding. It lay in the heart of a thick wood, the track leading to it barely wide enough for the silver Rover he'd hired for me.

The cottage had grey stone walls and a small garden, one bedroom, one kitchen, one living-room all furnished and decorated in greens, browns and greys. Faded cushions covered the slate seats of a deep inglenook fireplace.

A handwritten note lay on the mantelpiece. 'Firelighters in kitchen cupboard. Logs in shed outside. Chimney may need swept.'

The next few days were spent organizing. The phone needed reconnecting and the chimney was thick with soot. I bought more wood for the fire, food, some new clothes and footwear. When everything was done I looked for more to do, more mundane necessities. I was just putting off the moment when I'd have to do some 'investigating', but I didn't know where or how to start.

I recalled how I'd tracked down Kruger last time, driven by a manic need to kick the shit out of him for framing me. I'd just been running around crazed with revenge, asking, begging, bribing, threatening until I got what I needed. I couldn't work that way with this.

I sat down to think. It was dusk, windless, and cold. I built a fire and the clean chimney sucked at the firelighter flames and wrapped them round the ash logs. I washed the paraffin film from my fingers, poured a large whiskey, with ice, and settled by the hearth.

I drank and tried to plan. The only links at the moment apart from Harle were Bergmark and Rask.

They hadn't volunteered anything to McCarthy's people and there was no reason for them to treat me differently, but I had to try. I'd learnt from the file that Bergmark lived with his widowed sister, near Nottingham. I would visit him tomorrow then go to Kent the day after to see Rask.

Even if I came up with nothing, at least I'd have made a start. I drank some more and thought some more and wondered about what was to come. The fire burned hot and comforting and I eased off my shoes and closed my eyes.

Chapter 8

I found Bergmark at a run-down house on the outskirts of Nottingham. The broken gate swung both ways as I pushed through. Bergmark watched me from his wheelchair at the front door, a heavy coat and flat cap protecting him from the cold, an old blanket covering his footless legs. Allowing for his three or four days' beard growth, he looked to be in his mid-forties.

As I went along the path toward him his sister came out carrying washing in a red plastic basket with a vertical split in one side, which opened and closed like a fish's mouth as she walked down the short ramp.

When she saw me, she stepped in front of her brother's wheelchair, shielding him. 'What do you want?'

I stopped a few yards from her, 'Is it okay if I have a word with Mister Bergmark?'

'No, he's not seeing anybody,' she was big and serious, maybe five years older than her brother.

'It won't take long. I've come all the way up from London,' I lied.

'Well just turn round and go all the way back,' she said. Bergmark spoke, 'It's okay, let him in.' His fingers touched her hip, easing her aside. She scowled and stamped into the house. I offered my hand, 'Eddie Malloy.'

He shook it, 'Thought I recognized the face.'

A trace of a foreign accent, 'Walter, isn't it?'

'That's right.'

'How have you been?' I asked.

'I remember you. You were a fair jock.'

'Thank you. Look, I'm doing a favour for a friend and-'
'Used to ride Sandown well, as I recall.'
'Yes, thanks… Listen, Walter, I-'
'You got sent down, didn't you?' he stared into the distance, and hadn't looked at me once.
'That's right,' I said.
'Got you in the end, eh?'
He was miles away. I might as well not have been there, 'Walter, do you remember the man who did this to you?'
'I landed a real nice touch on your horse at Sandown once, Whitbread day it was.'
I sat on the ramp beside his wheelchair. Our eyes were on the same level, 'Look Walter, I'm trying to help catch these guys, I need-'
'Wasn't it the big race? You finished second, didn't you? Got it on an objection?' I spent another five minutes on similar lines with no result. Either he was putting on a hell of a good act or they'd screwed the guy's mind up. He rambled on as I walked away. 'They'd give her a gallop too many, too, by mistake and she still won easing up. Funny old game, eh?'

Yes, Mister Bergmark, a funny old game.

I decided to drive to Kent and find out if Kristar Rask would be any more helpful, pointless putting it off until tomorrow. The time with Bergmark had been a washout and I didn't want to waste any more.

It was a long drive down the eastern side of England. Rask lived right on the shore. I arrived just after 7 p.m. It was dark and the wind blew cold off the sea as I approached the unlit cottage, the curtains drawn on the front windows. The doorbell was a mechanical pull type, the chimes slow and hollow. I waited.

I rang again. Nothing. I went round the back. The rear windows were heavily curtained too. I sought gaps, looking for light, and quietly cursing this wasted day.

I was surprised Rask wasn't at home. From what I'd learned, he lived alone with his new guide dog. Mac's file said Rask had become a recluse since being blinded. He'd dropped what friends he'd had and if he went out at all, it was to walk with the dog on the nearby beach.

I decided to find a pub and pass a couple of hours before returning to check again.

The landlord of the Ancient Mariner had enough time on his hands to be throwing darts at the board in the corner. He had no opponent. Two other men were in the bar; one slumped in a chair by the gas-fire, either asleep or dead, and the other eating nuts and reading The Times. The owner put down the darts to pour me a whiskey, fold the fiver I gave him into a wad in his pocket, and give me change. He returned to my side and resumed his mechanical throwing.

'Fancy a game?' he asked.

'Don't play,' I said.

He threw, 'Pity,' he said, recovering the darts.

'Mmm.'

He threw again, 'We've got a good pub team here, y'know,' he said, dropping a dart as he pulled them out.

'Yeah?'

'Yep.'

Six more darts.

'On holiday?' he asked, throwing again.

'Visiting a friend,' I said.

'Local?'

'A mile or so down the front, Kristar Rask.'

'A close friend?'

'Why do you ask?'

'He killed himself yesterday morning.'

Chapter 9

The woman who'd been training Rask's guide dog had found the Labrador whining below his dangling feet as he hung by its chain lead from the doorway.

She told the police Rask had become depressed since his 'accident' and they said they would not be seeking anyone else in connection with Rask's death. No suicide note was found.

Rask was dead. Bergmark had a mental block. The only lead left was the jockey, Alan Harle, who'd been seen with the two men I was looking for. I hadn't wanted to approach Harle so early, in case he was involved. I had little choice now. I would just have to be careful.

I tried to contact him through a mutual jockey-friend who said Harle was in France, looking after some horses for his guv'nor and that he'd be home for the Champion Hurdle at Cheltenham in eleven days' time.

Eleven days with nothing to do but contemplate what it would be like to set foot on a racecourse again, Cheltenham, the track I'd loved above all others, back among the people I'd known so well. I wondered how I'd handle it, how I'd cope, how many would recognize me and turn away. I'd been an outcast since my teens, but racing welcomed my type. It had opened up and drawn me in and succoured me, or should that be suckered me?

I'd just turned twenty, heading for my first Champion Jockey title thinking I owned the world, believing I was King of Life.

Some of the old hands had warned me of the company I was keeping.

I'd laughed. Be careful? Why? Everybody loves me! I'm a

champion! I'm breaking no laws, what's the problem?

The problem was me. It was youth and inexperience and arrogance, and together they courted me away from caution, dissuaded me from defences, and Mister Kruger stepped right in through the widest of gaps and wounded me, mortally, it had seemed.

Until now.

Chapter 10

At last, the Cheltenham festival came round. I got there early and went to the Arkle bar. I found a space by the window and unfolded the Racing Post. The headline said: 'Spartan Sandal to Trample Rivals'. Their tip for the Champion Hurdle, the biggest race of the season for two-mile hurdlers. There had been a time when I'd have known every runner's form by heart.

I read on: 'Spartan Sandal looks to have a favourite's chance, in what appears a sub-standard Champion Hurdle, of landing the prize for the Essex stable of Jim Arlott.'

A piece near the end of the page took my attention. 'Castle Douglas, a long-shot, will be a first runner in the race for second season trainer, Basil Roscoe, who enjoys the exclusive patronage of the mysterious Louis Perlman, with whose horses he's done so well this year. A first Champion Hurdle ride for Alan Harle, Castle Douglas would have to show mighty improvement to figure here.

'Still, if the miracle happened, surely Mr. Perlman would at last come out of hiding to receive the trophy from the Queen Mother. Despite twenty-three winners this season, Perlman has not yet been seen on a racecourse, or anywhere else for that matter.'

I'd never heard of Perlman or his trainer, Roscoe. When I'd been riding, Harle wouldn't have had a mount in the Champion Hurdle. He hadn't been getting fifty rides a season back then.

Drifting around, I saw some old acquaintances. A couple of them stopped to talk; a few more nodded, embarrassed, and a handful ignored me. An owner I used to ride for asked if I'd be getting my licence back. I told him I doubted that very much and he touched my arm and looked sympathetic. Pity riled me, but I appreciated the gesture.

Twenty minutes before the off of the Champion Hurdle I bagged a good viewing spot in the stand. Spartan Sandal and Kiri jumped the last together and had a hell of a tussle until halfway up the hill, when Alan Harle swept through on Castle Douglas. Harle rode as though the devil hung on his tail, and he drove his mount past the battling pair and won going away.

Twenty-to-one winners of the Champion Hurdle are seldom greeted with cheers. He galloped past the post to cries of 'What the hell's that?' and walked back in to just a smattering of applause. Raising my binoculars, I focused on Harle's face. He wiped his nose on his sleeve and smiled, leant forward, slapped the horse three times on the neck and ruffled the delighted groom's hair.

People hurried to see the winner being unsaddled. I went against the flow, climbing to the top to look down on the paddock from the rear of the grandstand.

Harle dismounted to congratulations from a camel-coated man and a slim blonde in a tight black skirt. He was probably the trainer, Roscoe. The woman would be either his wife or girlfriend. I raised my binoculars. Roscoe looked fairly young, early thirties, and, from his styled hair to his brown Gucci shoes, impeccably dressed. Arms out of the sleeves, he wore his coat like a cloak.

A handful of pressmen surrounded him and the blonde, who looked older, maybe forty. I tilted the glasses slowly: good legs...good figure...good dentist. The MC picked up the microphone. 'Your Royal Highness, ladies and gentlemen, unfortunately the winning owner, Mister Louis Perlman, cannot be here today and so I now call on Mrs. Basil Roscoe to receive the Champion Hurdle Challenge Cup on his behalf.'

The blonde minced forward, her stiletto heels murdering a few worms as she crossed the lawn. Her husband watched, smiling smugly, and I wondered what kind of owner Louis Perlman was and what pleasure he took from his horses if he never came to see them run.

And what was Roscoe's history? He was a new one on me. The press bar was on the floor below so I put my binoculars away and went looking for some information.

Chapter 11

Approaching the press bar entrance, I saw Joe Lagota come out, head down, looking at his racecard. I quickened and bumped him and he dropped his card. I picked it up and smiled as I handed it to him, 'You'll be too old for bending down now,' I said.

He grunted and took the card, 'I heard you were back,' he said, 'never thought I'd see you on a racecourse again. What's the story?'

'What do you mean, what's the story?'

He pointed the red plastic tip of his pen at my face, 'Eddie, I know a desperado when I see one. I'd have bet a million that nobody could have hauled you back onto a racetrack when your ban was up unless it was to ride a horse.'

I hadn't reckoned on this. When I'd been riding, Joe was just one of the press pack, someone who'd gladly write another piece about the boy wonder.

He said, 'Come in and have a drink.'

I hesitated, but saying no would only confirm his suspicions.

He found us a quiet corner and ordered coffee and biscuits, and he spent ten minutes working me over, looking for an opening, trying to find out why I was putting myself through the torture of watching other men ride winners at Cheltenham.

I laughed, 'Torture? Come on, Joe. I was a kid when I was riding. Things change when you get older, you know that.'

He straightened, staring at me as though trying to find a way into my skull, 'You're telling me one thing and my sniffer is telling me something else, Eddie.'

I opened my arms: nothing to hide, 'Joe, I don't know how many different ways there are to say this, I'm here for a day out, for old time's sake. Okay, if I bump into some rich owner who wants to offer me a nice office job, I'd jump at it.'

His head went back and he frowned as though he'd suddenly smelled something bad, 'Office job, my arse! Now I know you're winding me up!'

I laughed. Joe said, 'Look, all I ask is that if you're working toward something, some kind of comeback or protest or campaign to get your licence back, give me a call first, will you?'

'Joe, that's crazy, but if that's what you need to put your mind at rest, then, yes, of course I'll call you.'

He nodded, short and sharp as if confirming to himself he'd been right, and he bit hard into a biscuit.

'Okay,' I said, getting up, 'I'll go and see if I can find Alan and congratulate him.'

'He's another one. If Harle gives you any clue whatever as to how he suddenly lands a job with some crackpot owner nobody's ever met, give me a call on that, too, will you?'

'Sure. I'd heard about this Perlman guy. He wouldn't be the first screwball to own a string of racehorses.'

'No, but he'd be the first to hand them over to no-marks like Roscoe and Harle.'

I took a step forward and put a hand on his shoulder and smiled, 'You are not having a good day, my friend. Think of the poor sods out there who'd kill for a job where all you did was watch racing and drink free beer.'

'They'd never stand the pressure of a deadline. That's why they're driving buses and emptying bins.'

'And reading your papers. Be careful never to write what you really think of your customers.'

He frowned and drank cold coffee.

There wouldn't be a chance of getting near Harle during the celebrations, so I walked on through to the ring, the bookmakers' stronghold. I knew a few of the bookies and some nodded recognition. None looked surprised to see me; if I ever found a horse that could move on a racecourse as fast as gossip did, I'd be a millionaire in a minute.

I moved to the rails where the big money guys bet. Most of their customers were known to them by name and bank account number.

At the end of this line, I spotted an old familiar face, which opened in a wide smile when it saw me.

'Eddie, my son, come 'ere!' The battered voice hadn't changed. I approached, smiling and greeted Wilbur Slacke. He clasped my hands in his, which were cold and white and blue-veined.

'Still skinning the punters then, Will?' I said.

'Just enough to keep the wolf from the door as usual, Eddie, though the bugger's getting a bit too close to the front gate recently!'

'Does that mean you'll have to sell one of the Mercs? My heart bleeds.'

He smiled even wider, showing his own teeth still. His eyes watered in the cold wind as he stepped rheumatically off the stool to lean on the railings. 'How's business?' I asked.

'Not so bad, Eddie. Can't complain really.'

'The big winner must have been a result?'

'Brilliant result. Best I can remember in the Champion for years. We all won a few quid except that bugger at the other end,' he nodded down the line of bookies toward a sour looking character handing someone a wad of notes.

'The big guy with the black hair?'

Will nodded, frowning now, 'You know, I saw him punching his clerk, right in the head, up at Sedgefield after a bad result, one time. Couldn't believe it.'

'I hope the guy punched him back.'

Will coughed raggedly and turned away to spit. 'Nah,' he said, 'Should've walked that day. I told him that. Still, the fucker's took a few doings with results recently so maybe he'll get skint soon.'

I'd never heard Will call anyone down. I looked at the guy again. He was taking money this time but didn't seem any happier.

'What's his name?' I asked.

'Stoke. Howard Stoke,' he began coughing again and I slapped his back. When he stopped, his face was crimson and his eyes watery.

'A nice glass of malt would quieten that down,' I said.

'Likely,' he nodded.

'Half a dozen would kill it stone dead.'

His smile returned, 'And me with it.'

Out on the course, the grass grew lush on ground that gave an inch under my heels, the feel of it unlocking whatever was shackling my memories of the glory days, and I knew I couldn't be among the throng at the last fence.

I set out to get as far from the crowds as possible. I stopped in the middle of the infield watching away in the distance as the starter let the big field go for the novice 'chase.

Then I had to move again, to get away from the PA system. Every word the commentator uttered seemed weighted with taunts about what I was missing.

I stood by the open ditch, on the far side of the track where only a whisper of the commentary remained. I gazed at the black birch between the white plastic wings, and the years tumbled away, exposing me to the raw hurt…I should have retreated, covered my ears, closed my eyes, ran…but I was transfixed as the runners approached. Sixteen thoroughbreds. Eight tons of horse-flesh galloping toward me at thirty miles an hour.

Me.

Here.

Rooted to the ground.

The leader, a big chestnut, ears pricked, primed himself for take-off, and I found myself counting the stride in with his jockey… one, two, three, kick – up, and over he goes.

The rest reach it now, closely grouped, colours mixing, meshing with speed as thunderous hoofbeats shake the ground and the birch crackles like a long firework sparked by ribs brushing through. Cameras click and whirr, jockeys shout, whips smack on muscle.

They land, front feet gouging the turf. Hooves slide and a big brown head goes low. The rider cries out…his mount recovers, but they are last by a length as the runners race toward the turn, carrying away my past, drawing with them my heart and soul, but leaving me behind.

Silence now.

Emptiness.

Hopelessness.

I shamble back to the car.

Chapter 12

At the cottage, in the cold gloom, I poured a drink stiff enough to splint a fracture, and downed it.

I lit a fire. After five minutes' spitting and crackling, the logs caught and began warming the room.

I stood staring at the burning wood then at myself in the mirror above the mantelpiece. The flames weaved and jumped, casting light and shadows on my face and shoulders. I looked tired… ghostly.

After another drink, I began to feel warm inside as well as out. Pulling the chair nearer the fire, I settled with a sigh. It had been a bloody melancholy day. Tipping the glass toward me, I gazed through the liquid at the soft yellow glow of the flames. All that looked back was my self-pitying face. Finishing the drink in one gulp, I shut out all the old pathetic thoughts and faced reality.

I was no longer a jockey. Maybe I'd never be a jockey again. There was a job to do and it would have to be done on the racecourse as much as anywhere else.

I had hated that place today because I wasn't the big shot any more. I would always despise going to racecourses now. I couldn't handle being just one of the crowd…Well, I would damn well have to get used to it.

I stood and put the drink down on the mantelpiece and stared stern-faced at myself in the mirror, 'Grow up, Eddie. Finally. Grow up for God's sake!'

The phone rang loud in the hard hallway and I watched what I looked like when I was startled, as my eyebrows rose and my mouth opened, and I laughed stupidly, nervously, as I hurried to pick it up,

'Hello, Mac,' I said.

There was a pause before he said, 'How on earth did you know it was me?'

'Well, you're the only one who knows I'm here.'

'True. How did today go?'

'Okay, I suppose.'

'What does that mean?'

'It means I managed to go to the Cheltenham festival as a bystander for the first time in my life and not slit my wrists. An achievement, trust me.'

'You'll get used to it. Did you find anything out?'

'I found out that God smiles not only on the righteous. How come Harle lands a job with this Perlman character after grubbing around the floor of the food chain so long?'

'Perlman is proving an utter embarrassment to the sport. There's a meeting going on about him, as we speak.'

'As in?'

'As in how the Queen Mother could be effectively snubbed by the owner of the Champion Hurdle winner.'

I was about to mention Joe Lagota's comments about Perlman, but thought it best not to let Mac know I'd been talking to the press. I said, 'What about this tailor's dummy, Roscoe? How did he get the training job? He's only been in the game five minutes, hasn't he?'

'Well, he's shrewd enough to say little and imply much.'

'What does that mean?'

'Roscoe's been building himself this mystical aura with the press. Lots of wise nodding and knowing smiles without actually answering any questions.'

'I find him getting such a big owner even more baffling than Harle. You don't just come from nowhere as a trainer into a job like that, do you? At least Harle has a few miles on the clock.'

'So, you're sticking with this Harle connection?'

'It's the only one I've got, Mac. If Harle's been talking to this pair who've done all the damage, he won't have been passing the time of day.'

'You said you know him pretty well, why don't you just call him and ask him out for a drink?'

'Because if he is into something with Kruger or with the two hit men, he's not only going to smell a rat, the stink will knock him out. We were never bosom buddies. Why would I call him after all these years?'

'Er, maybe because he's just won the Champion Hurdle?'

'Harle would know more than anyone that I'd be more likely to kill him for that than call him.'

Mac sighed, 'So, what next?'

'I don't know. I'll figure something out.'

'I'll leave you to get figuring then. Keep in touch, will you?'

'As soon as I've got something to tell you, I'll call.'

'Good luck.'

I lowered the handset slowly, and the click as it dropped into place seemed not so much to be turning off the noise of conversation, but switching on the silence once more. I returned to my seat by the fire.

Against the corner of the inglenook, a brass toasting fork stood. I reached for it, testing the prongs with my fingers, wondering how long it had sat unused.

I pushed it slowly into the flames to touch the end of the heaviest log, rocking it very gently, as my brain sifted and sorted and sought a way through the problems.

What would Harle be doing now? What would I be doing if I'd won the Champion Hurdle today?

I'd be partying. I remembered that partying was one thing Harle had been very good at…too good. His drinking had cost him some promising rides in his early days.

Harle might be staying at the Duke's Hotel in Cheltenham. The racing snobs never stayed anywhere else. Not that Harle was one, but Mr. and Mrs. Roscoe would be bedding down there and where Roscoe was, Harle wouldn't be far behind.

The Roscoes, with their designer gear, looked classic party types. They'd have arranged something. And if they were involved with Kruger, there'd be a few old villains there, even if the man himself wasn't.

I got the number of the Duke's and called and asked for Basil Roscoe.

'I'm afraid Mister Roscoe is not in his room, sir.'

'It was just to say I'm going to be a bit late for the celebration. I'm having some car trouble, but the last thing I want to do is miss the party.'

'I'm sure that will be fine, sir, people are still arriving for it. I don't think they intend to stand on ceremony.'

'Well, they never do with these, eh?'

She laughed politely. 'I'll see you soon,' I said.

'Should I mention to Mister Roscoe that you called?'

'No, no. It's pointless going to any trouble. It will be a nice surprise for him when he sees me.'

Chapter 13

The Rover's twin beams lit up the narrow, twisting, hilly roads leading down into Cheltenham town. The place was buzzing. The population must treble during festival week.

The white-fronted Duke's Hotel was illuminated by a row of floodlights in the gardens. This was my first time through its doors in six years. Inside, nothing had changed: twenty guineas a roll wallpaper and thirty quid a yard carpet. Teak, leather, brass and silk in dignified doses.

At reception, a dark-eyed, pretty girl told me Mister Roscoe had taken the Directors Suite on the third floor for the evening, and if I was Mister Glenn, I ought to go right up.

The suite looked big enough to hold fifty or sixty people but it was so crammed it pulsed like a living thing. Ten strides from the outer ring of the pack I could feel the body heat.

They had dressed for a party, some of the women with much care, but that had been hours ago, and the wear and tear of alcohol and smoke, of sweaty overcrowding, had peeled away the veneer: mascara smears from carelessly rubbed eyes, straggling tendrils escaping from a blonde bun, a vee-shaped frock front which had taken an uneven dive showing a tanned, wrinkled cleavage. If all the jewellery were real, there was a million pounds' worth.

I recognized a few jockeys, many conspicuous anyway by their short stature. The other men were all shapes and sizes and in varying stages of undress, some missing ties or jackets or both.

I sidled through the throng to where I'd guessed the bar was. Three staff in black uniforms poured champagne at a hot pace. I picked up a glass.

Someone spoke in my right ear. 'Take two.' A note in the voice zoomed straight into my memory bank and told me who it was before I turned around; a girl I had known when I was fifteen years old, a beauty I'd had such a crush on at school I'd barely been able to speak to her.

I turned. Charmain, her auburn hair pinned high showing small ears and the fine jaw line, those green eyes, the wide lips, just thick enough to give the impression of a permanent pout. She was lightly made-up, a natural flush colouring her cheeks.

I had never forgotten her. She'd been my first love and it hadn't mattered so much that it was one-sided. I had often lain awake, especially in prison, thinking about her, dreaming of meeting again and fantasizing about the outcome.

The scene had been well rehearsed in my mind; we'd look at each other for a long moment as we were doing now then she'd say, in a voice mixed with curiosity and desire, 'Aren't you Eddie Malloy?' All my old feelings for her surged back as I waited for her to speak. Her look turned to one of puzzled recognition, 'Don't I know you?'

I nodded, trying to look cool, 'I'm Eddie Malloy. We were at school together.'

Her eyes widened, 'Oh, I remember…of course.'

But I could see she didn't remember so I pretended I couldn't recall her name properly.

'And you're, eh, is it Carol…?'

'Charmain,' she said, 'Caroll used to be my surname but I'm married now,' she held out her left hand. The fat solitaire over a wide wedding band put the seal on my past like a trap-door closing.

I stared at the rings, 'When did that happen?' I asked, as though it were some kind of tragedy.

'Six months ago,' she said, smiling.

I caught myself about to ask if she really loved him. I was getting sillier by the minute. She made me feel even worse with her next question, 'What are you now?' I frowned. She said, 'I mean, are you a trainer or a jockey or something?'

Obviously just a something, I thought, in her eyes, anyway. 'I used to be a jockey,' I said.

'Were you good?'

'Yes.'

'Is that all?'

'What more do you want?'

'You don't just say yes to a question like that.'

'I do.'

She looked perplexed, 'You're funny,' she said.

'Thanks.'

'Why did you stop if you were good?'

'The authorities took my licence away.'

'Why?'

'They said I was involved with a doping ring.'

'Were you?'

'What do you think?'

She shrugged, looking hurt at my attitude, 'I don't think you'd have done it.'

I suddenly felt a great tenderness for her, but it was quickly snuffed out by a hefty bump from behind, which made me spill my drink. The offender pushed past without apologizing.

I recovered and looked round. A large man had his hand on Charmain's bare arm. Four thick fingers gripped her, the flesh between them showing white.

She looked surprised and embarrassed. He looked very angry.

About six feet two, fiftyish, his pale skin emphasizing how much dye was in his bluish-black hair, which looked greasy and hung over his collar. His sideburns were the same colour and stretched to two inches below his ear lobe. His eyes were grey.

He wore a fawn jacket over a stomach held in only by a large ego. His feet, in crocodile shoes, splayed badly.

He looked as mean as he had when I'd seen him earlier at the races paying out wads of money.

'Howard!' Charmain said, half pleading, reaching to try to ease his grip on her arm.

'Where have you been?' His voice was level but threatening. I guessed he'd had plenty of practice controlling a nasty temper in public. I was having some trouble controlling mine.

'I just came to get another drink, darling!' she looked up at him and turned on a full wattage smile, though he was still hurting her. I watched his fingers…they began to relax.

'Good,' he said and released her. Charmain's hand went up to cover the purple finger marks.

His ugly mouth smiled, showing teeth yellow near the gums and white at the biting end, but his eyes stayed mean.

Charmain introduced us, 'Oh, Howard, this is Eddie, he used to be a jockey.'

He looked down and his smile faded. He didn't offer his hand and he didn't say pleased to meet you. Charmain tried it from my side, 'Eddie, this is my husband Howard Stoke.'

I smiled my most pleasant smile.

'Who invited you?' The growl again.

'I'm a friend of Alan Harle's.'

'I should have guessed,' he said, 'you jockeys all have the same dumb look.' He smiled at his little taunt, watching me from his four-inch height advantage.

I drank, 'Are you always so nice to new acquaintances?'

He leaned forward and down, 'You won't ever be an acquaintance of mine, son.'

I feigned deep disappointment, shaking my head. 'And after we'd started on such friendly terms.'

He moved close. I could hear him breathe in his nostrils, 'And you won't ever be an acquaintance of this lady either, you randy little bastard!' The grey in his eyes darkened and I felt like saying, I've got news for you, mate.

Charmain clutched his sleeve, 'Howard, please come and introduce me to some of your friends!' He hesitated, glaring at me for another five seconds, and then he grabbed her arm and turned away. She didn't look at me as she followed him. I called out, 'Very nice meeting you, Mister Stoke.'

He turned and snarled, 'Up yours.'

'Likewise,' I smiled. They went into the throng and I watched his head bob away across the room as he dragged Charmain behind him. Beauty and the beast. How the hell had she got tied up with him?

Taking another glass of champagne, I went looking for Alan Harle and saw him standing by the entrance. When I was half a dozen steps away, he opened the door and left. I followed him.

Chapter 14

Six paces ahead and weaving unsteadily along the corridor, Harle stopped and pushed against a door. It swung open and he went in. I reached the door: Gentlemen, the sign said.

I was one of those.

The door of the middle cubicle was closed. Harle was behind it. I stood by the sink nearest the drier and waited. A minute passed. There had been no sound.

The door opened and Harle, fiddling with his jacket collar, took two paces out. He caught his breath in surprise when he saw me and, turning, flushed the toilet. When he came out again he looked calm and so pleased to see me you'd have thought I was his dinner date.

He walked up close and shook hands, 'Eddie! They told me you were back. Great news, eh? How've you been doing?'

I smiled. He was small, even for a jump jockey; about five three, but he had what bodybuilders called good symmetry. His face was chipped in places from racing falls and a crescent-shaped thick pink scar showed through his dark thinning hair.

'I've been doing okay,' I said, 'but not riding Champion Hurdle winners.'

'Magic, eh?' he beamed, drunk but looking lively.

'Fantastic,' I said, 'but no more than you deserve after all the dogs you've ridden in the past.'

He turned to the mirror, still smiling, and drew a comb from his pocket. Only the reflection of his head and shoulders showed as he combed his sparse hair. 'Yeah, you can say that again. And you won't see me on no dogs in the future either. It's going to be all top quality stuff from here on in.'

'Yes, I heard you'd landed a good retainer with whaddyacall'im?'

The comb moved in useless sweeps. 'Roscoe,' he said, 'Basil Roscoe.'

'That's right. I couldn't remember the name. He's a newcomer, isn't he?'

'After your time anyway, Eddie.'

'Yes, I've been out of touch.'

The comb stopped. Harle pushed it into his pocket, admiring its work. I turned and our reflections carried on the conversation.

'Any more like Castle Douglas tucked away?' I asked.

'We've got a couple of cracking novices. One runs in the Triumph on Thursday, Tourist Attraction, he's called.'

'Fancy him?'

'He'll skate up. Don't miss him.'

'I won't. Who owns him?'

He hesitated. 'Same owner as Castle Douglas.'

'Lucky man. Who is he?' I tried to appear open-faced and innocent. I don't know if he bought it because he paused again before answering and gave me a glance that said, is this guy kidding?

'Mister Perlman, he's Roscoe's biggest owner.' He straightened his tie, leaving the top shirt button loose.

'Perlman? Never heard of him either,' I said.

'He's only come into the game recently.'

I shook my head. 'Boy, I can't get moving for overnight success stories since I came back.'

Turning from the mirror, he glared at me. I smiled in apology and grabbed his arm. 'Hell! I don't mean you, Alan. You deserve every winner you get! You've worked hard for your success.' He seemed placated.

I followed up, 'But if you're honest, doesn't it make you sick when guys like Roscoe and Perlman flash a few quid around and suddenly they've got a Champion Hurdler when they haven't been in the game five minutes?'

He shrugged. 'That's the way it is, Eddie, money talks.'

'Where did Perlman make his fortune then?'

'Nobody knows,' he fished in his pockets. 'Any smokes?' he asked.

'Go in and ask Perlman for a Havana, I'm sure he can afford it.'

'I would if I knew what he looked like.'

'What are you talking about?'

He smiled.

I thought I heard the door open. Harle spoke. 'What I could tell you about Perlman...'

A squeak from the door spring...no footsteps on the tiled floor but Harle became alert. He gave a follow-me nod and turned to leave. Whoever had come in stayed behind the dividing wall. As we moved he began walking in and almost collided with us. He was short, neatly dressed and apparently stone-cold sober, and wearing thick glasses.

He looked surprised. 'Oh sorry!' he said and stepped aside to let us pass. 'Have to be getting the old eyes tested again, Alan.'

Harle nodded at him and smiled. We went out into the corridor.

'Friend of yours?' I asked.

'I've seen him around the racecourse. I didn't know he was here.'

We walked. 'Anyway, what were you saying about Perlman?' I asked.

We reached the door of the Directors Suite. 'Some other time, Eddie, eh?

'Sure. What about Thursday, after racing?'

'Fine, yeah, great.'

His eyes told me his mind was elsewhere. 'Okay,' I said, 'I'll meet you by the weighing room.'

'Definitely. Look forward to it.'

I headed along the corridor and returned to the toilet. All three cubicle doors lay open. In the one Harle had used, I found a plastic bag containing an empty glass phial and a syringe. It had been taped to the base of the cistern

Carefully, I put the bag in my jacket pocket, then I had second thoughts and I taped it back where I'd found it, just in case Harle developed a suspicion that our meeting had not been an accident.

I made my way to the car thinking there might just be a buzz playing amateur detective. It didn't deliver the thrills of my riding days, but it would do for now.

Chapter 15

All morning, McCarthy's office number rang out. At last, at noon he answered the phone himself.

'Can't you afford a secretary?' I asked.

'Who is this?'

'Malloy.'

He wasn't pleased. 'What do you want?'

'Some information.'

'On what? Is it important?'

'It is to me.'

'Look, Eddie, I'm under severe pressure over yesterday's Champion Hurdle. The Jockey Club wants a report by one o'clock today. There's no way -'

'What about the Champion Hurdle?'

'Well, nothing...nothing about the race itself anyway. But heads will be rolling because the Queen Mum was embarrassed at the presentation when the owner failed to turn up. She didn't complain, but the executive saw it as a deliberate insult by this guy Perlman. I told you last night there was big meeting about it.'

'You did. But you didn't seem half so worried last night. What's happened?'

'What do you mean, what's happened? Nothing's bloody happened!'

'Mac, you're blustering away like an old turkey. How am I supposed to help you if you won't be straight with me?'

I pictured his face deflating slowly as he considered. He said, 'You must not repeat what I'm going to tell you.'

'Mac. I'm not a schoolboy. Out with it.'

He sighed long and low then said, 'We sent someone to interview Perlman this morning. He can't be found. His house, or at least the address we have registered, is empty and has been for a while according to the locals who also say they've never heard of Perlman.'

'Wasn't he checked through the normal procedures before your people cleared him as an owner?'

'Of course he was! Couldn't have been more impressive. A million quid's worth of country house in Wiltshire, Rolls in the drive, we even sent the same guy this morning who interviewed him initially. The place is deserted.'

'What happens now?' I asked.

'Arses get kicked, our clearance procedure gets tightened and we keep looking for Perlman.'

'Have you called Roscoe, his trainer?'

'Yes. He claims he's never met Perlman nor spoken to him. He communicates with the stable only by email and pays his bills prompt on the eighth of every month. Obviously we'll be looking further into that but we're under the cosh.'

'If Perlman actually exists, then I know someone who might tell me a few things about him if I buy enough champagne.'

'What do you mean "if he actually exists"?'

'Oh, come on, Mac, how many owners don't turn up when they win the Champion? How many have never met their trainer? The name's got to be an alias, maybe somebody who's been warned off in the past.'

'For what?'

'How would I know? But whatever it was, he might be doing it again in the name of Perlman.'

There was silence at the other end. I went on, 'Anyway, I'll see if I can find anything out from Alan Harle.'

'Roscoe's jockey?'

'More like Perlman's jockey. Can you remember if Roscoe took Harle on at the same time Perlman appeared on the scene?'

'No, but I can find out. Call me here this evening.'

'Listen, I said. 'I'll see Harle at Cheltenham today and ask if he wants to go partying tonight. You find out what you can about him and Roscoe and I'll try to ring you around ten.'

'Right.'

Chapter 16

I missed the first three races that afternoon, and despite the melancholy it had caused the previous day, I forced myself to watch the fourth from the infield. What doesn't kill you makes you stronger, right?

There wasn't a single space in the crowd lining the rails at the last fence so I wandered down to the starting gate as the big field of novices lined up.

Harle was booked to ride Craven King for Roscoe and I tried to pick him out as the jockeys pulled goggles down on tense faces. The horses pricked their ears and strained at clinking bits, some rolling their eyes till the whites showed.

In a moment of almost eerie silence, I panned and turned the wheel on my binoculars to focus on the packed stands and twenty thousand pairs of glinting lenses looked back at me.

'Come on!' yelled the starter, breaking the spell. The tape snapped up, the riders let out an inch of rein and the ground shook as nineteen novice 'chasers set off to prove who was champion.

I walked toward the centre of the course away from the commentary, away from people. That feeling of desolation was creeping back and I was determined to fight it. I decided to concentrate on Harle and Craven King in Louis Perlman's pea-green colours. They travelled well for the first circuit but began to tire as they approached the top of the hill for the last time.

Harle wasn't hard on the horse, but Craven King repaid him by taking a crashing fall at the third last. I kept my binoculars on them to see if Harle would rise but he didn't. Nor did the horse. I was a couple of hundred yards from the fence. I ran.

Two medics stooped over Harle, looking back and waving anxiously for the ambulance, which sped toward us along with the vet's Land Rover and the horse ambulance. Craven King lay on his side panting as one of the groundsmen crouched by his head murmuring words of comfort.

I ducked under the rails. 'Is he okay?' I asked as I reached Harle.

'Concussed, we think,' said one of the ambulance-men as the other undid Harle's chin strap and raised his goggles. I looked down at the unconscious figure. A stranger.

'That's not Alan Harle,' I said rather stupidly. One of the medics glanced up at me but didn't reply. I checked the weight-cloth on the prostrate horse: number 6. I opened my racecard: Craven King, trained by Roscoe and due to be ridden by Alan Harle.

The doctor and the vet arrived at the same time. I hunkered beside the doctor as he eased the jockey's helmet off, 'Is he going to be all right?'

His fingers explored the base of the skull as he lifted the boy's head and turned it gently. 'I think so. Just concussed.'

'Who is he?'

'Greene, Philip Greene,' the doctor said as he signaled for the stretcher.

They loaded Greene into the ambulance and it trundled off toward the stands. I turned, hoping the horse was okay, only to see them erecting screens to protect the sensibilities of racegoers as the vet put a pistol to Craven King's head and squeezed the trigger. The horse shuddered briefly and lay still.

A man in overalls pulled a length of chain from the interior of the horse ambulance and looped it round the horse's neck. He pressed a button to start the winch and the chain clattered and heaved as it hauled the body across the muddy hoofprints in the grass and up the ramp into the darkness.

I felt an old sorrow, knowing that Craven King's tearful groom would be walking to the horse-box with nothing but a bridle to hang in an empty stall.

The vet hurried toward the Land Rover, pushing the pistol into a pouch as he went and talking to a man I recognized as Mr. Skinner, also a vet.

Skinner was thermometer-thin from smoking too much and eating too little. Dark-haired, maybe forty-five, Skinner had the blue face of a twice-a-day shaver. He'd been renowned as a compulsive gambler when I'd been riding and it had cost him his job. He'd been a racecourse vet until the Jockey Club decided his obsession with betting was not in their best interests. How the hell had he got back into racing?

I fell into step beside him. He glanced across and didn't look pleased to see me. 'What was wrong with him?' I asked.

'Broken shoulder.'

'It's a tough business.'

'You should know,' he said sarcastically, still walking.

'Wasn't Alan Harle down to ride him?'

'I'm not the bloody starter,' he said as he climbed into the passenger seat. The driver revved the engine.

'Any chance of a lift?' I asked, but the only acknowledgement was a cloud of blue smoke from the exhaust as they pulled away.

Chapter 17

Back in the stands, I made my way through the betting ring to where the reps for SiS were based. SiS is the racing news service, which relays information and live pictures from the racecourse to betting shops.

One person stood in the booth, a pleasant-looking bloke with brown hair and a moustache. He was speaking on the phone. When he finished I introduced myself.

'Eddie, I remember you well. Good to see you back. I'm Grenville Riley'

'Thanks, Grenville. I'm sorry, have we met before?'

'No, but I know a lot of people who don't know me.'

I smiled and clutched his arm, 'Then you're the man I'm looking for.'

He smiled, 'What can I do for you?'

'Do you know if Alan Harle has a mount today?'

He didn't have to consult any papers. 'No, he's not riding today or tomorrow. He was booked for two today and three tomorrow, but his trainer told me he wouldn't be riding for the rest of the meeting.'

'Roscoe?'

'That's right.'

'Did he say why?'

'Said he had a bad case of flu.'

Bad case of a hangover, I thought. 'When did he tell you?'

'About an hour before the first.'

'Did he say who'd be replacing him?'

'Young Phil Greene. The poor bugger just got buried in the last.'

'I know. He's all right. I've spoken to the doctor.'

He nodded. 'Didn't look too good for the horse though,' he said.

'Broke his shoulder. He's been put down.'

He frowned and shook his head.

'I don't suppose you know any of the vets?' I asked.

'Yeah, most of them,' he pulled a box of small cigars from his coat pocket.

'Skinner isn't back on the Jockey Club payroll, is he?'

'You kidding? With his reputation?'

'Exactly, but he was out there with the vet when he put Craven King down.'

'I heard he works for Roscoe now.'

'Skinner does?'

'Yeah, private vet to the yard so they say. If Roscoe's got any brains he'll be watching what Skinner jabs those horses with.'

I smiled. Many a true word…

'Smoke?' he offered.

'No, thanks.'

'My only vice,' he smiled, clicking his lighter.

'You're lucky. Listen, is Greene Roscoe's usual standby?'

'Not really. I've noticed he's been riding one or two in the last few weeks for him but before that Roscoe used anyone who was available.'

His phone rang. I slapped his shoulder lightly. 'Thanks a lot, Grenville, you've been very helpful.'

He smiled, 'Anytime, Eddie, anytime.'

I considered going to the trainer's bar and asking Roscoe how my pal Alan was, but thought better of it; Roscoe might be smarter than he looked. A phone call to Harle's hotel could pay dividends.

'Can you put me through to Mister Alan Harle's room, please?'

'Do you know the room number, sir?'

'I'm sorry, I don't.'

'Hold on please.'

I held on.

'Hello, sir, I'm afraid Mister Harle left this morning.'

'When do you expect him back?'

'We don't sir.'

I hesitated. 'Did you see him leave?' I realized it would seem a strange question from her point of view. She stayed non-committal. 'I didn't start till three o'clock, sir.'

'Of course. Did he pay his bill?'

'I'm sorry, sir, we're not allowed to answer questions like that about guests.'

'I understand. Thanks for your help.'

I hung up and headed for the paddock.

Standing around by the weighing room, I waited for a homeward bound jockey. The race in progress on the other side of the stands had most people's attention.

A figure came through the glass doors and started across the lawn. My height, my age, dark hair still wet from the shower. Falling into step beside him as he passed I said, 'Hello, John.'

He glanced at me but kept going, walking like a man with plenty still to do. 'Hello, Eddie. Heard you were back.'

Jockeys are a strange breed. When you're one of them, it's like being a member of some élite regiment in which your colleagues will do almost anything for you. It's a profession where you put your life on the line every time you pull on a set of silks. Your next ride might be your last and everyone knows it, but nobody discusses it. In a company of men who are all taking the same risks, there is comfort and camaraderie.

But as soon as you're outside that circle, unless through injury, you become a stranger again, a man in the street, a passer-by. It is nothing intentional or preconceived, that's just the way it is. The way I'd known it would be. But it still hurt.

I didn't feel like spouting any small talk and I knew John wouldn't care to listen to any. Quickening my pace to match his I asked, 'Where's Alan Harle staying now, is he still in Trowbridge?'

'As far as I know he's got digs near Roscoe.'

'He trains in Lambourn, doesn't he?'

'That's right, Benson's old place.'

'Thanks John.' I slowed to let him walk on. He stopped and turned. 'Harle owe you money, too?' he asked.

'Er, yes, he does. You too?'

He shook his head. 'Not me, but he's had a few quid from some of the others.' There was satisfaction in the way he said it, pride at not being as soft as those who'd fallen for Harle's promises.

I nodded, trying to look resigned.

'I wouldn't worry too much,' he said. 'He's paid all of them off in the last month or so. Maybe you'll be next.'

'I hope so. Thanks.'

'Okay, Eddie.' He smiled and I saw that sliver of pride, that edge of arrogance morph into what looked like pity in his eyes, and it made me sick.

Chapter 18

I arrived home at dusk and cleared ashes from the grate, and gathered logs and firelighters from the kitchen.

Fire crackling, one drink finished, I poured another and went to the telephone. Seven o'clock; I couldn't be sure if McCarthy would be home from Cheltenham. Best give him half an hour before ringing and spend the time trying to contact Harle.

A friend in Lambourn told me Harle lived about a mile from Roscoe's stables and gave me his number.

Nobody answered. I dialled that number every five minutes for the next half hour and then my phone rang.

'Eddie!'

'Mac. What's up?'

'I've been trying to get through for bloody ages!'

'Sorry, Mac, I've been calling Alan Harle's number.'

'Why?'

'You know he didn't turn up at Cheltenham today?'

The brief silence told me that McCarthy didn't know. He said, 'I've had a monstrously busy day.'

'That means no, then?'

'I can't keep on top of every tiny incident!'

'Cool it, Mac. I know you can't, I don't expect you to. Just don't be so defensive with me. It wastes my time and yours.'

'As it happens I've spent half the damn day getting the information you asked me for.'

'Okay. Okay.' I wasn't going to win this one.

Half an hour later, under the March moon, I drove southeast on the A40. I had washed, shaved and changed into dark comfortable clothes topped with a flat cap. The night was cloudless, cold enough for frost. I pushed the heater up a notch to blow warm air around my ankles.

The conversation with McCarthy replayed in my mind.

Perlman's horses had been with Roscoe for just over a year. Before that, Roscoe had trained under permit, which meant he could train only horses owned by himself or his immediate family. In Roscoe's case, his father had provided the horses, one of which remained in training along with ten of Perlman's.

No other owner had horses with him.

Harle had never ridden for Roscoe while he was a permit trainer. He'd been appointed stable jockey within a month of Perlman's horses joining the yard. Some said Perlman simply felt philanthropic; others suspected that Harle would be easier to manipulate than a top jock if the yard had skulduggery in mind.

Harle appeared to be doing all right from the arrangement. McCarthy discovered Roscoe paid him a retainer of twenty grand on top of his normal percentage of winning prize money.

Harle's rides for other yards had dried to a trickle over the last three months; he rode almost exclusively for Perlman now. McCarthy had made zero headway in discovering Perlman's whereabouts or his identity. The RSS man who'd screened him remembered only that he was short and round and he didn't talk much.

I told McCarthy I planned to go looking for Harle tonight, at his house, 'What do you think?' I asked.

'I think you should be bloody careful. If Harle isn't answering his phone, then it's likely he is not at home. Do not break into his house. Do not break the law.'

'Mac, I'll call you in the morning.'

'Eddie!'

'Good night.'

But Mac had read me well. I'd spent eighteen months in jail for GBH on Kruger, and a man in that jail had taught me how to pick locks. A year after my release he had contacted me seeking a tip for the Grand National. The horse I gave him won at twenty-five-to-one.

Three days later, I took delivery of a beautiful set of bone-handled lock picks. Now, ten minutes from Harle's house, the leather pouch of picks lay on the passenger seat.

I reached to touch them, and smiled.

Chapter 19

Most of the training yards in Lambourn are fairly close together, but Roscoe's lay high on the downs about three miles from his nearest neighbour. The Rover moved smoothly over the recently resurfaced track.

The moon shone so bright I was tempted to drive without lights. Somewhere along here was Harle's cottage. I kept my speed down and my eyes sharp.

The cottage lay back from the road. Turning off the new tarmac onto dirt, I cut the engine and killed the lights as the car rolled to a halt. The cottage was small, fronted by a neat lawn. Between two chimneys, the roof sparkled under a layer of frost. The place was in darkness.

Skirting the lawn, I walked up the centre path to the front door, which had a large brass knocker in the shape of a bull's head. The knocker hammered and bounced on the brass plate... silence, then, high in the trees behind me, an owl hooted.

Below the window ran a yard-wide strip of soil. Keeping my boots on the path, I leaned on the windowsill. My moonlit reflection loomed toward me as my nose went to the glass. The curtains were open but I could see nothing inside.

I returned to the car for my flashlight and lock picks then followed the path to the rear of the house.

There was one window and a door. I tried the handle. Taking the slimmest metal rod, I bent to the keyhole, slid it into the lock and silently counted. At eight, it clicked open. Not bad for an amateur.

The living room looked cluttered and untidy in the sweep of the flashlight beam. Newspapers littered the floor, a footstool lay on its side by the fireplace, two fat fireside chairs and a short couch faced different ways.

On the wall opposite the window, a glass display cabinet held a few trophies. Framed photographs hung on all walls: Harle on horses, Harle jumping, Harle galloping, Harle with friends – all Harle's pictures were here, but he wasn't.

I searched both bedrooms but found only an unopened pack of condoms.

In the living room again, I considered switching on the lights. It should have been safe but I felt nervy.

Best not.

Against the wall, opposite the fire, stood a big roll-top desk. The brass catch took a few seconds to click open. The wood-ribbed cover rode up quietly, revealing a broad writing surface and eight pigeonholes. Sitting in the leather-seated revolving chair, I went through Harle's stuff, and found four foil-wrapped syringes, which taught me nothing new.

Leaving by the back door, I relocked it.

The moon hung lower in the sky but still bright. Frost formed on the lawn. The cottage seemed to stare at me in cold, composed silence, pleased that it hadn't given up any secrets.

Harle stayed missing. I spent the next week looking for him, visiting racecourses, speaking to mutual friends - or should I say acquaintances, as it soon became clear that Harle had no real friends.

Nor had he any family. I remembered he'd been an orphan but thought there might be a brother or sister somewhere. If so, nobody I spoke to knew of them. The press had shown an initial interest in Harle's disappearance, but Roscoe told them Harle had walked out on him after an argument. He didn't know where he'd gone and 'frankly, didn't care'.

Someone did not want Harle found. McCarthy had wound himself up so tight his usual bass voice often hit soprano when we spoke on the phone. He told me he could fund just seven more days of my 'investigation'.

There was only one more thing I could think of to try to trace Harle, one last card. On the Saturday, I went to Ascot and played it.

Chapter 20

At Ascot it was raining. I sat in the bar. Next to me, munching her way contentedly through a smoked salmon sandwich, sat a regular race-goer known among jockeys as Walk-Over Wendy.

Wendy washed down the sandwich with champagne. I'd bought both. She was plumpish, fair-haired and pretty. No more than twenty, she didn't have the highest IQ in the world but she was always happy and obliging. Ex-jockeys, though, didn't qualify. She liked to stay in fashion that way. Has-beens got nothing except information, for which they had to pay.

She finished eating and wiped her hands and mouth with a paper napkin. Cocking her head to one side in what she imagined to be a coy pose, her eyes sparkled as she said, 'What is it you're after?'

'I want to know if Alan Harle has a girlfriend at the moment.'

She frowned. 'Oh, I haven't seen Alan for ages, weeks…I'd forgotten all about him.'

'Do you know where he is?'

She shook her head, looking serious. 'I haven't seen him since, when was it? Yes, Haydock, Greenall Whitley day.'

The girl's life calendar didn't run on dates, she tracked time by the passing of big races.

'Didn't you see him at Cheltenham?' I asked.

The smile returned to her chubby cheeks. 'Afraid not, I had Gary all to myself at the festival. I don't remember much else.'

She looked out of the window into the distance and smiled at the memory. 'Though he's the same as all you other jockeys, after sex,' she said, 'he just pats you on the neck and says, "Good girl! Good girl!"'

She grinned at me mischievously to see if I'd got the joke and I smiled and nodded, making her look very pleased with herself.

'Do you know if Alan was seeing someone when you last spoke to him?'

'Yes, he was.'

'Did he tell you her name?'

'He didn't tell me anything,' coy again. I poured champagne into her glass and she drank it. I waited.

'She told me,' Wendy said.

'Who's she?'

'Her name's Priscilla. Prissy by name but not by nature.'

'Do you know where she lives?'

'London. She goes racing quite a lot, met Alan at Kempton, I think. She said he was a real modern guy.'

I knew what she meant. 'Is Priscilla a friend of yours?'

'Mmmm, sort of. I've seen her around the tracks a few times.'

'Have you got her phone number?'

She lowered her head and puckered up her nose. 'I didn't think you were one for second-hand goods, Eddie.'

'Strictly business.'

'I'll bet. You want to take up where Alan left off, don't you?'

'How do you know he has left off?'

She sat up straight and looked serious. Maybe I was sounding too much like an interrogator.

'I don't. I was just thinking, if Alan hasn't been around for a few weeks…well.'

'Look, Wendy, I've got to get in touch with Alan. It's a business agreement we need to tie up and I'm under pressure.'

'Okay, okay! Keep your knickers on!' She dug around in her bag till she found her little black book and gave me Priscilla's number.

PRISCILLA WAS NOT enthusiastic about discussing Alan Harle. Cold would be a fair description. When I said I had some good news for him, her attitude changed. She agreed to meet me that evening in a pub near her flat.

'How will I know you?' she asked.

'What do you drink?' I said.

'Pernod and blackcurrant.'

'I'll order one. It'll be on the table beside me.'

Chapter 21

The lounge was quiet. Three men and two women sat drinking at the bar. I chose a table in the corner. The girl saw me when she came in and walked over without hesitating. The barman nodded and smiled at her.

She was tall, about five-nine, and would have dwarfed Harle. Her dyed black hair swung at shoulder length. She wore light makeup, and tight trousers as black as her hair. Her heels were three-inch spikes and a short red leather jacket hung on her skinny torso. She was at least ten years older than Wendy.

I stood up as she reached the table and held out my hand.

'Eddie Malloy,' I said.

She touched her fingers against mine. 'I'm Priscilla,' she said, with a false huskiness, and sat opposite me. I pushed the glass with the dark liquid toward her. She didn't say thanks, just sipped, half-sucked.

'You're looking for Alan?' she asked.

'That's right.'

'Does he owe you money?'

'No, but it'll cost him money if I don't find him.'

'How come?'

'A business deal we're working on. I need to see him to tie it up.'

'Not the smartest guy in the world, are you?' She drank again and looked coldly at me.

'Why's that?' I asked.

'Taking Alan Harle on as a business partner.'

'What's wrong with him?'

'He's a lying, scheming, unreliable bastard.'

I shrugged. 'Nobody's perfect. Can I ask when you last saw him?'

'What kind of deal is it anyway?'

'I can't tell you. Ask Alan.'

'No, thanks, I'm finished with him,' she sipped Pernod.

'What's he done to upset you?'

'More like what hasn't he done. He never turns up when he says he will, never rings, never buys you what he promises, screws around…' she hunched forward glaring at me as though it was my fault.

'So you'd fallen out?' I asked.

'Not as far as he was concerned, but as far as it goes with me we're finished,' she sat back folding her arms.

'Can you remember when you last saw him?'

'I haven't seen him since before Cheltenham.'

'And he hasn't phoned?'

She stared at me, weighing things up. Finally, she said, 'He phoned two days ago.'

'From where?' I asked.

'Fuck 'em Farm?' she waited for my reaction.

'Not a place I'm familiar with.'

'You sure? Never been to an orgy or anything there with your mate Alan?' her eyes widened as the anger built.

'Priscilla, I haven't a clue what you're talking about. What did Alan say?'

She stared at me. 'He said, "Help me, Priss, I'm at Fuck 'em farm." Then I heard him laughing and hung up on the bastard.'

'You sure he was laughing?'

She glared, maybe at the memory or at me questioning her interpretation of the call. She leant at me aggressively. 'Listen, he was screeching with laughter. Fuck 'em farm! Big joke, eh? He always thought practical jokes were funny. I didn't and that just egged him on with his piss-taking.'

'Why would he be laughing after asking you for help?'

'I'm telling you! That's what it sounded like to me. He was always taking the piss. Probably in bed with some bitch and thought he'd have a laugh at my expense.'

'Supposing he was in trouble?'

She looked uncomfortable. 'What kind of trouble?'

'I don't know. You said he was screeching?'

'He was…It sounded, well you know, that high-pitched kind of…'

'Did he sound scared?'

She hesitated then said, 'I suppose, if I didn't know what he could be like, I'd have taken it as sounding scared,' her face hardened again, 'is this something to do with this deal you mentioned? Has it got him in trouble?'

'It can't have done, it's a straightforward, upfront property deal. All above board.'

'He never did anything straightforward in his life,' she said, slugging down the rest of her drink. I pointed to her glass. 'Same again?'

She pushed the glass away, 'No, thanks.'

'Did Alan talk much about his job with Basil Roscoe?'

'I think you are not understanding our relationship, Mister Malloy. I didn't give a toss about his job with Roscoe so why would I ask about it?'

'And he didn't say anything about it?'

'If he did, he'd have got the rubber ear from me so I wouldn't remember.'

'You ever hear him mention a guy called Perlman?'

'Nope. You think these people have got something against him?'

I sighed, 'I don't know.'

'What are you going to do now then?'

'Try and find out where Fuck' em Farm is.'

For the first time, she smiled. 'You're serious?'

I shrugged. 'I've got nothing else to do, especially if this deal falls through.'

'So you think Alan will still be at this Fuck 'em Farm, eh? Like, mucking out the whores or something?'

It was my turn to smile. 'Maybe.'

'Good luck with that and do let me know if you find him so I can twist his little balls off,' she got up.

I looked at her. 'I thought you were worried?'

Hoisting her bag strap on the shoulder of the red leather jacket, she looked down at me and said, 'Life's too short.'

Chapter 22

Fuck 'em Farm. A nickname for some brothel perhaps? If Harle knew it by that name, other jocks would too. Most jockeys are highly sexed. Psychologists will tell you it's all linked to the danger and adrenaline and the 'today-could-be-my-last' culture. I rang three riders that I knew had the same appetite for women as Harle did. None of them had heard of the place.

I sat back and did some physical and mental head scratching. Supposing Harle had been abducted. I had to assume it was by the two men who'd smashed up Bergmark, blinded Rask, and maybe killed Danny Gordon.

Harle was last seen at Cheltenham races. If these guys wanted to get him, they'd have known they could intercept him on the way home from the racecourse. Harle lived in Lambourn but would have intended to stay over in Cheltenham for the three-day race meeting. I knew he hadn't because the receptionist had told me he'd checked out of his hotel on the Wednesday morning, the second day of the meeting.

Whatever spooked him must have happened at the party on the Tuesday night, or after it.

Assuming he ran for home after leaving the hotel, he'd have travelled southwest toward Lambourn. The area around Cheltenham had its share of quiet country roads and most jockeys knew the shortcuts. I needed a map to try to figure out his route. I headed for Cheltenham to buy one.

Driving into town, I saw the Library sign and quickly turned left. They'd have maps, and parking spaces. The smiling young man at the desk said they didn't have 'your standard road map', but the reference section did have ordnance survey maps for the UK.

Juggling a plastic cup of very hot coffee from the machine, I sat with OS Map 163, Cheltenham and Cirencester. I smoothed out the area to the southwest: the OS map charted every road, right down to a pig track. From the centre of town, I searched the possible routes Harle would have taken if he'd planned to go home. Three cups of coffee later I was bleary-eyed and no wiser, and I chided myself on the basis that I hadn't a bloody clue what I was doing.

They could have grabbed Harle anywhere; stepping into the car at The Duke's Hotel, arriving home at his remote place in Lambourn, or any point in between. I got up and began folding the map to hand it back when something caught my eye, an area to the east of Cheltenham coloured green on the map, shaped like a pair of thin legs wearing different size boots - Puckham Woods. Slowly, I sat down keeping my eyes fixed on the spot in case I lost it. Opening the map again, I traced with my finger a narrow dead-end road on the North West side of Puckham Woods. Where the road finished lay some small closely grouped buildings with the name Puckham Farm.

From the throat of a desperate man to the ear of an angry woman, how easily misheard? I noted the road numbers and directions and hurried to the car.

It was half an hour's drive away. Just after two o'clock, I drove through the last village on the map and out into open country. The road climbed and the surface worsened. Bushes on the overgrown verges scratched at the Rover as we sped along. In those twenty minutes, a blue van passed me going in the opposite direction, the only vehicle I saw.

It began to rain.

I turned at the no-through-road sign, knowing the farm should be at the end of it. The track dipped in the first fifty yards. It ran between trees and broken rusted barbed wire fencing. The tyres sloshed through the rain-softened surface.

The fields on either side lay empty. The woods grew denser the farther I went until I seemed to be in a tunnel. I broke out into daylight and a farmyard, so suddenly that I ran past and had to reverse to a point where I faced what looked like the main house.

I sat watching for signs of life. The yard, rutted and puddled, was about the size of two tennis courts and seemed to envelop the house in a grasping semi-circle of black muck.

The dark grey stone walls were pitted and dirty. Mustard-coloured curtains sagged in tatters behind the two windows, one of which had a smashed pane. The other was badly cracked. What remained of the glass was filthy.

Broken guttering channeled a thick rainwater stream onto the soil, pushing up a little active volcano of mud. Enough grey tiles were missing to make the roof look like a big wet crossword puzzle.

As I left the car, the wind snatched at my collar and rain peppered my face. I hurried toward the house, hands deep in pockets, gathering my jacket close around me. I stood at the door. The dark green surface was cracked and blistered, tiny pools overflowing from the open paint bubbles.

I knocked hard.

Nobody came.

I tried the handle. It turned just half an inch.

Going to the window, I squatted to look through the hole in the pane, but the dirty curtains did their job. In the glass I caught the reflection of something moving quickly behind me. There was a slapping, rustling sound. I spun to see a plastic rubbish sack blowing across the yard.

I realized I was holding my breath.

My pulse pounded.

The black muck sucked at my boots as I skirted the side of the building, trying to be cautious. I'd adopt the lost tourist routine if anyone was around but it wouldn't fit with the way I slunk along, so I straightened and strode out boldly till I reached the yard behind the house.

A barn-type block with a huge brown door joined the house at the far side. The door was fixed on runners top and bottom and I grasped the handle and leaned hard, pulling. It wouldn't budge. Using both hands, I tried again: solid. For a derelict property, things seemed pretty secure. I turned away, wondering what to do next, when I heard a noise. I stopped…it came again…moaning, like an animal, long and low and guttural.

Whatever was making the noise was behind the sliding door. I looked up at two small windows, too high to reach.

Along the wall beneath a broken drainpipe, a metal beer barrel lay in the gutter. I hauled it out, rolled it through the oozing soil toward the big door.

By the time I got the barrel across the yard, I was mud-splattered and soaked. My hair clung flat and rivers of water ran down my face and neck, inside my collar. My clothes and hands were filthy, and though my jacket was waterproof, the rain streamed from it onto my thighs till my trousers stuck to my skin.

I climbed up on the barrel with the thought that whatever was in here would get the fright of its life when it saw me. It also occurred to me that if anyone came out of the house now it was going to be tough pleading the lost tourist routine.

My hands clasped the ledge and I looked in…three stalls. Metal bars ran from the ceiling into the front wall of each. From the bars of the middle stall hung a cobwebbed hay net.

The moan again, long and painful and, I decided, human. I jumped down, arcs of mud splashing from my feet as I landed.

I looked more closely at the lock. The keyhole was large and empty. I ran to the car for the lockpicks.

The mechanism, though heavy, was crude and it clicked open in a few seconds.

Leaning back on my heels I pulled at the handle and the door trundled on its runners, noisy as a train in a tunnel. I took an anxious look round the yard before going inside.

The smell.

It grew worse as I left the fresh air, old and stale and dank. I followed the stench to the end box where my awareness of bad smells ceased, where my breathing stopped in shock and my eyelids forgot to blink, where, on a foul bed of straw, I found what remained of Alan Harle.

Chapter 23

He lay curled up against the inside of the wall below a torn hay net, naked, his flesh filthy with smeared shit. His knees were pulled up to his chin and his head lay in a patch of stale vomit and dirty straw which clung to his face and hair. From the bars above him hung a heavy dog chain, fastened around his neck. He moaned.

Kneeling beside him I reached to tilt his head toward me and what little light there was. The shock was fading, my senses regrouping and I gagged at the stench and turned away quickly, thinking I was going to be sick, but I held it down. He felt my hands on his shoulders and tried weakly to resist, drawing himself closer to the wall. I eased his head up and he whimpered. Small islands of flaked whitewash stuck to his forehead and a stream of saliva ran from the corner of his mouth down his chin. His eyes stayed closed.

'Alan!' I whispered it and didn't know why. No response. I slowly lifted the heavy links. He flinched.

The flesh was a raw ring. I supported his head with my left hand while my fingers followed the links to the nape of his neck. I found a small padlock below his left ear.

Easing the chain round as best I could without hurting him further, I picked the lock. The chain end slid from his neck and lay in the straw. I thumbed his eyelids open and saw the eyes of a sick waxwork dummy; pinhead pupils, the whites gone yellowish green. A sore festered in the corner of his right eye so I couldn't open it fully.

His knees were still drawn up and I turned him gently to try to straighten his legs. The movement released a potent puff of that rancid smell and I had to hurry to the door to suck fresh air.

His right thigh and lower left leg were badly scarred, but they were old wounds from pin and plate insertions after fractures. Shuffling through the straw, I manipulated his legs and feet one by one, watching his face for signs of pain. There was none, his joints moved freely. I worked back up checking arms and wrists.

The skin on the inside of his left arm at the elbow joint was black with bruising and needle punctures, some of which had scabbed.

His ribs were in one piece, which was easy to see because they lay like a toast rack. I doubted if he'd been fed anything but heroin since his capture.

So, no bones broken, but he was in a bad way. I decided to get him to hospital and worry on the journey about the story I would tell. I checked the yard; the last thing I wanted with my hands full of invalid was to walk into the men who'd done this to him.

The place was deserted. I opened the rear door of the car and went back for Alan.

I scooped him up and tried to support his head as I walked to the door but it hung over the crook of my elbow. His lower legs dangled and swung. I stopped and looked out again before going into the yard. It was raining so hard I could barely see the car.

Wading through mud, I tried cradling him from the worst but the big drops pelted his flesh and ran in rivers through the stinking brown smears, streaming down the vee shape of his rib cage and gathering in his crotch till a pool formed, covering his pubic hair.

When I arrived at the Casualty Department of Cheltenham General Hospital, steam rose from my clothes and the rank smell filled the car.

I spoke to the receptionist. Two orderlies came with me and slid Harle onto a stretcher, grimacing as they did so. They covered him with a blanket and hurried inside.

The triage nurse wanted particulars. I told her his name was Jim Malloy and that he was my brother, a heroin addict who'd been taking treatment at home but had disappeared weeks ago. I said I'd been searching for him and had just found him in a filthy squat, deserted by his friends.

She offered sympathy and said they'd do their best for him, but they'd have to inform the police of his condition. I told her to save herself a call as I was going to the police station next to update them, having originally reported him missing. She believed me.

I promised to visit next day, and I assured the nurse I would bathe and change, as she suggested, as soon as I got home.

DESPITE THE STINK in the car and my filthy, wet clothes, I felt a reassuring sense of achievement as I drove home. I had done what I'd been hired to do, or had at least partly done it, I'd tracked a man down. So, where did Kruger's men go next? Could Roscoe help me find them or should I put my name about as the one who rescued Harle and let them come straight for me?

The prospect of being the fox to their hounds didn't enthrall me, but it didn't petrify me either. They'd had the advantage of surprise over past victims but I would know they were coming. I was also angry that those two could go around maiming and killing without fear of retribution. They were due a little of what they'd been dishing out.

I decided to let slip on the grapevine what I'd done and take my chances when they came looking.

A visit to Roscoe's might prove fruitful though, especially if I called when he wasn't at home. I would have to plan it.

But first, I decided, a chat with Danny Gordon's widow might throw up something. I'd go and see her next morning.

Chapter 24

I called the hospital before leaving for Newmarket and learned Harle had suffered "a restless night". Not half as restless as his previous three or four, I'd bet. I rang McCarthy and told him about Harle.

'That's fantastic!' McCarthy said.

'Fantastic?'

'Well, you know what I mean. It's bloody grim what they did to him, appalling. But it looks like we have a proper breakthrough at last, doesn't it?'

'Well, we've got a man who was seen once with the pair that you think did Danny Gordon in. The cops would call it circumstantial, but it's all we've got it.'

'Talking of the police, did the hospital contact them?'

'I asked them not to,' I said.

'Why?'

'Because they'll drag things out for months or years. Look at Danny Gordon's death, are they any further along with that?'

'It's only been three months, Eddie.'

'I'll tell Mrs. Gordon that, shall I? I'm heading down to see her.'

He sighed. 'Look, the less the police get involved, the better for us too. We don't want the publicity. But we've got a relationship to maintain with them so we need to strike a balance.'

'You think Harle is going to tell on these guys? Did Bergmark? Did Rask? Come on Mac.'

'I know but, still-'

'Listen, would it be easier for you if I just didn't call you till I've definitely got something?' I asked.

'No. I need to be on top of what's happening. Just, well, just be a bit more circumspect.'

'What does that mean Mac, circumspect?'

'Er, discreet.'

'Why didn't you say discreet? I understand most short words. I'm only an ex-jockey, two syllables is my limit.'

'You're a lot smarter than you make out, Mister Malloy.'

'I hope you're right. Now can you find Mrs. Gordon's address for me?'

MRS. GORDON LIVED in an upstairs flat off the High Street, but either she was out or she wasn't answering the door to strangers. I turned to go down the stairs just as a plain, tired looking woman began climbing them.

She stopped and stared up at me, pulling her coat closed over what looked like a track suit. 'Morning,' I said, 'I'm looking for Mrs. Gordon.'

'I'm Mrs. Gordon.'

I walked down to where she stood and held out my hand. 'My name's Eddie Malloy. I wondered if you'd mind answering a few questions about Danny.'

She stared, frowning, unsure. I continued, 'I think the people who killed him are trying to do the same to a friend of mine.'

Still holding her coat closed, she reached out tentatively with the other hand and shook mine. 'Did you say your name was Malloy?'

I nodded, 'Eddie Malloy.'

'Are you the man who found Danny?'

My thoughts returned to that freezing morning. 'That's right.'

The frown disappeared, but she seemed to stoop as a long sigh deflated her. 'Come upstairs,' she said.

Mrs. Gordon put the kettle on a beat-up old stove, then moved around silently, picking up kids' clothes and toys and sweet wrappers. I sat in a chair by the unlit gas fire, on top of which was a half-empty Valium bottle.

'Milk and sugar?'

'Just black, please.'

She brought two mugs. Mine had a greasy smudge on the rim and I turned it and drank from the other side. Mrs. Gordon sat opposite me, still in her coat, and pushed the light brown hair from her face. She wore no make-up and sipped her coffee carefully to avoid a cold-sore on her top lip. Her hazel eyes should have been her best feature, but they looked lifeless.

'I'm sorry about Danny.' I said quietly.

She nodded, but said nothing. 'It takes a lot of getting over.' I said, feeling awkward and ashamed that I didn't want to be there.

'What was he like when you found him?'

I shifted, uncomfortable, uncertain.

She said, 'I never went to see him, to see his body. I wanted to, but they said it would be best if his father identified him. I lie awake now knowing I should have seen him…to say goodbye…I miss him.'

'I'm sorry,' I said.

'Tell me what he was like?' she persisted. Her eyes were vacant. I didn't know if her thoughts were on that frozen golf course or if the Valium had dulled her mind. And I didn't know how to answer.

'He was…' I began. 'It was very cold that morning…He was…white. The frost made him look peaceful.' I waited. She stared, but looked less tense. 'There wasn't much blood, was there?' she asked.

If I painted too bland a picture, she might berate herself more for not going to see the body. But I couldn't describe to her the real horror of it. 'No, there was very little,' I said, which was no lie as nearly all the blood had drained onto the frosty ground.

She shook her head, still miles away.

'I think you did the right thing,' I said. 'He wouldn't have wanted you to see him. He looked very calm, as though he'd made his peace with the world.'

'You think so?'

'I'm sure he did.'

She pursed her lips. 'You didn't find any letters in his pockets or anything?'

I shook my head, reluctant to tell her I hadn't looked.

'I thought he might have written one to me…to…to say goodbye?'

I nodded, desperately sorry for her. All the more so because the Valium seemed to have killed the emotion she should have been showing as she spoke. The drugs just channeled her feelings into a monotone.

'I asked the police,' she went on, 'but they said they didn't find anything either. They're fucking useless.'

The curse, completely lacking in anger, took me by surprise. She continued in that flat voice. 'I told them who killed him but they did nothing.'

'Who killed him?' I asked.

'I don't know exactly who did it but I know who had him killed.'

'Who?'

'Two men called Rask and Bergmark.'

I concentrated on keeping the excitement out of my voice. 'Why?'

'They'd been trying to blackmail him and Danny got his friends to beat them up.'

'Which friends?'

'I don't know. Danny didn't tell me their names.'

'Why were Bergmark and Rask trying to blackmail Danny?'

She sipped coffee. 'They said Danny had been sacked from the Tote in Sweden for trying to steal money. They said they'd tell his boss at the Lab.'

'What did they want from him?'

'They wanted him to cover up samples from doped horses.'

'Why?'

'They were doping them with a trainer… betting them.'

She reached in her coat pocket, brought out a packet of cigarettes and lit one.

'Any idea who the trainer was?' She shook her head and drew on the cigarette.

'You told the police all this?'

She nodded. 'They asked me for evidence, blackmail notes. I didn't have any. They told me they took Rask and Bergmark in for questioning but had to let them go. Useless bastards.' She flicked ash onto the carpet.

'You definitely don't know the trainer who was involved with Bergmark and Rask?'

'No.'

'And you've no idea who Danny's friends were, the ones who beat up Bergmark and Rask?'

She shook her head.

'Did anyone tell you Rask was dead?' I offered by way of compensation.

'Good. How did he die?'

'The police say he hung himself.'

I saw the first trace of a smile. 'Is there anything else you can tell me?' I asked.

'I've told you everything, the same as I told the police, only they didn't do anything about it.'

I wrote my phone number on her cigarette packet. 'Would you get in touch with me if anything else comes up?'

She nodded. 'Okay.'

Leaving the mug of half-finished coffee on the floor, I got to my feet. She pushed herself out of the chair. 'Who's the friend you're trying to help?' she asked.

'He's a jockey.'

'Was he involved with Rask and Bergmark too?'

'I don't think so. I'm not really able to question him just now.'

'You talk like a cop.'

I smiled. 'I'm not, but I know what you mean.'

She led the way to the door and opened it. 'If you find who killed Danny, will you come back and tell me?'

'Sure.'

'Do you have anyone to help you?' she said.

'One or two people.'

'Do you think you will catch them?'

I shrugged. 'I'll try.'

She stared at me and, finally, her tears welled. Reaching with one hand, I gently squeezed her arm then turned and left.

It was a relief to be in the sun.

On the long drive home, I tried to analyze the new information. When she'd started talking, I'd thought I had struck a rich seam, but trying to sift the nuggets from the dirt didn't clarify things a hell of a lot.

Danny was killed after the Swedes had been attacked. Had they organized it as revenge? If, as Mrs. Gordon claimed, Danny had arranged the assaults on the Swedes, then revenge made little sense, with both of them so afraid and so vulnerable. I began to feel some sympathy for the police.

Who was the trainer involved with Bergmark and Rask in the doping plot Mrs. Gordon had told me about? Roscoe? If he was tied up with Kruger in developing the perfect dope, then there'd be no need for an accomplice in the Forensic Lab since it would be pointless trying to hide what was undetectable. Or had they needed Danny to help get it to that stage?

A visit to Roscoe's had to be next, but I decided in the meantime to throw my hat visibly into the ring by letting it be known on the racecourse that Harle was back in circulation. That would flush out Kruger's boys.

Chapter 25

I phoned McCarthy and told him Mrs. Gordon's story. He said he'd check it with the police. When he learned I planned to leak a story about Harle as bait for the hit men he didn't like it.

He said the press would pick up on Harle and start digging dirt. I persuaded him it was a chance we had to take. I phoned Priscilla in London.

'Hello?'

I recognized the fake husky voice. 'Priscilla, it's Eddie Malloy.' She thought for a few seconds and I prompted her. 'Remember? I was looking for Alan.'

'Oh, yes, did you find him?'

'He's in Cyprus.'

'Cyprus! What the hell is he doing there?'

'He says he's sick of the British weather and he's going to ride there for the rest of the season. Don't be upset, he's thinking about you. He sends his regards.'

'I'll regards the bastard. He could at least have sent me some money.'

'I think he's a bit broke just at the moment.'

'Have you got an address for him?'

'No, I'm sorry, I haven't.' She grunted with anger and frustration and I guessed things were about to start getting thrown around her flat. 'I thought you'd appreciate the call anyway, Priscilla. If you do bump into Alan in the future, remember to mention my name. Goodbye.'

I hung up on one sore lady now guaranteed to blab around the racecourse how Alan had done her wrong and how Eddie Malloy had found him in Cyprus. It was just a matter of time till I received a visit.

I checked the Racing Calendar. Wetherby had a two-day meeting the following Tuesday and Wednesday and Roscoe had horses entered on both days, which meant he'd be away for at least one night, possibly two.

There was a strong chance his house would be deserted on the Tuesday night, just ripe for a visit with the lock-picks.

That evening I visited Harle in hospital. He was in the intensive-care ward heavily sedated and a doctor told me it would be days before he'd be well enough to talk sensibly. I said I'd come back soon.

Driving home, it occurred to me how vulnerable Harle was, lying almost comatose in a hospital bed. If the heavies discovered where he was, they wouldn't have too much trouble finishing him off.

But they'd have to find him first.

The smug smile still on my face, it dawned on me how stupid I'd been. Pulling over, I switched off the engine. There had been racing at Ascot that afternoon, a London track. Chances were Priscilla had been there mouthing off about Harle being in Cyprus. As soon as our friends tagged onto this, they'd be hotfooting it to Puckham Farm to check on Harle.

They knew his condition, knew he was beyond escape. If he wasn't there, he'd been rescued and if he'd been rescued, there was only one place for him: hospital.

And not just any hospital, the nearest hospital, the one I'd just left.

I turned back toward Cheltenham. If Harle stayed in that bed another twenty-four hours, he might leave it in a box. I'd put him in hospital, in danger, now I had to get him out.

I told the ward sister I felt bad about leaving my brother alone and could I stay with him until nightfall.

'Absolutely not,' she said. I pleaded, told her our mother was desperately worried about him but she wouldn't budge.

I couldn't get in but didn't doubt that Kruger's men would find a way, possibly a violent one, to gain access and kill him or abduct him again. His life was in danger and it was my fault for being so stupid as to make that call to Priscilla. I should never have done it without ensuring Harle was protected and, much as I hated the idea, the only way to make amends was to call in the police.

I'd been so used to going it alone, so determined to get the evidence needed to regain my licence that I didn't want others involved. Especially the police. I was an ex-jailbird; they were certain to treat me with suspicion. I was afraid they'd ask The Jockey Club to keep me out of it.

I tried to think of an alternative but with the exception of sitting outside the hospital with a gun, there wasn't one.

Best get McCarthy to make the call. I went looking for a phone-box, then the doubts set in again. Mac would be too anxious about how this would reflect on the Jockey Club. He'd probably want to have a meeting and prepare a statement before contacting the cops. I couldn't risk any delay.

I headed for the police station.

Chapter 26

A young female constable showed me into a small, brightly lit room and said that DS Cranley would be along soon. Ten minutes later, he came in with his notebook. About forty years old, five seven, twenty pounds overweight, reddish-fair hair, bad acne and an attitude that said he'd rather be doing something else.

He approached the desk. 'Mister Malloy?'

'That's right.' I offered my hand and he shook it reluctantly as he sat down. 'Detective Sergeant Cranley.'

'Pleased to meet you.'

He grunted. 'Now what's this about some friend of yours in trouble?'

'Alan Harle. He's a jockey. At the moment, he's lying comatose in hospital. Somebody's trying to kill him.'

He pursed his lips and stared at me. 'Who's this somebody?'

'I'm not sure.'

'Well, who do you think it is, Mister Malloy?'

This was going to be a long haul. 'I think a man called Gerard Kruger is behind it.'

'And why would this Mister Kruger want to kill your friend?'

'I don't know. That's what I was trying to discover when I found Harle.'

'Found him where?' he was making notes. I told him what happened at Puckham Farm.

'Why didn't you call us?'

'My first thought was to get him to hospital.'

'Well, what was your second thought?'

I bit back a sarcastic reply. 'Look, I only found him yesterday. I'm here now telling you about it. He needs some protection.'

'That's hardly for you to decide.'

'Well, who the hell is it for, then? Harle's life is in danger.'

He stared at me, frowning so hard his acne joined up. 'Keep your voice down, Mister Malloy, you're getting yourself all upset.'

'Look, Sergeant-'

'Detective Sergeant.'

'Listen, the guys who are after Harle-'

'I thought you said it was one man, a Mister Kruger?'

'He uses two hit men and they've already killed one man and maimed two others.'

'You've got evidence of this, I suppose?'

'No, I haven't.'

He held the pen horizontal above his notepad and stared at me as though I'd crawled from some hole. Then he dropped the pen from height and crossed his arms. 'You're sitting there naming names, accusing people of murder without any evidence? What are you all about, Mister Malloy?'

'If I had evidence I'd be talking to somebody higher up than you.'

Unfolding his arms, he clasped his hands. 'Is that right? And just who would you be talking to?'

I sighed in frustration. 'Look, I'm sorry, I shouldn't have said that. I'm worried about my friend. Everything I've told you is true. I'm just trying to convince you he's in real danger, that he needs some protection. Send one of your men to see what sort of state he's in if you don't believe me.'

'And you don't know why these people are after him?'

'No.'

'How did you know where to find him?'

'His girlfriend had an idea where he was.'

'Does she know who's trying to kill him?'

'She doesn't even know he's been injured.'

'A very secretive fellow, this Mister Harle.'

I put my elbows on the desk and leaned toward him. 'Detective Sergeant Cranley, the two men I told you about might very well be walking through the door of the hospital right now. I've signed Harle in under a false name, but they're clever and they won't take long to find him and when they do they'll probably finish what they started.'

He clenched his jaw and his nostrils flared.

'If Harle dies before your men get there, I will kick up the biggest stink in the press that you have ever smelt. My visit here is logged at your main desk. You yourself have made notes of what I'm here to ask for. It's your choice. If I turn out to be wrong on this, at least it won't cost a life. If you're wrong, it will.'

His face reddened and his next words came through almost gritted teeth. 'Which hospital is he in?'

'Cheltenham General.'

'Ward?'

'Intensive care, under the name James Malloy.'

He got up, almost kicking the chair aside. 'Wait here,' he growled.

Twenty minutes later, he came back looking no calmer. He didn't bother sitting down. 'Have you given your address and phone number to the desk sergeant?'

I nodded.

'You can go,' he said.

I stood up. 'What about Harle?'

'What about him?'

'Are you going to give him protection?'

'I don't discuss my plans with members of the public,' he baited me with a cold little smile.

'Only because they talk more sense than you do.'

His smile disappeared. He was being a bastard because I'd scared him into protecting Harle. We both knew it. I walked past him and headed home with the definite feeling that DS Cranley was the type of man to bear a grudge.

Sometimes I wished I could keep my big mouth shut.

Chapter 27

I skipped breakfast and went straight to the hospital. I wanted to see what Cranley's idea of protection was and I nursed a faint hope Harle might be fit enough to talk.

The ward sister told me a policeman had been with the man she now understood was called Harle, all night, though the patient had not yet regained consciousness.

The young constable sitting by the door of the small ward looked weary and bored. When he saw I intended to stop, he stood up.

'Good morning,' I said.

'Morning, sir.'

'I'm Eddie Malloy.'

'Uh-huh.'

'I brought Mister Harle in.'

He wasn't impressed.

'It was me that arranged protection for him. I spoke to DS Cranley last night.'

'That's right, sir, he told me.'

I put my hand on the door. He gripped my wrist. 'I'm afraid you can't go in there, sir.'

I looked up at him. The grip stayed tight. 'I've cleared it with sister, don't worry.'

'It's nothing to do with sister, sir, with respect.'

I let go the handle and he let go my wrist. 'Who is it to do with then?' As if I didn't know.

'DS Cranley, sir. No one is to see Mister Harle until we have a chance to take a statement from him.'

'But-'

'DS Cranley did mention your name in particular, Mister Malloy.'

I took a couple of steps back, trying to conceal my anger. I didn't want Cranley to have the pleasure of hearing I'd blown my top at the first obstacle. 'Okay. Do you know if Cranley's on duty just now?'

The constable looked at his watch. 'Shouldn't think so, sir. You'd get him around two this afternoon.'

'Thanks for your help, constable.' I turned and headed down the corridor.

'Don't mention it, sir. That's what we're here for.'

Very funny.

I stayed in town and rang McCarthy. He was at a meeting, try again in an hour, his secretary said. I had a feeling this wasn't going to be my day.

McCarthy was free when I called back. 'Mac, things are starting to get complicated.'

'What's happened?'

'I've had to bring the police in.'

'Why?'

'To give Harle protection. You were right. It was a bad idea to drop it on the racecourse that he was out. Even an idiot would know he had to be in the nearest hospital. There was no way I could stay with him day and night, so I had to go to the police.'

'I won't say I told you so. Did you mention us, The Jockey Club?'

'No. I told him Harle was a friend.'

'Who did you speak to? Maybe I know him.'

'God help you if you do. Detective Sergeant Cranley.'

'Never heard of him.'

'Lucky you, he's a major pain in the arse. He's already stopped me from seeing Harle. The police want a statement as soon as he's conscious. God knows what he'll say.'

'Eddie, listen, you will have to try to keep us out of this.' The stress he was feeling came through in each word.

'I'll do my best, Mac.'

'If you do anything to embarrass us-'

'Mac! I'm having a bad day and it's just started. Don't wind me up. I've told you, the last thing I want to do is involve you. Now take my word for it and let's leave it at that. If the shit hits the fan, just tell them I'm nothing to do with you. I'll go along with that.'

'Okay, well, we'll see. Just keep me fully informed, will you?'

'As and when I can, Mac. Did you find anything out about Mrs. Gordon's claims?'

'Not yet. I haven't had time. And this Harle stuff complicates any conversations I have with them now. I need some time to think.'

'Fine. Look, I might be at Roscoe's place tonight. I'll check tomorrow's declared runners at noon. Roscoe's got two entered at Wetherby. If they run, he'll travel up this evening and-'

'Don't tell me any more, Eddie. Just keep in touch and don't mention Racecourse Security Services to the police. Goodbye.' He hung up. I banged the phone down and cursed him.

Several coffees and a car wash later I went into a quiet little betting shop and checked next day's racecards: Roscoe's were running. I felt a brief thrill – tonight's visit was on.

But first, much as I knew I was probably stirring up trouble, I was determined to confront Cranley.

Chapter 28

At five past two, I was tapping on the enquiries desk at the police station. The desk sergeant returned. 'I'm afraid Detective Sergeant Cranley can't see you just now, Mister Malloy, he's rather busy.'

'When will he be free?'

'He said if you'd like to take a seat for an hour or so he'd try to fit you in but he can't promise anything.'

Bastard. 'I'll come back at three.'

Cranley was standing at the enquiries desk when I returned. He looked up, smiling sarcastically. 'It's Mister Malloy! To what do we owe the pleasure of today's visit, Mister Malloy? Wait, don't tell me, you've caught all those villains you were after, haven't you? Are they outside in the car? Would you like me to send some men?'

'What I would like is five minutes of your time, Detective Sergeant.' I was determined to keep calm.

'Five minutes! For a famous crime-buster like you? Certainly. No problem. Come this way.'

He led me into the same room we'd used last time. We sat down. His smile had gone and the sneer was back.

'I'm not here for a shouting match,' I said. 'All I want is reasonable access to Alan Harle.'

'What for?'

'Because he's my friend. I'm entitled to see him.'

'Why would you want to see him?'

'Because I'm interested in his welfare.'

'Oh don't worry about that, we're taking good care of him. That was what you marched in here demanding last night, was it not? That we take care of him?'

I stared at him. 'Why are you making things difficult for me?' I asked.

He smiled his cold little smile again. 'Because I do not like you, Mister Malloy. Because I doubt your motives. Because you think you're a real clever bastard.'

I fought my rising anger.

'Would I be right to doubt your motives?' he asked, 'why were you trying to find Alan Harle?'

'I told you, he's my friend, I was worried about him.'

'Very noble. Was that the only reason?'

'Yes.'

'What were you doing in Newmarket yesterday morning?'

I hesitated. 'I had business there.'

'What kind of business?'

'Personal.'

'Did you visit anyone there?'

'Yes.'

'A Mrs. Gordon, by any chance?'

'What if I did?'

'What did you talk about?'

'Nothing that would interest you.'

He smiled. 'You're lying again, Mister Malloy. See, that's another thing I don't like about you, you're a liar.'

'I found Mrs. Gordon's husband after he'd been killed. I was as much entitled to go and see her as I am to see Harle.'

'You're not entitled to interfere with police business and that's what you were doing in Newmarket, and that's what you're trying to do here, and I am not having any of it.'

'How am I interfering?'

'Because you told Mrs. Gordon you'd catch her husband's killer, and Mrs. Gordon passed that on to my colleague in Newmarket in no uncertain fashion. In fact, she raved and ranted so much at them in the station yesterday afternoon that she almost got herself locked up.'

'Maybe if they'd done their job properly-'

He raised a flat palm so quickly, I flinched. 'Don't get yourself in deeper than you already are, Mister Malloy. I am looking at this whole case and if I can find anything at all to nail you with, it will give me great pleasure.'

'You're in charge of it personally, are you?'

'That's right.'

'Well, I haven't much to worry about then, have I?'

His acne got redder. 'Listen, Malloy-'

'I'm finished listening.'

We stood. 'And you're finished with this stupid crusade or whatever the hell it is,' he said. 'What is it, Malloy, all this amateur detective stuff? Because you found Gordon's body and the police haven't caught anyone yet? Is it some personal vendetta to embarrass us?'

'You don't need me to do that, you manage fine yourselves.'

I walked past him to the door and out along the hall. He followed, calling after me. 'Listen, Malloy, stay out of this from now on! If you don't you'll end up back in prison, believe me. That's a personal guarantee!'

The doors swung closed behind me on his whining voice.

Chapter 29

Roscoe's place was in darkness. I had parked the car in a lay-by half a mile away and cut across fields and fences on foot to reach the stables. The house stood separate from the stable block and the lads' hostel.

Dressed in my best burgling clothes and wearing soft silent boots, I crept toward the front of the house and stopped at the entrance. It was like a porch with an American-type screen guarding the door.

The front was long with three windows either side of the porch. Stopping, I leaned against the wall and listened. The wind rustled the hedges and pushed clouds across the moon. In the stable-yard at the rear, a dog barked; another answered, louder and longer. Then they were quiet. Turning to the porch, I was through both doors and in Roscoe's hallway in less than a minute.

I stood waiting for my eyes to adjust. Shafts of half-light through the windows as clouds passed the moon gave me shadowy glimpses of the hallway.

Although I had a flashlight, I only wanted to use it when absolutely necessary. I started walking but the crepe soles on my shoes rasped off the floor at each step like the sound of sticky tape being peeled. I removed the shoes and carried them.

Passing the dark shapes of furniture against the walls, I was ten steps from the wall at the bottom when I froze mid-stride, the breath I'd just taken locked in my lungs.

Someone stood in the corner by the door…small, narrow, motionless. I waited, letting the breath trickle through my nostrils, hearing my heart beat, feeling the adrenaline racing…I was aware of my eyes straining, staring in complete concentration.

More than a minute passed. Neither of us moved. I could not hear him even breathe. The doubts crept in. Bringing the flashlight up, I pointed it at his eyes and pressed the button. A shiny painted face smiled back at me. A life-size statue of a jockey wearing red and blue silks. When the tension rushed out, I almost laughed.

I looked round the rooms, paying more attention to the study and the library than the others. In the library I used the flashlight again to examine the contents of a glass-fronted gun case. Inside it were three shotguns. I tried the handle; the case was locked. The guns looked expensive and very well cared for.

Many trainers took part in hunting, shooting and fishing, but Roscoe, with his Gucci shoes and coiffed hair, seemed about as far from that type as you could get. Maybe the guns were for show.

In the two rooms I found trophies, photographs, paintings and bronzes, copies of The Racing Calendar, entry forms, bills, vet's certificates for two new horses, expensive writing paper and a gold pen. On Roscoe's desk, ironically, sat a glossy brochure showing burglar alarms. Two separate systems had been ringed in ink and marked 'cottage' and 'house'. I wondered if the cottage was Harle's place.

Aside from the guns not sitting quite right with me, I found nothing that linked Roscoe to anything other than training racehorses. I sat at his desk for one final search through his papers and that's when I noticed the orange light blinking on his answering machine.

I pressed the play button.

The tone bleeped. I waited. An accented voice, anger barely subdued, said, 'Roscoe! Who the fuck is running this show? I want a meeting and I want it fast!'

The machine clicked. I sat there in the darkness smiling as I wondered what had upset the caller, the normally calm Gerard Kruger. I opened the tape door in the machine and levered out the mini cassette: the first solid evidence of a link.

I stopped. It was also evidence for Roscoe that someone had been in his house while he was away. But there was no way he could guess it was me. I looked in his desk drawer and found an opened pack of cassettes with three left in it. I loaded one of them in the machine and pocketed the tape with Kruger on it.

Time to go.

Standing by the porch door, I let the night air cool my face. Sweat ran from my armpits down my ribs.

Moving along the wall to the corner of the building, I listened before cutting across the narrow road. All quiet. The wind had dropped. The sky was clear.

I vaulted the fence into a small apple orchard, waking a pair of wood pigeons who flew off in panic, their wings slapping like rifle-fire, and I quickened my pace on into the meadows. They were grazing fields, though empty of livestock. I jogged in the direction of the car, casting a bobbing moon-shadow.

My mind buzzed. Just when it had looked like I'd get nothing on Roscoe, Kruger's phone call had implicated him. Roscoe had to know something about Harle's abduction.

Slowing to a walk as I approached the lay-by, I was breathing quite heavily, and sweating. I took my jacket off and threw it in the passenger side. Leaning over, I opened the glove compartment and put the flashlight inside. When I straightened up, someone in the back pushed a cold metal tube under my ear. It hurt my jawbone, and my heart almost burst through my shirt.

Chapter 30

The courtesy light was still on. I looked in the mirror; he wore a dark balaclava with two eyeholes and no mouth-hole. Someone sat beside him.

'Reverse,' he said. The voice was even, calm. I started the engine, switched on the lights and as I turned to look through the rear window, he moved the gun from my right ear to the same position behind my left. My heart hammered but I'd handled the initial shock. I reversed the car into the road, facing the way I had come.

Sliding the gear stick to neutral, I waited for directions. He moved the gun to its original position.

'Drive.'

I slipped into gear and drove, trying to force my mind to work on the problem, to analyze it, suggest a solution. But it kept veering off. How did they know I was here? Had they followed me? How long have they been watching me?

I tried to be conversational. 'Where are we going?'

No answer.

We were less than a mile from the main road when a warning light showed on the dashboard. The temperature gauge was in the red section and climbing. I clutched at the straw. 'We're overheating badly,' I said, 'we'll have to stop.'

'Stop,' he said, voice still calm and level. Pulling into the side, I switched off the engine.

The door clicked open and he began sliding out, but the gun remained in contact with my skin. He stood outside now, though his hand was still inside holding the gun against my neck.

'Get out.'

He stayed behind my door so I couldn't bump him as I opened it. I stepped out. His friend got out the other side. The gun went to the nape of my neck. 'Open the bonnet,' he said. I thought I detected a West Midlands accent but couldn't be sure.

'The lever is inside the car,' I said. He nodded to the other one, who got in the driver's door and fumbled under the dash until he sprung the lock. I walked to the front, released the catch and opened the bonnet.

'Prop it up,' he said.

I felt for the metal supporting rod and fitted it. The radiator hissed steam from tiny openings.

'Face the engine. Put a hand on each wing,' he said.

I did so slowly, wondering what the hell he was up to. He changed position behind me, moving to the right. I sensed him switching the gun to his left hand but it never lost contact with the upright hair on my neck. I could just see him reach into his army-style jacket and bring something out.

'Open your legs.'

I did. I was now half bent over the radiator, arms and legs spreadeagled. He pushed down on the back of my head with the gun. 'Bend.'

When I realized what he was going to do, I felt nauseous.

A man must have instincts to help him survive, especially when the brain is caught by surprise or unable to function, and as my face was forced nearer and nearer to the roasting radiator surface, instinct tried to take over from brain. But although my ears set off every alarm bell in my body as they heard the bubbling, spitting water, brain knew the consequence of resistance was a bullet in the head.

The gun barrel pressed against the protruding bone at the base of my skull now, hurting. My face was a foot away from the hot grey metal.

A bead of sweat fell from my forehead onto the radiator and I watched from six inches as it sizzled into vapour. My fingers gripped the wings of the car as my feet slid wider on the loose gravel.

My eyes were three inches away, already burning. I closed them. Gritting my teeth, I tried to turn my head sideways so my left cheek would make contact first.

He stopped pressing down.

He held steady.

I looked at the radiator cap an inch away, the steam under terrible pressure, hissing and bubbling; it seemed deafening.

'Stay away from Harle and Roscoe.' His voice was still calm. I had not heard mine for a minute. Mine would not be calm. I thanked God, or whoever was up there, that they were settling for a warning and not frying my face. I thought of Harle and how far from him I'd be staying in future.

I wondered when he would let me straighten up. Things were pretty uncomfortable.

Then I saw a hand.

The other man's hand.

It moved toward my face at eye-level. It was inside a thick grey industrial glove and it crept over the top of the radiator and came to rest on the cap.

The sickness returned.

An inch from my eyes, the hand pressed down, slowly unscrewing… The captive steam sensed freedom and the hiss became a roar in my left ear. The final seconds were a blur. On the last turn of the cap, the hand disappeared. The cap burst off and steam and boiling water rushed upwards as my face was pushed over the scalding eruption. I opened my mouth to scream, but I don't remember hearing any sound. I don't remember anything except the moments of searing pain before I blacked out.

Chapter 31

Consciousness returned as dawn broke. It was cold. I lay staring at a tyre a foot from my face. Pips of gravel stuck in the tread. I didn't move. Just my eyes. I became aware I was on my side beneath the front bumper, my right arm under my body. My eyes moved again and I saw the frosty spiky grass at the roadside. It was higher than my head.

Strange.

Very cold.

I tried to remember the season…spring. I was sure. Must be a cold snap.

My eyelids felt like dried, wrinkled leaves. My cheek and nose throbbed and stung as though someone had shaved me with a dry razor after my skin had been cooked.

My lips felt puffed. I prodded them with my tongue and regretted it immediately…tender, raw-flesh tender.

The sky grew lighter. I lay still. It wasn't the first time I'd lain injured on the ground. I had fallen from horses at speed more times than I could count.

I'd seen the green earth coming at me fast, felt it pound the wind from my body. I'd heard the crack of my own bones at impact. I'd shut my eyes and rolled my head on a pillow of mud and wet grass, counting out the pain with each turn of the head until the ambulance arrived.

And they always had arrived. I wished they were coming to get me now…pick me up from this road, wrap me in warm blankets, morphine the pain away.

Help me.

I lifted my right cheek and felt the gravel stick to my skin. Rolling over I looked at the sky. It was still grey but getting bluer. Slowly I tried to flex my arms and legs. A crow sat in the tree above me, watching as I moved like a dying spider.

My limbs were stiff and, though they weren't sore, the slightest movement anywhere in my body seemed to increase the pain in my face.

Very slowly, I sat up. My eyes reached the level of the radiator grille. Gripping the bumper, I pulled myself up…oh so slowly trying to keep my head still.

Every movement seemed to send shock waves into my skull to bounce around on the inside walls of my face, like some kid's computer game. Direct hits each time. No electronic beeps, only agony, agony, agony.

I held on to the front of the car for a long while. I stared into the black hole of last night's instrument of torture…the cap was nowhere to be seen and nature's overnight irony had applied to the rim a coat of ice.

The journey from the front of the car to the driving seat must have taken ten minutes. Moving in tiny steps, stopping till the pain was bearable for the next few inches, I heard the crow fly off. Bored, I suppose. If he'd been a vulture, I think he might have stayed.

The final small movements had to be made in bursts of held breath, squatting to sit on the side of the seat, sliding backwards, hauling my legs in and turning round to face the front. Each an individual stage.

Each, a dive from high cliffs, preceded by a deep breath. Each breath held till the stage was complete.

Finally, I sat. On the softness, the warm velour. No more gravel. No more cold.

I sweated. The drops ran out of my hair and carved paths down the burned skin. More and more of them. A big field. Many runners. Racing down my face…cutting it up.

I passed out again.

Chapter 32

The sound of an engine woke me. My eyes opened slowly. It was a horse-box, coming to a halt in front of my car. A door slammed. Boots hit gravel. I began to panic and was ashamed of my terror. If they'd returned for another session over the radiator…I felt very badly in need of a toilet.

I saw the boots running alongside the box. Small boots. Beautiful, small, undangerous boots. Their owner came into view, a girl. A loud involuntary sigh of relief groaned out of my body.

She came to the door and she bent and looked in. 'Have you broken down?' she asked in a lovely soft Irish accent.

I turned to look at her, and when she saw the full frontal, her brown eyes seemed to double in size in her freckled face. Her head went back with the speed of a rifle recoil. 'Fuckin' hell!' she said, her hand going to her mouth to hush it and cover her horror.

'Hello,' I said. Moving my lips was a big mistake.

'What in the name of God happened to you?' she asked.

'Accident,' I said, without moving my lips.

'How, what happened?'

'Later.'

'Will I fetch a doctor?'

There was nothing in the world I wanted more but doctors meant police and police meant, eventually, Cranley who would gloat and taunt.

'No.'

'But why? You're in an awful state. Have you seen your face?'

If it looked as bad as it felt, I didn't want to see it.

'You'll have to have a doctor.' She was pleading now.

'Please, no,' I managed to say. If I'd been able to use my facial muscles to help express how much I didn't want a doctor, perhaps she would have been more easily convinced. She was getting angry, maternal.

'Not here,' the pain was in my voice now. She softened and moved in closer, squatting. 'I see how sore it is for you to talk,' she puzzled for a few seconds then looked at my hands in my lap.

'Can you move your fingers?'

A cinch. I drummed on my thigh.

'Good,' she said. 'I'll just ask you questions and you can answer with your fingers. Right for yes, left for no.'

I raised my right forefinger.

'Are you hurt anywhere else except your face?'

Left hand.

'Can you move?'

I hesitated.

'With my help?'

Deep breath. Right hand.

'Can your car be driven?'

Left hand.

'If we go very slowly, can you make it to the horse-box?'

Right hand.

'Okay, I'll take you back with me, and then we'll get a doctor.'

After a million years, we reached the horse-box.

She climbed up and opened the door, jumped down. 'Wait,' she told me. Running round the front of the box, she climbed in the other side. Appearing above me in the doorway, she reached to help me up.

Breath-holding time again.

It wasn't a hell of a lot worse than the walking; the pain level had come down or my tolerance had increased. I reached the seat without blacking out again.

'I'll drive slow,' she said. And she did, but the road was bad in places. Every time we bounced, I sensed her glancing across at me and felt her grimace for both of us. I wondered how far we had to go and she read my mind.

'It's not far, another two miles or so.'

We rumbled on, slower than an old cart-horse

'The family are away just now though they may be back the morra,' she said. 'So you can have a bed till the doctor comes and maybe even stay overnight if he doesn't want to put you in hospital.'

It wasn't the doctor that wanted to put me in hospital, but I knew what she meant.

'Even if you're still here when the guv'nor gets back, he won't mind. He's a decent sort, so he is.'

I was glad of that.

'And Mrs. Roscoe's nice too.'

Sick time. Terror time.

The little straw-clutcher inside said maybe it wasn't the same Roscoe, but cold logic laughed him down. How common was the name? How many had horseboxes? How many had stables within two miles of where I'd been last night? Only one. Basil.

Chapter 33

I wondered if Roscoe knew yet that I'd been to his house last night. The hit men must have reported in to somebody, and if that somebody was Roscoe, he might be speeding my way right now.

I could only imagine his face when he walked in and found me being sympathetically tended to by his stable staff. The girl chatted on beside me while I tried to figure out what to do.

My main fear was passing out again and seeing Roscoe when I woke.

When we reached the stables, the girl drove to the rear of the buildings and turned into the yard. She looked across at me. 'I'll get help,' she said, and jumped to the ground, hurrying into the house I'd crept out of less than twelve hours before.

My vision was limited by the area my swiveling eyes could cover without moving my head, but I took in what I could through the windscreen and by using the big wing mirrors.

The girl reappeared and ran toward the stables behind me.

Seconds later I saw her in the side mirror hurrying back, followed by a lanky teenage boy. His lime-green sweater sleeves halfway down his forearms, and as he walked, his hands dangled and swung as though his wrists were broken. His face was long and pointed and looked like it hadn't seen soap and water since Christmas.

The girl climbed up and opened the door, and I turned slowly and painfully and came out backwards. They guided my feet to the rungs and helped bear most of my weight on the last big step to the ground.

Inside, they helped me to a chair in the kitchen, straight and high-backed, much easier to stand up from.

The girl went to the sink and tore two yards of pale blue tissue from a roll fixed to the wall.

She soaked the tissue under the tap and came toward me, water dripping through her fingers as she cradled the soggy mass.

'If I can dab some of this on your face it should soothe it.'

'No,' I said, fearing unconsciousness again if anything touched the skin.

'But you need something on it till a doctor gets here!' She was beginning to get frustrated with this invalid with the poached face. I decided to try one more request and prepared myself for another session of talking through unmoving lips.

'Have you called the doctor?' I asked.

'Not yet,' she said. The water dripped, making a pool on the tiled floor. I looked at the boy. He stared at my face with his mouth hanging open as though someone had removed the bolt from his jaw. The girl saw me look at him and turned.

'Thanks, Bobby. You'd better get back to the feed room and finish off that mash.' It was an order and Bobby looked used to taking them.

He drifted sideways, still staring at my face. I lost sight of him when he moved out of eye-swiveling range but I heard him speak for the first time.

'What you gonna do with 'im, Jackie?'

'Don't worry, I'll get him a doctor, he'll be all right.'

He didn't reply. 'Bobby,' she said sternly, 'go and finish the feed. I'll make sure he's all right.'

She turned to me. 'Don't tell me now you don't want a doctor!'

I didn't say anything. She stamped a foot, turned, strode to the sink, and dumped the saturated handful of tissue. It splodged and stuck by the sound of it. Back she came to me.

'Maybe I should just let you sit there till you die! Maybe you'd be happier then!' A flush spread under her freckles and her eyes sparkled. She was very attractive.

'Jackie,' I said. The use of her name puzzled her until she remembered Bobby had used it.

'Don't you Jackie me with any soft talk!'

I tried to look apologetic. 'Please do one more thing for me.' The m's were not coming out, but she understood.

'What?' Hands on hips now, ready for an argument.

'Call an ambulance.' I said. Her eyes went up to heaven. 'Thank God! You're coming to your senses.'

On a shelf by the window sat a white telephone and, picking up the receiver, she looked at me over her shoulder. The sun through the glass caught her face and hair; she was very pretty. Pity about my face. If they ever repaired it sufficiently I'd ask her to dinner.

'Nine-nine-nine?'

'Yes.' I said.

She began dialling. 'Tell them I had an accident in the boiler room.'

She turned, holding the receiver to her ear. 'We don't have a boiler room.'

'They don't know that.'

Shaking her head slowly, she dialled the last digit. Pacing the kitchen in silence, she asked again what happened to me, but I persuaded her the story would be best kept till some other time.

I heard the siren faintly, but when the ambulance came within clear hearing range of the stables the noise stopped. It took me a few seconds to figure out they'd switched the siren off deliberately in case we ended up with terrified horses kicking down their box doors and careering all over Lambourn.

Two paramedics breezed in cheery and efficient-looking. One had a beautifully kept beard and when he saw me, he whistled low and said, 'Nice one.'

The other man gazed at my face from about a foot away like he was looking in an aquarium for a lost fish. 'You won't be shaving for a week or two, old son,' he said. 'What happened?'

Jackie answered. 'The boiler blew.'

He straightened and looked at her. 'These burns aren't fresh.'

She didn't turn a hair. 'It happened last night when he was here alone. I found him this morning when I came back from the races.'

He turned to me again. 'Not the comfiest night you've ever spent, I'll bet,' he said. Then the bearded one said, 'I'll get the stretcher, John.'

'Okay,' John said. He smiled at me. 'We'll have you sorted out in no time, old son.'

He spoke to Jackie. 'What's his name?' He blocked my view but I could imagine the look on her face.

'Eddie Malloy,' I said, using my lips so he wouldn't ask for a repeat. It was very painful.

He turned his attention to me. 'You used to be a jockey, didn't you?'

'Yes.' I saw him reflect briefly on his use of the past tense. He must have remembered the circumstances of my warning-off because he looked uncomfortable. I wished I felt well enough to say something consolatory to fill the embarrassed silence.

His friend barged in with the stretcher, saving further blushes. They stood, one at either end, holding the stretcher and Jackie helped me lie on it. The bearded one faced me and John was at my head. 'All right, Eddie?' he asked.

'Yes.'

'Will you open the door, love?' he asked Jackie.

'Do you want to come with him?' the bearded one asked her.

'Not now, I'm expecting Mister Roscoe home soon. I'll telephone the hospital to find out how he is. Newbury General, is that right?'

'That's it, love,' John said. 'The number's in the book.'

'Thanks,' she said.

They carried me past her and when she smiled at me, it hurt too much to return it.

Chapter 34

They sedated me and I remember little of the first forty-eight hours in hospital. On the third day, things had eased enough to move me from pain-killing injections onto tablets.

The nurse who brought the medicine said, 'It's good to see you awake, Mister Malloy. Things should get easier now, day by day.'

'Thanks,' I felt angry and irritable.

She said, 'You've had a visitor yesterday, and the day before, a young woman, very pleasant. She said she'll be back today.'

A young woman? It had to be Jackie from Roscoe's yard. She was the only young woman I'd met in a year. 'Thanks,' I said.

She came in the afternoon, when I was lying, staring at the wall, tea cold beside me and sandwich uneaten.

She stopped at the foot of the bed and bent to get into my eye line, 'Hello! You're awake!'

I couldn't have smiled even if my injuries had allowed me to. I managed to say hello.

'Still sore?' she said.

I gave the briefest nod. She said, 'Mind if I sit down?'

I turned and nodded again toward the chair to the right of my bed and she adjusted it so she could sit almost face on. She looked clean, and fresh, and what struck me about her wasn't the sweet scent she wore or her beautiful eyes, but the flawless bright skin, especially on her cheeks.

'You must still be in a lot of pain,' she said.

'I'll live,' I said, hands crossed in my lap.

'You seem very low. I can sit quietly or I can come back another time. I just wanted to make sure you were all right.'

The me of a few days ago would have jumped at the chance to squeeze her for every ounce of information I could get about Roscoe and his associates. But the torture had seared my spirit as much as my skin. I just looked at her, hating the self-pity she would see in my eyes.

She got up and leant across the bed and softly placed her hand on my hands, 'It'll get better,' she said, 'Remember how brave you were to suffer so long lying on that road, and doing without a doctor. I know now why you did that.'

I moved my eyes to look at her and felt them fill. She squeezed my hand lightly, and deliberately turned away to save my dignity before the first tear spilled down my tattered face. The strange course the tears took, as they tried to find the easiest way through the facescape of blisters, deflected me for a while from my sadness. Then I laid my head back and closed my eyes.

Next day, Jackie came again, at the same time, and I guessed she was using up the gap that most grooms had to fill each day when they weren't racing, the blank hours before evening stables.

The pain had lessened. My mood remained low, but I owed her more than the grunts and neglect she'd faced yesterday. As she sat beside me, I tried to smile. She frowned and raised a flat palm toward me, 'Don't! No need. It'll hurt.'

I nodded my thanks, 'I'm sorry about yesterday,' I said.

'No need. It's a hard, hard thing.'

'You've got to be careful,' I said, 'if your boss finds out you're coming here- '

'He knows nothing about it. I found out what he's like now, I heard him talking about you that night, when he got home.'

'Who to?'

'I don't know who was on the other end of the phone, but Mister Roscoe was saying you'd need to be dealt with or everybody would be in trouble.'

'Bobby told him you brought me there? It is Bobby, isn't it, the kid with the long arms?'

'How did you know Bobby told him?'

'Because he thought I was a one-man freak show. No way was he going to keep quiet. How did you get out of it?'

'I told Mister Roscoe I was just about to come and tell him all about you but Bobby beat me to it.'

'Do you think he believed you?'

She screwed up her face, and her shoulders rose, 'I think so.'

'You might be best assuming he didn't believe you, and find yourself another job.'

'Why? Why do they want to harm you?'

I gazed at her. The shreds of my ego that remained wanted to offer arguments on my behalf, but it was easily overruled by my little self-hater, 'It doesn't matter. Not now.'

'Why not?'

'Because I'm done with it.'

'It wasn't something bad…' It was part question, part hope, and part reassurance.

'No,' I said.

She swallowed what was to be her next question, showing me how smart she was. She just nodded, and we sat awhile in silence.

She said, 'Do you know when you'll be going home?'

'Not yet.'

'Where is home for you?'

'A little place in a wood in the Cotswolds. But I'll be moving out soon.'

'Is there anyone you want me to get in touch with, to let them know you're here?'

'No,' I said, 'thanks.'

'Is there anything you need?'

I looked into her eyes for what felt a long time, long enough to silently say, yes, I need to erase the passing of time all the way back to Christmas. I need to say no to McCarthy on that black night in the caravan, I need to return to the silly belief that I was a man of courage, and confidence, and hope, and fire…it was a false belief, but I needed it nonetheless.

But all I heard myself say was, 'I need you to go away and be safe and go back home to Ireland, if you can, but get away from Roscoe.'

'I'm nanny to his kids. Him I could leave easily, and Mrs. Roscoe, too. But it would be much harder to leave the children.'

I laid my head back, but turned to look at her, 'He gets his money's worth from you, box-driver, groom, nanny.'

'I've never minded being busy.'

'Where is home for you?' I asked.

'Killarney.'

'You have family there?'

'My mother and my brother, on a small farm.'

'Could you go back there?'

'I suppose I could.'

'You should think about it.'

'I will.'

We sat again in silence, then she said, 'What will you do when you get out?'

'I don't know.'

'I could come and, and maybe help you settle back in, at home, I mean.'

I looked at the ceiling, at those tiles whose every whorl and bump I knew, and I wanted so much to say yes. I turned my head once more on the pillow and looked at her, 'Best not,' I said quietly.

'Will stopping be enough?' she said, 'Will it keep you from harm?'

'I don't know,' I said, and I looked away from her again, closing the subject.

She stood up, 'Would you like me to come again tomorrow?'

Our gazes held, locked in the certainty of the answer, 'Best not,' I said.

She nodded very slowly. Still our eyes held to each other. She said, 'I have your jacket. I meant to bring it today. I'll drop it in tomorrow.'

'Where was it?'

'In your car.'

The car. 'Is the car still there?'

'It was gone yesterday.'

I thought of Mac. He wouldn't know if I was alive or dead.

'Thanks,' I said.

'I will bring your jacket tomorrow. No need to see me if you don't want to.'

'Want doesn't come into it.'

Still she stood above me, looking into my eyes. 'Will you say my name?' she asked quietly.

I hesitated, then said, 'Jackie.'

She did not smile, just held my gaze and gave again that tiny nod, and left.

Chapter 35

I asked if I could have a bath, and, after much discussion, they agreed. I walked beside the nurse who carried my towels. She offered to sit with me for safety's sake.

'I'll be all right, thanks.'

'There's an emergency cord. Pull it if you feel in the least faint.'

'I will.'

When I closed the bathroom door, the first thing I saw was a stranger in the mirror.

The image you carry of yourself is so solid that even age seems to change it only imperceptibly. To see someone you don't recognize using your body is a hell of a shock. The first reaction is one of panic, and my brain battled to regain control.

The mirror was two paces away. After a long time fixed to the spot, I moved closer until my face was six inches from the glass.

The damage was bad. Nothing on my face looked like skin in either colour or texture.

It was made up of patches: livid pink, blood-red and colours in between. Small sections of tiny blisters bordered larger areas of egg-size blisters. My forehead and cheekbone on the right side were badly grazed. My nose and lips were grotesquely swollen.

On the remote islands of skin that had survived grew a week's stubble. It flourished on the large swathes of uninjured skin on my neck, making me even uglier.

I had never thought about my own looks, not in the way of pride, at least. I'd been called handsome. An abiding memory was of a visit from an aunt on my twelfth birthday: "You'll break many a heart," she had said, and I had felt an odd mix of pride and shame. It had seemed both compliment and insult.

In my glory days of the championship, there'd been plenty of women, but I had put it down to my position rather than looks or personality.

But confronted with such damage to my face, the truth of my vanity surfaced in a spurt of rage. How dare they? How fuckingwell dare they? In the mess of wounds my eyes suddenly burned. They burned much hotter than my skin as I stared at this alien, and I ground a gob of phlegm from deep in my throat and spat in the face of the stranger…and I watched it spread and slide and obscure him and I smiled, and it hurt, so I smiled wider.

No bath for me. Not now. Not yet. I had to call McCarthy. I went to the door and I had gripped the handle when it came to me that someone would have to clean away the sticky mess on the mirror, so I turned back.

Chapter 36

Two hours later, McCarthy marched down the ward, anger driving his swinging arms and his clenching jaw muscles. But when he reached my bed, the shock of seeing my face trumped all else, and his jaw muscles suddenly lost power and his mouth dropped open.

'Hello, Mac,' I said.

'Dear God…' he said quietly.

I nodded toward the chair, 'Sit down.'

He almost felt his way over to the chair, unable to look at anything but my injuries.

I let him settle until he was ready to ask the inevitable, 'How long have you been in here?'

'Almost a week.'

'A week!' The whole ward heard it. I glared at him, 'For God's sake stop shouting.'

He leaned forward, lowering his head and whispering harshly, 'Don't order me to stop shouting! I get a call from the hire company that the police have found your car abandoned in Lambourn, I'm wondering whether you're dead or alive and now you say you've been here a week and you haven't rung me before now. Why?'

I looked away again. 'I'll tell you sometime.'

'You'll tell me now!'

Slowly I turned to face him. 'Mac, sometime, if I ever feel human again, I'll let you know why I didn't contact you. I already feel like an idiot and a failure, I don't need you making it any worse right now.'

He shook his head and sighed, 'Okay.' He said, relaxing, crossing his legs, 'Can you tell me what happened then?' There was a note of sarcasm.

I told him, though when it came to the scalding I felt my voice go and had to stop and compose myself.

McCarthy listened in silence. When I finished he leaned forward and squeezed my arm. 'I'm sorry, Eddie. So sorry it came to this. I'll try and arrange some compensation for you. We have another meeting in the morning with the senior steward, I'll raise it there as part of your severance package.'

'Severance from what?'

'You won't be continuing, I assume?'

'Continuing is a very soft word, Mac. No, I won't be continuing, I'll be running these bastards down and doing to them what they did to me. I'll fry Roscoe's fucking face and whoever else decided to fry mine.'

'I'm afraid we don't have time for that, Eddie. We are under immense pressure. Immense. The senior steward has been told by the Palace to get rid of Perlman.'

'The Queen's put out a hit on Perlman? How I wish I was able to laugh.'

'No, the Queen has not put out a hit, as you very well know. Raleigh bloody Tredville, the Palace's press secretary, who seems to think he runs the country, has told the Jockey Club to find a way to warn Perlman off.'

'Well, you need to find him first, then find a reason to warn him off. And it's touching to know that Raleigh bloody Tredville is so upset about the attempted murder of Alan Harle.'

'Fortunately, there's nothing to suggest that was racing related.'

I looked at him. He concentrated on my eyes, seemingly embarrassed now at the revulsion my injuries caused him. I said, 'Are you for real? Fortunately? The people who did this to me tried to kill Harle. They warned me to stay away from him, and to stay away from Roscoe. Harle works in the sport that you help run. He's very probably connected to this guy Perlman who means so much to you and the senior fucking steward. And, fortunately, his attempted murder didn't embarrass you as much as Perlman not turning up to meet the Queen Mum?'

'That's not the way I meant it, Eddie, you know that.'

I shook my head, 'You need to choose your words more carefully, Mac.'

'Anyway, my team will take over now. Once you're out of hospital and fit again, we can see where we are.'

I bit back my protest and just nodded and looked at him and said, 'You planning to show your team a picture of my face?'

He shifted in his chair.

'Or to tell them what happened to me the other night?'

He crossed his arms and stared at his shoes.

'No, I didn't think so. Well, I know most of your guys, I'll be sure to say hello to them on the track in the next few days.'

'You're kidding! You won't be out of here for a month, by the look of you.'

'I'll be out of here tomorrow at the latest. Tonight if you'll take me with you.'

'No way will they let you out. Have you seen yourself?'

'I'll sign my own discharge. And, yes, I've seen myself. That's the reason I'm coming out of here.'

'What if these same people catch you again?'

'I'll be ready for them.'

'With what?'

'I'll be ready for them.'

He watched me. I said, 'Are you going to get me out of here tonight and back on the job?'

He leant forward, elbows on knees, 'Will you keep away from my boys on the track?'

'Your boys can stay in the office, Mac, same as they did at the start and for the same reasons you had to take me on in the first place. Because they were scared.'

He ran fingers through his deep wavy hair and sighed, 'I can't keep them off this job any more, Eddie. It's become a matter of pride for the senior steward that we nail Perlman, preferably along with the evidence to warn him off.'

'So, is it going to do any harm to have me out there, too? Especially when I'm now in shit or bust mode.'

He sighed long and loud this time, straightening, standing up, 'Let me raise it at this meeting tomorrow.'

'Okay, but I want out of here in the morning, no matter what. If you don't come and get me, someone else will.'

'Who?'

'Just be here, Mac, will you? You owe me that much.'

Chapter 37

Come the morning, much of the pain in my face had subsided. I asked the nurse to bring me whatever papers I needed to sign to get myself out, took my lecture from the doctor about the recklessness of my decision, though he was kind enough to order cream and painkillers from the hospital pharmacy.

I settled in the chair to wait for McCarthy.

An hour later, I was still waiting. I went to the nurse's station and got change for the payphone. I also wrote a short letter to Jackie to say thanks and would she mind posting my jacket to me. I put some cash in the envelope and left it with the nurse.

McCarthy's secretary said he'd left the office half an hour ago, but she did not know where he was going. I shook out another coin and I rang DS Cranley. His voice snapped down the line,

'Malloy! Where are you?'

'In a call box and I don't have much change so-'

'Where are you, Malloy?'

'Never mind that, is Harle all right?'

'Harle is not all right! And you're the man I need to talk to about it.'

'Where is he?'

'That's what I want to ask you. Now get to this station or tell me where you are!'

My gut sank. 'You took that guard off him, didn't you?' I asked quietly.

'Listen, Malloy-'

'You took the guard off him, Cranley, didn't you, you stupid, arrogant bastard?'

'Malloy!' He was almost screaming. 'I'll have you for this!'

I was so angry, I had to go outside or the staff might have had me sectioned under the Mental Health Act. I'd talked to Mac about Harle and assumed he was okay and still under guard. Mac had mentioned nothing about Harle's disappearance.

They must have gone for him after they'd got me. But they wouldn't have got him if that bastard Cranley had done his job.

I saw Mac's car turning in and I started for the car park. He only had the door halfway open when I grabbed the top of it and confronted him, 'Did you know about Harle?'

'Know what? What's wrong?'

I told him. He denied having any contact with Cranley or the police, and I believed him, 'He'll be dead by now, Mac, they'll have killed him.'

'Don't say that, Eddie.'

'He'll be dead.'

'Maybe that was why they warned you? Why tell you to stay away from Harle if they intended to kill him?'

'Because when they said it, he was still under guard in hospital. Then that dickhead Cranley left him wide to the fucking world!'

'Calm down, man, or they'll have you back in there. Why don't you go and get your things and I'll take you home?'

'These are my things, Mac,' I opened my arms on the clothes that seemed to hang strangely now.

'Get in.'

I strapped on the seat belt and opened the window. The breeze cooled my face as McCarthy pulled away. 'Mac, what would you say to a gun?'

He frowned. 'What do you mean?'

'If I wanted one.'

'No way.'

'Why not?'

'No way, Eddie, it's not on.'

'Why?'

'Because it's going too far. It's illegal.'

'So's murder.'

'What do you mean?'

'You know what I mean, for God's sake! The two guys who attacked me, who killed Danny Gordon and probably Alan Harle, it's called murder.'

'That's their problem. They'll have to face the consequences.'

'When? After they've killed me or somebody else, maybe even you?'

He was getting upset, shaking his head and rubbing the steering wheel with his left hand.

'No, Eddie, no. I'll get you anything else I can but no gun. I'd rather you packed it in altogether.'

'Mac, listen!' I clutched his arm but he jerked it free and kept staring at the road ahead muttering, 'No gun, Eddie, no gun.'

I'd been pretty sure he wouldn't wear it, but I'd had to try. At least it made him more amenable to my other requests: a faster car, more money and a renewal of the promise to help me regain my licence.

After half an hour without me mentioning guns, I think a trace of suspicion that he'd been conned into the other concessions was creeping up on him.

Searching for something to take his mind off the subject, I suddenly remembered when I last spoke to Harle, he'd given me a tip for the Triumph Hurdle.

'Mac, did Roscoe's horse win the Triumph?'

I could see the memory rewind in his eyes. 'No, thank God, it didn't.'

'Why thank God?'

'Because it would have been another embarrassment for us with Perlman.'

'You don't honestly believe this guy actually exists?'

'Maybe I don't, but what do I tell the senior steward? We're dealing with a ghost?'

'You can tell him that Perlman is Kruger. If he has trouble remembering the guy, just remind him he took my licence off me because he couldn't nail Kruger. Then you can tell him that Kruger and Roscoe are running some major scam, probably from Roscoe's place. Whether it involves heroin, horse-doping or both I don't know yet but I'm sure as hell going to find out.'

'Other than a hunch, how can you say Kruger and Roscoe are linked?'

I straightened my legs and dug into my trouser pocket, pulling out the tape from Roscoe's answerphone. 'Here,' I offered it. Mac glanced down, then held out his hand and returned his attention to the road. I told him what it was, 'Keep it safe,' I said.

We traveled a mile in silence, then I said, 'Couldn't you have one of your men go to Roscoe's? They must have something set up there. Did you know Skinner was Roscoe's private vet?'

He nodded, pondering. 'Maybe we should arrange a visit, maybe we should…'

It was late afternoon when Mac dropped me at the cottage. He came inside to make sure I had no unwelcome guests, and then left me with the address of his ex-colleague who'd recently retired. The man lived in Cheltenham and Mac told me to call there next morning and pick up my 'new' car, which was this guy's Jockey Club company car.

He said, 'And for goodness sake try not to lose this bloody car, will you?'

'Do my best, Mac. I'll do my level best.'

Chapter 38

Next morning, I took a taxi to Mac's friend's house. He gave me the keys to a black 2-litre injection Cavalier parked on a concrete standing at the bottom of his long drive.

When I reached the car, I began a routine I intended to make habitual. I checked every inch of the car. Where I couldn't see, I ran my hands over.

I was congratulating myself on thinking ahead and being clever when it dawned on me that, while I was poking my head under cars, somebody could be aiming at it with ten inches of lead pipe.

Still, I would have to learn as I went along and hope my next mistake didn't prove costlier than my first. When I was sure no one had stuck fifty pounds of gelignite on the chassis, I got in and shut the door.

It was quiet. Thinking of the last time I had driven a car, memories of the pain returned and scared me a little. But I shook them off. My mood was bright, positive. I was out, doing something, prepared to hunt this time, ready for trouble.

Taped to the steering wheel was a note from McCarthy: 'Eddie, remember, this is a Jockey Club vehicle, for God's sake take care of it.'

Slanting the rear-view mirror round, I saw my reflection. Still bad but getting better – even my face couldn't depress me today.

I headed for the police station to find out exactly how much damage Cranley had done.

After his usual bluster, he admitted he'd removed the guard on day four. By noon the same day, Harle had disappeared.

Fellow patients reported he'd been wheeled away on a trolley by two male nurses wearing surgical masks. Cranley said he was now pursuing a 'certain line of inquiry.'

He took a statement about the attack on me, and then told me I deserved all I got for playing amateur detective. The meeting ended in the usual shouting match. I walked away, my ears ringing with another warning to stay out of it.

I'd little hope of Bergmark talking, but I drove to Nottingham next to try to see him again. He sat in the same spot by the door in his wheelchair, wearing the same clothes, almost as if he'd never moved since I'd last visited.

I had to remind him who I was and he launched into the spiel about me being a good jockey, but as soon as I mentioned Danny Gordon's name he clammed up and sat staring straight ahead.

'You and Rask were blackmailing him, weren't you?' Silence. 'Answer a few questions and I'll leave you alone. I promise not to involve the police.' No response. 'The men who did this to you, did they work for Kruger?'

No reply.

I even tried a veiled threat, 'Rask's dead now.' But his expression remained blank. I gave up. It was late afternoon. I set off on the two-hour drive home.

Halfway down the track to the cottage I pulled over and parked in a small clearing. Locking the car, I crept through the woods. The place looked to be as I'd left it.

Staying in the trees, I circled warily to the rear. All the windows and doors looked secure. Moving to the front again, I stood behind a broad oak for five minutes, watching and listening. All quiet. My mind told me nobody was there, but my heart pounded as I crouched and hurried across the track for a close-up check of the building.

No signs of entry, no footprints in soft soil, nothing amateur. Turning the key in the lock, I hoped nothing professional waited inside.

I opened the door into the living room and immediately, instinctively, pulled it closed again as my brain registered someone sitting in the chair by the fireplace. In the time it took my heart to miss a beat, recognition followed and I looked inside again. It was Jackie.

Resisting the temptation to rush to her in case of a set-up, I cautiously pushed the door all the way in until it touched the wall. Nobody lurked behind it. The whole room was in view. No sign of anyone else.

The only sound was Jackie's steady breathing.

Moving through the house, I checked all the rooms and cupboards. None concealed any threat. I hurried to Jackie.

Holding her wrist in a pulse-taking grip I gently raised her chin. Slowly she opened her eyes and smiled. 'Hello,' she said, 'You had me scared half to death. How the hell did you get in?'

'The back door was open.'

'You're kidding!'

'I'm not! It wasn't lying open, but it wasn't locked. I just turned the handle.'

'Jeez!' I couldn't believe it. All those precautions I'd been taking with the car and creeping through the woods, and I'd gone out and left a door unlocked.

'At least you're okay, I said. 'I thought they'd done you in and dumped you here.'

'Who?' She was still smiling.

'The same people who did this to my face.'

'It's better than it was on Tuesday.'

'Not much.'

She stared at me, the smile fading. 'Does it still hurt?'

'A bit, but I'll survive. Listen, I hate to seem inhospitable, but what are you doing here?'

She reached for a soft basket-weave bag at her feet and took out my jacket. She said, 'I didn't want to trust it to the post.'

'It's a fair distance to travel, Jackie.'

'I hitched a lift this morning.'

'What did you tell Roscoe?'

'I had a few days off coming, so I told him my mother was ill and I had to go home and see her.'

'Home to Killarney?'

She smiled, 'You remembered.'

'My parents were from Ireland,' I said lamely, keen that she didn't misread my remembering as attachment.

'Whereabouts?'

'Donegal. I was born there.'

'So not only are your parents from Ireland, you are too?'

'I suppose so.'

She sat forward, smiling wider. Most of what I'd seen of her had been serious and sombre, she was a striking girl with rich chestnut hair and hazel eyes. She said, 'There's no supposing in it, Mister Malloy, is there?'

'I suppose not,' I tried to smile and she frowned watching the effort, and raised a soft hand, stopping just short of touching my face. She said, 'Shall I put some cream on that for you?'

Wary of how this was obviously going, a decisive no left my brain on its way to my tongue, but somehow came out as, 'Would you?'

'Where is it?' she got to her feet, and I went to the cupboard for the cream they'd given me.

I sat in the chair while she carefully smoothed the ointment on my wasted skin.

'Will you be badly scarred?' she said.

'Does it matter?'

'Only for your sake.'

'The doctor said he didn't think so. The liquid that forms inside the blisters can do more damage than anything if it seeps out but he said we're over that problem, though they weren't exactly delighted when I discharged myself.'

She nodded and after a few moments of silence said quietly, 'You should have told me when I found you that you were in trouble with Mister Roscoe.'

'Well, first, I didn't know I was in trouble with Mister Roscoe till somebody tried to boil my face and, second, how could I expect you to take my side? You've worked for him for a while, haven't you?'

'About two years.'

'And you hadn't known me two minutes. Besides, by the time I realized where you were taking me it was too late to do anything. Not that I was in a fit state to.'

'You should've said something.'

'There was no point, especially since I knew Bobby would have talked anyway.'

She nodded, still working with the cream. The scent she wore was very light, and I had to stop myself from drawing a long breath to sniff it. She said, 'I knew there was something wrong when you didn't want to stay in the house long enough for a doctor to get there, so I had decided not to say anything when Mister Roscoe came home.'

'Do you think he believed you when you said you had planned to tell him if Bobby hadn't beat you to it?'

'I think so, but I suspected right off there was something funny because he knew who you were even though nobody told him your name.'

'Does he know I'm out of hospital?'

'I don't know.' She stared at me, hesitant, concern in her eyes. 'I heard him talking about you on the phone yesterday afternoon and he was in a fierce temper. Whoever was at the other end was trying to calm him down, but he said you'd just cause more trouble and that they should have done more than just try to scare you off. That was the reason I came today.' She stepped back so she could see my reaction. I just held her gaze. She continued, 'And he said the man was now deciding if he wanted it done properly next time.'

'Who's the man, do you know?'

'No. I thought you might.'

I shook my head. 'Did he say when the next time would be?'

'No. What is it they're doing?' she asked. 'Why do they want to kill you?'

'I've half an idea, but that's all it is. And anyway, the less you know the better. For your own sake.'

'What about you?'

'I'll put some kind of plan together. Don't worry.'

'Is there anyone helping you?'

'Sort of. Look, don't worry, I'll be okay.'

She gazed at me again with those beautiful eyes. 'Let me help you.'

I stood up. 'Jackie, you've only just met me! I could be a crook or a murderer.'

She smiled and wrinkled her nose. 'What a crap line! What gangster movie did you get that from?'

I smiled and heard the slight smack of the cream, like a small kiss, as my skin moved. 'I give up.' I said and headed for the kitchen. 'Want some coffee?' I asked.

'I'll take some coffee if you let me help you.'

'Okay, you can wash the cups.'

'Very funny. You know what I mean.'

'I know what you mean and it's a crazy idea.'

She followed me through to the kitchen. 'How can it be crazy? I'm in the perfect place to spy for you.'

'That's what bothers me. You're also in the perfect place to have your face ending up like mine and then how would I feel, especially since yours is a damn sight prettier to start with?'

'Flattery won't put me off, Eddie.'

'I was already getting that impression.'

'Well?'

'Well, let's have a cup of coffee and talk about something else like how we're going to get you back to Roscoe's.'

'I can't go back till Sunday, remember? I'm in Ireland.'

I turned to her and put my hands on her shoulders. 'When I opened the door and saw you in that chair my first thought was, big trouble. Then I recognized you and said, thank God, it's only Jackie. I'm beginning to think the first impression was right.'

She smiled her soft warm smile again then, leaning forward, she closed her eyes and kissed me softly. I flinched. 'Does it hurt?' She asked.

I nodded. She frowned. 'But life's a compromise, I suppose.' I said and pulled her close.

Chapter 39

Maybe if I'd been physically and emotionally stronger, or if I'd been in a serious relationship during the last couple of years, I would have succumbed less easily to Jackie's determined seduction.

But I, or rather we, ended up doing nothing for the next three days but making love, indoors and out, walking in the woods, eating, drinking, sleeping, laughing, talking (the only taboo subject was Roscoe, Harle and associates).

At twenty, she was seven years my junior but she cooked for me, tended my face, bathed me, made me laugh, made me feel worthwhile and made me fall in love with her.

When McCarthy rang on Saturday to ask if Harle had been found, I was sorely tempted to tell him I was giving up. It just didn't seem to matter anymore. I was infatuated with Jackie, and she was, I think, with me.

She was due back at Roscoe's on Sunday morning. I told her we'd rise before dawn and I'd drive her there. On Saturday night, I took her to dinner. Jackie had made me forget all about my face and we breezed into the restaurant laughing, only for some of the ruder diners to stare open-mouthed at this Beauty and the Beast.

She gazed at me through the candle flame. 'Never mind, when your face is better we'll come back and show them!'

'They'll probably get a bigger shock than they just did.'

'What do you actually look like under all that, anyway?'

'A cross between Mel Gibson and Tom Cruise. It won't be my fault, of course, if I don't return completely to my former glory.'

She smiled and squeezed my hand. 'I'll never forget seeing your face that first morning. I almost fainted.'

'I was doing enough fainting for both of us, thanks.'

We ordered champagne. I reached for her hand. 'I'll miss you.' I said.

'I won't go then.'

'Seriously?'

'Seriously. It's not exactly the best job in the world. I'll miss the horses, and the children, but you would just about make up for that.'

I thought about it.

'We could leave here,' she said, 'go to Ireland. I know places where they'd never find us.'

'They…That's the trouble, that's what it would always come down to. They. Them. Looking over our shoulders all the time.'

'Why would it come to that? What have you done that would make them hunt you down?'

'I don't want to talk about it, Jackie. I don't want you involved.'

'Okay, so I won't get involved, I promise. I'm only asking you what you've done so far that means you can't stop now?'

I thought about it. 'Nothing, I suppose.' It was the easy way out, the way Kruger wanted me to take.

'Well, then,' Jackie said, 'why don't you forget it? You don't have any family ties, there's nothing to keep us here.'

Us. Me and Jackie, tucked away in some little Irish village. No more villains. No more scaldings. No more stupid cops.

'I could ring Mister Roscoe,' Jackie said. 'Tell him I'm not coming back because my mother's worse than I thought. We could leave tomorrow.'

She spent the next five minutes working on me, and much as the idea appealed on the surface, it was all the stuff underneath, everything we'd be running from, that would keep churning in my gut, never letting me rest.

She saw it in my eyes. 'I think I've lost this one, Eddie, haven't I?'

'Don't count it as a loss. We'll think back sometime and we'll be glad we didn't run.'

'We will or you will?'

'Both of us. I know I could never live with it and I'd take it out on you.'

'I'm strong, I can stand it.'

I smiled at her youthful optimism. 'Maybe for a month or a year, but not forever.'

'Try me.'

'Listen to the wisdom of an older man.'

'But-'

I squeezed her hand and shook my head. 'It's our last night, let's not argue.'

Pursing her lips, she nodded almost imperceptibly. Then she shifted to her other suggestion, spying for me. I was dead against it for her sake, but she persisted. On the drive home, we reached a compromise.

'Right, we're agreed,' I said.' You take no chances whatsoever. You don't go prowling, and you don't ask anybody any questions. All you do is listen and watch as you go about your normal daily business. All right?'

'Yes, sir.'

'Come on, Jackie, this is serious.'

'Okay! Okay! But I'm not a kid, Eddie!'

'I know you're not. You're twenty and I want you to live till you're thirty, and then forty and so on. That's why I'm going to keep drilling into you how dangerous this is. These people are killers and maimers. Think about it!'

She sat silent for a minute as we drove through the darkness, and then said, 'Tell me the story so far.'

Chapter 40

By the time we reached the cottage, I'd told her everything.

I didn't learn much new from Jackie about the people at Roscoe's, though the fact that Roscoe ran a couple of horses regularly at the small tracks in France was interesting. The runners were always accompanied on their travels by either Skinner or Harle. I'd bet they weren't there just for the racing.

Lying on the rug in the firelight, we finalized plans. 'I'm particularly interested in what Skinner's doing at the yard,' I said. I felt her shiver.

'Yugh!'

'Not your favourite person, I guess?'

'He's a dirty old bastard. Always trying to touch me up or making filthy suggestions.'

'He does look the part.'

'If I'm grooming or mucking out, he'll wait till my back's turned and, preferably, till I'm bending over, then he sneaks into the box under some silly pretext and tries it on.'

'You'd be amazed how much he'd probably respond to a well-aimed prod with a pitchfork.'

'I thought of that but up till now I've needed the job too much. Once this is over, I'll think of some way to fix him.'

'Let me know, I'd like to be there.'

'I will.'

'How long has he been at the yard?'

'Almost a year. I remember him first trying to grope me on Derby day.'

'Is he just doing normal vet-type things, apart from the groping, that is?'

'Yes, as far as I can see. He takes blood tests, checks legs, gives injections, that sort of stuff.'

'Ever seen him injecting what you thought was a healthy horse?'

'No, definitely not. I'd have noticed. Then again I don't see everything he does.'

'I bet you don't. Where does he live?'

'Mister Roscoe moved him into the head lad's cottage when he arrived.'

'Must have pleased the head lad.'

'He left shortly afterwards.'

'Does Skinner have a lab to analyze the blood tests?'

'I don't know.'

'Ever been in his cottage?'

'What kind of a girl do you think I am?'

I smiled. 'Come on, Jackie, stop messing about.'

'No, I haven't. Nobody goes up there because he keeps this big bloody Rottweiler and lets it roam around the house.'

'Does he spend much time in the cottage?'

'Can't say I've really noticed.'

'That's one thing you could start looking out for then, and do you have free access to all parts of the house?'

'Pretty much, with the kids running around.'

'You'll have noticed the shotguns in the library?'

'I often polish them for him.'

'Jeez, he gets his money's worth, right enough!'

'It's nothing to me, Eddie, I have plenty of energy,' she smiled mischievously.

'Those guns, does he ever use them? Does he go shooting? He just doesn't look the type to me.'

'I've haven't seen him take them outside, though that's not to say he doesn't. But I've never known him go shooting.'

'Would you be in the house every day?'

'I would.'

'Keep an eye on that case, will you. I'd like to know if a gun goes missing.'

'Why?'

'Because whoever has it might be coming in my direction.'

She looked serious for the first time that evening. I reached for her hand, 'What I want above all is for you to take no chances.'

She squeezed my hand and said quietly, 'I won't.'

'I mean it, Jackie!'

'Okay, okay, I know you do!' She leaned forward and kissed me. 'You're a terrible nag, Edward Malloy!'

'I've ridden some terrible nags, too, in my time.'

She grimaced. 'Your jokes are worse than your face!'

I grabbed her around the waist. 'But you love it anyway.'

'Oh, do I now?'

And we kissed. Then, in the glow of the dying embers, we made love, but not with the usual passion and energy. Thoughts remained unspoken but we knew the next time might be weeks or months away or, depending on the coming days, depending on Kruger and his thugs, maybe never.

On the drive to Roscoe's next morning, we went over the things she'd be looking out for and agreed that she would ring me from the pub each night if she could, at ten o'clock.

'What about you?' she asked. 'What are your plans?'

'Tomorrow I'm going to Kempton in the hope of seeing Harle's girlfriend. She's usually at the London tracks and there's a chance if he is still alive that he's tried to contact her. Where I go from there, I don't know yet, but I'll keep you up to date each time we talk. Remember, if you can't get me or if anything happens to me, you've got McCarthy's number. I'll speak to him tomorrow and tell him what we've planned.'

We stopped a mile from Roscoe's knowing it was safer if she walked the rest of the way. As dawn broke we stood holding each other tightly, then parted in silence.

Chapter 41

At Kempton I saw people I knew, but either they didn't recognize me because of my damaged face or didn't want to be seen talking to me.

I spotted Mac standing alone by a racecard kiosk. He watched me approach and looked nervous.

'I told you not to speak to me on the racecourse,' he said.

'Relax. As far as everyone's concerned I'm the invisible man anyway.'

'What do you mean?'

'It doesn't matter.'

He still seemed worried. 'Mac, there's a race going on, everyone is on the other side of the stand.'

'Okay, what is it?'

I told him about Jackie. 'That's a bad decision, Eddie.'

'How the hell is it a bad decision? She won't take any risks, she's just observing! She's an insider, for God's sake! It's the best break we've had.'

He stood shaking his head.

'What else can we do?' I asked.

Glaring at me he said, 'Look, Eddie, do what you want, just start getting me some results.'

I stared at him. 'What the hell's that supposed to mean?'

'It means I need some results from you! I told you that on Wednesday! I'm under pressure!'

'Results? Pressure? I just came out of the fucking hospital after getting my face fried for you and you talk to me about pressure!'

He looked around nervously. 'Calm down, for God's sake. I'm

sorry. Look, on top of the Perlman stuff, I'm getting calls from my boss now every time there's a major form upset. We're well into the Flat season, there could be a drugged horse in every damn race.'

'That's way over the top, Mac, and you know it.'

'Okay, maybe it is, but everybody's feeling it, not just you. Now look, I'll have to go. We'll talk soon when we've both calmed down a bit.'

The way I felt, that would take a while.

After half an hour spent searching the bars for Priscilla, I saw her walking toward me, deep in conversation with Wendy.

'Hello.' I said. They stopped and stared but didn't recognize me immediately. When Wendy did, her eyebrows went up and her hand clapped her open mouth. 'Eddie! What the hell happened to you?'

'It's a long story, as they say.'

'You look like you've had skin grafts from an old saddle.'

'I wish it were as tough.'

Wendy stepped to the side to see how far round the scarring went. I turned to her friend. 'Hello, Priscilla, remember me?' Priscilla seemed more bored than shocked. 'Not like that I don't.'

'Heard from Alan?' I asked.

She gave me a bitter look and shook her head. 'You told me he was in Cyprus.'

'I think he might be back.'

'He'd be riding if he was back.'

'Yes, I suppose he would.'

She sneered. 'Tell him when he does come back I hope he falls off his first ride and it kicks his balls up into his belly.'

'Painful.'

'Not half enough for the slimy little sod.'

Wendy had completed her inspection and was facing me.

She knitted her brows in a half-quizzical smile. 'You got scars anywhere else then, Eddie?'

'Nowhere you haven't seen before,' I said. She giggled. 'You coming in to buy us a drink?' she asked.

'Sorry, Wendy, not today. But if you hear anything of Alan Harle, ring me. There'll be a bottle in it for you.'

'Make it a magnum.'

'Give me a break.'

Her smile said it was worth a try. Priscilla's frown said let's get away from this freak. I said goodbye and went to see a couple of guys

I knew in the press bar.

The rest of the day was spent drifting, listening, trying to pick up any snippet leading to Harle, but I came up with nothing and left before the last race.

As I approached my car, I knew something wasn't right but couldn't nail what it was. Slowing down I looked around.

From what I could see, I was alone in the car park, though the high sides of the horseboxes could be hiding any number of potential attackers.

Ten paces from the car I realized what was wrong. It was parked nose up to a horse-box. I had reversed into the space when I'd arrived. Someone had been driving my car.

As I reached it, I peered through the windows. No unwanted passengers. I walked to the front and checked the bonnet-catch; no signs of tampering.

Squatting, I ran my hand along the underside of the car then decided that wasn't thorough enough. Lying down, I dug my heels in and pushed myself under the car for a proper look. I found nothing.

Sliding out, I got to my feet and dusted myself down. Close behind me someone spoke. 'Looking for something?'

I took a large step, almost a jump away from the voice and turned very quickly. My hand was raised to punch when my brain registered the uniform of the Metropolitan Police. It cancelled the message to my fist and began whirring frantically through the plausible excuse file.

I tried playing for time since I didn't think he'd quite believe I was looking to see if someone had stuck twenty pounds of explosive on my exhaust pipe. 'Do you always creep up so quietly on people?'

'Only suspects, sir.'

I watched his eyes registering the damage to my face, but he recovered quickly enough. I said, 'Suspect? Me? What of? This is my car.'

'What were you doing lying under it?'

'I saw a cat.' Jeez, I thought, what a lame excuse. 'A big black one. It was under the wheel. I saw it as I came up and I didn't want to risk running it over if it was trapped.'

'Animal lover, are you, sir?'

'Honestly!'

Unclipping the radio from his lapel, he asked HQ to run a computer check on the licence number.

That's when I remembered that the car wasn't registered in my name.

The tinny voice of the controller came through. The constable had his notebook out. 'The car is registered in the name of The Jockey Club, Portman Square, London.'

'Roger,' he said, pressing a period from his pencil into the book. I waited for him to speak. He looked at me. 'You a member of the Jockey Club, sir?'

Very droll.

'I have the use of the car for a while.'

'Do you have the keys?'

I pulled them from my pocket. 'Open the car, please,' he said. I pushed the key in, the lock clicked and I opened the door.

'Close it now, please.'

I closed it.

Walking to the back of the car, he looked again at the registration plate, notebook and pencil in hand.

'Will you open the boot, please, sir?'

'Sure.'

I pushed the key in. The lid came smoothly up, and I stared inside and wondered if the day was going to get any worse. There was someone in the boot. It was Alan Harle. He was dead.

Chapter 42

They took me to a small square room with a table and two chairs and a vase of daffodils on the windowsill, and kept me waiting with only a silent constable for company.

It didn't take Detective Sergeant Cranley long to get there, and the evil glee which had no doubt shone on his face throughout the journey was still obvious as he came through the door.

One of the London CID boys was with him and couldn't have failed to be impressed by Cranley's unbiased opening line. 'Well, well, well, Malloy, got you by the bollocks at last!'

I saved my reply. This already had the makings of a long night.

Cranley sent the young constable for a pot of tea, then he pulled a chair across for the CID man. They sat opposite me and Cranley smiled. He got up twice to make tiny adjustments to the position of his chair and when he finally settled he raised his arms, made guns of his fingers and thumbs and pointed both hands at me, 'Dead in my sights, Mister Malloy. I've got you dead in my sights now.'

I shook my head slowly. He said, 'Just the same as you had Alan Harle dead in yours. How long have you been hauling his body around?'

I said, 'You must have very little to do, if you're planning on baiting me all night with this crap.'

'Crap? Crap, is it? You almost kill him, then do your good Samaritan and rush him to hospital, all caring, and sharing your story with me. Remember, "Oh, please help my friend! He needs police protection. Big bad men are after him. Please hurry!" Well, Malloy, the big bad man was you, wasn't he? You're a decent actor, I'll give you that. You had me proper wound up.'

'Are you serious here, Cranley?'

'Never more so, Malloy, never more so.'

'You think I killed Alan Harle?'

'Not an unreasonable assumption given he's been a passenger of yours twice. The first time he went from your motor into the intensive care unit, the second, and, of course, last time, he went from your motor into the morgue. Oh, and just by the oddest coincidence, said motor is not registered in your name.'

I looked at the CID guy, 'Is this standard procedure?'

The man folded his arms and said, 'You're entitled to request legal representation at any time.'

Cranley leant forward, 'Oh, yes, Malloy, why haven't you asked for a lawyer by now?'

'Because I don't need a fucking lawyer! I haven't done anything!'

'You're a convicted criminal,' Cranley said, 'you cannot control your temper. You almost beat a man to death for which you spent eighteen months in prison. What did Harle do to you? Must have been much worse than this Mister Kruger, at least you stopped battering Kruger in time for doctors to save his life.'

I shook my head again. Cranley raised his left hand and pointed his finger gun at me, making as though he was pulling a trigger, 'Leopards!' He brought his other hand up and fired with that too, 'Spots!' then, slowly and theatrically he joined his palms, 'They go together, Mister Malloy. They do not change. The leopard does not leave his spots and the spots do not leave the leopard.'

I smiled, 'Have you any idea what you look like? Talk about me being an actor? Jeez, give it a rest, will you?'

He got to his feet and bent low across the table, 'Oh, there will be no rest. Not tonight, not until you tell us everything.'

The young cop came back in with the tea-tray. Cranley turned, 'Ah, sustenance. We're going to need it!'

He persevered, I'll give him that. All night he persevered, trying to extract a confession, screaming at me, pushing his sweaty pockmarked face into mine, breathing his garlic breath. At one point, he raised his fist, but then he looked in my eyes and what he saw made him think twice.

As dawn broke, they took my belt and tie and shoe laces and threw me in a cell. I'd had no food or drink and my head pounded from Cranley's screaming. I lay down and tried to clear my mind.

Who the hell were these guys of Kruger's? I'd been at Kempton no more than two hours. You don't just happen across a car and dump a body in it. How had they known I'd be there? How could they know which car I was driving? They began to seem somehow superhuman.

If they were that good, I'd better tell Jackie to forget what we'd arranged. She wouldn't be safe doing even that. Jackie…I thought about holding her the way I had on Sunday morning when we'd parted.

Trying to comfort myself, I replayed in my head our last conversation.

What are your immediate plans, Eddie? Well, tomorrow I'll be at Kempton…

Jackie…?

The longer I dwelt on it, the more my suspicion deepened. Surely everything we'd had during those three days couldn't have been false? Insecure as I was, I didn't believe I could be suckered so easily by a woman.

In the end, I convinced myself it was just tiredness and mental bruising making me suspicious of Jackie. After all, hadn't Kruger's men traced me before, followed me to Roscoe's place?

Or had they? Maybe they'd been on their way to Roscoe's and just happened upon my car. If they'd followed me, why hadn't they stopped me entering Roscoe's house?

My weary, battered mind tumbled the thoughts over in slow motion. I didn't know what to think any more, couldn't trust myself to be logical. Attempts at sleep resulted in a fitful two hours, punctuated by snatches of the same nightmare.

At ten o'clock, a policeman brought me breakfast, soap and a towel. 'Get that down you, then get cleaned up. There's somebody here to see you.'

Chapter 43

I was led to a room where McCarthy waited.

'You look awful,' he said.

'Thanks.'

'Have you been up all night?'

'Almost. Cranley was conducting one of his special interviews. You know, one of those where they tell you what you did rather than ask you?'

'Yes, he looks the type. I've just spent fifteen minutes with him. He is not your biggest fan, Eddie, I can assure you of that. What the hell have you done to upset him so much?'

'Nothing. We took an instant dislike to each other, you know, like the opposite of love at first sight? He's obsessed with my supposed involvement in all this, keeps saying he's going to get me.'

'Not this time he isn't. He's had the results of some of the forensic tests. Harle's been dead at least a week, which gives you the perfect alibi, since you were lying in a bed in Newbury Hospital when he was killed.'

'What was the cause of death?'

'Still to be confirmed, but they've detected Hepatitis B along with a massive quantity of heroin. Either he injected himself with an infected needle or somebody else did.'

'I think we can safely say it was somebody else, don't you? They'll be claiming he dumped his own body in my car next.'

He smiled.

'I guess that's how they got you involved, through the car?' I asked. He nodded.

'I'm sorry, Mac, I know that's really dropped you in it.'

'Don't worry, it turned out a blessing in disguise. It's made my people realize just how serious this is. There were a lot of heads in the sand, Eddie, a lot of people who didn't want to face the reality of what was going on, didn't want to admit you were on our side. Harle's body in the boot of a Jockey Club car at Kempton brought matters to a head. We had a very interesting meeting last night. If you're still up for it, I can tell you that you now have everybody's support. And I mean everybody.'

He sounded like he was knighting me. 'What do you want me to do, Mac, get down on my knees and thank the Lord?'

He shrugged and looked hurt. 'We've been skulking around in back alleys so long I thought you'd appreciate being, well, accepted.'

'How gratifying! I'm so pleased to know that Jockey Club members have now voted not to hold their noses and cross the street when they see me approach. I'm honoured, but did they say anything in passing about returning my licence?'

'I'm not going to bullshit you. That is still going to depend very heavily on getting a confession out of Kruger.'

'Well, surprise, surprise.'

He looked at me. 'Are you sticking with it?'

'Can you get me out of here today?'

'This morning.'

'Can you get Cranley off my back?'

'I've told him you are now officially employed by the Jockey Club…temporarily, of course.'

'Of course!'

'I said you'd be working on this case on the basis that the police, good as they are at their job, do not have enough time to dedicate exclusively to this particular problem.'

'And how did Detective Sergeant Cranley take that little speech?'

'Let's say he didn't applaud. I then told him that you would give the police all the help and information you could and that you'd expect the same from them.'

'Fat chance. What have the press got to say about it this morning?'

'Not that much in the racing papers who are closing ranks as usual, thank God, but a couple of the tabloids are featuring it, though that should soon blow over since Cranley intends to keep it low-profile.'

'Now, I wonder why that is? Could it be anything to do with the fact that so far he's made a complete balls of the whole thing?'

'Probably.' McCarthy looked at me expectantly.

'Well? Are you still in?'

I nodded. 'Either until they get me or the Jockey Club runs out of cars.'

Chapter 44

McCarthy found me another car, a white Granada ('It'll make you feel like a cop'), and I returned to the cottage to bathe and change.

Mac had underplayed the press reports. Harle's death hit the front pages in some papers. Roscoe was quoted as being 'devastated' by the news and repeated his story about Harle running out on him back in March and never contacting him since.

I slept for a while then prepared myself for another trip to Roscoe's. On the drive down, thoughts of Jackie occupied my mind. I was missing her, regretting I wouldn't be there for her ten o'clock call. I'd shaken off my suspicions of the previous night, though some dregs obstinately remained, making me feel guilty about harbouring them.

The gathering dusk closed around me as I crouched uncomfortably with my binoculars halfway up a tree, about three hundred yards from Roscoe's front door. Things were bound to be stirred up by Harle's murder and there was a reasonable chance Roscoe might be entertaining some interesting visitors.

It was midnight when I shimmied down to the ground, stiff, sore and cold. I could still smell the exhaust fumes of the car which had left Roscoe's and passed below me a minute before. The two men inside had been with Roscoe for almost three hours. One was my little bumbling friend from the toilet of the Duke's Hotel and the other was a young man I'd last seen lying unconscious on the Cheltenham turf – Phil Greene, Harle's stand-in. Somehow, I didn't think they'd been on a social call.

Resisting a brief crazy temptation to break into the grooms' quarters and find Jackie, I jogged to where I'd hidden the car and headed home.

I was in Cheltenham by nine next morning, drinking coffee in a restaurant overlooking the broad boulevard in the centre of town. Roscoe had announced the appointment of his new stable jockey, twenty-one-year-old Phil Greene. I doubted that all he was doing at Roscoe's last night was signing his contract.

And who was the little man who'd been with him, the same one who'd been shadowing Harle at the Duke's Hotel? The difference this time was that Greene obviously knew who he was. Harle hadn't, or so he'd claimed at the time.

I rang McCarthy's office and his secretary said sorry, he wasn't in, and who was calling?

'Eddie Malloy.'

'Oh, Mister McCarthy did leave a message that he'd be at Salisbury races this afternoon.'

'Fine, I'll see him there.'

It was the warmest day of the year so far, and when I reached the racecourse, I decided to have a beer before seeking out McCarthy.

Carrying the drink to the corner, I tucked myself in to watch the world go by. Part of that world was McCarthy, in a big hurry. I left my beer and followed him, catching him as he slowed approaching the weighing room. I touched his shoulder, 'Mac.'

He turned, looking flustered. 'Later Eddie, please. After racing.'

'Okay. I'll see you in the car park.'

Standing by the rails, I watched the next race, a decent sprint handicap. I was half a furlong from the winning post and as they charged past me, the whips cracking on rumps sounded like a busy rifle range.

All around me the crowds bawled at their horses to run faster, their jockeys to hit harder. As the winner passed the post, the roar collapsed to a murmur in seconds. I headed toward the winner's enclosure.

Walking steadily on the outside of the crowd flow, I saw Charmain crossing the lawn. Elegantly dressed and beautiful as ever, moving smartly and staring straight ahead, she looked pleased with herself.

Stepping out of the shuffling line, I turned and watched her walk away and thought about the last time I'd seen her; the Champion Hurdle party at the Duke's Hotel.

A fine party that. One worth reflecting on. Charmain had been there, so had Roscoe, and Harle and our little bumbling friend who'd visited Roscoe's with Greene last night. Had Skinner been at the party too, and Phil Greene?

I remembered Charmain's ill-mannered husband, although I couldn't recall his name. How had she escaped him today? I doubted he knew she was parading about at Salisbury races drawing lustful glances from every heterosexual man she passed.

His name came to me, Stoke, a bookmaker. Maybe he was here. I went to the betting ring to find out. He was standing on his stool, deep in conversation with someone else I knew, young Phil Greene, Roscoe's new jockey. Well, well, well, another ingredient. The pot was bubbling nicely.

Stoke was leaning over, his head close to Greene's mouth. His lips weren't moving so I guessed Greene's were. He talked with Stoke until they were interrupted by punters wanting a bet on the final race.

A twenty-five-to-one chance won it. The bookies smiled and got off their stools and the punters grimaced and made for the exits, dropping crumpled tickets on the way. Stoke jammed a wad of notes into the inside pocket of his jacket, peeled a few from another bundle to pay off his clerk, then walked with Greene toward the stands.

I followed them to the car park where they stopped alongside a big sky-blue Mercedes. Charmain was in the back seat, though neither of the men seemed to acknowledge her presence. Stoke opened the driver's door, took off his jacket and slung it in beside his wife.

He got in and looked in the mirror, fingering his too long hair and his too thin tie. Greene slid in. As they strapped on their seat belts, I made for my own car, parked near the exit.

The Merc's reversing lights glowed and Stoke swung it for the gate. I followed. McCarthy would have to wait.

Chapter 45

They kept a sensible speed, heading North on the A34 past Oxford. I found myself dropping farther behind as we got deeper into the countryside. The roads got narrower and other cars scarce. Stoke wouldn't have to be a mastermind to realize he was being followed. I tried to keep him in sight but it was a tricky game, the hedgerows grew high in places and if Stoke took a turn-off while he was out of view I'd lose him.

Just after seven, they stopped about a mile through a small village called Shipton-on-Cherwell. Stoke pulled up by a bridge near a neat white cottage on the canal and Greene got out. He turned and bowed to speak to Stoke who revved the engine, sending puffs of grey smoke from the tailpipe. Greene straightened and slammed the door and the Merc took off over the narrow bridge. He watched it go and was rewarded with a glance and a secretive wave from Charmain.

I carried on down the hill, slowing to a crawl approaching the bridge. Greene hurried along the canal bank by a line of four barges moored in the muddy water.

Two boats were covered by tarpaulins; another was a shiny varnished brown with brass fittings and a black chimney three feet high. Greene jumped onto the deck of the third barge in line, its yellow and green paint looking faded and cracked. The name on the side was Lickety Split.

The houses on the edge of the village were in view. I drove through the long evening shadows into Shipton. I stopped at a garage and asked the man behind the counter about the boat.

'I've passed it a couple of times,' I said, 'always fancied living on a boat for a year and that one looks like it wouldn't cost too much.'

'The guy who owns it lived on it himself for a few years. He just started renting it out at the end of last year when he got a new job down in Lambourn,' the garage man said.

'Think he'd be open to offers?'

'You can only try.'

'I don't suppose you've got his phone number?'

'Afraid not. Skinner's his name. A vet. I heard he'd got a job with a trainer after he'd had a few problems. Less said the better I suppose.'

'I know Lambourn. I've got a few mates there so I should be able to track him down. Thanks.'

'No problem. Hope to see you back here then, if you get the boat. Good luck with it.'

'Thanks. You've been helpful.' I said.

Really helpful.

I stopped at a phone box and called McCarthy.

'Eddie.' He didn't sound delighted.

'Sorry I missed you at Salisbury today, I got kind of sidetracked.'

'Anything worthwhile?'

I told him about Greene and the Stokes, and that Greene was staying in Skinner's boat.

'What do you make of it?' he asked.

'I don't know, but it set me thinking about Skinner. Can you remember him when he worked on the racecourse?'

'Remember him well. It was one of my lads who had to tell him his services would no longer be required.'

'For betting, wasn't it?'

'Yep. Compulsive gambling plus needles and horses are not a good mix.'

'How long ago did he lose his job?'

'Must be a couple of years now.'

'Was Howard Stoke around at the time? Making a book, I mean?'

'I can't remember, but I could find out. What's the connection?'

'I don't know that there is one, yet. But it would be interesting to know if Skinner bet with Stoke and if so, how much. There's obviously some tie-up between Stoke and Greene, and with Greene using Skinner's boat, well, there could just be a niche in Roscoe's set-up where we'll find Stoke fits nicely.

'And, last night I saw Greene leaving Roscoe's with the same bloke who was trailing Harle in the Duke's Hotel after the Champion Hurdle.'

'Are you sure it was the same man?'

'Positive. Small, chubby, very thick round glasses, unmistakable.'

There was silence for a few seconds. I thought the line had gone dead. 'Mac?'

He spoke. 'Remember I told you we interviewed Perlman before accepting his registration as an owner?'

'Uhuh. At his big house in Wiltshire, wasn't it?'

'That's right. Did I tell you the physical description as far as my man could recall?'

'Let me guess, small and chubby with very thick round glasses?'

'Got it in one.'

'Well, well, well,' I smiled.

'So it looks like there is a Perlman after all,' Mac said.

'No chance. The little guy has got to be a decoy. Kruger's the man, believe me.'

'Don't get stuck on Kruger, Eddie, you're too single-minded with him. You've got to allow for other possibilities.'

'Come on, Mac! I told you about the call Kruger left on Roscoe's answering machine. Let me remind you what he said, "Who is running this effing show, Roscoe?"'

'So who do you think Kruger was complaining about in that call? Who's trying to take over the show?'

'Roscoe. That's what it sounded like.' I said.

'That depends how you interpret it, doesn't it?'

That made me ponder. 'I suppose it does.'

'You shouldn't jump to conclusions, Eddie. Don't discount that little guy.'

'Okay, I'll keep him in mind.'

'I mean it!'

'Okay, okay.'

'So, what's next?' he asked.

'Well, Greene seems a cocky bastard. I think I'll pay him a visit under the guise of a journalist and butter him up a bit.'

'I'd say you were a hundred-to-one Eddie. Roscoe or Kruger or whoever is bound to have him briefed to give you a wide berth.'

'We'll see. Remember, officially, he's just signed with Roscoe so they might not have pulled him in yet to whatever racket they're running. Why, for instance, hasn't Roscoe moved him out of the boat

and into Harle's old place?'
　'Maybe he's afraid of ghosts.'
　'Maybe he is Mac, maybe he is.' I smiled.

Chapter 46

The following evening, I was back at the canal-side. I crossed the small bridge to the footpath. The water was so still I could see insects hopping on the surface. The boat with the brass fittings and polished wood had gone, leaving Skinner's and the other tarpaulin-covered boats, motionless as though the green slime surrounding them had anchored them to the bank.

I stepped onto Skinner's boat and it rolled under my weight. A little tattered red pennant hung limp from a thin six-inch pole on the roof.

Above a small entrance door was a Lucas headlamp the glass dirty and holed through the C. An air-gun pellet lay flattened behind the glass.

I tried the door: it was locked. Returning to the towpath, I moved along the side looking through the windows, but dingy curtains hid the interior.

As I walked to the rear of the boat, a man came down the towpath about a hundred yards away, running fast in my direction and accelerating as he closed on me.

He ran faster, sprinting. Reaching me, he went past and slowed down to stop at the front of the boat. He bent forward, hands on knees, and I walked toward him. He wore a black track suit of heavy cotton. Sweat dripped from his forehead and cheekbones and shone on the back of his neck. His face was red and he panted hard. His name was Phil Greene.

I sat on the edge of his boat. He didn't look up. All he would see from there would be my knees and shoes. 'In training for the new season, Phil?' I asked.

He nodded and pearls of sweat bounced and swung from his curly hair.

'Tough going,' I said.

He looked at me. 'I can handle it.'

I smiled. 'I'm sure you can.'

He straightened until he was looking down at me. 'What can I do for you, Mister…?'

He knew who I was. 'Malloy,' I said. 'Eddie Malloy.'

'I thought I'd seen your face somewhere.' His breathing had steadied. Squatting, he reached to the side of the path and plucked some of the longer blades of grass. 'You used to be a jockey, didn't you?'

Used to be…It always struck home. 'A long time ago,' I said.

'Couldn't have been that long ago.'

'Long enough. You can be a has-been in this game in six months.'

'If you're a mug you can.' He darted a childish little smile at me.

'Or if you get your neck broken.' I smiled back.

He didn't read the tone or he ignored it. 'That's for mugs too, riding dodgy novices. No more of that for me.' He smiled his smile again. I was beginning to dislike it.

'That's right,' I said. 'A cushy number for you this season, riding for Roscoe.'

'And for a few seasons after that if I've got anything to do with it.'

'Which is exactly what I came here to talk to you about.'

He looked up from where he was squatting like a kid, absent-mindedly rolling the blades of grass he'd plucked between his palms.

'How do you mean?' he asked.

'Ever read the profiles of racing personalities in The Sporting Life?'

'Uhuh.'

'How'd you like to be a subject?'

'Who'd want to read about me?' he asked in a silly, coy manner that filled me with an urge to throw him in the canal.

'People are always interested in the young hopefuls,' I said through gritted teeth.

He stopped rubbing the crumpled grass between his hands, opened them and let the small green cigar come to rest in his palm. Raising his hand to his lips, he blew a short hard breath and the grass disappeared. Only his eyes moved to stare at me. The annoying smile was still on his face but there was a sudden hardness, a greedily protective sheen. 'I'm no hopeful, Malloy, I've arrived.'

I didn't like the look and I didn't like him calling me Malloy, this punk who wouldn't normally last five minutes.

'Okay, you've arrived, I'm not arguing. But you must be thinking already of your first championship, riding a Gold Cup or a National winner.'

'That's only a matter of time.'

'One thing you need in this game is confidence and you're not short of that.'

'You bet I'm not. There's only one way I'm going and that's to the top.'

As if to reinforce it, he stood up. I stayed sitting while he walked the towpath, ten paces each way.

'A full page in the Life isn't going to do your career prospects any harm, is it?'

'I know it isn't. That's why I'm going to let you do it.'

'Good. When suits you?'

'Now, if you want.'

'Fine. Why don't you get changed and, we'll go and have a few drinks and outline the structure of the piece.'

'Okay,' he said and sprung past me onto the deck.

Chapter 47

The pub Greene chose was a short drive away, though it seemed a long one for me. He didn't stop talking about how well he was going to do in the new season, how much his riding had matured, how good horses would let him show his real worth.

Still, his boasting had benefits. If Roscoe had indeed warned him to avoid me, it seemed likely he'd ignore the trainer and rely on his own judgment. And he'd already decided I was a nobody.

We pulled in at a white-walled building with a thickly thatched roof. Greene nodded and smiled at a few people as we walked to the bar.

'What are you drinking?' I asked.

'Canadian Club on the rocks.'

'I'll have a bottle of beer, please.'

'Certainly, gentlemen,' said the barman, who was all dickied up with a nice white shirt and black bow tie.

He brought the drinks and I paid.

'Let's go out in the last of the sunshine,' Greene said.

'A bit noisy for interviewing.'

'Break your concentration?' he said snidely.

I sat at a table by the window and took out a mini tape-recorder.

'No, just might drown out your highly intelligent and interesting answers.'

He took it as a compliment, smiled and sat down. It wasn't difficult to fill a tape and we soon reached the stage where he was happy to keep talking, knowing the machine would pick it up, while I got us another drink.

He stayed with the clear-coloured whiskey and the more he drank the more he talked. Calling a halt around 9.30pm, I switched off the tape.

'Are you sure that'll be enough?' he asked.

'Could write a book from that, never mind a profile.'

He smiled, linked his hands behind his head and slouched in the corner of the sofa-type seat. 'Maybe someday I will write a book,' he said. 'Might even let you ghost it for me,' he nodded at his empty glass, 'if you buy me another drink, that is.'

When the closing bell rang, Greene objected, shouting for more whiskey. The barman ignored him and began clearing up glasses, putting towels over beer pumps and empty bottles in crates.

Greene was getting abusive. I reached across the table. 'Come on, Phil, we can go back to my place for a drink.'

As he stood up and gained his balance, he suddenly looked at me very seriously, 'Got any Canadian Club at home?'

'Plenty,' I lied.

He was surprisingly quiet for the first few miles of the trip, and I glanced across occasionally. His eyes were half-shut and he nodded unevenly like one of those rear-shelf toy dogs.

We must have been halfway there when he said, 'I've got a mistress, you know.'

I slowed but didn't respond. I thought 'mistress' an odd word for him to use.

'She's beautiful and I love her and when I'm champion jockey she's going to marry me.'

'What's her name?' I asked. His finger went to the side of his nose and tried to tap it.

'Secret,' he said, 'big secret.'

I didn't answer. Silence for ten seconds or so, and then he said, 'Her husband's a bastard, a real bastard.' He turned toward me. 'She married him for money, see, she never really loved him.'

'Sure.'

'Sure… Sure's right… Sure is absolutely right… She never did.'

I wondered if he looked on marriage for money as a virtue when he was sober.

'Can you take me to her now? He asked in a pathetic, begging tone. 'Please?' he added.

'Where does she live?'

'Suffolk. Somewhere in Suffolk.'

'Where in Suffolk?'

'Somewhere, okay? Somewhere…None of your business anyway.'

'I thought you wanted me to take you there?'

'I do want it but I can't. Her husband's home tonight. I am not allowed to go when he's there.'

'Back to my place then, you can have another drink and forget all about her.'

'I'll never forget her…Never!'

I thought I heard a sob. He dozed off two minutes later and didn't wake until I leaned in and shook him, having already stopped in the trees and checked the cottage for unwanted visitors.

I helped him inside and sat him down by the dead ashes of yesterday's fire. Taking off my jacket, I pulled on an old sweater and poured Greene a drink. His hand came up for it automatically. 'Is it Canadian Club?'

'Sure it is. On the rocks.'

'That's all I drink, you know.'

'So they tell me.'

'That's right.'

I cleared the grate, dropped in a couple of firelighters and some wood and set it burning. I washed my hands, poured a whiskey and sat opposite Greene.

I switched the lights off, and shadows flickered on the walls as flames circled the logs.

He sat in that loose way drunks do in easy chairs, as if his bones were an inch long and they'd folded and settled on one another.

Staring into the fire, he held the glass, although he seemed to be barely touching it.

'Take a drink, Phil.'

His arm brought the glass to his lips, his head ducked forward to drink, but his eyes never strayed from the flames. He gulped some whiskey and settled into his previous position.

'Romantic, isn't it?' I said.

He nodded. 'I miss her…I miss her badly…She's the only woman I ever loved…and she's in trouble.'

I let it ride for half a minute, but he wasn't adding to it. 'What kind of trouble?' I asked.

'Deep,' he said. 'Deep, deep trouble.'

'With the police?'

'Could be.'

'Why don't you tell me about it? Maybe I can help.'

He shook his head. 'I'll help her, I'm the only one.'

He went silent again for a while.

'Drink up,' I said, and he did, draining the glass. His arm swung down, the empty glass hanging between his thumb and fingers. I reached and refilled.

'We're going to buy a cottage by the sea when I'm champion.'

'You and Charmain?' I asked.

'Yes, just the two of us.' I watched as his memory tried to plough through the forty percent proof haze. His eyes moved from the flames and he looked quizzical, 'You know Charmain?'

'Sure met her a few times. Beautiful woman.'

'Beautiful…Beautiful…' He seemed happy. I played on. 'How's Howard, her husband?'

'A bastard's her husband, she married him for money…she didn't love him… understand?'

'Sure.'

He smirked. 'He's lousy in bed you know… she told me…Charmain told me he's a lousy lover.' He tried to raise his voice but it came out in peaks and troughs of sound. He giggled and his head swayed, though his body stayed relaxed.

'I thought Stoke was a big shot,' I said.

He stopped laughing and tried to stare at me. 'Big shot! Big shot!' He paused considering. 'Who cares? Who gives a toss about the big shot?'

'Aren't you scared of what he'll do when he finds out you've been seeing his wife?'

'Me? Scared? Of him? You don't know me mate…You don't know me!'

He was scared all right; even drunk you could tell. He drank, almost emptying the glass, and I reached for the bottle and poured him a double hangover.

'Do you plan to keep living on the boat, when you start your new job?'

His eyes closed, his head rested on the chair-back, the point of his chin aimed in my direction.

'Dunno…' he said, quietly.

'It's a nice boat, when did you buy it?'

'Not mine,' he mumbled.

'Whose is it?'

'Skinner's.'

'The vet?'

'Mmmm.'

His lower jaw sagged and his mouth opened a thumb's width.

'How well does Skinner know Stoke?' I asked.

He showed no sign of hearing me. I raised my voice. 'Phil, how well does Skinner know Howard Stoke?'

He answered with what was to be the first snore of many on the way to a king-size headache.

I waited five minutes, then moved across and eased him out of his jacket. He didn't stir. I rolled his sleeves up looking for needle marks, but both arms were clean.

I'd have bet he was up to the same games as Harle with heroin, but it looked like I was wrong. Still, there was the culmination of my little plan to look forward to.

Greene snored on. 'You enjoy your sleep, pal.' I said. 'To go with your hangover in the morning, I'm going to give you the fright of your life.'

I locked up and took the keys with me to bed.

Chapter 48

By dawn, I was awake and back in my chair facing Greene. Slumped asleep in the seat, chin on chest, a very stiff neck awaited him.

It was cold. The grate held only ashes and I had no intention of lighting a fire. I wanted Greene to feel as uncomfortable as possible when he woke. Heating my fingers round a mug of coffee, I watched him.

He was so pale he looked almost grey in the early light, his lips colourless, beard growth barely noticeable.

He moaned and tried to shift position. 'You awake?' I asked.

No response.

'Phil...time to get up.'

He frowned but didn't answer. I kicked the sole of his shoe and the frown deepened. Slowly, he pulled his foot away. I started kicking the other one. 'Rise and shine, Mister Greene, we've got visitors.'

He opened his eyes and stared at his lap trying to work out where he was and how he'd got there. I stopped kicking and stood up to look down at him.

'Some party, huh?' I said.

'Any water?' he croaked.

I got him some, and he pushed himself onto his elbow and drank all but a mouthful. 'What were you feeding me?' His voice still sounded hoarse, probably from talking too much about himself.

'Firewater,' I said.

'Shit,' he said, and tried to get up. 'My neck's killing me.' I helped him into the chair.

'Want some coffee?'

'Mmmm.'

I filled two mugs. He sipped his. It didn't seem to help.

'Your brain working yet?' I asked.

'No.'

'How many people do you know who carry guns and are built like brick shit-houses?'

His eyelids opened fully on bloodshot eyes. He stared at me. 'What are you asking?'

I repeated the question.

'Know anyone who fits the description?' I asked. He looked away.

'No.'

'You sure?'

He stared into his coffee. 'Yes.'

'That's funny, they seem to know you.'

His head jerked up. 'Who? What are you talking about?'

'The two guys who paid us a visit during the night.'

'Here? They came here?'

I nodded. He tried to smile but couldn't manage. 'You're kidding…You're just winding me up.'

'I've got better things to do. They asked for you in person.'

He sat forward. 'Just knocked the door and asked?'

'Not exactly. I heard them prowling around outside, trying the doors and windows, trying to get in.'

'What did you do?'

'I stuck a shotgun out the window and pointed it at the big one's head.'

He slurped some coffee but didn't take his eyes off me.

'I asked what he wanted and he said he wanted you. No trouble for me, just to send you out.'

Resting the coffee mug on his knee, he rubbed his bowed forehead with his free hand. I shrugged. 'Never mind, if you don't know these guys then obviously they've made a mistake and you can go right on out there.'

He looked up sharply. 'Are they still there?'

I nodded. 'They're in the woods…Waiting.'

'Oh, Jesus!' He bowed his head again and rubbed his eyes as though he was going to cry.

I got up and went to the window. Standing off to the side, I pushed open an inch of curtain. Greene was holding his breath. I sensed him watching my back intently. After a minute, I turned toward him.

'They still there?'

'It might not be as bad as you thought.' I said.

Relief crept across his face.

'I can only see one of them... having said that, it is the one with the gun...I suppose his sidekick could be anywhere.'

He slumped back in the chair, and some coffee slopped over and wet his trousers. I went back and sat opposite him. 'Want to tell me who they are?'

'I don't know who they are, not their names anyway. But they are bad news.'

'How bad?'

'Ask Alan Harle.'

'Did they kill Alan?'

'I don't know!' His voice was growing panicky again. 'Shit! What am I into here? I'm not saying any more.' He sat forward again. 'Do you hear me? Forget what I said about those blokes, I'm not saying any more.'

'Suit yourself.'

We sat in silence for a minute while he grimaced and fidgeted and sipped at his coffee. He would stare without blinking for a while then his eyes would be moving everywhere like a trapped animal looking for an escape route.

'Come on,' I said. 'I'll drive you home.'

'No way! I'm not leaving here. Not till they've gone.'

'You can't stay.'

'I'm staying!' he almost shouted.

'Okay, but you're staying on your own. I've got business to attend to and I'm not sitting nursemaid to you.'

His head snapped up and he looked at me again. 'You can't leave me by myself! They'll be through that door as soon as you go.'

'Too bad, Phil. Until I'm clear what I'm up against, I'm out of it.' I stood and reached for my jacket, pulled it on, and pulled out the car keys.

Greene got out of the chair, and made to stand up before realizing it put him in direct line with the window. He dropped onto all fours and crawled to where I stood. Safely out of the window-line, he got up.

His face was close to mine but not close enough for him to start whispering, which is what he did.

'Look, go out and tell them I've gone. Tell them I left by the back door while it was still dark.'

'They don't seem the type to believe it. In fact, the reason I can't see the other one out there is probably because he's covering the back of the house.'

He stood staring at me, expressionless. 'How the hell am I going to get out of here?'

'I can get you out but I want to know who those two guys are. You tell me that and I'll get you out.'

'Listen, I'll pay you. I'll waive the fee for the article, you can keep it.'

'There wasn't going to be any fee. You were doing it for the glory, kid.'

'Don't call me kid!'

'I'd have thought you've got more things to worry about just now than your ego.' I moved toward the window.

Trying to hurry, he stumbled round me and stood with his back almost to the wall. I squinted out of the corner of the curtain.

'Is he still there?' Greene asked.

'Yep, come and see so you can be sure it is who you think it is.'

'No way! God knows what kind of sights he's got on that gun.'

'It was only a pistol I saw in his hand. There was no rifle. None that I could see anyway.' He was quiet again, perplexed. 'How much do you want?' he asked.

'I'm not bargaining. I don't want paid. Just tell me who the hell Butch Cassidy and the Sundance Kid are?'

'Why are you interested in who they are? What's it to you?'

'What it is to me is that Alan Harle was a friend of mine and I want to know why he was killed and who killed him. If I don't know in two minutes, I'm going out that door, you're staying here and you can take what's coming from your visitors.' Greene's legs buckled slowly and his back slid down the wall until he squatted on the floor then, finally, sat. He stared at the ash-filled grate. 'Harle was killed dealing in drugs.'

'What kind?'

'Heroin.'

'What kind of deals?'

'Not the kind he wanted. He thought he was the big shot, moving among the internationals, the heavyweights. Some big shot.'

'You still didn't tell me what kind of deals.'

'He was trying to set something up with those two guys, but he tried to screw them and they found out…Goodbye, Alan.'

'What was he trying to set-up?'

'I don't know, some deal or other.'

'You keep talking about deals, do you have any details? Was he supplying heroin or smuggling it into the country or out of the country or what?'

'How the hell should I know?'

'You must have some evidence?'

'Look, give me a break, Malloy! I'm telling you what I think was happening, my opinion, right?'

'But without any evidence to back it up…Your opinion isn't worth shit, Greene. I think you're lying to try to get yourself out of trouble.'

'I don't have to sit here and listen to this garbage from you,' he said.

'Sure you don't.'

I moved to the curtain and looked out again. The sky was darkening. I walked through to the bedroom and heard Greene scramble to his feet and call after me, 'Where are you going?'

I came back in, zipping up my jacket. 'I told you, I've got business,' I said, turning toward the door.

'Good luck, Phil.'

He grabbed my arm. 'Wait!' I turned to face him. He loosened his grip. His eyes were tired, desperate.

There was some white matter in the corners of his mouth. We were close. His breath smelled bad. 'I'll tell you all I know. It may not be any good to you but I promise I'll tell you what I know.'

Chapter 49

I made coffee. We sat down and Greene talked. 'It was a kind of accident how I found out Alan was into drugs. I was still doing my two at Roscoe's. I was stacking bales in the hayloft one afternoon when I saw Alan come out of the house and cross the yard to his car. He always parked it behind the top block, out of sight of anyone in the yard. I could see him from the hayloft. He couldn't see me.'

Greene rambled on at great length filling in every detail down to how easily the veins showed in Harle's arms as he pumped up before an injection, but all it amounted to was that he knew Harle was a junkie. He tried to embellish the dealing side.

'One day I had a ride at Uttoxeter. Alan had three so we travelled up together. Alan, as usual, hardly spoke a word on the journey. He had a fall on his last ride and came back in the ambulance.

'I rushed down to meet it to check if he was okay. Not that I was worried about him, I just wanted to make sure he could drive so I could get home. Anyway, he was all right. My ride was in the last so he said to meet him at the car afterwards.

'Mine ran like a dog. When I'd showered and changed, I was one of the last out of the weighing room. It was getting dark but the rain had stopped. I walked to the car park. Alan had a green Saab and he was standing beside it talking to two blokes, big guys. I mean, most jockeys look small even next to your Mister Average, and Alan was short anyway, but these guys made him look like a toddler. Alan nodded toward me as I approached and they turned and looked at me. Then they said something to Alan, walked over to a black Merc and drove off.

'Alan was in the Saab by the time I reached it. I got in but he didn't speak. He looked pale but his eyes were bright. He set off, driving fast. I didn't ask who the guys were. I knew he wouldn't tell me.

'On the motorway he pulled in at the first services and told me to get myself a coffee as he was just going to the toilet. I got out and headed to the cafeteria, but when I looked, I saw Alan rummaging in the boot. He took something out and slipped it under his jacket then he headed for the toilet.

'As we drove back he started talking. He said he'd be retiring from the saddle soon. He was going places, going into business with his "Associates".'

'So you assumed he was dealing in drugs with these two guys?'

'Of course he was. What else could it be?'

'It could have been a million things. Did you hear the conversation with the two blokes?'

'I didn't but-'

'Did Harle ever say anything about dealing?'

'Well, no but-'

'Supposing he was dealing in heroin, that might not have been why he was killed.'

'Look, Mister, you asked me what I thought and I told you, so gimme a break!'

He hadn't told me everything, I was sure of that, and I considered questioning him to try to catch him out. I could have asked him about Roscoe, Kruger, and Skinner, but it was unlikely he'd tell me anything and it would only alert them further once Greene blabbed. If they believed I was just interested in Harle's murder, it might make things a bit easier. 'So you think the two guys in the car park killed him? I asked.

'That's my guess.'

'What was the motive?'

Greene shrugged. 'He must have double-crossed them.'

'How?'

'How the hell should I know? I'm only telling you what I think happened.' He finished his coffee. It didn't look like he wanted to hear any more questions. Leaning forward, he put the empty mug on top of the old mantelpiece and held his head again. 'You got an aspirin?' he asked.

I brought four from the kitchen with a glass of water. He took them all at once and managed to keep them down. I squatted to his level and took the glass off him. He looked at me, waiting for me to speak.

Spreading his palms upwards in an open 'honest' gesture he said, 'Look, I've told you everything I know. Can you get rid of those guys?'

'You haven't told me why they're after you. You say you don't know them. You say they killed Harle because he double-crossed them…what would they want with you?'

'I don't know, maybe they're scared I'll talk, just like I've done to you.'

'But if you didn't actually see them kill Alan then, as far as they're concerned, you'd have nothing to talk about, would you?'

He shrugged and tried the 'honest' gesture again. 'Look, I don't know why they're here, maybe they think Alan told me something about the deal they were setting up. Maybe they think I'll go to the police.'

I sat and stared at him for a while. 'Okay,' I said. 'Okay.' I went to the window again and looked out from the side. I turned away, pacing the worn rug behind the sofa, trying to look like I was thinking hard.

Greene was convinced. His anxious gaze followed me. I let him stew a while then told him what my plan was: to use a long coat I had in the back of the car to cover him as he dashed out.

I stopped pacing and looked at him. 'Okay?'

'Sounds a bit risky to me.'

'Would you rather stay here?'

His head dropped again. I returned to the window, looked out and then spoke to Greene. 'Ready?'

'Now?'

'I don't see either of them at the moment.'

'Okay.' He looked scared.

We went through the routine and Greene bolted into the car like a rat down a hole. 'Drive, for fuck's sake!' he yelped.

I accelerated away, wipers swishing, along the edge of the wood, leaving it to the birds, the badgers and the foxes.

An hour later, I eased the car to a halt in the lay-by next to the canal. Greene was still lying down in the back; he'd been fretting about being followed. 'You can come out now.' I said.

'Where are we?' he asked, still prone.

'Home. At the canal.'
'Anything behind us?'
Most of your nerve if you ever had any.
'Nothing.' I said.
'They didn't follow us?'
'Nope.'
The springs creaked as he sat up. Daylight on his face showed the effects of the heavy night and the tough morning.
'You all right?' I asked, not caring about the answer.
'For now I am but I've just been thinking, if they found me at your place, what's to stop them finding me here?'
'Nothing, I suppose.'
He frowned and ran his fingers through his hair. 'Do you think they could?'
'They seem smart enough.'
'Shit! I'd better start looking for somewhere else… I'd better tell Sk-' He stopped himself.
'You'd better tell who?'
'Nobody. Forget it.' He got out.
I rolled the window down. 'Who else is involved, Phil?'
He turned and headed for the boat. 'What about The Sporting Life piece?' I asked.
'Cancel it,' he called. 'I don't want it printed.'
'I'll save it then, it'll make a good obituary.' I thought he was out of earshot, but he faltered before stepping on the boat and disappearing through the green and yellow door.

Chapter 50

Half a mile up the hill from the canal lay the ruins of some buildings. I drove there, approaching them along a tangled, overgrown track. Mounds of tumbled sandstone and old broken bricks partially hid the shell of a burned-out barn. The uneven spars, charred a velvety black, looked like some crazy graph against the sky.

I picked my way through the rubble, grass and weeds and settled on the sandstone blocks.

The land sloped gently down, separated by hedgerows into small fields. I raised my binoculars and focused on Greene's boat. Just one barge floated beside Greene's, its grey tarpaulin gathering a spread of bird droppings.

I scanned the canal, the bridge, and the lock. Greene's boat, began rolling in the still water, then Greene came out, jumped to the towpath and hurried toward the bridge.

He crossed the road and went through the gate of the white cottage. As he walked on the paved path, it seemed strange, seeing him so close in these bright optics, not to hear his boot-heels click.

He knocked then drummed impatiently on the door until a woman opened it. She must have been almost seventy but stood ramrod straight, about four inches taller than Greene. He said his piece and she moved aside to let him in. Less than a minute later, he was back out. The old woman watched until he was through the gate and onto the road before closing the door slowly. Greene jogged to the boat, jumped on deck and went inside.

I waited more than an hour, shifting uncomfortably on the stone seat, my eyelids feeling bruised from the lens cups on the binoculars.

I laid them down and stood up to stretch.

A lime-green Renault approached the bridge and pulled in sharply on the grass verge. Skinner got out, raised the rear hatch and a large, thick-barrelled dog joined him. A Rottweiler.

He strode down the towpath to Greene's boat and the dog leapt on deck. Skinner followed, wrenched open the door and went in, slamming it.

He stayed inside for about twenty minutes and when the door opened again, the dog came out first.

Skinner and Greene followed, talking and gesturing. If they weren't arguing, they sure weren't trading compliments. Skinner edged toward the side of the boat. The dog took this as the off signal and jumped to the towpath, but Skinner stopped and turned on Greene again.

Greene spread his arms and shrugged in a 'what could I have done?' gesture and Skinner moved forward and poked him hard in the shoulder. Greene took a step back then did some finger-pointing of his own. He advanced on Skinner but faltered as he saw the dog bounding onto the deck. I panned down to see the big white wet teeth.

Greene backed off. Skinner spoke and Greene turned away and went inside. The animal stayed at Skinner's heel as they walked to the car. The vet swung the Renault, straightened up and sped off.

I lowered the binoculars…decision time. I could go home and change into suitable clothing, grab a flask of tea and some food, a flashlight and storm-lamp. I would be gone almost two hours.

Too long.

Greene might be anywhere by that time. He seemed panicky and probably wouldn't sit around much longer. I returned to my watchtower and settled behind the stone again. I'd burst the hornet's nest, I had to wait for the sting.

Chapter 51

Within fifteen minutes of leaving, the Renault came back. Skinner couldn't have gone farther than the village.

Greene emerged from the boat with a suitcase and hurried to the car.

Skinner screeched away and spun up the hill in my direction. I ran to my car, binoculars swinging round my neck, banging on my ribs.

I reached the top of the track in time to see the lime-green car blurring along through the trees and flying past the entrance.

I accelerated down the pot-holed strip, which battered the Granada's suspension into a series of clunks and bangs. Swinging onto the road, the tyres squealed as they tried to bite on tarmac. I straightened her and soon the only noise was the engine racing and the wind rushing past.

I had to keep Skinner in view but couldn't afford to get too close in case he spotted me, or Greene looked back. The straight stretches were the worst; it wouldn't take Skinner long to realize the car in his mirror had been on the same road for miles.

But the vet seldom dropped below eighty, meaning the road in front would need all his attention.

Whenever the opportunity arose, I'd let another car overtake for a while. But few travelled at my speed, and if I tucked behind anyone for more than a few minutes, the Renault got so far away it looked like a knot at the end of a grey ribbon. I was afraid he might head down some side road and be gone before I got there.

Skinner went east and after two hours, we reached the flat fenland of Cambridgeshire. The sun raised the temperature in the car until sweat prickled in my scalp and ran from my armpits. I opened the window and a rush of air and noise filled the car and seemed to slow it. I made do with the vents.

Sweat, excitement, adrenaline. Greene was obviously in something up to his neck and Skinner too.

They'd be running now to the next guy in line. I smiled, confidence growing, I'd been following them all this time and neither had sussed. I was entitled to feel pleased.

I should have known better.

The engine missed, picked up again, spluttered, and then died. The oil light in the dash lit up, I jabbed madly at the gas pedal, then looked at the fuel gauge – empty. I was pumping air.

The Renault disappeared round a bend.

Braking hard, I switched on the hazard lights, jumped out and grabbed the spare gallon I always carried in the boot. As the petrol glugged and burbled into the tank, I scanned the flat land through the rippling haze as the Renault, side-on, briefly came into view again before disappearing off the edge of the world.

The empty tank sucked slowly at the plastic spout of the can. I ran through my repertoire of curses, tempted to pour just half the contents in but at the speeds I'd been doing, even the full can would only take me another twenty-five miles. There might not be a petrol station for fifty.

The last few drops ran down the paintwork as I pulled the spout away and shoved the cap on.

The engine turned but didn't catch. I tried again. Nothing…the fuel wasn't through yet. I pumped the pedal hard and fast. Another turn…still not there.

I cursed myself for letting the fuel get so low. Trying to be patient, I counted to ten, quickening at seven, then turned the key again.

It started.

I let the clutch out and the car bucked forward. Within twenty seconds, I was doing eighty again but the tarmac stretched long, straight and empty.

Ten miles on, the road climbed almost imperceptibly over moor-like land, treeless except for a long, narrow wood in the distance.

The needle on the fuel gauge kept pointing at red, like some insistent schoolteacher trying to hammer home a lesson. The gallon hadn't moved it a fraction and what was left in the tank burned at a mighty rate.

If I didn't come on a garage soon, apart from never catching up with Skinner, I'd be in for a long walk.

The closer I got to the line of trees, the more obvious was their density. A hundred yards from them, I saw there were two broad rows of trees bordering a narrow road. I slowed as I passed the entrance. Something caught my eye and I braked and reversed.

At the turn-off, a tyre had ploughed a furrow through a patch of dark earth still soggy from the morning rain. In the middle of the furrow lay a rabbit, its back-end and rear legs crushed. Its ears twitched and it tried to raise its head as I walked toward it. The wheel had flattened it from just under the ribcage down.

A muddy tread-mark crossed the crushed white bob of its tail. I gently raised its head and broke its neck. It couldn't have lived more than a few minutes with those injuries, so someone had turned in here.

Decision time. There had to be a strong chance Skinner's car had done the damage. And if not? Well, with only about ten miles left in the tank it didn't seem likely I'd catch him anyway.

I drove into the avenue of trees, coasting out of gear when I could. Two hundred yards ahead, the road swung to the right and I looked for a gap to pull into.

There was none. The trees were so dense you couldn't have ridden a horse through them.

A hundred yards from the bend, I parked beside a solid border of Leylandii. Taking my binoculars, I crossed over into the trees and wriggled through in a slow slalom.

I cut across diagonally until I was stopped by a solid green wall of hedge about twelve feet high. On my side, the tree branches had been cut away completely up to that height so none could pierce it or alter its shape.

I pushed the toe of my boot into the hedge and though it gave a bit, it seemed strong and dense enough to let me climb. About five feet wide at the top, it easily supported my weight as I crawled across and lay flat to admire the view.

The road through the trees opened out onto a drive as wide as a motorway. It led to a big Georgian-style cream-coloured house with rows of green-curtained windows. Parked in front of the black double doors was a silver Rolls-Royce. Alongside it was the Renault. Both cars were empty.

The house was not.

With my binoculars trained through a ground-floor window, I saw Skinner and Greene. They were standing. Another man was pacing, talking, gesturing angrily. I wished I could lip read and work out just how hard a time those two were getting from Howard Stoke.

When it became clear from the body language this was no social visit, there was nothing more to learn. Harle, Greene, Roscoe, Kruger, Skinner and now Stoke – whatever this was, they were all in it.

I rolled over, leaving two dents where my elbows had rested, scrambled down and made my way back to the car.

At the junction, I turned left. The road to the right had no petrol stations for a long way. It was also the road Skinner would take to go home.

Within five minutes, I found a village and came upon what was little more than a wooden hut by the side of the road, fronted by two of the oldest petrol pumps I'd ever seen. They were pale blue with big lit-up lampshade tops. I pulled in, wondering if they were quaint display items for tourists, but a boy of eighteen or so skipped out of the hut with a sunny, 'What'll it be, sir?'

'It'll be a tank of four star and…' I went and got the empty petrol can and laid it at his feet 'one for the road.'

I made it home for Jackie's ten o'clock call and I told her everything.

Chapter 52

I spent the next three days at the races watching Howard Stoke. I wanted to find out how he ran his business, who bet with him and when and, if possible, in what amounts. I wanted to know who spoke to him but didn't have a bet. I wanted to see if Greene or Charmain would show up.

The start of the first race at Newbury on the Friday was delayed when a horse threw his jockey. Most riderless horses bolt, but this one seemed intent on doing damage, and kicked his fallen rider savagely before galloping off down the course. He covered a circuit of the track, slowing only occasionally to throw a kick at the running rails.

The rest of the runners circled at the stalls, their jockeys walking, leading them round. The loose horse had everyone's attention. The stands were two-thirds full and the bookmakers watched from their stools.

The horse was brown with one white stocking on his off hind and a star on his forehead. His number cloth said eight and I checked my racecard. His name was Castleford.

His lad and trainer were out on the course now and Castleford galloped toward them. He veered off, crashing through the plastic rails onto the steeplechase track. His lad hurried after him waving his arms as the horse spun and bore down on him.

The boy stood his ground and when Castleford was ten yards from him, he dug his feet in and stopped.

The reins had come loose and dragged on the turf. The horse lowered his head and crab-walked over to the rails where he turned his hind legs to the lad. The boy approached cautiously, his hand outstretched. A low murmur rose from the stands.

He got to the horse's head without being kicked and reached slowly for the loose rein, caught it and turned the horse gently back toward the paddock.

The animal went quietly with him, and as the crowd applauded, the boy turned to pat the horse's head.

Castleford opened his mouth and took the lad's arm between his teeth. The boy's cry could be heard high in the stands and the applause gave way to oohs and aahs.

Castleford pulled the lad off his feet, shaking him like a terrier with a teddy bear as the trainer and two groundsmen ran to help. One of the men, wielding a long-handled hoe, smashed it down on the horse's head. Castleford, stunned, let go his lad and the other man dragged the boy to safety His friend with the hoe hit the horse again, then the trainer grabbed one end of the rein and urged the groundsman to drop his weapon and get the other.

With a man each side, holding the rein tight at the mouth, Castleford walked off the course and away behind the stands. Two medics comforted the shocked and bleeding lad until the ambulance rolled up.

As soon as the race got under way, Stoke left his stool and hurried off in the direction of the unsaddling enclosure. It was the only time I'd seen him leave his pitch during a race.

The winner was being hosed down by the time Stoke returned. A handful of punters waited and his anxious clerk seemed pleased to see him. When he'd paid out, Stoke made a call from the telephone on the small shelf attached to the rails. The conversation was short and when he hung up, he smiled.

Three more races were delayed that day and the meeting ran over time by almost an hour. The last result brought a long queue at Stoke's pitch but he seemed calm as he paid them before stepping off his stool, leaving the bewildered looking clerk to pack up the gear.

I trailed Stoke to the bar, where he went in among the soft lights and the smiling faces hazed in blue cigar smoke.

I could have used a whiskey myself, chilled by two fat ice cubes. I decided to have it back at the cottage, as there didn't seem any point in hanging around watching Stoke drink his usual quota. Over the last three days, I hadn't learnt much, and the euphoria from finding the gang at Stoke's house was evaporating.

I got into the car, already anticipating Jackie's call. Maybe she'd have picked up something worthwhile today. She'd had nothing to report the previous two evenings and in a way I was glad; at least it kept her safe.

I reached the exit within a minute of leaving my parking space, which was bad news for Phil Greene. If I'd been delayed a while, I might have spotted him driving in. If I'd stayed for that drink, I'd have seen him meeting Stoke in the bar. If I hadn't gone home when I did, it's just possible I could have saved his life.

Chapter 53

Next morning, half my face was shaved when the phone rang. As I lifted the receiver, it slipped across the shaving cream on my fingers and clattered on the small table.

I picked it up again. 'Hello?'

'Eddie,' the voice was tense.

'Mac. What's up?'

'Have you see the papers?'

'They don't deliver here in the backwoods.'

'Phil Greene was killed at Newbury yesterday.'

Logic told me he was mistaken. I didn't answer.

'Eddie?'

'I'm still here. What happened?'

'He was savaged by a horse. They found him in its stable after racing, ribs smashed, liver punctured, both arms broken. The official cause of death was severe head injuries.'

It was beginning to come together. 'Was the horse called Castleford?'

'How did you know that?'

'I was at Newbury yesterday. I saw the horse take a mad turn and savage his jockey and his lad.'

'That's right. Do you know who owns Castleford?'

'I don't know who owned him when he arrived at the track, but I've a fair idea who owned him when he killed Phil Greene.'

'Go on.'

'Howard Stoke.'

'How the hell-?'

'I added two and two and got the right answer, for once.'

I told him about Stoke's behaviour and how he'd followed Castleford and his trainer as the horse was led away after being caught.

'Who found Greene?' I asked

'One of the groundsmen, checking boxes before leaving.'

'What time?'

'About eight.'

'Have you interviewed Stoke?'

'One of my men spoke to him late last night.'

'What's his story?'

'He claims he was having a drink in the bar when Greene arrived about six-fifteen and they got talking. He said Greene was boisterous, happy, and drinking large whiskeys. Stoke told him about the horse he'd bought, said it was absolutely crazy and there wasn't a man alive who could ride him and all that Wild West stuff. Stoke said he'd had a few too many himself. Anyway, according to him, Greene boasted there wasn't a horse alive he couldn't ride. He said he would get him out of his box and ride him bareback into the bar.

'Stoke says he stopped all the kidding at this point and told Greene there was no way he was to go near the horse. Greene wouldn't let up and Stoke, quote, had to get serious and threaten him to stay away for his own good.

'Apparently Greene then calmed down but ten minutes later he disappeared, supposedly to the toilet. He never came back. Stoke reckons he was determined to bring the horse out, just to show he could do it. My man said Stoke seemed very upset.'

'Did he ask Stoke why he bought the horse?'

'Yes. Stoke claims he didn't want to see the horse put down, but he didn't want it to race again either, in case it savaged anyone else.'

'Did your man believe him?'

'I think so.'

'You've got some gullible people working for you, Mac.'

'That's not exactly fair comment, Eddie, we had no reason to suspect Stoke was involved.'

'Listen, as soon as Stoke bought that horse the first thing he did at his pitch was make a phone call which was, very probably, to arrange for Greene to come to Newbury.'

'Eddie–' He started back on the defensive.

'Mac, I'm sorry. You're right. Your man didn't know enough of what was going on. Forget what I said.'

'Okay.'

'Have the police interviewed Stoke?' I asked.

'They saw him last night. I spoke to them just before I called you. They said it's unlikely they'll be looking for anyone else but they'd wait for the verdict from the inquest.'

'Hmmm.'

'As far as they're concerned, Stoke's alibi, if he needed one, is cast iron. There were at least thirty people in that bar when Greene went out and with all the noise that had come from the table most of them would have noticed he'd left and Stoke was still there.'

'And why do you think Stoke was generating the noise?'

'Well, that's a thought.'

'A thought! Do me a favour, Mac, if I'm still in one piece when this is over, point me in the opposite direction from Racecourse Security Services and tell me not to stop until I clear the horizon.'

He didn't reply.

'Do you know when the inquest is?' I asked.

'Probably early next week. I'll contact you as soon as I have the details.'

'Okay.'

'Right, I'll leave you to it then.'

'Mac, before you go, how did Greene get access to the racecourse stables, where were Security?'

He cleared his throat. 'We've identified a breach there, which is being investigated.'

'Cut the official crap, Mac. What happened?'

'Last day of the meeting. Stoke's was the only horse still there.'

'And?'

'The guy on the gate skived off for a beer.'

'One of your people?'

'It'll cost him his job.'

'It cost Greene his life.'

Chapter 54

The inquest was on Tuesday: death by misadventure. They buried him on Thursday, a warm afternoon under a cloudless sky. The heavy scent of wildflowers from the field next to the small cemetery drifted over the wreaths.

The Roscoes and Stokes attended, and Skinner was there. Half a dozen jockeys turned up.

After final prayers, the mourners drifted off in small groups. I made my way over and fell in behind Skinner's gathering. I deliberately caught Stoke's eye. He looked smug. Roscoe ignored me and Skinner's returned glance was evil.

I scanned the Life each morning for word on Roscoe's new stable jockey. His announcement after the funeral had been, 'We'll have to wait and see. It's hardly the first thing on our minds at this sad time.'

How touching.

And, the reporter had asked, would Mr. Perlman, have a say in the choice of new stable jockey?

'Mister Perlman,' Roscoe told him, 'leaves the handling of all his racing affairs to me. I will choose the new jockey.'

As yet, he hadn't.

Stoke was responsible for Greene's death. I wondered if he'd organized Harle's, or had Greene been telling me the truth about Harle being killed by his 'business associates'?

If Stoke controlled the hit men, why hadn't he used them to kill Greene instead of taking a chance himself? I needed more information on Stoke's background.

One person who should know Stoke better than anyone was his

wife Charmain. I wondered if she'd talk. She'd looked drawn and haggard at the funeral. If Phil Greene's drunken boasts of her being his mistress were true, that might explain why she'd seemed so stressed. But the strains of living with Stoke couldn't be helping her either if he often behaved as he had with me at the Champion Hurdle party.

He probably beat the hell out of her if she looked the wrong way at the milkman, and when he went racing she'd be shut in that big house in the middle of nowhere with nothing to do but watch the trees grow.

I reckoned she'd be sick of Stoke's idea of domestic bliss. I remembered what she'd been like as a teenager; she wouldn't have stood Stoke's treatment for two minutes back then. How had she got herself involved with him? Why? How much did she know and what would she be willing to tell?

I checked The Sporting Life classified ads and found that Stoke planned to be at York next Tuesday, Wednesday and Thursday. A long way from home. On at least one of those nights his wife would have my company.

Chapter 55

At ten o'clock on Friday night, the day after Greene's funeral, my phone rang. Thinking it was Jackie, I hurried to answer.

'Hello.'

'Eddie Malloy?'

'That's right.' I didn't recognize the accented voice immediately.

'I have information you may want.'

The same voice I'd last heard shouting on Roscoe's answerphone. 'Kruger?' I asked

'Yes.'

'Information on what, Mister Kruger?'

'On the doping ring you are trying to break.'

'Why should you want to give me information on something you are running?'

'I am not running it, not anymore.'

'They threw you out?'

'Wrong. I am stepping out. I came into this to make a profit, not to have people killed. You know that, Mister Malloy. I am not a murderer.'

'So who is the murderer?'

'You must meet me tomorrow.'

'Sure, so I can be next in the morgue.'

'Mister Malloy, you do me a disservice, I told you-'

'You did me a pretty big disservice yourself five years ago.'

'That was business. There was nothing personal.'

'And isn't this the same business, Mister Kruger, only for higher stakes?'

'They told me there would be no killing, now three people are dead. I will not take any further part in it.' His voice was calm and measured and he sounded, God help me, sincere. 'So what do you get out of it by giving me information?' I asked.

'I will give you evidence to convict the madman in charge and you will keep me out of it. I will be leaving the country tomorrow.'

'Why not just leave anyway? Why give me evidence?'

'Because I want to sleep easily in my bed. I will be able to do that if I know this man has been locked up for a long time.'

It was beginning to sound plausible. I knew Kruger wasn't the type for murder. A con man, fraudster and all-round crook, but he wasn't into violence on that scale.

'If you say I'll be safe at this meeting tomorrow, then you won't mind me bringing someone else along, will you?'

'No police.'

'No police, but a member of the Racecourse Security Services.'

'That is the same.'

'It's not. He has no powers of arrest other than as a citizen and that's not what I want him for.'

'Why, then, do you want him?'

'I want him to witness a sworn statement from you that I had nothing to do with that doping ring five years ago.'

'I can write that statement and sign it and bring it with me.'

'No. Without a witness, I'd be accused of forging your signature.'

'I will write the whole statement by hand. You could not forge that.'

'No deal. I want to bring my own witness, and I want you to speak the confession into a tape recorder. Then I have a witness and your voice too, admitting everything. No arguments then.'

'Mister Malloy-'

'Those are the terms, Mister Kruger. If you want this lifelong safety, if you want me to deal with this man, those are the terms.'

He was silent. I thought he had gone, 'Kruger?'

'All right. I will see you and your friend tomorrow.'

'Where?'

'You know the field which is used as a car park at Stratford racecourse?'

'Yes. What time?'

'Ten o'clock.'

'Okay.'

He hung up.

I stood staring at the phone, trying to take in the prospect of getting back my licence, of riding racehorses once more, of a second chance at life.

Was he bluffing? Was it a trap? I walked to the window and stared into the deep woods. If I told Mac the truth, he'd insist on having a squad of armed cops there. Was I entitled to keep it from him, that Kruger was the man we'd be meeting?

If it turned out to be a trap, was I justified in risking McCarthy's life as well as my own?

I sat by the cold fireplace, head in hands. Everything I knew about Kruger chimed with what he'd said. He'd had no taste for violence. Even all those years ago when my rage had driven me to beat him savagely, there had been no comeback, no revenge attack on me, even though Kruger could've organized that with a one-minute phone call.

No, I must dump the doubts and believe what he had told me. A decision had to be made, and this was it.

I called McCarthy. 'Mac, I need a big favour, two big favours.'

'What?'

'Number one, meet me at Stratford tomorrow morning at ten. Number two, don't ask me any questions on the phone, I'll fill you in when I see you.'

'There's no racing at Stratford tomorrow.'

'Meet me in the field they use for the public car park. And bring your Dictaphone.'

I POURED a drink and began to let the pictures of me, in silks once again, on horseback, begin trickling back into my mind.

I was on a real high when Jackie phoned at ten-thirty. She sounded anxious. 'Eddie! I've been trying to get through for ages, is everything all right?'

'Couldn't be better. The reason you couldn't get through was that I had a call that's given me the best break of the case. In fact, it'll probably crack it completely.'

I told her everything, blabbing like an excited schoolboy. She said, 'Eddie, I don't like the smell of this.'

'Look, don't worry! I won't take any chances. Mac's agreed to come.'

'What time will you be home? Can I phone to make sure you're all right?'

'We're due to meet him at ten at Stratford racecourse but depending on how it goes I might not come straight back here. Chances are I won't. Listen Jackie, don't worry. Ring me tomorrow night if you can.'

'Okay.'

We talked for a while. There was nothing to report at her end except a noticeable lack of grief at Roscoe's about Phil Greene's death. Plans for our future took up the rest of the conversation, and I went to bed confident we would be together again soon.

Chapter 56

McCarthy was at Stratford at ten. So, it seemed, was Kruger, as the only other car was a black Vauxhall parked two hundred yards away in the empty field.

McCarthy pushed open his passenger door for me but I declined. 'Let's walk. It'll give me time to tell you what's happening.'

We went through the gate toward the big black Carlton, which faced us head-on.

'You got the whadyamacallit,' I asked, 'the recorder?'

'The Dictaphone. It's in my pocket.'

'Let me see it.'

He stopped and frowned. I clenched my jaw and stared at him. He sighed and drew the small beige machine from his jacket pocket.

'Good,' I said, 'In that black car is Mister Gerard Kruger.'

Mac grabbed my arm, 'You are kidding me!'

'I'm not kidding you, Mac, and he's here to do us a big favour.'

We were fifty yards from the car. Mac stooped, trying to see who was in there, 'Well, it looks like he's on his own.'

'He is on his own,' I said, 'and he's promised to tell everything so long as he can then walk away.'

'Why?'

'Because he didn't sign up for any killings, and he wants the man who is carrying out those killings locked up for a long time so he can sleep safe in his bed.'

Mac stooped again and stared. I said, 'Mac, you're going to spook him. His engine is still running. It won't take much for him to hit that gas pedal and take off. Come on.'

We walked. Mac kept his eyes fixed on the black Carlton, he was getting edgy again. 'I don't like this Eddie. He's seen us. We're walking toward him. Why not switch off his engine now?'

'I don't know, Mac. Maybe he's cold and likes to keep his heater on.'

'Or maybe, as soon as we're close enough, he'll accelerate and run us down.'

'If he does, you go left and I'll go right. One of us'll survive.'

'Don't be flippant, Eddie, for all you know-'

'Mac,' We were ten yards from the car now, 'what's that sticking through his window?'

'Shit!'

We ran to the car. McCarthy yanked the rubber hose pipe from the small gap and I pulled the driver's door open to haul Kruger out. But his skin was cold, his limbs stiff.

My jockey's licence, within an arm's length last night, had not so much receded over the horizon as disappeared into space. I had to turn away, fighting a sudden urge to punch Kruger's cold, dead face.

McCarthy switched off the engine and looked at me. 'Suicide?' he asked.

'Suicide, bollocks!' I said. 'They doped him, knocked him out or something and stuck him in there. Probably did it somewhere else and drove him here. His phone must have been bugged.'

McCarthy looked distressed and I began to wonder if this was the first corpse he'd seen. He leaned on the bonnet, staring down at his big reflection in the shiny paintwork and said quietly, 'We'd better get the police.'

'You get the police, I'm going.'

His head snapped up. 'What are you talking about, going? You're staying here to give a statement to the police.'

I marched over to face him across the bonnet and just stopped myself from grasping the wing and leaving fingerprints all over it. 'Mac, who was there when Danny Gordon was found dead?'

'You were.'

'And Alan Harle?' He didn't answer. 'And now Kruger?'

McCarthy shrugged. 'No matter, Eddie, you'll have to stay. It's not fair-'

'Not fair! Mac, grow up! Have you forgotten Detective Sergeant Cranley and what he thinks of me? Just tell the cops you'd arranged to meet Kruger here to get information on something you were working on. What the hell difference does it make if I'm here? Kruger's dead, he won't care!'

'All the same-'

'All the same nothing, Mac! If I'm here when the police arrive, Cranley will lock me up for a month just for questioning! I'm sick and tired of the bastard who's doing this and I'm going to find him and kick the fucking shit out of him!'

'You're shouting, Eddie.'

'Who cares!'

'Now look-'

'You look, McCarthy! Look at me leaving. You tell the police what you like when they get here but don't mention my name! I'm off. I am going to get whoever is doing this and the next call you get from me will be to tell you I'm holding the bastard by the balls!'

I ran, got in my car and drove home at high speed.

I spent the rest of a long day knowing it must be Stoke. He had to be the top man. Skinner and Greene had been in terror of him, he'd engineered Greene's death and probably ordered Harle's. The only one I couldn't positively tie him to was Roscoe but I was certain he was involved with whatever was going on at Roscoe's yard.

I had to keep control of my rage until I'd got some evidence. Surely, Charmain would know something? And surely, if she was fully aware just how evil he was, she wouldn't protect him?

I'd have to get into that house and see her. Stoke would probably leave for York on Monday. This was only Saturday morning…Jeez, how was I supposed to hold out?

The anger bubbled and fuelled frustration and when Jackie rang, full of hope and excitement, I was sharp with her and we had a row. In the end, she hung up. Disgusted with myself I sat down and tried to get drunk. Half a bottle of whiskey later I was still sober, angry and bitter.

I went to bed and lay in the darkness regretting the argument with Jackie and thinking how happy we'd been last night on the phone when I'd told her we were going to meet Kruger.

Coldness descended on me…I'd told her who and I'd told her where. I thought back again to my suspicions of her when Harle's body was dumped on me at Kempton, and the coldness turned to nausea as I faced the logical conclusion – she was working for Stoke and Roscoe.

I lay awake for hours trying to talk myself out of it but the rationale was undeniable. I should have guessed on the very first day. Why had she appeared out of the blue at the cottage?

After less than half an hour, she'd launched a deliberate seduction, which I was vain enough and stupid enough to be flattered by. And how hard she had tried to get me to pull out completely, to go with her to Ireland…

My last thoughts before sleep were that I deserved everything I'd got.

Chapter 57

Next morning, I rang McCarthy to warn him about Jackie. I expected an argument first over me running out on him yesterday, but he was calm, 'What are you going to do about her?' he asked.

'I don't know. Maybe we can use this to our advantage.'

'How?'

'I don't know yet. I'll have to think. I'm heading for Suffolk tomorrow to try to see Stoke's wife. We'll just have to wait and see how things play out after that.'

'How will you get to see her with Stoke around?'

'I'm counting on him leaving for York tomorrow. He should be away for at least three days.'

'What are you hoping to get out of her?'

'She's an old girlfriend of mine, leave it to me.'

'You're the original eternal optimist, Eddie.'

'Show me someone in racing who isn't an optimist?'

'True. Maybe I should have said delusional.'

'Listen, I know one thing now that Kruger's dead, there's no chance of getting my licence back. But promise me a half-hour interview with that senior steward when this over. At least I can tell him what I think of him.'

'I'll see what I can do.'

'What did the police say about Kruger?'

'What do you think? That it looked like a suicide was what they said.'

'But you told them otherwise?'

'I told them he had a criminal record and it might not be as straightforward as it seemed.'

'Let's hope they value your opinion more than they do mine,'

'We'll see.'

'Sounds like you had calmed down anyway by the time they arrived.'

'Well, after you'd gone, I began to see things more from your perspective. You were right, I was at no disadvantage without you.'

'See? Sometimes it's better to act on instinct.'

'You're never too old to learn, I suppose. Let me know the outcome of your visit to Stoke's house. And please be careful, Eddie.'

'Aren't I always?'

I moped around for the rest of the day knowing Jackie would phone at her usual time. When she did, I'd have to apologize for last night's argument and I'd have to sweet talk her, to keep her believing I suspected nothing.

That would stick in my throat but it was necessary if I wanted to turn her treachery to my advantage at some point. She rang at five to ten and I managed to hide the bitterness in my voice and play the part well.

Before she hung up, she told me she loved me. Like Judas loved Jesus, I thought, and went miserably to bed.

Chapter 58

Across the flat fenland, I saw the trees when I was still miles away, the long rows of trunks curving when they reached the big house, enveloping it. Scrawled on the sky above them was the silver swelling vapour trail of a jet.

It was just before three o'clock when I turned out of the sunshine into that dark avenue. Stopping about thirty yards before the road curved round to the driveway of the house, I got out and locked the car.

Skirting the edge of the dense wood, I jogged to the main gates. All looked quiet around the house.

The gates were about twelve feet high, the bars ornately plaited, topped by black spikes. No padlocks, just large keyholes: one in the centre, one at the bottom. I reached for the lock-picks in my jacket and went to work on the higher lock. Three minutes later, I was still fiddling with it and getting anxious. Had Stoke put in some special mechanism?

I was as comfortably dressed as a man can be for climbing gates: cords, a loose cotton shirt and strong, stiff-soled shoes. Up to the centre column where the gates met, there were enough footholds to reach the top.

Crossing the spikes was the tricky part but I couldn't afford more time working the locks.

I began climbing and halfway up had the sudden thought someone might be watching from the house two hundred yards beyond. I glanced across. The view was partly blocked by the big, silent, waterless fountain in the middle of the lawn and I felt a bit more secure.

The prospect of climbing this side as a stallion and ending up on the other as a gelding made me very careful as I reached the top and stepped across the spikes onto the bar welded to the inside. Footroom was two inches and bringing all my weight down I swung my left leg over, uttering a short prayer that the welder had been a time-served tradesman with a pride in his work.

As my right leg cleared the spikes, I pushed off, twisted in mid-air and landed with everything intact.

Away from the trees, I felt very exposed on this long tarmac drive. I wondered about servants. The place was big enough to need a gardener and a maid, at least. But there were no signs of life, the only sounds distant birdsong and the gravel dust crunching beneath my shoes.

The double doors at the front of the house were closed. The two door knockers were of the same dark metal, and I picked up the one on the right. It clattered down, sending an echo into the hall then out toward the dry fountain behind me.

I waited a minute before trying again. The same clatter, the echo seemed quieter. Nothing. No footsteps in the hallway, no turning of handles.

I walked backwards and looked up at the windows: three rows of four on each side of the doors. All the curtains were the same shade of pea-green, a distinctive colour that scratched at my memory. I saw nothing in the windows but reflections of white drifting clouds. I wondered if Stoke had taken Charmain with him.

I went round the back to look for a tradesman's entrance, and found the tidiness and uniformity of the front giving way to a paved yard of broken flagstones with high weeds flourishing in the cracks. A stable block had both half-doors of the end box lying open. The bottom door of the centre box had a deep semicircular gap where a crib-biting horse had gnawed the wood. There were no other signs of horses, not even a strand of straw.

Beside the stables was an electric mower, big and shiny, the blades clogged with dried cuttings.

Against the handle of the mower, a pitchfork rested and, on the ground, spikes up, was a rake.

The windows had net curtains that needed cleaning, or maybe the glass was dirty. There was only one narrow single door, stark black against the once-white walls.

I lifted the metal knocker but it was stiff and useless. I banged four times with my hand. No answer.

Another four thumps, this time I thought I heard a noise. Standing close I put my ear against the wooden panel…silence. I listened hard, taking half a lungful of air and holding it to stop the sound of my breathing.

I heard something.

The hairs on the back of my neck began pricking. I could feel them almost as if they were rising one at a time, stiffening from the nerve ends at the sound.

The noise had not come from the house.

There it was again.

Behind me.

Very close behind me. From low in the throat of what sounded like a large, fiercely hostile animal.

Slowly I turned, bringing my weight square onto my heels. Before I could see what it was and where it was, it growled again, longer this time, deeper, more drawn out, more savage. I finished turning. My back was touching the door, hands by my side, head motionless on a rigid neck.

Only my eyes moved. They scanned down and to the right and focused ten feet away on the beast watching me, on the blackness of it, broken by the tan-coloured right leg. A creature I'd last seen bounding into a lime-green Renault. Skinner's car…Skinner's dog…Skinner's big bloody Rottweiler.

Chapter 59

We looked at each other, no doubt in either of our minds who was more afraid. His growl grew constant. The dark eyes sparkled and narrowed. The fleshy lips drew back. His teeth shone so white I could have believed they were false. If only. If only a swift kick would knock the whole set from his mouth onto the cracked paving.

The growl grew louder and the dog began crouching, slowly shifting weight to his haunches, gradually coiling. My brain searched crazily for a way out and suggested I start talking softly to him. But I rejected it, convinced that the slightest sound or movement would trip the switch and set him at my throat.

The dog was ready, fully coiled, the growl steady and loud. I realized my left wrist was resting against the door handle. Slowly, I raised my hand, clasped the handle and turned it…a click, and the door opened.

The relief trickled out silently through my nostrils with the breath I'd been holding.

I considered turning quickly and pushing through, but I couldn't be sure I'd be inside before he caught me. If I could just ease it open a few inches at a time until it was wide enough to slip through…I started. One inch…two inches…the growl deepened…three inches…it barked and snarled…four inches…a noise from behind me, close to my left ear, metal on metal, the terrible spirit-sapping sound which meant there would be no five-inch opening…the sound of a security chain taking up the slack links, tightening, closing off my escape route.

The dog was ready.

One chance. I stepped away from the door, turned and slammed my shoulder against it, high up, as close to the chain as possible. The door held. I bounced and turned as the dog sprang.

I dodged, twisting to my left. His head loomed, jaws open, and he tried to snap them shut on the junction of my chest and shoulder at my right armpit. My body was still turning and the jaws closed on fresh air leaving the arm of my shirt wet with slavering mucus.

When the dog landed, he lost his balance and rolled over.

I ran.

The stable block was ten long strides away. I hoped to dive into the middle box through the gap left by the open half-door at the top.

The snarl of rage and the rough pads of his feet and claws scraping the concrete in pursuit spurred me.

About three yards from my take-off point, he caught me and bit deep into my left leg and along with the pain I felt the corduroy binding tight at the front as he gathered the loose material in his jaws. He let go my leg to rip free the rest of the cloth.

I heard it tearing as the tightness gave way to flap loosely and I waited to feel the teeth again in my bare flesh. I stumbled, nearly went down, tried to catch my balance by grabbing at the handle of the mower, missed it and caught the wooden shaft of the thing leaning against it, the pitchfork.

I couldn't stay upright, but kept hold of the pitchfork and pulled it out to the side as I automatically tucked my head in and rolled as I landed. I whirled the pitchfork at about two feet above ground level.

Somewhere in the swinging arc the dog should be.

I heard the thud as the shaft hit him, and the snarl of pain and anger. I came to rest sitting in a cloud of dust. The blow knocked the dog over but he was up again and running at me. No time to get to my feet. I swung the fork again and cracked him hard on the side of the head. He yelped this time, almost like a pup, and broke off to the side to recover. I rose. He stared at me, warier now.

Dazed, I backed toward the open box at the end of the stable block, limping badly, blood cold on my leg as the air reached it through the torn hole.

I retreated slowly. His growl was guttural now, drawn out. He crouched again, low, stalking. I held the pitchfork straight out, the spikes about four feet from his open jaws. I reached the box, backed in and, raising the fork about the height of the half-door, kept him at bay while I dragged the bottom half of the door closed.

It was almost five feet high with a big thick safe bolt at the top. I pushed the bolt well home then continued, for some reason, moving backwards until the rear wall of the box stopped me. With my back against it I slid down, all my energy draining as I did so. Sitting on the floor, knees bent to keep the wound off the dirt, I felt exhausted. My hands barely had the strength to shake.

I stood the pitchfork against the wall…rested my head against it…tried to calm myself. The box was dark and empty. Some bundled old newspapers lay heaped in a corner. Nothing else. Nothing but daylight coming through the top half of the door.

The sun's rays warmed me and I almost smiled. Then a big black shape blocked the light as the dog cleared the bolted door and I nearly died.

From somewhere another surge of strength came, and I was on my feet as he landed. For a few moments, he didn't seem to focus on me, a couple of seconds' adjustment from daylight to half-darkness. I was only going to get this chance. Grabbing the pitchfork and throwing all my weight on my good leg, I turned, bringing the sharp prongs round and upwards in a scooping motion.

The points pierced the black hair under his big ribcage, and he yelped again and snarled as he tried to turn and bite at the wooden shaft of this thing stabbing his guts. I bent low to keep the fork in him and drove, stumbling and crying with exertion and fear, into the corner of the box. His head met one wall and his tail the other and his body curved in the middle as I forced the tines in all the way to the U shape until his ribs cracked and gave way. I knew I would never forget his dying howl.

The certainty of safety came with the points sticking into the wood as they broke through the other side of his body. I held him there impaled until I was sure his breathing had stopped. Even then, I left the fork in him, pinning him to the wall. I was panting hard, as much from nervous reaction as exhaustion. I released my grip on the fork and turned away toward the door, sickened but safe.

I heard a crack behind me and the terror surged back. I turned. It was the pitchfork handle hitting the floor as the weight of the corpse pulled the tines from the timber. I limped from the box and, to be doubly sure, bolted the door.

Outside again in the sunlight I breathed deep and long and leaned heavily on the mower. The dog's howl and the cracking of his ribs echoed in my head.

I was parched, and couldn't raise spit as I hobbled to the door of the house.

As I lay against it, more through weakness than anything else, it opened as far as the chain would allow. Resting my head on the black wood, I closed my eyes against the sunlight. Through the gap, from somewhere inside the house, I heard a call for help.

Chapter 60

The call came again, faint, but very real. I turned, weight on my good leg, and examined the security chain.

The plea echoed, louder this time.

Three yards along was a window at ground-floor level. I hobbled across to get the rake and smash the glass.

My leg was stiffening badly. I couldn't straighten it without stifling a cry of pain. Using the rake for support, I made my way to the window.

Holding the rake like a rifle, I was about to smash a pane of glass low down when it occurred to me to try opening the window first. It shuddered stiffly up for the first eighteen inches then smoothly till it slotted under the upper sash. The gap was big and the ledge low enough to sit on and swing my legs through.

I was in a kitchen.

Crossing the threadbare rug, I opened a door into a narrow corridor. I stopped, my hand on the cool wall, and listened…the cry came again. I started moving and heard the sticky pull of my shoe on the linoleum. Blood rimmed the outer heel leaving a horseshoe of red. I wouldn't be hard to track.

A door led to a large wide hallway, well carpeted and ornately furnished. The walls held paintings, mostly of racehorses in the style of seventeenth and eighteenth-century painters; animals with small narrow heads and stretched bodies on stick-like legs.

Halfway along the hall was a staircase of around thirty steps, fairly steep, the carpet bordered on each side by polished wood. I began climbing, listening…no more cries. Squeaks. Every stair squeaked.

My leg hurt. I was bleeding on the carpet. After ten steps, my wounded left thigh would no longer push my body up. I resorted to one step at a time.

It took me a while to reach the top floor. I checked every room. Most were empty of even a chair, many had no carpets and, even in this early summer, they seemed damp and cold. I wondered why Stoke didn't just move to a smaller house and furnish all of it.

As I opened the door of the next room, I heard a sharp intake of breath. Charmain Stoke stood by the bed looking at me. She wore a silk nightgown. Her hair, long and loose, shone as the sun caught it through the window behind her.

Her face was perfectly made up and her fingernails and toenails were painted pink.

On her left ankle was a broad gold bracelet, on her right ankle a steel manacle. The chain attached to it lay in coils, its tail anchored to a square steel plate bolted to a side wall. The green curtains, the pale pink of her gown, the yellow of her jewellery and the silver glint of the chain and manacles were the only things in the room that weren't white.

The bed was a white four-poster with white linen. The carpet was white and deep…a dressing table, two high-backed padded chairs, a chest of drawers, a wardrobe and a footstool…all white.

Charmain stood motionless, staring blankly at me. A man she obviously didn't recognize was in her bedroom, bleeding on the white carpet, yet she seemed perfectly calm.

Her brow creased, quizzical, though her mind seemed miles away. She spoke quietly, 'I know you.'

I nodded. 'We've met before.'

She turned to face me full on. 'Why are you here?'

I shrugged. 'I want to ask you some questions.'

Chapter 61

Charmain stared at me, her eyes going blank again. I wondered if she was in shock. Taking two steps back, she sat on the bed. Pushing her hands under her thighs, she swung her legs back and forth, as a child might, the chain clinking lightly.

After a long silence, she glanced sideways at me and the patch of carpet I stood on.

'Is that blood?' Her voice still carried the flat tones of disinterest.

'I'm afraid so.'

She got up and walked toward me, the chain swishing through the carpet like a pet snake. 'Let me see,' she said.

I turned and leaned against the door, resting my leg on the toe of my boot to expose the injured thigh.

She squatted and gently parted the torn material. 'Did the dog do that?'

'Yes.'

'Where is it?'

'The dog?'

'Mmmm.'

'In one of your stable boxes.'

'Did you lock it in?'

I hesitated. 'It isn't your dog, is it?'

'It's Mister Skinner's.'

'Well, it's dead.'

'Did you shoot it?' Still her voice showed no emotion.

'I stabbed it with a pitchfork.'

She stood up and I turned to face her. She was smiling. 'I'm glad,' she said. 'I'm glad it's dead.'

She wandered over to the window and stood perfectly still, staring out. The sunbeams pierced her gown outlining her body. I spoke quietly, 'Was it Howard who chained you up?'

She nodded, 'And Howard brought the dog,' she said.

'When?'

'Yesterday.'

I limped over and stood by her side. 'Does he always do this when he goes away?'

She looked through the window at the high gates and the dark trees, the prison grounds. The sun highlighted the fine down on her profile, more noticeable as her top lip quivered. Her eyes glistened wet.

'It's been worse for a few weeks.' It came out thickly past the lump in her throat.

'I'll help you if you want to get out of here,' I offered. She didn't reply, didn't turn to look at me, but the water built up in her eyes till finally she blinked, forcing out a big tear which rolled into the ridge between her lips. The tip of her tongue licked it away.

Quietly, I asked again. 'Charmain, do you want me to help you get away?'

She nodded slowly and on the third nod, her head stayed down and she sobbed softly. Six inches beyond Charmain's reach with the chain fully extended Stoke had hung the manacle key on a small hook. I gave her the key, and putting her foot up on the bed, she freed herself.

She was suddenly brighter, more positive. 'Can we go now?'

'You'd better get dressed. I can wait outside.'

'I haven't any clothes.'

I looked at the thin pink gown.

'It's all I have left. Howard burned all my clothes two days ago.'

'Okay, we'll have to find you something when we get out.'

Charmain supported me as I hobbled down the stairs. I pictured her climbing the big gate in her nightgown. I pictured me climbing it in a bandage and a lot of pain.

'Is there a key for the main gate?' I asked.

'I think there's one on the ledge of the mailbox'.

There was.

We walked round the bend under the dark trees to the car.

'Should I drive?' Charmain asked.

I gave her the key. She adjusted the seat and rearranged her gown as I lowered myself into the passenger side.

Mechanically, she checked face and hair in the mirror. Some level of confidence was coming through, replacing the quiet resignation she'd shown when chained up in her room. She turned to me. 'Ready?'

For the first time in months my sense of the ridiculous took over and I laughed, albeit quietly, and rolled my head on the headrest. Charmain didn't speak, she just looked at me, waiting for an explanation.

'Sorry,' I said. 'I can't make up my mind whether this is a murder mystery or a farce.'

'What do you mean?'

'Me bleeding through a hole in the seat of my pants, you wearing nothing but a silk nightgown ready to drive us to God only knows where and you don't even remember my name.'

'I do. You're Eddie Malloy. You used to fancy me at school.'

'How did you know I fancied you? I never told you.'

'You didn't have to, I...'

'You what?'

'Nothing. It doesn't matter. But I do remember you from school.'

'But that was years ago, I could have turned into a madman for all you know, I could be taking you anywhere for any purpose.'

She glanced down. 'I doubt you'll be doing much in your condition,' she said. 'I think I can cope.'

She started the engine, and released the hand brake. Then she pulled it on again. Reaching to the floor below her seat, she brought out a small pink nylon case, something between a purse and a cosmetics bag.

I hadn't noticed her carrying it from the house. She looked inside, closed it again, stuffed it under the seat then picked slowly away into a neat turn.

'Where are we going?' she asked.

'I don't know. Let's just get away from here.'

She didn't look back. I did, at the big white prison with the green curtains and I remembered where I'd seen that colour before – on the jockey who rode the Champion Hurdle winner, Alan Harle. The colours belonged to the phantom owner who retained him to ride all his horses, Mister Louis Perlman.

The sun, though sinking, was still bright, the road clear and straight. We decided to visit the nearest hospital so I could get some treatment and Charmain, wearing an old raincoat I always carried in the boot, could call a friend whom she reckoned would take her in 'until the heat died down'. God knows when that will be, I thought. Once Stoke discovered she'd gone, the temperature could only rise.

'Doesn't Howard know this friend?' I asked. 'Won't he go there looking for you?'

She shook her head confidently. 'Doesn't know her. I haven't seen her myself for ages.'

The Greenlands Hospital Casualty Department was empty when we arrived and the doctor saw me within five minutes. Half an hour later, I returned to the car and sat tenderly on eleven stitches and an anti-tetanus injection.

Two paracetamol were supposed to have made things easier, as yet they hadn't.

Charmain looked much more anxious than when I'd left her. She stared straight ahead through the windscreen, biting ferociously at her lip.

'What's wrong?' I asked.

'Kate's gone to Italy.'

'Your friend?'

She nodded.

'When's she due back?'

'Next month.'

I cursed silently, selfishly, knowing what the outcome of this would be. 'Is there anyone else?'

She shook her head in short sharp jabs.

'Don't worry,' I said, with more confidence than I felt. 'We'll find somewhere.'

She turned to me, the hunted look already etched deep in her face. 'Where?'

I shrugged. 'With me, if needs be.'

It didn't ease things for her. 'But doesn't Howard know you?'

'He knows me all right but he'd have no reason to suppose you were with me.'

Eyes vacant, she nodded, not really taking it in. 'Okay,' she said, starting the car. 'Which way?'

'That way.' I pointed west and we lowered the visors against the setting sun.

It was all I could think of. Returning to the cottage for any length of time was out of the question.

Stoke's men would eventually come looking.

Chapter 62

During the next hour, Charmain grew increasingly agitated, biting her nails and rubbing her mouth hard with the back of her hand like she was wiping saliva away.

When she let the car stray over the central white lines on the road for the second time, I spoke to her. 'You okay?'

She looked round suddenly at me, as though I'd just appeared beside her. 'Yes...yes. I'm okay.'

Her skin was pale. She didn't look okay. 'Will your husband be at York till Friday?'

'I think so.'

'What were you supposed to do for food while he was away?'

'He leaves a supply of fruit in the cupboard.'

'Fruit! For three days?'

She was rigid in the seat, neck stretched, arms dead straight on the wheel as though trying to hold a runaway horse. 'Howard said it helped me keep my figure.'

'Why didn't you leave him?'

'I had my reasons.'

I waited.

'He's not an easy man to leave,' she said.

'Has he always used Skinner's dog as well as the chain?'

'Today was the first time. He told me it was there but I only half-believed him.'

'What has he got on Skinner?'

'Skinner owes him a lot of money. Howard lets him run up big debts then calls in his favours.'

'What kind of favours?'

She shrugged. 'I don't know specifics, but Howard's seen a lot of Skinner lately.'

The talking seemed to relax Charmain and she leaned forward into a more natural driving position. Her next question surprised me.

'Is it Skinner you're after, or Howard?'

'Who do you think?'

She kept staring at the road. Since we'd started the conversation, she hadn't looked at me. She shrugged and frowned. 'Well, I don't know.'

'But I should be after somebody?'

'You must be. People don't go around killing dogs and breaking into houses for nothing…And asking questions.'

'I'm trying to find out who killed Alan Harle.'

Our speed dropped suddenly as her foot eased off the gas then surged as she realized what had happened. Her knuckles were white on the wheel and she bit hard at her bottom lip.

'You knew Alan.' I made it a statement. Still she wouldn't look at me.

'I'm very tired,' she said. 'I feel faint. Can we stop a while?'

'Okay, pull in at the next lay-by.'

That suggestion seemed to stress her even more. 'No, not a lay-by, somewhere with a toilet, somewhere I can eat. Maybe a cup of sweet tea, something like that.'

'Fine, wherever you want.'

She nodded, but the tension didn't ease and by the time we stopped at a small transport café, her concentration had deteriorated so much she couldn't have driven any farther.

The place looked all right for truck-drivers but not for pretty women in pink nightgowns. Charmain didn't seem to mind. If anything, her stress diminished as she reached for my old coat in the back.

'Can I use this again?' she asked brightly.

'Why don't you wait in the car and I'll go and get some food?'

'No!' She almost shouted. 'I can't wait in the car…I have to go to the toilet.'

I looked at her. She avoided my eyes. 'Okay, you go to the toilet. I'll get some food and drinks.'

She nodded, stepped out, pulling the coat round her shoulders, picked up her little pink bag and hurried off toward the white pebbledash buildings.

Suspicion had been growing, but I knew then she'd return calm, smiling and self-assured.

I was right.

Charmain sipped tea but wouldn't eat. The colour had returned to her cheeks and she was bright and chatty. Her eyes shone.

'Pretty uplifting toilets, those,' I said.

'Mmmm.' She smiled.

'Take away hunger and tension and tiredness. Think a visit would do my leg any good?'

She just kept smiling, reached for the handle and reclined the seat, perfectly relaxed.

'I know where I can stay,' she said.

I waited.

'A friend of mine has a boat. It's on the Oxford canal near a little village.'

I wondered for a moment if she meant Skinner but I didn't think so. 'What's your friend's name?'

'Phil Greene, he's a jockey.'

'You've got a short memory, Charmain, Phil Greene's hardly cold in his grave. You were at his funeral.'

Eyes still closed, she frowned for a few seconds then smiled again. 'It's all right. I've got a key.'

'For what?'

She looked at me. 'The boat.'

'So, it doesn't matter that Phil Greene's dead as long as you have a key to his boat?'

'I'm not saying it doesn't matter. He was a sweet kid and he would have wanted me to stay at the boat if I was in a spot.'

'So why didn't you think of that first before you rang your friend?'

She shrugged. 'I forgot.'

'You forgot or you didn't realize how short of heroin you were?'

It didn't faze her. 'What do you mean?'

'I mean that until you went into that toilet and shot some of the stuff into your arm you didn't realize how little you had left.'

She looked at me, her smile replaced by a hardness.

'So?' she said.

'So, you obviously think Phil had some on the boat somewhere. What was he, your official supplier, by appointment, after Harle disappeared?'

She lay back again, closed her eyes and smiled. 'What's it to you?'

'Nothing to me. It's your life. Why should I care if you screw it up like Harle and Greene and end up the same way?'

'Don't worry, Mister…I've forgotten your name?'

'That's all right. You won't be seeing me again anyway, once I've dropped you at the boat.'

She opened her eyes and sat up. 'You said you'd help me.'

'Don't give me the Little Miss Helpless act. I'll help you hide, help you keep away from your husband for as long as I can, but I won't help you kill yourself.'

'You're overreacting.'

'Maybe, but that's the way I feel. I'm sick of all this crap. Of being scalded and bitten and shit on by idiots like Harle and Greene and you. You're not worth it.' I opened the door, struggled out and went to the driver's side.

'Move over,' I told her. 'I'll drop you at the boat.'

'But your leg!'

'Move!'

'It's a long drive! It'll be dark soon!'

'Move or get out!'

She moved.

Chapter 63

Someone was on the boat. A thin beam of pale yellow shone through a gap in the curtains as we drove down the hill. I cut the engine and the lights and coasted silently, steering by moonlight, until we stopped by the white cottage.

Eyes wide, Charmain tensed in her seat.

'Who do you suppose it is?' she asked, whispering.

'I don't know.' I slid the key from the ignition, 'Wait here,' I said.

She grabbed my arm 'Hold on!' A harsh whisper now. 'Leave me the car key!'

I tried to shrug her hand off. 'No.'

'Yes!' She gripped harder. I turned to face her. She was corpse-pale. 'No,' I said.

'You must!'

'Why?'

'They might get you…I'd be stuck…they'd get me too.'

'Too bad. I'm taking the key. I don't trust you.'

'I'll wait for you. Honest, I will!'

Putting the key in my pocket, I prised open her grip. 'If you weren't a junkie, Charmain, I might believe you. Stay here and keep quiet. I'll be back soon.'

I hobbled down the path to the side of the boat. The night was cool and cloudless. The boat lurched gently from side to side, the water lapping rhythmically with the sway.

The window at the end was open. I heard the rising and falling tones of conversation. Crouched below the window I could hear the voices clearly. Two men. Recognizable accents: one West Midlands, the other a West Country burr.

'I thought Stoke said there was a watercock?'

'He said he thought there was. Try the kitchen.'

'The galley, you mean.'

'Bollocks.'

The boat rolled as he walked along.

'Don't see anything.'

'Have to be the acid then, won't it?'

The steps moved to the middle of the boat.

'How we gonna work it?'

'I told you, when he's out for the count we uncork the bottle and tip it over. It'll burn a big enough hole within a couple of hours to let the water in.'

'The cops won't wear the acid once they've dragged this thing up. What would Malloy be doing with acid?'

'Could be anything, how would they know? It's not as if Malloy's gonna be here to answer questions. Obvious accident, innit? Four hundred milligrams of alcohol in his blood, pissed out of his brain, what else can they call it?'

'I dunno.'

Glass clinked on glass.

'Careful!'

'No sweat.'

'What do we do if Malloy ain't home?'

'We wait. Stoke said do it before he gets home. That gives us three days.'

'He could have been out of the way ages ago when we had him over that radiator.'

'That was just a fright job. That was all we got paid for. One of my better performances too, I'd say.'

'Yeah, really effective, Bill, the guy's caused nothing but trouble since.'

'Can I help it if Malloy ain't got the brains to keep his nose out of other people's business? I'll still bet he won't forget the night I nearly roasted it off his face.'

Bill, you never spoke a truer word.

The pain in my leg didn't matter anymore. Heading home, I drove at speeds of up to a hundred, headlights picking out the bends just in time. I felt excited. Scared, but excited.

The relief Charmain had shown when I returned to the car had disappeared. The tension was back, and the fear.

I told her what I wanted her to do when we reached the cottage, repeating it over and over to make sure she understood. 'I'll park deep in the trees but facing the road they'll have to come down to reach the cottage, either by car or on foot. If they walk, you should be able to see them by the light of the moon, but they'll probably drive. Especially when they see the cottage is in darkness.

'Driving or walking, you'll have to be alert. If you miss them and my plans don't work out, they'll kill me. If they kill me, your protection has gone. I'm all you've got now. Do you understand that?'

She nodded.

'Say yes,' I said.

'Yes. Yes, I understand.'

I stared at her. 'If they kill me, you're next.'

Her eyes were wide. I said, 'If they pass you on foot, give me thirty minutes. If you don't see the lights come on in the cottage by then, go to the village and ring DS Cranley at this number. Tell him the men who killed Alan Harle have got Eddie Malloy and tell him where we are. Okay?'

She nodded.

'If they pass you in a car, cut the time to twenty minutes maximum. Got it?'

'Yes, but what if they see me in the car as they pass?'

'They won't. If they do, then slip out into the woods and try to get to the village.'

She began shivering.

Five hundred yards from the cottage, an old cart path led off into the wood. In winter, you couldn't drive along it, but on this summer night it was manageable.

I drove well down, turned off into a clearing and parked facing the road. We got out and dragged broken branches and ferns across the windscreen and side body. 'You'll have to roll down the windows in case the moon glints on the glass.'

'Okay.'

I looked toward the road. A moving car would be easily visible through the thin pines. I just hoped the same didn't apply to this stationary one in the woods.

I opened the passenger door for Charmain. She got in and sat clenching her left fist inside her right hand. I thought she was going to cry and I hunkered down and took her hands in mine. The moonlight filtering through the trees showed the goose bumps on her arms spiked with tiny hairs. Cold or fear, I couldn't help with either.

'We'll make it,' I said.

She nodded, holding back the tears.

Chapter 64

In a cupboard in the kitchen were some wire-cutters and a pair of heavily padded industrial gloves. I worked without light. In fifteen minutes, I was ready for them.

Ready and waiting.

Waiting in the alcove in the living room twelve feet from the cold fireplace, six feet from the back of the worn sofa. Waiting. Tense in the darkness. Cold. Leg aching.

On the mantelpiece the clock ticked, steady and reliable…the only sound, the only beat. Tick-tock. Tick-tock. Two men. How long? Two men. How long?

Twenty minutes passed…half an hour. How was Charmain holding out? Maybe they'd seen her on the way past. What if they'd caught her? What would she tell them? What would they do to her?

I heard a noise. On the roof. Someone was on the roof.

My heart rate doubled.

Another noise above – scrabbling, scratching, like fingernails clawing their way up the tiles. I stopped breathing…I heard wingbeats, passing the window, then silence. Thirty seconds…a minute. No more noise.

I realized what had happened; a bird had dropped his catch then swooped low, talons open, to snatch it as it slid down the tiles. Breathe again…Beat easy, heart.

The lungs breathed but the heart kept pumping fast. It must have known something because it was then that I heard them.

Footsteps. In the loose gravel by the road, coming closer, so close I waited to see them pass the window. They didn't. Noises to my right, through the kitchen. They were round the back. Prowling.

I hoped they wouldn't try the back door. If they came in that way my chances were down by fifty percent; they had twice as much floor-space to cross. Twice the chance of seeing me in the narrow alcove.

I waited.

How long had it been since they passed Charmain? The longer they took coming in the less time I'd have before she headed for the village.

No more noise at the back. They must be circling the building making sure no one was at home. I was at home. So was the clock. Two men. They're here. Two men. They're here.

I heard no more footsteps, just the thin sound as the lock-pick slid into the mechanism. The click as the lock turned. The creak as the door opened and two spiders walked into the web of the fly.

Chapter 65

They were three steps from where I stood. Everything depended on them taking those steps in my direction. They didn't. They did something even better. They sat on the sofa.

'Let's make ourselves comfortable till our little friend comes home.'

Their little friend was a yard away thinking how much their heads above the sofa resembled coconuts on a shelf. I didn't even have to step forward. In each hand, I held a double loop of barbed wire, two feet in diameter.

The padded gloves protected my skin as I reached and slipped one loop over each head. They cried out. One full twist tightened the barbs.

'If you even swallow I'll rip your throat open.'

I stepped in close behind them.

'Start working your way in very slow movements to the end of the sofa.'

When they reached the end, I moved to the side so I could control them more easily when they stood up.

'You're going to stand up very slowly and you're not going to do anything silly. It'll take me a tenth of a second to twist this little necklace one more time, so best behaviour unless you want to become a blood donor via your jugular. Stand up.'

They stood. 'Which one is Bill?'

'Me.' said the one on my left.

'If you raise your left hand to that wall, Bill, you'll find a light switch. Press it.'

He did. The light came on and I pictured Charmain sighing in relief.

I twisted the wire, forcing him to turn his head to look at me, and I smiled as our eyes met. 'Hello, Bill. Remember me?'

He nodded very carefully.

'I thought you might. What's your friend's name?'

'Trevor.'

'Hello, Trevor.' I smiled. He wasn't reassured. 'I believe you were at the open-air barbecue too, the night my face was on the menu?'

Swiveling his eyes, he looked at his partner. 'I'm not hearing you, Trev,' I said.

'Yes,' he croaked.

'Well gentlemen, never let it be said that I don't return hospitality. As soon as I've made you comfortable I'm going to put the kettle on.'

I bound them together, back to back with thirty feet of barbed wire, double twisted the ends and crimped them with pliers. Then I went to the kitchen and filled the kettle, lit the gas, and put it on to boil.

I made them stand in the alcove while I leant on the mantelpiece. 'Why did you kill Alan Harle?'

They didn't answer.

'I don't know how much of your physics lessons you remember, but you've got as long as it takes to boil two pints of water on a full gas flame. If you're not talking by then, well, I've always supported the eye-for-eye theory…Though I think boiling water is even more painful than steam.'

They flinched.

'I'll remind you of the question. Why did you kill Alan Harle?'

Silence.

'Fine. I can wait.'

I started whistling, lightly, watching them as they wondered if I'd do what I'd threatened. Whistling on in a deliberate monotone, I kept it up until the kettle whistled low, then steadily higher.

'Catching, isn't it?' I said, smiling.

They didn't seem to find it funny.

I carried the kettle through. Bill saw the towel wrapped round the handle. I smiled at him. 'Don't want to burn myself, it's very hot.'

His eyes widened.

I stood very close to him. The streams of blood stained his white collar like tiny red rivers on a hillside, and the wire was so tight on his chest he wasn't taking full breaths. I stared hard and cold and unblinking into his eyes. He knew I held the kettle somewhere below but he couldn't bend his head to look down.

'Why did you kill Alan Harle?'

He looked unsure but he obviously thought I wouldn't do it because he decided not to answer. It was a gamble. He lost.

I splashed about a cupful on his thigh and he screamed. Trevor's body stiffened at the sound.

'My aim was out a bit. I'll get it this time.'

I swung my arm.

'No! No, I'll tell you!'

'Start telling.'

'It was a job. Just a job, a contract.'

'Who paid?'

He hesitated. I swung again.

'Stoke! Howard Stoke!'

'Why did Stoke want him dead?'

'We don't ask for reasons.'

'Why?' I shouted in his face.

'He was screwing around with Stoke's wife.'

'Bullshit!'

'Honest!'

'How did you kill him?'

'Injected him with something Stoke gave us.'

'After chaining the poor bastard up in a filthy stable for weeks!'

'That was the way Stoke wanted it.'

'And the customer's always right, huh?'

He didn't answer.

'Harle was already injecting heroin, wasn't he?'

'Yes.'

'Where did he get it?'

'We don't know.'

'Was he dealing in it?'

'We don't know.'

'Was he dealing in it?'

'We didn't ask him any questions!'

'Don't get smart, Bill, you're on the wrong side of the wire to get smart.'

He avoided my stare. I spent another five minutes pumping them but I learnt little. They didn't know much because they hadn't wanted to know. Their only interest had been money.

'Is it just Stoke you've been involved with or have you done jobs for anyone else?'

'We take it where we can find it.'

'Took.' I told him. Then I remembered the others who'd been attacked. 'Was it Stoke who gave you the contracts on Bergmark and Kristar Rask, and Danny Gordon?'

No answer.

I lifted the kettle to eye-level. 'Tell me!'

Bill looked at me. His voice was strained, 'They were just jobs, nothing personal.'

'Nothing personal! You crippled Bergmark, as good as killed Rask and murdered Danny Gordon and you say it was nothing personal! You fucking bastards!' I swung the kettle and splashed another half pint of water on Bill's thighs, then did the same to Trevor. They screamed.

My control was going and I put the kettle down in the hearth, because I was sorely tempted to pour the rest over their heads and they were already writhing. The barbs punctured their skin and blood ran from their throats and wrists.

I went to the phone. 'I'm just about to ring the cops but I hope you fuckers bleed to death before they get here.'

I called the station and they said Detective Sergeant Cranley was at home. They wouldn't give me his number, so I told the duty sergeant where I was and what had happened and warned him if he didn't send a squad car within an hour they'd be picking up two corpses.

I left them groaning and gasping and went to get Charmain.

She'd gone. So had the car.

Chapter 66

I stared through the silhouettes of the trees against the big moon wondering how long ago she'd left. Wondering if she'd waited to see the light going on, to see me safe. Wondering if her nerve had simply failed or if she'd just been desperate for another fix.

Whatever, she'd be heading for the boat where the heroin was, and the whiskey and the acid. I was beginning to regret freeing her from the ankle chain.

I hurried back to the cottage where Bill told me, in a strangled voice, which pocket his car keys were in. The barbed wire spiked him twice before I got them out. I switched the lights off, making it even more risky for them to move around. I couldn't see their faces but as I closed the door, I heard them curse.

Chapter 67

In the boat cabin, the syringe was on the table. Charmain lay sprawled on the narrow bunk, her right hand over her head idly fingering the curtain, a half full glass of whiskey in her left.

One knee pointed at the low ceiling. The other leg lay flat. Both were bare. The hem of her nightgown was round her waist exposing white underwear.

She smiled at me. 'Home is the sailor, home from the sea and the hunter home from the hill,' she said.

High as a kite.

I sat opposite her, wincing as the hard edge of the bunk caught the leg wound. 'And the junkie?' I asked. 'Where's she home from?'

Still smiling she raised the glass and drank. 'Who cares? Who cares where the junkie's home from? Who cares? Home from the woods, the junkie's home from the woods.'

'Is this why you left?' I asked, picking up the empty syringe.

'Left what? Left where? I've left a lot of places, Mister Malloy, a lot of places.'

Her face was pink from the warmth of the cabin. The three small gas fires along the length of the boat glowed.

'Left the woods,' I said. 'Where you were supposed to be watching out for me.'

'I watched out. You were okay,' the smile was dropping, 'you didn't need me anymore after the light went on, you were the big hero then, weren't you? The big hero.'

Letting go the curtain, she began rubbing her thigh. She drank again then closed her eyes and laid her head against the paneled wall. She looked almost serene.

Six feet to the side was a step down to the kitchen area, where an old fridge and cooker and a sink unit with a dented draining board sat on a floor of cracked and curl-edged vinyl tiles. Limping over, I got myself a glass from the shelf above the sink. Charmain opened her eyes again as she heard the whiskey being poured.

'Help yourself to a drink,' she said, not looking at me, 'plenty for everyone.'

I sat down again, more carefully this time, and hauled my bad leg up straight on the cushions. Raising her glass, she said, 'Cheers! Here's to the hero.'

She took a big slug. 'And here's to the heroin.' I said.

Lowering her glass, she half sneered, half smiled at me, wrinkling her nose, 'Very witty, Mister Malloy, very witty. You must be the smartest person out of everyone I know.' She held her glass up in mock salute.

'Smart and brave and virtuous,' the glass came down, the smile dropped away and she stared up at the ceiling and said, just loudly enough, 'Arsehole.'

I let it pass. She was feeling guilty about leaving me at the cottage. The fact that she also felt obliged to me for 'rescuing' her from Stoke made her feel worse.

If you ever want someone to resent you for life, do them a big favour.

She wouldn't let it be. Turning on me again she said, 'What is it with you, Malloy? What do you get out of all this?'

I shrugged. 'My licence back, I hope.' That silenced her for a minute. She must have been expecting me to spout some high moral reasons she could ridicule and taunt me with.

I drank, flushing the golden liquid round my mouth, burning my gums, and waited for the next assault.

But her frown told me the drug-clouded whiskey-soaked brain was struggling to come up with anything logical.

'What do you know anyway?' She said, staring at the wall.

Closing her eyes, she rested her head against the panel, her hair rasping on the rough varnish.

'Charmain, I need your help.'

Her head snapped up, eyes blazing. 'Don't fucking patronize me!' I shrugged. 'I didn't intend to.'

She made a face and mimicked me. 'I didn't intend to. I didn't intend to…You bastard!'

'To hell with this,' I said and swung my leg off the sofa. Her pink heroin bag rested by her side. I grabbed it. Her face froze, open-mouthed, as I sat back again clutching the bag. She reached out. 'Give me that.'

'Shut up.'

She stared at me, knowing she'd pushed me too far, just as she'd done in the car that afternoon.

'I need it.' Pleading now.

'Too bad.'

Unzipping the bag, I took out a thumb-size, half-full phial of clear liquid. 'Where did you get it?' I asked. The nightdress hem tumbled to her knees as she stood up quickly, clutching her drink. 'Give me it.'

The tone was strident. Her free hand reached toward me.

'Was it part of Greene's supply or did you bring it with you?'

'It's mine! Give it to me!'

Rolling it on my palm, I said, 'It's not yours. If it was yours, you'd have used it in the car in the woods and saved yourself a long drive. It's Phil Greene's, or it was Phil Greene's. Where was it hidden?'

She lunged at me. Clutching the phial, I pushed her away. Losing her balance, she lurched backwards and landed awkwardly on the bunk, splashing her drink on the green cushion. Struggling forward she tried to get up again.

'Sit still,' I said. 'Or I'll pour this down the sink.' She glared then threw her glass at me. It hit the panel behind me, but didn't break.

Charmain sat clutching her drawn up knees and staring out of the small window into the darkness.

'Where's the rest of the supply, Charmain?'

She ignored me. She began rocking slowly, back and forth. I got up and went to the sink. Unscrewing the lid, I tilted the phial. 'Where's the rest of it?'

She stopped rocking and stared at me wide-eyed, unbelieving.

'Don't! There isn't any more!'

'I don't believe you.' I tipped it until it was horizontal. 'Where is it?'

The horror-stricken face had me almost convinced she was being truthful. But I had to make sure. I let out a trickle and she screamed and ran toward me.

Falling to her knees as she reached me, she hammered on the dirty tiles with her right fist.

'Please, please, please...that's all there is! I need it...for tomorrow!' She was sobbing, staring at the floor, she wouldn't look up at me.

She stopped hammering and pushed her forearms under her forehead and rocked back and forth on her knees like some demented jockey. 'Please, please, please...'

Screwing the cap onto the phial, I helped her up. Standing in front of me with bloodshot eyes, tear-stained face, runny nose and flakes of dirt in her hair she seemed utterly dejected and beaten.

Reaching for her limp right hand, I brought the open palm up and placed the phial in it. She gazed at me like a grateful animal newly relieved of pain, and two big tears spilled. Opening her arms, she slumped forward, head on my chest, and pulled me toward her. I put an arm round her waist then gently stroked the hair at the nape of her neck.

I felt, as much as heard, her deep sigh, and her warm tears soaked through my shirt.

It took Charmain a while to calm down. She'd dry her eyes and try to smile and say she was fine then burst into tears again. But at least the spite was all out of her. She looked apologetic and extremely sorry for herself, though the feminine wiles still worked as she decided the troubles were ours rather than hers.

'What are we going to do?' she asked, sipping a fresh drink.

I could play that way too.

'Before we can plan anything I need to know more about Howard and his business...and his connections.'

She nodded and after some gentle prompting, told me how she'd met Howard at Sandown three years ago when she'd backed a winner with him. Okay, he was much older, but he had money and big cars and nice houses. She wasn't embarrassed about admitting she was a gold-digger.

She said Howard kept his business affairs to himself. Very few people visited him at home and when they did, he'd never discuss things in front of her. All had been fine for the first two years. He'd taken her out, bought her jewellery, and treated her well. It started going wrong when Harle came along.

'What happened?' I asked.

She shrugged and stared at her feet. 'We became lovers.'

'You and Harle!' I hadn't meant to sound so incredulous but when I thought of them together...Harle's small greasy slyness and her, well, I suppose beauty was too strong a word, but she was very attractive, though when it sunk in that she'd slept with Harle she seemed a lot less so. Maybe I was just jealous. And mad with myself. The girl I'd thought too gorgeous to even approach at school falling for the likes of Harle...At least she'd taken Stoke for money.

She caught the tone in my voice and looked hurt, then defiant. 'He was good in bed,' she said, almost accusingly.

'You don't have to explain to me.'

'It sounded like I did.'

'My bad manners showing again. I'm sorry.'

She pouted and drank. 'You men think sex isn't important to a woman...well, to some of us it is. I didn't love Alan, didn't even care all that much for him, but he was brilliant in bed.' She drank again, angry, then repeated, 'Brilliant.'

I stayed silent, waiting for her to get it out of her system.

'Howard was impotent,' she said, staring at her empty glass. 'From the day we were married. It terrified him.'

I bet it did. It went a long way toward explaining his crazy jealousy and manic over-protectiveness of her. 'Did he know you were sleeping with Harle?'

She nodded. 'I think he did, but he'd never have challenged me. He was too afraid of the truth.' She spoke quietly, with no hint of satisfaction.

'But not too afraid to make sure Harle never saw you again.'

She stared, unblinking, into her empty glass. I filled it with what remained in the bottle.

'How did you meet Alan?' I asked.

'Howard introduced us at a party. He kept calling Alan his boy, his best boy.'

'When was this?'

'New Year's Day. We'd been to Cheltenham.'

'What was Alan doing for him? What was the connection?'

'I don't know. I assumed he was just a friend, or maybe a hanger-on. I didn't ask questions.'

'Didn't Alan tell you anything?'

'Sometimes he'd ramble on when he was drunk about how rich he was going to be, how everything was going to work out.'

'Drunk or high?'

'I don't know.'

'Was he injecting?'

Tilting her head back, she closed her eyes. 'What does it matter? Alan's dead…What's the point?'

I let it rest for a while. 'You know Alan rode for a very rich owner?'

She nodded.

'Nobody seems to have met this guy Perlman. Didn't Alan talk about him?'

Wearily she shook her head.

'Did he ever even meet him?'

'I don't know.' She sounded very tired.

I changed tack. 'Alan was injecting. I only asked you to see if you knew.'

She nodded.

'How often?' I asked.

'I don't know.'

'Did he offer you any?'

She hesitated. 'He didn't offer…I asked if I could try it…he didn't want me to.'

She gazed down and fingered her glass.

'But you talked him into it?'

She sighed deeply. 'In the end… I tried my first fix the week he disappeared.' She seemed to be going on a downer again. I kept up the questioning. 'Was Greene injecting, too?'

'No.'

'You seem pretty definite.'

'He wanted to stay clean. He'd seen Alan's behaviour when he needed a fix. Phil Greene didn't want to do anything that would stop him being champion jockey.'

'You seem to know a lot about his personal ambitions.'

She leaned forward far enough to sip her drink then lay back again. 'Phil had a crush on me.'

'And?'

'He agreed to help me after Alan disappeared.'

'You mean he agreed to get heroin for you?'

She nodded.

'Who paid for it?'

She stared at me, looking hurt but too tired to raise any real fire in her voice. 'What the hell does that mean, Malloy?'

I shrugged. 'Heroin costs a lot of money. I just wondered who paid for it.'

'I paid. All right?'

'Okay.'

She settled again, closing her eyes. 'How did you meet Phil?' I asked.

'Howard brought him home for drinks after Alan disappeared.'

'Did Alan know Skinner?'

'They were connected in some way, but Alan didn't like him.'

'Phil Greene was connected to Skinner too, wasn't he?'

'I think so.'

'They were at your house together last week.'

She didn't comment. 'So, we've got Alan and Phil and Skinner and Roscoe and Howard, all connected in some way, Alan and Phil more than anyone else because they're dead, murdered, by your husband.'

I wasn't sure how she'd react. Deep down she must have known Stoke was behind Harle's death and I suspected she knew he'd engineered Greene's. I watched her. She didn't even blink.

'Charmain, did you hear what I said?'

She nodded.

'Am I right?'

'Aren't you always?' she murmured and turned her head away.

'When did Howard find out about your heroin habit?'

She stared into the fire. 'A couple of weeks ago, when Phil brought the stuff. I had no money. I gave him my watch to pay for it and to get some more. He said he'd wait for payment but I told him to take the watch. He shoved it into his pocket. Last week, when he came with Skinner to see Howard he accidentally pulled the watch out. It fell on the floor, right at Howard's feet. Howard bought me that watch as a wedding gift.'

She drank.

'Phil gave him some stupid story about finding it outside in the driveway and Howard pretended to believe him. Later, he punched the truth out of me.'

I looked at her. 'As much motive as Howard would have needed to kill him, I'd say. He probably also knew that Greene had been drinking with me and had talked too much.'

Charmain's chin dropped onto her chest. Maybe the realization of the part she'd played in the deaths of Harle and Greene was beginning to sink in. She seemed drained but I needed the answer to one more question.

'Charmain,' her head stayed down. 'Do you know what Skinner's working on at Roscoe's yard? Is he making heroin or horse dope or what?'

She shook her head slowly, still not lifting it. I persevered. 'He's using the head lad's cottage, working on something secret. It could be the key to all this to Harle's and Greene's deaths…Charmain?'

She was sobbing again in that soft way she'd wept when I'd taken the heroin from her. I went across and stood above her, my hands on her shoulders. 'Charmain, please tell me what Skinner is doing at Roscoe's?'

She leaned forward, throwing her arms around my waist, weeping. 'I don't know! I don't know! Oh, Eddie, what are we going to do?' She forced me to take a step back as she stood up and cradled my face in her hands.

I stood holding her for what seemed a very long time then her tear-stained face tilted and her big sad eyes drew me in. As she arched her neck, her pink swollen lips parted showing the tip of her tongue and she closed her eyes and kissed me, long and wet and warm.

She swept the cushions off the bunks and arranged them on the floor. Pushing at the shoulder straps of the nightgown, she wriggled out of it and, bending gracefully, slipped her panties off. She knelt, pulling me down with her and we kissed again as she undressed me. Unresisting, I let her lead, still wanting, childishly, to believe she was doing it because, deep down, she loved me, but knowing it was a reaction to what we'd been through tonight. A crazily overheated libido was one of the after-effects of coming safely through danger.

Mine was as hot as hers.

She was also doing it because she hoped to gain control, as she'd tried to do with Stoke and Harle and probably Greene. She lay flat now and pulled me alongside her. 'Oh, Eddie, this is what you wanted, isn't it?' This is what you were dying for when you came into my bedroom…and when I was in the car…This is what you wanted in the woods…isn't it, Eddie…isn't it?' She was moaning softly.

Maybe it's what I wanted, but it's not what I'm going to have, Charmain, not when you've been with scum like Stoke and chancers like Harle and idiots like Greene. I don't play fourth in a field like that.

I'd rather try to remember you the way you were.

Then Jackie's image loomed in my mind, Jackie the traitor, and my vengeful streak showed through.

Why shouldn't I have sex with Charmain? I could tell Jackie about it and watch her face…How does it feel to be betrayed, Jackie?

I watched Charmain, writhing, moaning, longer and louder, 'Now, Eddie…please…come on!' And I let her go and slowly and silently got to my feet and stood over her, looking down.

She lay still, staring at me, quizzically at first then her eyes focused on mine and she saw how much, at that moment, I despised her and she seemed to crumple as she turned on her side drawing her knees up, her hands covering her face as the tears fell. 'You bastard,' she murmured softly through her weeping, 'you dirty, rotten bastard.'

And I stood there for a minute surprised at my feeling of triumph. I'd just paid her back for ignoring me at school, for not wanting me when we met again, for all she'd ever done to me or could do to me in the future.

It was illogical and unfair and childish, and I knew I was a bastard. But I felt good.

Chapter 68

Plagued by nightmares I awoke after little more than an hour's sleep. Charmain still slept. The sun was up but the boat felt cold. I made a mug of coffee and took it outside.

On the untrodden grass bordering the towpath, the dew lay heavy. The cars we had driven, mine parked half on the road and half on the towpath by Charmain, were also wet with dew.

The cars would be spotted if any of Stoke's cronies were out searching and I decided to take them into the village.

I went to get my jacket. It would be best to move them now while the area was quiet. Anyway, I had to phone DS Cranley for an update.

Charmain was sleeping when I left. I locked the door and took the key.

It was after 7 a.m. when I parked the second car, probably a bit early to catch Cranley, but I spotted a phone box so it was worth a try. He was at his desk.

'Where are you, Malloy?' he asked.

'A little place in the country.'

'Where?'

'I can't tell you. I might not be here after today. I'll let you know where I am as soon as I'm sure it's going to be reasonably permanent.'

'That's not good enough. I want a full statement from you about last night.'

He was being remarkably polite. 'Fine, I'll call in at the station.'

'When?'

'As soon as I can.'

'Malloy!'

'Sergeant, look, tell me you'll pick up a bookmaker called Stoke for questioning and I'll come to the station right now.'

'For questioning on what?'

'For at least three of the murders that you and I have been fighting about since we met. Those were his two guys you picked up last night. They were out to add me to their list.'

'They're claiming you abducted them.'

'Oh, come on, Cranley! Even you can't believe that?'

'I'm not saying I do.'

'Look, arrest Stoke. I can get people to testify if he's safely locked up.'

'Come and see me, Malloy, then we'll talk about it.'

'I can't! Not now. I told you that.'

'Then it looks like I'm going to have to let your two friends here go.'

I heard a click. 'Cranley! Cranley! You bastard!'

Charmain was up when I got back, spooning coffee as the kettle whistled. The covering of make-up didn't completely hide the dark rings round her eyes but she looked reasonably bright. It was hard to tell if she'd had her first fix of the day.

'Coffee?' she asked.

'Please. Black, no sugar.' I sat on the bunk.

'Just as well. There's no milk.'

She brought it and sat opposite me, clasping her cup. 'Where've you been?'

'I took the cars into the village.'

She looked puzzled.

'In case Howard's got a search party out.'

She sipped. Neither of us spoke for a minute. She seemed almost friendly and was acting as if last night hadn't happened.

'Do you think Howard will know I'm with you?' She asked.

'I hope so.'

'Why?' She looked nervous.

'Because I need him to come looking for us.' My stomach heaved as I said it. I was afraid.

'Jesus.' she said, quietly, and I knew she was scared too. 'Then what?'

'I don't know. I'm still thinking.'

She sipped her coffee. I blew on mine. We were silent again for a minute then she spoke, gazing over the rim of her cup at the floor. 'How long will it take him to find us?'

'I don't know.'

'It might be days,' she said.

'Maybe.'

'Or even a week.'

We looked at each other.

'I don't think I could stand that,' she said, 'just sitting here knowing it could be any minute or it could be days and days.'

I nodded. I didn't think I could stand it either.

'What do you think he'll do when he gets here?' she asked.

'Charmain, I don't know yet. I'm trying to plan something.' I felt irritable though she didn't seem to notice. I went to the window. The hedge by the towpath blocked the view of the road and made me start worrying that Stoke might already be on his way and I wouldn't even see his car pull up.

I went outside. The air was warmer now, the low mist lifting. I watched the road, grey and empty.

Charmain was right. Neither of us would stand days of waiting, especially if her heroin supply ran out.

Rather than hide the fact we were here, I should have been advertising it. The sooner Stoke knew, the quicker he'd come.

I'd get my car back and leave it at the top of the towpath. It could only be a matter of time before one of Stoke's buddies passed by. I told Charmain but her relief seemed marginal, about the same as a condemned man shows when you tell him his sentence has been brought forward.

I bought groceries in the village, and a pink track suit and yellow training shoes. The last two items were for Charmain, but by the time I got back to the boat I'd decided not to give them to her.

'Why?' she asked, as I stashed them in a small locker.

'Because when Howard does come,' I shut the clasp lock and straightened to face her, 'I need him to think you're being held prisoner.'

'By you?'

'Yes. And there's a hell of a lot better chance of him believing it if you're dressed just in your nightgown with no shoes.'

'Why do you want him to think that?'

'To protect you. So you'll have to do your bit to convince him from the moment he comes through that door.'

She was looking nervy again. 'What will you be doing?' She asked.

'I won't be here.'

She stared at me. I went to the sink, filled the kettle again, and lit the stove. 'Did you notice the old barge moored behind us?' I asked. She nodded.

'When he comes down the towpath I'll be in there. When he gets through this door, I'll slip out and ring the police from the lock-keeper's cottage.'

'What if the lock-keeper isn't in?'

'We'll just have to hope he is, otherwise I'll have to drive into the village.'

'Then what?'

'You convince him I kidnapped you. Tell him I've gone to buy some booze and that I'll be back any time. I'll speak to DS Cranley. He'll make sure the police come quickly and quietly.'

I rinsed the coffee mugs. 'When the police get here I'll come back on board and make Howard incriminate himself loudly enough for the police to come in and get him.'

'That's silly.'

I shrugged. 'It's the best I can come up with.'

'Howard won't come alone, you know,' she said.

'We'll have to wait and see. As long as they all come on board then I can still make the call.'

She stood, arms crossed, clutching her elbows tightly, 'What if he doesn't believe me?'

The kettle bubbled. I poured and stirred, 'You'll have to make him believe you.' I carried the drinks over and we sat down.

She looked across at me, 'What if he shoots you as you walk through the door?'

I sipped the coffee and shook my head, 'He won't, Howard will want to see me squirm, make me suffer.' I looked at her, 'don't you think so?'

Despite the warmth from the fire and the hot coffee, she shivered and looked away. She knew I was right.

I locked her in, ducked through a gap in the hedgerow and set off across the field up toward the ruined farm I'd watched Greene and Skinner from. The binoculars swung from my shoulder.

Reaching the rock I'd used before, I settled down knowing I could wait days for one of Stoke's men to come along.

Earlier that afternoon I'd gone to the lock keeper's cottage and asked to use the phone. In the general small talk, I found that the couple who lived there had no plans over the weekend. At least there'd be a phone available when the 'emergency' came.

It was a fine, warm, windless evening. A tractor, orange light flashing lazily on its roof, chugged up the hill and turned off into a cornfield. The only other vehicles I'd seen after half an hour were six cars and a laundry van.

I'd been there forty minutes when I heard noises from the direction of the canal. I focused on the boat.

It was rolling heavily and unevenly in the water. Faint sounds of breaking glass or crockery reached me.

What the hell was she doing down there? No one got could have got on board without me seeing them. She had to be making all that noise on her own.

My first inclination was to run down the hill, but what would I be running into? The noise got worse. A metallic banging echoed as though she was hitting the draining board with a cooking pot. Was she trying to get out? Had a fire started?

A curtain moved. I concentrated on the window and saw her grip the curtain and tear it down. I set off half-limping, half-running toward the boat.

Chapter 69

Charmain sat cross-legged on her bunk. A corner of the torn curtain lay over her shoulder, tucked under her chin, which was sunk deep on her chest. Her hair had fallen forward hiding her face. Her hands, white-knuckled, were clamped to her sides as if she were holding her ribcage in place. She was rocking to and fro making a tuneless sound somewhere between a moan and a hum, as though hoping to drown out something she didn't want to hear.

The damage around her couldn't have been worse if the boat had overturned. Every internal door was open; lockers, cupboards, fridge, cooker, toilet. Some of the smaller ones hung only from one hinge. All looked empty, their contents on the floor: books, magazines, towels, bedding, clothing, pictures, mirrors, twisted coat hangers, light bulbs, crockery, glasses, cutlery.

Many things were broken, bent, torn, mangled, smashed, spilled.

In the kitchen area, a mess of food lay over and among the wreckage. A slab of butter spread wide by her foot, blobs of corned beef with jelly clinging, raspberry yogurt bleeding from a cracked carton, a burst loaf, bruised apples, torn teabags, a trail of coffee grains, puddles of milk and orange juice, hundreds of loose matches, most with spent black heads, and, scattered over everything like corn-coloured snowdrops, thousands of cereal flakes.

The only object not on the floor was a plant pot on its side on the small table next to me; the contents, a short, vicious looking cactus, had been dragged out. Some of the spikes at the tip were bloodstained. I righted the pot. What was left of the soil inside bore Charmain's scrabbling, desperate, heroin-seeking finger marks.

I went over to where she sat rocking.

Rolling back and forth with her, in the dip made by the nightgown between her open knees, was the empty heroin phial. I squatted in front of her to look up into her face.

'Charmain, what happened? I thought you had enough to get you through?'

She didn't answer, just kept rocking. Delicately, I reached for the phial, which had dropped into a fold between her thighs. Empty. I looked closely at the cap. It was cracked. By her side were the tattered remains of her little pink bag, the lining had been torn out. Gently, I parted her hair. A piece of the lining, sucked dry of the leaked drug, hung from her mouth like a desiccated tongue.

Whether it was shock or the beginning of withdrawal I don't know, but I couldn't rouse her. She was locked away, eyes still open, in her own little world. I thought of cleaning the place up then decided Stoke would be more easily convinced by our story if I left the mess.

I stayed by the window to keep watch as best I could while Charmain rocked and swayed on her bunk, hour after hour.

Come early evening she began moaning and whining.

I gripped her knees. 'Tough it out. We'll soon be away from here.'

She shook her head. 'Can't.'

'You can.'

'No! Get me some stuff!'

'Charmain…' I tried to make her look at me but she wouldn't. I touched her chin, tried to bring it up.

'Charmain…' Slowly she straightened and looked at me with red, pained, pleading eyes. 'Please…' she moaned.

'There isn't any, Charmain. There's nowhere I can get it. We're in the middle of the countryside, it'll soon be dark.'

She kept staring like a frightened child. 'Just a little…' The whine again. This was no good. I couldn't face many more hours of this, never mind days. Somehow, I had to let Stoke know we were here. An idea came to me. I checked my watch.

'Charmain, try to take in what I'm saying to you.' I cupped her face in my hands. 'Listen, concentrate. I'm going out for a while and for your own good, I'm going to lock you in. Try to stay calm and don't call out, because I can't come to you.'

She didn't look up, didn't make a sound. I squeezed her shoulders and turned, picking my way through the debris. Locking the door, I stepped onto the towpath, made for the car and headed for home. Leaving Charmain alone for a couple of hours was a gamble I had to take.

Back at the cottage, the place was cold but I couldn't bring myself to build a fire, that would be too cheery. I sat silently under the light of a small lamp, accepting I was making the final admission to myself, knowing I was extinguishing the last dregs of hope for our relationship.

At 9.55pm, Jackie called and we spoke lovingly and I left her with the news of exactly where I was and who I was with. If she did her job as well as she had with Harle and Kruger, Stoke would soon be coming.

Chapter 70

When I returned to the boat there had been no change in the pitch of Charmain's whining. I tried to get through to her that Howard could be on his way and it was essential she stuck to the story we'd agreed. I was wasting my time. She took nothing in.

I doubted Stoke would come that night, Jackie couldn't be that blatant about betrayal.

If he did come, I'd have real problems between Charmain and trying to rouse the lock keeper so I could use his phone. But I couldn't take any chances, so I prepared for a night on the old barge. The only consolation was I wouldn't be in the same room as Charmain and her moaning.

By midnight, the only life I'd seen was a fox trotting along the towpath. He'd stopped alongside Charmain's boat, lifted a front paw and cocked his ears at the pathetic whingeing from inside. She'd kept it up non-stop for two hours. The fox trotted on out of earshot. He was lucky.

I spent an uneventful night disturbed only by the cold and Charmain's moans.

When dawn came and Stoke hadn't showed, the tension eased a notch and I was sorely tempted to try to get some sleep. But it was too risky.

I wanted a cup of coffee to warm me and keep me awake but I was apprehensive about going back inside the boat. There had been no noise from Charmain for over an hour. I guessed she'd fallen asleep so I didn't want to wake her and find myself subject to another desperate pleading session.

And, Stoke might still arrive at any minute. As soon as I walked through that door, he could come coasting down the hill in his big quiet Rolls. I thought about it. I thought about the hot coffee. To hell with it, I'd make some.

Hoping not to wake Charmain I crept in quietly but she wasn't asleep. She sat on the floor by the bunk, her knees drawn up to her chest.

As soon as she saw me, she scrambled up and stumbled forward, grabbing at my lapels, staring up into my face, her hair matted with stale sweat, her skin aspirin-white, making the rings around her bloodshot eyes look even darker. Her breath smelled bad.

'Did you get any?' she whined, eyes wide and wild.

I tried to ease her grip. 'No, Charmain.'

'Yes! You must have!'

'I haven't been anywhere! I've been in the boat behind you all night freezing to bloody death.' I held her shoulders and turned her toward the bunk again. 'Come on, I'll make you a coffee.'

She tore herself away and pushed me so hard I overbalanced and fell against the table, the leg wound getting the worst of it.

She stamped once and clenched her fists and leant forward, her face inches from mine. A vein swelled in the centre of her forehead and a dozen sprung on her neck and, screaming every word at me she said, 'I don't want a fucking coffee! I want a fix!'

It might have been through some desire to calm her down, but I think it was mostly anger that made me stand up and slap her face. Reeling, she staggered back against the wall, tears welling in her mad pathetic eyes. Slowly, she let herself slide until she was sitting, knees up, on the floor. She stayed there, weeping quietly.

I made the coffee, brought a mugful for her and set it down by her side. 'Black only. You spilled all the milk.'

Looking up at me, she shifted into pleading mode again. 'Let me go…please!'

I leaned against the table. 'Where to? Where would you go, Charmain, in that state?'

'Roscoe's.'

'Why?'

'There'll be some stuff there, I'm sure there will. Alan could have left some, or Phil. Roscoe's probably got some.'

'And do you think he'll give it to you?'

'I'll make him.'

'Sure you will. How are you going to get there?'

'Just gimme the keys, I'll drive.'

I hunkered in front of her. 'Charmain, you can hardly walk, never mind drive.'

With both hands, she rubbed her forehead, then her eyes. 'I can,' she wept, 'I can.'

'Charmain, listen…listen to me. You've got to be here when Howard comes. You've got to go through with what we agreed.' She wouldn't look at me. I said, 'He'll come before midnight tonight. I'm sure he will. Then we'll get you away from here, get you sorted out.'

She just shook her head slowly and the quiet weeping gave way to heavy sobbing. I was fighting a losing battle and couldn't spend any more time trying to console her. For all I knew Stoke was standing outside.

I turned and headed back to the old barge, locking Charmain in.

By noon, a combination of boredom, silence and a night without sleep had me dozing on my feet. I decided to risk another confrontation with Charmain for the sake of a coffee and something to read.

Anyway, she'd been quiet for a while, maybe she was sleeping.

Unlocking the door, I tiptoed in, wary of waking her. I heard the metallic clunk at exactly the same time as I felt the blow and I remember marveling stupidly at how synchronized it seemed as I slumped to the floor and sank into unconsciousness.

Chapter 71

I opened my eyes and didn't know where I was. My head hurt. I stared at a long narrow ceiling. Was I in a hallway in some big house? Rolling onto my stomach I slowly pushed myself up until I was kneeling. I looked around. I was still on the boat.

It was deserted. No Charmain, no Stoke, no bad men. Beside me, upside down on the floor, was the steel cooking pot I'd been hit with. It wasn't even dented. Tenderly, I fingered my skull and found a painful lump over my right ear.

I got to my feet. The dizziness was slight. I walked a few steps toward the door…balance was okay. I went outside. Dusk was falling. The car had gone.

I remembered the other car parked half a mile away in Shipton and felt for the keys in my pocket.

Found them.

I set off in a running limp for the village.

I thought of Charmain as I drove. She'd be there by now, easily. How was she planning to find the stuff at Roscoe's? Would she wait until dark and try to break in? She couldn't wait. She'd be growing more desperate by the hour. What if she hadn't told me everything? Maybe she was tied in with Roscoe too, the same as she'd been with Harle and Greene.

I drove fast, my leg wound pulsing at every ridge and pothole. Driving the route that led the last couple of miles to Roscoe's brought scary memories of the scalding. The black shape of each large tree I passed reminded me of the one I'd woken up under, lying on the frosty road.

Half a mile from Roscoe's I stopped, got the flashlight and lockpicks and quietly closed the car door. I felt only minor twinges in my leg as I climbed the small fence and set out across the fields.

No lights showed in Roscoe's house, but I took a line toward the small cottage sitting alone on an incline about two hundred yards from the main stable block. The head lad's cottage, where Skinner was living now - it too was in darkness.

The door was unlocked. I checked the area before going in. Down to my left was the stable yard, dark and almost silent. The only sound came from a box in the corner where a shod hoof worked through straw bedding to scrape at the concrete floor. Softly, I turned the door handle.

My flashlight flared in the narrow hall, showing a door either side. I chose the one on the right and eased it closed behind me. I moved the beam a yard forward and in the spotlight was a foot. The yellow training shoe hung only on the toe. Above the shoe, the pale pink leg of the track suit, bought new the day before.

As the light moved upwards, something glinted on the floor: an empty glass phial. Her left sleeve was rolled up. Still hanging from her bare arm was the syringe, the plunger pushed fully home.

Her eyes were closed. No more cramps. No more shivering. No more loneliness chained up in the big house. Life's agonies ended.

As I knelt in the darkness to ease the syringe from her arm, someone switched the light on. I was dazzled for a second then I turned round and Howard Stoke stood by the door, his hand still on the light switch. Roscoe, looking strained, was at his shoulder. Switching off the flashlight I slowly got up.

Stoke and Roscoe hadn't spoken. Stoke's fingers remained on the light switch. I considered yanking the door open and running, and then Stoke took his hand from the switch, put it into his coat pocket and brought out a gun.

Chapter 72

Stoke pointed the gun at my head and I thought he was going to shoot me without saying even one word. I wanted to look at Roscoe to see if there was anything in his face to give me hope, but I couldn't make my eyes leave Stoke's trigger finger. Something told me that if I looked away he'd fire.

His lips drew back from his teeth.

'Tell me how it feels, Mister Malloy?' Stoke said. The level of control he needed to steady his voice frightened me much more than the silence had.

'How what feels?' My own control had almost gone.

'How it feels to be living the last two minutes of your life.'

'What do you want me to say? That I'm sorry about Charmain? About Phil Greene and Alan Harle?'

His reply started under control, but each word jumped ten decibels. 'I want you to say you're sorry for fucking up my life!'

The gun quivered in his hand. I fought to keep cool. 'It wasn't my doing.' I said.

'Whose was it,' he yelled, 'the man in the fucking moon?'·

I stayed silent. Whatever I said, he was going to shoot me. I'd never seen such rage. The volcano had started erupting and it was only a matter of minutes, maybe seconds, before it blew completely.

'Look at her,' he said. I kept my eyes on the gun. 'Look at her!' he shouted. I turned and looked at Charmain.

'The stuff in that syringe, the stuff she squeezed into her arm cost me half a million pounds…Two liquid ounces…One single ampoule…Five hundred thousand pounds.'

And four lives, I thought.

'And that bitch shot it into one dirty vein. But don't think you've beaten me, Malloy…I'd hate you to die thinking that. Skinner didn't fuck up completely, he did remember to write the formula down, so we will be back in business very soon. Very soon, Mister Malloy, and without you this time.'

He stepped forward and motioned Roscoe into the room. 'Where's Skinner?' Stoke asked him. I glanced at Roscoe. He looked very wary of Stoke.

'He's outside.'

'Get him in here.'

Roscoe went out and returned with the vet, who darted a frightened glance at Stoke.

Stoke looked at me. 'I believe you've met Mister Skinner?' he said. I didn't reply. 'He's nearly as bad as you, Malloy. You know how these guys with degrees are supposed to be brainy? I mean, they told me this man was a genius when I took him on. He was smart enough to work on the ultimate drug, completely undetectable. A drug that will make me millions, give me control over all the arseholes in racing, like you, Malloy. Pretty smart, then, you'd say, eh?'

He turned his attention to the scowling Skinner.

'But not smart enough to remember to lock the fucking door behind him!'

That was how Charmain had got in.

Stoke glared at Skinner, who looked away quickly. Stoke turned again to me.

'What did McCarthy tell you? You'd get your licence back if you cracked it? The Jockey Club would reconsider and all that fucking garbage? And you believed it? They took you for a mug, Malloy, and look where it's got you.'

I kept watching his finger. Slowly he lowered the gun and held it out to Roscoe who'd moved away.

'Roscoe!' Stoke almost screamed. 'Take this!' Roscoe, pale-faced, hurried forward and took the gun. 'If he even moves, shoot him,' Stoke ordered.

Stoke put his hands on his hips and smiled at me. 'Cool, Malloy, very cool. I thought I'd have you begging, thought you'd have been on your knees. You must have known I wouldn't shoot you.' He took off his coat and walked to the sink unit, talking as he went. 'No way…I couldn't just kill you without you suffering any pain.'

'Bad for your reputation,' I said, and wished I hadn't.

'Very cool, Malloy, but very true.' His voice was much lighter. He seemed to be enjoying the prospect of whatever he had planned.

Lifting a phial of dark liquid from a shelf, he held it up. 'This is what's going to kill you, Malloy, and it's going to take weeks, maybe longer. I'm going to lock you away and come every day to watch you die, to see you suffer.'

I stared at the liquid. My brain had stopped working.

'Sit down beside my wife, Mister Malloy, make yourself comfortable. And before you do, take off your jacket.'

I took it off.

Stoke took his off.

'Now sit down like I told you.'

I eased myself down beside Charmain's body, which was already cold.

'Now let's roll our sleeves up.' He rolled up his shirtsleeves. 'Come on!' he yelled.

I rolled them up.

Carrying the liquid, he came toward me, moving like the eighteen-stone slob he was. As he walked, he said, 'Did you know what your friend Harle died of?'

'Heroin overdose.'

'Nope.' He stood over me, blocking out the light. I looked up at him. He smiled. 'Ever heard of Hepatitis B?'

I kept staring. He kept smiling. 'Harle had it. We did give him an overdose, two syringes full, in fact. Both needles were infected.'

My eyes were going to the glass phial as he asked, 'Guess what this is?' He held up the dark brown liquid.

I knew.

'A clever fucker like you will have sussed that it's a blood sample from Harle's corpse taken shortly before we dumped him in your car.'

He bent and pulled the syringe from Charmain's arm. 'She was still alive when we got here, you know. Told us you'd be coming…To rescue her…She always was a poor judge.'

Taking the liquid to the sink unit, he dipped the empty syringe in it and drew the plunger until it filled.

He turned to Roscoe. 'If he moves an inch either way, shoot him.'

Roscoe raised the gun. I looked at his face. It told me nothing. I didn't think he'd shoot, but couldn't be sure.

Stoke came for me, holding the syringe up. He stopped at my feet and stood open-legged. 'Arm out.'

I didn't move.

'Hold your arm out or I'll inject it through your eye.'

Slowly I straightened my arm. Stoke bent forward. I glanced at Roscoe, grim-faced, still aiming. Stoke was astride my legs. He reached for my wrist, bending, slightly off-balance. I leaned toward Charmain, bent my right leg and smashed a kick so hard between Stoke's legs I felt his balls separate as the toe of my boot hammered deep into his scrotum. He screamed and dropped the syringe, which turned once in mid-air like a dagger, then stuck into Charmain's thigh.

Stoke clutched his groin. I reached and grabbed the collar of his shirt and hauled him down to shield me from Roscoe. Pulling the syringe from Charmain's leg, I held it to Stoke's neck. He was groaning, gasping.

Roscoe, gripping with both hands, still had the gun leveled. His knuckles were white as he held it at arm's length.

'Drop it or the needle goes in,' I said, trying to sound calm.

He said nothing but I could see the panic rising in his eyes. From beneath the perfectly set fringe, beads of sweat began popping. There were dark patches, too, under his arms. His lips were parted, teeth clenched. The jaw muscles swelled then relaxed, beating like steady pulses.

Skinner glowered at him. 'Don't let us down, Roscoe.'

'Come on, Roscoe…' I urged. Stoke was still fighting for breath, gasping, spluttering, very close to the needle.

'Shut it!' Roscoe cried.

I tried to weigh up the look in his eyes again and hoped it was panic rather than madness. I played on.

'What's the point? You'd have to kill us both.'

He sniffed hard. Sweat broke on his top lip.

'Where would you go?' I asked. 'Do you think you could leave three bodies here? How will you explain all this stuff? And Harle and Greene? Why take the blame for everything Stoke's done? That's where they'll pin it.'

He stared at me.

'Put the gun down and call the police, tell them about Stoke. Hire a top lawyer, and you'll get off with five years, three, with good behaviour.'

He wavered.

'Roscoe! Shoot him!' Skinner shouted.

'Don't listen to him, Roscoe. Okay, you'll lose your training licence, but so what? Stoke here, or Perlman, or whatever you call him, won't be sending you any more horses anyway.'

That seemed to do it. Slowly he straightened up and lowered the gun. The tension eased from his face to be replaced by tiredness and defeat.

Skinner moved quickly and smashed his elbow into Roscoe's cheekbone, grabbing the gun from him as he fell. Skinner came at me looking a lot more determined than Roscoe and almost as crazy as Stoke, who was still gasping for breath.

I held the needle closer to Stoke's throat. 'Another step, Skinner, and it goes in.'

'Who cares? Kill the bastard, I never liked him anyway, but you're dying with him, you smarmy little shit.'

He moved sideways, toward the open door, aiming the gun at my head.

'You've got too much to lose, Skinner.'

'Shut it! That doesn't wash with me! I'm not some fucking wimp like Roscoe! You are going to die, so say your prayers and say goodbye to your pretty little face that all the girls thought was so fucking cute when you were a big-time jockey!' He bent forward holding the gun straight out. 'Because I'm going to blow your head right off your shoulders.'

I watched his finger tighten on the trigger and closed my eyes. Then I heard a sweet soft Irish voice,

'Don't even breathe, Mister Skinner. Drop the gun.'

The pistol clattered to the floor, and I opened my eyes to see Jackie resting the barrels of a shotgun just below Skinner's ear. The vet had gone very pale. 'Lie down on the floor next to Mister Malloy,' she said.

Skinner obeyed, and she took the gun and rammed it hard between his buttocks. 'Now, Mister Skinner, you tell me how it feels to have something unexpected stuck in your arse.' She looked at me and we smiled.

Chapter 73

Jackie said, 'I'll call the police.'

'No, not yet,' I said, 'can you put your hands on some rope? I want to tie them up.'

Jackie brought rope from the tack room and we tied Stoke and Skinner together. She covered them with the gun while I took Roscoe outside, and round the gable end of the sandstone building, 'Against that wall,' I said, 'facing me.'

Roscoe backed up until his heels touched the wall. He looked terrified, and his cheeks reddened. I don't think he realized he was holding his breath. 'You'd better breathe,' I said.

He did.

The night on the road came back to me and I had a fierce urge to punch him full in the face and hear his head bounce off the wall and back for more punches. But I needed a deal. I said, 'I'm not calling the police, I'm calling Jockey Club Security, Peter McCarthy. When he gets here, you are going to tell us everything, every little detail. Every single thing Stoke has done, and Kruger and Skinner.'

'You said you'd get me off, then.'

'I said the cops might take an easier view. Don't start putting words in my mouth because I'm an inch away from punching you till my knuckles break.'

He held his breath again. It was irritating me. 'Breathe!' I yelled.

He breathed. I said, 'I'll get McCarthy to negotiate with the cops on your behalf. He's got a much better chance of getting a deal for you than I have. But you leave out nothing, right?'

He nodded. I said, 'I've put it all together now anyway, so I'll know if you leave anything out.'

He nodded more eagerly this time. I took him back in and tied him up in a separate room. There was a telephone on the bench in the lab. I called Mac and told him what had happened, 'Bring two of your guys, three if you can get them, and bring that little Dictaphone thing. Don't speak to the police.'

'Have you called them?'

'No. I'm leaving the glory for you.'

Chapter 74

In the hour it took Mac and his team to get there, Jackie could no longer listen to the groaning and crying from Stoke, who writhed constantly, driving Skinner crazy. Skinner bitched and yelled. Stoke moaned and howled and Jackie couldn't stand it. I could. I watched with satisfaction.

Mac's three men took over the watch while he and I went into the big house. Jackie said, 'I'll make some tea.'

I caught her by the arm, 'No! Your days of running after people are finished. I want you with me. We're a team.' We sat at Roscoe's kitchen table, under the bright lights. Mac said, 'What's the proposal you mentioned?'

'What I said. You get the glory. For you, for your department, for your senior steward. A payback for all that mighty pressure you keep telling me you've been under for so long.'

'And what do you get?'

'My licence back.'

'We'd agreed that was conditional on an admission from Kruger, so-'

I grabbed his arm, 'Mac! it doesn't matter what we agreed! The game's changed. That was the old deal. This is the new one.'

'I don't think it will-'

I squeezed his arm hard, 'Mac! Come on. You owe me here!' I pointed to my face, 'Look! Look at this!' I watched his eyes move from hairline to chin, and he said, 'But-'

'No more buts, Mac! This is the deal. You get on the phone to the senior steward and sell it to him. He'll lap it up, you know he will.

What difference does it make returning my licence for this rather than for the Kruger confession? There's no difference, is there? It's a technicality!'

Mac glanced at Jackie, then looked down at the table, 'Okay', he said, 'I'll ring him.'

He got up and asked Jackie where the phone was. 'I'll show you', she said.

I called after him, 'Tell him what I'm giving up here, Mac, remind him of all the shit I've had to take from Cranley, and now I don't get to rub Cranley's nose in it. That's a biggie for me, a big sacrifice. He gets the headlines, your man. Tell him that. He'll be the hero. He'll win-'

Mac turned and raised a hand, 'Okay! Okay! I get it!'

Jackie smiled.

Chapter 75

We untied Roscoe and led him to the house. I'd wanted Jackie with us again for this, but it was too hard for her, and she opted out.

We sat Roscoe down in his own kitchen. Mac set the Dictaphone going and one of his men stood in the corner as a witness.

I said, 'Right, take it from the start Mister Roscoe.'

He rubbed his mouth, and then his chin and looked down at the table before muttering, 'I'm trying to remember…'

'Who assaulted Bergmark and Rask?'

'Stoke's boys.'

'Bill and Trevor?'

He looked sharply at me. The message had got home; I already knew the answers to many of these questions.

'Why?' I asked.

'They'd been blackmailing Danny Gordon. Kruger wanted Gordon to work with him and Skinner on the new drug, but Gordon was afraid it would give the Swedes something else on him.'

'On top of what?'

'A Tote fraud Gordon had been in on.'

I was tempted to run through the rest of the story myself, but realized it would all need to come from Roscoe. 'So what was the deal for Gordon?'

'Stoke would get the Swedes off his back, then Danny would be free to help.'

Mac said, 'So who killed Danny Gordon?'

Roscoe glanced at me, then at Mac, 'Stoke's boys.'

'Why?'

'He reneged on the deal. Once he knew the Swedes were completely out of the game, he told Skinner he wasn't doing it.'

I said, 'Kruger wouldn't have signed off on Gordon's killing. He wasn't into violence.'

'Stoke told him Bergman and Rask had put the hit out on Danny.'

'And Kruger believed him?' I said.

'Stoke can be very persuasive. Kruger came round to it but the crazier things got…well, Kruger knew then.'

I said, 'Was Rask murdered or did he hang himself?'

'He hung himself.'

'How did Stoke get into this in the first place?' I asked.

'Skinner. Skinner owed him a lot of money from gambling, and this was his idea to pay it off and make everybody rich.'

Mac said, 'So Stoke bought all those horses for you?'

'That's right.'

'So he was Perlman?' Mac said.

'I suppose so.'

I said, 'I warned you about telling everything.'

Roscoe looked sideways at me, then down at the table. I said, 'The little guy with the glasses who was here that night with Phil Greene. The same guy who was at your Champion Hurdle party in the Duke's. What's his name?'

He hesitated, then said, 'Louis Perlman. But he didn't own any horses.'

'So what was he doing, apart from being a decoy?'

I could see by Roscoe's face he was considering his answer. He said, 'He spent a lot of time following people, watching them.'

'Who?' I said.

'Danny Gordon, Alan Harle, Greene, Charmain…you.'

Much of what I had been putting down to Jackie's deception had been my stupidity in not knowing I was being trailed.

Mac said, 'Where is he, Perlman?'

'He'll be at home. I can tell you where.'

I said, 'Why was Harle killed?'

'Mostly, for trying to rip Stoke off on heroin income.'

'Mostly?' I said.

'He was sleeping with Stoke's wife.'

Mac said, 'Go back to the heroin income.'

'Harle had been dealing in it small time. He already knew Stoke. Stoke was paying him for information, and for arranging the odd bent race.'

'So that's why he got the job riding?'

Roscoe nodded.

I said, 'And how did you get the job training?'

'I knew Skinner and Alan. Alan had been providing cocaine for us.'

'Who is "us"?' Mac said.

Another hesitation, then, 'Me…and my wife.'

'Where is your wife?' Mac asked.

'Staying with friends.'

'Since when?' Mac said.

'Yesterday. We knew we were very, very close to the breakthrough. Skinner had got all the stuff he needed and all the information from Kruger, and he'd been working day and night. My wife knows nothing. I always sent her away when anything was happening here.'

I said, 'How did you know Kruger was meeting me at Stratford?'

Roscoe came alive for the first time with a protest, 'It wasn't me! I didn't kill Kruger! It was Stoke's guys!'

'How did Stoke know?' I said.

'Perlman bugged Kruger's phone.'

Mac nodded and put a finger to his chin, 'Take me back to this heroin income, was it significant?'

'It helped Stoke pay a lot of the expenses. It was easy to make and sourcing it in France was simple. I'd send horses over with Harle when we needed more supplies. They were smuggled back in the horse box, and Skinner blended everything in the lab.'

'And Harle sold it?' I said.

Roscoe sighed, nodding, 'Until he got too fond of it himself.'

'And too fond of Charmain,' I said.

'That was what fucked everything up. He was a fool. We'd have made it through but for that. It got too personal for Stoke, and he started making poor decisions.'

'Like buying savage horses to kill his young stable jockey?'

Roscoe looked away, and said, 'That was bad. But Greene was almost as stupid as Alan.'

I leaned forward, 'Tell me this, who was it who came up with the methods, the ways to kill and torture?'

'Stoke. He'd spend a lot of time on it.'

Mac said, 'You must have been scared yourself if he was that bad?'

'He's a psychopath.'

We spent another ten minutes going over everything again, then Mac went to call Cranley. He returned to the table and looked at me, 'Your nemesis is on his way.'

'I'm his nemesis, Mac. I just wish we could find a way of sticking it to the bastard and letting I'm know who the smartest guy was in the end.'

Mac said, 'Well, we can always go back and talk again about the deal?'

I got up. 'No way, Mac! The deal's done now. I'm going home. Jackie's coming with me. Neither of us has been here today, okay?'

Mac said, 'Have you agreed this with Stoke and Skinner?'

'I'm sure when you go in and tell them what the arrangement is, it'll save them considerable embarrassment. What's the saying, adding insult to injury? I think they'll be only too pleased to claim it took most of the Jockey Club Security team to nail them rather than an ex-jockey and a young girl.'

Mac reached to shake my hand, 'I'll call you tomorrow.'

'You'll meet me tomorrow, Mac. I want you to drive up to Mandown gallops and see me on a racehorse for the first time in more than five years. I want you to hand me a piece of Jockey Club headed paper on which will be a lovely letter from the senior steward confirming I am once again a licensed jockey. I will show that piece of paper to a trainer I am about to call, and he will have a horse ready for me to school.'

Mac smiled, 'You've got it all worked out to a T, haven't you?'

'You bet.'

'I'd hate to play you at chess,' he said.

I smiled. Mac raised a finger, 'But I'd love to play you at poker.'

'Don't be so sure.'

'We'll see sometime.'

'You are on!'

Chapter 76

We didn't go home. I hadn't realized that it was almost midnight. We made the short trip to the Malt Shovel in Lambourn where they found us a room and a bottle of scotch.

Jackie had brought me a pair of riding boots and a helmet from Roscoe's place, and I put them on the floor by the wardrobe.

She said, 'I thought you'd leave them in the car until tomorrow?'

'Too precious,' I said. 'I want to look at them.'

She smiled wearily.

We sat on the bed in quiet companionship and I tried to accept it was all over. I'd expected to feel elated, to be buzzing with the satisfaction of revenge, but none of it was there.

All I felt was a deep contentment that Jackie was with me again, a massive happy relief that she hadn't betrayed me and a steadily burrowing guilt at having suspected her.

There was no lovemaking. When the trauma hit Jackie she got very weepy, and I spent half the night comforting her, and the other half coping with my deepening guilt over doubting her. Knowing she would never forgive me if she learnt of my suspicions, I overcame the urge to confess.

In the morning, I left Jackie asleep, and went downstairs and made the call I'd planned to make the night before. It was to Grayson Lassiter, an old friend who was in the twilight of his training career.

'Eddie! How good to hear from you! How are you?'

'Never been better Grayson. I thought I'd do you the honour of legging me up on the first racehorse I'll have sat on since I was warned off.'

'I'd be delighted! What's happened?'

I explained, and Grayson agreed to bring a nice young gelding he thought highly of, and meet me on the gallops at half ten. I called Mac then to confirm everything, 'You got the letter?'

'It's being faxed to me as we speak.'

'Good. How was my friend DS Cranley when he pitched up?'

'All flashing lights and business. I'll tell you about it when I see you.'

Jackie and I had breakfast in Lambourn, 'You look miles better after that few hours' sleep,' I said.

'I'm sorry,' she said.

'What for? No need to apologize.'

'I must have been running on pure adrenaline. It felt like something out of a film. It was only when you and Mister McCarthy marched Mister Roscoe inside that it all actually hit me.'

I motioned with my hand toward the café window at the bright morning, 'New day, new start, new world.'

She smiled and nodded and reached to clutch my hand before I put it down. I said, 'A bit early for arm wrestling,' and we laughed.

Chapter 77

High on the gallops we looked out on that fresh morning across the thousands of acres of grass, at the criss-cross patterns made by the white railed sections. Rows of schooling fences ran along hedge lines. Most horses had finished their morning work, but a few dozen cantered or trotted, most heading toward home.

Half a mile down the track, I saw a lone horseman and recognized the half-slumped style of Grayson Lassiter in the lemon, knitted polo neck he'd owned as long as I'd known him.

Coming up the tarmac road, with perfect timing, was McCarthy in his Volvo. I smiled and turned to Jackie, 'Funny how when everything comes together everything kind of comes together!'

She laughed.

Mac waved as he pulled in beside us. Grayson was two hundred yards away. He too raised a hand in greeting and I waved to him.

Mac got out and smiled at me, 'Aren't you the cat that's got the cream?'

'So long as you're the cat that's got the letter.'

He pulled it from his inside jacket pocket with a flourish, and he bowed, and handed it to me.

"Edward Malloy Esquire" the envelope read.

Jackie said, 'You're an esquire now. Open it!'

I did. It was worded exactly as I'd wanted it and signed in broad dark ink by Peregrine Huntley, senior steward of The Jockey Club.

I read it again, smiling, then looked at Mac, 'I never thought this day would come.'

He smiled, nodding, 'Oh, it would have.'

I stopped waving the letter and looked at him, 'What do you mean?'

He took out another envelope and gave it to me. The envelope was blank. I looked at him, puzzled. 'Open it,' Mac said.

I pulled out a photocopy of a handwritten letter. It was Kruger's statement, his confession that I'd had nothing to do with the doping that had cost me my licence. I read it twice, then looked up at McCarthy. He was smiling.

'How long have you had this?'

'Remember that morning at Stratford, when you so selfishly ran off and left me to explain everything?'

I nodded slowly.

'The police found it in his jacket pocket, in an envelope addressed to the senior steward. You'll see that it's unsigned.'

I looked again at it and said, 'When I spoke to him on the phone the night before Stratford, this is what he offered, to write it longhand and sign it in front of you. I told him no.'

'Well, he didn't listen.'

'But he never signed it.'

'I took it to the senior steward a week ago and argued your case. The Jockey Club have accepted that it's his handwriting and the fact that the police found it helped the approval of my request to have your licence returned.'

'You've known since that morning at Stratford I'd get my licence back?'

He nodded. 'If you'd been less of a hot head. If you'd stayed behind when I was almost begging you to, you'd have saved yourself an awful lot of trouble.'

I stared at him. I was confused, angry, dizzy... 'Mac, I almost lost my life last night,' I held the letter up, 'and I could have walked away from this weeks ago.'

'No you couldn't. You were in it up to your eyes. You wanted revenge, and you wanted to prove to Cranley that you were no fool, and you didn't want to let down Danny Gordon's wife.'

'Maybe. But you used me.'

He put his big hand on my shoulder and smiled, 'I harnessed a runaway, Eddie. I did my job. And I tried to give you the chance last night to keep the glory, to get your own back on Cranley. But you wouldn't let me get a word in, wouldn't give me a chance to tell you about this.'

I nodded slowly, raised my eyebrows, and looked at Jackie. She smiled and gave me a "never mind" shrug of the shoulders. I reddened as I looked at McCarthy. He smiled and said, 'When would you like that game of poker?'

We laughed, as Grayson pulled up alongside us on a shining bay gelding with a lovely head and honest eye. He slid off gracefully and walked round and hugged me without saying a word and I felt my eyes fill up.

'Put your helmet on,' Grayson said.

I offered him the Jockey Club letter, 'Do you want to see this?'

'Nope.'

Jackie fastened the helmet buckle for me and I walked slowly round to the side of this fine-tuned sixteen hands of muscle and bone and very slowly, I drew the reins along his neck until my fingers grasped the saddle. Grayson leaned down and offered his hand as my leg bent naturally so he could clasp my shin and up I went lightly, softly, beautifully, to sit once more on a thoroughbred racehorse, to look away into the distance, to the horizon where the earth ended and the sky started and my life began again.

Hunted

Copyright © 2015 by Joe McNally and Richard Pitman
All rights reserved.

No part of this book may be reproduced in any form or by any electronic or mechanical means, including information storage and retrieval systems, without written permission from the author, except for the use of brief quotations in a book review.

Authors' note

This is a work of fiction. Names, characters, places and incidents are either a work of the imagination of the authors or are used fictitiously, and any resemblance to actual persons, living or dead, business establishments, events or locales is entirely coincidental.

Chapter 1

As I was leaving the changing room at Haydock, things went suddenly quiet among the group to my left, eight or nine jockeys in various stages of undress. Con Layton's Irish accent rose from their midst. 'And did yer mammy iron your nice clean underpants for you before you came out? I'll bet she still wipes yer bottom too? Is that right…? Don't be shy, you can tell your Uncle Cornelius …'

I could only see the back of Layton's head. Squinting through someone's crooked elbow I saw the reddening face of the Irishman's latest target, a newcomer named David Cooper. The boy was only nineteen and had the makings of a top jockey. Well, he had the skills; I wasn't sure his heart was in it.

He was a quiet kid, didn't mix and didn't speak much, mostly I suspected because he was painfully self-conscious about the distinct 'th' for 's' lisp which made his upper-class accent sound staged and effeminate.

Strained chuckles rose from Layton's audience as he tormented the boy. The Irishman wouldn't be doing it just for fun. The lad had a fancied ride against him in the big race; this was Layton starting to psych him out.

Since my comeback I'd had little to do with Layton. He threw the occasional taunt my way, as he did with everyone else, but he'd been careful not to bait me too fiercely.

He stooped close to young Cooper, almost nose to nose. He said, 'D'ye still sleep with yer mammy?' The boy flushed, unable to hold Layton's gaze. His eyes flitted sideways and upward at the ring of faces watching him, begging without hope for someone to intervene.

Layton said, 'What does she look like with no clothes on?'

Tears welled. No more chuckles from the audience. Some turned away, shaking their heads. The room was silent waiting for the kid's reaction. A few would want to step in, but knew the youngster had to handle it himself if he wanted to survive.

Layton said, 'Come on, son, what does she look like? All the boys would like to know.'

I was twenty feet away. I said, 'That how you get your kicks, Layton?'

Everyone turned. Layton pushed through them. Young Cooper watched, unable to hide his relief.

Layton stopped a couple of paces in front of me. About five seven, three inches shorter than me, he was rat-like. His reddish-brown eyebrows met over his big nose. His white T-shirt was blotched with water, and he had a hand on each end of the yellow towel hanging round his neck. He said, 'A voice from the gallery, Malloy. I didn't quite catch what you said, now?'

'I said is that how you get your kicks? Is that what turns you on, asking young boys about their mothers? Or is it just bullying that gives you the big charge?'

Layton's turn to redden. 'You sayin' I'm a bully, Malloy?'

'A bully or a pervert, take your pick.'

His fists balled, jaw muscles clenched, brow furrowed, but I could see he was uncertain. It must have been the first time in years he'd been challenged. Even worse, he didn't know the strength of his opponent.

A fight could leave him with a broken jaw which, aside from the humiliation, would mean he wouldn't be riding for a while.

Feet apart, arms folded, I stood calmly watching him try to make a decision. Though I'd told no one yet I was quitting, if it came to a brawl he had more to lose.

His hands relaxed and he clasped them behind his back and put on a sly smile. 'You've an awful insolent mouth on you, Malloy.'

'I can live with it. Better than a mind like a sewer.'

Now he knew he wasn't going to win a battle of words. Taking a couple of steps toward me he leaned forward until I could see the tiny blue veins in the whites of his eyes. He said, 'You and me must get together some time soon.'

I held his gaze. 'Anytime. Just give me a couple of days' notice so I can arrange a vaccination.'

A few laughed. There was one outright guffaw and that triggered him; he knew he had to do something. With our faces so close, I guessed it would be a head-butt and I moved just as he tried it, stepping aside as he over-balanced.

I hit him in the ribs, then in the kidneys. He grunted and went to his knees. Grabbing the towel, I looped it around his neck and pulled a tight stranglehold while I stood on his left calf to stop him rising.

He gurgled, clutching. I leaned close to his ear. 'How does it feel, Layton? What's it like to be on the receiving end?' I jerked the towel tighter and his tongue came out.

I let go. He slumped forward, head on the bench, saliva dripping. I stepped away. There were maybe twenty people around us, most watching me, some staring at Layton.

I turned to leave and heard him trying to rise. Sprawled against the bench face up, he was breathing hard, glaring at me. 'You're a fucking dead man, Malloy.'

'Top marks for perception.' I said.

Layton looked puzzled, as one of his buddies, Meese, helped him away to the toilets.

The buzz of conversation resumed. Colin Blake squeezed my arm. 'Nice one, Eddie, but you've done yourself no favours there, mate.'

I smiled at him. 'You'd be surprised.' The confrontation had boosted my self-esteem, though I wasn't sure how much of the bravado had come from the knowledge that after today I would never be in a changing room with Layton again.

On my way out a couple of the lads slapped my back and said well done. I felt as if I'd won a race.

In his father's luminous yellow and red colours young Cooper was sitting on the scales, weighing out for the first. Still embarrassed, he glanced at me, his discomfort obvious.

Not wanting to make him feel obliged, I smiled briefly and walked on, but he stuck out a hand to grip my arm as I passed. I stopped. 'Thank you,' he said, avoiding the shortened version so he wouldn't have to lisp the 's'.

'Forget it. Good luck today.'

He smiled weakly and nodded, causing the scale needle to bob between ten stone ten and ten twelve. I left him with his troubles and took mine outside.

Chapter 2

The oval horsewalk was empty but the runners for the first would soon be in and the crowds would form around the rails to watch them parade. Then the bell would ring in the changing room and the jockeys would come out and make their way through the admiring throng into the arena.

They'd huddle with trainer and owner and friends and talk tactics, discuss plans. Then they'd mount and be led out, staring straight ahead above the crowds, feeling that tight thrill that comes from being different from the masses, from knowing that among the millions who love racing you are one of the main players.

And I wouldn't be there.

Not after today. Hopelessness weighed heavy in my gut, and I suddenly knew how drug addicts must feel when they realize there's never going to be another fix.

When someone touched my elbow and spoke my name I turned.

Her face was thin, hair dark and luxuriantly thick, eyes brown and distinctly oval, good mouth with well-shaped lips, my height, she looked at me. 'You okay?'

I nodded, dredging up a half-smile. 'Sorry, I was miles away.'

She said, 'Carter told me what you did to Layton. I just wanted to say I wish I'd been there.'

Lisa Ffrench was being pretty forthright. I didn't know her much beyond saying hello. Her job barred her from 'consorting' with jockeys and she was probably leaving herself open to criticism even talking to me now. Lisa was a stenographer. She worked for The Jockey Club, noting everything that was said during Stewards' Enquiries.

I shrugged. 'I didn't really do anything ... just put him in his place.'

'Well and truly, the way I heard it.' Her smile was wide.

I said, 'You're not a member of his fan club then?'

'Watched him lying through his teeth too many times, and sucking up to the stewards.'

I nodded, anxious to be alone again so I could be as miserable as I wanted. I said, 'Well, it won't take him long to bounce back, nasty as ever.'

'No doubt, but his ego will stay bruised for a while so you'd better watch yourself.'

'Shouldn't be too hard. This is my last day.'

'Last day at what?'

'Race-riding. I'm quitting.'

'Why?'

'Because I can't make a living at it anymore.'

She shook her head slowly. 'That's tough. Bad luck. You're a good jockey.'

'You think so?'

She nodded.

'Pity you don't own a string of twenty.' I looked away across the parade ring expecting her to politely excuse herself before the conversation got embarrassing. 'What are you going to do?' she asked.

I shrugged. 'I don't know yet, but I know what you'd better do before your bosses see you talking to lowlife like me.'

'Is it safe to leave you?'

Puzzled, I turned toward her again. She said, 'I'm scared in case you overdose on self-pity.'

That made me smile. She headed for the weighing room walking athletically in her flat shoes, skinny bottom swinging in a tight knee-length skirt.

I watched her go through the door. Two minutes later she came marching straight for me again. Half surprised, half apprehensive, I waited.

When she reached me she offered a piece of information that could save my career and ruin hers.

'Why are you doing this?' I asked.

'Because I don't want you to quit.'

'What does it matter to you, you don't even know me?' It sounded hostile and she raised her hands in surrender. 'Okay, okay, sorry for interfering.'

'Look, Lisa, I'm sorry, I didn't mean to sound ungrateful. I appreciate what you're doing …' I tailed off lamely.

She looked perplexed. The wind caught her heavy shoulder-length hair and lifted it to show a small gold earring. Her brown oval eyes told me her patience was waning. She said, 'Fine, do what you like.' She walked away with that confident head-up stride.

Hubert Barber trained Cragrock, the favourite in the big race. His stable jockey hadn't turned up and Lisa had overheard Barber tell the clerk of the scales that he planned to withdraw the horse.

She'd just been trying to persuade me to approach Barber and ask him to run Cragrock and let me ride.

I had ridden for him a few times during my Championship season and we'd got on okay, but he'd never offered me anything since my comeback. Watching Lisa disappear into the crowd I thought, what the hell, I might as well try. With no confidence and little hope I went looking for Barber.

I found him outside the main gate, shuffling impatiently, peering at cars coming in, squinting into taxis as they pulled up.

Barber was an easy man to recognize: in his mid-sixties, heavy, maybe eighteen stones, big red nose, prominent ears, moist blue eyes and a clump of pure white hair tucked under a tweed cap. Superstitious like many racing folk, he wore the same huge army-issue overcoat he'd had on when he trained his first winner.

'Mister Barber,' I said. He turned, suddenly hopeful, but his features sagged when he saw it wasn't his stable jockey.

'Hello, Eddie,' he said gruffly, then went back to scanning incomers who were becoming scarcer as the first race drew near.

I was hopeless at asking for rides at the best of times, and there had been so many refusals in recent months my confidence was shot. The fact that this was my last gasp didn't make it easier.

'Mister Barber, I heard Tommy Gilmour hasn't turned up.'

He gave me his full attention. 'Who told you that?'

'Well, we sort of noticed it in the weighing room.' I lied.

'Any of you lads see Tommy last night?'

'I don't think so. Nobody mentioned it.'

He stared down the long tree-lined drive again and said, 'Can't understand it. He's always been a hundred percent reliable.'

'It's not like him,' I agreed. 'Have you rung his hotel?'

'Rang his hotel and his house. The owner's husband even drove to his hotel to see if he's broken down on the way.'

'Mister Barber, if he doesn't appear, have you thought about a replacement?'

He looked down at me, blue eyes watering in the wind. 'Eddie, I've thought about nothing else, but the horse's owner won't have it, she wants to withdraw.'

'Why?'

'Because the silly cow's convinced that nobody but Tommy can handle the horse. He's a difficult ride and takes a bit of knowing, but we've had a right few quid on ante-post, her husband and me, and we're desperate to run him.'

He really got going then, gesticulating, jerking at his cap. 'She's a nice lady, Loretta, but she's wrong on this one. Thinks because Tommy is Champion Jockey he's a stone better than the rest of you. Someone else rode him last year and Cragrock fell and didn't get up for a long time. Loretta was hysterical, threatened to take the horse out of training altogether. Crazy woman.'

'Where is she now?'

Barber dabbed at his big nose with a tissue. 'In her private box. Paul, her husband's trying to talk her into accepting a substitute, but he's fighting a losing battle. I had to get out of there before I strangled her.'

'Do you think she'd accept another Champion Jockey as replacement?'

He stared down at me. I shrugged, 'Okay, so it was five years ago,' I said, 'but it's worth a try.'

Still morose, he shook his head then suddenly his face lit up. 'You might be right, Eddie! You might just be right! Come on!'

Checking his watch, he turned and hobbled into the course. An accident had left him badly lame in his right leg. Barber always claimed it happened when he came off a horse on the gallops but Muriel, his wife, said he broke it when he 'fell down the stairs, pissed'.

I walked alongside him conscious of the steep rise and fall of his left shoulder as he tried to hurry through the puddles. The commentary on the first race pulsed from the speakers. Barber, face beaming, kept saying quietly, 'The very man! The very thing!'

He told me to stay by the paddock as he disappeared into the main stand.

I waited, trying not to hope too hard. Within five minutes Barber hove into view, his face telling me all I needed to know. Smiling wide he slapped my shoulder and said, 'We're back in business! I'll send someone along with the colours and I'll see you in the paddock.'

Stunned, surprised, delighted, I grasped his hand. 'Hubert...this means a hell of a lot to me.'

He gripped my forearm with his free hand. 'Me too,' he said, 'me too. Listen, do me one favour, Eddie, try to make sure the TV cameras don't catch your face before the race starts.'

I stared at him. 'Why?'

He smiled. 'Just do it. I'll explain later.'

It took me a minute to figure out what he'd done, then I sussed it. If I lost Barber would be in deep trouble with Loretta Whitehead.

Chapter 3

Emotions bubbling, brain buzzing with plans and hopes, high on the prospect of showing thousands of racegoers and TV viewers I could still cut it, I strode into the changing room, grabbed Tom, my valet, by the shoulders, shook him and said, 'I ride Cragrock in the big race!'

He stared at me. 'By the looks of you you'd think you'd already won it!'

Wearing green and blue colours, Bill Keating, a veteran, saw my smile as he passed and said, 'You look as if you've won the pools, Eddie.'

I fought to contain my excitement. 'Hubert Barber's asked me to ride the favourite in the Greenalls.' I had tried to say it calmly but it came out loud and boastful. Most of the jocks heard me.

Bill looked puzzled. 'Where's Tommy Gilmour?'

I shrugged. 'Hasn't turned up. They weren't going to run him but they've had a few quid on and decided to have a go.'

'Good luck to you,' Bill said. Then Con Layton piped up. 'Gilmour could handle that horse, Malloy, but you couldn't hold one side of him. You'll make an arse o' yersel.'

I turned to face Layton, it hadn't taken him long to recover from our earlier scrap. I stared at him and got the usual taunting look from his pale close-set eyes.

I said, 'Well, you'd certainly recognize an arse before most people, Layton, since you see one when you're shaving every morning.'

The place went silent. They watched Layton who'd lost his mischievous look and was glaring at me. He spoke, trying to sound menacing. 'Pretty full of yourself, Malloy, on the strength of a single ride, ain't you? Pretty full of yourself for a has-been.'

I smiled warmly. 'I'd sooner be a has-been than a never-was.'

'Listen, Malloy –'

'You listen! How long does it take you to learn a lesson? How many second prizes have you got to get?'

He growled, 'You'll get yours, Malloy!' and marched out. His sidekick, Ben Meese, a swaggering little runt, tried a bit too theatrically to fill the silence by pointing the end of his whip at me and saying, 'You'd better be very careful, Malloy!'

Taking two strides toward him I bent over until our noses were almost touching and said, 'Meese, if the organ grinder doesn't scare me, what chance has the monkey got?'

He didn't care for that, or for the burst of laughter from the lads. He reddened, glared at me, then turned and whacked my saddle hard with his whip before scuttling away after Layton.

Ten minutes before the off, three of us huddled in the paddock feeding off each other's tension. I was edgy, aware it was my big chance. Barber's money was on the line along with his judgment. Paul Whitehead had a sizeable financial stake, too, and he stood close as Barber gave me riding instructions, Paul repeating them, nodding, tugging at his ear lobe.

'Where's Mrs. Whitehead?' I asked.

Barber said, 'Eh, we persuaded Loretta to watch it on TV. Muriel's under instructions to keep her occupied.'

I smiled. 'You told Loretta Tommy had arrived, didn't you?'

Barber said, 'Ask no questions, hear no lies. A Champion Jockey's a Champion Jockey. Just get out there and ride like you used to.'

At the start, Fred Harbour, the assistant starter, went among us checking girth straps, which always worked loose as horses stretched on the canter down the track. Fred was an ex-jockey staying in touch with the game as best he could. Accumulated injuries had forced him into early retirement. Fused vertebrae and dislocated shoulders had slowly curled his nine stone body up until he looked sixty rather than forty.

It was the horses he loved; he spoke little to the jockeys, resenting the fact that he wasn't one of us anymore. He walked toward me and I pulled Cragrock to a halt. Fred twanged the girths to test for slack. 'How are you doing?' I asked.

'Okay.'

From up here you only ever saw the top of his cloth cap. His injuries made it difficult for him to straighten his neck. Fred grunted as he strained to get my girths a hole tighter then, head still down, he said, 'Watch yourself, I think Layton and Meese are going to try and put you out of the race.'

It was the first time he'd spoken more than two words to me.

'Thanks,' I said. He didn't acknowledge, just patted Cragrock's neck and moved on. I looked around. The others circled, chatting, trying to discover each other's tactics, who was going to make the running, who would be dropping out early. Layton and Meese were together. Layton laughed harshly, rolling his head back. Meese smiled up at him.

The starter called us into line. I moved Cragrock toward the rail. Someone barged up my inside, shoving me to the right. I glanced across. It was Layton, pale smiling eyes watery-looking behind his goggles. I glimpsed to my other side. Meese was there, smiling too.

They knew Cragrock had to be held up in the middle of the field and they'd obviously decided to waste no time in trying to intimidate us. I had a little surprise planned.

Chapter 4

I watched the starter. His fingers tightened on the lever and as he opened his mouth to call 'Okay, jockeys!' I kicked Cragrock hard in the belly. The tape flew up, Cragrock's ears pricked, Layton cursed, and after the first six strides we were four lengths clear of the rest.

Cragrock was confused. Used to his jockey fighting to hold him, his ears flicked as he tried to figure out why he was being not only given his head but pushed along. He was still thinking by the time we reached the first fence, and he took off a stride and a half too soon, but we sailed over and landed just as far the other side, balanced and running.

We went ten lengths clear.

Coming to the second, his blood was up. Going too fast. No time for adjustment. He took off way too soon. Jesus! His front hooves barely cleared it and his hind legs hit the fence, smashing birch twigs out like feathers from a shot pheasant. I sat back, expecting him to pitch forward, but the effort of the leap and staying upright brought only a short grunt from him as he sucked in air.

Before he could regain full steam, I took a determined hold of the reins and managed to break his stride. He slowed to the easier pace I wanted. We were beginning to get an understanding.

Initial exuberance gone, Cragrock settled to a steady pattern, his fluid stride beating out a rhythmic thud on the turf, all the more noticeable in the eerie silence afforded a front-runner. Each leap brought a brief suspension of the hoof beats and another fix of the exhilaration which had made an addict of me.

As we approached the last in the back straight, four from home, they came after us. It sounded like a group of three. Ten strides from the fence Cragrock sensed them closing and suddenly his rhythm altered and he guessed at the take-off. There was nothing I could do. At full stretch I saw the birch coming up fast to meet us...

We ploughed into the guts of the fence. Cragrock's shiny black front hooves were higher than his head as he stretched, trying to save himself, then came that awful vacuum as his half-ton body hit the tight packed birch...the weird feeling of being in a snapshot, waiting for the punch of the momentum to catch up...as always, it did.

And it smashed Cragrock onwards and downwards, thumping the air from his lungs in a long rasp. A fraction of a second before being catapulted forward, I saw a blurred mesh of bay, chestnut and grey horseflesh flash past in a graceful arc. Cragrock, still doing everything to stop himself crashing, was trying desperately to get a leg out...the effort caused his big frame to buckle, then straighten, throwing my legs and backside higher than my head as my face was forced into his mane. No brilliant recovery, I was on my way out frontward when suddenly he found a foothold, got his undercarriage down, then scampered along like a crab before raising his neck, belting me in the face with his head and pushing me back into the saddle.

Stunned and bloody-nosed, I tried to collect my senses as the horse found his stride again and galloped on.

My head cleared. Three to jump. We lay fourth twelve lengths off the leader. But Cragrock was getting his second wind. He rallied as we rounded the bend into the straight. Ahead of me three pairs of white breeches pumped in union.

Because of their crouch, I couldn't see the colours but you get to know a rider's style and build. One of those in contention, Meese, I recognized by his weightlifter's thighs.

Halfway round the home turn, Layton ranged alongside, his almost toothless grin telling me he still thought he had plenty of horse under him. The running rail was on my left, Layton on my right. He moved his horse, Machete, a big powerful grey, across to lean on us. Cragrock faltered.

'Layton! You bastard!'

He looked across, boring harder into us now and spat at my face. The wind carried the gob, splattering it greasily on my goggles as we were forced into the rails. The white plastic shattered, sending out a spray of shards. Cragrock broke stride and Layton, laughing, eased his horse away and kicked on toward the third last fence.

I pulled my smeared goggles down and hauled Cragrock off the rail. He came quickly onto an even keel approaching the fence and met it on a beautiful long stride, landing far out on the other side, feeling as though he'd never left the ground. After going at such a hectic pace, maybe the enforced breathers had helped him.

I was closing, though Meese was travelling best of those in front. Layton, seeing his friend creep through on the rail approaching the second last fence, eased his horse right handed, squeezing the chestnut in the middle onto Meese's bay as they all took off. Unbalanced, the bay scrambled over then disappeared for a moment before I saw his hind legs come up as he somersaulted.

Cragrock soared over and I looked down to see Meese lying under the rails as his horse slid on its side along the grass.

Ahead, Layton was working on his next victim, intimidating the little chestnut alongside him.

We were three lengths off them, and closing. With Layton still squeezing out his rival, they were flat to the boards and drifting coming to the last, close together, leaving me more than half the fence. Layton met it spot on. His challenger finally chickened out putting in two short strides, losing impetus.

Cragrock met it dead right, jumping with no wasted effort, and landed running at Machete's quarters. Layton looked over his shoulder, cursing as he saw me. I smiled.

He knew he was in trouble. The shape of the run-in at Haydock forces jockeys to quickly take a diagonal line left after jumping the last, or risk galloping into a set of wooden gates dolling off the no-entry section.

Layton, believing he was home free, had left himself little time and space to get across. Now I was blocking him.

As the gates loomed, Layton hauled violently at his tired horse, Machete, trying to pull him across.

Machete was tired. So was Cragrock. Both breathing hard, sides heaving, muscles straining, nostrils flaring as they snorted huge lungfuls. I was running out of energy too, panting as I scrubbed and pushed.

But Cragrock ran straight. Machete, with Layton pulling hard on the left rein and desperately hitting him down the neck and shoulder, was unbalanced.

And we closed in on those black and white gates.

I was a neck behind, which gave him a few final seconds of hope before he realized he was trapped. They ran into the first gate and by the sound of his curse and howl, Layton's right leg had taken the impact. He hit the next three like skittles, only they didn't fall down.

He stopped riding. I went a length up, feeling a pang of sympathy for Layton's brave horse. The race was over. I eased Cragrock past the post becoming aware for the first time of the roaring crowd.

Glancing round at Layton as we pulled up, I saw him slip his feet tenderly from the stirrups. His right boot was torn, blood dripping from the toe, staining his horse's grey foreleg.

I was elated. A couple of hours ago I'd been almost suicidal, now I'd won one of the biggest races of the season, and beaten Layton at his own game.

Barber hobbled to meet us, showing a mixture of relief and annoyance. He said, 'What were you silly bastards up to?'

'All down to Layton,' I said. 'He did me on the home turn.'

Barber said, 'And you tried to get your own back! On the bloody run-in of all places!'

'I held my line, Mister Barber, that's all.'

Still looking surly he said, 'You shouldn't have retaliated.'

'If I hadn't you'd probably be leading in the second.'

He nodded then looked up at me again. 'Other than that,' he said, 'you rode a bloody brilliant race!'

I smiled and shook his hand. 'Thanks.'

We entered the winner's enclosure to loud applause. I'd forgotten just how sweet it was. As I dismounted, the loudspeaker's message of "Stewards' Enquiry" turned the welcoming cheers into sighs.

Barber, seeing his stake money once more in jeopardy, looked worried. 'I don't need this, Eddie. Don't need it,' he said, as we stopped in the winner's berth.

I undid the girths and the saddle pad squeaked keenly as it slid from the sweating horse. Turning to Barber I smiled confidently. 'See you soon for the presentation,' I said.

'Let's hope so.'

Chapter 5

Con Layton sat smoking in the corner of the changing room, his feet on the bench, drying blood crusting around the tear in his boot. A valet said, 'Better get that seen to, Con.' Layton, smiling at me, said to him, 'That'll count in the Enquiry. You wouldn't be wanting me to cover it up.'

I sat across from him. My cold stare met with a smug smile and a blown smoke-ring, which broke up as it looped and twirled like a tossed coin.

Between smoke-rings, the smile stayed fixed on his thin lips. 'What're you starin' at, Malloy?'

'I'm trying to work out why the little arguments we had earlier make you think you've got the right to try to kill me.'

He smiled. 'Ah it's a big bad world out there, Malloy, where clever words are of no use to you. You must learn to be tough.'

I leaned forward. 'I think I'm tough enough to handle an idiot who blows smoke-rings that are bigger than his brain.'

'Malloy, you've an awful smart mouth.' He flicked the cigarette at my face.

I ducked, then rose, ready to lunge at him. Layton was rising to meet me when a stern voice brought us up short. 'Malloy! Layton!' We turned. One of the stewards' secretaries stood in the doorway.

'Come with me,' he said, 'the stewards will see you now.'

Like a frustrated child I considered shouldering Layton aside and marching out first, but I decided I'd rather have the bastard in front than behind me.

He headed for the door. I followed and said, 'Listen, if you come near me in a race again I'll break your legs.'

'What was that, Malloy?' asked the stewards' secretary.

'Nothing, sir, I was just asking Mister Layton if he was riding in the next.'

'Neither of you will be riding in the next if you keep the panel waiting much longer!'

The stewards' secretary was a tall man, maybe six three, and very thin. His shoulder blades swung at our eye level as we followed him. His name was Claude Beckman. He stopped outside the stewards' room and told us to wait.

Beckman knocked and took off his hat as he went in.

We stood in silent animosity. This was my first Stewards' Enquiry since coming back. Nothing would have changed. Beckman would be briefing the stewards, re-running the video, telling them where he thought the fault lay.

The stewards were unpaid local volunteers, mostly from society's fortunate section, lovers of the sport, but not as well versed in race-riding techniques, as they should have been considering our livelihoods depended on their decisions.

Beckman was a paid official. Stewards' secretaries were appointed because of their in-depth knowledge of racing. A few had race-riding experience as amateur jockeys. Their brief was to help the stewards reach a fair conclusion. Many secretaries had military backgrounds. Far too few were ex-professional jockeys, who did the best job of all. But the stewards tended not to trust the ex-pros and preferred the principle that a new broom sweeps clean. Though old ones, I thought, glancing at Layton, knew where the dirt was.

They called us in. Layton led, limping theatrically. Beckman, impatient, nodded at us to move quicker. The room was almost square; high roof, tatty decoration, poor lighting and bad ventilation judging by the musty smell.

Two men and a woman sat behind a long table: Lord Cumbernauld, John Carnduff and the Honourable Clarissa Cover who bred and raced jumpers with some success.

Sitting to Miss Cover's right, fingers poised over a grey machine, was the stenographer, Lisa Ffrench. I watched her from the corner of my eye.

Beckman was looking down on us. He was fortyish and totally bald, although it added to his imposing look which bordered on fierce. He spoke. 'We are here to enquire into careless riding in the last race. You will answer the stewards' questions truthfully and without the usual tiresome embellishments.'

Video evidence during Enquiries usually pinpointed the main culprit, but when guilt wasn't clear, it tended to be the more articulate jockey, the best salesman, who won through. Embellishment was understating it; often it was pure fiction. But it was part of the trade.

Lord Cumbernauld cleared his throat and asked us to explain our actions. Layton got in first, bowing and scraping, lying. He blamed the problems on his horse hanging badly.

I told them it was deliberate. Layton, who'd been chummily calling me Eddie, acted horrified at this claim.

'May I suggest we see the film, sir?' I said. Every race is filmed from a camera patrol and from a head-on view in the straight. It was rare for film evidence to be poorly interpreted, and I was confident they would find in my favour.

The chairman glanced at Claude Beckman who reddened as he said to me, 'It is not a jockey's place to decide when a film should be viewed, that option rests with the stewards. Unfortunately, in this instance, we've had a technical problem which means the film will not be available. This case will be decided on the evidence of our own eyes and the testimony of those involved.'

Pompous bastard.

I noticed that Lisa Ffrench's fingers stopped on her keyboard before Beckman finished speaking. I glanced at her. She looked bewildered for a second as she stared at Beckman before tapping in his final few words.

They listened as we put our cases: I as quietly and sensibly as I could, and Layton increasingly dramatically as he felt the verdict slipping away. At one point he asked if he could sit down as his injured foot was killing him.

They sent us out while they debated. I'd been confident going in that the video would clear me. The main thing in my favour was Layton's reputation. Many of the Stewards believed he was crooked; they just couldn't prove it.

Five minutes later we were still waiting. Jockeys weighed out for the next. The officials milled around, anxious to present the prize for the Greenalls. People were getting worried.

The door opened and Beckman motioned us in. He didn't look pleased. I stood in front of the panel trying to guess from their faces. Deadpan.

Lord Cumbernauld spoke. 'Without video corroboration we've had to take both your stories with a large pinch of salt and have reached a decision on our own' – he glanced, rather coldly I thought, at Beckman – 'and Mister Beckman's recollection of the race. There is no doubt, Malloy, that you made the best of the situation after the last and that you had no intention of allowing Layton a clear run. However, you did keep a straight course and we've concluded that Mister Layton's problems were of his own making. The result stands.'

Layton breathed sharply through his nostrils. I smiled at the panel and said, 'Thank you.' The chairman nodded and as we turned to leave said, 'And Layton, since your injured foot is causing you so much pain we've also decided that you must pass the doctor before riding again.'

Layton swore quietly. I managed to suppress my laughter until I got outside where Layton ran through his repertoire of curses.

Pulsing with energy, feeling great, I changed into the black and red colours of my next mount, pausing only to shake hands and accept congratulations from the lads, especially the little team in my own corner. Hope for one meant hope for all.

Amid the laughter and horseplay and leg pulling, I felt as good as I had for five years. Gradually, over ten seconds or so, I was aware of the room becoming steadily quiet. From near the entrance, all the way down to where we were, the noise dried up like taps being turned off.

Along with everyone else I looked toward the main door. Bob Carter, the senior valet, a big imposing man, stood white-faced, mouth open, looking at us. When there was complete silence Bob said, 'The police just found Tommy Gilmour's body. He's been murdered.'

Chapter 6

Tommy had been shot once, between the eyes. A jogger had found his body in thick woods a mile from his hotel. It was a morbid group that filed out to ride in the next.

I'd been away from racing for five years. All I knew of Tommy Gilmour was that he was a nice guy, a solid pro who'd worked hard for the breaks. A quiet family man, who rarely socialized, he was liked and respected by everyone, but nobody seemed to know him well.

As we lined up at the start, my feelings were confused. I was the only one who'd benefited from Tommy's death. I should have felt dreadful but didn't.

There was sadness for him, but I couldn't make it overcome the pleasure I felt from winning, and the new hope it had brought. And the schemer in me was hatching plans to try to take Tommy's place at Barber's.

The least I should have been able to find was a helping of guilt, and I realized how desperate I'd felt these last few months, how much my character had changed, how right Jackie had been about me.

Jackie. I hadn't even phoned her with the good news. Maybe she'd have seen it on TV. I hoped not, that would make things worse. I resolved to ring her as soon as I got back in.

The starter raised his flag and we raced off into the gathering gloom.

Mine finished a distant seventh, and I dismounted the weary chestnut and headed for the warmth of the weighing room. The jag from stones through my paper-thin boot soles reminded me I'd had so few rides this season my feet hadn't toughened. Perhaps all that would change now. Today might be the turning point.

Halfway across the tarmac, I saw someone approaching in a hurry. A couple of strides from me he said, 'Eddie Malloy?'

I stopped. 'That's me.'

'Good. I'm Clive Bannatyne from The Globe. Can I ask you a few questions?'

'What about?' I asked.

'Winning the Greenalls.'

'Sure.'

He said, 'How does it feel to have won under such circumstances?'

'Under what circumstances?'

'The murder of the bloke who was supposed to ride the horse, you know, Gilmour, Tommy Gilmour?'

'Who did you say you work for?' I asked.

'The Globe. Big circulation.'

Among those that liked sleaze with Sunday breakfast, I thought, but I would have to give him an answer. 'I feel terrible for Tommy and his family. We all do, but we're professionals and the only satisfaction I take from the race is that I did my job well.'

'But it takes the shine off, is that what you're saying?' He stared at me, smiling and nodding in that inane way that reporters think encourages you to talk.

'Of course it takes the shine off! You don't see anybody celebrating, do you?'

He was scribbling. 'Why would anyone want to kill Tommy Gilmour?'

'How should I know? Why don't you find who did it and ask him?' I walked away. He fell in beside me and asked, 'What do you think of the guy that did it?'

I stopped and glared at him, but he just stood, pencil poised, like a robot waiting for the next component. I said, 'What do you think of him? He must be a lunatic!'

He nodded. 'And do you think he'll strike again?'

'If he does I hope you're there to witness it first-hand, which should save you asking people silly questions.'

I showered and changed before heading home. The victory party had, understandably, been cancelled. I concentrated on blocking thoughts of Tommy and decided to pick up a couple of bottles of champagne to surprise Jackie. It would be surprise enough for her to see me come in with a smile on my face. I'd phoned her before leaving the course, but the line was engaged. At least that meant she hadn't left me.

We lived in an old hunting lodge in Leicestershire, leased to us by Henry Kravitz, an owner I rode for occasionally. He'd been very understanding about the rent.

The Lodge lay in flat countryside about three hundred yards off the main road. The wide drive leading to it was uneven and badly pot-holed in places. I bumped along through the darkness, pulling up quietly by the side wall of the building.

The only light through the windows was from a lamp in the living room. Softly I turned the handle on the heavy door. It was locked. That wasn't like Jackie. I reached for my key.

The silence told me she'd gone. The phone was off the hook. The note was under the lamp, her looping handwriting in a pool of yellow light. "I looked in the mirror, Eddie, and a thirty-five-year-old woman stared back. You were killing me. I didn't know it until this morning, and maybe you didn't know it, but it was happening. I just want to be twenty-one again. I don't have to be happy, I just want not to be dying. Jackie."

Over the top as usual, typical Jackie. I smiled and folded the note, letting it flutter onto the table. She had an awful temper and became overwrought about the smallest things. Then she'd recover and go the other way, smotheringly loving. The mercurial highs and lows had troubled me at first, but I was getting used to them. Confident she'd return in a day or two, I poured a drink, flopped into the chair and thought of our nine months together.

Last summer, we'd met when she'd discovered me lying in the road, badly wounded. I'd been helping The Jockey Club Security Department in a criminal case, one that helped me win back my jockey's licence. She was eight years younger than me, and I'd warned her I could be a sullen bastard, hard to put up with when life wasn't going right, but she reckoned she could change me.

I sat in the pale lamplight, in the cold of that big twelve-roomed house, consoled by the silence. I'd grown used to Jackie fussing around, usually in an effort to cheer me up after another bad day, but I found the hush, the peace, surprisingly welcome. I was alone again as I'd been for most of my life. Normal service resumed.

Then I felt guilty. She hadn't much money…where had she gone?

To her mother's in Ireland? Did she have the fare? I could ring her there. It might be best to wait a few days, until we were missing each other. It would be easier then.

As I opened a fresh whiskey bottle, the phone rang.

Chapter 7

The caller was Lisa Ffrench, the stenographer. 'How'd you get my number?' I asked.

'Mutual friend. You heard about Tommy Gilmour?'

Her tone put me on the defensive. 'Yes,' I said, 'I couldn't believe it.'

'Nor can Susan, his wife.'

'You've seen her?'

'I'm with her now. At her house. I came straight here from Haydock. She's under heavy sedation.'

'I didn't realize you knew the Gilmours.'

'I knew Susan before she met Tommy. We were at school together.'

I felt awkward. 'I'm sorry,' I said, 'it must have come as a hell of a shock. They've got a couple of kids, haven't they?'

'One's four, the other's only two. We haven't told them yet.'

We?

'God help them,' I said.

'If there was a God, He would've helped them before their daddy got shot, don't you think?'

'Maybe.'

'Maybe?'

I said, 'Lisa, if you want to be mad at someone, go ahead, I owe you one.'

'I'm sorry, I didn't mean to snap.'

'It's okay.'

Calm again, she said, 'Listen, did you hear any rumours about

Tommy, about the murder?'

'Not a thing. All anybody could say was that he was a nice guy. I don't think anyone even knew him that well.'

'I heard it might have been something to do with someone trying to stop the horse running, because there'd been a big ante-post gamble.'

I considered it, knowing that ante-post bets, those placed prior to the day of the race, were lost if the horse didn't run.

'A bit drastic, I'd have thought,' I said. 'It would have been easier to get at the horse than kill the jockey.'

'Did you know the horse had been under a twenty-four-hour guard for weeks?'

'No, I didn't. But they tell me it's not uncommon these days with fancied horses. And Cragrock's owner, Loretta Whitehead, treats the horse like a, well, like a baby.'

'So you wouldn't read too much into that?'

'Personally, no. Others might, I suppose.'

'I'm going to tell the police about it anyway.'

'Have the police been to talk to, uh…?'

'Susan? They wanted to but I told them she was unfit. They're coming in the morning.'

'Best tell them then,' I said lamely.

'Yes. But will you keep your ear to the ground for me, let me know if you hear anything?'

'Sure,' I said.

'Okay, I'll give you my number here and my number at home. You'll catch me at one or the other if we don't meet on the racecourse.'

I picked up a pen.

'By the way,' she said, 'you know in the Enquiry today when Claude Beckman said the video wasn't available?'

'Yeah, technical problems.'

'Not when I saw it there weren't.'

'You saw the tape?'

'I saw Beckman watching it before the stewards arrived. He hadn't heard me come in, and as soon as he realized I was there, he switched the VCR off and muttered something about a faulty tape.'

'Did he tell the stewards beforehand it was faulty?'

'I didn't hear him.'

'He must have. They didn't look surprised when he told me,

though you did.'

'I know.'

I said, 'Could it have been faulty in places you didn't see?'

'I doubt it. I think Beckman's got it in for you in a big way. He was really having a go before you came in, trying to convince the panel you were to blame and should be disqualified. And when you were cleared he was absolutely fuming.'

'Any idea why? Why he's got it in for me, I mean.'

'I thought you might know.'

'Haven't a clue. Hardly know the guy.'

'Well, you'd better watch out.'

'I will, thanks.'

'Okay, ring me if you hear anything, will you?'

'Sure, and Lisa, thanks for today. For pushing me toward Barber.'

'That's all right.'

'No, I mean it. I wouldn't have done it myself. Confidence was gone. Shot to shit.'

Lisa said, 'You've had a few bad breaks, you just needed a boost.'

'Maybe.'

'Look, Eddie, I've got to go the baby's crying.'

'Okay. Good night.'

She hung up.

When I realized I'd written her phone numbers on Jackie's goodbye note, I felt a sudden pang of guilt, of unfaithfulness.

It took me ten minutes to finish my drink. Nine of them were filled with thoughts of Lisa and what she'd said. Jackie crowded back in for the last one, and as the wind picked up outside, I imagined her wandering in the darkness or huddled miserably in the corner of some bus shelter.

After a restless dream-filled night, I was looking forward to hot coffee and some good publicity in the papers, though I knew Tommy's murder would take the headlines.

I jogged along the big hall. Approaching the foot of the stairs, I noticed an envelope on the mat. Unless the Royal Mail had started a Sunday service, someone must have delivered it by hand.

Perhaps it was from Jackie.

'Malloy' was written on the front in neat block letters, and I ripped it open as I walked to the kitchen. Inside was a thin racing diary. Tucked between its pages were two pieces of paper: one was a cutting from a morning newspaper headlined, Champion Jockey Murdered. A section of the text had been highlighted in bright yellow: 'Malloy said that the killer must be a lunatic.'

The other piece was plain white; printed in block letters was: 'The lunatics have taken over the asylum.'

Below that was: 'Numbers 32:23.'

I opened the diary. It was Tommy Gilmour's.

Chapter 8

My first thought was that it was a sick joke. Layton maybe, still mad from yesterday. But how the hell would he have got hold of Tommy's diary? Was it Tommy's? It would be easy enough to fake a diary.

How did this guy know where I lived?

The note was obviously meant to be either a warning or a threat. If it was genuine then for my sake as much as Tommy Gilmour's, I had to call the police.

If I reported it and it turned out to be Layton or someone winding me up, then I'd be laughed out of the weighing room. So what? It wouldn't be the first time I'd been made to look foolish.

I didn't want to over-react. I would ask McCarthy's advice. He worked for The Jockey Club Security Department. We'd helped each other in the past. I found his number. He was out. I left a message.

Sipping coffee, I scanned the newspapers. The racing writers mourned Tommy and wrote warm obituaries, while the tabloid hacks speculated on the motive. A police spokesman said forensics were taking Gilmour's hotel room apart and stripping his car. They appealed for anyone who thought they could help.

If the note had come from the killer, there would be a chance he'd also left one at the murder scene. It would give the police corroboration. If the diary wasn't a fake it could be a vital clue. I picked up the phone.

An hour later DS Latimer from the local CID turned up at my door; slightly built with thinning sandy hair, his sheepskin coat bulked him out a bit, but his neck was scrawny, his wrists thin.

'Well tucked away here, aren't you?' he said, wiping his feet on the mat. 'I was beginning to think somebody was winding me up.'

I made coffee. He gulped it noisily, Adam's apple bouncing, as he took my statement, and then gave me a receipt for the diary and the note. 'Any thoughts?' I asked, as he rose to go.

He shrugged and smiled. 'Glad it's not ours. The City boys can add it to their pile.'

'Who?'

'The Manchester plods, or possibly Merseyside. Haydock racecourse comes into this new Greater Northern Police Area. You'll get a Manc or a Scouser on it.'

'I'll wait to hear from them then.'

'Don't hold your breath. They'll hate this one. Nobody wants fruitloops like this guy. Too unpredictable.'

'You're filling me with confidence.'

He smiled and opened the door. 'If it was this bloke who delivered the note and he's got a grudge, I can offer you a bit of off the record advice, kind of, with my experience but don't quote me, if you know what I mean?'

I nodded, waiting.

'Get yourself the fuck out of here. Find a small flat in a big city. You'll be much harder to track down.'

'Eh, thanks, but my name's in the racing section of the papers every day telling the whole world where I'm riding.'

He looked at me with a mixture of pity and curiosity. 'Anything else you're good at?' he asked.

'I can drink a fair amount of whiskey before I fall over.'

He smiled and buttoned his coat. 'That qualifies you for the CID. Straight in at DS level.'

I walked with him to his car. He said, 'I gave you a tip, got any for me?'

'I'll give you a double…Be Wise and Don't Bet.'

'Ha! Very good.' He got in and wound the window down. 'Seriously Mister Malloy, get yourself out of there. This place is far too remote with shit like this going on. You got a family?'

'Just a girlfriend.'

'She live with you?'

'Sometimes.'

He shook his head. 'Get out until they catch this guy.'

I nodded. He drove off. I stood for a while listening, watching the fog, trying to quell my instincts to hurry inside and barricade the doors. The phone rang, giving me an excuse and I hurried in, hoping it was Jackie. Young, pretty, feisty, determined Jackie. She of the auburn hair and hazel eyes, the freckles and the squint-toothed smile.

But it turned out to be the old, white-haired, lame Hubert Barber, asking me to ride two at Hereford for him next day and three at Sedgefield on Tuesday.

I hung up knowing I'd now need to adjust to trainers calling me rather than the other way round. And maybe I'd have to adjust to Jackie not being here too.

I lay awake wondering where she was.

Chapter 9

I travelled home from Sedgefield on Tuesday with a winner and a third to add to my two winners at Hereford the previous day. Barber's stable was in cracking form, and I'd got in at the right time. Apart from missing Jackie, I was happier than I'd been for years and finding it tough to feel guilty about it.

Maybe if I'd known Tommy better I'd have felt worse, but his death had given me a break, a new chance. I had to snap it up without agonising, but maybe I was making too good a job of that because people were shunning me.

A few jockeys who would normally have passed the time of day had cold-shouldered me at Sedgefield. I could live with that, but on the way to the car park, four potential sources of rides, three owners and a trainer, had walked straight past, ignoring my greeting.

I knew some were pissed off about me getting Gilmour's rides, but these reactions just didn't tie up. Race-riding's a hazardous occupation. If a jockey gets injured someone else takes over. That person could easily break his neck the following week, letting in another substitute. It's a tough game and racing folk accept that. Somebody had to take Tommy's rides. These people were acting as if I'd murdered him myself.

I still hadn't spoken to McCarthy, The Racecourse Security Services man, about the note and the diary. We kept missing each other, leaving messages.

It was dark when I reached the Lodge. I switched on the lamps, built a fire, and pushed a packet meal into the microwave. Despite being five-foot-ten, I could eat what I wanted. I rarely had weight problems, and I found the microwave meals palatable and convenient.

I closed the curtains and poured a drink. When the oven bleeped, I emptied lasagne onto a plate, turned on the big 1950's Bush radio in the corner and sat down to listen to the news as I ate.

I slung a few more logs on the fire, and started going through the next day's runners at Southwell. Chris Brydham had booked me to ride two and, after Saturday's big win, there had to be a chance of landing the odd spare ride too. Things were looking up. I felt comfortable and relaxed.

I must have dozed off. I woke convinced I'd heard a noise outside. Sudden thoughts of Tommy Gilmour, the note, and the policeman's warning stirred a surge in my gut. In stockinged feet, I moved quietly toward the window and listened.

Through the crackle of burning logs, I heard a car pull up. A few seconds later the door-knocker fell, pounding an echo along the hall.

Hanging from the coat stand was a metal baseball bat. I'd bought it the day after DS Latimer had advised me to move out. Unhooking it, I moved behind the door as the knocker fell again. 'Who is it? I asked.

'Eddie? It's Mac.'

It didn't sound like him. McCarthy had played a big part in my comeback. Almost six years ago I'd been Champion Jockey, until I'd lost my licence after being falsely implicated in a doping ring. I'd served a five-year ban, then McCarthy recruited me to help him nail the guy who'd framed me. We caught him, I got my licence back, and McCarthy won promotion. Maybe I was still drowsy but I wasn't sure it was Mac on the other side of that door.

'Come on, Eddie, stop messing about, it's bloody freezing out here. Let me in.'

That was Mac.

Wearing coat and scarf, he sat by the fire. The glow haloed his dark curly hair. Pulling a small container from his pocket he grimaced as he dropped sweeteners into his mug of coffee. 'Hate these damn things,' he said. 'Always leave a bitter taste.'

'How's the diet going?'

'Lost seventeen pounds but it's killing me. Jean won't give me a break. Not even at weekends.'

'Good for her.' Jean was his wife who'd recently decided that after fifteen years of marriage to a slob, it was time to sort him out.

McCarthy's boss was retiring soon and Jean was determined Mac would get the post when it came up. She had set about decreasing his waistline and improving his appearance.

McCarthy was forty-one, six foot two, fifty pounds overweight and bloody good at his job. It was Mac who'd persuaded his bosses I could help them break the doping case, though his motives at the outset were not selfless; I took the chances, he got the glory.

Sipping coffee, he glanced around the room. 'Nice place,' he said.

'Cold place. You ought to try sleeping in it.'

'Buy yourself a hot-water bottle from Saturday's prize money.'

'Maybe I will.'

Mac was silent for a while, shifting in his seat and generally looking awkward.

'What's up?' I asked.

'Kello gave me the Gilmour case.'

Kello was his boss. I suspected he was putting Mac through a final test as his potential successor. 'And?' I asked.

'I wondered–'

'Wonder all you like, Mac, but leave me out of any little scam you're planning. I've told the cops what I know, done my duty as a citizen and all that.'

He played the wounded look. 'Eddie, I appreciate you want to get on with your career, there's no way I'd ask you to get involved in anything that didn't concern you.'

'Good. What can I do for you then?'

'Relax! I just wanted to ask you a few questions since you were indirectly involved.'

I bristled. 'How do you work that out?'

'Well, you got Gilmour's ride in the Greenalls, didn't you?'

'What the hell is that supposed to mean?'

'Take it easy, I'm not accusing you of anything.'

'What are you doing, then?'

'I'm only stating a fact. When Gilmour disappeared, you rode the horse.'

'So?'

'Who offered you the ride?'

'Nobody. I asked for it. I asked Hubert Barber if I could ride.'

'When did you speak to him?'

'Just before the first race.'

'Did he mention that the owner initially wanted to withdraw?'

'Mac, how is all this relevant?'

He half sighed, half blew on his coffee. 'It probably isn't, but I have to start somewhere. I've got nothing.'

I said, 'Okay, Barber did say that Loretta Whitehead was thinking of withdrawing the horse, but her husband and Barber persuaded her to run. They'd had a few quid on ante-post.'

McCarthy, pudgy cheeks reddening now from the fire's heat, looked troubled. 'That's the only possible motive I can think of, the betting side, someone trying to stop the horse running, but it seems a bit desperate.'

'I think you're right. Killing the jockey wouldn't have guaranteed anything. It's too easy to get someone else to ride.'

'But maybe they planned on that. Knowing Cragrock was such a difficult ride, perhaps they didn't care who rode him so long as it wasn't Gilmour. Every time Cragrock won this season the papers were full of how nobody but Gilmour could have won on him.'

'Yeah, the press boys did Tommy a favour there, eh?'

McCarthy shook his head slowly. 'Poor bastard. I hear his wife's taking it really bad.'

'Been to see her?'

He stared at the flames. 'Haven't been able to pluck up the courage. I must do it soon.'

I nodded in sympathy. 'You checked out the betting side?' I asked.

'All the way back. No bookmaker was offering Cragrock at a significantly higher price than his competitors, and nobody had huge liabilities. Barber and his owner had some chunky bets but they'd already told us that. There's nothing to support the betting side as a motive.'

'Just as well you've been up there before, Mac, you're going to need the experience.'

Puzzled, he looked at me. 'Up where?'

'Shit creek without a paddle.' I went to get a drink.

He called after me, 'I might not be the only one in the canoe, Eddie.'

I returned, ice cubes swimming in my whiskey, and sat across from him.

'What about Saturday's race,' he asked, 'I heard you got a rough ride?'

I nodded. 'Con Layton and one of his cronies. Nothing I couldn't handle.' I told him about our confrontation in the changing room and how the Irishman had lied at the Enquiry.

'You want to watch Layton,' he said, 'he's your original nasty piece of work.'

'So they tell me.'

'His party trick is biting the necks off beer bottles and swallowing lit cigarettes.'

'That kind of sums up his mentality then, doesn't it?' I said.

'Maybe, but he's a wily bastard. We've been watching him for the past two years, trying to catch him at one of his dodges. He can be smart when he wants to.'

'As long as he's smart with someone else and not me, I won't be too bothered. I'll be happy to be left alone to pick up my career.'

He gazed at me. I looked away, staring into the fire, and he said, 'That means left alone by me as much as Layton, doesn't it?'

'Mac, the reason I helped you last time was to get my licence back. Okay, sometimes it was great playing detective, but when I found myself on the receiving end of beatings and threats, when I had to handle idiotic cops and junkies and psychos, it began losing its attraction. And on top of everything else, I was shit-scared most of the time.'

He smiled at me. 'But you got the job done. You were good.'

'As the Chinese stamp collector said, philately will get you nowhere.'

'So you're sitting this one out?'

'If it's all the same to you.'

He sipped coffee and put on his grave face, but behind those dark eyes, devilment glinted. 'I don't think you'll be able to, Eddie.'

He loved this.

'Out with it, Mac.'

'I was at Windsor yesterday... There was a rumour going round, one I first heard on Sunday evening.' He paused, and drank.

'And?' I said.

'They're saying you had Tommy Gilmour murdered.'

Chapter 10

I stared at McCarthy, conscious of holding my breath. 'You're winding me up, Mac?'

He shook his head. 'Wish I was.'

'Come on, why would I want Tommy dead?'

'They're saying you did it to get his rides.'

I laughed, half-manic, half-nervous, though I felt relieved as I slumped in the chair. 'Is that all? Is that my sole motive for having Tommy Gilmour murdered?'

He shrugged. 'As far as I know.'

'Well that's all right then.' I held my glass up, 'Cheers.'

McCarthy stared at me. 'Look, you could be in very deep trouble here.'

'Mac! For God's sake, it's too ridiculous for words!'

'I know that and you know that, but you can't just write it off so easily for others.'

'Look, I'm a jockey. I ride horses for a living. I go racing, then I come back to this big house and eat and sleep then go racing again. I'm a jockey, not a bloody Mafia man!'

He was irritated. 'So people are supposed to just ignore your criminal record, your history of violence?'

'My history of violence, as you know, is confined to kicking the shit out of the guy who framed me which, as you also know, was what earned me my criminal record, so stop exaggerating.'

'What about your little barbed wire episode last summer?'

'It was them or me, Mac, come on!'

He squirmed a bit. 'I'm only trying to play devil's advocate, Eddie.

These are serious allegations.'

'Mac, think about it! Anybody with half a brain would laugh you off the racecourse if you repeated all this. Me, having someone murdered just for his rides? What do I do if Barber's horses go down with the virus, murder someone else?'

McCarthy put his cup down and hauled himself out of the chair. 'Well,' he said, 'you're obviously determined to write this off without any more thought.'

'It doesn't deserve any more thought,' I said, standing up. 'Who started these rumours anyway?'

He shrugged. 'Who knows?'

'Well who did you hear it from?'

'Half a dozen people.'

Resting my elbows wearily on the mantelpiece, I cradled my head in my hands. Then, remembering the note and Tommy's diary, I told him about them.

'Who sent them?' he said.

'How the hell do I know? They were meant to look like they'd come from Gilmour's killer. That's what I rang you about.'

'You think it was meant as a threat?'

'Or a warning. If it's genuine.'

'Why would he warn you?'

'Maybe he was upset at me calling him a lunatic.'

Mac shut his eyes and frowned deeply. '"The lunatics have taken over the asylum…"' He mused, then, 'What do you suppose the numbers meant?'

'Haven't a clue.'

'What were they again?'

'Thirty-two and twenty-three.'

'And they mean nothing to you?'

'Not a thing. What struck me as curious was that he'd written the actual word "numbers" before the figures themselves.'

Eyes still closed, Mac shook his head. 'Beats me.'

'Shouldn't the police have told you I gave them this stuff?'

'In theory, yes. Seldom works in practice.'

'But you will make sure the rumour-mongers get to hear about them, the note and the diary?'

Massaging his face wearily with his big hands he looked at me, 'Think it'll make any difference?'

'It had better!'

He shook his head, 'Eddie, if they think you're guilty of something, they'll just see this as an attempt to cover-up.'

'By me?'

He raised his eyebrows, 'Who else?'

'Jeez! I give up!'

'Come on, Eddie, your friends will see the rumours as nonsense, but you know what this game's like!'

'Listen, just call me with the name of the next person you hear it from, OK? I'll take it from there.'

By way of closing the subject, I marched across to the drinks cabinet and poured myself another large defiant whiskey. 'Cheers,' I said coldly to McCarthy.

He looked at me. 'So you don't want to help in tracking this guy down?'

'This is what all this is about, isn't it? You make me feel threatened, I get involved in looking for Gilmour's killer and you have an easier life.'

He shrugged. 'I'm not denying I could use your help, but I think you owe it to yourself to take-'

'Look, Mac, don't give me that crap. I'm staying well out of it.'

'Okay.' He put his hat on. I followed him out to the hall and opened the door. 'Sorry you've had a wasted journey.'

He looked at me from his four-inch height advantage. 'Eddie, I think you're badly underestimating the feeling that could build up if Gilmour's killer isn't found soon. Take a minute to look at the full picture from a stranger's point of view - you've been out for five years, remember, there aren't that many people around now who remember you well.'

He was right about that.

'And as far as they're concerned you're an ex-Champion Jockey with a grudge against the establishment for taking your licence away and almost killing your career. It's your first year back and you're having a terrible season. Everybody knows you're up to your eyes in debt. As I said, you've got a criminal record, you can be ruthless and you can be violent. And don't forget, who was the only jockey who went and asked for the ride on Cragrock?'

He stepped outside. 'Think about it,' he said. I watched him drive off then slowly closed the door.

Chapter 11

The 10 a.m. news had finished and I was ready to leave for the races when the phone rang. It was Chris Brytham, the trainer who'd booked me to ride at Southwell. 'Eddie, I'm sorry, but I'm going to have to cancel these bookings for today.'

'Aren't they running?'

He paused and cleared his throat. 'They are running but...well, the owner's asked me to find another jockey.'

'Why?'

Another pause, then, 'I'm sorry, Eddie, it's not my decision. If it had been, you would have kept the rides.'

It was my turn to be quiet. Brytham tried to fill the silence. 'I was just hoping I'd catch you before you left to save you a trip. I'm sorry.'

Everything Mac said last night came back to me. 'I appreciate the thought, Mister Brytham, but I'll be going to Southwell anyway. And listen, thanks for the call. I can think of a few trainers who would have replaced me without even letting me know.'

'I wanted to tell you it wasn't my choice, Eddie. I daresay you've an idea what it's all about and personally I think it's a load of rubbish. If things weren't so tough, I'd tell this owner where to go but, well, you know how it is.'

I knew how it was, too many trainers chasing too few owners. Chris Brytham wasn't the only one having to lick boots.

'Yeah, I know. Forget it. Thanks again for the call.'

'I hope it all gets sorted out soon.'

Well, well, well, it looked like Mac was right. There were people out there prepared to believe these rumours.

Common sense told me to ring Hubert Barber and ask if the stories had reached him. If Barber pulled the plug I had two choices: hang up my boots and saddle until the cops found Gilmour's killer, or find the bastard myself. The way I was feeling, the latter was very much favourite. But in calling Barber, I was afraid of what I'd hear, so I left it.

I was determined to go to Southwell, even if I had to spend the day doing nothing. To stay away would only fuel the rumours. I slung my gear in the car and accelerated viciously down the drive.

I eased out on to the long straight road and quickly pushed the needle up to seventy. Flashing headlights glinted in my mirror. Five or six hundred yards behind me was a big white saloon, cops maybe. I dabbed the brakes and checked the speedo.

The car closed quickly, still flashing. No police livery, no light on the roof, two men in the front seat. I didn't like it. I pressed the gas pedal and got up to ninety. They followed effortlessly, a big white Rover 820, lights flashing, horn honking, the bearded passenger, angry, signalling wildly that I should pull over.

I kept going, sweat prickling on my scalp. Who the hell were they?

At a hundred, steering wheel vibrating in my hands, they pulled out and moved alongside me. I glanced across. The bearded guy was holding something up to the glass. I checked in front and glanced again. It was a small open leather wallet showing what might have been a police badge.

We were a couple of miles from a village. If I could hold out, at least there'd be someone around when I stopped. My pursuers had other ideas and as they quickened past, they crossed in front of me and the brakes were steadily applied.

Ramming was an option, but it was unlikely to do enough damage to stop them, and if it was the cops I'd be even deeper in the shit. I braked hard and skidded to a halt at the edge of the road.

Chapter 12

They came toward me. I got out and stood by the door. They wore shirts and ties and walked like cops, and they also had that look about them of trying to remember whose turn it was to do the wisecracks. The honour fell to the clean-shaven one, the driver. Stopping by the front bumper he said, 'Mister Malloy, is it?'

'Who's asking?'

At arm's length, he held out his little wallet. 'Detective Sergeant Kavanagh.' Tall, fair hair, blue eyes, the gauntness of his face highlighting the small scar on the ridge of his right cheekbone; white shirt, navy tie, dark trousers, black shoes. I stepped forward and looked at his credentials.

'This is Detective Sergeant Miller, who was rather having doubts about your name for a few minutes. We knew it began with M-a. I was pretty sure it was Malloy, but my colleague here swore it was Mansell.'

Very droll. At least it told me they were genuine cops who'd read up on their motorist gags before leaving the station.

'I'm afraid,' I said, 'that when a big car with no markings comes buzzing up my arse at a hundred miles an hour, it tends to make me nervous.'

Kavanagh smiled and said, 'Now with your background, Mister Malloy, I can understand that.'

'Good,' I said, ignoring the jibe. 'Now what can I do for you?'

'You can join us in the nice warm car out of this nasty wind. We just want a little chat.'

'I don't mind the chat, but I'd just as soon have it out in this nasty wind if it's all the same to you.'

He smiled again. 'Fine. Where were you last Friday evening?'

'Was that when Gilmour was killed?'

'Maybe you can tell me that?'

'I had dinner with some friends.'

'Where?'

'Southport.'

'And after that?'

'Had a drink in the bar of the Hotel and went to bed.'

'Alone?'

'That's right.'

'What time?'

'What time did I go to bed?'

Kavanagh nodded.

'I don't know, somewhere between eleven-thirty and midnight.'

'What time did you have breakfast?'

'Eight o'clock.'

'So between midnight and eight you have no alibi?'

'Alibi for what?'

Kavanagh grinned apologetically. 'Sorry, poor choice of words. What I meant was nobody can account for your whereabouts between midnight Friday and 8 a.m. Saturday.'

'I told you, I was asleep.'

His smile dropped, bony face turning sinister. 'You told me you were asleep. Alone. No one was with you, which means you might be in very deep trouble.'

The serious look was supposed to make me nervous, but he was bluffing. I shifted my weight, resting a foot on the sill of the open door. 'Listen, Mister Kavanagh,' I said, 'I'm going to Southwell races. I need to get there for the first race. You've chased me along the road at a hundred miles an hour, scaring the shit out of me, you're firing questions at me like I was on Mastermind, and now you're saying I might be in trouble. I think you forgot something? You still haven't told me what the hell this is all about?'

Miller, the bearded one, spoke. 'Stop being a smartass, Malloy, you know fine what it's about. Instead of going to the races why don't you just turn your car around and follow us back to the station.' The dark beard on his pale skin was thin and well-tended; his hair was slicked with gel, though a tendril had worked loose by his right temple and swung in the wind.

'You asking me or telling me?' I said.

Kavanagh said, 'We're asking you, Mister Malloy, asking you nicely.'

'Then you won't mind if I decline, just as nicely.'

They weren't pleased. 'Look,' I said, 'I've heard about the garbage being talked on the racecourse and I'm just as anxious as you to clear it up. I'm happy to give you what you need. I'll sit and talk all night if you want, but you've caught me at a bad time. If I don't turn up at Southwell today, all the assholes who are already talking will say I've gone to ground. Contact the local CID, they've already taken a statement from me, then if you still want to speak to me I can meet you somewhere after racing.'

I didn't mention the note and diary in case they led to further questioning.

Kavanagh looked at Miller. I pressed on. 'Look, put yourself in my place. What would you do? I've got to be at Southwell. Tell me where you guys are based and I'll come and see you after the races. I'll drive straight there.'

Miller wasn't happy but Kavanagh said, 'We're at the Griffin Hotel in Leicester.'

I nodded. 'I know it. I can be there around eight.'

Kavanagh's smile returned. 'We can have a nice cosy dinner.'

I didn't reply. Kavanagh headed for his car. Miller glared at me. 'You'd better be there, Malloy.' I smiled, just to annoy him.

As I pulled out to pass them, Kavanagh stuck his head out and motioned me to stop. I pressed the button to lower the passenger window. Kavanagh was smiling big now and shouted, 'Any tips for today?'

My eyes said to him, cheeky bastard, and he laughed as I drove off.

Chapter 13

Acting normal at the races was not going to be easy, especially as I had no booked mounts. Scavenging spare rides wasn't my style at the best of times. Now that people would be finger-pointing and bad-mouthing me behind my back, I found the prospect even less endearing.

Standing by the door of the weighing room, I watched the comings and goings of a sparse crowd. Small track, cold day, midweek meeting, moderate horses - they'd be lucky to get five hundred through the turnstiles.

At the approach of anyone I recognized, I waited to see if I'd be acknowledged or ignored. Everybody I knew spoke or nodded. A few held eye contact longer than normal as though hoping to discover something. Others grunted and avoided looking at me at all.

Feeling out of place in suit, shirt and tie, I moped around the changing room as jockeys and valets busied themselves with colours and saddles and boots. All was hustle and bustle. Except me. I went outside.

Just after the second race Bobby Watt, a trainer I used to ride for, hurried across the parade ring. 'Eddie!' he called as he approached. He looked anxious.

'Mister Watt,' I said, 'How are you?'

'In the shit. You don't ride in the fourth, do you?'

'No.'

His narrow flushed face was tense. 'Can you ride mine?'

'I'd be glad to.'

'Great, I'll be back shortly.' He scampered off toward the

weighing room. A forty-five-minute final deadline was enforced before each race for the declaration of jockeys; I reckoned Watt had about three minutes to declare me.

Pulling out my racecard I checked its name: White Hart, due to be partnered by D. Cooper, the kid Layton almost had in tears on Saturday. Young Cooper had been pushed into the game by his multi-millionaire father who was, I'd heard, a major pain in the arse. Daddy, apparently, was trying to buy success for the boy and had twenty horses in training. White Hart was one of them.

So why wasn't David riding it? I checked to see if he'd had a fall in either of the first two races but he had no other mounts. Maybe he was sick.

Bobby Watt came back, moving at a more sedate pace. 'You make it okay?' I asked.

He nodded. 'Just. Clancy's got the colours.'

'Fine,' I said. Clancy was a valet. 'What's happened to young Cooper?'

Watt shrugged. 'Nobody knows. He hasn't turned up. His old man's going crazy.'

I had immediate uncomfortable thoughts of Gilmour. I tried not to let it show. 'Has he done this before?'

'Missed a ride? Never. Keen as mustard. Well, once he's on a horse he is, otherwise you wouldn't know he's alive, especially when his old man's around. Poor kid's scared to breathe in case he gets a bollocking.'

'Where is his father?'

Watt nodded toward the main stand. 'In the bar. You ever met him?'

'Never had the pleasure.'

'It isn't one, believe me.'

'So I've heard.'

I wondered if Cooper senior had heard the gossip yet. 'Does he know you've asked me to ride?'

'Does it make a difference?'

'Not to me it doesn't, but depending on what rumours-'

'You mean that crap going round about you and Gilmour?'

I nodded. He smiled, showing small discoloured teeth. 'Load of bollocks and everyone knows it!'

'Everyone?'

'Anyone with any sense.'

'I wish I had your confidence, but I can do without the publicity of taking another ride from a jockey who's disappeared.'

Watt patted my shoulder as we headed for the weighing room. 'Don't worry about it, his car's probably broken down or he's dirtied his nappy.'

Half an hour later, I had the misfortune of meeting the boy's father. I'd always considered the stories about him grossly exaggerated. I was wrong. Cooper had made millions in the hotel and property business and believed that his money meant he could do and say as he pleased.

A watery sun hung over the parade ring where little groups stood chatting, corralled by their circling horses. Everyone was well dressed and reasonably sober.

Just to prove that no one dictated what Jack Cooper wore to the races, he came striding across the lawn in jeans and an open-necked denim shirt. He moved fast in a straight line toward us, pinched, high-cheek-boned face grim and determined looking. I glanced at Watt; he whispered, 'Shit, he's in a temper!'

Cooper stopped in front of us: early fifties maybe, light-brown hair suspiciously short of grey, dark eyes, my height but leaner, wiry. I was struck by his skin texture: very thin, almost parchment-like, making him look unwell.

Watt said, 'Jack, this is Eddie Malloy.'

Smiling, I held out my hand. Cooper ignored it, and leaning at me like a Regimental Sergeant Major, he said, 'Watt says you're a hotshot. You'd better be. You get one chance with me, that's all. I've had a very big bet here,' he jabbed a finger at me, 'so don't fuck up!'

Watt saw me redden and said, 'Eddie's good, Jack, he won't let us down.'

'I'll do my best.' I said, through gritted teeth.

Cooper said, 'Do better than your best, Malloy. Win. I've got a lot of money on this horse. You cut slices off him if you have to.'

I'd sooner cut slices off you, you bastard. I needed the breaks but not this bad. I unbuckled my helmet and said, 'I'm a jockey, Mister Cooper, if it's a butcher you're after, try the High Street.'

Bobby Watt, pulling nervously at his earlobe, intervened. 'Eddie, I'm sure Mister Cooper meant -' Cooper thumped him on the shoulder, knocking him off-balance.

'Don't fucking apologise for me!' Cooper shouted. Among the little cliques around us, a few heads turned. Watt straightened, trying to regain his composure. 'Sorry, Jack, I was only-'

'Shut it!' Cooper barked and turned back to me. 'Are you saying you won't ride this horse?'

'I'm saying if you want me to ride, I'll do my best, but I won't knock him about if he's struggling.'

The loudspeaker sounded: 'Jockeys, please mount.' Each lad led his horse off the tarmac to the lawn as jockeys moved toward them.

Cooper turned to Watt. 'You said this bastard was desperate. You said he'd do what he was told.'

I looked at Watt. He shrugged and half smiled apologetically. 'Well, he was wrong,' I said. 'Now do you want me to ride this horse, or will I go and take these colours off?'

Cooper sneered. 'The stewards would do you for refusing to ride.'

'Not if I told them the reason.'

'You wouldn't dare!'

I stared back at him. The skin around his eyes creased as he squinted at me, trying to weigh things up. A substitute at this stage wouldn't be allowed. If I refused to ride, the horse couldn't run, and the stewards would want to know why. Also, Cooper wouldn't have the chance to land his bets.

The others were mounted. White Hart's lad looked anxiously in our direction. Cooper said, 'You think you've got me by the balls, Malloy.'

I nodded. Watt was almost wetting himself.

'Get on the horse!' Cooper said bitterly.

Knowing it would be my last ride for him anyway, I pushed my luck and said, 'What's the magic word?'

'What did you say?'

'What's the magic word to get people to do what you'd like them to do?'

Face reddening, eyes bulging, neck veins straining he slapped his fringe away from his forehead. 'Malloy! If-'

'Ah-ah.' I smiled, determined now, nothing to lose. 'The magic word?'

'Please!' He spat and strode off, steam-driven, across the parade ring.

Laughing quietly, I walked toward the horse. Watt, pale and sweating so much his hair was damp, followed me shaking his head and saying again and again, with different inflexions each time, 'Jesus Christ Almighty!'

Although 6/1 with the bookies, the horse was clearly the best in the race. Watt must have been cheating with him all season to get such a decent price. We were going easily throughout and could have won by ten lengths, but I decided to give Cooper a few palpitations by holding my challenge until the last few strides before winning cheekily by a head.

Cooper met us in the winner's enclosure. You'd have thought his successful bets would have cooled his anger, but he still bubbled at high temperature. The sparse crowd's applause as I dismounted couldn't drown his words: 'Get weighed in and get those colours off, you'll never wear them again.'

I undid the girths and said quietly, 'Mister Cooper, my memory suffers when people don't talk nice to me. Sometimes makes me forget to do things…like weigh in.'

Every rider has to report to the scales after each race and have the clerk check that he's come back with the same weight he went out with. If I failed to do that, it meant automatic disqualification, all bets lost.

Until I weighed in I still held the whip hand. Cooper had forgotten that. Instead of trying to be polite, he reverted to threats. 'Malloy, if you don't weigh in, I'll make sure you never ride in Britain again. I might even fix it so you never fucking walk again!'

Saddle over my arm I sidled up to him. The crowd probably thought we were exchanging pleasantries. 'Listen, Cooper, I'd have thought a smart man like you would have guessed by now that I don't like being threatened. It doesn't scare me, just rubs me up the wrong way. Now, you might think that because you've got tuppence less than the Aga Khan it buys you the right to abuse people, but it cuts no ice with me. I need the rides and I need them badly, but if all the owners in racing slithered out of the same hole as you, I'd go and shovel shit for a living.' Leaning close to his face, I said, 'Comprende?' I walked away.

Not weighing in would have sorted Cooper out nicely, but it would also have deprived me, and hundreds of honest punters, of a winner, so I did my duty.

I hung around until the last race hoping for more rides, but worried too about David Cooper. By the time I left he hadn't turned up. If he too was found murdered, at least they couldn't accuse me of trying to curry favour with his father.

Reviewing the day as I drove home, I should have been depressed: no word of Gilmour's killer, the rumours about me were gathering pace, and to top it all I'd sacrificed another good source of rides in Jack Cooper.

But I felt fine. My run-in with Cooper had given me back some self-respect, a quality I'd been pretty short on for a long time. So I'd lost a few rides, what the hell? I felt good about myself, and I'd forgotten how much that meant to me.

On the way to Leicester to meet the cops, I stopped at home to dump my gear. The phone was ringing as I went in.

It was Hubert Barber. 'Eddie, something's come up, we need to talk.'

His tone was serious so I didn't need three guesses. 'Sure, Mister Barber, I'm free just now.'

'Not on the phone. You're at Stratford tomorrow, aren't you?'

I took a deep breath. 'If you still want me to ride those horses, I am.'

'Can you meet me in the car park around half eleven? You know my car, a blue Range Rover.'

Rides neither confirmed nor denied.

'Mister Barber, is this about-'

'I'd sooner we discuss it tomorrow, Eddie.'

Fine. One more try. 'Is it worth bringing my riding gear?'

'Bring it. See you tomorrow.'

I hung up. At least I wasn't jocked off. Yet.

Chapter 14

On the drive to Leicester to meet the two cops, I forced myself to accept that my three rides next day would probably be my last for Barber. He wouldn't sack me because of a few rumours. Either he'd heard something else or his owners had blown me out.

It was time to take things more seriously.

The Stockwell lounge in the Griffin Hotel was big, high-ceilinged, softly lit. The place was about a third full, maybe thirty people. Their conversations hummed just above the tone of the music.

Miller and Kavanagh sat in the corner where crimson curtains provided a quiet backdrop to Kavanagh's sweater of multi-coloured squares. The guy certainly liked to be noticed. When he saw me approach, he smiled in a way that said, "Here comes this evening's amusement".

I nodded a silent greeting and sat down. Kavanagh kept smiling. Miller glowered. No fancy duds for him; dark blue polo shirt and navy chinos.

'You made it,' Kavanagh said.

'Like I said, I'm anxious to co-operate.'

His blond head nodded slowly, easing the smile a few watts.

'Want some grub?' Kavanagh asked.

'I grabbed a sandwich when I dropped my gear off. I'm okay.'

'Good.'

Miller bought drinks, then they both set to work on me. Skirting around at first, messing about, trying to make me believe they had proof I was involved. After half an hour they saw I wasn't biting and got on with the direct questions. Four brandies down the line, it was obvious they had nothing to go on, though they weren't happy to concede.

I said, 'Can I ask a few questions?'

'Ask away,' Kavanagh said.

'Have you spoken to the local CID?'

Kavanagh nodded, 'They told us about the note you said you'd got.'

'What do you mean, I said I'd got? It was pushed through my door early on Sunday morning.'

Miller said, 'Who pushed it, you?'

'Come on! Have you guys seen the note? If I was cooking up a story, I think I'd have come up with something a bit more credible than that.'

Kavanagh smiled. 'Seems pretty credible to me.'

I said, 'You think it's genuine then? You think the killer wrote it?'

'I'd say it's odds-on the killer wrote it,' Kavanagh said.

I turned to Miller and said, 'So?'

Kavanagh said, 'Doesn't mean to say you're not the killer, Malloy.'

'Oh, come on! What about the diary?' I asked.

'What about it?' Kavanagh said. 'Who'd be most likely to have a murdered man's diary…the murderer?'

'Exactly!'

'So who had it, Malloy? You did.'

I shook my head. 'I'm pissing in the wind with you two, aren't I? It's a complete waste of time.'

Miller said, 'It's you that's wasting our time, Malloy.'

Trying to contain my anger, I said, 'No. You bastards are wasting my time and your own. Gimme your boss's name, maybe he'll give me sensible answers.'

Unfazed, Kavanagh said, 'To what questions?'

'Questions like, was a note found on Gilmour?'

'If there was, it doesn't really help you out, does it?'

'Did you find a note on Gilmour? In his car? In his hotel room?'

Kavanagh said, 'What do you think, Eddie? Would you bet on it? What d'you reckon the odds would be?'

'I'd reckon it was long odds on. If the same guy that wrote my note murdered Gilmour, then I'd say there'd be every chance he'd have left one. Somebody who acts that way, well, it's just what I think he'd do.'

Miller said, 'He didn't.'

I turned to Kavanagh for confirmation. He nodded and said, 'That's right.'

I said, 'He didn't leave one or you guys didn't find one?'

Miller gave me his cold look. 'He didn't leave one.'

I stood up and put my jacket on. 'I don't believe that. I don't think your people looked hard enough.'

Miller glared up at me. 'Malloy, we don't give a flying fuck what you think.'

I said, 'Well that's been pretty obvious since I sat down. Now, if you don't mind, I'll say goodnight.' I edged my way around the table, saying 'I'll ring your boss tomorrow, see if I can get any sense out of him.'

Miller raised his feet, lodging them on Kavanagh's seat, blocking my way. I looked down at him, his chin resting on his knuckles, gold pinkie ring gleaming in his dark beard. His eyes swiveled upwards as he bit at the loose flesh between thumb and forefinger. He said, 'Be sure and tell him how kind and considerate we were to you.' I stepped over his legs and went home.

Chapter 15

It was late when I got in. I was anxious about young Cooper. I rang Bobby Watt, who, after moaning about the way I'd talked to Jack Cooper earlier, told me the kid arrived home around eight. He'd got lost on country roads after his car broke down.

I'd just pulled the cold bed-sheets over me and was reaching to turn out the lamp when the phone rang. Ten past midnight. I hurried downstairs. It was McCarthy. No apology for the late call.

'You saw Kavanagh and Miller tonight.' A statement.

'That's right.'

'You talked about the note and the diary.'

'Mac, did you get me out of bed to tell me what I did tonight?'

'Their boss called me.'

'Kavanagh's and Miller's?'

'Yes. They should have told you not to mention the note to anyone.'

'Well, they didn't.'

'I know. They've had a bollocking. But Inspector Sanders wants to make sure you don't discuss the note with anyone until we find out more about it.'

'Tell Inspector Sanders that doesn't fit with my plans. I'm meeting Hubert Barber in the morning, and unless I can convince him I had nothing to do with Gilmour's murder then I ain't going to be riding for him anymore. I need to tell Barber about the note.'

'Eddie, this could mean the difference between catching the guy or not.'

'Too bad.'

'Come on!'

I stayed silent.

Serious now, Mac said, 'The note's sub judice. If you discuss it or comment on it in any way you're breaking the law.'

'Mac, gimme a break with all the Latin crap.'

'Sorry, Eddie. Sanders said to ask you nicely then to tell you your feet won't touch the ground.'

'If I can't talk about this note, the ground's the only thing my feet will be touching. They certainly won't be in a pair of stirrups!'

'Eddie-'

I hung up. Bastards. They had me all ways.

It was dull and drizzly next morning as I pulled up next to Barber's Range Rover in the members' car park at Stratford. Through the rain-covered windshield, Barber's head with his icing-white hair was like a melting pudding. When I climbed in, he looked stern.

'Your lights are on,' I said.

'Thanks.' He flicked a switch then turned, looking solemn. 'Have you heard these rumours about Tommy?'

'I've heard I'm supposed to have had him killed.'

He gazed at me for a long time. Maybe he was waiting for me to glance away or look nervous. I held steady. He obviously wanted to trust me. The prospect of having to interrogate me didn't sit well with him. I tried to make it easier.

'Hubert, listen, you don't owe me anything. You're as entitled as anyone else to be suspicious. Ask whatever you want, I won't take offence.'

He sighed, hung his head and ran his fingers through his hair until it stood up. 'I don't want to ask you questions. I don't feel I have to. I've always considered myself a fair judge of a man and I think this whole bloody thing is a piece of nonsense.'

'But?'

He looked at me. 'Some of my owners are getting a bit windy.'

'They don't want me on their horses.'

Looking uncomfortable and apologetic, he said, 'It's one chap in particular, been ringing the others up, getting them at it.'

'Who?'

'Delaney. I don't think he has anything against you personally, he's a bit of an old woman, listens to too much gossip. He keeps saying he's got inside information on you from the stewards' room.'

'Like what?'

Barber shrugged. 'He won't say. He's pretty close to one of the stewards' secretaries, Claude Beckman.'

It was Beckman who'd given me a tough time in the Enquiry after the Greenalls. Beckman who'd withheld the race video. 'What's Beckman saying about me?'

'I don't even know if it is Beckman, Delaney won't tell me.'

'Maybe I should talk to Delaney.'

'No. Leave it for now. I've persuaded them to hold off for a week to see if the police come up with anything on Tommy.'

'So I'm still riding for you?'

He nodded.

'Until when?'

'Next Thursday morning.'

'And if my name's cleared before then?'

He smiled. 'You'll be riding for me as long as you want.'

I looked at the big open face, knowing how hard he'd probably had to fight to keep me on. Offering my hand, I said, 'Thanks, Mister Barber.'

He shook it. 'I'm only sorry it's worked out like this, Eddie.'

'Forget it. I'm sure something'll turn up in a week.'

'Hope so.'

Opening the door, I stepped to the ground. 'See you later, Mister Barber.'

'Eddie…'

I looked at him.

'…we've decided to run Great Divide in the Gold Cup. If the police find Tommy's killer by then, you ride.'

I smiled, nodded, not sure what to say. Pushing the door closed I raised a hand in acknowledgement and saw Barber's smile widen.

I sat in my car listening to the rhythm of the rain on the roof and thinking about a week today. The Cheltenham Gold Cup was the biggest steeplechase of the year, and Great Divide had a strong chance of winning. That would put me right back in the spotlight.

Perhaps the cops could use a little assistance.

I rang McCarthy. We arranged to meet at Sandown next day.

I spent half the evening going through cuttings in the offices of the Gloucester Crier. I knew their racing reporter, Guy Webster.

Tommy Gilmour, an Irishman, had lived in Gloucester since getting married seven years previously. A local hero, there were numerous articles on him, most written by Webster and all churning out the same adulatory prose.

Webster had gone to the pub, though I had strict instructions to return the cuttings to Benny in the Library. Benny was small, thin, bald and doleful looking. He took the folder from me. 'Find what you wanted?'

'Afraid not.'

He moved away between the racks and slid the folder back onto its shelf. I called after him, 'Tell Guy Webster I said thanks, will you?'

He nodded, turning. 'Was it Webster's stuff you were going through?'

'Yeah, some articles on Tommy Gilmour.'

'The bloke that was murdered?'

'That's right. Did you know him?'

Benny stuck his hands in the pockets of his brown cardigan and pulled out a tobacco tin. 'I didn't myself, but Webster knew him well. Gilmour was the reason he got his job here.'

'How come?'

'Webster's predecessor wrote a story on Gilmour and they spiked it. He took the hump and walked out.'

'Spiked?'

'Binned. Not published.'

'Why not?'

He shrugged. 'Dunno.'

'What was the reporter's name?'

'I can't remember. He was an Aussie. I heard he went back there shortly after chucking the job.'

'Back to Australia?'

'So I heard.'

'Why did he get so upset about one story not being printed?'

He shook his head, frowning as he concentrated on rolling a cigarette. 'Don't know. All hush-hush.'

'You must have heard a whisper of what the story was about?'

The tip of his tongue came out and he drew the paper along, put the cigarette in his mouth and stood up patting at his pockets. 'What did I do with those matches?'

I waited. He found them and lit up, then said, 'I think it was something to do with the IRA.'

I went to the pub to find Webster. He remembered the story.

'Why wouldn't they print it?'

'Tommy was our local hero and the piece was just tittle-tattle. Tommy had been stopped by the cops at Fishguard once after he'd been home to Ireland for a family party. During the visit, he'd stupidly gone to see a cousin of his who was supposedly linked with the IRA.'

'Supposedly?'

'More than supposedly, I guess,' said Webster, 'the cousin was in the Maze when Tommy went to see him.'

'The Maze prison?'

'The Maze, Long Kesh, H Blocks, whatever you want to call it.'

'Was Tommy's cousin in the IRA?'

'He'd been convicted of ambushing a military convoy.'

'So what happened to Tommy?'

'They held him for the weekend under the Prevention of Terrorism act, took his car apart searching for weapons or drugs or cash then had to let him go.'

'When did all this happen?'

'Hmm. Would be about four years back.'

'Any follow up by the police?'

'Not to my knowledge.'

'His cousin still in prison?'

'Who knows?'

Chapter 16

My ride at Sandown next day finished unplaced, and I didn't hang around the weighing room afterward. I was hoping McCarthy would have something for me. We sat in a little office-cum-store-room, uncomfortably warm. McCarthy, sweating, tried to open a window but it was jammed. He took off his jacket, loosened his tie and sat down, belly straining at his shirt buttons.

'Thought you had clout,' I said. 'Couldn't you get a better place than this?'

'It's not mine. We don't have an office on-course, we need to take whatever's free.'

'Only winding you up, Mac, take it easy.'

He looked tense.

'So the cops have nothing to go on?' I asked.

'Not a jot. Most murders are domestic, committed by someone known to the victim. If they can't pin it down within that framework, it gets pretty tough for them.'

'Hence the reason they've been hassling me.'

'I wouldn't take it personally.'

'You would if you were the one getting hassled.'

'Don't get paranoid, Eddie.'

I hadn't told him about Gilmour and the IRA story. There seemed to be nothing in it and exposing it would probably stir up trouble for Tommy's widow.

I said, 'I think you should ask Inspector Sanders to run his fine-tooth comb over Gilmour's belongings again. His car, his clothes and bags, his hotel room.'

'What for? It's all been done.'

'Because until such time as it is proved otherwise, I'm assuming the note through my door came from the murderer. And, as I said to the cops, a guy who writes cryptic notes for one quite probably does for all.'

'I don't disagree with you, Eddie, but they've looked and can't find.'

'Tell them to look again.'

'I'll try.'

'Wasn't there anything else?' I asked. 'What was the exact gun model? Was he only shot once? Had he tried to fight back?'

McCarthy, sweating freely, said, 'They found ether in his lungs. His right leg had been broken at the knee.'

'Had been broken or was broken in the struggle?'

'Broken deliberately, they think, with a blunt instrument, a few minutes before he died.'

Frowning, I looked at Mac. 'What the hell would anybody want to do that for?'

Mac shrugged. 'Who knows? Maybe Gilmour was fighting back?'

'So why didn't the guy just shoot him?'

'I don't know.'

'I mean, if he wanted to make Gilmour suffer for some reason, why not break his leg a few hours before shooting him?'

'Eddie, I don't know. I wish I did.'

'What about the ether, can't the forensic boys trace the source?'

'Ether's ether. Tell me a brand name you know?' Mac ran his shirtsleeve across his hot wet brow. 'God, I need to get out of here.'

'Lose some weight,' I said. 'You wouldn't sweat so much.'

'Give me a break, you're as bad as Jean.'

'Did I ever tell you that story about the country hick who became an American football star?'

'The one where he says, Gee, you sure don't sweat much for a fat broad?'

'I told you it.'

'More than once.'

'It's a true story.'

'Apocryphal, Eddie, apocryphal.'

'Bless you.'

'Very funny. Are you ready?'

'As I'll ever be.'

I smiled. Mac rose and reached for his jacket. He said, 'You're pretty jaunty for somebody holding a threatening note from a murderer.'

'I'm planning to get him before he gets me.'

'Well you'd better hope he doesn't have that Beretta stuck in his waistband.'

'I'll be careful.'

We went out into the March wind and Mac sighed with relief at the cool air. Together we walked to the car park.

I said, 'Have you seen Mrs Gilmour yet?'

'I'm seeing her on Tuesday.'

'Have the police spoken to her?'

'Of course.'

'Bet they didn't ask if Tommy got a strange note in the post during the past few weeks.'

Mac, flush-faced, looked at me. 'I'll find out.'

Driving home, I cursed myself for my stupidity in handing over that note and diary. I should have photocopied every page. There could have been something in there, something as cryptic as the note itself, and I had barely skimmed it.

Where were Gilmour's things, his clothes and stuff? Maybe they'd been returned to his wife. Would she let me search them? What about the hotel room, perhaps I could get in there for a look around? If McCarthy introduced me to this big shot inspector, that might help.

I phoned him when I got in. He said it couldn't do any harm and that he'd arrange a meeting.

Chapter 17

Detective Inspector Sanders agreed to meet McCarthy and me on the Sunday. Mac picked me up and we headed north.

Sanders was macho and handsome; six foot two, fiftyish but athletic looking, with short iron-grey hair and matching precision-trimmed moustache, perfect eyebrows, square jaw, high cheekbones and eyelids one-third closed over striking brown eyes. I'd bet he'd had some women trouble in his time.

He led us into his office which was immaculate and smelled of polish. Above his desk was a picture of Sanders shaking hands with the Prime Minister. He took my coat and hung it on a wooden stand in the corner. He wheeled two comfortable seats up for us, then a young cop brought a silver tray with tea on it.

Sanders, smiling thanked the kid then, anxious to reinforce his "I might be a big shot who looks like a movie-star but I'm really just one of the boys" image, he poured tea for us, insisting on doing the milk and sugar too.

McCarthy explained about me and how I was involved, and Sanders, finger and thumb stroking his moustache in opposite directions, smiled and nodded, sharing his attention between Mac and me as he listened.

Sanders said to me, 'I believe you've met two of my men, DS Kavanagh and DS Miller?'

'I've had the pleasure twice,' I said.

'Fine policemen,' he said.

'I was impressed,'

He nodded, ignoring the sarcasm. 'And you're giving The Jockey

Club some help on this one from their side?'

Which meant be a good boy and stay out from under our feet. Mac and I glanced at each other and I said to Sanders, 'I've got a vested interest as you probably know, but we were sort of hoping that the police and The Jockey Club could work together.'

He straightened and tilted his head back. 'Of course. We'd be glad to have any input from you.'

Mac, to his credit, stepped in. 'Absolutely, Inspector, but we would be seeking reciprocation. Two heads, after all, are better than one, even if they're sheep's heads, that's what I always say.'

The inspector's eyes hardened. I don't think he cared for the farmyard comparison. Just as well McCarthy hadn't made it pigs. He dug up a condescending smile and said, 'We'll help wherever we can.'

I said, 'Can I ask if you've had a chance to go over Tommy Gilmour's things again?'

'Ah,' he said, 'in search of the elusive note?'

I nodded.

'If your involvement with this case lasts any great length, Mister Malloy, I think you'll find that I have one of the most thorough and professional teams in the country.'

'I don't doubt it, but you wouldn't expect them to be perfect, would you? Something could have been missed first time round.'

He considered me. The smile was still on his mouth but his eyes hardened. 'I don't think so, Mister Malloy, but I'll bear your suggestion in mind.'

I sat up, leaned forward and said, 'I hate to be a nuisance but I'm convinced there's a very strong chance that there is another note. Would you have any objection to me going through Gilmour's things? His car, hotel room?'

He looked at me, long and hard. Mac shifted nervously. Sanders said, 'I don't think that would be the best idea right at this moment.'

'With respect,' I said, 'I don't have a lot of time to waste. Unless I can do something by Thursday morning to prove I was not involved with Gilmour's death, then I can probably say goodbye to what remains of my career.'

That made him smile properly. He said, 'You have my sympathy but my career depends on catching criminals, not rehabilitating jockeys back into the community.'

Police-speak for helping ex-jailbirds and he knew I knew it. I didn't see much point in humouring him or trying to be Mister Nice-

Guy anymore. I said, 'Well, I hope I have the chance some day of influencing your career.'

He smiled, 'I do think that's most unlikely, Mister Malloy.'

The meeting ended shortly after that with Sanders, courteous again, accompanying us to the main door. Halfway along the corridor, I realized I'd forgotten my coat and went back for it.

Hurrying through the rain to the car, we set off toward the M6. Mac's car was at my place. I was driving.

'Well,' I said, 'bet that was worth coming all the way from Lambourn for?'

'The only decent bloody meal Jean cooks these days is Sunday lunch. To think I missed it to sit listening to that pompous bastard. And you did your usual, wound him up. He might not have been so bad if you hadn't.'

'What'd you expect me to do? He's sitting there as though he has all the time in the world to catch this guy. What am I supposed to say? Come on, Mac!'

'You'll have to learn some diplomacy.'

'Bollocks.'

'Enough said.'

Mac moped. The only sound was rain on the roof and the sloshing of tyres, then he realized we were travelling east. Spotting a road sign through the swinging wipers, he said, 'You're going the wrong way.'

'I know.'

'We want to go south.'

'Not yet we don't.'

He said wearily, 'Eddie, where are we going?'

'To a place that does a very nice lunch. And if you promise not to moan at me too much, I won't tell Jean you broke your diet.'

'I haven't.'

'You will.'

Chapter 18

The Green Manor Hotel was only a couple of miles from Haydock Racecourse. It was the last place Tommy Gilmour had stayed. As I turned the car through the gates, tyres crunching across the gravel, Mac said, 'Please tell me you're not planning what I think you're planning?'

Swinging the car into a parking spot, I smiled. 'Needs must when the devil drives.'

He moaned softly and got out.

McCarthy ordered lunch while I found a phone and called Lisa Ffrench.

Over thick, grilled fillet steaks, McCarthy tried to convince me it was most unwise trying to get into Gilmour's room.

'It might not be a good idea but I'm going to do it, and if I don't find anything, I'm going to Tommy's house tonight to check out his car and his personal gear.'

'The police will still have that stuff.'

'Uh-uh,' I mumbled, mid-chew. 'They returned it to Mrs Gilmour last Friday.'

'How do you know that?'

'One of the lads told me.' I had to keep Lisa out of this, for her sake.

He shook his head. 'There's no way they'll let you into Gilmour's room.'

'Want to bet?' I smiled.

'You've got one of your stories cooked up.'

'Better than that.'

He saw the mischief in my eyes and said, 'I don't think I want to know.'

I chuckled. 'How's your steak?'

'It tastes great. It's the indigestion that's worrying me now.'

'Relax, I'll make sure you come out squeaky clean.'

'I make a point of being wary of people who advise me to relax.'

'Could've been worse. I might have said, trust me.'

He chewed in silence until his curiosity beat him. 'How do you plan to get in?'

'You still carry that nice big fountain pen?' I asked. Puzzled, he nodded slowly. 'Can I borrow it a second?'

'What for?'

Reaching into my jacket pocket, I took out a piece of folded paper and pushed it across to him. He shook it open; it was blank except for the official heading of the Greater Northern Police Force. McCarthy closed his eyes for a few moments, his head sinking steadily.

When he looked up again I smiled and said, 'Remember when I forgot my coat?'

'You stole this from Sanders' office?'

I shrugged. 'It was lying around. I was tidying up.'

'I didn't see anything lying around.'

'Top drawer, right hand side,' I said, smiling.

Eventually I persuaded Mac to lend me his pen. He gave it to me with his ritual 'I am washing my hands of this' look.

Leaning on the wine list I wrote the request to the Duty manager, and signed it "Inspector Eric Sanders".

'Want to see this?' I asked McCarthy.

'No, thanks. If you get caught, you're on your own.'

'Mac, whatever happens, you know I wouldn't drop you in it.'

He got up, 'I'll be in the bar.'

I was wearing my only suit with a white shirt and navy tie. Clean-shaven and sombre looking, I handed the note to the duty manager whose badge said his name was Christopher.

He turned to the girl behind the desk, 'Anyone in two-ten, Joanna?'

Joanna checked her screen, 'No Mister Cheeseman.'

'Would you hand me the key, please?'

He smiled and asked me to follow him.

The room wasn't that big. I started at the window end, working through the desk drawers, wardrobe shelves and base, the floor, skirting boards, under the beds, methodically checking the least likely places, trying to cover every inch.

The telephone table: nothing stuck under the phone. The table had one narrow shelf, dark and quite deep and, apparently, empty. On my knees I reached inside and felt a book. I slid it out: The Bible. I shook it, riffling the pages with my right hand. A card, a white card with writing on it fluttered to the floor.

I bent quickly and grabbed it: 'This Bible was placed here by the Gideon Society.'

Shit.

I put the card down then noticed something on the back. It looked like the neat block writing that had been on my note, in the same black ink. It read 'Hebrews 9:22.' I searched the bible hurriedly: "Without shedding of blood is no remission."

I just stopped myself from kissing the card as though it were a winning lottery ticket. It let me off the hook, left me free to ride all of Barber's horses, including his Gold Cup runner.

McCarthy rang Sanders, who arrived within the hour, hot and bothered. Kavanagh and Miller followed him up the steps to the front door as we watched from the bar.

We tried to be amiable, but none of them spoke until we reached the room. I told them what I'd done and showed them the card. Miller turned me by the shoulders, forcing my hands against the wall. He searched me, then Kavanagh read me my rights and they marched me out.

I was thrown in a cell and told they intended to charge me with the murder of Thomas Gilmour.

Chapter 19

They locked the door at ten to five on Sunday afternoon. Between then and the next morning, I saw no one except the silent cop who brought me a dried-up meal around seven thirty.

The cell had cream-painted brick walls marked with smudges where someone had tried to remove graffiti. Curl-edged brown tiles pocked with cigarette burns covered the floor. There was a bed and a chipped washbasin. The place smelled of Jeyes fluid.

I spent an uncomfortable though not particularly stressful night, since I was confident I'd be released as soon as Sanders considered he'd given me a big enough fright. If they really suspected me of Gilmour's murder, they'd have been interrogating the hell out of me.

Parched scrambled egg and toast arrived at eight. Kavanagh and Miller arrived at eight-thirty, Kavanagh frowning and tutting at me and Miller wearing his usual aggressive stare. They took me to 'the interview room'.

We sat on metal chairs opposite each other across a table; two against one. Kavanagh talked. Miller clicked a tape-recorder and took notes.

Kavanagh said, 'You've been a very silly boy, Eddie.'

'Slap my wrist, then, and send me home.'

Kavanagh said, 'I don't think you'll be going home for quite a while.'

'Then you'd better charge me with something.'

'Where do you want me to start?' Kavanagh asked. 'Stealing police property? Forgery? Impersonating an agent of the Greater Northern Police Force? Murdering Thomas Anthony Gilmour?'

'Come on, Sergeant Kavanagh, why don't you just admit that you and your boss are a bit peeved that I found something you guys should have found a week ago?'

Kavanagh went cold-eyed and said, 'It wasn't there a week ago.'

He waited for that to sink home. I smiled and said, 'You honestly expect me to believe that you think I wrote that note myself?'

He shrugged. 'You said it, Eddie, not me.'

I laughed and sat back, shaking my head. Kavanagh said, 'You were in the room alone, you could have done anything. You gained fraudulent access. You were desperate to get in there.'

'I was desperate to get in there because, as I kept telling you, your boss and anyone else who'd listen, there had to be a note. You were too pig-headed to go and look again. I was the one taking all the shit, what did you expect me to do, sit quiet and watch my career slide down the drain?'

He waited, knowing he was getting me riled then said, 'Did you ask McCarthy to come to the room with you?'

'You know I didn't or you wouldn't be asking.'

'Why didn't you?'

'Because it wasn't his problem.'

'He's in charge of the case for The Jockey Club.'

'McCarthy does things his way, I do things mine. In theory, with the letter and stuff, I was breaking the law; if I'd pushed Mac into it too his employers wouldn't have been pleased. I can take my chances. I've no one to answer to.'

He smiled. 'Except us.'

I sighed in frustration. He said, 'Convenient that McCarthy wasn't with you. Did the hotel manager ask if you wanted him to wait in the room?'

'You obviously know damn well he did.'

'But you sent him away.'

'Look, Kavanagh, this is a load of crap. I'm not going to answer for every little thing I did yesterday.'

'You're above the law now, are you?'

'I'm above being wound up by you guys. This makes your Monday morning, does it? Helps beat the depression of coming to work?'

'We're just trying to do a job.'

It was obvious the tape-recorder was on, Kavanagh talking official and acting all hurt. First chance they got they'd be back to their smartass remarks and threats.

I said, 'Trying is the right word because you haven't been too successful so far, have you? Doubting me on the note, missing the one in Gilmour's Bible. Now you want to hide your embarrassment, turn the screw on me with all this nonsense, it's bloody pathetic! You know I had nothing to do with Gilmour's murder! So does Sanders! But you're obviously going to take whatever childish satisfaction you can get by messing me around as long as possible!'

Kavanagh tutted, 'The bluster of a guilty man.'

He had me well on the boil and I had to fight to control myself. I was tempted to goad him with missing Gilmour's potential IRA connection too, but it would have meant a grilling for Susan Gilmour who would never stand the strain. I said nothing about my booked mounts at the Cheltenham festival which was twenty-four hours away. I had to be out by early next morning to keep those rides.

Kavanagh persevered, attempting to wear me down, to get a confession, but I was convinced his heart wasn't in it; he knew it was a sham.

I had an idea. 'What have you done with the note?' I asked.

Kavanagh said, 'It's gone to forensic with your fingerprints on it.'

I said, 'It's also gone to forensic with ink on it that's at least a week old.'

'So...you brought the card with you. When did you write it?'

I stared at him. 'You really expect me to dignify that with an answer?'

'It's a formal question, Mister Malloy, and a perfectly sensible one under the circumstances.' He folded his arms, looking smug.

I leaned across the table. 'It's only perfectly sensible to someone with no sense. This guy is very very confident that he's a lot cleverer than you, though that wouldn't be hard. He's already proved it. His calling card's been lying here for a week, waiting for someone who's smart.'

Kavanagh reddened, looked at his watch and said, 'Interview ended, seven minutes past eleven.' He clicked off the tape and they left.

I saw no one else except the cops who brought food. At lights out, I lay down to torture myself into the small hours of day one of the Cheltenham festival, the burial place for my career.

Chapter 20

I woke to daylight through the tiny window, and soreness in my muscles from the bad bed. It took me ten seconds to realize where I was, and I'd just pulled my thoughts together when I heard the key turn in the corridor door. I prayed it would be Kavanagh. I reckoned I'd a reasonable chance of getting through to him, of persuading him to let me make a call.

It was the silent breakfast cop, tall and skeletal, an inch gap at the throat of his shirt, his bony wrists like pistons coming from his cuffs as he laid the tray down. I asked him to get Kavanagh for me, or Sanders or even Miller. He just stared back. I pleaded with him to call McCarthy. Eventually he spoke. Shrugging his narrow shoulders apologetically he said, 'I'm sorry, mate, I can't.'

I paced the cell, dragging the minutes and seconds behind me. They'd taken my watch but every time I turned toward the door I saw through the bars the black clock high on the wall.

I tortured myself with thoughts of Cheltenham, the biggest National Hunt meeting in the world. The place where it was an achievement for owners, trainers and jockeys just to have a runner. Where riding any winner over the three days left memories which lasted years. To be connected with the winner of one of the two major championship races was to bask in the glory of it for the rest of your life and be spoken of, even after death, as the man who rode, owned or trained a Gold Cup or Champion Hurdle winner.

Forty thousand racegoers, some from halfway round the world, would be on their way to the course now in cars, trains, buses, on foot…those in helicopters would look down on streams of humanity converging from all directions like people who'd found the end of the rainbow and were certain the gold was there.

I tried to drive it from my mind, but I couldn't. The clock hands crawled to eleven-thirty. At the course, horses would be coming down the ramps out of their boxes, looking around, ears pricked, excitement building, knowing why they were there, heading for the stables, coats gleaming, muscles showing hard and smooth, fit to run for their lives.

The crowds would be buzzing, moving past shouting newsvendors, heather-pushing gypsies, cockney ticket touts. They'd be queuing for racecards, filtering down to look at the course or hurrying toward the bars which would be full of noise and anticipation, whiskey fumes, champagne bubbles and cigar smoke.

Bookmakers would be setting up their stands, opening satchels, counting money into them, thousands of pounds. They'd be cleaning boards, sorting race sheets, smoothing the pages of their big field books, bantering among themselves, boosting collective morale knowing they were seen by almost everyone else there as 'the enemy'. Only a hundred or so of them against forty thousand, but favourites for victory even though all they had for ammunition was luck.

Ten to twelve.

The main players would be gathering around the weighing room: Jockey Club members, millionaire owners, movie stars, pop singers, trainers, jockeys…

Jockeys…they'd be discussing prospects, exchanging information, finalising plans, enjoying that delicious high of anticipation that can only be savoured before your first ride of the day, before the disappointment of a loser snuffs it out.

I flopped on my bunk almost crying with frustration. Then I heard a key turning in the corridor door…footsteps. I looked up. A sergeant I hadn't seen before, McCarthy behind him looking serious. The cop opened the door and left without locking it. McCarthy stared at me, still unsmiling, as I stood up.

'What is it?' I asked.

'Come on, you're out.'

'Out? How?'

'Good news and bad news.'

I waited.

He said, 'You know Dermot Donachy?'

I nodded, 'What about him?'

'They found him dead last night. Same gun that killed Gilmour, leg broken, bible quote, the whole nine yards.'

'Jesus!'

'The manager of a Cheltenham nightclub discovered his body in the toilets.'

I looked at the clock: five to twelve. Grabbing McCarthy's arm I hauled him through the door. 'Come on, I can still make Cheltenham. You can tell me the rest later.'

Sanders didn't turn out to say goodbye, nor did his two wise monkeys. We stood at the desk waiting for the sergeant to get my things together. A thought occurred to me and I said to Mac, 'Have they checked what the bible quote was?'

'Too much blood and brains on the note to be certain just now. It was rolled up and stuck into the exit wound in his head.'

Chapter 21

We left the station at twelve-ten. Cheltenham was one hundred and twenty miles south, and I had a mount booked in the two-fifty, but would have to be there half an hour before that. McCarthy offered to drop me at the Green Manor Hotel to pick up my car.

'Mac, we don't have time for that! Get on the motorway and put your foot down.'

'Come on, Eddie, you've got no chance of making the second race.'

'We'll make it if you drive fast enough.'

'Even if the motorways are clear, we'll never get through the jams around the course.'

'Let's worry about that when we get there.'

He looked across at me and said, 'No way am I driving at a hundred, I've already got a speeding ticket.'

'Pull over. I'll drive.'

He grimaced. 'You're not insured, Eddie.'

'Mac! I've just spent the last forty-eight hours locked in a cell wondering if I'm going to be charged with murder, and you're whining about speeding tickets and insurance! It's the Cheltenham festival, for God's sake, and I've got the biggest break of my life! If you're not going to let me drive, then I'll find some other way of getting there.'

He stopped and got out, mumbling something about being sorry he ever got involved with me. I slid across, and did everything through the city traffic except loop the loop.

We hit the motorway, moved into the fast lane, and I pushed the needle of the big Peugeot up to a hundred and twenty, flashing the poor law-abiding drivers in front to move over. I prayed for no road works, no hold-ups, and no police.

Mac kept quiet during the journey, more, I think, out of self-preservation than anything else; he didn't want to break my concentration.

A56, M6, M5, few delays, no police patrols. We left the M5 and hit a three-mile tailback. It was one forty-five.

McCarthy looked at me with ill-disguised smugness that said, "What are you going to do now, big shot"?

I got out, threw my jacket and tie on the seat and said, 'See you at the course.'

Since I hadn't been riding enough to keep fit, I'd been doing a lot of running, and had turned in some reasonable times in the fields and lanes around the Lodge. Leather shoes weren't the best for it, but the grass on the verge showed some give and I soon built up a good pace.

I drew my share of laughter and comments as I passed along the crawling line of car-bound racegoers. Their exhaust fumes didn't help my breathing.

It was a fine crisp day. I hit a nice rhythm and could have been enjoying it if I'd had time.

Hard pavement now beside the dual carriageway. My feet began to hurt. Three long rows of vehicles queued at the lights about a mile from the course. Five back from them on the inside was a long haired, leather-clad motorcyclist revving a big Harley. I stopped in front of him. He looked at me and eased off the throttle. 'You know where the racecourse is?' I asked.

'Why?'

'I'll give you thirty quid to take me there.'

'Jump on.'

We roared past the rest of the traffic on the outside, and were at the entrance five minutes later. Sweaty and windblown, I must have presented a wild picture to Hubert Barber when I found him by the weighing room.

'Where have you been?'

'It's a long story, Mister Barber, can it wait?'

'I suppose so,'

'I'm sorry,' I said, 'but I've got no kit with me. I'm going to have to dash off and make some arrangements.'

'Go on then, I'll see you before the race.'

Before turning away, I said, 'Did you hear about Donachy?'
He nodded, grim-faced.
'Am I in the clear?'
He paused.
I waited.
'Ride me a winner and I'll tell you.'
I didn't. We finished fourth of fourteen in the Arkle Chase, but the horse, Leandering, ran up to his best form and gave me a brilliant spin, flying every fence and turning into the straight in line with the leaders, only to weaken on that long climb to the post.

Barber came hobbling to meet us. The pre-race tension gone, his face told me he was pleased with the performance. 'You've got yourself a horse for next year,' I told him, and he smiled and clapped Leandering's foam-flecked shoulder.

McCarthy sent in my jacket and tie with one of the valets, and the clink of keys in the pocket reminded me I had to arrange for the car to be picked up. I made a few calls.

I found Barber and asked again if I was in the clear with his owners. He said, 'We only heard the news this morning. I'll talk them round. Don't worry.'

I told him what had happened since Sunday, and he said that was a hell of a way to get myself an alibi for the latest killing.

Donachy had been based in Ireland and seldom rode here, so his murder had less impact in the changing room than Tommy Gilmour's had.

The murders added further drama to the festival and, as the day wore on and people moved around, meeting friends, drinking, exchanging gossip, embellishing tales, boasting of Irish contacts, theories became rumours and rumours became facts. In the end, I must have heard a dozen different versions of what 'really' happened.

None mentioned the biblical notes.

The favourite story was that Gilmour and Donachy had reneged on 'arrangements' to give the IRA information on planned betting coups. Someone said Gilmour had been 'knee-capped' before being shot.

Another theory was that the guy was a psycho, killing jockeys at random. He'd done a couple of Irishmen in a row just to lull the English boys into a false sense of security. He'd get one of them next. This set a couple of the lads flapping a bit, and by the time I left there were some worried faces in the weighing room.

I headed for the car park with one race still to go, intent on beating the traffic jams.

Outside the weighing room McCarthy fell into step with me, and as we went toward the gate he said, 'The forensic boys deciphered Donachy's note.'

'And?'

'Another quote from the Bible: Romans six, twenty-three: "The wages of sin is death".'

I shook my head. 'This guy is going to take some catching.'

As we reached my car, Mac said, 'They've had another look at the note you got. Remember what it said? Numbers, thirty-two twenty-three?'

I said, 'There's a book in the Bible called Numbers, isn't there?' He nodded.

'What does it say?'

'"Be sure your sin will find you out".'

'Which one? There's plenty to choose from.' I said.

'I hope you feel as light-hearted as you're trying to make out.'

'I wish I did, Mac.'

'You can expect a visit from Kavanagh this evening.'

'What for?'

'He wants to dig a bit deeper into your background to try to find a link with Gilmour and Donachy.'

I sighed heavily, tired of all this. Mac said, 'Want me to come along for moral support?'

'Or to stop me punching the bastard.' I said.

Chapter 22

Kavanagh stayed for two hours. Mac sat in. Other than the fact we were jockeys, I could think of nothing to tie me in with Gilmour and Donachy. I argued that if I was on the list, why hadn't he tried to kill me the day he'd brought the note? Kavanagh said the killer might not have delivered it.

The police were dissecting Donachy's history, and when I told Kavanagh my parents came from Dublin he renewed his grip on the 'Irish link'. I didn't like talking about my family and this reluctance rekindled Kavanagh's hunch about some terrorist connection.

'Not in my family,' I argued.

'Not as far as you know,' he said. Things got heated then, and Mac suggested we adjourn overnight.

The terrorist angle resurfaced in next day's papers. One of them had picked up on Gilmour's twenty-four-hour detention by the police at Fishguard, the incident the Aussie had written about. The only person I'd told about that had been Lisa, and I was concerned in case she thought I'd dropped Susan in it.

At nine o'clock I rang Lisa at home. She answered, sounding out of breath. 'You okay?' I asked.

'Fine... Been out running... Just came through the door.'

'Do you want me to call back?'

'No, it's okay... have you found something?'

'Not really, I was wondering if you'd seen this morning's papers?'

'The bit about Tommy?' she said.

'I just don't want you thinking they got that from me.'

'I didn't. I knew it was only a matter of time before they dug it up. So did Susan.'

'Have the press been pestering her?'

'They might have been trying to, but they won't find her. She's gone to stay with a friend in France for a few days. What about you? Are you any further forward?'

I hesitated, then said, 'Put it this way, I've had a few little adventures since we last spoke.'

'Anything you can tell me about?'

'How long have you got?'

'If it's to do with Tommy?'

'More myself than Tommy, I suppose,' I said.

'Maybe we can meet?'

'Thought you weren't supposed to hang around with bums like me?'

'Well, if you don't tell, I won't.'

'Okay. How about Saturday night?'

'Sorry, Susan's due home Saturday evening, promised I'd pick her up.'

'Sunday?'

'Depends how Susan is on the Saturday. I'm on leave for a couple of weeks after that. Can I call you?'

'Sure.'

'Fine.'

Sounded like she was anxious to get away. I felt awkward. Apart from Jackie, my contact with women in the past six years had consisted of occasional one-night stands. Developments in sexual-social manners had passed me by. I wasn't confident any more about interpreting signals.

Lisa said, 'I've got to go. Good luck in the Gold Cup.'

'Thanks,' I said lamely as the line went dead.

Chapter 23

Great Divide was my only ride of the day, and potentially the most important one I'd ever have.

The changing room was alive with jockeys and valets checking and double-checking, shouting, laughing nervously as the tension built.

People send good luck messages: used to be telegrams, now it's cards or faxes, and Simpson, one of the valets, was calling names and handing them out. Everybody had at least one. Mine was in an envelope with my name printed in block capitals.

The folded piece of paper stuck together as I tried to open it. I eased the corners apart. The message was typed, the print faint and uneven. It said: "Vengeance is mine. I will repay, sayeth the Lord."

I read it twice, then shoved it into the zipper pocket of my kitbag. Bob, my valet, approached and began tying the blue silk cap onto my skullcap. 'Ready for it?' he asked. I nodded.

I had been ready, now I was in a mild panic. Bob stepped back, looked me over, spun me by the shoulders, put a playful arm around my neck and said, 'You should've been one of those male models, Eddie. You'd have made more money.'

I smiled, miles away as Bob slapped my shoulder and wished me luck. I'd need plenty of it if this madman was going to try something during the big race. I'd had a written threat once before, warning me to fall off at the first in the Champion Hurdle or I'd be shot. I'd ignored it and finished third.

Should I ignore this? Should I tell Barber? If I did, he might withdraw the horse. Then again, it hadn't been a direct threat to do something during the race. But why send it just before the off?

The bell rang, signalling time to leave for the parade ring. I had to make up my mind. We filed through the big glass doors onto the veranda where the privileged people posed: trainers, owners, Jockey Club members and their celebrity guests.

As we broke through the pack and entered the parade ring, the impact of the occasion hit me as it always did. The crowd rose away fifty deep up the steps to the right of the large oval, and you could feel their reaction to our entry. No cheers or clapping but an almost tangible increase in the tension round the whole arena.

We cut through gaps in the circling horses and split up to join the tight little groups scattered across the lawn. Barber stood over a party of six, none of whom I'd met before. He introduced me: only two were the owners of Great Divide, Mr and Mrs Carfax. The others were friends of the family who kept saying, "Isn't it exciting!" Too exciting for Mrs Carfax whose heavy jowls swayed as she jigged from foot to foot.

Barber legged me into the saddle, squeezed my ankle and wished me luck. The blonde groom, Natalie, who'd led me in at Haydock was almost pulled off her feet as the powerful 'chaser surged forward.

Watching on TV during my prison sentence, I'd studied the camera angles and favoured shots at Cheltenham determinedly, promising my mates I'd give them a wave when I rode in my next Gold Cup.

Face on to the camera at the top of the ring, I smiled and tipped my cap and thanked God I was out here riding and not in there watching.

Natalie led the horse round, walking fast, patting his neck regularly I called down to her, 'Do you get all the good horses?'

She turned, smiling nervously. 'I'm lucky, I suppose. Divvy's my favourite. You will look after him, won't you?'

I nodded, fighting thoughts of someone out there with a high-powered rifle. Aiming at a racing target, he was much more likely to hit the horse.

She turned to me again as we left the parade ring. 'God, I hate this. I wish we could just keep them in the stable and ride them in the mornings. I wish they never had to race. I can't watch. I have to lock myself in the loo.'

Throughout the slow parade in front of packed stands, my mind was on the note. Why use a typewriter this time? The others had been hand-written. Why no reference to chapter and verse like the previous ones? This had been a direct quotation. The other notes, apart from my first one, had been found with corpses. Why not wait until he'd killed me?

Natalie slipped the lead rein off as we turned and Great Divide lunged forward, getting the run on me, galloping to the start more quickly than I'd have wanted.

Even though our mounts were veterans, we urged them toward the first jump to remind them of what they faced. As Great Divide peered over the beautifully built four-foot-six fence, something caught my eye.

About a hundred yards beyond the inside rail, near the centre of the course, a man in a dark suit stood alone. He seemed to be holding an object at eye-level, and my first thought was that he was sighting something. The sunlight glinted on it. He noticed me watching and quickly slipped whatever it was into the inside of his jacket. He walked slowly toward us…he was wearing a roman-collar.

Priests. Bibles.

Decisions.

I could tell the starter and have the horse withdrawn, although if the assassin was determined to shoot me he'd do so much more easily as we stood alone as the rest galloped off.

I was over-reacting. Priests are not an uncommon sight at Cheltenham, with so many Irish racegoers attending. It could be a priest who was simply checking his binoculars. The glint could have been off the lens.

Why did he stuff them so quickly into his jacket then?

If I asked the starter to have the police pick him up and he turned out to be innocent, I'd be laughed off the racecourse.

Circling at the start I looked to see if he was still there. He was moving down the dirt track on the inside of the rails. Which fence would he stop at?

I tried to reason with myself to quell the rising panic. Maybe I could just stay on the outside of the pack throughout? But there were only five other runners.

Girths checked, small talk finished, starter mounting his rostrum. 'Ready, jockeys?' Nobody answers, the lever cracks down, the tapes hiss skywards and we're off in the Gold Cup.

All abreast, we make the short run to the first at a speed that leaves little room for adjustment. We land safely, though at full gallop, and each of us knows we'll have to settle our horse down a gear or two to survive.

Even a race as pressurised as the Gold Cup can become an enjoyable romp on top-class horses, if the ground is good and the field small. Closely packed, the banter is sharp and relaxed among the others, now that we're racing.

Tucked in the middle of the group I keep quiet and concentrate on settling my horse. After the fourth jump he's moving in a nice steady rhythm on the bridle, listening to my signals. I ease him to the tail of the field, ready to gain ground on the outside as we come down the hill for the first time toward the jump where the priest waits.

We approach the fence tightly bunched, hoof beats drumming, biceps straining, boots touching…I see the man, his arms resting on the rails, no weapon visible. I switch Great Divide to the outside, hiding. We clear it and gallop away.

Still in a tight group, we set off on the second circuit, all going well and jumping soundly. Five from home, the long shot, a grey horse, begins to labour, and drops away as the pace picks up.

We five remaining jump the next and as we land, Bomber Harries on the second favourite, Tuscany, kicks for all he's worth as the rest of us get our horses balanced.

Turning down toward the third last where the priest waits, Bomber's gone four lengths clear.

We trade glances, knowing that if anyone goes in pursuit we'll put our mounts under pressure, accelerating downhill where bodyweight alone causes a natural surge, making the jump even more dangerous.

Blakey, the most experienced, and swinging along nicely, says, 'He's gone too soon.'

The others look doubtfully at Blakey who says, 'I'm telling you, the bastard's gone too soon!'

He's wrong, I'm sure, but if I go after Bomber alone, my man at the fence will have the clearest of targets. If I wait, if I hide again on the outside of the others, I won't win the Gold Cup.

Do I blow my career or give this guy a free shot?

I shout, 'You're wrong, Blakey, he's nicked it! We'd better get after him!' The others say nothing. Blakey says, 'Believe me, he'll come back to us!'

Bomber's five lengths clear, travelling strongly. I change hands on the reins, kick my horse in the belly and go after him, out into the open.

Galloping hard now, a hundred yards from the man in black…Bomber goes over…silently I count down my final strides, the man straightens from the rails, I crouch lower, he reaches inside his jacket, the black birch looms, Great Divide's quarters coil, he springs, the man's hand rises holding glinting steel, I cringe as we land…and the priest drinks from a whiskey flask.

I laugh as the terror evaporates, replaced by a massive surge of vitality. I whoop like a Red Indian and the horse's ears flick back. I shout, 'Let's go and win this!'

Bomber is seven clear leaning into the final bend, with no sign of him weakening.

We find our rhythm. I twirl my whip, then smack Great Divide's quarters. He surges, chasing Tuscany's black tail as I duck and push, my pelvis urging him forward.

Tuscany blunders through the second last. I set mine up for a long one as we approach, and he flies in a low accurate trajectory, hardly breaking stride.

We gain a length to Tuscany's lost length. Just two more lengths to find.

Both horses begin to struggle approaching the last, Bomber's, maybe, a bit more than mine, and we reel him in slowly, a foot or so a stride.

I'm on the inside, a length behind as we hurtle to the final fence. Crouched, I see the winning post like a tiny gun-sight between my horse's ears. If we jump clean we'll win.

Tuscany rises in front of us, Great Divide comes up at the same time, tired, mistaking the long shadow of the fence for the take-off point…we crash through the packed birch, and I feel the spirit go out of him as his ears drop with exhaustion.

Through the tunnel of crowd noise, Tuscany crosses the line four lengths ahead.

I shook Bomber's hand as we returned to the winner's enclosure. I acknowledged the applause, and smiled at Barber as he walked out to meet us. I exaggerated the effect of the error at the last to Barber and the owners, and retreated to the safety of the changing room. The exhilaration at getting safely over the third last had drained away, leaving me feeling empty and stupid. My overheated imagination had probably cost me the Gold Cup…Me, Hubert Barber, the Carfaxes, and young Natalie.

Barber sent a message telling me we'd been invited to join the winning owners at home that evening for a celebration.

My inclination was to give it a miss. I was on a downer and would probably depress people. First is first, second is nowhere. I slipped quietly out while everyone was concentrating on the next race, wandered off into the car park, and locked myself in the car.

I wound the recliner and lay almost flat so nobody passing could see me, and spent fifteen minutes berating myself for losing the Gold Cup and cursing whoever had sent that note.

I was sure now it hadn't been genuine, which meant somebody was leaking information about the murders. Either the police or someone in McCarthy's department. The more I dwelt on it, the angrier I became.

Thinking McCarthy's people the more likely source of any leak, I set off looking for him. My frustration grew when I couldn't find him, and I decided to go home. Before leaving, I spoke to the valet who'd handed me the typed threat. He had collected all the messages from the secretary's office. No one there could remember who'd delivered it.

Chapter 24

By the time I reached the Lodge, I'd committed to finding the murderer. I knew I was useless when undecided about things. I was sick of the stops and starts in my life, tired of the uncertainties. I felt poisoned by the toxins that grudges and shame and bitterness had brewed in my mind and in my soul, and I cared little about being killed. It was preferable to living with this shit day in, day out.

I thought today's note was fake but couldn't be sure. Even if it was, until it was known why this guy was shooting jockeys, I might still be on his list.

I needed a meeting with McCarthy to find out who was coordinating the police work. Donachy had been killed in the south-west, Gilmour in the north. I hoped Sanders wasn't in charge.

Should I go to Ireland and dig into Donachy's background? What if that revealed an IRA connection too? Would I really want to go on? Looking for a madman who was acting alone was one thing; taking on a terrorist organisation was a completely different kettle of piranha.

No, I couldn't believe the IRA had anything to do with it. Leaving Bible notes was hardly typical of their operation. Sure, religion was in there somewhere, but this had to be an individual.

Shouldn't be that hard to find. I'd tracked down the last lot of villains for McCarthy, hadn't I? That thought brought Jackie to mind.

She'd been gone less than two weeks. The longer I waited before trying to contact her the more difficult it would be. Although I still missed her, I was kind of scared she'd want to return. I knew we'd start fighting again.

I tried McCarthy's number again. It rang out. I cursed and went to open a bottle of whiskey. The phone rang and I spun and grabbed the receiver.

'Eddie, aren't you coming to this party?' It was Hubert Barber. I'd forgotten about the Gold Cup winners' party.

'Sorry Mr Barber. I ran into a few unexpected, er, things after racing. Delayed me a bit.'

There was a pause. He said, 'Anything I should be worrying about?'

'No, not at all. Not in the least. Family stuff, you know.'

'That's a shame. I wanted to talk to you.'

'In a good way or a bad way?'

He chuckled. 'You should have been here, then you'd know!'

'Well, I'll see you at Wolverhampton tomorrow… If you still want me to ride for you that is?'

'I most certainly do. And I'd like you to ride for me next year.'

'Sure, 'I said, 'I'd be glad to.'

'I mean as my stable jockey. Under retainer.'

Stable jockey. Retainer. I'd misunderstood. The best I'd hoped for was that he'd still give me a few rides. A retainer brought security. It meant riding good horses, being able to turn down bad ones. And the strength of Barber's yard would bring a serious chance of becoming Champion again, in only my second year back.

He said, 'Eddie, what's the problem?'

'No problem,' I said, 'no problem, Mister Barber. Sorry I, I just didn't expect it. Of course I'm bloody delighted to accept! Brilliant!'

'We'll talk about money soon, get it tied up before the end of next week'

'Great.'

'Good man. We'll show that little bastard, Delaney.'

'So he's still got a problem with me riding for you?'

'Claims you're not to be trusted. Says Claude Beckman told him it's only a matter of time before you're involved in a major fuck-up.'

I said, 'Beckman's opinion's probably shared by about ninety per cent of his colleagues.'

'Well it's up to us to prove them all wrong then, eh?'

'It is, Hubert. We will.' My decision to stay involved in the hunt for Tommy's killer suddenly pricked my bubble of enthusiasm, reminding me that detective work and trouble tend to be close partners. 'Mister Barber,' I said, 'before you commit yourself there's something I'd better tell you.'

Chapter 25

On Friday morning I set off for Wolverhampton with Barber's job offer still intact. I'd told him about the note being delivered just before the Gold Cup, and he had accepted that I had to act to help the authorities find this guy. One proviso: if I got involved in anything that affected my riding, I was out.

I won the first race for Barber on a novice hurdler in which he himself had a half-share. He wasn't at the races. Maybe his Gold Cup hangover was too heavy.

My next ride, a handicap 'chaser called Hair Trigger, had an excellent chance and had been backed heavily by his owners, a four-man syndicate. My confidence was high and if he lost I knew it wouldn't be for want of a good ride.

Standing in the corner of the changing room, I pulled the blue and yellow jumper on. The neck was tight and when my head finally popped through, Con Layton was six feet away smiling at me.

I smoothed my hair back.

'Do you fancy yours here, Malloy?' he asked.

My first thought was to tell him to piss off, but I didn't need another confrontation. I had to keep a faultless discipline record or Delaney would be saying 'I told you so' to Barber.

'The connections expect him to run well,' I said.

'Ah and I wouldn't want to see them disappointed,' Layton said, still smiling, 'but there's a difference between running well and winning.'

A five-horse contest, a small track, it looked like Layton had one of his bent races in mind. Adjusting my breeches and boot-tops I said, 'Look, Layton, whatever your plans are, count me out.'

He sat down opposite, trying to reflect some friendship from his small pale eyes. 'Eddie, there's other things in life than riding winners. What about the little luxuries, the things you can't afford with your ten per cent?'

'I'm not interested. Go away.'

'Clarkie will win this and you'll be on the odds to a grand.'

'Fuck off.' I started checking my saddle and girths. His voice went very cold, 'Malloy, look at me.'

I ignored him.

'Look at me!'

I looked at his hard eyes. He said, 'Clarkie wins this race. You get paid.'

I stood up and stared down at him. 'I don't care who wins, but mine runs on his merits so you can shove your money up your arse.'

'Malloy, it's four against one. Your horse wants holding up so you'll be among us. If you're going out to do your best, then we'll do our best to make sure you come back in an ambulance.'

Hard as I fought to stay cool, he was making me angry. I took a couple of steps toward him and said, 'Look, what did I tell you last time? You or your cronies come near me during a race and I'll break your fucking legs. Now move!' I pushed past him and went out.

The size of the field gave me the advantage; dirty riding would be hard to disguise. My girths were being checked as the others circled at the start. Layton and Clark talked quietly. The lack of pre-start ribbing and the cowed expressions of the other two jockeys told me Layton had them in his pocket.

We lined up. Layton pulled down his goggles and smiled at me. 'It's make your mind up time, Malloy.'

I glared at him. 'You've had one warning, Layton, that's all you're getting.'

The starter pulled the handle. The elasticated tape flew up. We were off.

My first thoughts were to have plenty of daylight between myself and the rest, race wide of them. It should prompt the stewards to keep watching me.

Off a very slow pace, I raced on their right flank like a dog herding sheep, my horse enjoying himself free of hassle and flying divots. We just kept popping the fences nicely, behind and wide of the others.

Onto the second circuit and they quickened, hoping to draw me in, knowing if I wanted to scuttle their plans I'd have to join the race soon. Equally, if they continued to crawl along, they'd all still be full of running at the finish, making their intentions to fix the result obvious.

Two couldn't maintain the increased gallop beyond the third last, and I passed them in three strides. Up ahead, Layton and Clark were talking. I was closing fast but the wind carried their words out of earshot.

Mine, Hair Trigger, was travelling easily. We could pass them when we wanted. The problem was which route to take. If I went outside Layton he'd run wide, carrying me off-course. Up the inside and Clark would have me through the rails. Between them would be suicide.

But they were both coming under pressure and in the scramble of the first few desperate strides after landing over the second last, they moved apart, trying to tempt me through.

I kicked Hair Trigger forward as if to dive between them but at the last moment yanked his head to the left, almost running into the back of Clark's horse.

The first move panicked Clark into leaning right-handed, shutting the gap but leaving a big opening on the rails. Clark had bought the dummy and Hair Trigger's head slotted nicely into the space on his inside.

'Rails! You thick bastard!' Layton rasped. 'He's gone for the rails! Stop him now!'

Violently changing direction on half a ton of galloping horseflesh twice in a few seconds is a lot to ask, and although Clark's horse responded, I was away, leaving nothing to cushion him from colliding with the wing of the last fence.

The shattering crash, Clark's anguished cry and the horse's grunt made me wince. Layton's antics had cost him several lengths and his horse was struggling. He drew his whip and laid into the poor beast under him, more to relieve his anger than raise another challenge.

Hair Trigger jumped the last with the energy of a horse going to the start and galloped past the post well clear. As we pulled up, I thought briefly of Clark and how badly he might be hurt, then dismissed twinges of guilt. He'd brought it on himself.

As we walked in 'Stewards Enquiry' boomed from the loudspeakers and I suddenly felt a mixture of rage, elation and relief. Layton had been out to maim or kill me for the sake of a few thousand pounds. Should I take my revenge privately or try to get him warned off?

If I told the stewards he'd approached me with a bribe before the race, I was sure they'd view the video with a different perspective. Then again, Layton would deny it and accuse me of smearing him. No doubt the other three would back him up, though the way Clark crashed through that wing, he'd be giving no evidence today.

My memory echoed his scream as the horse came down, but sympathy was the last thing he deserved. Or maybe he did deserve some; Layton had probably bullied him into it. Layton might have had something on him, and on the others. As soon as you accepted a bribe, the first time you took part in a bent race, the moneyman had you in his pocket.

Why was it that Layton always came out without a scratch? Maybe a private comeuppance was just what he needed.

Chapter 26

Hair Trigger's owners were incensed that their horse and their cash had been endangered, and I had to hold the biggest of them off when he tried to reach Layton as he dismounted. 'It won't help in the Enquiry,' I told him. 'Calm down. I'll sort Layton out.'

As soon as we'd weighed in, Beckman came for us. 'The stewards' room, now!' he barked. We followed. Neither of us had spoken since weighing in. I'd decided to play it cool and let the video evidence speak for itself. Accusing Layton of attempted bribery without proof was pointless. It was important, too, to let Layton think he was out of his league with me, that nothing he tried would bother me. Then he'd slink back into his own division and stick to people who were afraid of him.

No waiting outside the stewards' room this time. Beckman, who looked pretty angry himself, marched us straight in and slammed the door, which earned him a reproving glance from the chairman of the stewards, Simon Fullmore.

I was glad to see Fullmore. He was known for being firm but fair with a sound knowledge of race riding. Narrow-faced with slate grey hair and blue eyes, he was pushing sixty but looked ten years younger.

Fullmore was flanked by Clarence Heaton, an amiable old buffer who hated disagreeing with anyone, and John Chalmers, a man I knew little about.

Beckman started by having a real go at me, accusing me of 'disgracefully dangerous riding'. The chairman shut him up and turned to Layton and me.

Layton told them I'd been cursing at him and Clark, threatening them throughout the race, telling them I'd had a big bet on my horse, knowing, as we all did, that jockeys are not allowed to bet. He said I'd barged into them deliberately, trying to bring them down.

I put my case calmly despite frequent interruptions from Layton and Beckman who glared at me throughout. This was the guy who'd tried to screw me at the Greenalls Enquiry and who'd been badmouthing me to Barber's owner, Delaney. What the hell had I done to upset him so much?

Chalmers asked me, 'Why would Layton and Clark want to stop you winning?'

'If you you had witnessed a changing-room conversation between Layton and me before the race, you would know, sir. But since I can't corroborate what was said there, it's probably best that I ask you to draw your own conclusions. I was riding the favourite and you may want to bear in mind the results of previous four and five horse races on the smaller tracks which Layton and Clark have ridden in.'

I sensed Layton wanted to say something, but he'd be wary of incriminating himself. The results were in the form book.

Chalmers said, 'Are you saying that Layton and Clark are responsible for fixing races?'

'I'm not sir, as I can't prove it. I'm sure the stewards are more than capable of interpreting the results of a series of races without any help from me.'

'Indeed, Malloy,' said Fullmore, 'but we're here to discuss an allegation of dangerous riding. Much as we might wish to take account of previous incidents', he glanced at Layton, 'we cannot. Have you anything else to say, Malloy?'

'I'd like to see the film, sir.'

'Layton?'

'Just to say, sir, that Malloy is a very dangerous man to be riding racehorses and I think he should be taught a lesson.'

Fullmore said, 'By the stewards?'

Layton spluttered, 'Of course, sir!'

Fullmore said, 'Well thank you for that advice. Mister Beckman, do you have any more questions?'

Beckman looked at me. 'Malloy, do you have any idea where Clark is now?'

'I should think he's on his way to hospital, Mister Beckman.'

Beckman said, 'That's right. He's going there for treatment to a broken arm, concussion and possible internal injuries.'

I said, 'Some people only learn from experience.'

He didn't care for that. 'You don't consider yourself responsible in any way?'

'Not in the least.'

'Listen, Malloy-'

Fullmore intervened. 'Gentlemen, I think it best if we adjourn for the moment to watch the film of the race. Malloy, Layton, the stewards will view the race in private first. Please wait outside.'

Layton followed me out and closed the door. He looked at me with his sly little half-smile. 'When are you goin' to learn your lesson, Malloy?'

'When will you learn yours? You're never going to get a result out of me and you'll never get one from the stewards. They all know you're bent.'

'We'll see,' he said.

'And I'll tell you another thing, Layton, I'll spell it out since you're too thick to take the hints. You don't scare me. I've gone through more shit in the last five years than you've ever seen, and if you think I'm going to let a prick like you fuck things up, you've got a lot to learn. Stick to playing with the second-raters and stay out of my way.'

He smiled. 'Ah, you've a lot to learn yourself, Malloy.'

We sat silent until they called us in five minutes later. Beckman's florid face, his white-knuckled grip on his notebook, told me all I wanted to know.

Fullmore spoke. 'We have looked at the race and the incident in question a number of times, and have come to the conclusion that no blame attaches to Malloy. Clark appeared reckless, and, as such, was the architect of his own problems. You, Layton, also appeared careless in allowing your horse to bump Clark's and you'll be suspended from riding for a period of three days from the twenty-fourth of March.'

Fullmore continued, 'The result stands, but before you go, gentlemen, it is perhaps appropriate to warn you that the stewards will be taking a particularly keen interest in future races where you are opposing each other.'

I said, 'Thank you, sir,' then glanced at Beckman, whose returned stare was hard and hateful. You'd have thought either Clark was his brother or that Beckman was in league with Layton and had just lost a fortune.

My mount in the last finished second, rounding off a nice day. I showered and changed and headed for a restaurant for a celebratory meal with the owners of Hair Trigger. They were a decent bunch. I found myself laughing with them and, on the drive home, realized I'd been behaving like a normal human being for an hour. Some people, with their lack of intensity, their capacity for easy relaxation, intrigued me at times.

The Lodge was in total darkness, my headlights swinging on the windows as I bounced along the drive. Car lights off, I reached into the glove compartment for my flashlight and clicked it on, following its narrow beam to the door.

I juggled my keys, and found the main one. I clicked the hall light switch. Nothing. No popping bulb. I stepped into the living room and reached for the switch there. Clicked it. Darkness. Shit!

I went to the cupboard under the stairs, my beam searching for the main fusebox. There was a sudden strange smell. Sweet. Pungent. The beam found the box. Someone had turned the power off. I backed out quickly. Sweet smell stronger. A cold metal tube pressed against my neck. Something clamped on my mouth and nose. The flashlight tumbled...rolled noisily along the hall...shadows loomed. Odour overpowering now. Consciousness going. Slumping... Sweet air... Ether... Jesus Christ. I'm dead.

Chapter 27

The cold woke me. Shivering. Freezing. Pounding headache. The wind blew hard outside. Every time it gusted, an icy draught cut a line down my spine. I lay on my side. My shirt must have ridden up out of my trousers. I reached to pull it down. Nothing there. No clothes. Naked.

Consciousness returning, making me feel even colder. I was lying on damp wood. There was something round my neck, something on my face. I reached up. A heavy chain, a hood sewn into the steel links. I followed the chain with my fingers. Two feet from me it looped around a big square piece of timber, the leg of a table, a bench maybe. A fat padlock clasped the links.

I tried to lie on my back but the chain tightened, stopping me. I edged closer to the padlock and tried again. Made it this time, though something crunched below my left buttock and jagged my flesh. Easing my hips up, I reached slowly. It came away in my hand, cold and slimy with brittle shards. I flicked the dead snail from my fingers and heard it stick to the wall.

I was in an outhouse or a shed, or an old garage; not a stable, no stable smell. Total darkness. Faint tang of creosote and dampness. Sweet and sour odour of dying vegetation.

Dreadful headache. Nausea. The worst of hangovers.

I checked my limbs, flexed my arms and legs, wrists and ankles, fingers and toes, felt my face and skull through the rough cloth hood, reached hesitantly and hopefully between my legs; everything still there. Chilled to the bone, but from what I could tell in the dark, healthy, apart from the headache, which was of hammering intensity.

Must have been the ether. No bumps on the head. No signs of him having hit me.

The wind gusted again sending an icy slice down my side. My teeth chattered. I had to get off the floor. Turning slowly in the direction of the padlock, I lay on my front. Tried pushing myself onto my knees but the chain was anchored low. I felt for where it looped round the wood - very little play but I began working it upward. The strain on my shoulder muscle meant I had to stop and rest every minute or so, but eventually I made it to my hands and knees. The exertion warmed my head inside the hood. The rest of me shivered.

I rested.

As full consciousness returned, it scared me into immobility. Maybe I could lift the bench and free myself. Out there in the darkness there might be a hammer, a chisel, a crowbar, something within reach to break the chain links.

But I was afraid to stretch out and feel for them in case nothing was there, terrified to haul at the bench for fear it wouldn't move. Then, there would be no escape. No survival. I would be here when he came in with the gun.

A condemned man now, the events of the past two weeks loomed in my mind, leaving just the rest of my life to flash before me.

I'd never thought of facing death anywhere but on the racecourse. I couldn't come to terms with the prospect of dying naked and alone in a bitterly cold outhouse. There had to be some way out.

Running my hand up the thick timber, I felt the horizontal section where it stopped. I was chained to a bench of some sort. A heavy workbench or an old butcher's block. If I could lift it and slip the chain clear of the leg… I ran my hands downward again. The leg was bolted to the floor through metal brackets.

I worked on the loop, pushing it upwards until I could get to my feet. Got there. Couldn't straighten because of the chain, but at least I was off the floor. I stood hunched, draught cutting my ankles.

I eased my head down to rest it, and felt along the bench surface. There might be tools around. But all that my fingers found was a big steel vice, too far away, impossible to get the chain into it.

Pushing toward the back I worked as far up the wall as I could, which was only a couple of feet…nothing. Resting my forearms on the bench, I stretched my right foot out, feeling the floor with my toes. My foot found some sackcloth and I dragged it slowly within finger reach, shook it hard to clear insects and debris, and pulled it across my shoulders. It was damp, but I couldn't be any colder than I was, so it was worth wearing for a few minutes to see if it improved things. If it didn't I would be in danger of hypothermia.

Hypothermia...I'd have to stay alive long enough to catch it.

Where was I? Where was he? Why hadn't he finished me off like Gilmour and Donachy? Why the hood? If he planned to kill me, what did he care if I saw his face?

The little straw-clutcher inside me reached out...was this a lesson, a reminder that I shouldn't have ignored his note? Maybe he'd just hold me for a couple of days then let me go. Or keep me locked up until he'd finished the killing.

Shit, what about my rides at Chepstow tomorrow? What day was it? He'd got me on Friday evening; I was assuming this was somewhere in the early hours of Saturday morning, but there was no way of telling. I didn't know how long I'd been unconscious. I couldn't tell if it was day or night. It could be Sunday or even Monday. Bloody hell, Barber would be cursing me. Delaney would be in his element.

This was ridiculous. What was I worried about? I probably wouldn't be seeing Barber or anyone else again.

Even Lisa. She was supposed to call me on Saturday.

I should have told her my plans, rang her every night to tell her my movements, warn her that if I disappeared suddenly, it wouldn't be through choice. Maybe she couldn't have done much to help find me, but at least she'd know I hadn't let her down. And she could have told Barber I hadn't let him down either.

Uncontrollable shivering took me, vibrating the headache against the walls of my skull.

Still hunched, leaning my hooded head on my arms, I tried to jog lightly on the spot in an attempt to get warm. It was tedious and tiring, but it began to work. I kept it up until my calf muscles burned and made me forget my headache for a minute. Eventually I warmed from freezing to plain bloody cold.

I don't know how long I kept it up. All sense of time faded. My mind became separate from my body, laughed at it jogging stupidly, going nowhere. Look at that fool, Malloy running pathetically, half naked, wearing that silly hood and sackcloth. I mocked myself cruelly and enjoyed it. All my thoughts seemed pleasant. The pain went away. So did the chill, and I ran myself into an exhausted trance.

Chapter 28

I thought I heard a key click. Couldn't be sure.

Awake, slumped on the floor against the bench leg. Or was I? Maybe I was dreaming or still hallucinating…daylight through the hood. Door opening. Closing. Four footsteps. Big fingers on my back, gripping my sides, turning me onto my hands and knees. I submit easily. No fight. Must be a dream. Someone pulls the sackcloth off my shoulders. A hand grasps my hair through the hood, pulling my head up and back…chain tightening. Agony. No dream. Don't think so…

…Something pushed through my legs. Long and thin. Between my balls and thigh. Like a pencil high in my crotch. Drawing it back… a foot, two feet, three. Leather. Yes, leather. Moving slowly. A tab catches me, cuts into my penis. A tab… a flap. A leather flap. A riding whip. That's it, a… aahhh… aahhh, hitting me now. My back. Stinging. No dream.

No dream.

The whip bit into my back, my shoulders, thighs, buttocks; I cried out. He hit faster, harder, grunting with the effort, no aim, any piece of skin. My arms and legs gave way and I crumpled onto my stomach. He thrashed, grunting, the leather-covered whalebone singing through the air then smacking tightly into my flesh. I was yelping, almost squealing. I tried to stuff loose cloth from the hood into my mouth so I could bite it. Didn't make it. Tried to turn. To fight. Couldn't. Could hear him. Breathing hard. Trickles from my wounds warm on my freezing skin. Blood. And pain. And blood and pain and grunts and whacks and pants and cuts and screams…

A noise woke me. A voice. It was dark again. Was I awake? The pain was there. What was the voice saying? Same thing. Over and over. What was it?

"Work out your own salvation with fear and trembling." "Work out your own salvation with fear and trembling" "Work out…"

It was on tape. On a loop. Same thing. Deep, forced sound. Which part of the Bible was it from?

Who cares?

I settled on my front, joints and muscles stiff and sore, but scared to move. The burning throb in my back was worse. My neck was raw from the chain. My head pounded. My gut ached from hunger.

But I was alive. Pain, glorious pain, told me he hadn't killed me.

Outside, the wind had died down. The draught chilling my right side was steady. Trying to relieve the stiffness I moved a couple of inches to the left and flinched as I felt a cut creak open, the wound edges tearing themselves slowly apart.

I lay still, panting, waiting for that eruption of pain to subside to bubbling point along with the rest. I tried to think what to do. Something positive. I couldn't. Nothing came.

The loop ran: 'Work out your own salvation with fear and trembling.'

I'm trying. Honest to God, I'm trying.

Maybe if I could get to my feet again.

Huh? Big laugh. As much chance of that as flying.

Must try.

I sucked the hood, caught some cloth between my teeth and bit down. Forced my arms up under my face. Heard the dried blood cracking and parting on my shoulders, letting the pain weep through the wounds. Felt the cold, sticking, oozing wound under my right buttock as I drew my leg up. I got as far as my hands and knees, breathing hard through my nose, blubbering through the snot, sweating in the hood, eyes crushed closed, trying not to faint with the agony, battling to control my movements, my thoughts, block out the taped voice taking over my mind…I bit through the cloth and passed out again.

Darkness when I woke. Pain still there. Tape playing. Same words. Interminably. Filling my head. Where was it, the player? On the floor somewhere. By my feet. Near the door. I stretched a leg slowly toward the sound. Felt the plastic casing with my toe, the handle. I kicked.

Pain-burst.

The machine fell over. The voice stopped. The tape was off. In its place some music. Then a terrible screeching interference. Must have knocked it to radio. Local station, maybe. Find out where I am. Searing white noise. Worst I've known. Wish I'd left the tape on.

Blacked out again.

It was daylight when he returned. I didn't hear the door open or his footsteps. Only knew he was there when he switched the radio off and there was silence.

Heard him breathe.

Would he speak?

No. No words. Just a sound. A quiet sound. Swish. Swish. Swish. The deadly singing of the whip.

Terror grabbed my gut. A pathetic groan of fear and shame escaped my throat, making me rage at this man who'd reduced me to a petrified child. 'Who are you?' I asked, a desperate plea, raising more anger, at myself, my fear and humiliation. 'Who are you?!' I screamed it this time.

No answer.

Guessing where he'd be, I kicked out grunting through the searing ache and effort in a weak attempt to fight him, to show him he hadn't beaten me.

My body turned as I lashed out, the back wounds grinding splinters from the floor. Before I could turn onto my stomach again, he whipped me twice on the chest and groin.

I stifled a scream, determined to go out with some dignity.

I cringed, anticipating the next blow, heard him stretch as he raised the whip then jerked silently as it bit like a red-hot saw blade. I waited for the onslaught.

It didn't come.

Just the swishing noise close to my ear. The stretch as he raised it…no hits. The swish again. Then three heavy horrific smacks in quick succession.

I lay praying, begging God to make him stop but all the time…swish… waiting…for the next one.

He would hit me once in two minutes then twice in ten seconds. The agony of not knowing when the next stroke would come was worse than the blow itself. Then, like last time, the grunting started.

Hitting faster. Grunting to a sexual intensity.

Now the frenzy. Almost a relief. No more teasing. No more waiting. Exquisite pain. Quickly bringing blessed unconsciousness.

Chapter 29

I woke up in heaven. Or that's what I thought. No pain. Warm bed. No voices. No whips. Just quiet. A pleasant, groggy peace.

A nurse came. A beautiful nurse who smiled like my mother.

'You're awake,' she said.

'I think so.'

'Somebody did a right number on you!'

Liverpool accent.

'Afraid so.' I said.

'What did you do to upset him?'

'Wish I knew.'

She hadn't stopped smiling. 'Try and get some more sleep. If the pain comes back, I'll give you something for it.'

'Where am I?'

'Hereford General Hospital.'

'How did I get here?'

'The ambulance brought you in early this morning. Somebody found you in the car park of the local supermarket…without a car, and without much else either.'

'What day is it?'

'Monday.'

'What date?'

'Eighteenth of March.'

'Oh shit.'

'What's wrong?'

'I need to make a phone call.'

'I'll bring you the phone trolley.'

The nurse lent me some money for the call. When I got through Mac said, 'Lots of people looking for you, Eddie. Where've you been?'

I told him where I was and he started firing questions. I said, 'Come and get me out of here and I'll tell you what happened.'

He agreed. And I asked him to bring a few things. 'Mac, have you seen Barber?'

'Saw him at Chepstow on Saturday.'

'Was he mad?'

'About you going missing?'

'Yeah.'

'Well he was before racing, but he seemed a bit happier afterwards. Both his runners won.'

'Oh no! Who rode them?'

'Jimmy Crane. Two bloody good performances. Don't want to depress you, Eddie, but I think you might be out of a job.'

An hour later, much of the pain was back. I'd refused more morphine, settling for some tablets, so my head would be clear enough to let me ride at Nottingham next day.

I'd spoken to Barber. When I told him I was ringing from a hospital pay-phone, he said he'd best ring me because we needed to have a 'long talk'.

I didn't tell the full story, only enough to get his sympathy. If I'd told him how badly injured I was, there's no way he would have asked me to ride so soon. I said I'd give him all the details when we met at Nottingham. He said Delaney was stirring things up again, and that if anything else happened to stop me riding, the job offer would be withdrawn.

After speaking to him, I told the ward sister I planned to discharge myself as soon as McCarthy arrived with some clothes and money. She wasn't pleased. Five minutes later, a doctor appeared with some advice.

His name tag said Doctor Mason. He was square-faced and bearded with light brown hair and angry-looking eyes 'I really don't think it would be wise of you to voluntarily remove yourself from hospital care, Mister Malloy.'

'I wouldn't argue with you, Doctor, I'm sure it's pretty unwise myself, but needs must when the devil drives and all that.'

'You do realize that the hospital cannot accept responsibility for any deterioration in your condition should you leave here without our approval?'

'I do.'

Like wedding vows in the marriage to my career.

'May I ask why you're so anxious to discharge yourself?'

'I need to be back at work tomorrow.'

'No job is that important, Mister Malloy.'

'This one is.'

'What do you do for a living?'

'I ride horses.'

'What sort of horses?'

'Mostly slow ones, unfortunately.'

He stared at me. 'You're not a jockey?'

'I know a few people who'd agree with you, there.'

'Are you telling me that, in your condition, you plan to ride racehorses tomorrow?'

'Over jumps.'

He sagged and sat on the end of the bed. 'You're in the wrong hospital, Mister Malloy, you want certifying.'

I nodded. 'I know a few people who'd agree with you there, too.'

'Seriously,' he said, 'do you know how many stitches we put in those wounds this morning?'

'The nurse said sixty-two.'

He nodded in confirmation, gravely waiting for it to strike home. I said, 'I hope they're flexible ones.'

He wasn't amused. 'Mister Malloy, if you take a fall, you are looking at permanent severe scarring at best. At worst, you could get blood poisoning so bad it could kill you.'

'I'll be careful.'

He looked at me for a while then said, 'Your flippancy doesn't impress me, you know. I don't see your attitude as brave. It's foolish.'

'I told you, Doc, I agree with you. I'm not trying to impress anybody. Look, it's a long story. It's the story of my bloody life and if I had time to tell you it.... look, what I'm saying is, if you knew what was behind it all you'd probably understand why I've got to ride tomorrow.'

He shook his head slowly. 'I doubt it. Whatever it is it will be downright bloody stupid and irresponsible of you to ride in a horse-race tomorrow.'

'I'm sorry, Doctor, that's the way it is. It's my life.'

'Oh it's your life all right, but when you're back lying in hospital again tomorrow night as you undoubtedly will be, it's my colleagues and I who have to patch you up again, which can be just a little bit galling. And it's the man in the street, the taxpayer, a man who has a humdrum job and an average wage who'll be paying for you to lie in that bed. A bed, incidentally, which you will probably be depriving someone else of. Someone who might have been suffering on an NHS waiting list for some considerable time. Think on that, Mister Malloy!' And he set off down the ward stopping after five paces, brows like storm clouds. 'Have the police been to interview you yet?'

I shook my head.

'I'll ring them again and remind them. Maybe they can talk some bloody sense into you!'

He went away, leaving me feeling very small indeed.

At 9 p.m., along with McCarthy, came Kavanagh and Miller. Kavanagh, unbuttoning his raincoat, smiled and said, 'Long time no see, Eddie.'

I looked at him. 'Yeah, I missed you.'

'Me too,' he said.

I glared at McCarthy. He said, 'I thought it best to call Inspector Sanders since you're the first, uh, survivor.'

'And witness,' Kavanagh added.

I said to Kavanagh, 'Isn't this out of your patch?'

'Special arrangement with the Hereford lads.'

Miller, more satanic looking than usual in black coat and matching polo neck, spoke from the bottom of the bed, 'We told them you were a difficult guy to deal with.'

I nodded. It hurt. 'The doctor will confirm that,' I said.

'So, what's the story?' Kavanagh asked.

'Look, can't it wait? I'm tired and sore and it's a long way home.'

Kavanagh said, 'You're not going home tonight?'

'I've been through all this with the doctor. He's left me in no doubt that I'm a silly, selfish bastard. He's right. You're right. Everybody who disagrees with me is right. I'm not arguing. But I am going home tonight, and tomorrow I'm riding two horses at Nottingham for Hubert Barber. It might kill me but I'm doing it. I hope I've made myself absolutely clear because I'm not talking about it anymore.'

'Oh,' Kavanagh said, 'we are a bit tired and emotional.'

I turned to Mac. 'Did you bring some gear?'

He nodded. 'But no way will it fit you.'

'It's just for the journey.'

He put a leather hold-all on the end of the bed, took out a pair of brown corduroys, held them up and said, 'You could probably get into one leg of them.'

Kavanagh chortled, 'Failing that, you can always blow them up and hire them out as a bouncy castle.'

Miller laughed. First time I'd heard him. A girlish giggle. McCarthy was embarrassed. He said, 'They're far too big for me now too since I started my diet!'

'For God's sake,' I said, 'we'll be here all night. Just leave me the bag and draw the screens so I can get changed.'

Kavanagh's face hardened. 'We need to talk to you Malloy.'

I struggled to push myself upright. Half-grunting, I said, 'I know you need to talk to me, Kavanagh. I'm going home. Either follow us or come and see me after racing at Nottingham tomorrow. Even better, why don't you travel with me in Mac's car and you can do all your questioning on the way over? Help take my mind off the bumpy roads.'

He looked at McCarthy. 'That okay with you?'

Mac shrugged. 'Makes no difference.'

They left me to get changed, an exercise which made me think again about leaving hospital. Though my shoulders, back and thighs were heavily strapped and dressed I could feel the wounds pulling and straining at the stitches. Sweating and swearing, starting and stopping, I eventually got myself into Mac's old cords, a tee-shirt and a jumper.

There was no mirror, but I felt as though I'd lived quite comfortably in these clothes then somebody forgot to feed me for three years. Too sore to open the curtains, I slipped through a gap and shuffled up the ward in a pair of old training shoes. Eyes swiveled from pillow height on either side as the other patients watched me weave along the floor, stooped like some demented hunchback, trying to hold the trousers tight at the waist without them touching my wounds.

I signed the discharge papers and, flanked by my visitors, started slowly down the long corridor, with them hoping silently, no doubt, that they wouldn't meet anyone they knew and have to explain what they were doing with this ragged shambling lunatic.

Chapter 30

Mac drove. Kavanagh slid in with me. Thankfully, Mac had remembered to pack the thick blanket I'd asked for to help pad my wounds on the journey. The pain itself was a throbbing pad, and when we hit a bad piece of road I had to stifle a moan. Mac would say sorry and I'd say don't worry.

I was sweating again, and each time we passed under a street-lamp the orange light showed Kavanagh my twisted glistening face. 'You okay?'

I nodded, not trusting my ears any more to keep me from crying once they heard how pathetic my voice sounded. Kavanagh said, 'I'll wait until we hit the motorway, before I ask you any questions.'

Jaw muscles clenched, I thanked him with my eyes, wondering if I'd stay conscious long enough to reach the motorway. I did and the smooth surface made things, if not painless, a good deal easier. Kavanagh looked at me. 'Can we talk now?' he asked.

I nodded. He said, 'Mister McCarthy said the guy caught you at home, that right?'

'Yes.'

'Friday night?'

'Yes.'

'How did he get in?'

'I don't know. I'd just got home. There were no lights. I thought a fuse had blown, but when I went to check I saw the power had been switched off at the mains. Then, like, all at once I smelt the ether and felt a gun in my neck and a pad being clamped over my mouth. He was strong.'

'Big?'

'I think so.'

'He say anything?'

'No.'

'Did you get a look at him?'

'He put a hood on me, tied it to a chain collar.' I swallowed, feeling a mild panic.

Kavanagh said, 'How long were you unconscious?'

'I don't know. I woke up freezing cold, bollock naked…something made me think it was the early hours of Saturday morning but I couldn't be sure.'

'Tied up?'

'Chained by the neck to the leg of a bench or a heavy table. Somewhere outside, an outhouse, a shed, or an old garage, maybe.'

'You hear any sounds? Traffic? Trains? Aircraft?'

'Nothing like that, though I was unconscious a lot of the time so there might have been. Just small animal noises, mice, birds and the smell of rotting vegetation. I remember that, you know that sort of sweet sickly smell?'

Kavanagh nodded, though I could see he was clueless. 'Somewhere in the country, I'd guess,' I said.

'Why'd he dump you in a car park in the centre of Hereford, then? He could easily have been spotted. Why not on a country lane? A field? An old barn?'

'Maybe he didn't want to shit too close to his nest.'

'The countryside's a big place, Eddie.'

'Look, I don't know why he didn't dump me, as you put it, somewhere else, I just don't know!'

'Okay, okay, no problem. When did he start on you with the whip?'

The burst of fear I felt when he mentioned it took me by surprise. I swallowed hard. My mouth dried up. I had to detach myself from the memory of it before I could tell him about the whippings. And about the tape loop.

'What did it say?' McCarthy asked.

'It said, "Work out your own salvation with fear and trembling."'

Mac said, 'Is that from the Bible?'

'It's worth checking,' Kavanagh said, then, 'We've got a real weird bastard here. What was the voice on the tape like? Would you recognize it again?'

'Yes, but it wouldn't count for anything, it was one of those put-on voices, like an impersonation of the devil, deep and sort of growly at the back of your throat. Something you'd do to scare the kids.'

Kavanagh said, 'And the guy himself never spoke once?'

'Not a word. Just grunts. He grunted hard and fast when he was really going at me, just before I passed out each time. I couldn't make up my mind whether it was exertion that was making him grunt, I mean, or, well, it sounded almost sexual.'

'A deviant,' Kavanagh said.

'Look, I'm just telling you the impression it left on me, which might not be all that dependable on account of me thinking I was being beaten to death. You could hardly say I was of sound mind at that particular point.'

Kavanagh nodded slowly and was quiet for a while. Then he said, 'Know what? I don't think this is our man.'

Mac said, 'He's got to be! Exact same modus operandi as Gilmour and Donachy. The note, the ether, the biblical stuff. Nobody else could have known about that. None of it's been released to the press, has it?'

Kavanagh said it hadn't. McCarthy asked me, 'Have you mentioned it to anyone, Eddie?'

'Not a soul.'

'Well,' McCarthy said, 'the only person I've told is my boss, who probably told the senior steward. So unless it's one of those two beating the shit out of you over the weekend then it's got to have been our man.'

Kavanagh said, 'A major difference in the guy's m.o. from Gilmour and Donachy...he didn't break Malloy's leg and put a bullet through the middle of his forehead.'

'There must be a reason for that,' McCarthy said.

'Yeah,' Kavanagh said, 'the reason is it's not our man.'

McCarthy said, 'No I just can't agree with you. What do you think, Eddie?'

'I'll tell you one thing, when that ether pad went over my mouth and I remembered Gilmour and Donachy, I thought it was him all right! I thought I'd breathed my last.'

Kavanagh asked, 'You still think it's him?'

'I don't know. Did I tell you about the threat I received before the Gold Cup?' They looked mystified. 'The note?' I prompted. Nothing. Obviously I'd forgotten to mention it. I filled in the details.

Kavanagh was angry because I hadn't called them as soon as I'd read it. I was too sore and weary to argue, but we discussed the note and none of us could make up our minds whether it was connected with the murders, my abduction or anything else. Things were becoming more confusing.

Mac favoured the theory that it had been the killer who'd kidnapped me.

Kavanagh shook his head. 'Nah, sorry, but it just doesn't fit.' He looked at Mac, catching his eyes in the rear-view mirror. 'Do me a favour, Mister McCarthy, and just check with your boss and the senior steward if you can, if they've mentioned the notes or the ether to anyone else.'

Mac said, 'I'm sure they won't have.'

'I'd be grateful if you'd check, all the same.'

I couldn't see Mac's lips in the mirror, but his eyes told me they'd be pursed.

Kavanagh asked Mac to stop at a service station. Miller followed us in and Kavanagh transferred to his car, promising he'd send the forensic boys to the Lodge in the morning to pick up the Cheltenham note, and check the place over. He warned us to disturb as little as possible when we got back.

It was dark when we drew up at the Lodge. I cursed as I remembered I had no key, but Mac clicked the thumb-latch and the door, undisturbed since Friday night, creaked open.

My stomach turned over; I had to steel myself to follow Mac in. I told him where the mains box was and he fumbled his way forward, leaving me holding on to the door jamb in the blackness.

A heavy click then flaring lights blinding me. I narrowed my eyes and looked around. Nothing disturbed. Bag on the floor where I'd dropped it. No signs of a struggle. Then again, I hadn't put up much of one.

It was cold. Mac built a fire and offered to make tea. I settled for a glass of water and some painkillers. Mac had agreed to spend the night in the Lodge. It was too far to drive to Lambourn, I suggested, but the real reason was that the memory of Friday made me scared. I needed someone with me.

Mac searched all the rooms and found a broken window at the side.

He got me upstairs and helped me undress. I was grateful for that and for his company.

He offered to sleep in the chair by the bed but he'd only have nagged me about wanting to ride next day so I sent him to his own room, took a sedative and slept restlessly until 8 a.m.

Chapter 31

Along with my riding gear, I packed strong painkillers, determined not to take any until just before my first mount. After half an hour's driving I was so sore I couldn't lean against the soft velour.

I stopped, adjusted the seat and set off again perched on the edge, grimacing and sweating like a chronic constipation case. My pig-headed self was insisting I ride today, while my logical self laughed uproariously at the absurdity of the idea.

Nottingham racecourse is a flat, fair course with no tricky fences. I reckoned I had a good chance of getting Barber's two horses home safely; maybe not in front but in one piece.

If I did have a fall, I hoped it would be soft. A fall I'd get up and walk away from, one which wouldn't make the course doctor want to examine me. If he saw the state of my skin he'd ground me until it healed, and once I was grounded I was out of a job.

Standing by the weighing room I sipped black tea and watched my hot breath mist the air. From the top of my spine to the lowest wound on my right calf the soreness was pulsing now and I was trying to take my mind off it.

Things around the weighing room were getting busier; most of the jockeys and valets had arrived and I set about planning the best way to hide my injuries from them.

Tipping the last half-inch of tea onto the grass I turned to go inside when I heard Barber's voice.

'Eddie!'

Slowly I did an about-face and saw him hobbling toward me, his over-long white hair billowing like hovercraft skirts beneath his cap.

He looked anxious. I cranked up what I hoped was a disarming smile.

He was red-faced, puffing, unbuttoning his long army coat to let the cooling wind in. 'You okay?' I asked.

'Put in a bad weekend, Eddie, a bad weekend.'

I waited.

He went on. 'I feel as if I've been fighting battles for you for years rather than bloody weeks and you're never there to support me. Delaney's been mouthing off again. He's ringing round my other owners. They know what he's like, which is lucky for you, but some of them are beginning to question my judgement.'

Up until now I'd been prepared to wing it, give Barber enough bullshit to try to get his commitment again, but I saw in his face hurt and puzzlement that I should keep letting him down. It was hardly my fault but Barber wasn't to know that.

It came home to me that he had a life too, a career which no doubt meant as much to him as mine did to me. I was helping wash his down the tubes along with my own.

A combination of guilt and the brutal pain pushed me into a full confession. We went and sat by the empty parade ring and I told him exactly what had happened over the weekend, along with most of the other stuff, though with Kavanagh's warning in mind I didn't mention the notes or the ether.

As I talked I watched the trainer's expression change down through aggravation, wonderment and relief, to sympathy.

He said, 'Jesus, Eddie, I knew there had to be good reasons. I knew you wouldn't just have let me down.'

'It's the last thing I'd want to do. Look, you'd better book someone else for these two of yours today.'

'You're feeling that bad?'

I nodded. 'I could just about stay on them, I think, but there's no way I could give them a proper ride. I've messed you about long enough, Mister Barber, you've got yourself and your owners to think about.'

The relief in his eyes, the acknowledgement that he needn't argue me out of it, told me I'd done the right thing.

He gently squeezed my arm. 'Take some time to recover, Eddie, I'll keep the job open. How long do you think before you heal?'

'A week maybe, I don't know.'

'No problem. A week, two weeks, whatever, don't worry.'

'Thanks, Hubert.'

I'd no doubt he meant it, but the man who said a week's a long time in politics ought to be told it can be a bloody eternity in racing. In the course of a week, Barber might have twenty runners. If whoever took my place rode a few winners, Barber would be under strong pressure from his owners to keep the new guy on.

He was still holding my arm, looking sympathetic. I smiled, 'Go and book someone for those two horses, Mister Barber, or you'll be too late.'

'Right. Fine.' He stood up, glad to be escaping. 'Let me know if there's anything I can do, Eddie. Keep in touch.'

I sat still, the pain fading as the realization of what I'd done sunk in. Unless Barber's yard suddenly hit a bad patch, I'd probably just offered my resignation as stable jockey.

Back to square one. And what a bloody lonely square it would be.

I felt better having come clean with Barber, but even that satisfaction was tainted with the knowledge that by race time I wouldn't have been able to get into the saddle anyway. As the day had worn on, the pain had worsened, bringing cold sweats at visions of someone back slapping to wish me luck or congratulate me.

Slowly, I stood up. What the hell, I was alive, still breathing. Square one wasn't exactly unfamiliar territory. I'd survive.

Wearily, achingly, I set off to pick up my kit, swallow some painkillers and try to gee myself up for the drive. My skin creaked and stung as I walked and I promised it two days of me lying motionless on my front if only it would ease off.

I told my valet I wasn't feeling too good. He helped me get my stuff together and I thanked him by deftly dodging his sympathetic hand aimed at my shoulder. Mumbling something about a jarred collarbone, I apologised and headed for the door. As I reached to open it, someone came through from the other side. It was the course doctor. He was in a hurry.

'Sorry!' he said as he rushed past then, stopping quickly, 'Eddie! You're the man I'm looking for.'

I knew Doctor Donnelly well enough to recognize his suspicious look. I had a brief stab at a defence, 'Sorry, Doc, but I was off home... can it wait?'

He half-smiled. 'Just a few minutes of your time, Edward.'

I walked alongside the doctor to the ambulance room. He had hollow cheeks and a wide, light brown moustache stained in the centre by nicotine. He spoke. 'Unlike you to leave early, not feeling well?'

'Felt better.' I was about to plead flu but realized it was hopeless.
'Where are you living now?' he asked.
'Leicester. Henry Kravitz's old place.'
'God, I haven't seen Henry for ages, how is he?'
'Haven't seen him myself for a while.'

We went into the warm room, all drab greens and browns rather than hospital whites, but the smells were there. Doctor Donnelly closed the door.

'Sit down,' he said.

Trying to hide the pain, I lowered myself into a hard plastic chair, resting on the edge. He looked at me. 'Sit back, Eddie, relax.'

I looked at him. 'All right, Doc, who told you?'
'That's not important.'
'It is to me.'
'It's for your own good, Eddie.'
'I know what's for my own good, that's why I'm taking a couple of days off.'
'From what I've heard you might need longer.'

He sat comfortably, legs crossed, arms folded, honest brown eyes waiting for my next weak offering.

'I'll be okay in a day or two,' I said.
'You sure?'
'Positive.'
'You won't mind if I take a look then?'
'Doc, listen-'
'Eddie,' his voice softened, 'it's my job. Your job is riding horses, mine is trying to make sure you don't kill yourself in the process. Jockeys are not of sound mind. You know that and I know that. Now, I have to take a look at your back.'

I hung my head, rubbed my eyes, stared at the floor. 'I don't think I can get my shirt off.' I said quietly.

'I'll help you.'

I'd put on two shirts in case blood leaked from the bandages. It had, in big patches on both shirts and through to my sweater. After calling me a crazy, crazy bastard several times, he managed, with the help of a pain killing jab, to change my dressings.

Then he took my medical book and stood me down for fourteen days, no argument. 'Get a lot of rest, make sure the dressings are changed every forty-eight hours, and come and see me in two weeks.'

The Grand National was in two weeks. Not that I was likely to be offered a ride. Not now.

'Doc, do me a favour, tell me who reported me?'

He shook his head. 'Someone who obviously had your best interests at heart.'

'I doubt it.'

'Some day you'll be grateful.'

The pain killer got me home without me having to stop. I parked, and the wind across the flat land ripped the car door open as I sprung the catch, then cut icily through my sweater as I made for the door.

The identity of Doctor Donnelly's informer had bugged me throughout the drive, and it still gnawed as I clumsily built a fire, piling it high in case I couldn't move too well later.

It had to be the doctor at Hereford Hospital, he'd been angry enough with me. I washed up, made coffee and rang him. He remembered me, said he was glad I'd been stood down but denied contacting the racecourse doctor: 'I've better things to do with my time than continuing to care for patients who have foolishly discharged themselves.'

The other man who'd crossed my mind was Barber. Although I'd asked him to keep it quiet, maybe he'd let it slip. If not, that left McCarthy and the two cops; they were the only others who knew, but I couldn't see a motive for them other than Miller's obvious dislike of me.

I rang McCarthy's office. He told me he hadn't spoken to the doctor or anyone else.

I raised Kavanagh next. He'd mentioned my injuries to nobody, nor had Miller to the best of his knowledge though he'd check.

I said, 'Barber's the only other person I've told. If he didn't report me there's only one more guy who knew the state my back was in.'

I rang the racecourse and managed to speak to Barber just before he left.

'How'd your horses do?' I asked, not sure if I wanted to hear the answer.

'Stuffed, both of them.'

'Sorry to hear it for your sake, Mister Barber, though I can't say I am for mine.'

'At least you're honest.'

'Mister Barber, did you speak to anybody today about, about my injuries?'

'Not a soul, Eddie. You asked me not to.'

'Of course, I know but, well, I had a run in with the course doctor, he stood me down for fourteen days.'

Silence for a while, then, 'I'm sorry to hear that, Eddie.'

'Me too, but there could be a clue in there somewhere that might be useful to the police. I just wanted to be sure you hadn't let anything slip, even by accident.'

'Definitely not. Absolutely not.'

'Mister Barber, I had to check, no offence intended.'

'None taken.'

'Good, thanks again, I'll keep you in touch.'

'Do that.'

I rang Kavanagh and told him.

'Did you ask this doctor who tipped him the wink?' he said.

'Several times. He's not saying.'

'Well he'll be saying when I ask him. Do you know where he'll be tomorrow?'

'Southwell maybe, possibly Worcester. If you ring the track in the morning they'll tell you.'

'Where will you be?'

'I'll be here by the phone. Probably lying flat on my belly trying not to move, but I'll be waiting for your call.'

Chapter 32

As the night wore on and the wind howled around the Lodge, the pain returned, slowly, like small biting animals hatching all over my back. I rejected the paracetamol in favour of a half bottle of whiskey, which dulled the soreness in my body in exchange for a spreading melancholy.

Fractured thoughts floated, ruined career, screwed-up comeback, broken relationships, nobody to turn to… I wallowed a while, then something that had been nagging at me all day finally surfaced. I hadn't spoken to Lisa. She'd probably be thinking I was trying to avoid her.

I found her number. It rang eight or nine times before she answered. 'Eddie. How are you?'

'Okay.'

'Listen, can I ring you back?'

'Tonight?'

'Five minutes, give me five minutes.'

'Sure.'

I hung up, feeling better already. She sounded fine, not mad or anything. I thought about pouring another drink, considered what fourteen days of inactivity would do to my weight, then said what the hell and half-filled the glass.

The phone rang. I reached for it. 'God, that was quick! Thought you said five minutes?'

Silence.

'Lisa?'

Nothing.

'Hello…?'

'Eddie…?'

That sweet soft Irish voice, sounding hurt, unsure.

'Jackie! Where are you?'

'Who's Lisa?'

'She's just a friend. Tell me where you are.'

'No. I just wanted to make sure you were okay, but obviously Lisa is seeing to that.'

'Jackie, come on!'

'Barely two bloody weeks, you bastard!'

'Jackie, listen for God's sake!'

She hung up.

Shit! What a day this was turning out to be. I laughed with frustration and relief. At least Jackie was all right. It had been a good clear line, maybe she hadn't gone to Ireland after all.

The phone rang again. Jackie or Lisa. I answered carefully, 'Hello?'

'Eddie.'

McCarthy, sounding tense.

'What is it Mac?'

'David Cooper's disappeared.'

'When?'

'Yesterday. He didn't show up to ride at Fontwell today.'

'He's done that before.'

'He was due at his mother's house in London last night for her birthday party. Didn't turn up.'

'Maybe he doesn't like parties.'

'Don't be facetious, Eddie, I've spoken to the police, they're treating it seriously.'

'The kid's probably just got sick of his old man's bullying and buggered off somewhere.'

'You know the boy's father?'

'Unfortunately, yes.'

Mac said, 'He's just been ranting at me for the last ten minutes. He wants to put up a fifty grand reward. Both the police and I have advised against it in case he gets into a ransom situation with this guy.'

'And?'

'He's going to do it anyway.'

'Good for him. Gives me something to occupy myself with for the next two weeks. And, there's nobody I'd rather take fifty grand off than Jack Cooper.'

Mac seemed baffled. I reminded him I'd been stood down by the doctor. Mac said, 'If you're unfit to ride, what makes you think you can charge around the country looking for David Cooper? What if the killer has got him?'

'Mac, my career is sliding swiftly down the pan. The prospect of no job and no money makes fifty grand worth taking a lot of risks for.'

'So now you think the killer's got young Cooper?'

'I hope not, for his sake.'

'Yours too. The reward is for the boy's safe return only. No payout on corpses.'

We talked a while longer, and Mac wasn't pleased when I said I thought there was a leak on his side. Somebody had reported me to the doctor at Nottingham. Somebody knew about the notes and the ether. As if the prospect of being on the killer's list wasn't bad enough, somebody else was out to end my career.

Mac said, 'That's wild speculation, Eddie. You'll have to name suspects.'

'Okay. I'll give you two.'

I told Mac it had to be either Con Layton or Claude Beckman. Both had major grudges against me; Layton for obvious reasons, Beckman's motive I'd yet to discover. Mac disagreed. Accepting my theory meant admitting there was a problem in his department. We didn't say goodnight on the best of terms.

Next morning, I sat down to plan the practicalities of searching for David Cooper.

Money: I'd paid the most pressing bills and was still owed my five per cent of second prize money in the Gold Cup, fifteen hundred quid.

Transport: wouldn't win any Formula Ones but was fast enough to get me out of most trouble spots.

Health: not good. Wounds still sore, driving long distances looked out. Have to do what I could on the phone for the first couple of days and hope for improvement.

Thoughts of the telephone made me realize Lisa hadn't called back last night. Maybe she'd tried a few times. I called her number. No answer.

Straight-backed and suffering, I shuffled to the kitchen for coffee and toast then sat down to list people who could tell me things about David Cooper.

Might as well start at the top. I found his father's office number in The Directory of the Turf and phoned him. His secretary told me he wouldn't take my call, and did so in such a casual way that I realised she'd never had to offer the standard 'he's in a meeting' euphemism.

'Tell him it's about David,' I said.

'His son?'

'That's right.'

Seconds later his familiar bark came through, 'Malloy! What do you know about David?'

'That he's missing. That I think I can find him, and that I need the reward money.'

'Well, you should have thought of that before you decided to be so fucking insolent last time you saw me.'

'You only thought it was insolence because you're not used to people standing up to you. You think your money makes you free to behave as you like, when all it does is trap you into thinking everyone agrees with you all the time.'

'Well, you've come running back like all the rest.'

'I'm not running back. I've suddenly found I've got time on my hands. And I like David. As it happens, I'd go looking for him for nothing, but there's nobody I'd rather take fifty grand from than you.'

He laughed. I got the job, but it didn't make him amenable during my follow up questions, which he answered more with irritation than enthusiasm. I made notes while he talked about his son's background - education, friends, places they'd lived. I asked about girlfriends. Cooper couldn't name any ('He's not fucking queer, if that's what you mean!'). The Coopers had divorced when David was twelve. Was he still close to his mother? Cooper said the kid never talked about her.

I'd expected at least a couple of nostalgic reminiscences about the boy's childhood, but Cooper kept it practical. It seemed to me he hardly knew his son. Memories of my own father loomed; our relationship had been no better. Makes you wonder why people have kids.

Cooper quickly grew impatient, and told me to get cracking and to assume the boy had been abducted by the killer.

David had last been seen by his father's trainer, Bobby Watt, visiting his yard on Monday to school a couple of horses. Watt's place was near Uttoxeter in Staffordshire.

The trainer wasn't that helpful when I phoned. 'The kid looked okay, quiet as usual. He arrived about eight, schooled three for me, had breakfast and buggered off.'

'Did he say where he was going?'

'Nope. He wasn't racing that day was all he told me.'

'And he seemed all right?'

'I told you, the boy's so quiet you wouldn't notice any difference. He could be suicidal and you prob'ly couldn't tell.'

'He finish his breakfast?'

'As far as I know. I don't wet-nurse him.'

'He was supposed to be going to his mother's birthday party that night, did he mention it?'

'Not to me he didn't.'

'Is he close to anyone in the yard, any of the lads?'

'I think Pauline's got the hots for him but I doubt it's mutual.'

'Can I talk to her?'

'She's out with the second lot just now.'

'Ask her to ring me, will you?' I gave him my number and asked him who would ride Cooper's horses while the kid was missing.

'Nobody. Jack told me to withdraw two today and two tomorrow and not to make any more entries until the kid's found.'

'So you will be suspending his training bills out of sympathy?'

'Fat fucking chance.'

Pauline called within an hour. She was hard work. All I learnt was that David wasn't happy living with his father, and had talked vaguely about moving to France with his mother sometime soon. He had mentioned his mother's birthday party and intended going on the evening he'd disappeared. He hadn't said what he'd planned for the rest of that day and no, Pauline didn't walk him to his car, so couldn't say if he had a suitcase with him.

I thought the next best lead would be David's mother. If he was close enough to her to talk about moving to France, then he wouldn't have run away without telling her. If he'd absconded to escape his father, there was every chance she'd be in on it.

I rang her, introduced myself and asked if she'd mind answering some questions.

'I don't know you from Adam,' she said, 'you could be anybody.'

'If you'd like to call your husband, he can -'

'Listen Mister Malloy, Jack Cooper hasn't been my husband for a long time. I haven't spoken to him for even longer. If you want me to answer questions, come and see me, and bring some ID.'

She gave me her address in London. I said I'd be there by eight that evening.

Lisa had left a message on the answer-phone.

I called her. 'Not working today?' I asked.

'On leave for two weeks.'

'That's right, I forgot. How's Susan?'

'Not at all well, I'm afraid. They took her into hospital last night.'

'Jeez. That bad?'

'On the edge of a complete breakdown.'

She sounded strained. I said, 'Are you okay?'

'Fine. I just feel so sorry for her.'

I sympathised and we talked for a while. I told her what had happened over the past few days. She reacted with anger and incredulity. When I reached the part where the doctor stood me down, she told me she'd been at Nottingham and overheard a discussion between the racecourse doctor and Claude Beckman.

'Beckman was saying something like, when he does come back I'll have him in front of the stewards. I hadn't a clue who they were talking about.'

'Can you remember what time it was?'

'It was after racing. I was on my way home. Why?'

'I was just wondering if Beckman could have been the guy who tipped the Doc off, but there's no way he could have known.'

'That man does not care for you at all,' Lisa said.

'It's getting to be mutual. What do you know about him?'

'Not much. Was a bit of a mummy's boy. He travelled abroad for a few years from what I hear. Moved in with his mother when he returned and looked after her until she died. Lives on his own somewhere in the Welsh Borders now, I think. Never married.'

'Gay?'

'Does it matter?'

'Not to me, but the more I know about him, the better chance of me finding out why he hates me.'

'Well if he was gay, he'd probably fancy you.'

That shut me up for a moment. 'I don't think I'd be his type.'

'Whose type would you be, Eddie?'

The conversation was taking a turn which felt more like a skid. I was losing control of it, unsure whether Lisa was coming on to me or not. 'I don't think I'm the one to ask about that. Can we concentrate on Beckman?'

'Sure.'

'Does he bet?' I asked.

'I don't know.'

'Maybe he lost a lot of money on one of my horses, and that's why he can't stand me. In fact, I'm wondering now if he's in with Layton on the bent races. He was raging at Wolverhampton after that race that was supposed to be fixed.'

'I don't think he does bet. He's not supposed to, as you know, but I'd have heard it on the grapevine if he was a gambler.'

'He's beginning to bug me.'

She said, 'Let me nose around and see what else I can find out about him.'

'Be careful. You've got a job to protect.'

'Least of my worries.'

I told her I was heading for London to see David's mother, and that I'd keep her in touch.

She said, 'What about your back? Can you drive?'

'A bit like Quasimodo in a milk-cart but I'll get there.'

'Why don't I drive you?'

'To London?'

'Wherever. I'm doing nothing for the next ten days. Pick me up.'

'You might need to pack an overnight bag.' Unsure if I was reading too much into the ensuing pause, I added, 'Just as a precaution. It's not a come-on.'

'Of course not.'

Again, I couldn't read her tone and wished I could see her face. She said, 'See you when you get here.'

Chapter 33

Lisa must have been watching from the window. As I parked, she came striding toward me in that easy athletic gait. I tried not to grimace or groan as I eased myself out of the car and straightened slowly.

We both smiled. Her hair shone, the whites of her brown eyes were luminously clear beneath a dark fringe. I couldn't see a trace of make-up. She smiled; her teeth gleamed. Standing close to me on this bright cold afternoon, I thought she was the healthiest, most vibrant human being I'd ever seen.

'You look… very well,' I said awkwardly.

She smiled wide and said, 'Thanks, I wish I could say the same for you. You look like shit. Your back must be killing you.'

'Is it that obvious?'

'You're an awful colour.'

I smiled. 'I can see this is going to be a really uplifting trip.'

She touched my arm. 'Sorry, I should keep my mouth shut.'

'Forget it.'

I moved my makeshift backpad to the passenger seat, Lisa adjusted the driving position and mirrors and we set off south.

We talked about Beckman and the killings, young Cooper and his father, Susan and the children (staying now with their grandparents in Devon) and about things in general. Nothing too personal, but by the time we reached the outskirts of London we seemed reasonably familiar and comfortable with each other.

We stopped for coffee. I rang Kavanagh to find out if he'd spoken to Doctor Donnelly.

'Funnily enough, I just got back from interviewing him.'
'Did he say who reported me?'
'Yes and no.'
I waited.
'His informant was anonymous. Left a note.'
'Saying what?'
'Saying, take a look at Malloy's back, he's badly injured and shouldn't be riding.'
'Don't suppose it was hand-written?'
'You don't suppose correctly, type-written.'
'Any clues there?'
'We're working on it.'
'Couldn't be the same typewriter that produced the Cheltenham threat?'
'You are very perceptive this evening, Mister Malloy.'
'It's the same?'
'Might be. The jury's still out.'
'And if it is?'
'Another clue, isn't it? Another piece in the jigsaw, another pattern in the great tapestry of justice.'
'You been at the cooking sherry again, Kavanagh?'
'How can you tell?'
'Sharp perception, like you said. Will you let me know as soon as something's definite?'
'You'll be the first on my list.'

David's mother lived in a nice big house in Kensington with three Birman cats. She was dark, slim, pale, elegant and much less aggressive than she'd been on the phone. David took his looks from her.

'Please sit down,' she said, 'Can I get you a drink?'
'No, thank you.' I eased myself into the low chair as she watched.
'Are you all right, Mister Malloy?'
'Injured my back a few days ago. It should be better in a week or two.'
'Did you break it?'
I looked at her, wondering if she was being sarcastic, but she was open-faced and seemed concerned, 'No, it's not broken. Skin damage mostly. I'll try not to be bleed on your furniture.'

She smiled and settled in the chair facing me. She said, 'I worried about David when he wanted to become a jockey, but I didn't think he'd last. He's surprised me.'

'What about his disappearance, has that surprised you?'

She nodded, almost imperceptibly, as though admitting that I'd hit home, 'I'm not that surprised, if I'm totally honest, hence my lack of obvious motherly concern. I never believed David would last with his father. Nobody lasts long with Jack Cooper, as you will discover, though I suspect you already know?'

'We've had words. I don't like him, and he doesn't like me, but we both know it, and that makes the working relationship about as straightforward as you could get.'

She sighed, 'I suppose that would be an advantage. Jack dispensed long ago with the notion that any kind of social lubricant was necessary in the conduct of day to day relations with humanity.'

'David seems very different from his father.'

She seemed suddenly wary and looked at me as though trying to figure out if I was being offensive, and I realized the implications of what I'd just said, 'I didn't mean to suggest anything improper. It's just that David and his father are polar opposites.'

Some warmth returned to her look, 'David gives the lie to the nurture beats nature theories. If anything, his father's behaviour has taught him what not to do. The only passion David ever shared with Jack was horses. Jack couldn't wait for him to graduate, as he put it, from ponies to horses, and David loved those ponies. Anyway, I suspect David's finally had enough. He'd never have been able to tell Jack to his face that he was leaving.'

'Has he told you?'

'David?'

'Yes. Has David been in touch with you?'

'No. No he hasn't. Don't mistake my less than panicked reaction at David's disappearance as some sort of collusion with my son. David was always at great pains never to take sides after the separation. But I know my son, Mister Malloy. I'd have bet an awful lot of money that he would do this one day.'

'Do it like this? Just walk out? Disappear?'

She nodded, 'He'll take what time he needs to come to terms with this, then he'll call me. What happens after that, well, I won't tempt fate.'

I watched her in her cool composed certainty that David was fine, and had not been abducted, and I subdued an urge to give her the full details about the killings so far.

We talked on, but I learned little more about David than his father had told me, and I left her house with the feeling that either she was holding out on me, and David had been in touch, or that in his parents' long years of back and forth battles, he'd been of no more notice to them than a net to two tennis players.

I settled beside Lisa in the car. 'Worthwhile?' She asked.

I sighed. 'I don't know. Time will tell… and other clichés.'

She smiled. 'You'd have been antsy if you hadn't come.'

'You've sussed me already.' I said and leaned against the pillows drained of energy. She said, 'You're not fit for this trip home, are you?'

'A couple of painkillers and I'll be okay.'

'You won't. You're shattered.'

Pivoting my head against the seat, I looked across at her and managed a weak defeated smile. 'I'll find us a hotel,' she said.

It was a small place, softly lit. Lisa wouldn't let me carry her bag. I asked at reception for two single rooms. The man behind the desk said, 'Sorry, only one twin room left.'

I said, 'Thanks, we'll find somewhere else.'

Lisa, standing beside me, said, 'No, we won't. We'll take it.'

She wore cream silk pyjamas with teddy bears on. I wore blood-stained bandages.

'Didn't you bring fresh dressings?'

I looked at her. 'Couldn't have changed them myself.'

'You knew I'd be with you.'

A tiny shrug was all I could manage. 'Didn't want to appear presumptuous.'

She shook her head slowly, but I thought I saw a spark of gratitude in her eyes. She got dressed again, went downstairs and returned with a first-aid kit.

An hour later she was asleep in the bed nearest the window.

Chapter 34

Next morning, I called Kavanagh. He wasn't in, nor was Miller. I rang Mac to ask if they'd been in touch with him.

'Haven't heard a thing. Not from them anyway...'

'Meaning?'

'Are you still on the trail of young Cooper?'

'I saw his mother last night. Didn't learn much, why?'

'I just heard the boy was seen with your favourite steward's secretary early on Monday afternoon.'

'Claude Beckman?'

'Uh-huh.'

'Where?'

'At a service station on the M6.'

'Doing what?'

'Drinking coffee and chatting amiably, according to what I hear.'

'So Beckman could have been the last person to talk to the kid?'

'Very likely.'

'Any objection to me paying him a visit?'

'None at all, but the chances of him answering questions from you are about the same as me getting a ride in The Derby.'

'At least I'll get the pleasure of being the interrogator for a change. Can I challenge him about being seen with David Cooper?'

'Sure, just don't say it was me who told you about it.'

'Who told you?'

'Oddly enough, Doctor Donnelly. But don't mention him either.'

'I won't, Mac. Did Donnelly speak to them?'

'No. He thought it a bit strange so he left it.'

'Where is Beckman tomorrow, do you know?'

'He's on a week's holiday. Want his phone number?'

'So he can hang up on me? I'd sooner turn up at his door.'

'And have it slammed in your face?'

'I'll be persistent.'

Mac gave me his address and we set off west. Beckman's home was an old cottage at the foot of the Black Mountains in Wales. McCarthy could offer no directions, claiming Beckman always said he lived 'in the middle of nowhere'.

Two hours later, we pulled in at the Red Lion pub in Llangorse village, the only habitation of any size in Beckman's postcode. The landlord knew of Beckman, though he'd never met him, but he provided directions which brought us to the bottom of the steep track leading to Beckman's place. I prepared to get out of the car.

'Best if you drive a mile up the road out of sight, Lisa. If Beckman hunts me off his property and sees you, the last thing we need is him reporting you to your boss. Give me half an hour.'

'What if something goes wrong?' She asked.

'Like what?'

'Like you not being here when I come back.'

'If I'm not here, maybe you could head to the Red Lion. Wait there another hour then phone Mac. Don't tell him who you are, just say you dropped me off at Beckman's and I haven't come back.'

'How are you going to play it?'

'Straight. Tell him I'm working for Jack Cooper while I'm laid up and that I heard he'd been seen with David.'

She looked at me. I tried to appear confident and would have been if I wasn't hurting so much.

'Eddie, be careful.'

'Don't worry. See you in half an hour.' I stifled a grunt as I lurched out of the car, and started up the path.

The landlord had warned that it would be a wet climb. He said it had been raining heavily for days. Deep ruts in the steep track funnelled noisy streams past my feet. My shoes and trouser bottoms were quickly soaked and the ache in my wounds worsened.

The white-walled red-roofed cottage sat at the end of a drive bordered by young trees. I went through the gate and along the path, but stopped suddenly as a familiar smell reached me. I stood sniffing lightly, trying to place it.

A breeze carried the scent down the narrow tunnel formed by the side of the cottage and a high fence. It came to me: that sweet sickly odour of dying vegetation, all the more pungent now as the sun warmed the rain-sodden ground. I'd last smelt it lying helpless and naked and covered in whip wounds.

That made me reconsider. It could be a complete coincidence; that smell must be rising from a million overgrown gardens, fields and woodlands all over the country. Or it could be that this was the place I'd been held. It wasn't such a long way from Hereford where I'd been dumped.

If Beckman was the man who'd abducted me, if he was home just now and I walked blithely in not only unarmed but seriously unfit to put up a fight… I looked around for a concealable weapon, a rock, a short heavy stick… but what if he was watching? If he saw me pick anything up, he'd know I knew and that would probably make him a hell of a lot more dangerous. If I lingered much longer, he'd get suspicious too.

Just for show I patted my pockets and looked forgetful, as though I'd left something in the car, then I moved on toward the door.

It was open. Just slightly ajar, maybe an inch. I pressed the big enamel weather-stained bell button, and all I heard was a series of sharp taps as though the bell was made of wood.

I waited a minute. Nothing. I reached forward again, more tentatively now, and gave the button a short stab. Another minute… silence.

Putting my ear to the gap, all I could hear was the faint ticking of a clock. I pushed the door. It swung noiselessly. I went in.

Slowly and quietly down the hall on the worn wrinkled carpet. All the doors wide open: kitchen and toilet on my left, two bedrooms on my right, and the living room at the bottom where I could see the side of the big ticking grandfather clock.

Stopping outside the living-room door, I peered through the narrow gap at the hinge side to make sure nobody stood behind it. I saw only a thin slice of the room: yellowed wallpaper on the ceiling, dark curtains, old brown sofa, mother-of-pearl tiled fireplace over an unlit gas fire, brown carpet…no occupant…silent…not a breath.

Leaning forward I looked in.

Empty.

An old TV on splaying legs in the corner, a wooden magazine rack stuffed untidily full. Three watercolour landscapes on the wall. On the mantelpiece, a brass frame held a black and white photograph of Beckman at his graduation with, alongside him, his mother aged around forty. The resemblance was striking. I also felt that I knew her.

In the kitchen, a shrink-wrapped chicken lay in a glass dish, defrosting instructions uppermost. Beside it a bottle of red wine had been opened.

Wherever Beckman had gone, it looked like he'd intended to return soon.

From the kitchen window I could see a long garden, badly overgrown. At the bottom stood a large shed. A bunch of keys hung from a rusting hook. I took them and went out.

That smell was strong now.

A dirty, beat-up green Land Rover was parked at the far corner. I moved past it to the shed, which rested on railway sleepers. Sackcloth tacked inside covered the windows. The door was padlocked. The smallest key on the ring turned slickly in the lock.

The door creaked open, letting in daylight. Against the rear wall was the heavy bench. On top of it lay the hood with the chain sewn in, and on the floor I saw my bloodstains.

I felt a terrible urge for revenge. No curiosity, no 'why me?' just a violent impulse. If I could rescue David Cooper at the same time, all the better, but my main aim was to find Beckman, get him into to this cold wooden torture chamber and give him exactly what he'd given me.

Returning to the house, I searched as neatly and methodically as I could through drawers, in cupboards, even in the hollow body of the grandfather clock. I found nothing to link Beckman to either of the murders. Two scrapbooks filled with press cuttings gave me hope for a while. I was convinced when I opened them I'd find evidence relating to the murder of Gilmour or Donachy, but there was nothing, just press reports and pictures on racing.

One odd item in the scrapbook: a defaced black and white picture of the finish of a race at Sandown where the second horse and jockey had been slashed beyond recognition. Why put a ruined picture in an album? On the table I found a scrap of yellow paper with the words, 'check Ruger' and what looked like a phone number. I pocketed it.

Suddenly remembering Lisa, I checked my watch; I'd been here almost half an hour. One job remained, the Land Rover.

Its doors were unlocked. On the passenger seat was an old typewriter without a cover. I opened the glove compartment…just a few odds and ends. I hauled the typewriter out. Someone shouted, 'Leave it!'

I turned. At the end of the overgrown garden, about a hundred yards away, Claude Beckman was raising a shotgun.

Chapter 35

I heard a blast, then the hedge to my left being peppered by shot. Back pain forgotten, I raced down the track, clutching the typewriter, scared to look round in case I slipped in one of the watery ruts, I prayed the car would be there.

It was. Lisa saw my panic in and started the engine. I jumped in and she pulled away, my door swinging open. I looked up the track, expecting to see Beckman taking aim, but he'd gone.

We stopped in the car park of the Red Lion. I tried to calm myself. Sweat prickled my scalp. Lisa lit a cigarette. Her brown, almost-oriental eyes looked at me as her cheeks hollowed, sucking in smoke. 'Think he'd have killed you?' she asked.

'Put it this way, I wouldn't like to give him another shot.'

'My guess is he'll be packing his bags and heading in the opposite direction.'

'I hope you're right.'

The landlord was in the hall, trundling an old manual carpet sweeper to and fro. He was small and round and his fat shiny face showed no surprise at seeing us for the second time in an hour.

He stopped and leant on the handle of the sweeper and said in his strong accent, 'Not lost again, are we?'

'Just want to use the phone.' I said.

McCarthy listened in silence, broke off to call the cops then phoned me back. He said, 'So it looks like we might have a little PR problem on top of everything else?'

'What are you talking about?'

'The Jockey Club, I mean, with Beckman being, well, an employee.'

'Big deal. He'll need more than a PR man once the police catch him.'

Lisa smiled at me. Mac said, 'What do you plan to do now?'

'I plan to ask you to find out as much as you can about Beckman, especially his past, and to get me names of his friends and acquaintances, find out his religious leanings, what he does in his spare time, and who his psychiatrist is.'

'He's got a psychiatrist?'

'He's a fucking madman, he should have.'

'Mad men don't usually know they're mad, Eddie.'

'I was kidding, Mac. Just find out what you can, will you? The cops are going to ask for all the info anyway.'

'When the mess clears from the shit hitting all the fans here in Portman Square, I'll see what I can do.'

I hung up, and pulled out the slip of paper with the number written on it that I'd taken from Beckman's telephone table.

It rang six times then an answerphone clicked on and someone thanked me for calling "Sparky's" apologised for his absence and said that opening hours until April were six until ten weekdays and ten until ten weekends.

Sparky's. What kind of business were they running? What did Beckman have to do with it and who was Ruger? The landlord was standing by the exit. 'Does the name Sparky's mean anything to you?' I asked.

'There's a place on the south side of Llangorse Lake called Sparky's,' he said, 'it's a gun club.'

On the journey home, Lisa suggested she ought to stay with me for a few days.

'The Lodge is hardly the safest place for you to be.' I said.

'And it's no safer for you. That's why you need somebody with you.'

'The police will give me a bodyguard if I need one'.

'Good. That'll make it safe for me to keep you company then, won't it? Somebody has to change your dressings, and I don't think that's in the job description for bodyguards.'

'Neatly argued.'

She smiled. We called at her house and she packed a few more things. I spent the remainder of the drive home worrying that Jackie would be sitting waiting when we walked in.

All that waited was an answer-phone message from Mac saying

that when the police reached Beckman's place, he'd gone. The shed I'd been held captive in was a heap of ashes. They had alerted other forces to be on the lookout for Beckman.

Delving into my dwindling stock of packet meals, we ate dinner and shared a bottle of wine then settled down by the fire to plan the next day's moves. Lisa called the hospital. Susan remained under sedation.

I remembered Sparky's and got the number out again.

'Sparky's.'

'Can I speak to Mister Ruger, please?' I asked.

A few seconds' silence then, 'You winding me up?'

'Not intentionally.'

'Mister Ruger?'

'That's who I was told to ask for.'

'Somebody's winding you up then.'

'How come?'

'Ruger is a make of gun.'

Just to make sure he hadn't misheard me, I said, 'Different from a Luger?'

'Completely different.'

'Oh, well, I guess Claude Beckman was pulling my leg.'

'That'd be a first.'

I hesitated, wondering how far to push my luck. 'Oh, he finds his sense of humour sometimes.'

'I'll take your word for it. Listen, are you going to be seeing Mister Beckman soon?'

'I hope so.'

'Tell him the gun's arrived, will you, and we've paid for it up front.'

'That'll be the Ruger?'

'The Ruger Blackhawk.'

'Will do, thanks.'

Although the puzzle pieces seemed to be coming together, the picture wasn't getting any clearer. I rang McCarthy. He said he'd let Kavanagh know about the gun club, then told me he'd dug up some stuff on Beckman.

'Two different sources are saying the same thing but can't support it with any evidence. I'm trying to get verification,' he said.

'What is it?'

'Beckman studied law at Oxford for three years, then dropped out to take a job as a management consultant in London. After a year in the UK, he moved into international management consultancy which turned out, according to my sources, to be a cover for what do you think?'

'I don't know. Drug running?'

'Try gun running. He was an arms dealer.'

'Hardly looks the type, does he? Anyway, that's not illegal, is it?'

'Depends. If you get proper end-user certificates and export-import licences, then you're okay. It seems Beckman stuck to the shady side, forging certificates, bribing officials; he's supposed to have made a few quid and got out. Bought his mother a couple of racehorses, got himself a boat, took a respectable job with The Jockey Club.'

'Didn't your people check him out?'

'Of course. Rock solid. Impeccable references.'

'Probably wrote them himself. How long was he gun-running then?'

'Maybe as long as seven years.'

'Was he involved in Ireland?'

Mac hesitated. 'Do you think he had something to do with the deaths of Gilmour and Donachy?'

I sighed. 'I don't know what to think. If Beckman's the killer, why didn't he shoot me when he had me locked up? To beat me the way he did he must have hated my guts but not badly enough to kill me. How could he have killed the others?'

We kicked it around a while longer and Mac said he'd see what else he could find out.

A lamp glowed in the corner of the big room and the fire roared like a small furnace. Lisa sat on the rug; I lay on my front, the heat warming away the ache on my right side. Lisa sipped wine. I had whiskey and balanced my chin on the rim of the glass.

Lisa said, 'That'll break and you'll have more scars.'

'Hmmm.'

We were silent for a while, staring at the flames. Lisa said, 'When I was a kid, I always dreamed of living in a place like this, big and old in the middle of nowhere, a roaring fire in a dark room, making toast with a long golden fork and drinking hot chocolate… listening to the wind and rain rattling the outside, making me feel cosy.'

Chin still on glass I mumbled, 'Bit short on golden forks, I'm afraid.'

'You're not overflowing with hot chocolate or bread either,' she said.

I smiled.

'What did you want to be when you were a kid?' She asked.

'A jockey.'

'Always?'

'Well after hearing the shattering news, when I was about three, that I couldn't be the king.' I raised my elbows now to prop up my chin and looked at Lisa. I said, 'I'll always remember that, the first time anyone had ever asked me what I wanted to be when I grew up. It struck me that kings and queens had a pretty fine life of it, and that's what I'd set my heart on. My mother laughed and said it was impossible, you had to be born into the proper family. It was the first time I can recall feeling a sense of injustice.'

'At three?'

'Around then…maybe five or six.'

'You don't get much more precocious than that.'

'Nah, first signs of an incurable romantic, that was all.'

'What about family?' she asked and waited in open-faced anticipation for the start of my life history. I thought about changing the subject but ploughed on reluctantly.

'My parents are still alive and I've got a sister somewhere, but I don't see any of them.'

I wasn't looking at her. She hesitated and then said, 'Family feud?'

'Sort of.'

She saw I was uneasy. 'You'd rather not talk about it?'

'Not tonight.'

We were quiet for a while then she said quietly, 'Do you want to talk about today?'

I knew what she meant, but tried to dodge it. 'Which particular part?'

'When you opened that shed.'

I felt a lump rise in my throat and took a drink to disguise the swallow I had to make. 'I don't know what I felt.'

Lisa stayed silent.

'It was a bad mixture of fear and…shame. Rage. Humiliation. A gut need for revenge. Anger at myself for letting anybody do that to me, especially Beckman who thinks he's better than me anyway. Fucking bastard.'

She watched, intense but silent, studying me.

'If he'd been in that shed when I opened it, armed or not, I'd have torn his fucking head off. I'd have bit him and butted him, smashed his bones and stood on his face…jumped on his face, kicked it, raged and howled at him, battered him and when he was dead I'd have pissed all over his body.'

Still she was silent. She didn't say, "Feel better now?" No platitudes. I was grateful. After a minute, she raised her glass. 'Here's to quick healing,' she said.

Chapter 36

Next morning at seven, Jack Cooper's call woke me. He was looking for news of his son. I mentioned he'd been seen with Beckman, though I decided not to tell him Beckman had disappeared.

I didn't think Beckman had the boy or he'd have been locked up on his property somewhere. And Cooper senior would go into meltdown at the inference of a homosexual relationship.

'So you haven't really got anywhere?'

'I suppose not.'

His language made me glad he wasn't employing me direct.

'Did David have his own place?' I asked him.

'I bought him a nice flat in Sutton Coldfield.'

'I'd like to see it.'

'Fine. Pick the keys up at my office.'

'You carry a set?'

'Why not? It was my money that bought it!'

'Only asking. You been there since he disappeared?'

'I was there yesterday.'

'Was all his gear still there, clothes, shoes, passport, stuff like that?'

'How would I know?'

'I thought you might have looked. Why did you go there?'

'To see if he left a note or something.'

'And did he?'

'Don't be so bloody silly! I haven't got time for this. Come and pick up the keys, they'll be with my secretary. Let me know what's happening.'

He hung up.

Lisa was impressed with David's flat. She assured me the décor was straight from Vogue. There was a narrow floor-to-ceiling bookcase with few spaces, and watercolours above big pot plants.

Lisa said, 'Well there's your answer about the girlfriend, he's got one.'

'You think so?'

'Definitely. This is a woman's house.'

'So all men have bad taste in decor?'

'Maybe not bad, but not as good as this. Look at the lighting arrangement, the plants.'

'Interior designer?'

'Possibly. A female.'

I shook my head. 'I'm going to have a wander round.'

Young Cooper had always dressed well, and if he'd gone of his own accord, he'd left plenty of stuff behind; his wardrobe was full.

In the bottom drawer were two padded envelopes, three feet by two, unsealed. I slipped them out and eased framed watercolours from the open flaps. Both were country scenes, very well done. And very similar in style to the ones on Beckman's walls.

Why weren't these on David's walls? I looked closer. David Cooper's signature was on both. I called Lisa through.

Returning to the living area, we checked the pictures on display: all David's.

We nosed around a while longer but found nothing important; no passport, no wallet, no toiletries even, though that meant little. If he'd left on Monday with the intention of travelling to his mother's house, he would have taken an overnight bag.

'We'd better get moving,' I said.

Lisa said, 'Just let me finish the plants.'

She hurried through to the sitting room and picked up a half-full plastic jug. 'You never know how long he'll be gone, don't want them to die of thirst.'

David's flat was in a block of four. Hoping for a clue, we tried all the neighbours: nobody home.

On the drive back, I told Lisa how similar David's paintings were to those in Beckman's house. She said, 'So their relationship could have been as simple as buyer and seller?'

'Exactly.'

We wondered if Beckman had friends among the other members of his gun club, someone who, at least, might have been able to confirm where he'd got the watercolours. Failing that, I'd ask the police if we could go back to Beckman's place for another look around.

'What time does the gun club close?' Lisa asked.

'Ten.'

She looked at her watch. 'We could be there for half eight if I drive.'

'It's a long way, Lisa.'

'Are we doing anything else?'

'I suppose not.'

The club, about fifteen miles from Beckman's cottage, was a just a floodlit rifle range with a sort of log cabin attached as a clubhouse. As we approached the doors, two men came through them: Kavanagh and Miller.

At his syrupy best Kavanagh said, 'Mister Malloy, what a small world!'

I tried to remember if he'd met Lisa before and hoped he hadn't. I introduced her as a friend. Even Miller smiled.

'Afraid we beat you to it tonight, Mister Malloy.' Kavanagh said.

'Looks like it,' I said. 'Find out anything useful?'

Kavanagh kept smiling, darting show-off glances at Lisa. 'Plenty.'

'But nothing you can talk about?'

'Not to the, uh, general public.'

'Fine. I'll bear that in mind next time I have some information.'

'Don't be childish,' Kavanagh said, 'it doesn't suit you.'

'What about Beckman's house?' I asked, 'you been there?'

'Hours ago.'

'Did you notice the watercolours hanging in the living room?'

'Can't say I did. Why, thinking of setting up as an art critic?' He flashed a little aren't-I-clever smile at Lisa.

'Forget it,' I said, and turned away.

Kavanagh said, 'Goodnight, ma'am, nice meeting you.'

Suddenly remembering Beckman's typewriter, which was still in my car, I called Kavanagh back and gave it to him.

'Try not to lose it,' I said, 'you'll probably find that my Cheltenham threat and the tip-off to Doctor Donnelly were typed on it.'

Kavanagh sneered. 'How very clever of you.'

I ignored it. Lisa and I went inside.

We wasted half an hour talking to several people. No one there had known Beckman socially. He was a regular on the range but a loner. Nobody could remember him even having a drink in the club bar.

I said to Lisa, 'We'll get a break soon. We're due one. You'll see.' I was trying to persuade myself rather than her.

Back late at the Lodge, fed and watered, wounds tended, sitting together again by the fire, I phoned McCarthy and told him about meeting Kavanagh and Miller at the gun club. 'Heard anything from them?' I asked.

'Their boss rang me. Beckman was a long-term member there. He had a case full of guns.'

'All kept at the club?'

'Yep. Strictly legal.'

'I'm sure.'

'Among his collection was a Model Ninety-two F Beretta, the same type that was used to kill Gilmour and Donachy.'

'How significant is that? Statistics-wise, I mean.'

Mac sighed. 'That's the trouble, forty per cent of their members have that gun and the club owner says that would be a fair reflection countrywide. But we'll soon know. The police have Beckman's gun and it's being sent for tests.'

'Does Inspector Sanders believe he killed Gilmour and Donachy?' I asked.

'He won't commit, but I get the impression Beckman's becoming chief suspect.'

'I've a feeling Sanders will find himself on the wrong trail.'

I told Mac about the watercolours then asked if he minded me doing my own thing over the next couple of days, talking to Beckman's colleagues and maybe a few of the stewards, sniffing around discreetly in high places.

'What's the point? You said you don't think Beckman's the killer?'

'That's right, but I'd still like to know why he bears me such a grudge. Anyway, he's the only link I've got to David Cooper.'

'Okay, just try to upset as few people as possible.'

When I hung up, Lisa said, 'Have you still got that note with the gun club's telephone number on it?'

I fished it out and showed her it.

'What were the numbers on the note you got through the door, can you remember?'

'Three, two, two three. They were chapter and verse numbers from the bible.'

'Can you recall what the handwriting was like?'

'Square, blocky, even, like typed characters only they were definitely written.'

'See the two in this number.' She handed me the piece of paper. 'It's curly, with that little looped ring on the foot of the two.' She said.

She was right. These numbers were uneven, in a rounded hand with loops and twirls and a continental stroke through the figure seven. 'Nice one.' I said. I was conscious the note I'd got could have been deliberately disguised, but I was reluctant to say so. Lisa had done well to think of this and I didn't want her to feel I was crabbing her.

She said, 'Of course, we don't know if Beckman wrote it. It might have been written for him.'

'True.'

'I can probably get hold of some of his handwriting from an Enquiry report,' she said.

'That would be a big help.'

'I know it rules nothing in or out, but it might kind of change the odds a bit.'

I smiled at her. 'You should set up workshops to train the likes of Kavanagh and Miller. You're good.'

'Aww shucks!' She said.

Chapter 37

Saturday and Sunday were spent making appointments by phone and driving fast to keep them. I spoke to a number of Beckman's acquaintances from racing, none of whom could help. We even traced a couple of David Cooper's old school-friends, though we'd nothing to show for it.

Sunday evening found me dispirited, and my mood began seeping into Lisa. The combination of a lack of success and confusion, in my mind at least, about how we really felt about each other made me think we needed a break.

I suggested she might want to go home that night and take Monday off, then maybe we could both come back with a fresh approach. She seemed relieved, packed her things, kissed me lightly on the cheek and said to ring right away if anything came up.

Watching her drive off, I had mixed feelings. But when I closed the door, I knew I was glad to be on my own again. I'd been a loner most of my life, acutely so in the last six years. I didn't believe I'd ever adjust to the idea of a regular partner. On this dreary Sunday, I didn't much care.

At six-thirty next morning, the phone rang. I hurried downstairs cursing Jack Cooper and making a mental note to leave it off the hook at night.

It was McCarthy. I could feel the tension in his voice when he said my name.

'What is it, Mac?'
'Another corpse.'
'David Cooper?'

'Garfield Rowlands.'

I couldn't place him.

'Used to be a trainer,' Mac said, 'retired two years ago.'

'He wasn't Irish?'

'English through and through. Retired to his home village near Barnsley.'

'Shot?'

'Centre of the forehead, shoulder broken this time rather than his leg.'

'Bloody hell! Any note?'

'Pinned through the flesh of his throat with a sharpened nail; usual chapter and verse numbers.'

'Which translate to?'

'"And I looked, and behold a pale horse; and the name that sat on him was death."'

'Was the same gun used?'

'We don't know yet. No whip weals, by the way, and no sign of a hood being used.'

'They checked him for that? Kavanagh and Miller must be catching on.'

We were silent for a few moments. I said, 'It's not Beckman, is it?'

'I doubt it. He did a copycat on you for some reason. Listen, I'm heading for Yorkshire now. Want to meet up there?'

I pondered. 'Mac, I don't know what to do. I'm supposed to be trying to find David Cooper and it now looks like the killer doesn't have him, which, if I want this reward, kind of sends me off in another direction.'

'But the boy could be anywhere! It could take you years to find him!'

That was an argument too. 'Look,' I said, 'let me ring his father. I'll call you back.'

'Eddie, remember, you're still in this guy's book somewhere.'

'What's that supposed to mean?'

'He paid you a visit, didn't he, the day after he killed Tommy Gilmour? You won't be off his radar, so I wouldn't be getting complacent.'

'Well, thanks, Mac. Is there any depths you won't stoop to so I don't pull out of this?'

'I'm only saying...'

'I'll call you back.'

I think Jack Cooper was quietly impressed at me ringing him so early in the day. I told him about Rowlands and his groan of relief that it hadn't been David was the first emotion, other than anger, I'd witnessed in him. I explained about Mac and how my loyalties were divided.

He said, 'Listen, Malloy, go after this crazy bastard. If you're right and he hasn't got David, then at least I can assume the boy's probably safe.'

'And what if David turns up while I'm helping try to track the killer down? I've suddenly done fifty grand, haven't I?'

'Tough titty. What is The Jockey Club paying you to help out?'

'Peanuts. It might feed me for a month or two, but I won't retire on it.'

He was quiet for a moment then said, 'Look, I'm feeling generous. If David turns up safe and you help catch this maniac, you get paid.'

'What if I help catch him and David doesn't turn up?'

'Too bad. You get nowt. Whole duck or no dinner. Fair enough?'

'Fair enough.'

I rang McCarthy. 'Where do you want to meet?'

We had an appointment with Jeff Rowlands, the dead man's son. His house was in Middleham, a sort of Newmarket of the north. I considered calling Lisa in as driver again, but if Mac caught sight of her she'd be finished in her job. I got behind the wheel. It felt strange to be driving again.

Mac was waiting when I reached the Rowlands' place. He got in my car to brief me, and I learnt that Jeff Rowlands was well known to the Security Department as a big punter on the racecourse. He'd been in financial trouble more than once and only just escaped being warned off for gambling debts. Mac suspected him of shady dealings with jockeys but had never been able to prove it.

He had agreed readily to the meeting when Mac had phoned, though he seemed less than agreeable by the time we knocked on his door. Shushing three barking dogs, he ushered us into a large kitchen, apologising for his temper.

'Fucking press!' he complained. 'Driving me crazy. The phone's been non-stop. I had to take it off the hook. Six of the bastards are roaming around outside like jackals...try to be civil with them then it's "When did you find him? Where was he? How bad were the wounds? Was it a burglary? Did he have any enemies?" ... Stupid bastards!'

We stood, nodding, trying to be sympathetic. Rowlands Junior was about forty; good thatch of fair wavy hair, strong jaw and nose, only his bulging blue eyes stopped him short of handsome. Slim and fit looking, he slid two chairs out from the oak table and we sat down.

He made coffee, having to stop at times to concentrate on where the cutlery, the milk and stuff were.

We offered condolences. He sat opposite us and a black Labrador sidled up for a comforting pat. Rowlands looked at the dog and rubbed its broad head. 'Even the animals are fucking shattered.' He said.

Then resting his elbows on the table, he massaged his face with both hands and sighed, which seemed to settle him a bit, 'I'm sorry,' he said. 'What can I tell you? How can I help?'

From then on he was cooperative and focused. We explained about the other murders and how we thought they were linked.

Was there anything in his father's past that could possibly have set him up for this? Anything that could have riled some lunatic sufficiently?

No, nothing.

The only time his father had ever upset anyone was when his head lad had been caught embezzling. The guy, Nick Canning, had helped himself to over twenty grand in a two-year period, earning himself three years in jail. Despite promises by Canning to repay him, and pleas from Canning's wife not to leave their child fatherless, Garfield Rowlands had testified at the trial.

Jeff Rowlands did stress that at no point had Canning threatened his father, and that Canning, although involved in fraud before, had no history of violence as far as he knew. He suggested we ask around, as Canning had been in racing most of his life.

Thinking of Gilmour and Donachy, I said, 'Do you know if Canning might have had a grudge against anyone else?'

'Not to my knowledge. I think you're on the wrong track there anyway. I heard he'd got converted in prison, born-again Christian and all that.'

Mac and I hesitated, waiting for him to realize the implication in what he'd just said. It didn't seem to sink home. I said, 'Who told you about this supposed conversion, can you remember?'

Massaging his forehead, he said, 'Christ, no, it was ages ago.' Then it reached him and he stopped the tired rubbing and stared at me. 'Did the others have these Bible quotes attached to their bodies?'

Mac, in a particularly bold move for him, admitted, 'Yes, they did, but the police are especially keen to keep that quiet.'

'So Canning might have had something to do with it?' Rowlands said.

Mac said, 'Put it this way, we'd certainly like to speak to him. I'm sure the police would too.' Mac left him a card and he promised to get in touch if he heard any news about Canning.

I asked Rowlands if the quote found on his father meant anything to him: "And I looked, and behold a pale horse: and the name that sat on him was death."

He frowned for a while, staring at the floor, then shook his head. 'Not a thing.' He said. We shook hands and he quickly closed the door behind us.

We sat in my car. Mac said, 'What do you think of young Mister Rowlands?'

'I don't know what to make of him. If all that Canning stuff was an act, planting the suspicion, pleading on the guy's behalf then carelessly dropping in the born-again bit, well, he's an awful ham. It was so bad it makes me think he might be genuine.'

'I checked with a few bookies this morning, Rowlands owes almost eighteen grand, he is in severe trouble.' Mac said.

'And he's an only child and sole heir to the farm?'

'Correct.'

'Do the cops know he's got gambling debts?'

'I haven't told them.'

'But you will?'

He nodded.

'Kavanagh and Miller on this one too?'

'Yep.'

I shook my head. 'No wonder so many villains are running loose.'

Chapter 38

Two messages were on my answer-phone tape, Lisa, and Jack Cooper's secretary. I returned Lisa's call first and told her about Rowlands. I'd expected her to be annoyed that I hadn't rang her before I'd travelled up to meet Mac, but she didn't mention it.

We talked about Jeff Rowlands, and Beckman, and David Cooper until I was tired of it. I said, 'We're covering the same ground over and over as though somehow something's going to jump out and shout This Way Please!'

'You sound well pissed off,' she said.

'I am. I can't get my head round anything. Motive's the key, but what is it?'

'Hmm.'

We were quiet again a while, both thinking. I said, 'Do you know the most puzzling part for me?'

'Go on.'

'This bone-breaking thing. With Tommy and Donachy he did it less than an hour before killing them. I'll bet the autopsy on Rowlands will prove the same thing. What's the point? If he wants to cause people real suffering before pulling the trigger, why not beat them senseless? Why not break both legs and leave them in agony for hours? I'm sure it's a ritual of some sort, the same as the Bible notes are a ritual, but where the hell do they tie together?'

Lisa said, 'And it was Rowlands' shoulder he broke?'

'His left shoulder.'

'Why? Why not his leg like the others?'

'Wish I knew.'

She was quiet for a moment then asked, 'Was it the same leg with Donachy and Tommy?'

'I don't know.'

'That could be relevant.'

'How?'

'If it's some kind of ritual.'

'I'll ask McCarthy.'

I called Cooper's secretary. She told me her boss was in hospital, intensive care. He'd collapsed with a heart attack just after speaking to me this morning, and his secretary wondered if I'd given him some bad news on the phone.

I said I was sorry to hear it and told her what Jack and I had discussed. She said he was still critically ill. I offered my sympathies again saying I sincerely hoped he'd pull through. I had no great love for the man, but the practical side was that if he died there'd be no reward money.

I phoned McCarthy to tell him about Jack Cooper. He said he'd heard news from Kavanagh about the ex-Rowlands groom, Nick Canning.

Mac confirmed that he had become a born-again Christian in prison. I said, 'I wouldn't read too much into that. I think a lot of these guys do it to help their parole chances.'

He said, 'Maybe, but listen, Jeff Rowlands got it wrong. Canning has a number of convictions for violence, one of them GBH. He broke a guy's arm with a hammer.'

I waited.

'They've found out where he's living and they're going in at dawn tomorrow.'

'Any chance we can tag along?'

'Four thirty kick off. They wanted to do it at six until I told them most of Lambourn would be well awake by that time.'

'The whole shebang then, a truckload of cops with battering rams and guns?'

'Sanders will want to make it as dramatic as possible, so, probably. But they won't let us within a mile of it.'

'Is it far from your house?'

'Forget it, Eddie, leave them to it. It's too dangerous.'

I hated missing anything that generated adrenaline but I knew Mac was right. 'Okay. Call me when they get him.'

Chapter 39

The breakfast news on radio carried a short piece about the police firing two shots in a house in Lambourn in the early hours. No one was injured but an animal had died. The Independent Police Complaints Commission had been informed. I called Mac. He said he was waiting to speak to Inspector Sanders for the full story, but the word in Lambourn village was that there had been a major balls-up by the cops.

An hour later Mac rang. 'Red faces times ten for your friends Kavanagh and Miller.'

'I'm listening.'

'Canning wasn't there when they burst through the door of his flat this morning.'

'Uh-huh.'

'The reason he wasn't there is that he's been in jail for six months. Assaulted a barman in Newbury. Got a year for it.'

I couldn't suppress a smile.

Mac said, 'And, they shot his girlfriend's dog, a pedigree poodle she used for breeding. She's suing.'

'Why did they shoot the dog?'

'Kavanagh claims it took them by surprise when it ran out from under the bed.'

I laughed. 'That pair wouldn't even get into the Keystone Kops. What's their excuse with Canning?'

'They say an informant let them down.'

'Badly.'

'Anyway,' Mac said, 'Canning's out of the running. We're left with Beckman.'

'You might be and the cops might be, but he's not for me. The killer's a psycho, a "man with a mission" type. I'm sure of it.'

Mac said, 'So, what's the mission?'

'If we find that out we've nailed him. There's something in his mind that links the victims so far, some definite tie-up.'

We dissected things again for the umpteenth time and I suggested we'd been looking too closely at the personal lives of the dead men, searching for a connection in their nationalities, their family problems. The only solid link they had was racing.

'Why don't we have a really close look at the form book?' I said.

'What for?'

'I don't know, but at the moment we've got nothing else. We might turn up some connection.'

Mac said 'You're talking about a mountain of work. Where the hell do you start?'

'Weatherbys. They'll probably have everything on computer.'

'They will but they're administrators. Slow, meticulous, detailed.'

'Maybe, but they're your administrators, the Jockey Club's. I'm sure your boss can persuade them to be fast, meticulous and detailed.'

'Let me make a call.'

Next morning, Lisa and I sat in the reception area of Weatherbys in Northampton waiting for our contact, Colin Tindall. He came smiling toward us, offering his hand three strides away. Mid-thirties, short and thin, about nine stone; a jockey's build.

Lisa had assured me no one here knew her by sight. I introduced her as Linda, just to be safe. I explained to Colin we were there simply to do some research into certain trainers and jockeys.

'How far back do you want to go?'

I thought of Rowlands. 'Could be twelve, fifteen years.'

He made that teeth-sucking noise which pleases people who know something you don't.

I said, 'You're going to tell me it's not on computer.'

'Most of it probably is.' He smiled. 'But the system's down at the moment, I'm afraid.'

Lisa asked, 'When is it likely to be up again?'

'This afternoon, hopefully.'

We sat at a long table in a room brightly lit by neon strips, one of which buzzed so annoyingly that I stood on a chair and removed it.

'Let there not be light.' Lisa said.

I said, 'Let there be peace.'

Blue-covered form books were stacked around us, sandbagging us in with their weight of information. Each contained a full season's worth of results. Every runner in every race listed right down to last place, every faller, every horse which started but failed to complete. All we needed was hidden in those tissue-thin pages, but where should we begin?

Ideally we wanted a huge database where we could key in: list full information on all horses ridden by T. Gilmour, i.e., owner, trainer, breeder, finishing position, betting fluctuations, etc. The same then for Donachy and Rowlands, and we could even have tried David Cooper in there in the hope that some link would be thrown up.

That was what we wanted.

What we had were thousands of galloped miles and forests of jumped fences filtered clean of the bruises and sweat, the shouts and the whip-cracks, the joy and the sadness; just dry records, names and places, dates and starting prices.

Lisa said, 'Maybe we should start with Horses in Training, find Mr Rowlands' horses then start checking them one by one in the form books.'

I sighed, 'Okay.'

'At least it's a start, Eddie, cheer up.'

'I'm cheered, I'm cheered,' I said, reaching for a copy of Horses in Training. 'I'll take his final year training if you do the year before that.'

'All right. Do you know how long he trained for?'

'Around fifteen years, Mac said.'

Opening her book, she raised her eyes. 'They'll find our skeletons in here covered in cobwebs.'

After a while I put my pen down, shoved a space among the pile of books and laid my head wearily on the desk, encircling it with my arms. 'God,' I said, 'talk about needles in haystacks.'

Lisa said, 'Eddie, an ounce of persistence is worth a pound of talent.'

'So I hear, but there's got to be an easier way.'

Lisa said, 'Let's list everything we know again.'

'We've done that a hundred times!'

'Maybe we overlooked something.' She was admirably, annoyingly calm.

Pushing myself wearily upright, I reached for my notepad and flipped to a fresh sheet. We went through it all again: victims, names, cause of death, which limb was broken, what the Bible quotes said, traced the last runner each had had, mixed and matched, stood things on their head... nothing.

Back to the grind.

Three fruitless finger-licking cross-eyed hours later, McCarthy rang. 'Find anything?' he asked.

'The computers are down and we're not far behind them.'

'We?'

'Me and my fingers,' I improvised. 'It's going to be a very long job, Mac, I think I'll chuck it until the computer's working again. It's like ploughing a field with a fucking fork.' Suddenly conscious of the inadvertent curse, I glanced at Lisa. She didn't even look up.

'When will it be fixed?' Mac asked.

'God knows. This morning they said this afternoon. It's almost four o'clock. I'll give it another hour.'

'Listen,' he said, 'I've been checking the sort of people who use ether regularly...'

He did his usual tail-off, waiting for the prompt. 'And?' I said.

'... the most common users these days are Animal Research labs.'

He left it hanging in the air for my instinct to sniff at. 'What else?' I asked.

'That's all.'

'They use it as an anaesthetic?'

'On small animals. They also use it as a cleaning agent.'

'Mmmm...' My mind sieved the facts, automatically trying to shake out the relevant pieces... fragments tumbled around, dead jockeys, broken limbs, animal research, crazy quotes... Scraps of Rowlands' Bible verse came back to me: A pale horse... the name on him was death... horse... death...

'Mac,' I said, 'I think you've cracked it.'

Chapter 40

Lisa had put her pen down and was watching me. Mac said, 'You think this guy works at one of these labs?'

'The opposite,' I said, 'I think he raids them. Probably burns them down.'

Mac said quietly, 'Animal Rights.'

I sat smiling, cradling the phone and doodling. Lisa's questioning frown asked if she could be let into the secret. Teasing her a while longer, I said to Mac, 'Makes sense, doesn't it?'

'Maybe.'

'No maybes. I'll bet each of the victims has been involved with a horse being killed on the racecourse.'

'That's not saying much,' Mac argued. 'If he was killing people on that basis, we'd be piling the corpses pretty high.'

'Maybe he's just started, Mac.'

I could almost hear him shiver down the line. 'Don't say that, Eddie.'

I said, 'Look at the evidence. Let's assume for a minute I'm correct. What happens when a horse breaks a leg?'

'It gets destroyed, shot.'

'Where?'

'Between the eyes.'

'Right. Now suppose this madman has decided someone is directly responsible for each horse death. What would be his idea of perfect revenge? Letting them suffer the exact same fate! Break a limb, leave them writhing in agony for about as long as it would take to get a vet there, then put them out of their misery with a bullet in the forehead.'

Knowing it was the best theory so far, we kicked it around a while longer, aware that we had to narrow the field. Mac had a point; anything up to a thousand horses had probably died on racecourses in the past decade. Somehow this guy had to be fining it down. We had to uncover his method of selection.

Watching Lisa as we talked, I saw she'd picked up the thread. She started working through the form books.

Mac asked me to ring Hubert Barber and find out if any of his recent fatalities had been ridden by Tommy Gilmour. He said he'd contact Jeff Rowlands and Donachy's main retainer with the same question.

He hung up. I held the receiver, ready to phone Barber. I smiled at Lisa. 'Guess you caught the gist of that.'

'Uh-huh,' she said, not looking up from her book.

I said 'What are you doing?'

She looked at me from beneath her dark eyebrows. 'Sleuthing,' she said, 'Is that what you call it?'

I nodded, smiling, and dialled Barber's number. He was out. I put the receiver down waiting for Mac to call. Lisa was engrossed in the form book.

'Sleuthed anything?' I asked.

'I have, actually.'

I smiled again, relaxed in her company, happy in the glow of success. Lisa glanced up. 'You look like the cat that's got the cream,' she said.

I nodded. 'Double helpings.'

She turned another page, tracing a finger down it and said, 'Shouldn't start licking my chops just yet.'

'Why not?'

She closed the book, threw back her hair, tidying it with her fingers, then rested her chin in cupped hands. She said, 'You want to know how this guy's targeting people?'

'Mac should be calling in about two minutes with that info.' I said.

'I'll tell you now, if you want, who he's going for and in what order.'

'I'm listening.'

She tossed her hair again. 'Well, it's sort of good news and bad news.'

I waited.

'His target is people involved with horses killed in the Grand National. He's taking them in chronological order, in reverse.

Tommy last year, Donachy's horse was destroyed the previous year, and one trained by Rowlands, a grey incidentally, hence the "pale horse" quote, the year before that.'

I was staring at her now. 'Brilliant!' I said, and moved quickly down beside her. She showed me the pages, carefully marked. I read through. She was right.

'How did you twig it?' I asked.

'The Grand National's only about ten days away, it was in my mind. There's always some sort of protest there anyway, so it was a good bet for the first shot. I hit lucky.' She smiled, pleased but not triumphant. I'd have been doing handsprings. I felt like kissing her but thought she might consider it patronising.

I tried to get back to a business-like tone. 'So we also know who's lined up next?'

'That's the bad news.'

I could tell by her eyes. 'Me?' I asked.

She nodded.

'Can't be,' I said, lifting the books again. 'I didn't ride the year before Rowlands or the year before that.'

'No fatalities in either of those Nationals,' Lisa said. 'In the previous race there were three. You rode one of them.'

My mind rolled through six years... Mylah, big black beast, took a horrible fall at Becher's, broke his neck.

Lisa arms folded, watched me. 'Who were the other two jocks?' I asked.

She glanced at her notes. 'A. Crawford and M. Pelham.'

I remembered. 'Alan's retired,' I said, 'Mark is still riding.'

'Well we'd better get in touch with them pretty damn fast.'

I dialled McCarthy's number - no answer. I rang Kavanagh while Lisa scanned the paper to see where Pelham was riding today. Kavanagh, as usual, was about as receptive as a rubber lightning rod. I said, 'Look, it's the best theory we've got by far.' I told him Pelham was at Sandown and that he'd better organize protection.

Finding Alan Crawford was going to be more difficult. Many ex-jockeys stay in racing but, from what I could remember, Crawford had disappeared altogether. I told Kavanagh what I knew of him, which wasn't much, and said I'd try and get more info from McCarthy.

I rang him – no answer.

Lisa had the form books open again. I said, 'Take a break. You've done enough.'

She didn't look up. 'Might as well keep tracing through the Nationals, see how long a list we're facing.'

'I'll give you a hand,' I said, and hauled another decade of books off the shelf.

Opening the first one near the middle, I sprayed page-edges off my thumb at a hundred a second until I reached early April and the three-day Grand National meeting.

The next half-hour of searching was interspersed with companionable mumbling and throwaway comments that sought no response stronger than a grunt or an 'Mmmm'. When another name was added to the list I'd picture the face. Very few were unfamiliar to me. Lisa knew her fair share too.

I rang McCarthy again. Still nothing. Back to the books, silent for a long spell. Lisa stopped once and said, 'You know Rowlands? I wonder why he killed the trainer rather than the jockey?'

It was a good point. We ploughed on. Making notes, and passing quiet comments. After a while Lisa said, 'Eddie, I'm tempted to quit my job and take this work up full time.'

I smiled. 'It doesn't pay too good. What would you live on?'

'How about half of the reward money for finding David Cooper?'

'And how long do you think that's going to take?'

She brandished a form book. 'Not long at all because, courtesy of this little book, I know where he is …well, not his exact location, but he's with the killer.'

I waited.

She said, 'He abducted David by mistake.'

'Who did he mean to get?'

'Rowlands' horse wasn't the only one to die in the race three years ago. A Mister D. Cooper's horse fell at Valentine's and broke a shoulder. Cooper was an amateur in his early forties. I remember reading an article about him. He retired at the end of that season.'

I stared at her. 'He's got the wrong man.'

'That's why his corpse hasn't turned up.'

'Yet.'

Lisa said, 'Think he knows about the reward money?'

'Bound to.'

'Fifty grand buys a hell of a lot of ammunition.'

Chapter 41

We had a meeting that evening at the Lodge. McCarthy, Kavanagh and Miller came.

It went smoothly apart from the occasional belches of sourness from the two cops, pissed off at being beaten to it. Protection had already been arranged for Mark Pelham. Alan Crawford was tracked down working in a stud in Dubai. The Sheikh who owned the place promised him two bodyguards. Lisa had come up with seven more names from the last ten Grand Nationals; Mac's department and the cops were trying to trace them.

The debate was whether to give all of them police protection. If the killer stuck to chronological order everyone else was safe until Pelham, Crawford and I were dead.

Kavanagh said with some satisfaction, 'You'll need a babysitter too, Malloy.'

Resisting a sarcastic reply, I nodded, 'Fine.' Kavanagh rang Sanders, his boss, and told him we wanted to keep the Animal Rights connection from the media for the moment. Sanders gave us forty-eight hours. He was being pressed for results and was anxious to publish news of progress.

We decided not to tell Jack Cooper about his son in case he hired a posse to round up every known AR activist in the country.

Beckman's name was mentioned, but McCarthy was confident he'd never shown any leanings toward Animal Rights.

Miller told us about a special department at Scotland Yard which had a file called ARNI, Animal Rights National Index. ARNI held details of all AR people known to the police. Miller and Kavanagh planned to go there next day for a full briefing.

'Can we have another meeting after you've been there?' I asked.

Kavanagh said, 'We'll see,' but his cold look meant, no, we can't. I suggested asking Mark Pelham to help us trap the murderer by pulling his bodyguard away and having a team follow him unobtrusively.

'Why don't you be the stool-pigeon, Malloy?' Miller asked, 'you're pretty good at volunteering others for dangerous jobs.'

I said, 'I'd be happy to, but if the guy's working in strict chronological order backwards then he'll try for Pelham before me. He was last to fall.'

Mac said, 'You really think he'll be that thorough?'

I shrugged. 'He's been pretty precise so far. Breaking the exact bone each horse had broken, leaving them to suffer for about as long as it would take to get a vet there. He even chose a quote for Rowlands that fitted the colour of the dead horse. I think we're dealing with a very picky man.'

Overruling my protests that they might at least consult Pelham, they threw the idea out, though they did agree to my shadowing Pelham for the next few days.

McCarthy thought that was a bad move. 'You're offering the killer two birds with one stone.'

'There'll be a bodyguard there too, Mac,' I reminded him, 'it won't be easy to take three of us.'

'But you obviously think he'll try, or you wouldn't be tagging along.'

I shrugged. 'It'll pass a day or two until we've got some solid information together on the Animal Rights people.'

He didn't like it any better, but said no more. He was tired and hungry and wanted to get home. By eleven, they'd all gone. I called Lisa to give her an update and mentioned I felt guilty she'd had no credit for her detective work.

'Don't be daft,' she said, 'you sussed what the motive was, not me. I only filled in a few blanks.'

'Still,' I said, 'I'd like to have told them tonight how brilliant you were. I'm, well, I don't mean this to sound patronising, but I'm proud of you.'

There was silence for a moment then she said quietly, 'I know what you mean, Eddie. I'm proud of you too. I've had more satisfaction, I was going to say fun but it's not really the right word, more… fulfilment out of this than from anything I've done in my life.'

'Well, I'd still have been blundering blindly if it wasn't for you.' I was about to tell her she was a wasted talent sitting typing out the crap that's spouted in Enquiries, but it wouldn't take much to push her into quitting her job, a dangerous decision to make on the back of seventy-two hours of adrenaline.

'Do you intend to stay with Mark Pelham, sort of, twenty-four-seven?' She asked.

'Probably. We'll need to see how it goes. I'll keep you up to date as best I can.'

'I'm not worried about that. I've got some plans. I'll spend tomorrow morning with Susan and in the afternoon I'll ferret out, if that's the right word, my local Animal Rights Group and see if they want a new member.'

'Lisa, no, look-'

'Eddie. Shhh! I'm doing it. I'm in now. I faxed my resignation across this afternoon.'

Chapter 42

I drove to Haydock next day, reaching the course as Mark Pelham went out for his third ride.

I watched him throughout the race, crouched nervously behind his mount's head in a much lower style than usual. Vehicles using the M6 were easily visible from the far side of the track, and the thought of what a particularly loud backfire might do to Pelham's sphincter brought a smile.

He finished third, and I moved down from the stand to walk in alongside him. Seeing me he nodded briefly. His tightly strapped riding helmet gave him premature forehead wrinkles and squeezed a few dark curls out behind his ears. Nervously, he studied the faces in the crowd. A couple of times he turned to glance behind. Veins stood out in his neck, and I could see the clear beat of a pulse there. His white breeches bore mud and grass-stains, which told me he'd had a fall.

Standing by the entrance to the winner's enclosure, Kavanagh watched Pelham come in on the dark, steaming horse. Then Kavanagh saw me and looked perplexed, though he didn't speak. Pelham guided his mount into third spot and vaulted down. His trainer and the horse's owner asked him how it had gone, and must have been surprised to find him clutching their arms and gathering them around him in a human shield.

I hoped for Pelham's sake that whatever was in store would happen soon. His nerves wouldn't take many more days like this. I drifted over and stood beside Kavanagh. He spoke from the corner of his mouth looking at me.

'What do you want, Malloy?'

'Just wondered if all was quiet on the Western Front. Pelham looks a bit nervous.'

'And you're so cool.'

'That wasn't what I meant.'

'Listen, you shouldn't be talking to me. For all you know the killer could be watching.'

'So?'

'He might suss that I'm a cop.'

'Think that would make any difference?'

'Piss off, Malloy.'

'What about my protection?'

'Stick with Pelham until we get a chance to talk. His bodyguard's the guy across there in the dark coat and glasses.'

'With the silvery tie?'

'Uh-huh.'

'Fine. I'll stay by the weighing room and wait for Mark.'

I stood it for about two hours then realized why Pelham's nerves were shredded. Kavanagh and the bodyguard behaved as though they expected the gunman to walk round the next corner, step from a doorway, spring from behind a tree, drop from the roof, pop up through a drain. The tension stretched between them like a fraying hawser. Sooner or later it had to snap.

If this was what protection did to you, I told Kavanagh, I didn't want it. He made me sign a disclaimer and I left at five and returned to the Lodge.

I rang Lisa. No answer. Something else for me to worry about. I moped for a while wondering about the wisdom of refusing a bodyguard. With Pelham being watched closely, the murderer might take the easy option and come for me.

He had a gun. At least one. What did I have? A metal baseball bat. It could crack your skull, cave your ribs in, but I wouldn't swing it quite so fast with a bullet in my head. Or with my lungs full of ether.

The sweet pungency came back to me.

Where was Beckman?

Why did the killer use ether? You stick a gun in someone's face, they tend to be reasonably obedient. Why knock them unconscious?

Maybe he had to set them up in a certain position for limb breaking. What did he use, a hammer? He'd have to put his gun down then, I suppose, to hit them. Was that why he used the anaesthetic?

I unhooked the bat from the coat stand, comforted by the heft of it in my palm, squeezing the rubber grip. Opening the door, I took it outside and walked to the rear of the building twirling the bat as I went, watching the sun glint off its swollen stainless-steel end.

Only twitches of pain now from the ten-day-old wounds. I widened the arc of the swing, gripping one-handed then double, turning and crouching, imagining a bone-rending connection with the murderer, or Beckman. I had to get Beckman whatever else happened.

By the shed in the garden lay a heap of bulging black refuse sacks. I brought the bat down hard on the top one and it burst, spraying out long-dead leaves.

The wind helped suck them through the gaping hole, then blew them in all directions. I spun and whirled, turned and dived, swinging the bat at the flying leaves like a maniac trying to swat a swarm of locusts, keeping it up until all the leaves had gone.

I stood panting, laughing, half-moaning as my back ached and the wind ruffled my hair then patted it down as though saying, try again some other time, little boy.

Evening. Alone in the Lodge. Waiting. I couldn't settle. It seemed strange without Lisa. Where was she? How was she? How was Pelham?

This was hopeless. I couldn't suffer it, the hanging around, the tension. I rang McCarthy to tell him I was home.

'Who's with you?' he asked.

'Nobody.'

I told him about dumping the bodyguard and signing Kavanagh's disclaimer.

'You're crazy,' he said.

'I know, but I've decided to take my own precautions.'

'If they're illegal, I don't want to know.'

'They're not. I'm just going to make myself hard to find. I'll move out of here for a while, stay off the racecourse. If this guy wants me he'll have to come looking.'

As we discussed the best place for me to go, I realized it wasn't where I was that was screwing me up, it was the fact that I was doing nothing.

'Heard from Miller today?' I asked Mac.

'Not yet.'

'So you don't know if he saw these ARNI people at Scotland Yard?'

'I'm assuming he did.'

'They're taking the piss, Mac, you realize that? Miller and Kavanagh and your man, Inspector Sanders. We give them leads, they promise to keep us informed, and then we get nothing.'

It didn't take long to persuade him I was right. He had connections at Scotland Yard, and I talked Mac into arranging a meeting for me with one of the ARNI people.

'Give me half an hour, I'll ring you back,' he said.

Chapter 43

The ARNI man's name was Kevin Sollis. I was to meet him at ten next morning. Intent on avoiding any midnight visitors, I set off for London that evening.

Sollis, one of two guys on the ARNI unit, was friendly looking, thirtyish, with a big square face, light brown hair, thick moustache, skin pitted ruggedly but evenly, like orange rind. He wore a checked lumberjack shirt loose over khaki army-type fatigues with loads of pockets, the bottoms tucked into high Timberland boots – a regular backwoodsman who'd been born in the wrong country. He was very helpful, didn't seem at all miffed about me being a 'layman', and he had a general demeanour of quiet patience and inner calm that Kavanagh and Miller could have learnt from.

He'd spent some time with Miller the previous day and said he was happy to give me the same info and advice he'd dished out to him.

First, he gave me a potted history of the Animal Rights Movement in Britain. Set up in the mid-seventies, they operated in individual cells with no overall structure. They raided Animal Research establishments, farms, pet shops, butchers, burger bars, department stores, and fox-hunting yards.

They carried out rescues or arson attacks, their main tactic being economic sabotage of any business they thought was involved in animal abuse.

Of late they'd started branching into 'consumer terrorism', threatening to contaminate food and drink manufactured by companies whose policies they disapproved of. The police reckoned around two thousand activists were operational in the UK.

To combat them, ARNI had been set up in 1984, and officers from the unit had made a number of arrests, securing convictions and jail sentences in some cases.

Only a handful of activists had been convicted of individual acts of personal violence, and Sollis had concentrated on those in drawing up a list of possible suspects for Miller.

He had pinpointed the four most likely and graded them on an educated guess basis as to which we should aim for first.

I said, 'Only four? I thought there'd be a few.'

He smiled, teeth hidden under the big moustache. 'It's a funny game, you know. Most of the people involved realize they've got, if not the support of the general public, then a grudging sort of sympathy. As long as they stick to raiding research labs, burning down furriers and disrupting fox-hunts, then they know they'll be looked on as crusading outlaws. Once they get involved in violence, it's a different story.'

I argued that the movement, by its very nature, must attract fanatics, but Sollis said they're quickly weeded out.

'Then where do they go, the weeds?'

He shrugged. 'Who knows? A few are just violent for the sake of it and find somewhere else to practise it…gangs, football terraces, pub fights.'

'But the true Animal Rights fanatic, maybe one who's tired of what he sees as peaceful protest, might well blow a gasket and go on a spree like this?' I asked.

'Every chance.'

'So, if the movement itself is eager to keep a non-violent image, there's a possibility someone there would blow the whistle on this guy if they knew who he was?'

Sollis said, 'Your real problem would be getting them to admit any association with him.'

'But if I could convince them he was definitely on an Animal Rights kick?'

He smiled his slow smile. 'It's worth trying.'

I asked what Miller's thoughts had been on this list. Sollis said he'd just taken the names, along with a note of their last known whereabouts, and headed north saying he'd be in touch.

'A dedicated detective.' I said sarcastically.

Sollis shrugged, refusing to rise to it. 'Some like using different methods.'

I left it at that.

The Animal Rights Movement had no recognized leader, but Sollis told me my best bet for information was a guy all the other AR people looked up to.

He'd just been released after serving five years for arson and was living in a London flat provided by a sympathiser. He was known simply as Buck, a name he'd adopted in memory of the ill-used fictional dog hero in The Call of the Wild.

Buck's flat was in North London, halfway down a shabby backstreet. I pressed the bell. A minute later the door was opened by a thin, pallid man in a white T-shirt and blue jeans. He was barefoot, his toes long and pale, fair hair cropped short, a day's beard on his narrow jaw and wearing glasses so thick that each blue eye seemed to fill the lens. He blinked, almost startling me. I said, 'I'm looking for Buck.'

'Who are you?'

'My name's Eddie Malloy.'

'What do you want with Buck?'

I was trying to place the accent but couldn't.

I said, 'I need his help.'

Buck stared a while longer, blinked again then led me inside.

He sat on the edge of a square table, sharing the space with a big blue typewriter and piles of letters, half of them unopened. Smoking roll-ups and drinking strong black coffee from a panda-badged mug, he talked about Animal Rights with the controlled passion of a fanatic tutored by a PR man, a mixture of persuasive reasoning and colourful sound bites: 'Vivisection labs and factory farms are the concentration camps of the Human Reich.'

When I steered him round to what I wanted to discuss he said, 'Everyone involved in horse racing is a fucking moron.'

I said, 'Well all these morons are building themselves a nice fund of sympathy in the public eye because this bloke is going around knocking them off. He must be setting your cause back years.'

He stopped halfway through a slug of coffee and said, 'Don't try and con me with that shit, man.'

I shrugged, 'Nothing to do with conning you, it's a simple fact. Racing folk are involved in sport, they're not vivisectionists or factory farmers, they're innocent people trying to make a living and this guy is murdering them.'

He loosed off then about whipping and making horses jump

fences, and I listened without interrupting too many times, but I kept driving him back to the point because he knew I was right. I mentioned the names Sollis had given me and Buck smoked a while and thought.

He said, 'I'd have to make a phone call. You want to come back?'

'If it's privacy you want, I'll wait outside.'

'Okay, gimme five minutes.'

After a few minutes, he opened the door and said, 'Reid moved to the Shetlands a few months ago, he's either studying seals or working on the rigs, depending what story you believe. Craven's hanging around with some of the so-called New Age Travellers, last heard of in Dorset about three weeks ago.'

'Where in Dorset?'

'Dunno.'

'What about the other two?'

His magnified eyes stared at me blankly, saying he thought he'd done enough. 'No information,' he said.

'You haven't got it or won't give it?'

'Haven't got it.'

We exchanged mistrusting glances for a few seconds. 'I'd appreciate a call if you do find out anything about them.'

He took my number without comment, a hint of sourness creeping in; regret, maybe, that he'd helped me. I left. He didn't say goodbye.

I rang McCarthy and asked him to speak to Dorset police and find out the movements of whatever convoy Craven was with.

He said, 'Maybe we should get Kavanagh to do it.'

'Maybe we shouldn't. Listen, Mac, Kavanagh doesn't give a toss; the guy is a bad policeman. So is Miller. He took the same list as I've got and buggered off without giving it any more thought. If Kavanagh finds out about Craven, he'll either ignore it completely or go barging in among those travellers like Geronimo attacking a wagon train. They're sure to point him toward Craven then, aren't they?'

He gave in with a sigh but no further argument. 'Okay, Eddie, I'll ring you as soon as I've spoken to the Dorset people.'

While waiting, I studied again the briefing sheet Sollis had given me on Craven, and the picture. Very dark, blue-black hair long and thick, heavy eyebrows over deep-set dark eyes, leathery complexion and, in this picture anyway, a moody scowl.

Thirty-three, divorced, convictions for violence going back sixteen years, twelve of which he'd spent in jail for murdering a man who'd kicked his dog (the judge had allowed for a certain degree of provocation).

Most of Craven's troubles could be blamed, it seemed, on his terrible temper. He could take offence at the mildest comment and lash out immediately with whatever was to hand, which, given his taste for drink, was often a beer glass.

He had a soft spot for animals, stemming from his childhood in Cornwall where he was raised on a farm, often trading pocket money or payment for work in exchange for the life of a lamb or pig, despite his father's mockery.

At seventeen he'd joined a hunt saboteurs group but was banished by them after frenziedly attacking a huntsman who'd been left behind when his horse went lame. It had taken five of Craven's fellow saboteurs to drag him off the unconscious rider.

When told by his 'colleagues' he was no longer welcome, he'd set about them too, putting three in hospital.

Jailed for murder just as Animal Rights Groups were setting up their economic sabotage operations, Craven had supported them from his cell in the form of a stream of letters to newspapers, few of which were printed.

He looked a sound bet from a violence point of view, but there seemed to be no Bible connection, and the only link with horses was that first incident at the hunt. Why would he have latched on to racing?

Mac got the information I needed and I headed for Dorset.

In the small village of Castle Combe, it wasn't hard to discover the pub favoured by the travellers. It was even easier to unearth where Craven was. At the cost of a few pints of beer and a story from me about trying to contact Craven with regard to a legacy left to him by a recently dead animal rights sympathiser, I found out he was no longer at the camp.

He'd been travelling with the convoy in an old estate car since the previous autumn, but hadn't wintered well. After spending the cold months with a worsening hacking cough and spitting gobs of phlegm 'the size of fried eggs', Craven had been admitted, six weeks ago, to a Bristol hospital, suffering from tuberculosis.

It was too late to get to Bristol and see Craven. I booked in at a small hotel, phoned Sollis and Mac, and told them I planned to visit

Craven next day. I tried Lisa's number. We hadn't spoken for three days. It rang out. My answer-phone at the Lodge had a remote playback and I'd agreed with Lisa we could leave messages for each other if there was anything important. I'd given her the access code. I called it, hoping to hear her voice, even if there was nothing to report. The tape was empty.

Chapter 44

I was Craven's only visitor. He sat propped up on pillows, wheezing gently, looking much less threatening than in his photograph. The thick dark hair was stringy and grey-streaked, the cheeks sunken, the eyes dull. His thin lips were clogged at the corners with white sticky matter. A shallow enamel bowl curved to fit the chin lay on his bedside table, its bottom coated with red-speckled phlegm. Beside the bowl were two get-well cards.

I sat down and introduced myself as a journalist, but I could see from the start he didn't buy it. I told him I was working on the jockey murders and had got on to the Animal Rights angle and that there'd be a few quid in it for him if he could give me an inside story.

He said nothing. I might as well have been talking to his pillows. He lay staring at me as though he pitied me, shaking his head slowly at what I said. When for the third time I asked if he thought any Animal Rights supporter could be capable of these murders, he spoke: 'Fuck off, you prick,' he said weakly, his eyes finally showing an edge of hardness.

I stood and lifted the cards from his table. He frowned and wheezed as I opened them. One was from Mary and urged him to get better for the summer. The second said, 'Get fit and come out fighting!' It was from Buck.

I headed for the car knowing Buck had put me away and wondering how significant it was. In saying Craven was with the travellers in the West Country, he'd given me sufficient information, if I was smart enough, to track Craven down to his hospital bed.

Why hadn't he simply said he didn't know where he was? Why

hadn't he told me Craven was in the Shetlands along with the other guy, what was his name? Reid. Was he just trying to keep me off Reid's tail? Was Reid our man?

I stopped at a payphone in the reception area and dug the cop's card out: Kevin Sollis. I rang and persuaded him to join me for a drink around ten o'clock. It was eightish now; I could get to London for ten. He said to meet him at The Yard.

Sollis, still wearing his backwoods gear, waited outside on the pavement idly throwing soft kicks at a lamppost and whistling quietly. The same lazy smile was there under his moustache as he reached to shake my hand. 'You like real ale?' he asked.

'Don't think I've ever tried it.'

'Want to?'

'Sure.'

He turned me with a hand on my shoulder. 'There's a good place about five minutes' walk away.'

'Fine.'

We ambled companionably down the wet street, Sollis telling me lovingly about the qualities of real ale, stopping occasionally to expand on a point, never once asking why I'd invited him out. By the time we reached the pub he'd made me feel I'd been his friend for years.

I guessed he had a gift for doing that with everyone. A few more of his kind in the police force in exchange for the Kavanaghs and Millers would improve its image.

Comfortably settled in a smoky corner of a busy bar, I told him I thought Buck had conned me and that he might be hiding the real killer. 'What would be the chances of a phone tap?' I asked.

He turned, raising an eyebrow, 'On Buck?'

I nodded.

'Got one,' he said and sipped beer.

'Now?'

'Uh-huh.'

'Who monitors it?'

'We tape everything and play it back each morning.'

I felt the sudden tension of expectation. 'So who did he call to get the info he gave me on Craven?'

'Nobody. He was just bluffing you.'

'But there must be something. He must make some calls?'

'Oh, he makes calls and he gets calls but it's all domestic stuff. He knows we're listening in.'

'So what's the point of tapping the line?'

Sollis shrugged. Reaching for his glass he said, 'Procedure, I suppose.'

'Sounds a bit daft to me.'

He shrugged again, happy to accept my judgement. I said, 'He must make calls from elsewhere, I mean he must have some contact with these other Animal Rights people.'

Sollis said, 'I'm sure he does. He'll get a call asking him to ring back and he goes out and rings from a call-box.'

'So why don't you bug the call-box?'

'He always uses a different one. Anyway, we'd have trouble getting clearance for that. Buck's been squeaky clean since he came out.'

A woman sat down at the piano in the corner and tried to start a sing-along. Sollis looked across at her and smiled. I said to him, 'Why didn't you tell me on Wednesday about the phone tap?'

'You were enthusiastic. I didn't think Buck would give you anything, but I couldn't be certain.'

I looked at him. 'I was thinking of trying again tomorrow,' I said, 'confronting him with the fact that he knew Craven was in hospital.'

Sollis drank and shook his head. 'Pointless. He'd just laugh at you.'

'So what do I do next?'

'We can try to locate the other three on your list.'

'How long is that likely to take?'

'No way of saying but we can start in the morning.'

I sighed and nodded slowly, downcast. Sollis punched my shoulder gently and smiled. 'Cheer up. It's not the end of the world.' He started singing along with the pianist, as tuneless as he was jolly.

I went to the payphone to call Lisa. No answer; I was beginning to worry. Meeting Craven and Buck had given me a taste of what some of the extremists were like, and I'd always been uneasy about Lisa's blithe intention to infiltrate an Animal Rights group.

I called the Lodge and pictured the phone ringing out in an empty house. The answer-phone clicked on and I entered the playback code.

Lisa's voice was there telling me she was just checking in. No real news, though she had joined an Animal Rights Group which she said, so far, was 'the bore of the year'. I smiled.

After Lisa, another female voice played back, a stranger. Identifying herself as a Mrs Pritchard she carefully gave her contact details, saying she had some urgent information on Claude Beckman.

Chapter 45

Next morning, Sunday, I returned Mrs Pritchard's call. She was nowhere near as keen as she'd seemed on the answer-phone, saying that she wasn't sure it mattered much anymore. Eventually she agreed to see me at her house near Finsbury Park around ten-thirty.

On my way to North London a newspaper banner caught my eye. I stopped and bought three papers. Inspector Sanders had released the Animal Rights 'line of inquiry', saying he felt confident the public would respond positively with any information.

With the Grand National less than a week away the press, predictably, made a major story of it with most of the tabloids carrying it on the front page. I wondered how the killer felt as he read it over his breakfast.

Mrs Pritchard watched from behind a curtain as I climbed half a dozen steps toward her door, and waited without knocking. She was tall, even in her flat shoes, maybe forty-five, pale skin, long face, sad eyes. She didn't invite me in and suggested we have our chat in the open spaces of Finsbury Park.

It was cold and drizzly. She wore a grey herringbone coat and carried a black umbrella. I turned my collar up.

Between splay-footed strides on the wet pavement, she spoke little, though the noise as buses and cars splashed past would have drowned conversation anyway. We went through the gates and took the diagonal path across the park. In a grove of trees by the railed-off duck pond she said, 'I am Claude Beckman's sister.'

I waited for more.

She said, 'I was concerned when some of the papers were alleging

Claude might have been involved in those jockey killings.'

She'd obviously become a lot less concerned when she'd seen this morning's headlines, hence her sudden backtracking. I said nothing. She continued. 'Claude couldn't kill anyone; it's not something he'd be capable of, much as he may sometimes like to think he would.'

We walked on past a kid throwing bread to the ducks. Mrs Pritchard said, 'Claude had a large chip on his shoulder about you, but he had no quarrel with the men who were killed and the newspapers shouldn't have implied he was involved. He hated you because you took a race away from Mother just before she died, the Whitbread Gold Cup.'

I'd finished second in the Whitbread, one of the biggest races of the season, about six years ago. But I'd been awarded the race after objecting to the winner for bumping me on the run-in. I couldn't even remember the name of the horse who'd originally 'won.'

Mrs Pritchard said, 'Mother had always wanted to win the Whitbread. She'd been ill for some time, but had gone to Sandown that day with Claude. When her horse passed the post first she told Claude she could die happy. Then you objected and they took the race away from her. She died two weeks later. Claude doted on her.'

I recalled Mrs Beckman's picture on Claude's mantelpiece. Now I knew why she'd seemed familiar. I also remembered the defaced photo in his racing album and realized the slashed, scarred jockey was me.

'Do you know where Claude is?' I asked.

'I haven't seen him for more than three years. We were never particularly close, but I felt I owed it to the family name to try to clear it in his absence.'

'So how do you know he hated me so much?'

'Because for ages after the Whitbread, he talked about getting revenge on you, then within a year you'd lost your licence and your livelihood and Claude was ecstatic. Then, last summer when I read you'd got your licence back, I knew Claude would be raging. I thought of warning you but I knew he was working for The Jockey Club and I didn't want to jeopardize his position.'

'But you didn't mind jeopardizing mine?'

Offended, she stopped and looked down at me. 'If I'd have thought you were in any real danger, I would have warned you.'

'A bit late for that.'

A jogger passed us, panting, squelching across the grass.

She said, 'What do you mean?'

'Just over a week ago he drugged me, locked me up in his garden shed, stripped me and laid into me with a horse-whip until he was too tired to lift his arm. Then he dumped me naked in a car park.'

She stared, frowning, thinking, then said, 'But he didn't kill you.'

'So that justifies it?'

'Of course not. I'm sorry he did that, but what I meant was, he's not a killer.'

She turned and slowly started walking again. Producing a linen handkerchief from her pocket she tried, as elegantly as her long nose allowed, to clear her sinuses.

'So why doesn't your brother come out and defend himself against these allegations in the papers? Where is he?'

'I don't know.'

We walked a few strides in silence then she said, 'Did you tell the police he assaulted you? Are they looking for him?'

'They know what he did, and they're sort of looking for him in a half-hearted manner.'

'So they don't really believe he killed those men?'

'I don't think they do. They can't make their minds up.'

'So,' she said indignantly, 'why are the papers allowed to publish these allegations? How can they get away with it?'

I shrugged. 'If you look closely you'll see they're not really alleging anything, not outright anyway, it's the way it's written – for those who read between the lines. They use terms like "confirmed bachelor" which is libel-free doublespeak for homosexual.'

She said, 'They used that expression for Claude.'

'And is he?'

She looked at me like I smelled bad. 'He is a confirmed bachelor. He is not, as far as I know, a homosexual.'

'As far as you know?'

'We were never that close. I didn't keep tabs on his private life. What has Claude's sexuality got to do with it? It would hardly give him reason to murder people.'

She was right, and I realized my mind kept returning to the intensity of his grunts as he beat me. The nakedness and helplessness adding to what I was seeing as the sexual edge of the assault.

On the walk back I learnt she was a widow and ventured out seldom, preferring a quiet life with her cats. Two of them were in the window as though waiting for her, and it was the only time I saw her smile. She went up the steps without a goodbye and, duty done, conscience clear, stepped through the door back into her own private little world.

I called McCarthy and updated him on Beckman.

'So what's your next move?' he asked.

I sighed. 'I'm going to stay away from the Lodge for a few more days. Sollis has been helpful. Says he'll get to work today on tracking down the other three names on my list but we're running out of time, Mac. This guy must have something big planned for Saturday, some major fireworks.'

'Probably. I've got a meeting with the Aintree executive tomorrow morning to discuss security.'

'Better tell them to get the army in.'

'Cheer up, Eddie, we still have a week to get this guy.'

'And he has a week to kill a few more people. Me included.'

'Stop being pig-headed then, take the offer of police protection.'

'I'll tell you, I wouldn't mind Sollis as a minder. He's built like the proverbial brick shit-house and he's an all-round Mister Cool.'

'If he's had firearms training, I could probably arrange that.'

'Okay, see what you can do.'

Next I rang Lisa and felt a slight nervous flutter as, this time, she answered. She sounded glad to hear from me. I told her what I'd been doing and asked how Susan Gilmour was.

'Improving. Very slowly, but she is better.'

Lisa had joined an Animal Rights Group in Cheltenham and quickly befriended one of the most dedicated members, a young girl called Lucy.

Lisa said, 'She's only eighteen. You'd be amazed at the number of kids in these groups. Some of them are only about fourteen!'

'The idealism of youth.'

Lisa had only been to one big meeting but had spent a lot of time with Lucy. She said, 'They have quite an effective recruitment campaign. Once someone shows a spark of interest, they bombard them with statistics on factory farming, research labs and stuff. They hand out horrendous pictures and show videos of fox-hunts and horses taking some terrible falls in races. I'm trying to find out if they have any footage specific to the Grand National. Maybe somebody in the movement specialises in it.'

'Lisa, you've just given me an idea.'

Chapter 46

We sat in Sollis's office. He'd just brought in a box of videotapes and was pushing one into the VCR. He said, 'Aintree last year, that was where you wanted to start, wasn't it?'

'Might as well.'

Pressing the play button, he settled back. 'Got loads of these, you know,' he said, 'fox-hunts to fashion shows. See a lot of the same people in each film. Mostly peaceful. A few skirmishes but no violence on the scale you're talking about.'

The tape opened on about a dozen protesters on the road outside Aintree racecourse. Their banners had pictures of fallen horses under big slogans like YOU BET: THEY'LL DIE and they could be seen appealing to racegoers, though there was no soundtrack.

Most racegoers ignored them; a few openly taunted them. When the camera closed in on faces, Sollis leant toward the screen and pointing with his pen ran through a few names and gave brief biographies of each.

'You'd make a good racecourse commentator.' I told him.

He smiled and continued until a teenager appeared on the screen. Reaching quickly for the remote control he froze the picture. I looked at him. He'd gone serious. He said, 'I'd forgotten about this.' Nodding toward the shimmering freeze-frame he said, 'A few hours after this was taken that kid was dead. Crushed under the wheels of a horsebox.'

I tried to see the boy's face. It wasn't clear. 'What happened?' I asked.

'This protest was on the Friday, the day before the National. Early next morning they appeared farther up the road to try and prevent horseboxes driving into the stables. They had a sit-down protest and our lads had to drag them away to let the boxes through. This kid wriggles free and runs after one of the boxes, tries to jump up on the driver's footplate, misses, and goes under the wheels.'

I cringed. 'You got film of it?'

He nodded. 'But you don't want to see it.' He stopped the tape, ejecting it. 'How about the previous years?' he asked.

I shook my head slowly, still thinking about the dead boy. 'How old was the kid?'

'Sixteen, I think.'

'Was there an inquest?'

'Death by misadventure.'

'Were you there?'

'At the inquest? No. My mate was, had to show this tape and give evidence.'

'Can I talk to him?'

Sollis looked at me. 'Think you're on to something here?'

'Knowing a bit about the likes of Craven now, I'd be pretty sure one of the AR people would have threatened revenge. Didn't you hear of anything?'

'You'd be better talking to Polly, he was dealing with it.'

'Polly?'

'Jim Perkins. We call him Polly.'

Sollis got him on the phone and we had a long chat. The boy's name was Christopher Roe. Roe's mates had tried to attack the box-driver straight after the incident, and the driver had subsequently received death threats by post and telephone, though all that calmed down after a couple of weeks.

The only family the boy had was his father, who he'd lived with on a farm near Hereford. His mother had been killed three years previously in a traffic accident.

'Was his father at the inquest?' I asked.

Perkins said, 'Yes. I remember watching him as the box-driver gave evidence. Now from what I'd heard, if anyone was cut out for taking revenge it was Victor Roe. Ex-SAS man, tough as nails, supposed to have killed half a dozen terrorists in his time.'

'But he was as calm as you like. You'd almost've thought he was in church. Peaceful looking? I'd have called it serene. Not a hint of animosity in his face. Just sat there clutching his Bible.'

Chapter 47

Perkins was confident that after the inquest Roe had returned to his farm to get on with his life as best he could. I was more of a mind that he'd found justification in his Bible to avenge his son's death.

It was mid-afternoon. Sollis was still awaiting official approval to take over as my bodyguard. I rang McCarthy again to tell him about Victor Roe, and to ask him to press hard for Sollis's clearance.

While we waited, I discovered the name of the box-driver involved in the kid's death and rang his stable. I was put on to Tony Greenaway, the head lad, who I knew well. We exchanged pleasantries and I told him as much as he had to know before asking him if I could speak to Sampson, the box-driver.

'He left last year, Eddie, around the beginning of July.'

'D'you know where I can find him?'

'We've already tried a few times. He's called us once, that's all we've heard, and he was in a bit of a state then.'

He told me Sampson had said in that call that he wouldn't be back, that he couldn't forget the kid's death. Sampson had worked there for five years. A recovering alcoholic and ex-vagrant, he'd made a lot of friends at the stable. Tony reckoned he was drunk the night he rang and might have ended up on the streets again.

He said, 'Every month or so one of the lads goes to London and spends a night trawling the streets and soup kitchens to see if we can find him.' He sighed, 'No luck so far.'

'You were sure he was drunk the time he called?'

'He was pretty emotional, crying. That wasn't like him. It was a bloody shame. I remember him saying to tell Liz, that's our cook, that he loved her and that he was sorry he'd never got round to telling her that himself. Terrible…'

'And not a word from him since? Not a sighting?'

'Nothing.'

I thanked Tony and told him I hoped Sampson would turn up, though I had grave doubts.

I tried ringing the police to give them the info on Roe. Kavanagh and Miller were both in London. Inspector Sanders wouldn't speak to me.

Over a quick lunch in his favourite pub, Sollis and I worked on the best and safest way to approach Victor Roe. Sollis wondered how much his ex-bosses in the SAS would be willing to tell us.

Nothing, was the answer. We rang a captain at the Hereford barracks who denied ever having heard of Roe. Sollis pressed him without mentioning that Roe was suspected of involvement in the killings.

The captain insisted he knew nothing of Roe, and that if we wanted more information, we would have to request an interview by letter with his superior and provide details of when Roe was supposed to have served at Hereford.

Sollis called Perkins, who said he understood Roe had left the SAS four years ago after his wife had been killed. He didn't know what rank Roe had held nor could he confirm the 'terrorist killing' stories. He admitted the information on Roe had come from a man at the inquest claiming to be Roe's neighbour. He couldn't recall the man's name.

'Brilliant,' I said. 'How the hell do we corroborate it?'

Sollis smiled. 'Don't worry. We'll get an interview fixed up. They'll have records at the barracks. Standard procedure in the SAS to disclaim all knowledge of individuals.'

We sent the letter by fax to SAS HQ then spent the afternoon waiting for a response, and for approval for Sollis on the bodyguard front. That arrived at six o'clock. We waited another half-hour for a reply from the SAS. None came.

I said, 'Let's go up there. This is a waste of time.'

After completing paperwork in triplicate in three different offices, Sollis checked out a Smith & Wesson pistol, fifty rounds of ammunition and an unmarked Range Rover with a car-phone installed.

I spent the first twenty minutes of the trip marvelling at the technology that allowed you to call somebody on the phone while travelling at eighty miles an hour. 'How much do these cost?' I asked Sollis.

He smiled at my wonderment. 'I heard they're close to two grand.'

'Jeez!'

'Our tech guys say they'll get cheaper. They told me everybody will be carrying one in their pocket in five years' time.'

'They'll need bloody big pockets.'

He smiled again.

I felt better than I'd done since this thing had started. For once, I wasn't on my own. Sollis was more than co-operative. He was friendly, trustworthy, and he was armed.

It's amazing the confidence you have when you've got a gun on your side.

It was dark by seven. We were forty miles from Hereford when the car-phone rang. 'Get that, will you?' Sollis asked.

It was confirmation from his office that a fax had arrived saying someone at the barracks would see us. I used the phone to call Lisa, telling Sollis I had to update her but really just wanting to boast to her that I was calling on a two grand car-phone. She wasn't home. I rang my answer-phone to leave a message for her and to play back whatever had come in.

Lisa had left a long message: 'Eddie, tried to reach you earlier. No luck. Listen, we were wondering why Rowlands was killed and not the jockey? It seems Rowlands ran the horse after it had taken a bad fall in the Gold Cup a couple of weeks before. There'd been a few protests in the press after the Gold Cup, saying the horse should have been retired for the season rather than risked again in the National.

'Rowlands obviously ignored everyone and the killer seems to have taken the view that he was to blame for the horse's death. Anyway, the point is it set me thinking about the others, your race for instance. What if the guy was hunting around for someone other than the jockey to blame?

'Don't know if you've heard of a vet called Digby Craddock, but I found out today that he was responsible for giving the horse that Mark Pelham rode a clean bill of health when it was sold a week before the National. The horse died of a heart attack, and the gossip is that Craddock must have known about it. Some think he did it for a backhander from the vendor.

'I've tried to talk to Craddock on the phone to warn him but he thinks I'm a crank, so I'm driving up to see him. Not far, Bromyard in Worcestershire. I'll try you again on the number you left, once I've spoken to him, or I'll leave another message here. Take care.'

I put the phone down feeling panicky. Lisa's instincts had been a hundred percent sound so far. If she was right on this one too... 'Is it OK to make a call?' I asked.

'Be my guest,' said Sollis.

I phoned McCarthy, and he read the unease in my tone.

'Eddie, what's wrong?' he asked.

'You heard of a vet called Digby Craddock?'

He thought for a few seconds. 'Name rings a bell but I can't say I know him. Why?'

'Lisa thinks he might be involved in all this. She says he had something to do with a dead horse in the National.' My voice was tight, tense.

Mac murmured, 'Craddock, Craddock, Craddock... no, can't think.'

'He lives somewhere in Bromyard. Find out exactly where and get the police there as fast as you can.'

'Eddie-'

'Listen, Mac, Lisa's gone up there to see Craddock. The killer could be making the same trip, now do me a favour, will you? Humour me. You owe me one.'

'Eddie, look-'

'Do it, Mac!' I gave him the car-phone number.

Sollis looked across at me. 'Want me to head for Craddock's place?'

I nodded, staring, bug-eyed, mind racing. He accelerated.

About fifty minutes later, I reckoned we were no more than a couple of miles from Craddock's house when McCarthy rang.

'Eddie...'

I could tell by his voice. 'Lisa?' I asked and held my breath.

'Craddock...he's dead.'

'And Lisa?'

'She's not there.'

'Thank God!'

'Eddie, they found her handbag in Craddock's house.'

Chapter 48

There was still some heat in Craddock's body, which lay on the cold tiles of the kitchen floor. The cops were waiting for their medical man, but a grey-haired sergeant reckoned the vet had been dead less than an hour. The corpse showed no obvious cuts or bruises or broken limbs. The note in the pocket of his pale blue shirt read: Jeremiah 17:9. No one had tried to find a Bible.

Lisa's handbag had been discovered under the kitchen table. The worktop bore signs of a struggle: a pool of coffee spilled from a broken mug, a small bunker of sand which had burst from a shattered egg timer, jagged slivers of a shattered whiskey glass in the stainless steel sink.

I told the sergeant Lisa was my girlfriend. He said, 'Tough break.' He wouldn't let us nose around. 'Nobody touches anything until SOCO get here.'

'Scene of Crime Officer,' Sollis said.

Kavanagh and Miller were also on their way. The sergeant said I'd best wait until they got there. I didn't think so.

I rang Mac from the car and updated him, then asked, 'Have you got a Bible?'

'Somewhere, hold on...'

I heard drawers being opened, stuff being shuffled around then he picked up the phone. I gave him the details and he mumbled quietly as he leafed through the pages. 'Found it. "The heart is deceitful above all things, and desperately wicked."'

I said, 'Mean anything to you?'

He pondered. 'Something's clicking with Craddock... can't pin it down.'

'The key word in the quote is heart. Lisa found out Craddock knew the horse had a dicky heart, but he passed it okay to run in the National. You can tell the pathologist to start the autopsy by looking at Craddock's heart.'

Sitting in the darkness, I thought about Lisa and felt angry at her foolhardiness, then guilt at allowing her too much rope.

Worry followed, twisting maliciously in my gut, sending nasty little questions as to why he'd taken her, feeding images of brutal rape to my mind's bulging eye, then murder. I couldn't switch it off. The more I tried, the more vivid the show became.

Sollis tried to reassure me. 'Maybe she escaped.'

I shook my head. 'Her car's still there. He's got her all right.'

We sat in silence.

Sollis said, 'What's she like? Will she handle it?'

I sighed. 'As long as she stays alive, she will.'

'If it is Roe, he might be heading back to Hereford right now. Want to try to keep this appointment?'

I looked at him. 'Be ten o'clock before we get there. Think this captain guy will see us?'

'I'll drive. You ring him.'

The captain said he'd be there. Sollis pushed the car up to eighty and made me feel better by offering the pistol to load.

Mac rang with confirmation of the rumour Lisa had heard about the dead vet.

'No proof then?' I asked.

'None or he would have been struck off.'

'How widespread was the rumour, Mac?'

'From what I can find out, it seems not that many people had heard it. It was no big deal really, compared to some of the other stuff that goes on.'

'Doesn't it make you wonder how our man got hold of it, then? He'd have to be pretty heavily involved in racing to have heard it first-hand, wouldn't he?'

'I suppose so.'

'Unless he has a ready source of inside information.'

Mac paused then said, 'You think somebody's setting people up?'

'A ready source, Mac. David Cooper. Under duress of course, but that must be why he's holding him.'

'You think he's maybe torturing the boy to get it?'

'Big possibility. Who was the vendor who knew that horse had a dicky heart?'

'I don't know.'

'Well you'd better find out, because he might be next.'

Mac said, 'With Mark Pelham off the hook, you maybe better face the fact that you could be next.'

'Mac, the way I'm feeling, the sooner this bastard comes for me the better. I'm ready.'

'Just stick close to Sollis,' he said, then, 'By the way, if it helps with your Victor Roe theory, the gun used to kill Gilmour and Donachy is among those on standard issue to the SAS.'

We sped on, headlights cutting through the rural dark, my anger and frustration bubbling as I tortured myself with the thought that we were probably driving in the tracks of the killer, following him, never knowing what turn-off would lead in a different direction.

At the SAS camp, two armed soldiers took away Sollis's pistol and ammunition and escorted us to a sparsely furnished office in the basement of a darkened building. They left us alone there for about twenty minutes.

Quickly sussing we were either being watched, listened to or both, we stuck to talking about Roe and the killings.

The door opened and a soldier came in, introducing himself as Captain Gavin: early thirties, slim, quiet looking, nothing rugged or square-jawed about him. Not what I'd expected.

He listened carefully and almost silently to our story as we listed piece by piece why we suspected Roe was involved. When he'd heard us out, I asked, 'Can you confirm that Victor Roe was part of the regiment here at one time?'

'Yes, I can.'

'And that he left when his wife was killed around four years ago?'

'About six months prior to that actually.'

'Do you know why he left?'

'Religious grounds.'

'Can you be more specific?'

'He became one of those born-again people, renounced violence.' The captain seemed contemptuous.

I said, 'Did you know his son also died in an accident this time last year?'

'Oh I know that,' he said, 'but what you gentlemen obviously don't know is that Victor Roe killed himself three months later.'

Chapter 49

Roe had been found dead in his living room, a shotgun on the floor nearby and half his head blown off. He'd left a note saying he couldn't go on after the death of his son.

Having built up my expectations of raiding Roe's place tonight and freeing Lisa, I felt angry and frustrated to the point of tears. After all the disappointments and wrong turnings over the past three weeks, I was raging against fate. I couldn't accept that we were back at the start with nothing.

I'd have bet Jack Cooper's fifty grand reward money Roe was the killer.

We booked in at a pub offering accommodation, and ordered drinks. Sollis had beer. I sipped whiskey. I'd been ranting for a while and I was aware of Sollis watching me.

I said, 'It could be an SAS cover-up, you know, to protect an ex-member. Maybe it wasn't suicide. Maybe he is still running around.'

Sollis nodded, but I could see he just wanted to avoid an argument. He was happy to listen to me sounding off until all the steam had gone. He said, 'We'll go and see the local police in the morning, get full details. See if anything funny shows up.'

'Thanks for humouring me, Kevin. I appreciate it.'

He looked mildly hurt. 'I'm not! It's worth a shot. We're here anyway. It won't do any harm.'

Next morning, we visited the local police station, more because we didn't know where to turn than in any real expectation of finding something. Sollis charmed the desk sergeant into letting us see the file on Roe's suicide. Sitting in the small interview room, we worked our way through it.

On 7th July last year, Roe had placed a shotgun under his chin and blown the front of his head off. The body hadn't been discovered until almost a month after his death when a social worker visiting Roe to help him get over his son's death had discovered his badly decomposed corpse in the living room. Reading the report of the officer in attendance, the first thing Sollis noted was that no swabs had been taken of Roe's hands.

He explained: 'In any shooting there'll be some blow-back, some chemical discharge from the gun onto the hand holding it. It's a simple way of proving a suicide. No trace of discharge, then somebody else pulled the trigger.'

'Would it be standard procedure to take a swab?' I asked.

He shrugged. 'Not exactly standard, I suppose. Depends on the officer in charge.'

'Would the swab still show something after a month?'

'Oh yes. Would be faint, but it would be there.'

Flipping the report over, he picked up the next piece of paper, read it and passed it to me. 'Suicide note,' he said. 'Probably the reason they didn't take a swab.'

I looked at Roe's blocky handwriting: '1472 days since Isobel's death. 83 since Christopher's. Along with my God they both await me in Heaven.'

The figures were a neat uniform height. Sollis flicked a picture across of Roe's wasted, insect ridden, unrecognisable corpse. I gazed at it for a while then at the numbers again and I smiled.

Sollis frowned at me. I said, 'He faked it.'

'What?'

'He's still alive.'

Fifteen minutes later Sanders faxed a copy of the other notes Roe had left on his victims, as well as the one he'd sent me. We sat comparing the figures on the chapter and verse numbers with those on Roe's 'suicide' note. To my eye, they matched exactly.

Sollis although not as convinced, agreed there was a very strong chance my theory was right.

To help build my case, I got the number of Roe's social worker and rang her. She confirmed what I'd suspected, that Roe had known the exact date she was due to drop in. In the three weeks after his son's death, she'd gone there once a week, then Roe had said that a monthly visit would be fine.

'So what was his thinking there?' Sollis asked.

'To make doubly certain the body was unidentifiable…by sight anyway. First he makes sure the shotgun blows the face away, then to cover any discrepancies in build, he gives the corpse maximum time to rot, knowing it unlikely that anybody except the social worker will call at the farm for a month.'

Sollis nodded slowly, then said, 'So who's the dead man?'

I leaned back, comfortable with my thoughts, happy that I'd put everything together correctly. I said, 'Who do you think? Who'd be most likely?'

Hands in pockets, Sollis shrugged. 'A jockey? Trainer?'

'How about Sampson, the box-driver?'

He frowned, puzzling. I said, 'Roe's a religious man. He has to find justification for killing. Who would he have felt justified in killing within twelve weeks of his son's death under the wheels of a horsebox?'

The big man's frown dissolved. He smiled.

I said, 'The guy's supposed to have conveniently disappeared and returned to the anonymous life of a vagrant a few days before Roe kills himself. He rings the stable in a very emotional state to say he won't be back, which means, theoretically, nobody will be looking for him.'

'I'm warming to it. Go on.'

I said, 'How'd you like to bet Roe had a pistol at the poor bloke's head as he spoke?'

The more we went over the whole thing, the more convinced I was that I was right. Sollis was on my side. Mac too, when I rang him. He decided to drive straight up.

By the time he arrived, we'd read the contents of Roe's will. He'd asked that the animals be given free to good homes and that the farm be sold and all proceeds donated to the RSPCA. He'd added an interesting rider: 'As a memorial to my wife and son, the farm should stand empty for a period of one year before being sold.'

I looked at my companions. 'Guess where Mister Roe is based?' I said.

Chapter 50

The farm lay five miles north of the town. Sollis had persuaded me that we had to wait until nightfall before going in. We were on our own. Kavanagh and Miller, acting on information from Buck, were scouring the flatlands of East Anglia trying to find their new 'chief suspect'.

Inspector Sanders was of the opinion that we hadn't a shred of solid evidence to justify a raid on "a dead man's house".

British summer time had begun the previous night and I had to suffer the additional frustration of waiting an extra hour for darkness. If anything happened to Lisa between now and us going in, it would take a lot of living with.

As dusk fell, Sollis and I crouched on the crest of a small hill about five hundred yards from Roe's farm. McCarthy had volunteered to stay with the car 'in case we needed to make a quick getaway'.

One light showed in the farmhouse through a downstairs window. Sollis checked his gun for the tenth and final time, and darkness wasn't quite on us when we started creeping down the hill.

Reaching the corner of the house, I peeped out across the yard. All was still and silent.

I turned to Sollis. 'I'm going to work my way along that wall. If he's inside the house, he won't see me. If he's outside, he can only be in the big barn to your left or by the gable end at the top. Can you try to cover those areas?'

'I will. Be careful.'

'I'm only going to take a look through the window, no heroics.'

'Good luck.'

I slunk out, crouching, and scuttled toward the corner. Staying close to the rough sandstone wall, scrutinising doorways and the deep windows of the barn opposite, I felt my senses so keenly tuned I could have seen an atom or heard a feather land on snow.

I reached the lit window and peered in: an empty kitchen, bare ceiling bulb casting a harsh glow on the sink unit, table and chairs, dirty dishes, a toppled cereal box and various packets and tins. Glancing behind toward Sollis, I saw his silhouette against the last of the light of the evening sky. I moved on.

In the shadow of the doorway, as I reached for the handle, the door was opened from the inside. Sollis shouted, 'Down, Eddie!'

But I stayed upright, and saved the life of David Cooper.

The boy said Roe had left two hours previously, then he led us to where Lisa lay in a bedroom. Hearing footsteps, she got to her feet looking defiant. When our eyes met she tried to smile, but her face crumpled and she slumped. I caught her before she fell.

He'd kept her tied up, using blue and yellow mountaineering ropes threaded through heavy metal rings fixed to wall-beams. Her wrists and ankles were raw from rope-burns.

She clung to me, head on my shoulder, weeping quietly and I was perversely happy that her cool efficiency, her hundred per cent competence had finally broken down.

Sollis said, 'Eddie, he might come home any time.'

Lisa jerked upright, her wet wide eyes staring at me. 'You haven't caught him?!'

Half-puzzled I shook my head. 'No, he left two hours ago, according to David.'

Lisa looked horrified. She said, 'He's gone to kill Vanessa Compton!'

Vanessa Compton was an owner who lived in Richmond, Yorkshire. Roe had told Lisa that although Compton had been warned of her horse's failing eyesight, she'd forced her trainer to run it in the National where it had fallen, breaking its neck.

When talking about it, Roe had kept quoting to Lisa, 'If the blind lead the blind then both shall fall into the ditch.'

Sollis rang the Richmond police suggesting they might be able to trap Roe, and asked them to contact us at Hereford police station as soon as they knew anything. He and McCarthy took over control of operations, organising a welcome party of armed police at the farmhouse in case Roe aborted the Richmond attack.

Before leaving to take Lisa to the Lodge, I reminded young Cooper to call his mother and father. He nodded, looking a bit perplexed by everything. He told me he'd found Roe waiting in the back seat of his car the day he set off for London and his mother's party.

Roe soon realized he had the wrong D. Cooper, but couldn't let him go and kept him locked in the basement below a heavy trap door. The night we turned up was the first night the kid had tried to open the trapdoor, and succeeded only to narrowly avoid having his head blown off by Sollis.

Chapter 51

Roe never appeared in Yorkshire, nor did he return to his farm. That worried Lisa enough to talk me into moving out of the Lodge again. Roe had told her how frustrated he was that he'd failed to trace me and keep to his strict chronological killing order.

He'd known too that I'd been trying to track him down, though Lisa couldn't say how he'd got that information or how he'd learned about the rumours surrounding Digby Craddock and Vanessa Compton.

Mac had checked out the Compton 'blindness' thing and, as with the vet, confirmed that it had been a tightly kept piece of gossip. I asked David Cooper if Roe had been pumping him for information. He denied it.

Sollis shadowed us discreetly over the next three days. We stayed in Southport, close to Aintree, and moved each night to a different hotel.

Lisa was sure Roe was still after me, and by Wednesday evening she almost had me convinced too. But he'd have his work cut out.

His face was all over the newspapers and the TV bulletins. There had been numerous reported sightings in the last forty-eighty hours, all of them investigated by the police, none leading to anything other than increased media hysteria.

We heard that David Cooper had paid a brief visit to his father, who was now off the danger list but barred from attending the National in which David was to ride his horse, Gospel Oak. Jack Cooper sent me a message via McCarthy, congratulating me on finding the boy and promising a cheque soon.

I told Lisa we'd have a fortnight in Antigua when the money arrived, but she'd have been happier just to come to terms with what she'd gone through. I'd been unsure how she would react to the ordeal; I'd thought she'd be depressed and weepy for a while. But there seemed to be an air about her of suspended belief, and until late that night, when we were in bed and the lights were off, she'd refused to talk about her time in captivity.

Now, here in the dark, her body tense and sometimes rigid beside me, she began opening up, 'Everybody seems to think Roe's dangerous because he was in the SAS, and he can shoot, and plan things. But he's dangerous because he's angry…because he feels guilty…guilty enough to look forward to dying, to be put out of his misery.'

I turned toward her, but said nothing. She went on, 'I felt sorry for him in the end. How can you not feel sorry for someone who's lost all they have, a wife and a son? That night he caught me, he sat talking about them for ages. Just watching his face was worse than being tied up and locked in and deprived of freedom. He blamed himself at first, for both deaths. His wife's car had come off the road on an icy stretch and dropped down the valley. Roe said he'd been meaning to fit snow chains that morning, but got caught up in a long phone conversation. And he'd promised Christopher, his son, he'd join him at Aintree for the protests, but he got there too late.'

She went quiet for a while. My eyes had adjusted to the dark, and I could see her profile as she stared at the ceiling. She said, 'And he told me he felt guilty too about killing the horsebox driver. His original plan had been to kill himself, but he couldn't "leave the world," as he put it, without something to remember him by.'

'Well, he's done that all right,' I said.

'He said human beings were the worst things to happen to the planet. Animals were the only creatures worth space and time. "Humanity's poison," he said, "me included."'

'Meaning you, or himself?'

'Himself. He made that clear. He asked me nothing about myself, other than how I could justify being involved in racing.'

'What did you say?'

She hesitated. I heard her swallow. She said, 'I told him he was right, and that he'd made me see the truth…I crept and I crawled because I was afraid he would kill me.'

I reached to touch her bare shoulder, 'I'd have done exactly the same.'

She turned and smiled sadly, 'No, you wouldn't. But thanks, anyway.'

By morning, I regretted that we hadn't made love before all this happened, for I'm not sure it was me she wanted. I couldn't rid myself of the impression she was clinging to me for comfort and for the promise that life, someday, would return to normal. She was especially tender with the still fresh scars on my back, treating them almost as old friends, reassuringly familiar.

I lay awake, cradling her as she slept, sad now for her and maybe for me too that her shell had broken, and the confidence, the independence, the pure zest for life was leaking out.

The Aintree management declared they were taking unprecedented security arrangements for the whole meeting, and intended to search every racegoer by using scanning machines. They also said that armed police would be on duty strategically placed around the course 'to deal with any situation'.

Neither of us was really in the mood for Thursday's racemeeting, and we went wandering on foot along the coast. On Thursday evening, Mac called to tell me Jack Cooper's trainer, Bobby Watt, was trying to contact me. I rang him.

'Eddie, I just had a call from Jack Cooper's secretary saying I should offer you the ride on Dunstable in the first at Aintree on Saturday. Interested?'

'I'll be interested if the doctor gives my back the all-clear.'

'What's wrong, been lying on it too much?'

'Yeah, very funny. I'll see the doc tomorrow. I should be okay. Will you be there tomorrow?'

'I've no runners, but I'll be there.'

'Can I tell you then?'

'Sure.'

'How's your National horse going?' I asked.

'Great guns, if the kid ain't been screwed up with this bloody kidnapping caper he'll have a fine chance.'

'Jack Cooper had a big bet?'

'I don't think so. Got to keep his excitement levels down.'

'You'll be glad he's on the mend, anyway.'

'Damn right. He's a bloody nuisance at times but I know which side my bread's buttered.'

'See you tomorrow.'

On Friday morning, Lisa did one final clean up on my back and we packed our bags and headed for Liverpool.

Chapter 52

More than the usual number of fallers at Aintree on the Friday meant that the course doctor was kept busy, and when I persuaded him to spend a minute examining my back, he hiked my shirt up, and passed his hands over the healing scars and said, 'You'll do.'

I hadn't expected it to be that easy, and was now faced with the prospect of my first ride in a fortnight. I sat on the scales: ten six. I'd put on three pounds. No matter, Dunstable was set to carry eleven seven. No sauna session would be necessary.

Lisa and I spent the rest of Friday in a private box as guests of Frances Crosbie, a race sponsor and an owner I rode for occasionally. We drank too much champagne, though it seemed to make Lisa forget things for a while.

In our bedroom, alone with me again, Lisa became moody and depressed as the alcohol effects wore off. The hotel was full of people we knew, and I persuaded Lisa it was best if we sought out as many of them as possible. Their company would keep our thoughts off tomorrow.

In a crowd of a dozen or so we had a great night, spiced with the delicious anticipation of every Grand National eve. Four of the lads had rides in the National and three owners with us had runners.

Comparisons were made, bets were struck, information sought, plans revealed. It was everything I'd remembered, and the only bitterness came from the fact that I had no ride in the race.

But even that resentment wasn't nearly as strong as I'd feared. Maybe, after the events of the last few weeks, my values were finally changing.

We went upstairs at one o'clock and Lisa flopped down on the bed looking sad again. I felt a sudden responsibility for her, a deep tenderness that caught me unawares. Taking my jacket off, I sat beside her, pulling her toward me. She linked her arms weakly around my waist and rested her head on my shoulder. I stroked her hair, the side of her face, then felt the warm tears through my shirt.

She cried herself softly to sleep and I laid her down, gently eased her dark velvet dress off and drew the covers over her. Quietly undressing, I switched off the light and got in beside her. I lay for a while watching her pretty face, thankful for the peace sleep had given her.

If the demon of Victor Roe was going to be exorcised, we wouldn't have much longer to wait. In his mind, he'd feel he had little to lose. With his picture in every paper, it was my guess he'd try to go out with a major bang, and tomorrow had to be it. Grand National day – the first anniversary of the death of his son.

Chapter 53

I'd been looking forward to the Saturday and my first ride since coming back, but Lisa's emotional and mental condition was making me wonder if it was safe to leave her on her own. Sollis stuck close now and accompanied us to Frances Crosbie's box.

Frances promised to keep an eye on Lisa, and with Sollis at my shoulder, gripping the loaded Smith & Wesson in his coat pocket, I went to get changed for the first.

Fighting our way through the crowds, reading newspaper headlines like Murderer's National Threat, hearing racegoers discussing Roe, seeing armed police at every doorway, perched on roofs, riding heavy horses, listening to the tense communications on security staff radios, noting the glint of excitement in the eyes of ordinary people who, having been electronically searched for weapons, sensed that for once they could be as much a part of the drama as the jockeys and horses, the real impact of what Roe had engineered came home to us. We looked at each other earnestly and Sollis said, 'I wonder where the hell he is?'

There had been no reference in the press to my part in freeing Lisa and David Cooper, yet Roe knew I was after him. I was still next on his list as well.

It came home to me as I pulled on the pink and yellow colours, that Roe couldn't hope to stay free much longer, whatever happened today. And he was already going down, so another murder would make no difference to him.

If there was going to be one more killing, it had to be me, this afternoon. The ideal race, for maximum publicity, would be the National itself. But I wasn't riding in it, so if he wanted to shoot me, he had about ten minutes.

We trotted around the parade ring, the stable lad on my right, Sollis, wary of the slavering mouth and prancing metal-shod hooves, on my left. The jogging motion threw my churning stomach into greater turmoil.

I looked from face to face then across the rooftops where, realistically, Roe would have to be for the chance of a decent shot, with a rifle anyway. I counted the armed police up there: twenty at least, watching from the rear of the stand. The same number, I hoped, would be at the front.

What if he was down there in the crowd, Beretta in pocket? A couple of quick shots then he disappears in the panic; I pictured Sollis bending over my bleeding corpse.

I tried to force it from my mind as we cantered to the start.

The race passed without incident. I finished third, panting hard. Sollis met me as I came in, no smile, eyes everywhere, stress tightening his face.

When I reached the safety of the changing room, my adrenaline, which had been pumping like a burst hydrant, slowed to a steady stream. I promised myself a stiff drink as soon as I got back to Lisa.

The happy tension was steadily increasing in the weighing room among those with a ride in the National, and I would have liked to have stayed and shared it even though I had no more mounts. But thinking of Lisa again and that drink, I showered and changed and returned to the box.

Lisa was much calmer. We watched the second race together and she bet the winner; fizzing with excitement she turned to me, waving her ticket, 'Sixteen to one!'

'Brilliant!' I said and kissed her. She hugged me, eased her grip then hugged me again. She was smiling, vitality and intensity back in her face. I said, 'You seem better.'

She nodded. 'I think I'm going to be all right now... I'm sorry about last night.'

'Forget it.'

Her hand on my shoulder she guided me to the door. 'You go to the weighing room. I'll be fine here.'

'It's okay, it's not as if I've got a ride.'

She looked at me. 'I know you want to be there, go on.' She gave me a push. I turned. 'You sure?'

'Sure I'm sure, I'll be fine, see you after the race.'

Sollis put down his orange juice and we hurried to the weighing room. Sollis stood guard outside. I went in to soak up the atmosphere. With forty-five minutes left before the off, the place was buzzing. There are two changing rooms at Aintree and both look as ancient as the race itself, with their high ceilings, wooden walls and metal saddle racks worn smooth and shiny.

I sat in room two watching the nerves working on jockeys and valets. They each had their own way of handling it: some joked incessantly or played pranks, others went abnormally quiet, a few became surly and uncharacteristically abrupt or developed high-pitched laughs, almost everyone mocked any colleague who appeared on the TV above them doing one of the stream of live interviews.

Looking at the screen, someone said, 'Oh-oh, here comes the boy wonder.'

Most of us glanced up. The presenter was introducing David Cooper, wearing his father's luminous yellow colours with crimson sleeves.

The presenter turned to David and said, 'David, nineteen years old, first ride in the National, the weight of family expectations on your young shoulders and, if that wasn't enough to be going on with, earlier this week you were literally snatched away from the clutches of a madman. Tell us about it.'

David Cooper, not at all awkward, stared his questioner in the eye and said, 'It was no big deal really, I learned a lot from it.'

'Like what?'

'Well, like what really matters in life, what it means to have proper values, how important it is to have the courage of your convictions.'

This was far from the youngster's normally tongue-tied performance, and the atmosphere gradually quietened as people paid attention.

The presenter smiled and said, 'I think everyone would agree with that, but how do you feel about the man who, allegedly, murdered your colleagues, who kept you locked up in fear of your own life?'

'I admire him.'

The smooth presenter suddenly looked flummoxed, he said, 'You admire him?'

'That's what I said. Victor Roe is a man with total commitment to his convictions. The Grand National cost him the life of his only son. He considers the race barbaric and murderous and has had the courage to do something about it.'

Sensing a real news story, the presenter perked up again. 'David, forgive me, but you sound as though you almost agree with the views of Victor Roe.'

The changing room was now completely silent. This interview was going out live all over the world.

Cooper said, 'I agree wholeheartedly with them.' He turned to face the camera which went in close on his face. He said, 'All of you out there are contributing to barbarism, to the practice of forcing dumb animals over huge fences. You are all condoning cruelty of the most horrific kind…'

At this point, I heard the clerk of the course at the doorway say, 'Jesus Christ Almighty!' in a voice that suggested the world had come to an end.

'… a cruelty I will no longer be party to…' At this he ripped his silks off, the cameraman zooming out quickly to catch him throwing them to the ground. I thought of Jack Cooper watching this and his nurses trying to get his heart rate down.

The boy went on, 'Every one of you should be ashamed of yourselves. If Victor Roe had got his way, this race would never have gone ahead. There is still a chance that it might not and I sincerely hope that will be the case.'

Without any acknowledgement to the now speechless presenter, the kid turned and walked away, dumping his whip in a bin as he passed.

The director cut to a betting show. We all looked at each other; Bomber smiled, shaking his head and said, 'Never thought the kid had it in him.'

For the next couple of minutes, everyone forgot their National nerves as they discussed the interview. Suddenly I heard my name called by a weighing-room official. I went to the door. The man said, 'You're wanted.'

Looking over his shoulder I saw a frantic Bobby Watt beckoning me. I went over and he handed me the silks the kid had discarded. 'Get changed! We're trying to get special permission from the stewards for a late change of jockey.'

I just nodded, dumbfounded; I'd been so wrapped up in David Cooper's performance it hadn't occurred to me that the horse would need a new rider. I hurried back into the changing room and found myself a valet who quickly replaced the buttons ripped from the silks by young Cooper.

Drawing my boots on, I became aware of another pair of boots stopping in front of me and heard Layton's furtive voice. 'You're a jammy bastard, Malloy. Wouldn't be surprised if you put the kid up to that just to get his ride.'

I didn't reply, didn't even look up, and Layton, no doubt smiling his snide smile, started to move off. I poked my toe out to catch his heel and he tumbled forward, crashed against a bench and landed prone at the brown-brogued feet of Sir Marcus Talland, the senior steward.

Looking down, Sir Marcus said, 'No need to grovel, Layton, this is not a Stewards' Enquiry.' Everybody laughed except Layton.

Chapter 54

The bell rang; time to leave the warmth and safety of the changing room. We all got up and filed through the exit like paratroopers committed to jump, though unsure if our chutes would open.

Sollis stepped in beside me and we walked, shoulder to shoulder, to the parade ring. I glanced at the police marksmen on the roof. If Roe was somewhere up there with a rifle, had he heard the jockey change being announced? Did he know I was now on Jack Cooper's horse? If he did, he'd have no trouble picking me out in these dazzling yellow silks.

Watt legged me up onto Gospel Oak, a big iron-grey gelding. Detailed riding orders were pointless in the National and Watt restricted himself to, 'He stays all day. Don't be afraid to use his stamina, even if it means doing the donkey work over the last two miles.' I nodded and the stable girl led me round the ring abreast of another horse. Sollis walked alongside, out of kicking and biting range. Forty horses and their excited mass of human connections made things cramped.

The majority of my rivals had known of their intended rides for months beforehand, which left me at a disadvantage. Knowledge of the strengths and frailties of others can give you quite an edge in the National, and I'd had no time to make any detailed assessments.

Still, I was beginning to get a feel for Gospel Oak's power from the way he used himself, his long swinging walk, and springy muscular jog.

Suddenly, there was a sharp crack. Women screamed and the crowd scattered as a horse went down three ahead of us, his jockey rolling into the foetal position on the grass. Sollis drew his pistol and aimed in the direction of the sound.

People were ducking, staring wildly around. Two policemen came rushing in from the far side. All TV cameras swung toward the spot. Some jocks had leapt from their saddles. I watched, trying to understand what had happened. The fallen animal was scrambling, attempting to get up, but its lad sat on its neck gripping the reins, immobilizing it.

The rifle-crack noise had come from the horse lashing out with a rear leg and catching one of the stanchions with a shoe, shattering its pastern. When calm was restored, they wheeled the screens in to shield the stricken horse and its weeping connections, and waved us out onto the course.

Sollis was white-faced and wide-eyed.

The jocks who'd dismounted, diving for cover, were looking rather sheepish as we circled at the start. All the horses were well on their toes. Equine and human nerves seemed intertwined, taut as twisted stirrup leathers.

The stands behind us, and the enclosures on either side, were packed solid. I wasn't the only jockey anxiously scanning faces on the rails, looking for some sign of madness, searching for the face of Victor Roe which stared out from the front page of every newspaper.

As much to ease the tension as out of habit, a bunch of us broke off and cantered to the first fence. Gospel Oak immediately took hold of his bit and set off, gliding over the turf. Crossing the cinder-covered Melling Road, he half-jumped from instinct without breaking his stride, and when we halted by the jump he had the cheek to plunge his head into the belly of the fence, coming away with a mouthful of spruce.

In the last few minutes, he'd told me all I had to know about him, and I had no complaints.

As the starter called us in, I emptied my mind of everything except tactics. I'd decided to go down the inside where the steepest drops lay. This would let me keep my eye on the leaders while hopefully avoiding the crowding and trouble which was inevitable at the first three fences.

We lined up, and when we were all still, and facing the right way, a momentary hush fell over the racecourse, then a huge roar as the tapes shot skywards.

Above the noise I imagined I could hear Sollis's sigh of relief.

Chapter 55

We were off, the crowd noise quickly fading in the mad rush for a good take-off position at the first, most going too fast in the desperate quest for what seemed the same eight yards of fence.

I heard the crashing noises before seeing the signals of trouble in front of me. The leader of the trio just ahead must have come down, because the tails of the two following him were erect and waving like flags as they tripped over the rolling faller.

Three horses thrashing around on the other side, but where exactly? There was no way of knowing and I pulled violently on my right rein to force Gospel Oak over at an acute angle. At full stretch, the horse grunted in mid-air and landed inches from Bob Jenner, who'd fallen toward the middle of the fence.

The horrified look on Bob's upturned face told me he'd lost his nerve, the worst thing that can happen to a jump jockey. Once your nerve goes, you've gone, and as he caught my eye we both realized, he with embarrassment, me with sadness, that he'd soon quietly retire.

We raced on, my horse and I sharper for the close call. Taking a good hold of his head, I guided him over the next four without getting near another horse. Becher's Brook loomed and that cold little blob of extra tension tightened my gut.

Seeing a good stride from a long way out, we met the take-off bar spot-on and soared over, the thrill as strong as it was when I'd last jumped it, six years ago. That additional second you're airborne over Becher's seems like a moment frozen in eternity.

We were nearer last than first approaching the right-angled Canal

Turn, and I decided to take my chance to reduce the deficit. Pulling ten yards off the inner, I then asked Gospel Oak to veer sharply left, attacking the fence at an acute angle.

His grey head missed the upright end of the fence by centimetres, and we passed at least fifteen others who'd been forced to jump straight before being yanked around the right-angled bend to confront Valentine's Brook, the next jump.

Having improved our position so dramatically with little effort, we settled into a rhythm, conserving energy for the same spot next time round.

The spruce tops seemed to slip easily underneath, and when Gospel Oak flew over the huge Chair fence, real hopes of running a very good race crowded my mind. With a circuit to go, fate couldn't be tempted by thoughts of actually winning.

As we came to the first again, now the seventeenth jump, I was glad to see Bob Jenner on his feet by the rails, a broken bridle hanging from his hands, horseless maybe, but in one piece. He looked up as we jumped past, knowing he'd never be with us again, and shouted, 'Good luck, lads! Good luck!'

Surviving the first circuit offers confidence mixed with reminders to be careful: holes torn in fences, equine casualties hobbling to the stables, loose horses careering across the centre of the course, jockeys being attended by medics, broken stirrup irons, deeply gouged furrows... drawing a breath I checked the others, about twenty still galloping, some beginning to labour.

Approaching the Canal Turn again, we lay fourth. I glanced behind, maybe fifteen or sixteen remaining, most of them showing signs of weakening. Nothing looked to be going better than us. It would soon be time to kick on and try to break them.

Taking the fence less acutely than on the first circuit, I glanced back again at those still jumping it. Among the cavalcade of vehicles following on the tarmac road inside the rails, something struck me as not being right. The horse sensed my concentration drifting and his stride faltered for a moment.

We faced Valentine's, the first of four jumps in the long straight before the turn for home. Still unsettled, a hundred yards before the fence, I looked over my shoulder again: the usual vehicles tracked us, camera cars, ambulances, stewards, vets... then I realized what was strange the ambulance was weaving in and out as though trying to overtake the others.

I turned my attention to Valentine's, saw a good stride and we sailed over. I glanced back, one was coming after us, black colours, could be Layton.

Three more fences in the straight. From the corner of my left eye, I saw the ambulance drawing alongside me on the road. He should be at the tail of the field waiting for casualties, not up with the leaders. I turned to look directly at him.

The driver's window was down. He looked terrified. Upright beside him, leaning against the passenger door, was a man with a rifle. He was aiming it at me.

Instinctively I crouched low, the horse's action changed as he guessed at what I wanted. The fence was close. I stayed low, no help to Gospel Oak, and he rose a stride too soon…only the gap punched in the fence on the first circuit saved us.

We raced to the next. I looked at the gunman, the ambulance swayed, the weapon swung in a ten-inch arc and he fired. The bullet zinged over my head. The horse didn't falter. Jesus! What do I do? Slow down? Speed up? Stop? Couldn't stop, that would be like shooting fish in a barrel.

He drew slightly ahead of me, looking for a broader target, aiming at me front-on. I moved to the inside, narrowing the angle. He slowed and widened it again. I ducked below the horse's neck… another bullet went singing past as I heard the rifle-crack.

How long before he gets his range?

Over the fence. Flew it again, the horse travelling strongly, not yet sensing my terror. Where the fuck were the police? They must have suspected something was wrong by now.

One to jump before the home straight. The ambulance level again. The incongruous sight of a man in a St John's uniform aiming a rifle at me, the poor driver crying with terror and struggling to keep the vehicle straight. After this fence, he would run out of road. Either he turned away or came crashing through the rails to follow me.

Hoofbeats behind, getting closer. I glance round; it's Layton, driving his horse on, grimacing, shouting at me, seemingly unaware of the ambulance. At my heels now, trying to force his way up the inside and I'm so tempted to let him come through and give me cover.

He yells, 'Give way, Malloy!' and barges through, knocking me off balance as we rise at the fence. Mine hits the top and starts to topple. I let go the reins and instinctively pull my feet from the stirrups…going down, almost slow motion, a gunshot, Layton screams, the earth pounds the air from my horse in a cavernous grunt and I'm over his head, rolling clear, spinning forward, Layton's horse slumps in front of me, see-saws once then comes to rest lying on my legs.

    I can see the clouds, and hear Layton moaning. I turn my head, but can't move. The screech of brakes, boots running on tarmac, horses landing either side of me, their jockeys trying with wild disbelief to take in the scene; then Victor Roe above me, blocking out the sky, a terrible murderous madness in his wet eyes as he levels the weapon at my face. 'You made me kill the horse, Malloy!' Then screaming it, 'You made me kill the fucking horse!' I stare up at him, blank-faced, a baby at the mercy of a giant. He rests the rifle barrel between my eyes and squeezes the trigger and I hear the sound but feel no pain.

Chapter 56

I opened my eyes and the rays of the afternoon sun made me think I was in Heaven rather than a bed in Walton Hospital. McCarthy was there, and Lisa…she smiled at me. I could see she'd been crying and she started again when I smiled back.

McCarthy said, 'You okay?'

'Am I alive?'

He nodded. 'And in one piece.'

'What time is it?'

'Quarter to one, Sunday afternoon. What do you remember?'

'I remember Roe pulling the trigger and I remember hearing the shot.'

'As he was pulling the trigger, half a ton of sweating steeplechaser landed right on top of him. One of the amateur-ridden stragglers determined, luckily for you, to finish the course.'

'Roe dead?'

'Badly injured, but he'll live. You were luckier than you thought too. The horse that took Roe out kicked you in the head. Your skullcap's holed.'

'My head could have been holed by a bullet, so I'm happy. What about Layton?'

'Roe shot him in the knee, his career's over. The bullet went straight through and killed his horse.'

'That's what Roe was screaming at me,' I mumbled.

Mac said, 'What?'

'Nothing. Who won?'

'Santa Lucia, the favourite.'

'Punters would've been pleased.'

Mac nodded. Lisa was squeezing my hand. I smiled. 'Must've been fun at the Stewards' Enquiry.'

Between them Mac and Lisa filled in the rest of the story. David Cooper was helping police with their enquiries on the basis that he'd conspired with Roe in giving him personal details about two people: Digby Craddock and Vanessa Compton.

It seemed Roe had treated the boy kindly from the start, explained his beliefs to him, even sought comfort from the kid over the death of his own son. I felt stupid at being duped by young Cooper's excuse of escaping from the cellar that night.

David, with Jack Cooper as a parent, had taken to Roe as a worthwhile father figure, someone to whom money meant nothing, but the lives of defenceless creatures meant everything. This had blinded the kid to Roe's madness. They reckoned a good lawyer would keep David out of jail, and that maybe even Roe would escape it for a mental institution.

And Roe's big plan for the Grand National? He had intended to release David Cooper on the Wednesday and have the boy claim he'd escaped. Cooper was then to help smuggle Roe into the weighing room on Saturday, where he would hold all the jockeys at gunpoint and give his anti-National speech direct to camera at the off time so that the broadcast went all over the world. With Roe's face in every newspaper and TV broadcast, they'd had to settle for Cooper's mini-version.

Beckman has yet to be sighted.

I was on my feet in a couple of days, and almost a hundred per cent within a week. The season was nearly over, I was tired and so was Lisa. Jack Cooper's cheque arrived with the message that he was giving up his racing interests to spend more time with his son. Lisa and I decided to go away for a month and return refreshed for the new season.

We did some spring-cleaning before we left for Antigua, and I found the Bible which had been kept handy these last few weeks. Browsing through I discovered what looked like a suitable quote for Victor Roe. I scribbled out the chapter and verse numbers on a scrap of paper – "John 19:30" – and dropped it in an envelope addressed to the prison hospital.

We mailed it from the airport.

Blood Ties

Copyright © 2015 by Joe McNally & Richard Pitman
All rights reserved.

No part of this book may be reproduced in any form or by any electronic or mechanical means, including information storage and retrieval systems, without written permission from the author, except for the use of brief quotations in a book review.

Authors' note

This is a work of fiction. Names, characters, places and incidents are either a work of the imagination of the authors or are used fictitiously, and any resemblance to actual persons, living or dead, business establishments, events or locales is entirely coincidental.

Chapter 1

In the dying days of the old jump season, after the toughest five months since my comeback, I got a phone call.

'Malloy?'

'Yes.' I didn't recognize him.

'You don't know me, but you'll get to know my voice.'

I hoped not. It had a sniggering, know-it-all tone. I said nothing.

He said, 'You're riding right through the summer?'

'Who's asking?'

'Just listen. You're riding through the summer.' No longer a question.

'Maybe.'

'No maybe. You will be.'

Stern. Commanding. Certain. I felt a nervous ripple in my gut.

He said, 'Over the next few months I'm going to call you a few times - probably on the evening before you ride something fancied. I'll give you riding instructions and you'll stick to them.'

Trainers gave riding instructions, and very occasionally, owners would; complete strangers were a new one on me.

'You listening, Malloy?'

'Keep talking.'

'I know something about you. You do what you're told or I give it to Kerman.'

Jean Kerman was a ruthless tabloid journalist specializing in dirt digging in sport - she'd ruined at least a dozen careers.

I'd been shamed and scorned enough in my life. There was only one thing left, one secret, and I said a brief intense prayer against his knowing it.

He spoke again.

He didn't know it.

The sudden relief cushioned the shock of what he did say. I stayed silent, trying to gather my thoughts.

He said: 'You've gone all quiet and shy, Malloy.'

'Run it past me again.'

'Don't mess me around! You heard.'

'I just want to be sure I've got everything right.'

There was a pause then he repeated everything in an impatient monotone, like a teacher with a backward kid. 'You and Martin Corish are conning breeders. Town Crier isn't covering the mares you say he is. You're using a cheap ringer and charging the full fee. Now, if that gets out, do I need to tell you how it will affect your little business, not to mention your career?'

A year ago, I'd invested everything I had in becoming equal partner with Martin Corish in the stud he had started. I hadn't a clue what this guy was talking about, but he sounded very convincing. I said, 'I think we'd better meet.'

'I think you'd better get your cheating boots on. I'll be in touch.'

'Listen...'

He hung up.

I rang Martin. His secretary-cum-groom was evasive, defensive. She told me he wasn't around.

'When will he be around?'

'Emmm. I'm not really sure.'

'Where is he?'

'Maybe if you call this evening.'

'*Where is he?*'

'I'm sorry Mister Malloy, I can't say.'

'Look, don't make me drive all the way down there.'

'I'm sorry. I'm just to say he's uncontactable. That's what I was told.'

'Where's Caroline?'

'Mrs. Corish isn't well. She's lying down.' The girl was agitated, her voice rising. It was unfair to take out my frustrations on her. There was obviously something wrong at the stud. I told her I'd see her in an hour, clicked the answerphone on, grabbed my jacket and pointed the car toward Wiltshire.

I'd been sucked into enough whirlpools in recent years to sense another one when it was still some way off. I was already feeling the pull of its vortex.

Chapter 2

It was close to nightfall when I reached the farm. As I swung the heavy wooden gate open, insects hummed in the greenery and swarmed around the headlights that illuminated the sign reading: THIS GATE MUST BE KEPT CLOSED AT ALL TIMES. It wasn't unusual for a horse to get loose somewhere on the enclosed three hundred acres. If you could keep them off the roads, you stood a chance of getting them back unharmed.

Martin Corish and his wife lived in a big farmhouse close to the stable yard. The house was unlit. I pulled in by the low wall and stepped out into the deepening dusk. The outlines of mares and their foals in the nearby paddock merged into single shapes. No dogs barked.

Something was wrong.

I stood, listening. Nothing but the sounds and smells of a warm June night in the country. Insects. Musky flower scents. Quiet whickering from horses. Away across the fields, the eerie cry of a vixen.

I walked into the yard. A phone rang. After half a dozen rings, a light came on inside the office in the corner and glowed yellow through the barred window. Along with the moths and their brethren, I moved quietly toward it.

The top part of the uncurtained window was open. I listened to Corish's secretary. She sounded much more aggressive with this caller than she'd been with me an hour and a half ago.

'When? Soon's not good enough. It's been "soon" for the past nine months! Oh, it's different all right! It's worse!'

She was shouting. The other party must have told her to cool down.

'Why should I? I won't wake Caroline! She's out of her head as usual, and I can see why she does it! Why should I? Give me one good reason!'

It had to be Corish on the other end and he must have given her a few good reasons, because she shut up and when she spoke again, all the fire had gone out of her.

'But what do I tell Eddie Malloy? But what if he does turn up, Martin, what do I tell him?'

Melodramatic by nature, I was tempted to burst in and grab the phone so he could tell me personally, but I'd learn more by staying put.

She said, 'When? Where? What if he asks for your number? Martin! Martin!'

He must have hung up. The girl did the same then worked through a string of curses in a steady monotone, as though reciting tables at school.

I went in. She was sprawled in a swivel chair, long red hair unkempt, blue eyes tired and puffy. She gasped and reached toward her groin, pulling frantically at the open zip on her tight beige jodhpurs, trying at the same time to get to her feet and turn her back on me.

In a TV sitcom, it might have looked funny, but I felt an instant pang of regret and shame, almost as though I'd assaulted her. I didn't even manage to redeem myself by catching her as she collapsed in a dead faint. On the way down, her head smacked against a metal filing cabinet.

By the time I was on my knees beside her, she was already bleeding.

The wound was on her scalp and not dangerously deep. Blood trickled across her temple, forming a pool in her ear. Her pulse was steady, her breathing even.

Making a pillow of my jacket, I gently raised her head and eased the makeshift cushion underneath. In the corner of the office was a small sink. As I got up to fetch a wet cloth, I noticed her white swollen belly exposed by the gaping fly of her jodhpurs. Red pubic hair curled over the pink waistband of her pants. Looking around for something to cover her, I scooped a purple fleecy jacket from the swivel chair and laid it on her midriff.

I checked her pulse again, wondering whether I should call an ambulance, when her eyes opened and tried to focus on me. I moved aside, not wanting to seem threateningly close. I sat on the chair. Her face remained calm. She reached to feel her head.

'Fiona, are you all right?' I asked.

She looked at the sticky blood on her fingers.

'Just a flesh wound,' I said.

Puzzled, she stared at me. 'You hit your head on the cabinet,' I explained. 'My fault for barging in like that and scaring you. I'm sorry.'

She made to get up. I was caught between helping her and saving her embarrassment as the jacket covering her bare middle slipped. She grabbed at it. I stood up. 'I've got a first-aid kit in the car - won't be a minute,' I said, and went out into the cool darkness.

When I returned, she was sitting at the desk sipping water from a cracked cup and sobbing quietly. I said, 'Fiona, look, I'm sorry for scaring you like that. I didn't mean to.'

She wiped at her eyes with the bloodstained cloth I'd been using. Opening the first-aid box, I handed her a dry pad. She took it and carried on wiping.

'Got some painkillers here,' I offered.

She raised a hand, pushing them away.

I spent the next fifteen minutes asking questions. Where was Martin Corish? Where was the rest of the staff? Who was tending the horses? I told her I'd overheard her telephone conversation - where had he called from?

I thought it best not to question her about the stallions, Town Crier especially. Martin Corish was the man with the answers, but if Fiona knew his whereabouts, she wasn't saying. She stayed silent, dabbing at the now dry wound and staring at the desk. Her Snoopy watch read eleven o'clock when I gave up.

Footfalls deliberately heavy on the cobbles, I crossed the moonlit yard, wanting to convince Fiona I wasn't coming back. I started the car, drove a few hundred yards then pulled in, and ran back.

Outside the office once again, I listened for the frantic return call to Corish, but all was silent. Either she'd made it after I'd left, or she genuinely didn't know where he was.

I waited twenty minutes. Nothing.

I was tempted to visit Town Crier's box. I knew the horse well, and reckoned it would take a pretty good ringer to fool me. But like a number of stallions, he could be unfriendly toward humans;

particularly, I suspected, those who intrude in the hours of darkness. I decided to leave it till next morning.

With no clouds to blanket the day's heat, it was quickly growing cold. I returned to the car, wondering where to spend the night.

The nearest hotel that would let me in this late was about fifteen miles east. But my credit card was swipe-weary and battle scarred. Basic guesthouses would already be locked up and I had no friends in the vicinity.

I sat looking through the windscreen at the stars, knowing the overnight sleeping arrangements were a choice between kipping in the car or seeking a warm corner in Corish's hay barn. The prospect brought a smile to my face as I remembered past conversations with people who envied the glamorous life of a professional jockey.

Last season's glamour for me had included a virus-stricken stable, three periods of suspension for 'irresponsible' riding, and a series of damaging falls, leaving me with a fractured wrist, a broken collarbone and, most recently, four smashed ribs and a punctured lung. Not to mention severely dented confidence and a badly bruised bank account.

Just when I thought it was safe to get back in the saddle, this had to happen. The partnership with Martin Corish was the only investment I'd ever made. No jockey can ride forever, and the stud was supposed to provide me with some security when I hung up my boots, a notion I'd entertained often lately. I sighed, fighting off self-pity.

I'd find a lay-by and get what sleep I could before returning in the morning. The ignition fired and the buttons on my mobile phone lit up as it beeped into life. Before setting off, I went through the motions of ringing home to my answerphone, though it had been a while since there'd been any worthwhile messages on it.

Tonight there was one and it drew me home at speed.

Chapter 3

I reached the flat at 2 a.m. and stopped barely long enough for tea and a sandwich. I replayed the message again: 'Eddie, Barney Dolan. If you get this in time there's a winner waiting for you tomorrow, er, that's Wednesday. I heard you passed the doctor and thought I'd give you a winner. The bad news is it's up at Perth and it's in the two o'clock. I'll hold off till nine in the morning to hear from you.'

Good old Barney. He was one of a handful of trainers I rode for when it was mutually convenient. My retainer was with Broga Cates, whose flat I was sitting in now. Broga owned a string of twenty-two, trained by Charles Tunney, whose Shropshire yard my flat overlooked. Broga paid me a reasonable retainer to ride his horses, and when the stable had no runners, I was free to take rides elsewhere.

Many of our horses had been down with a virus last season and we'd had just eleven winners - a disastrous total that had shaken Charles's confidence. He'd closed the yard for the normal summer break, and buggered off to Alaska for a month's holiday, leaving his secretary to feed the dogs and keep things ticking over.

Until this season, jump racing had always stopped for two months in the summer, but the British Horseracing Board had decided to grant a few fixtures to courses wanting to hold meetings during the summer. Most of the top jockeys had said they wouldn't ride at these meetings; eight weeks was little enough break from the daily grind of driving, dieting and injuries.

I could have done with the holiday - at least my battered body could have - but my bank balance dictated otherwise. So, after an hour's restless sleep, I left rural Shropshire in the early hours of Wednesday morning for the long drive to Perth, a course lying so far north it never risked racing during the winter months.

Every minute on the road took me farther from where I'd planned to be at first light, the Corish Stud.

My thoughts returned to the mystery caller. If my partner was doing what was claimed, how had the guy found out? And how had he discovered my involvement with Martin Corish? We'd kept it quiet. And what was the caller's link with Jean Kerman, the tabloid hack with the poisonous pen?

I'd count myself lucky to have twenty rides through summer, but that would be twenty opportunities for the blackmailer to get at me. And it was unlikely he'd stop at summer's end. What would I do if he asked me to ride a bent race?

I didn't know.

I'd never pulled a horse. Ethics aside, my belief is that as soon as someone gets something on you, you're prisoner for life. Even one guilty little secret will stay fixed to you like a choke-chain - a very long chain maybe, but one that would snap you backward and haul you in to face either justice or another demand.

As dawn lit the hills of the Scottish borders, I was no nearer a solution. The choices were: find Corish and get the truth or track down the blackmailer and deal with him. Even if Corish was guilty, I'd still have to trace the blackmailer. I had to face the fact that this Perth ride might have to be my last until I caught this bastard.

The only way to stay clean was to make sure the blackmailer had no leverage. If I wasn't riding, he couldn't influence my performance.

But how many rides could I refuse before trainers stopped asking me?

It looked like my first decision in the battle, to go north for one ride, was the wrong one. The time would have been better spent trying to find Martin Corish, but I was committed now and at 8.15, I rang Barney Dolan and told him I'd be at Perth by 11.

'Good man, Eddie. You won't regret it.'

I had a very strong feeling that I would.

Chapter 4

Perth Racecourse lies in the fertile grounds of Scone Palace on the banks of the River Tay. Early mist rose from the water on this hot morning. I was first into the jockeys' room and sat wearily on the varnished bench, dropping my kitbag and saddle at my feet. I hadn't been here in almost eight years.

It was quiet inside the antiquated wood-paneled room. Faint sounds of birdsong came through the open window, and I laid back my head and thought of the days when being in a room like this had brought me only pleasure. Every new changing room, every new course, had been a wondrous adventure to a wide-eyed and breathless teenager, drinking in the history of these old places, sitting on every inch of every bench so I could be sure to have sat where all the champions had sat before me. That teenager was long gone. It seemed a lifetime ago.

The sweet pine-scented air had come from an aerosol. Motes hung in the long sunbeam that warmed my legs. I must have dozed.

I woke feeling stiff. Sitting opposite me, crunching crispbread and sipping black tea, was Keith Allardyce, who'd been born in Stirling, 'two doors down from Willie Carson' as he always said. Cheeks full of soggy crispbread, he still managed a wide smile as I stretched awake.

'Tired?'

'It's all right for you locals. Probably just fell out of bed ten minutes ago. I bet you've even had time for a plate of fried haggis before leaving home.'

'Haggis season doesn't start till August. We're not allowed to shoot them till then.'

'Contact the British Horseracing Board,' I said. 'They'll get it brought forward.'

Keith swallowed. His smile widened and we chatted about what had been happening while I'd been laid up these last five weeks. The northern racing fraternity moved in their own separate world from the rest of the UK, so I picked up some new gossip.

'Have you got a paper?' I asked.

Keith hauled a rolled up copy of The Sporting Life from his bag and threw it to me.

'How many in the first?' I asked as I opened it.

'A few, I think. Your old buddy's got a ride, you'll be pleased to know.'

I looked at him.

'Tranter.'

'Oh, Tranter the Ranter, that's all I need!'

Billy Tranter didn't like me. His antics had earned me two suspensions last season just for trying to keep him at a safe distance during races. The animosity stemmed from a successful objection I'd made to a winner he rode at Newbury in November. Nothing personal on my part - Tranter's tiring horse had leant on mine on the run-in; it was arguable whether or not it affected the result, but I owed it to the owner and trainer to try an objection and it was upheld.

Tranter the Ranter lived up to his nickname that day.

Since then he'd had a go at me numerous times during races, using various dirty tricks. I'd responded accordingly in the hope he'd soon tire of it and lose the taste for revenge, but all it did was increase his appetite. My fuse burns slowly these days but eventually, for practical reasons, I'd laid him out flat and stone cold on the weighing-room floor at Bangor.

Next time we rode against each other, he tried to put me through the wing of a fence. Grassing on colleagues isn't done, but after that incident, I told Tranter that if he persisted, I'd make sure he got warned off for a long time. It didn't cool the fire in his eyes. Today would be the first time we'd met since that conversation.

I scanned the race; twelve runners. Dolan's horse, Cliptie, was down to be ridden by his son Rod who, Dolan had told me this morning, had been hospitalized for a few days after a crash with the family tractor yesterday evening. The first that people would hear of the jockey change to E. Malloy would be when it was broadcast to the betting shops shortly before racing.

That suited me. It meant the mystery caller wouldn't have the opportunity to ring me and make suggestions.

I left Keith Allardyce to the remains of his lunch and went out into the sunshine to call the Corish Stud. George, the stud groom, answered the phone but was reluctant to answer questions about Martin Corish. He was hiding something. I resolved to leave after my ride in the first and head back down there to get some answers.

The sun was high as we filed out for the first and my dark colours, black with scarlet crossbelts, held the rays, slowly cooking my upper half. Sweat ran from my armpits over the heavy rib strapping from my last injury. Eager for a cooling breeze, I cantered to the start more quickly than normal. Cliptie, a neat bay gelding, moved nicely beneath me. Well-balanced and alert, he seemed the perfect type for this tight track.

Circling at the start, I watched Billy Tranter with concealed amusement. He'd dismounted and was adjusting his mount's bridle. Tranter's face had been a picture when he walked into the weighing room and saw my head popping through the neck of Cliptie's colours. His smile disappeared as though his facial muscles had been sliced.

Women thought him good-looking, which I suppose he was in a gunslingerish sort of way: high cheekbones, narrow deep-set eyes, strong jaw, and prairie-coloured hair. He could frame a mean look but at five foot five, he was more Alan Ladd than Gary Cooper.

He didn't speak to me, didn't have to. It was obvious that hostilities would be resumed as soon as possible.

Tranter remounted his horse, a big brute, its coat so black the sun glinted blindingly from it at times. It was a long shot in the betting and that made me especially wary. If Tranter felt he wasn't expected to win, he would concentrate on doing me damage. He kept glancing behind as we walked round at the start, both playing a slow game of cat and mouse before lining up.

Dolan was confident we'd win and had told me to lie fifth or sixth and bring him to lead at the last. Tucking Cliptie away in this sort of field shouldn't prove difficult, but if Tranter was determined to be in there scrimmaging with me, he'd have plenty of cover from the eyes of the Stewards.

It was a two-mile hurdle and the starter called us in and snapped the tape up quickly, letting us go to race clockwise for almost two circuits. I jumped Cliptie off smartly and led for the first furlong. He was keen and I had some trouble restraining him. After such a long layoff from riding, I felt my shoulder and back muscles stretch and resist as I gently wrestled Cliptie into submission, playing the bit in his mouth as an angler would play a salmon.

After we jumped the second, he settled and we swung along nicely six from the front with a horse either side. I peeked under my armpit to see Tranter three lengths behind, moving his horse toward the rails. As we turned into the straight for the first time, I heard angry shouts then felt my horse take a heavy bump on the quarters.

I looked round. Tranter had barged up the inside, forcing others to move out quickly. We'd been caught in the domino effect. But Cliptie seemed okay and galloped on. Through clear goggles, Tranter's narrowed eyes were fixed on me. Jaw muscles grimly clenched, he ignored the curses as he continued barreling forward.

Kicking Cliptie through a gap, I moved to the wide outside to keep at least one horse between Tranter and us. It would also give the Stewards a clearer view as we turned to race away from the stands.

But Tranter reined back to come round and move inside as we rounded the bend, at which point he bumped my horse hard, forcing us into the middle of the track.

He followed.

I glared across. 'Tranter, what the...?'

He bumped us again, and then with an exaggerated show of trying to control the big black gelding, he forced him onto mine, leaning and boring diagonally toward the river.

'Straighten up, you bastard!' I yelled, but he was half-standing in the stirrups, pretending to haul at the reins while carrying me off the course. Looking at the bridle, I saw the bit had come right through the horse's mouth. Tranter was without brakes or steering.

We were feet from the white rails and I tried desperately to pull Cliptie up, but Tranter's horse carried us through in a crackling shower of plastic shards as the rails shattered. We were on the downward slope of the riverbank, travelling too fast for an emergency ejection. I made do with getting my feet out of the irons just before Cliptie burst through the glinting surface of the peaceful, slow-flowing Tay.

The sound of half a ton of galloping thoroughbred hitting deep water was like a bomb blast, shaking me almost as much as the shock of the temperature change and the sudden confusion of my senses. Cliptie's momentum carried me under as he overturned in the water.

Temporary panic. Sucked down by the horse. Very cold. Goggles filling through the tiny air holes. Water swilling darkly. On my back now. The sun a watery molten disc above. Terrible memories.

A heavy punch hits my shoulder. Must be Tranter. Mad bastard. I turn, in fear.

No Tranter but Cliptie, kicking out, beginning to swim. The reins move like dark skinny eels. I grab at them and pull myself toward Cliptie's strong neck, which I clasp in a hug, forcing tiny bubbles from his coat. Could use some of them. Not much air left in my lungs. But Cliptie's paddling strongly. Best rely on him.

We break the surface.

Cliptie blows through his nostrils as though applauding himself. I cough and splutter and try to look up. Blinded by the light.

Chapter 5

The horses were okay. We'd been lucky to miss the rocky shallows and plunge into a deep pool in the river's curve. At the Stewards' Enquiry, Tranter looked suitably shocked and penitent. The patrol film 'showed clearly', according to the Stewards, that the loose bridle had caused Tranter's misfortune and therefore mine. Although he swore the bridle had been correctly fitted, they fined the baffled trainer of Tranter's horse £200.

Now I knew why Tranter had been fiddling with the bridle at the start, a point he quickly raised in his defense, claiming it had felt loose and he'd been worried about it.

I was certain he'd sabotaged the bridle. I'd considered Billy Tranter nothing more than a bad loser, a small-minded guy who harboured grudges. But if he had deliberately loosened that bridle then he'd endangered himself as well as me, not to mention two racehorses.

I wondered what I had to do to stop him. I'd tried being tough on the track, I'd decked him at Bangor, I'd threatened to have him warned off. What next? He was rushing to ride in the second race and I was in a hurry to get back to the stud. I had to settle for tugging his sleeve and speaking quietly. 'When are you going to give up, Billy? When we're both dead?'

He grinned coldly and triumphantly, and I was left unsure as to whether that meant his 'honour' had now been satisfied or if he was already planning the next round.

By the main gate, Cliptie's lad was walking the steaming horse in a circle. Cliptie seemed bright and refreshed for his cool bath. Barney Dolan, his trainer, looked shell-shocked.

He leant against the fence, watching Cliptie with unblinking eyes. He didn't see me until I stopped beside him. The sun filtering through his loose-weave Panama hat cast a tight pattern on his face, making his booze-reddened nose even darker. The knot of his tie hung six inches below his sweat-stained shirt collar and a heavy sports jacket was draped across his forearm. On the grass at his feet lay his battered binoculars case.

'You okay?' I asked.

He pulled his mind to the present and focused on me. 'Mmmm.'

'You don't look it.'

He reached in his jacket for cigarettes and matches, then dropped the jacket beside the binoculars and lit a cigarette. 'He would have won that, Eddie. Pissed up.'

'I'm sorry.' It was pointless telling the Tranter story. I let him believe it was just bad luck.

He nodded again, slowly, not looking at me. He drew deeply and blew smoke into the hot still air. 'We needed that, Eddie.'

Gently I clasped his arm. 'There'll be another time. I'd love to ride him again.'

'Mmmm.'

More smoke. That faraway look again. 'Gimme a call if there's anything,' I said.

He didn't reply.

After an hour's driving, I was yawning at regular intervals. My ribs ached too. After my ducking, the doctor at Perth had restrapped them but the bandages felt tight. And I was hungry. To hell with it. The mystery of Martin Corish could keep until tomorrow. I turned off and headed west toward home.

Chapter 6

I left after breakfast next day and reached the stud just before ten. I parked by the wall of the house as Fiona came out of the yard, leading a mare whose bright chestnut foal followed anxiously, tottering on too-long legs like a child in high heels. Fiona didn't acknowledge me as I got out. 'Good morning,' I called after her.

'Morning,' she said without turning.

'Is Mrs. Corish home?'

'Try the garden.'

Following a side path, I came to a gate in a high hedge. The big sandstone house cast a long shadow over the kidney-shaped garden, only the top third of which was in sunshine. Two white patio chairs stood in the centre of the lawn. Another white chair and a matching table had been moved into the sunny spot. On the chair, her back to me, sat Caroline Corish.

She stirred slightly as she heard the metal latch click when the gate swung closed, but didn't look round. I called out, 'Good morning!'

She turned, saw me through her sunglasses but said nothing. I crossed the lawn, lifted a chair and put it down by Caroline's table.

She wore cream-coloured calf-length leggings, which were stained, and what looked like one of her husband's shirts, blue-striped and open-necked, showing a sunburned V of skin. She was shoeless. Her feet were dirty. Cracked dried blood showed on the toes of her right foot.

On the soiled tabletop lay a packet of cigarettes, an expensive lighter, a half-empty bottle of white rum and a litre of cola. She drank from the fat glass in her hand. It wasn't yet 10.30.

Even behind the dark glasses Caroline looked haggard. Fortyish, she was naturally slim but looked gaunt. As she raised the glass, her wedding ring slid an inch along her bony finger. I'd known them for years and had never understood what Martin had seen in her. Most times I'd met her, she'd had something to whine about. Her commitment to drowning sorrows this early told me that Martin was causing plenty trouble.

I kept it light. 'Sunbathing?' I asked, as I sat down.

'Do make yourself comfortable, won't you?' she said sarcastically.

'How are you?'

'Drunk. Cheers.' She emptied the glass in two long swallows and refilled it, the cola frothing and running over the edge.

'What's the celebration?'

She turned petulantly and I was glad I couldn't see her eyes. 'Surviving another night alone in the fucking Ponderosa,' she said, nodding toward the house.

'Where's Martin?'

'Screwing stablegirls, probably.'

'He's been away for a few days?'

'I couldn't give a toss if he never comes back.' She shook a cigarette from the packet and lit it, killing the scent of the flowers with the smoke flaring down her nostrils.

'Caroline, it's important that I speak to Martin soon. Have you any idea where he's gone?'

'Why don't you go and ask that little whore, Fiona? Ask her if he plans to be there to hold her hand when she's in labour?'

Oh dear. My thoughts returned to Fiona's open jodhpurs and protruding white belly. And her haranguing of Martin on the phone. I guessed he had more problems than just Town Crier.

In the yard, red-haired Fiona looked almost as rough as Caroline did, though considerably plumper. She was yelling at two lads to get some tack cleaned. They wandered slowly out of the feed-room, chatting as if she didn't exist.

'Glad to hear you've got your voice back,' I said.

She stared at me, flushed from shouting. I asked where Martin was and she continued the silent treatment, which was really beginning to piss me off. I said, 'Fiona, if you want to have a job this time next week then answer me when I talk to you.'

She half-sneered, 'You can't sack me.'

'Martin's disappeared. I'm applying to have the business assigned to me.'

She seemed uncertain. 'You can't. He'll be home to...' She stopped herself.

'When? Tomorrow?'

'I'm not to say.'

'Okay, pick up your things. I'll pay you a month's wages in lieu of notice and send your cards on.'

I turned and went into the office. She yelled after me: 'You can't! You can't!' I brought out a jacket and a shoulder bag. 'These yours?'

She crossed her arms. 'I won't accept them!'

I laid them on the ground. 'Anything else you want to recover from the office?'

She scowled. 'You can't do this!'

I checked my watch. 'It shouldn't take you long to walk to the main gate. Be off the property in half an hour.' I returned to the office. A few minutes later, I was going through the contents of the filing cabinet when the door creaked open. Fiona stood there, the sun haloing her carrot hair. Staring at her feet like a little girl, she said, 'Martin will be here in the morning.'

'What time?'

'First thing.'

'Fine. Come in and start explaining how this place has been running.'

She worked confidently through the paperwork, showing me the accounts. I learned little either way. I was not enough of a financial gourmet to detect the whiff of cooked books and Fiona probably realized this.

Although I knew where Town Crier was stabled, I asked her to take me there to see if that shook her confidence, but she led me to the box without hesitation.

In front of me was a long strong bay horse, well ribbed up with straight hocks and good legs, a fine head with large ears and a bold eye. The only marking on him was a touch of white no bigger than a thumbprint on his forehead. I was sure within a minute this was the genuine Town Crier, and equally certain that physically at least there was not a thing wrong with him.

I asked Fiona when he'd last covered a mare.

'Er. A week ago today, I think. Yes, last Friday.'

'Were you there?'

'What?'

'Did you see him covering?'

'No.' She looked puzzled.

'Who was there?'

'Martin.'

'Who else?'

Her brows knitted. 'A couple of the lads, I think.'

I dropped the subject and told her I was heading into Marlborough to book a room for the evening. I warned her that if she rushed off to ring Martin she'd better tell him that if he wasn't here first thing in the morning, she'd be out of a job and I'd be out looking for him.

Chapter 7

I rang home to my answerphone. No messages.

I found a small hotel, removed my rib strapping, had a cool shower and lay wet and naked on the bed, letting the air from the open window dry me. I thought about Martin Corish. He had been my boyhood hero, champion jockey when I was a teenager. It hadn't been just his brilliant riding that had bewitched me: he was interviewed often on TV and always seemed to have a twinkle in his eye and a joke ready, usually told against himself. He was handsome too, but seemed to manage that rare balance of attracting women while not alienating men.

By the time I started riding, Martin's career was winding down, but I'd made no secret of how much I admired him. Admiration which increased when he accepted me immediately as his equal, as a man and as a jockey. He made me feel special and it took me a while to realize that was how he made most people feel. It wasn't contrived on his part; he was simply a charismatic type of guy.

After retiring he'd spent some time working on TV and radio before setting up as a trainer, something I felt he'd put off deliberately till the highs of his riding days were more of a memory. To achieve the same success training would have been a tough enough task without carrying the burden of other people's expectations.

Martin never reached higher than middle rank when he was training, and when that position started slipping he packed up, unwilling to wait for the humiliating slide to obscurity. That's when he set up the stud, which had been going for three years when he'd approached me last summer, offering me a fifty-fifty partnership for £200,000.

In any normal season I'd be lucky to have a twentieth of that in the bank, but I'd come into some money via an insurance company reward. My share had been a hundred and seventy-five grand. I had ten of my own in cash and I'd borrowed another fifteen and gone in with Martin. I guess I'd never really lost that desire to impress him, to win his approval.

It hadn't made me a millionaire but it hadn't proved disastrous either. I'd managed to make the loan repayments quite comfortably and start rebuilding modest savings from the director's salary the stud paid me. But I was a long way from getting my money back.

I lay staring at the ceiling, promising myself I'd resist Martin's charm in the morning, wouldn't be calmed down by layers of bullshit. I'd be as hard with him as I had been with Fiona.

I swung my legs off the bed and stood up in front of the full-length mirror fixed to the open wardrobe door. Fresh bruises added to the colourful display on my ribcage, shellbursts of yellow and blue. On my left shinbone, a familiar old pink scar, legacy of a pin insertion years ago, ran diagonally through the dark hair. My muscle definition was good, but I noticed a thickening round the middle and more flesh on the upper thighs. I'd never had a weight problem but last season a pound or two extra had somehow lodged itself on my frame.

I decided to skip dinner.

After the nine o'clock news, I made a final call to my answerphone. The first message was from Barney Dolan, Cliptie's trainer. He wanted to meet me at Worcester tomorrow to discuss something important.

The second call was from the blackmailer: 'I see from the papers you took a little bath up at Perth yesterday. Most amusing. Don't ever accept a ride again after the overnight stage. I'll be in touch.'

Arrogant bastard.

Jockeys declared at the overnight stage were guaranteed to have their names appear alongside their mount in the morning papers. If this guy didn't know where I was riding, he couldn't ask me to stop one. I was seething as I worked through my diary in search of Barney Dolan's number. He sounded anxious when I explained to him that I had no plans to be at Worcester tomorrow. I had no booked rides and, more importantly, I had pressing business elsewhere.

There was a long pause then Barney said, 'Eddie, I've got to see you. I'm in deep trouble. Fierce trouble. I need to see you tomorrow.

Chapter 8

I was at the stud by 5.30 a.m. in case Martin decided to pay a fleeting morning visit. In the paddocks, mares and foals grazed. Mist rose from the river and dew lay thick on the front lawn of the big house. The yard was empty of people, though equine heads looked inquiringly over box doors, a few whinnying at the prospect of an early breakfast.

The office was locked. I sat on the red-leaded windowsill and watched the sun rise slowly over the pitched roof of the stable block. Just after seven, as the lads arrived on foot and by bike, I heard a car and walked out to see if it was Martin. The car had stopped two hundred yards along the road beside the cottage where Fiona lived. Martin drove a gunmetal grey Rover and the car was the right shape, though the angle of the sunlight made it hard to distinguish colour.

I reversed my car along the drive and blocked the exit road. I'd thought the whine of the fast gear would bring him hurrying to investigate, but he stayed inside for almost ten minutes and didn't look surprised when he came out and saw me.

Many ex-jockeys quickly bloat as they indulge themselves after years of self-deprivation, but Martin had never been more than half a stone over his riding weight. Standing on the steps of the cottage, he looked a stone under it. His five foot ten was stretched and gaunt. With his hunched shoulders, curved spine and drooping head he resembled a jockey off one of the old cigarette cards.

He stood like a prisoner in the dock waiting to be taken down, eyes on the ground as I approached.

I'd spent much of the morning rehearsing angry words, but when

I saw his face all I could say was, 'Are you okay?'

He raised a warm but very tired smile, and once again, maddeningly, I felt somehow privileged. It was almost as if he had only three of those smiles left to get him through the rest of his life, and he'd spent one on me. He put a hand on my shoulder. 'Come in and have some breakfast.'

I stopped him. 'I'd rather we spoke alone.'

'It's okay, Fiona's just leaving.'

She must have been standing inside the open door for she appeared on cue, kissed Martin lightly on the cheek and came down the front step where he ruffled her hair affectionately before she walked up the dusty road in the direction of the yard.

The cottage kitchen was untidy. Dirty clothes lay on the floor by the open door of the washing machine and the sink was full of dishes. Old newspapers and office books were strewn on the table, which had a pine bench on either side. Martin cleared a space. 'Sit down, Eddie. Coffee?'

'You sit down. I'll make the coffee.'

He did so without argument, and I found the makings of coffee and toast which he refused. I persuaded him to eat it.

Martin was forty-five. Not only did he still have all his hair but it seemed to be growing wild, out of control, thick and greying and alive. Framing his fine-boned unshaven face, it made him look more like a refugee or half-crazed artist than one of racing's former heroes. But there was none of the usual fire in his blue eyes, which were bloodshot, exhausted-looking, lifeless. If the body had its own hospital, they'd have been in intensive care.

When he'd forced down the last mouthful of toast, he looked at me and said, 'I'm sorry, mate.'

There was no need to start barking questions at him. He went through everything from the beginning, punctuating the story with regular apologies. 'I should have thought more about it, should have called you. I just sort of panicked. It had been building up for weeks and when the guy phoned, I just blanked, panicked.'

The blackmailer had contacted him on Monday, claiming he knew another horse, a ringer, was being used to cover for Town Crier. He suggested Martin approach me to say 'the game was up' and that we'd better co-operate, which meant he would tell me which races not to try in. Martin couldn't pluck up the courage to ring me, and when the blackmailer called on Tuesday and again on Wednesday, only to find Martin was avoiding him, he'd phoned me direct.

I said, 'So he's right in what he says about Town Crier?' Martin nodded slowly, thick tendrils of hair swinging across his eyes.

'What's wrong with him?'

'He's lost it. Just lost it.'

'Lost what?'

'His fertility.'

We looked at each other.

'Completely?' I asked.

He nodded again. 'Went from an eighty-eight percent success rate to zero.'

'What, just like that? Overnight?'

'Almost. Three or four days maybe.'

Stallion fertility is measured in how many mares each horse gets in foal. Town Crier's had always been consistently high. 'You should have called me.'

His shoulders tensed, hunching again as he moved awkwardly in his seat. 'I thought he'd come through it, Eddie. I thought it might be a virus or something.'

I shook my head slowly, rubbing my face as the impact sank home. 'You should have told me, Martin.'

'I'm sorry, Eddie, I didn't know how to tell you! What was it going to sound like less than a year after you put everything you had into the business? After I had persuaded you to invest all that money? What was I supposed to say: "Look, Eddie, sorry but our major asset has collapsed, our top player has just drawn stumps?"'

I was angry and avoided his eyes to hide it, then got mad at myself for being so protective of him. Almost afraid to ask I finally said, 'What about this ringer stuff, that's not true, is it?' I don't know why I asked, because I knew it had to be true or he wouldn't have run away. Like battling on from two fences behind in a steeplechase, you're always hoping for that little miracle, and maybe I thought that Martin had scarpered purely because of the pressure of Town Crier's problem being revealed to the public. Maybe that was all it was.

It wasn't. He'd been using a stallion called Acapella to cover the Town Crier mares. Acapella stood at a thousand pounds, half the fee we charged for Town Crier.

That wound up my sympathy and patience to breaking point. 'For God's sake, Martin, they're not even the same colour!'

'Close enough. There's plenty bay in Acapella's family. We'll be okay.'

'He's black!'

He hunched his shoulders again and hung his head. His reasoning was that the colouring wouldn't be a big issue, and maybe we would sort Town Crier out for next season. The fact that Acapella was also less likely to sire a horse of the same ability as Town Crier's offspring didn't matter to Martin at the moment. Most were bred for jumping and it would be five years before they'd see a racecourse. Again, he argued that Town Crier would have overcome his problem long before then so half a dozen or so sub-standard progeny would do little damage to his reputation as a sire.

I said, 'And what do we do when the blood samples from the foals are analyzed for Weatherbys?'

The Jockey Club's administrators, Weatherbys, operated a checking system to prevent the very thing Martin had been doing. As soon as a thoroughbred foal is born, a vet takes a blood sample to send there for testing. The sample proves the mating that is on paper is the one that produced the offspring.

Running nervous fingers through his wild hair, Martin said, 'That won't happen for months. We can sort something out by then.'

'Like what, a miracle?'

'We can say there was a mistake here, or maybe we can get hold of the samples before they get to Weatherbys, or bribe a vet or something.'

I stared at him. 'You're kidding me now, Martin. Tell me you're kidding?'

He clamped his head between his hands and squeezed his eyes shut. 'My head's gone, Eddie. I'm sorry.'

I wondered what he'd told the staff. For each covering there would have to have been at least one other person present. A mare has to be held steady while the stallion is led up and sometimes helped to enter her. Unwilling mares can have hobbles fitted to stop them trying to escape or kicking the stallion, so often there will be three people at a covering.

'What did you tell the staff?' I asked. 'Would they have known who the mares were booked to?'

He shook his head and muttered, 'They thought it was a simple booking to Acapella.'

'And nobody questioned why Town Crier hadn't covered for so long?' He shook his head again.

'What about the insurance? Why don't we just claim on that?'

Insurance was available against a stallion's losing fertility and most breeders took sufficient cover.

In a quiet voice he said, 'I didn't take it out.'

'You what? We agreed it! It was part of the budget!'

He couldn't look at me. 'Didn't think it was worth it. His fertility rate was so high.'

I sighed. It was pointless getting any angrier. I tried to figure out what we could do to start repairing things.

I asked, 'What are the vets saying?'

Still gripping his head, he said in a tense voice, 'I took a sample of blood and sperm to a vet in Ireland, top bloke. The blood's fine. The sperm is a hundred percent sterile.'

'Temporary or permanent?'

'No way of knowing.'

'What about a second opinion?'

'Who from?' There was an edge in his voice now.

'One of the Newmarket guys.'

'Who'll then know that the Corish Stud has a useless stallion. How long before that gets out to breeders?'

'Martin, how else are we going to solve this? We can't keep it covered up.'

'We've got to keep it covered up, Eddie! Make no mistake about that!' There was some fire in his eyes at last, sparked by desperation. But it was blinding him to logic.

'Martin, we're in a hole, let's stop digging, please?'

He rounded on me, slamming his open hands on the tabletop.

'You stop digging! It's all right for you! If the business goes under you've done a few quid. Fine. You go back to riding. You're young. You'll be okay! What have I got? Fuck all!'

His fists and jaw muscles clenched and unclenched. 'I'll tell you what I've got, Eddie, I'll tell you what I've got coming at me from all points of the fucking compass! Divorce proceedings. My first child who'll be born just after my forty-sixth birthday. No business. No money. Nowhere to live. And I'll tell you what else I don't have that you don't think about now but by Christ you will when you get to my age, I don't have another ten or fifteen years to pull the whole fucking thing back together again!'

He was reaching across to me, arms extended. If I'd been directly in front of him, he'd have had me by the lapels. His head was low, chin almost touching the table, tears welling. And I was sorry it had taken this much to make me understand why he'd crashed and burned in the past seventy-two hours.

I stayed until noon, comforting him, trying to persuade him we'd come through, that we'd get the blackmailer before he did any damage.

Chapter 9

I drove at speed to Worcester races, where I'd agreed to meet Barney Dolan behind the main stand after the second race. Waiting for him, I watched the boats on the Severn, which flows so close to the track that there has never been a winter when it hasn't flooded the racecourse. Watching the wide muddy river, I was glad Tranter hadn't barged me into this one.

Barney appeared, looking as though he'd just come from our last meeting at Perth; same clothes, tie hanging loose at the same length, identical expression, cigarette freshly lit sending smoke trails up through the weave of his hat rim. We shook hands and when he glanced furtively around the way they do in B-movies, I thought it was all a wind up, though he'd sounded pretty desperate on the phone last night.

'Why all the secrecy?' I asked.

'I don't want us to be seen together. You'll know why in a minute.'

A rowing crew surged past sweating and grunting. Barney and I were the only ones behind the stand. I said, 'Barney, if anybody does see us round here, they'll think we're up to something. Whatever it is you want to talk about, let's do it out front. Okay, people will see us but you're a trainer and I'm a jockey, they're much less likely to be suspicious.'

He didn't say anything, just turned and led me along the single track. Among the crowds once more, we passed a line of glum bookmakers paying out on the second race, and walked on toward the parade ring, which we skirted then came back, travelling the route four or five times while Barney told his tale.

It seemed that my bathing partner at Perth, Cliptie, had been carrying a large amount of cash, carefully placed in betting shops around the country. So large that if the horse had known, he'd probably have sunk without trace. Most of that stake money, thirty grand of it, had belonged to one of Barney's owners, Joe Dimokratia, Joey the Greek. And herein lay the crux: Joey the Greek did not know Barney had used his cash.

Joey was spending the month of June in his home country before returning to collect from Barney the proceeds of the sale of two of his horses, proceeds that Barney no longer had. Barney made it clear that Joey was unlikely to take this news gracefully.

If it hadn't been for the pallor of Barney's complexion and the nervous pitch of his voice, I would have found the whole thing comical. 'So what do you plan to do?' I asked.

'I've got to get the money before he comes back.'

'And what do you plan to use for stakes, if it's any of my business?'

'I've sold another one of Joey's horses.'

'You're kidding. Without him knowing?'

He nodded, shrugged. 'He can't do any more to me if it doesn't come off.'

'Where do I come in?' I asked.

'I want you to be at Market Rasen on Saturday and to leave yourself free for the second race.'

'I'd hardly have thought I was your good luck charm, Barney.'

'You're trustworthy and reliable, Eddie, and you can keep your gob shut. We just got a bad break on Thursday.'

He didn't realize how bad a break and I was tempted to tell him that I thought Tranter had sabotaged the bridle. But I wasn't certain that he had. But supposing Tranter rode against me again when Barney's money was down? I settled for telling him that Tranter held a grudge against me and that while Thursday's incident might have been an accident, Barney shouldn't risk putting me up on Cliptie again if Tranter was in the same race.

'Don't worry about Tranter, I'll sort him out.' He said it in such an offhand manner - almost like, 'forget about the fly, I'll swat it' - that it worried me and made me realize how desperate he was. I'd expected him to blow his top and demand more details about Tranter and the Perth race, but that faraway gaze was in his eyes again, though this time it looked like single-mindedness rather than despair. He could see the target a week away and wasn't going to be deflected.

Clutching his elbow lightly, I stopped and turned him toward me. 'Barney, if I want him sorting out, I'll do it myself.'

'Leave it to me, Eddie.' He made to walk on again. I held him. 'Barney. I'll sort it out.'

Barney's big red nose made him appear jolly in a music-hall sort of way, but his grey eyes were cold and hard and I wondered how afraid he was of Joey the Greek. He said, 'Eddie, I can't afford another fuck-up.'

'Listen you won't put Tranter off easily, I've been trying to do it all season. Play safe, book somebody else.'

'I want you, Eddie.' He didn't voice it but the look in his eyes said, "You owe me one."

'Fine. Let's say I'll ride. Just make sure you've got a standby in case Tranter turns out to have a mount in the race.'

Barney looked down at me, gripping my shoulders with both hands. 'Eddie, you're the standby.'

It turned out that Rod, Barney's jockey son, had suffered no accident on Wednesday. The plan from the start was to declare Rod, an inexperienced claiming jockey, as the rider at Perth to discourage the public from betting on Cliptie so his price would drift. The last-minute substitution of E. Malloy would have gone pretty much unnoticed in the country's betting shops. If I'd been unavailable for the ride on Thursday, Barney said he would have withdrawn the horse and held off until I was free.

Now he planned to try the same ruse at Market Rasen next week. Trouble was the blackmailer had warned me last night never to take another unbooked ride. Barney was staring hard at me, stiff with tension, and I saw in his face a reflection of Martin's haggard features. I couldn't tell which was the devil and which the deep blue sea.

At least it gave us something to work to, a deadline. We had exactly one week to find the blackmailer.

Chapter 10

As arranged, Martin came to see me on Sunday afternoon and we walked to the pub for a late lunch. On the way there, the storm that had been brewing for days broke with a lightning bolt and thunderclap that made you believe in God. We ran but were drenched in seconds by a deluge that left us gasping for breath, then laughing stupidly, and finally splashing like children through the water overflowing the road drains.

By the time we reached the pub, it had rained itself out. We sat at a white table in the beer garden, steaming gently in the sun.

Martin drank beer. I sipped mineral water as we waited for sandwiches. We had agreed yesterday that Town Crier had to be officially taken off the market so that we weren't compromised further. Martin was to phone the two breeders with mares booked in and tell them the horse was carrying a slight injury, nothing permanent, but the vet thought he'd be off for a few weeks. It was close enough to the end of the breeding season for them to be unlikely to request a new date.

'How did they take it?' I asked.

'Mrs. Sansome was annoyed and moaned like hell but she's a bit of a cow at the best of times. Parsons was okay. I got the impression he might even have been a bit relieved.'

I nodded, watching him. He looked much more positive, alive again. I'd persuaded him that things would come good if we worked through them. First priority was identifying the blackmailer and persuading him he'd been misinformed. The second was to find out what was wrong with Town Crier and fix it. And the third was to offer the owners who'd had a 'fraudulent' covering by Acapella a free nomination to Town Crier next year.

This was the one Martin was most nervous about. 'Eddie, can't we avoid that, somehow?'

'How?'

'I don't know.' He squirmed uncomfortably, shaking water drops from his hair. 'I just don't think we can tell them it was a mistake. How incompetent are we going to look when that gets out?'

'As incompetent as you can get, but our honesty in admitting it will go a long way in mitigation. And we'll be better off admitting it before the blood tests from the foals force our hand.'

'It's not going to be as easy as you think.'

'Listen, it's the least of our worries. We made it bottom of our list yesterday. Let's keep it there until we've sorted out the others. Now who else knew about Town Crier's fertility problem?'

'Nobody.'

'Nobody? You didn't tell a soul?'

He avoided my eyes.

'I told Caroline.'

'Right. When?'

'End of March.'

'Did she know about Fiona at the time?'

He shook his head. More droplets. It turned out Caroline had found them in bed together a few weeks later, though Martin said it did nothing more than confirm what she'd been accusing him of for years. 'She almost enjoyed it. Finding the evidence which would save all the cross-examination in the future.'

'Who else knows?'

'Fiona.' He lowered his gaze.

I sighed. 'Why didn't you just take out an ad in the local paper?'

'Fiona wouldn't breathe a word. I'd bet my life on it.'

'So it must have been Caroline.'

'Couldn't have been.'

I leaned across the table. 'It must have been, Martin! You can't have it both ways!'

He threw his hands wide and the waitress bringing the sandwiches had to jig quickly sideways. He apologized and turned on his most charming smile, but she'd been looking curiously at us dripping oddities all the way down the path and seemed keen to get back indoors. Martin paid and she hurried off.

I lifted a thin ham sandwich. Martin continued gesturing. 'Carrie would have absolutely no motive for giving the game away.'

Between bites I said, 'Never heard of "hell hath no fury" and all that?'

'Look, all she cares about is screwing me for as much as she can in the divorce settlement. Why should she risk.' he sought the word 'devaluing my only asset? Our only asset?'

He had a point. 'Have you asked her?'

'What, if she's told anyone?'

I nodded.

'That's the last thing I need - for her to know I'm being blackmailed!'

'We are being blackmailed.'

'We, I know. It's the only reason she's still there. She knows we won't be able to sell the business until Town Crier's back on song, so she'll have to sit and suffer till it's sorted out. Or rather I'll have to suffer the constant bloody nagging.'

'I thought you were in the cottage with Fiona?'

'I am but she summons me every day for a bloody progress report.'

He bit fiercely into a sandwich. I said, 'You're going to have to ask her.'

'What do I say?'

'Just ask if she's mentioned it to anybody.'

'And if she has, do you think she's going to tell me?'

'I don't know, but if you don't ask, we won't find out.'

He sipped beer and sulked. I was learning more about him all the time. I said, 'Martin, it's the only card we've got at the moment. You have to play it.'

'I'll speak to her tonight,' he said quietly.

'Don't accept the first thing she says,' I warned.

'Unless it's yes.'

I smiled. 'If it's yes, make sure you get the name of the guy she told.'

'That'll probably cost me another ten grand on the settlement.'

We moved on to priority two - could Town Crier be cured? Any vet we used would have to be discreet and totally trustworthy. If word got out about the stallion, I doubted we'd ever restore breeders' faith in him.

Town Crier had been three or four pounds short of top class

when racing over a mile and a half on the flat. When breeders are trying to get jumping stock, there aren't many reliable stallions. As most 'practicing' jump horses are geldings, there is no stud career waiting after retirement. No matter how talented they've been on the racecourse, the chance to pass on genes had disappeared, commonly in their formative days, along with their testicles.

So for ex-flat stallions to establish themselves as good sires of jumping stock normally takes years, as their early crops are usually tried on the flat for a couple of seasons at least. If they don't prove successful, they're often put over jumps where it might take three or four seasons for them to shine. Even then, breeders will be cautious and wait a few seasons more to check if the rest of that stallion's progeny also show talent over hurdles or fences. By the time a jumping stallion does make a name for himself, he can be sixteen or seventeen - or, more likely, dead.

Town Crier was twelve and could easily have another decade at stud, covering approximately a hundred mares a season. Multiply that by his fee, which would rise in accordance with the success of his stock, and you could see what a blow it would be to the stud if his infertility proved permanent. It was this simplified breakdown of figures and prospects that drained the colour from Martin's face.

I'd called an old friend and fellow jockey who also happened to be an excellent vet. His name was Brian Kincaid, and I'd arranged to meet him while he was at work in Gloucester next day. Martin was very anxious about it. 'Can't you just give him the samples? He doesn't have to know what stallion they've come from, or even the stud.'

'And what's the likelihood of his learning anything more from the samples than your man in Ireland did?'

He had no answer for that.

'He's going to have to examine Town Crier, Martin.'

He clasped his head, fingers pushing out thick wings of almost dry hair, and stared at his feet.

'Martin, I trust this guy. I've known him for years. He's one of the old school.'

He nodded, head still in his hands. 'Okay, okay, Eddie.'

'I'll ring you as soon as I've spoken to him.'

He finished his beer and stood up, soggy trousers sucking noisily at the chair. 'I'd better get cracking.'

As we returned to my flat, he had one more go. 'Couldn't we

bring Town Crier to him, tell him it was something else?'

'Then expect him to give us one hundred percent trust?'

He hunched his shoulders again and stuffed his hands moodily in his pockets. We walked the last half-mile in silence.

Chapter 11

Next morning I found Brian Kincaid in a stall at a Gloucester stud, with his arm so far up a mare's backside his right cheek rested on her buttock. He winked and smiled at me. I nodded. He was watching a small monitor, pointing with his free hand to what looked like a white UFO on the black screen.

'Cyst, I'm afraid,' he said to the man holding up the mare's tail. 'It may look like an embryo but it's another cyst.'

The man swore. 'Bad luck,' said Kincaid, withdrawing his arm and a thin cable. The cable was attached at one end to the computer and at the other to an egg-sized rubber ball. He placed the ball in a white bowl on the table, peeled off the long dirty rubber glove, dropped it in the bin and reached over to shake my hand. I took his rather gingerly. The smell of fresh horseshit rose from a brown plastic bin beside him, and the apron he wore was heavily soiled with shit and blood and membraney type stuff. 'How're you doing, Eddie? Nice to see you.'

'And you.'

He introduced me to the disgruntled tail-holder, the stud manager, who was anxious to get the next mare in. Kincaid said, 'Just one more to do and we'll have a cup of tea.'

I nodded. 'Sure. No hurry.'

The mare with the cyst was led out and the rear doors slid open to reveal another mare waiting in the yard with her foal. A lad half-pushed, half-carried the foal in and placed it in the stall beside its mother, who walked quietly after them. Kincaid swung the half-doors closed to stop her kicking and a groom held her halter while the stud man pulled her tail aside.

Kincaid bent low, plucking a fresh blue glove from a box of disposables and pulling it onto his right arm, which he then eased inside the mare. A few seconds later, he drew out eighteen inches of shit that seemed moulded beautifully to the shape of his arm all the way to the crook of his elbow. A deft flick saw the load dumped in the bin. Two more excavations, carried out while chatting congenially to the tail-holder, and he was happy enough to pick up the scanning bulb and go back in.

His eyes turned in my direction. 'You'll have seen this before, Eddie?'

'Once or twice.' I'd been raised on a stud farm, but had never quite come to terms with how casually vets took this part of their job.

Kincaid passed the scanner over the top of the uterus, and watched the ultrasound waves paint a picture on the screen, which seemed clear to Kincaid and the stud man but looked like it always did to me - abstract.

'Twins,' Kincaid said.

The stud man swore again. Thoroughbred mares showed a high incidence of twins, which might at first seem like good news for the breeder. But mares rarely carried healthy twins successfully; if they went their full term, they tended to be born weaker than single foals, which made them poor investments.

This meant that in almost every case the vet would decide which embryo should be killed in the womb to allow the other to develop. The vet simply 'popped' one embryo, squeezed it between his fingers, but a wrong decision by him could prove the most expensive pop in the history of the turf. What if that squashed embryo held the genes to be a Triple Crown winner?

The vets were in the happy position that nobody would ever know how that embryo would have turned out. They based decisions on whatever evidence was available from a fourteen-to twenty-day-old blob. Inevitably, the smallest or most misshapen one would be popped and then everyone just hoped for the best.

Kincaid withdrew his arm and put on another fresh glove before gently pushing his way along the vaginal tract. No scanner to help now, everything done by feel. The mare shifted uneasily and the lad at her head cooed and comforted her. Her ears and eyes were back, almost as if she sensed what Kincaid was trying to do in there. He spoke quietly to her. 'It's for your own good, old girl.'

He eased out his arm and said to the stud man, 'I'll have another look at her on Thursday.' Using clean cotton wool and soapy water, he spent a minute thoroughly cleaning the mare's vagina and the surrounding area before she was led out through the sliding doors at the front.

The stud man didn't look too happy. Kincaid put an arm across his shoulders. 'Good days and bad, Stan, good days and bad.'

Stan nodded.

Kincaid said, 'Any chance of a pot of tea?'

Stan wandered off to fetch it. Kincaid smiled and stretched, yawning. 'How goes it, Mister Malloy? What's the big mystery this weather?'

Kincaid was a six-footer and strong looking. He had to waste hard to ride at ten and a half stone. His natural weight would be over twelve. He only rode as an amateur with maybe forty or so mounts a season, but was one of the best amateurs I'd ever seen and well respected in the weighing room.

In his early-thirties, he was fair-haired and threw quite a distinctive profile with his hooked nose and prominent, slightly upturned chin. The lads called him Mr. Punch, often in a puppet-show voice, and he took it with good humour - but what a ribbing he'd got last year when he married a girl called Judy. He had smiling blue eyes and was very even-tempered. I don't think I'd ever heard him complain, but he always had a sympathetic ear for others who wanted a moan.

And like most vets I'd known, Kincaid was a true animal lover. One of the things he'd always claimed had stopped him becoming a professional jockey was the expectation of a number of owners and trainers that the whip be used to maximum effect on their horses. 'No way do I want my living to depend on that,' he'd told me once.

He stood now, hands on hips, smiling at me as smelly steam rose from the bin between us. 'You look well,' I said.

'Bloody tired.' And he yawned again then took a couple of steps into a gloomy corner and reached out. On a shelf was a shiny platter of sandwiches. Kincaid swung it toward me, resting the edge against his soiled apron. 'Sandwich?'

'No, thanks.'

He started munching happily, enjoying my expression. 'God, you'll catch beriberi or something.'

Smiling, he shook his head. 'Beriberi's caused by a thiamine deficiency. Plenty of thiamine in blood and shit.' He waved the platter and I turned away in disgust. Kincaid laughed.

The stud man brought a tray with tea on it and I took it from him. We headed across the yard to sit on a low wall in the sunshine. Kincaid brought his sandwiches and as I laid down the tea tray, he reached for the pot and said, 'Will I be mother?'

I grabbed at it. 'Will you hell! Poison yourself if you like; I prefer tea minus the germs!'

He laughed again.

We spent quite a while on that wall; our shadows had shifted noticeably by the time we got up. I outlined the problem, missing out the ruse Martin had pulled on some breeders. Kincaid talked me through the reproductive system of the stallion in detail but the bottom line was that never before had he heard of such a sudden loss of fertility, not without an obvious physiological cause.

He agreed to come and see Town Crier on Wednesday afternoon.

Back at the flat, I checked my answerphone - nothing of consequence. I called Martin and told him when Kincaid was coming. 'Did you get anything out of Caroline?' I asked.

'Dog's abuse.'

'She hasn't told anyone?'

'Definitely not.'

'Do you believe her?'

'I'm inclined to. She went ballistic when I even suggested it.'

'Guilty conscience, maybe?'

'Well. I don't think so.'

He questioned me on everything Kincaid had said and I dressed things up a bit.

I asked how serious Caroline's drink problem was.

'She never drinks while she's asleep.'

'So it's pretty bad?'

'Morning till night, most days. Very steady though, can shift a couple of bottles before blacking out.'

'Is there any way she could have told someone about Town Crier while she was drunk?' 'Like who?'

'I haven't a clue. It was just a thought. That might be the reason she doesn't remember saying anything.'

He was silent for a few seconds. 'Could be,' he said. 'But how do we find out?'

'Who does she see? Does she drink with any of her friends?'

'Friends? Eddie, all of Caroline's friends are forty proof and don't talk back.'

'There must be somebody she sees outside of the stud. What about a hairdresser, a local shopkeeper or something?'

'On the odd days she goes out she manages to be relatively sober, which means she'd most probably remember what she'd said. Anyway, she wouldn't discuss stud business outside. Shit, she doesn't know much stud business to discuss!'

Except that Town Crier's a dud, I almost said. I left it at that and told Martin I'd see him next day, and we could go through the list of breeders whose mares were carrying what they thought were Town Crier foals.

I spent the rest of the evening hoping the blackmailer would call. Finding him was top of our priority list, and I had nothing to go on. I'd copied his last message from the answerphone on to a normal audio tape, and played it repeatedly in the hope that something would trigger my memory.

London accent, voice pitch on the high side, suggesting he was fairly young. I had to assume he was quite deeply involved in racing; he knew the implications of using a ringer at stud and he seemed to have the know-how to set up whatever betting coups he was planning. I resolved to start the process of elimination tomorrow, involving Caroline if necessary.

Chapter 12

'I'll say one thing, Martin, you don't mess about.' I was examining the list of 'conned' breeders. On it were two prominent Jockey Club members and the wife of the High Sheriff of Wiltshire.

He shrugged, half-smiled.

'You'd better start thinking up a convincing story for when you have to go back and tell them a mistake was made,' I said.

'No problem. So long as Town Crier's okay, that's the main thing. I'll come up with something.'

Martin brewed tea while I got my portable radio-cassette from the car. We sat at the kitchen table in the cottage playing the blackmailer's tape. Martin concentrated, brow furrowed, right ear inclined toward the sound. He said, 'There's something familiar about the voice.'

Pressing the play button again, I watched him. He looked frustrated. 'I can't say I know it.' He gestured with his hands. 'It's not somebody I know, if that doesn't sound daft, but it's familiar, I've definitely heard it.'

'Recently?'

He shook his head, listening again. 'It's like someone I've heard but I don't know the person. Like somebody on TV, a newsreader or something, know what I mean?'

'Sort of.'

His frustration was almost painful to watch and the tip-of-the-tongue element was getting to me too as I silently urged him on. I said, 'You're lucky I don't have my whip with me. I'd be sorely tempted to give you a smack to make you go through with your effort.'

He laughed, easing the tension.

We played that tape until it squeaked, drew up lists of people Martin had met recently, tried to plot Caroline's movements, but came up with nothing. I wanted to confront her, but Martin asked for one more day to try to pin down the voice.

Brian Kincaid was due down next day and Martin offered me the spare room. I refused as politely as I could. The presence of the sour-faced Fiona (boy, could Martin pick 'em) and the thought of spending the night in that dismal cottage held no appeal. Maybe I was getting too used to my own company. Anyway, I went back to the small hotel in Marlborough where I'd stayed last week.

Skimming through the Racing Post I checked the entries for Market Rasen on Saturday. Cliptie, my synchronized swimming partner from Perth, was entered in the second race. Sure enough, the jockey's name was given as R. Dolan, Barney's son, and I wondered how the poor kid felt about being used as a stooge in betting coups.

If Barney was to pull this off and the Corish Stud was to stay out of the weekend scandal sheets, then we had four days to find the blackmailer.

On Wednesday, Kincaid spent more than an hour with Town Crier, giving him as full an examination as was possible without anaesthetic. Martin anxiously followed him, asking questions which Kincaid handled good-naturedly. He took away more samples and left in an ill-concealed state of excitement, which raised Martin's hopes till I told him Kincaid was simply thrilled at being involved in such an unusual case. 'It's the scientist in him coming out. If he finds the cure he'll want it named the Kincaid Serum or something.'

Watching the vet's car disappear along the drive, Martin said, 'He can call it the Kincaid Master Triumph Total Genius Cocktail if he wants, so long as he cracks it.'

We returned to the yard. The phone in the office was ringing. Martin hurried over but it stopped as he opened the door. 'Damn!'

He picked up the receiver and dialed a short number, listened and noted something down. He dialed again. 'Tom, you rang me...Uhuh. Yeah, Friday's fine.' He hung up and said to me, 'Blacksmith.'

'Makes a change from blackmail. What did you just do? How did you know it was him that called?'

'Just dialed one four seven one, that tells you the last person who called you.'

'When did that system start? Do you have to apply to have it installed?'

'Don't think so. We didn't. It was Fiona who showed me how to do it. You don't need it anyway, your answerphone's always on.'

'Answerphones don't tell you the number of the last blackmailer to call.'

Chapter 13

On Thursday morning, Barney Dolan rang, sounding nervous. I assured him I was okay for Saturday. If we hadn't nailed the blackmailer by Friday night, I'd been prepared to tell Barney I couldn't take the ride. It wouldn't have been worth exposing the stud just to do Barney a favour. But now that we had an ideal opportunity to get the guy's number, I was happy to ride, knowing I'd get an angry call from him after Cliptie ran.

Priorities one and two were coming along nicely, and if over the weekend I could bail Barney out of trouble with Joey the Greek, it could yet turn out to be a productive week.

The rest of Thursday and Friday proved quiet, frustrating and boring. In the blackmailer's hall of fame, our guy must hold the record for the smallest phone bill. I began wondering if something had happened to him. Maybe blackmail was his stock in trade and another 'client' had sorted him out.

At noon on Friday, I checked the next day's declarations and I cursed when I saw Tranter's name against a runner in Cliptie's race.

I was about to call Barney Dolan to warn him when the phone rang. The pause before the caller spoke increased my heart rate and stopped my breath for a second.

'Eddie?'

It was Martin. I almost swore at him. He said, 'I think I've got our man.'

'The blackmailer?'

'Yep.'

'He called you?'

'Nope.'

'Come on, Martin!'

'I'm looking at a picture of him.'

Martin arrived that evening and produced a cutting from a monthly racing magazine called Bloodstalk. It was a full-page story about the Corish Stud and what a fine establishment it was. The writer's name was Simon Spindari. There was a head and shoulders picture of him at the top of the page - young, dark-eyed, olive-skinned, smiling. Your original Latin lover.

Martin explained that the feature was commissioned as 'Advertorial': the magazine had been paid £1,250 and had written the piece in a very positive light.

Martin said, 'I twigged when I noticed the cutting on the office wall. That's where I'd heard the voice before. He came twice to interview me and I found out this morning he came once when I wasn't there and spent the afternoon with Caroline, boozing.'

'Who told you?'

'Fiona.'

'Why didn't she tell you before this?'

'She said she didn't want me to think she was telling tales on Caroline, trying to turn me against her.'

'Telling tales? A journalist having a few drinks and a chat?'

Martin looked uncomfortable. 'Well, Fiona thinks it was maybe more than just a few drinks. Which is fair enough, Caroline's got her own life to lead now.'

But I could see that in his mind it wasn't fair enough. The thought of Caroline with someone else hurt him, and perhaps he now saw why she might have betrayed him and told Spindari about Town Crier and what a bastard her husband was. She could have been drunk or simply vengeful. 'Have you asked Caroline about it?'

'Thought it best not to in case she warned the guy.'

I nodded, thinking. 'Are you sure it's him?'

'Positive.'

'Okay.'

Martin watched me. 'What do we do now?' he asked.

'I don't know. It'll take a bit of thinking out.'

'Why don't we just ring him up, tell him we know who he is?'

'Where does that leave us though? He's still got damaging information.'

'He's always going to have that, isn't he? Doesn't matter what we do.'

'Unless we can make him believe Caroline was lying to him,' I said.

'How do we do that?'

I told him what I thought we should do, and when he called me a genius, my thoughts went back to the days when he was my idol. His praise always made me ridiculously proud.

Before Martin had sussed the identity of the blackmailer, the plan had been for him to come to my flat and wait for the call while I was at Market Rasen. Now he had to make a quick return trip to the stud to put plan B into action.

Before leaving, he begged me to ring Kincaid to ask about progress on the Town Crier samples. The vet had a ride at Market Rasen and we'd agreed to meet after racing. I promised Martin that if Kincaid got a breakthrough, he'd be on the phone quicker than you could say 'sperm count'.

I spent most of the journey to Market Rasen trying to figure out how I was going to cope with Billy Tranter in the second race, which was tailor-made for more of his villainy.

Cliptie had fourteen opponents and was a twelve to one chance in the betting forecast. If he won, Barney would recover Joey the Greek's cash and more besides. But such a big field on this tight undulating track would have Tranter slavering with anticipation.

The best way of staying safe and getting a clear run would be to jump him off in front and try and hold on to the lead, but horses are individuals and need riding in different ways. Dolan had told me Cliptie did best when covered up and delivered very late. A tricky horse, and, in Tranter, a tricky rival.

Chapter 14

The past few days had been cooler, and it was grey and overcast with dark clouds rolling in from the west as I headed for the weighing room. We could have done with some rain earlier in the week to soften the going, though the management had been watering and claimed to have produced perfect ground. Against Tranter, I feared I'd be hitting that ground hard at some point between 2.45 and 2.50, and had my doubts about how 'perfect' it would feel then.

But trainers seemed convinced as there were more than ten runners entered in each race, a rare thing these days. This meant the weighing room would be busier than normal. There were the usual calls of welcome and jocular abuse as I worked my way through valets and jockeys in various stages of undress till I reached my peg.

In the changing room, there is an unofficial pecking order based on success and experience and everyone observes it. The top jocks always got the positions closest to heaters, toilets, saunas, etc., then the scale slides to the bottom, the dingy corners where you find the humble conditional jockeys, their eye as firmly fixed on that number one peg as it is on a Grand National victory.

The place smelled of leather and sweat and tobacco smoke, liniment, saddle soap, boot polish and hope. And we treasured it as the sanctuary it was. No trainers or owners allowed, no matter how rich or how well connected. Valets, jockeys, racecourse officials only. It was our own little Wendy House where the baddies couldn't get us and where most of us hoped we'd never have to grow up.

I knew Barney Dolan liked a drink, but I hadn't seen him drunk. Not until I walked into the paddock. Sweat beaded his forehead and each cheekbone, as though his red nose was radiating heat. His eyes were bloodshot, his pupils the size of confetti. He stank of gin and slurred his speech as he gave me instructions. I squeezed his arm. 'Cool it. We'll be okay.'

He just nodded stupidly and tears welled but didn't fall, as his face seemed to freeze with the terror of losing. You could have transferred the picture straight into a Gamblers Anonymous leaflet and captioned it 'Addict at the end of his tether'.

I'd been pretty tense myself for the past hour. Tranter hadn't turned up. I'd sat in the changing room, waiting to see his face as he came through the door. I would know by his first look if he intended to try and do me again today, but he didn't arrive and minutes before the deadline a substitute jockey was declared.

I knew now I could ride the race without constantly watching my back. I'd been looking forward to giving that good news to Barney Dolan in the paddock but his mind was no longer open for business, closed down for the afternoon by that well-known racecourse firm, Fear & Booze.

The mounting bell sounded. Barney stood rooted. I went over to Cliptie and the lad legged me up. Cliptie flicked an ear and rolled an eye toward me, probably wondering which little adventure I had in store for him today. I clapped his neck as we walked round. 'Relax, I forgot to bring my swimming trunks.' The blond lad looked up at me and smiled.

As we left the paddock, I looked toward the car park to see Billy Tranter running for the weighing room as furiously as his saddle and kitbag would allow. I whistled loudly through my teeth, which wasn't the smartest thing to do as Cliptie jibbed in surprise and jumped sideways, but I caught Tranter's eye and gave him a wide smile and a high wave. I saw his mouth form a curse as he slammed the saddle to the ground and kicked it.

We cantered to the start.

My stupid antics had stirred Cliptie up, and he wouldn't settle to walk round. He jogged and skittered and generally worked himself into lather, and I was glad that Dolan wasn't capable of holding up a pair of binoculars. By the time the tape rose, Cliptie was in such a sweat, I could hear my boots squeak against his sides as I fought to settle him. He fought, throwing his head about, pulling hard, so determined that he barely took off at the first hurdle then almost tied himself in knots as he hurried to overcome the stumble and resume his headlong gallop.

I hadn't managed to rein him back an ounce as we approached the second and I stopped wrestling and just concentrated on getting him over safely. He jumped it cleanly, eager to return to fighting me.

If trainers give riding orders, most jockeys try to stick to them, even if they think they are wrong. It's better to lose a race you could have won than to disobey orders. If the horse gets stuffed then at least the blame can't be laid on you. The reverse side of this is the fact that a large number of races are decided by decisions taken during running, and I was about to make one for good or bad.

Cliptie needed holding up in the pack then brought with a late surge to give his best. If he tried to lead all the way, he'd run out of puff or enthusiasm and pack it in before the finish. On the other hand, he was using so much energy fighting my efforts to settle him he'd have nothing left at the finish anyway. So I stopped pulling against him, sat as still as I could and talked softly, sending messages down the reins to say, 'Okay, you win, no more battles, I promise. Take it easy now, do your own thing.'

And he understood. The frantic attitude disappeared. The pace didn't ease much, if any, but the gallop became rhythmical, smoother, not so taxing. The less I moved, the more his excellent balance was apparent. We jumped the third. I glanced round. We were twenty lengths clear. Five to jump.

How was Dolan coping with this?

Cliptie held together beautifully over the next two. Unfaltering. Three to jump.

Attempting to lead all the way is different from any other race-riding tactic. Normally you'll have a calm, settled horse who's a proven stayer, who enjoys being out there on his own, who relishes the battle when challengers come at him late in the race. But even on those types there's always a little spider of doubt waiting to unravel its web, anticipating that blip in the stride or breathing that tells you it will be a miracle if you last home.

And it's not only getting home, returning in one piece, puttering into the petrol station on your final whiff of vapour. On a thoroughbred, there is a pack after you. A pack of animals. And you have a fierce desire to win. Not just for you, often for the horse, for your partner, the one who's done everything he can to stay ahead of that pack. Sometimes you can almost feel the primal fear from him as he falters and tries to keep going, to keep living.

The worst feeling of all is the helplessness. That was the sensation I dreaded most and that was what I found myself expecting as I went to the second last on this horse who was trying to lead throughout for probably the first time in his life.

I forced myself to look round again.

They were coming.

The dark pack closed like some shaking eraser deleting the distance between us.

Ten lengths behind. Two to jump. Three furlongs to go. Six hundred and sixty yards. How much was each worth in pounds to Barney Dolan?

But Cliptie was holding together. Then, a hundred yards off the hurdle, he went... faltered. The tiniest of tremors but one that I knew signified the beginning of the earthquake.

He cleared the jump but failed to get away cleanly, lost his stride. I gathered the reins, sat lower, gently tried to bring him onto an even keel. His breath rasped, ears came back. I talked to him. 'Come on! Stay with it! Not far. One more jump.'

I daren't look behind. The simple turning action could easily throw him off balance again. I didn't know how near they were.

Then I heard the hoofbeats.

Approaching the last, he was almost exhausted and hit the top, stumbled, but somehow got his legs out in front and stayed upright. I was now a passenger. Dead freight. I was convinced that if I started riding a finish Cliptie would go to pieces.

Hoofbeats right and left. Loud panting. Then in the periphery of my vision a dark stretching nose each side of Cliptie's quarters, both gaining, reeling us in, foot by foot, reaching our breast girth, jockeys like dervishes, every instinct in me screaming to kick and scrub and push but my brain overruling, forcing me to sit still and stay balanced, letting Cliptie do everything for both of us. Ninety nine percent of onlookers would think I was throwing the race.

The winning post seemed eerily fixed, never coming nearer, the only movement from those other two snorting, sweating, whip-marked animals, their heads at Cliptie's shoulder now, at his throat, his jaw, his nose.

Then past him.

And the post.

'Photograph,' the PA blared.

'Photograph.'

In most tight finishes, you know if you've won or not. Normally you'll glance across as you hit the line, but I'd been so afraid to move for fear of unbalancing Cliptie that I'd kept staring straight ahead. He pulled himself up very quickly, exhausted. I jumped off and led him toward the unsaddling enclosure.

A few punters by the horsewalk asked me if I'd held on and that made me more hopeful; others cursed me for not riding out the finish. Dolan waited in the enclosure. The colour had gone from his face though his nose stayed stubbornly red, making the surrounding skin look even paler. He swayed gently as though just holding on for the result before keeling over.

He lumbered across, almost blocking my way as I led the horse in, and tried to ask silently but the intended quizzical expression resulted in one slightly tilted eyebrow and crossed eyes. At least if we'd lost he'd feel no pain till he sobered up. I looked at him and shrugged. It was as though we had a pact of silence. The lad took Cliptie and I clapped the horse's lathered neck. Cliptie's sides heaved and his head hung.

I watched the two other jockeys involved ride in; neither entered the winner's spot.

The PA crackled slightly and breaths were held. 'Ladies and gentlemen, the judge has called for a print before deciding the outcome of the second race.'

Unless it was desperately tight, the judge could usually nominate the winner from the negative. We'd now have to wait a few minutes more for a full print to be produced. I went to weigh in then hurried back out. Beside me, Barney stared straight ahead and kept swaying, rhythmical as a metronome.

After five minutes without an announcement, there were murmurs of 'dead heat'. Finally, the PA crackled again. 'Ladies and gentlemen, the result of the photo finish... the judge has called a dead heat between number three, Cranston Hall, and number seven, Cliptie.' I grabbed Barney's arm. 'Will that do?' Bets on dead heats are settled to half the stake. Cliptie's Starting Price was twelve to one. I wondered how much Barney had bet. But he smiled stupidly and nodded then said, 'Fixed Tranter, too. Fixed Tranter.'

I smiled. 'What did you do?'

Comically, he bent over and swung his arm, releasing a phantom bowling ball. 'Old spud up the arse trick!' he bellowed. I later found out he'd got someone to block Tranter's car exhaust with a raw potato. Barney bowled again in a demented action replay then fell over and lay on his back, cackling at the sky.

Chapter 15

Brian Kincaid turned up half an hour later, and we took Styrofoam cups of black coffee outside and stood by the empty parade ring during the running of the next race. Kincaid's hooked nose touched the edge of the narrow cup and he had to tilt his head back as he drank. He had no news of any breakthrough on the Town Crier samples, and told me that progress would be quicker if we would allow him to contact the Equine Fertility Unit in Newmarket.

The lab had some ultra-sophisticated equipment but much of their work came via the Jockey Club, and I was as nervous as Martin about any involvement with them. From the beginning, Kincaid had taken the view that if he asked no questions he'd hear no lies, so when I confirmed we wanted the EFU guys left out he didn't push it, just told me we'd have to be patient.

I watched Kincaid ride in the last, admiring how stylish he looked for such a tall man. He rode a brilliant race to catch Tranter's horse close home, and that made victory all the sweeter for me. Although Kincaid had never given up hope on his horse, Tranter's had been well clear on the run in then started idling so badly that Kincaid caught him in the shadow of the post and won by a neck.

I went to applaud Brian Kincaid as he came in. Riding toward the winner's enclosure Kincaid wasn't smiling, he was grim-faced and obviously very angry. Jumping from the saddle, he forced a smile for the winning connections and managed a few terse words with the trainer before hurrying inside the weighing room. I followed him.

He got up from the scales and strode into the changing room, dumped his saddle and whip on the bare wooden table and wrenched open the buckle of his helmet strap. The way he tore the helmet off must have hurt his ears and as he turned to face me, his fury made him almost unrecognizable. Kincaid was the most relaxed guy you could meet, and if anyone had offered to bet me I'd one day see him in such a rage, I'd have lost a lot of money.

I'd been anxious to ask what had happened, but as I stopped a few yards from him he moved forward, eyes burning through me, and pushed me firmly aside with both hands. I turned to see who his target was, and as a scowling Tranter appeared carrying his gear, Kincaid took two more steps, drew back his right arm and unleashed a punch Tyson would have been proud of.

The only sound that came from Tranter was the crunching grind of gristle giving way to a hammerhead of knuckle. His mouth opened half in surprise, half in protest, but before a word could form, he was hurtling backward, scattering tack and dropping his own gear as he fell. A dozen men, jockeys and valets, stood still. Through the doorway, an official moved forward inquiringly. Kincaid stepped over Tranter and slammed the door.

No outside observers now.

Grabbing the dazed Tranter, Kincaid hoisted him up and tore at his colours until much of Tranter's flesh was exposed. Grunting, he lifted him off his feet and half-laid, half-threw him down on a long trestle table. Kincaid picked up Tranter's own whip and started thrashing him, high hard strokes across his pale skin. Weals rose in instant red ridges as Tranter, still semi-conscious from the punch, groaned and tried to turn.

We all looked at each other, nobody sure what to do. From time to time, scores were settled in the privacy of the changing room. It was usually short and sharp and soon forgotten about but Kincaid was out of control. He started shouting: 'If you ever do anything like that again I'll kill you, you fucking despicable little turd!' He was grunting with the effort of beating Tranter.

'Brian, enough!' I said, grabbing at his elbow. He wrenched free and raised the whip again. I seized the collar of his silks from behind and jerked him back, off balance. 'You'll kill him!'

He stared down at me. He was red-eyed with rage. I took the chance of reaching up to grip his shoulders. 'Brian, for God's sake, calm down! Calm down!'

He stared at me and I thought he'd gone permanently mad. He was panting, and blobs of spittle had appeared at the edges of his mouth.

With a mixture of gentleness and firmness, I led him slowly away from a prostrate Tranter as the others watched. They moved aside to let us through. Quietly I said to Colin Blake, 'Get the doctor.'

Blakey moved quickly toward the door as I sat Kincaid on the bench. He stared straight ahead but his breathing eased and the rigidity seeped from his body until he was half-slumped, elbows on knees, head drooping, gazing at the floor.

Two hours later, Kincaid's demeanour had changed to one of deep depression. We were in a small country pub, looking at glasses of whisky that neither of us had any real appetite for. His all-out assault had been triggered by Tranter's abuse of his horse after being caught on the post. As they'd pulled up Tranter had steered himself behind Kincaid's mount so that he couldn't be seen from the stands and thrashed his own exhausted horse savagely with his whip around the head and neck. Brian described it graphically. Tranter lashed across the velvety muzzle and, more painfully, down the horse's last rib so the leather flap wrapped under the soft part of the belly to bite into the fleshy purse that held his penis. Kincaid said Tranter gave the poor beast a welter of vicious strokes before he'd managed to reach him and almost wrench him from the saddle.

But the vet was disgusted by his own behaviour and lack of self-control, and no matter how much I tried to reassure him it was justified, his mood grew blacker. I told him Tranter had never lost consciousness and that the bewildered doctor had said he didn't think there would be any permanent damage.

Nor was there any danger of Kincaid being disciplined. No witness would snitch and, spiteful as he was, it was highly doubtful that Tranter would either. 'You'll have to watch yourself though,' I warned Kincaid, 'the little bastard won't forget it easily.'

Kincaid and I left the drinks unfinished and went our separate ways.

Back at my flat, Martin confirmed that the first part of our plan to beat the blackmailer had been carried out. As agreed, he persuaded Fiona to call Spindari and warn him that he was being set up.

Spindari had denied he knew anything about the blackmail attempt, but Fiona told him that Caroline, with Martin's knowledge, had deliberately fed him false information on Town Crier in the hope that Jean Kerman would print the story and leave her newspaper open to a huge libel suit from the Corish Stud.

When Spindari asked what Fiona's interest in it was, she'd said she was pregnant by Martin who had reneged on his promise to marry her and gone back to his wife. The simplest of motives: revenge.

Martin had spent the evening waiting to see if our plan had worked. The blackmailer would be aware by now that I'd ridden a winner at Market Rasen, having accepted exactly the type of ride he'd warned me against. But he hadn't called. It looked like he'd swallowed Fiona's story.

Chapter 16

Martin stayed overnight and next day we travelled to Worcester to visit Kincaid to try to cheer him up. The vet's mood had improved greatly since the previous evening; Judy, his wife, had told him he'd done exactly the right thing and that she'd have thought less of him if he hadn't given Tranter a beating.

As we drank tea, Judy moved around the big kitchen preparing lunch and joining in the general conversation. Martin was growing increasingly impatient to ask questions about Town Crier. Kincaid noticed and suggested that we might like a conducted tour of the facilities.

As soon as we were outside, Martin pressed for news of progress on the samples. Kincaid explained he was still waiting for some results on the blood and sperm specimens.

'Results from where?' Martin asked nervously.

Kincaid smiled. 'Don't worry; they don't know which stallion the sperm is from or why I've asked for the analysis.'

'Who are they?' Martin asked.

'Specialists, Casper and Denbourne, a big lab. Lots of vets use them for analysis.'

'Thoroughbred specialists?'

'Specialist analysts, all animals. Look, the samples should be here by Tuesday at the latest. I'm as anxious as you guys to crack this. I don't like mysteries.'

Martin nodded and ran his fingers through his grey mop, pushing it away to reveal that telltale gauntness, as though all the worries in his head were sucking at the skin, stretching it tighter over the fine bone structure.

Kincaid reached out and squeezed his shoulder gently. 'I'll ring you as soon as the results come through.'

The best that could be said about the next three days was that Spindari failed to resurface. It looked like we'd beaten the blackmail threat.

Kincaid called me just after nine on Tuesday morning: the lab could find nothing in the sperm to offer a clue as to the cause of the sterility.

'Where next?' I asked.

'Can you give me till the end of the week?' He sounded serious, thoughtful.

'Sure. What're you thinking?'

'Ask no questions, Eddie.'

'Brian…'

'Eddie, listen, I won't drop you in it, I promise.'

'Okay. Can I make one stipulation?'

'Shoot.'

'No Horseracing Forensic Lab.' The Horseracing Forensic Lab dealt mostly with security issues - the last thing we needed.

'Fine. I'll call you. Oh, are you at Stratford on Friday?' He asked.

'I've got nothing booked, but I'll probably be there mooching around. Better than sitting here in this heat looking down on a one-horse yard.'

'Dust in the mouth? Tumbleweeds outside the saloon?'

I smiled. 'Something like that.'

'See you on Friday.'

I had to ring Martin with the bad news, but I decided to dress up the facts a little. I told him the samples had highlighted something that required more investigation, further tests, and that Kincaid had asked us to hold on till the end of the week.

Martin took it well and quizzed me for details. I told him Kincaid had been talking medical terms and I hadn't really taken it all in.

When I saw Kincaid at Stratford on Friday, he seemed very positive. He told me he expected to have some results by Monday at the latest. I'd agreed to ask no questions and I held to the deal, content to wait a few days more. Kincaid had been very upbeat and wasn't the type to raise false hopes.

He was at Stratford for a ride in the last. We stood talking just inside the changing-room door. I suggested we have dinner somewhere before driving home. He smiled ruefully. 'Afraid not, Eddie. I haven't eaten since yesterday morning. Got to do ten eight in the second at Southwell tomorrow.'

'On what?'

'Tubalcain.'

'They must fancy it.'

He nodded, smiling.

'Excuse me!' A voice from behind us. It was Tranter. We'd been half-blocking the doorway. We moved aside and there was a sudden yelp. We turned to see Ken Rossington, a valet, clutching his right foot and hopping about in apparent anguish. Kincaid had stood on his toe, and although he was most apologetic, Rossington made his usual show of it. One of the changing room's jokers, he'd milk any potential laugh for all it was worth.

Tranter looked in poor shape; bruised eyes, nose still swollen and misshapen. He sat on the bench. Kincaid followed him and it seemed for a few seconds he was going to approach him; there was an air of conciliation about the vet. Kincaid took a couple of steps inside the room, hesitated, then turned and strode out, a trace of anger back in his face.

Tranter didn't watch him leave. Unpacking his kitbag, he showed no emotion.

I rode in the second race and the fourth, both unplaced, and loitered till after the fifth on the chance some poor bugger might crock himself and let me in for a ride in the last, but they all returned safe and I headed for the exits to beat the crowds. Driving home, I speculated on the chances of Kincaid's coming up with something by the time I saw him at Southwell next day, but Kincaid didn't make it to Southwell. He never left Stratford alive.

Chapter 17

I heard about it next morning driving to Southwell. It was an item tagged on to the end of the news on Radio 5: 'An amateur jockey and prominent vet has been found dead in what is believed to have been an horrific accident at Stratford Racecourse. Mister Brian Kincaid, who was married with a baby daughter, apparently collapsed in a sauna and died of severe hyperthermia. Mister Kincaid's body was not found until early this morning. Racecourse officials say there will be a full inquiry.

'And now the weather.'

And now the weather.

I must have imagined it. Nobody could report the death of a friend of mine and simply say 'And now the weather'. Impossible. A hoax or something. It had to be. I pulled over, mounting the grass verge. I was vaguely aware of a lorry thundering past, horn blaring, shaking the car. I sat gripping the wheel, staring straight ahead, replaying the news clip over and over in my mind.

I don't know how much time passed before I reached for my phone and found the number of Stratford Racecourse in my diary. I asked for the clerk of the course. Unavailable. Could they confirm the news report? Not prepared to comment. Where could I get confirmation? Sorry, couldn't help.

I had a friend in Jockey Club Security, Peter McCarthy. We'd helped each other over the years. I knew he tried to avoid working Saturdays, so I rang his home number and held for ten rings before he answered.

'Mac, Eddie Malloy. I just heard a news item that said Brian

Kincaid is dead. Is it right?'

'Eddie, yes, I'm sorry. Only heard myself about half an hour ago. You knew Brian quite well, didn't you?'

'What happened?'

'The theory is, apparently, that he went into the sauna for a half-hour session after the last race and collapsed in there, by which time everyone had gone home.'

'Collapsed?'

'It seems he'd been wasting quite hard to make the weight at Southwell today. Tragic, isn't it?'

My mind overloaded temporarily with doubts, questions, and images of how Brian would have looked after lying in a sauna for hours.

Mac said, 'Eddie, are you all right?'

'Mmmm. Surely the sauna cabin has some sort of safety cut off?'

'I don't know, Eddie. There will be a full inquiry.' I simply couldn't think straight. Had to get off the phone. I told McCarthy I'd call him later.

I got out of the car and wandered over to a stone wall hemming black and white cattle into a big field. Resting my hands on the wall, I stared across the field into dark woods, trying to pull my thoughts together.

Brian Kincaid was dead. An accident in a sauna.

No way.

Not Brian. He was a highly intelligent man with considerable medical experience. Light-headed from fasting maybe, but he would have been more aware than most of the dangers of losing consciousness in a sauna. At the first sign of dizziness, he would have got out, I was certain of it. But he didn't get out, so either somebody knocked him unconscious in the box or prevented him from escaping.

Logical progression: who?

Logical answer: Billy Tranter.

I leaned against the wall, trying to close down my emotions and think objectively. After the chances he took at Perth and the persistence he'd shown in persecuting me, it had occurred to me that Tranter might have the germ of a psychotic disorder. Whether it could have mutated into psychopathic was another matter. I needed to know more.

I got back on the road to Southwell. The last thing I felt like doing was riding horses, but Tranter would be there and I wanted to see him. Watch him. Study his behaviour. Analyze it. That's what the logical side of me wanted to do. What the rest of me wanted to do was find him guilty without trial and beat him until he died.

The news at noon ran the same item on Brian's death; no further details. Two minutes later, my phone rang. It was Martin. 'I just heard on the news, about Kincaid.'

'Uhuh.'

'Tell me it's not true, Eddie?'

'It's true.'

'Ohhh. Jesus Christ! What are we, jinxed or something?'

'What are you worried about? The samples? Town Crier?' I was just in the mood for an argument. Ready to take my anger out on somebody.

'Eddie, what are we going to do?'

'What are we going to do? What the hell's Judy Kincaid going to do? She has a three-month-old kid with no father! We've got a mangy fucking stallion firing blanks! Whose shoes would you rather be in?'

There was a long pause, and then Martin said quietly that he would call me later. I told him to be more bloody respectful to Brian Kincaid's memory when he did. Memory. God, you'd think he'd been dead years. Yesterday I'd spoken to him. Yesterday. In the corridor in the weighing room. He'd been telling me he was wasting hard for this ride.

And who was behind us when he said it? Who was listening? Who could have made a reasonable assumption that Brian might use the sauna yesterday afternoon?

Billy Tranter.

I pressed the accelerator to the floor, speeding dangerously, stupidly, toward Southwell.

Chapter 18

My temper had cooled by the time I reached the course. The guys in the weighing room weren't as subdued as I'd expected and it made me angry, made me want to preach a sermon telling them they ought to be grieving for Brian Kincaid. But the fact that he was an amateur meant that he was never really part of the 'brotherhood'. It wasn't a matter of not being accepted, simply that most professional jockeys see each other almost every day in the same way as soldiers in a small elite unit do.

We know each other's characters and weaknesses and share the same dangers daily. Amateur jockeys are tolerated and grudgingly respected if they are good. Brian had been respected but there seemed little emotion at his death, only shock at the manner of it. There was a lot of speculation about how terrible it must have been, and some juvenile nominations of the ways of dying some of them would prefer.

Bill Keating came in and told everyone he'd spoken to the caretaker at Stratford, the bloke who'd found Brian's body

'He said it was like a potato crisp.' That silenced everybody. Tranter was in the corner. I watched his face but saw no emotion. I was sorely tempted to approach him and ask him to account for his movements every minute of yesterday, but had to settle for watching him whenever I could: observing, looking for some flicker of satisfaction when Brian's name was mentioned. But I saw none. And paranoia crept in. I imagined him congratulating himself as he cantered to the start, pictured him locking himself in the toilet so he could gloat and have a good laugh.

I resolved to wait in my car after racing and follow Tranter, but as the afternoon wore on realized that would be a foolish thing to do. Pointless.

Where did I expect him to head for, the scene of the crime? Or did I think he'd go home and erect a banner saying 'I killed Brian Kincaid'?

Half-disgusted, wholly frustrated, I left after my ride in the fourth and drove to Worcester to see Judy Kincaid. The dread of facing her grew mile by mile but I felt I had to go there, pay my respects, and trot out the standard, 'If there's anything I can do'.

She was in bed under sedation; the baby was sleeping in the arms of her sister, who slowly paced the kitchen floor as her husband made coffee. All three of us sat for half an hour in that collective daze that descends on the newly bereaved and suspends social conversation, excuses long silences.

They promised to tell Judy I'd called in. As we said goodbye, I had the strongest of urges to stroke the baby's forehead. I reached out and rested my hand softly on the warm pink skin. A tiny smile flickered on the round sleeping face, and I thanked God she wasn't old enough to understand how much she had just lost.

Chapter 19

I slept on my suspicions, and they were stronger when I woke. Once again, I rang Peter McCarthy, the Jockey Club Security man.

'Eddie, how come I don't hear from you for months then the only time you can find to call me is at weekends?'

It was warm-hearted banter. In the humour market, Mac and I usually traded at about the same exchange rate, but this morning it was the last thing I felt like and I steered him straight on to Brian's death.

'I know very little about it, Eddie.'

'Well, do yourself a favour and get some sniffing around done.'

'You mean, do you a favour?'

'Mac, there's no way that was an accident.'

'How do you know?'

I argued my case for Brian's medical expertise, which Mac accepted as a reasonable foundation, then told him everything that had happened with Tranter.

'You ought to be very careful who you mention this to, Eddie. That's a pretty serious allegation.'

'That's a fact, Mac! I'm not alleging anything. I'm telling you what happened between Tranter and Brian, and I'm telling you that Tranter heard us talking on Friday and could have made a reasonable assumption that Brian was going to be in that sauna.'

'Ah, but—'

'Ah, but nothing! You came to the same conclusion I did just then when I laid out the facts.'

'It's obvious the slant you're taking.'

'Because it's the logical bloody slant to take!'

There was a pause and I pictured him shaking his head slowly.

He said, 'I think you'd best wait and see what the inquiry comes up with.'

'Which will be when? Weeks? Months?'

'I don't know. Let's see what the police have to say. The coroner's report might throw up something.'

'Like what? What evidence is going to be left in a desiccated corpse?'

'That's not for us to say, Eddie.'

'Come on, Mac, don't go all superior. The cops have to be persuaded, as from now, to treat this as suspicious.'

'I wish you luck in your persuading.'

'It would be easier with your help and you damn well know it. And you know that's what I'm asking for.'

He sighed, long and deliberate, straight into the mouthpiece.

'Okay, after the beating last week, did Tranter say he was going to take revenge on Kincaid?'

'Well, I didn't hear him say that.'

'Did anyone?'

'I don't know.'

'Can you find out?'

I can ask around, sure, but—'

'Perhaps you could also ask if anyone knows what time Tranter left Stratford on Friday, and were there any witnesses to his leaving, and did anyone know where he was going, and can anyone at his ultimate destination give him a credible alibi?'

That cooled my ire. Mac was being sensible and logical, while chiding me gently for not being the same. He'd just set off a train of simple deduction, a straightforward elimination process that I should have gone through before even picking up the phone to him.

Chastened, I told him I'd press on with it and get back to him soon. I paced the flat trying to concentrate, to clear my mind so I could start again using calm logic rather than anger and emotion.

The flat was uncomfortably hot. The heat wave persisted. I went outside, scrambled over the big five-bar gate and walked up onto the gallops. The sun threw long shadows across the grassy slope. I spent more than an hour roaming the open spaces, spooked a couple of hares, heard skylarks above and steadily ordered my thoughts.

Back in the flat, I sat down with my diary and began making calls.

The first was to Bill Keating, the jockey who'd spoken to the caretaker at Stratford. The caretaker was a friend, and Bill said he thought he'd speak to me quite freely if I called. His name was Charlie Kenton and he answered at the first ring.

'That was quick,' I said.

'I was just about to make a call myself! My hand was on the bloody phone! Didn't half give me a fright. Who is it?'

I introduced myself as a close friend of Brian's. Kenton was happy to talk, with the performing instinct of an accomplished gossip. I let him warm up with a gruesome rendition of how he found the body and what he'd told the police. When I got the chance, I asked questions.

'How come he wasn't found till next morning?'

Kenton blustered about not being able to be everywhere at once, that his duties were different on racedays, and that generally it was nothing to do with him that Brian's body had lain in that sauna all night.

'Did nobody see his car left in the car park?'

'Ah, there, you see! He didn't bring his car. He got a lift with a mate.'

'Who? Which mate?'

'Scotty Fraser, so they tell me.'

'And wasn't he travelling with Scotty?'

'Apparently not.'

'How did he plan to get home?'

That stumped him. 'Er, I'm not sure on that one.'

I pressed him on whether he himself had been around the weighing room after racing. I was hoping to find out if Tranter had been among the last to leave. But Kenton admitted that he'd been on 'traffic duty', which amounted to directing cars out of the public car park. He gave me no further useful information.

I called Scotty Fraser and was glad, in a sad way, to find him as depressed about Brian's death as I was. Scotty felt guilty about not giving Brian the promised lift back.

'What happened, did you forget about him?'

'No, I was heading to the weighing room after the last to meet him and I was told he'd already left.'

'Who told you that?'

'Billy Tranter.'

My second call of the day to McCarthy interrupted a late Sunday lunch. He wasn't pleased.

Scotty Fraser had gone on to explain that he'd called Tranter yesterday, demanding to know why he had said Brian had left Stratford. Tranter told him he'd done it to get back at Brian after the beating. He'd overheard Brian mention he was getting a lift home and thought it would be a nice little touch to leave him stranded. I told Mac all this.

'Well, there you are then,' he said smugly.

'Mac, come on! Tranter would say that, wouldn't he? He's hardly going to admit killing him.'

'Equally, if he intended to kill Kincaid, he'd have to be pretty bloody stupid to drop himself in it now the way you're suggesting.'

'Why not? He had to make sure that Fraser didn't go looking for Brian.'

'Perhaps, but he could have done that just as easily by forging a note or something.'

'And who'd have delivered it to Fraser?'

'Wouldn't have been a big problem.'

'Mac, why are you being so negative? How come you can't see the obvious?'

'How come you've got tunnel vision? Tunnel vision trained on Tranter?'

'Because he's the only one I know with motive. And he's crazy.'

'Motive for what? You're seeing demons round every corner, Eddie. At the moment, we have nothing more than a very unfortunate accident which, with hindsight, some might say was waiting to happen. We have a jockey who's probably malnourished to some extent, already riding more than a stone below his natural weight; he's ridden that day having taken no sustenance at all in the previous twenty-four hours. It's quite probable he's drained and light-headed then he goes and bakes in a sauna. What price a collapse? You wouldn't get big odds.'

We fenced for another ten minutes and Mac said he'd speak to the police officer in charge and raise the possibility of 'foul play'. I urged him to tell them to have a word with Scotty Fraser.

Then I rang Kenton, the caretaker back at Stratford, and he said he'd be happy to show me around. We agreed to meet early next morning.

Chapter 20

I was at Stratford before 8 a.m. Kenton was holding the main gate open as I came up the drive. The sauna was situated at the end of a row of showers. Kenton told me it was less than two years old. I went inside the box while he chirped on, pointing to where he'd found Brian and how he'd looked like 'some little alien'. I wanted to yell at him to shut up and get out. Not once had he mentioned Brian's family or expressed sympathy for my loss of a friend. I needed time to look around. I asked him if he'd mind returning to the car and bringing me my mobile phone. He took the keys and hurried off.

Trying to block out the image of Brian's corpse, I examined the sauna box: standard, nothing unusual, two benches either side, one above the other, the coals corralled in the corner, water bucket on the floor nearby. I pulled the door closed from the inside, feeling an unexpected wave of trepidation as it clicked shut on the ballbearing catch.

I pushed it. It needed a little weight behind it but gave quite easily. I repeated the action then went outside and did the same; opened and closed it half a dozen times. The handle was of wood, shaped like a bow, about a foot long. Crouching, I looked closely at it, ran my hands down the soft pine. Relatively new, it had its share of dents and grazes though it gave slightly even under the pressure of a fingernail.

Where the bottom of the handle met the door, just on the underside of the curve, a ridge ran across. I traced it with my finger; no deeper than a millimeter, it had smooth edges. Facing the door, maybe six feet away, was a solid wall tiled in white glaze. I knelt and looked up at the ridge, but the light wasn't good.

'May I ask what you are doing?'

I turned slowly to see a well-dressed, white-haired man - the clerk of the course, Gilbert Grimond.

'Saying a prayer for Brian Kincaid.' On my knees, it was the first thing that came into my head and it was enough to throw Mr. Grimond temporarily. 'Oh,' he said. I didn't think it was the right time to tell him that what I was really doing was trying to figure what had been wedged against that handle to keep Brian Kincaid from escaping. What had been used to cover the end of the instrument so that the ridge it left was soft, barely perceptible.

I decided the real reason could wait until I'd spoken to McCarthy, told him what I'd found. Bad decision.

McCarthy was in meetings all day Monday. I left several messages for him but it was late evening before he called me at home. He sounded weary at first, giving the impression that I was the final one on his 'to do' list and all he wanted was to tick off my name and get a decent night's sleep. When I told him about the door handle, he wakened up a bit. 'I'd better go up there in the morning and have a look,' he said.

'I'll meet you there.'

'No, that's a bad idea. You're much too close to this without having any real reason to be so. Not to the outside world, at least.'

'Mac—'

'Eddie! If there is a case to be investigated here, the police are going to be touchy enough about me bringing it to their attention. If they think you're the one behind it all, driving things along, they'll make life difficult.'

'But—'

'Also, what they will see is a vendetta against Tranter. Leave it to me. I've got no axe to grind, and apart from anything else it is my job.'

'So you say, but how come you always clock on when the rest of the shift have done the donkey work?'

'The craftsmen always come in after the labourers, Eddie. Like the stallion that finishes the job after the teaser's done the dirty work.'

I smiled. 'The stallion? Getting a bit above yourself, aren't you?' But he was probably spot on. I'd been involved with various police forces in the last few years and if there was a right way to rub them up I'd yet to find it. I contented myself with the thought that evidence was beginning to build - circumstantial maybe, but it was early days and the outlook was promising.

In a more positive mood, I made a sandwich and sat down to listen to the radio news, half-hoping for some breakthrough by the cops. But there was nothing at all on Brian's death – a stale story, filed away and forgotten. I wondered how Judy was bearing up, whether she was still under sedation.

The phone rang. Martin, sounding strung out. 'Eddie, I'm sorry about your friend, but we've got to do something about this horse!'

'What's the big hurry? The stud season's almost over.'

We got into a long argument about the urgency of solving Town Crier's problem. I got the impression that Martin was feeling neglected because Town Crier was no longer my priority. I told him if he felt so strongly about the problem, he should solve it himself. He said that was just what he would do and slammed the phone down.

Ten minutes later, I called him back and arranged to meet next day. He promised to be at my flat early and was true to his word, getting me out of bed.

Even allowing that I was unshaven and bleary-eyed, I still looked better than he did. That terrible concentration-camp gauntness and desperation were in his face. I made coffee. Martin paced, unwilling to sit down.

'What's wrong, Martin?'

'We can't let this slip, Eddie. We've got to sort Town Crier out.'

'I know but there's no big hurry any more, is there? We've got seven months before the start of the new season.'

'We've got nothing like seven months! If the story gets out and we have to submit to tests on him, we're fucked!'

I couldn't understand the sudden desperation. 'Martin, what's happened? Has Spindari been back in touch?'

'No, but—'

'So how is the story going to get out?'

He marched up to me, shoving his face in mine, shades of madness in his bloodshot eyes. 'It could! It just could! And you don't care anymore! You don't give a monkey's fuck! What am I supposed to do, eh? Tell me!' Then he broke down in tears, deep racking sobs. He sank to the floor, crying uncontrollably.

An hour later, with a pint of coffee inside him, he was calmer. He admitted he'd been drinking far too much and that Caroline and Fiona were putting 'unbearable' pressure on him. The bills were mounting, Kincaid was dead, and my attention was elsewhere. He said he just felt everything was slipping away from him and that if he could only be sure Town Crier would recover, that would give him strength.

I looked at this hero of mine, slumped at my table, beaten by his own doubts and fears. This hero, this man, this child. And I promised I'd make everything better for him.

He suggested we visit Brian Kincaid's partners and try to find out what had happened to the samples Brian had sent off. He seemed in no fit state to meet anyone but he promised he'd be okay. Foolishly, I believed him and set up a meeting that afternoon with John Brogan, the senior partner in Kincaid's surgery.

I found a clean shirt for Martin and persuaded him to have a shower and a shave. Just as he closed the bathroom door, the phone rang. It was McCarthy. I looked at my watch: 10.25. I'd assumed he'd be travelling to Stratford as promised but the call was on a clear line, no mobile. I said, 'I thought you were going to Stratford?'

'I'm at Stratford.'

'So what do you think?'

'I think we've got problems.'

'The cops might have problems,' I said with some satisfaction, 'not us.'

'We've got problems, Eddie.' A serious tone I should have recognized sooner.

'What's wrong?'

'The sauna's gone.'

'What?'

'Somebody burned it down in the early hours of this morning. And the weighing room with it.'

Chapter 21

I was driving as fast as my brain was working which wasn't sensible on these country roads and the tyres screeched complaints at each bend. Martin stared straight ahead. He'd just lost the argument about concentrating on Town Crier rather than Brian's death, which I was now almost certain was murder. He paid me back by not responding to the questions I threw out as we headed south. Few needed answering. But I could have used some murmurs of encouragement now and then.

'I mean, if Tranter's done this where does he stop? He kills Brian, burns down the weighing room to get rid of the evidence, the whole weighing room, mind you... I wonder if it was anything to do with McCarthy going there this morning. How could he have found that out?'

I asked Martin to get Mac's number from my diary and dial for me. Silently he did it and handed me the phone. Mac's mobile was switched off. Martin tried the racecourse number. It rang out unanswered. I cursed and returned to one-sided speculation about Tranter and his psychological history, motivation, private life, etc.

Finally, as we sped down the slip road onto the M5, Martin spoke. 'What if it wasn't Tranter?'

'Well, if it wasn't, I wouldn't want to be the cop who's got to solve it. I never knew anybody else who disliked Brian. Who could have a motive besides Tranter?'

'You talk like you and Kincaid were blood brothers or something. I mean, how close were you? He might have been up to all sorts of stuff?'

'Like what?'

'I don't know. Could be anything!'

I was angry with Martin. But he and McCarthy had now said I should be more objective about possible suspects, so I kept quiet for the next few heat-hazed miles and concentrated on trying to come up with alternatives. I failed, but it set me wondering if Brian's partners had an opinion on it.

The practice was located on the Worcester/Hereford border, and we got there twenty minutes early and waited in a small hot yellow room where an oscillating fan riffled the dog-eared pages of old Sunday supplements.

The meeting was disastrous. Brogan knew nothing of Kincaid's work for us and hadn't the faintest idea where any samples might have been sent to. Martin quickly lost the place completely and started berating Brogan, accusing him of being incompetent, of being in collusion with some unknown enemy. In the end, I had to apologize and almost drag Martin out. We had a serious argument in the car. Serious but pointless. His sole focus was Town Crier's fertility problem and he was obviously willing to batter and bludgeon his way through all obstacles in his attempt to find a solution. He saw no reason to make allowances for others.

'You simply can't go around behaving like you did in there!' I said. 'Brogan owes us nothing. He'd've been well within his rights to have slung you out of there…bodily!'

'Eddie, what you can't seem to understand is we don't have the time for anything else! Hear that? We! You're in this with me but you're too fucking busy being nice to people! You're only interested in everyone thinking you're a nice guy! We're bleeding to death, man!'

We travelled in silence for the last hour, and as soon as we reached my place, Martin got straight into his car and roared off without saying a word. Back in the flat, I wondered what to do next.

What a bloody mess.

I grabbed the whisky bottle and sloshed some into two inches of water. Sipping methodically at the scotch, I waited for it to seep under the door marked 'Inspiration' in my brain and open it from the inside. Come evening, I was on my second drink, watching the moonrise. I'd spoken to McCarthy. He'd told no one why he was going to Stratford, so unless the caretaker had twigged that I suspected foul play, and he'd blabbed to someone, then either the timing of the burning was coincidental or it lent even more credence to the murder theory.

Mac had told me the police were waiting for the Fire Department's forensic report so he'd reserve his opinion until that came through.

I tried to figure out how I could learn more about Tranter's movements on Friday evening, but the only people likely to know were his friends, if he had any. If he did, then they'd probably know exactly what he thought of me.

Another hour of pondering brought no ideas, though Martin's mind had obviously been at work on the drive home. Just as I was falling into bed, he called me with a ruse of his own.

Chapter 22

By noon next day, Martin had compiled a list of the labs equipped to carry out the analysis required on the Town Crier samples. We'd agreed to split it and ring them posing as a partner from Brian's practice - further deception. I took three numbers and left Martin with four and a warning not to lose his temper.

Forty minutes later, I had scored a blue line through all of mine: negative. Martin was waiting for one to return his call, which they did within the hour: zilch. None had received samples from Brian or his practice. Martin got edgy again and started slagging Brian off, saying he'd done nothing with the samples, claiming he'd been stringing us along. I knew Martin was under severe pressure, but couldn't listen to another tirade. I hung up on him and left the phone off the hook.

It was hot and I was hungry. I had little to eat but plenty to chew on. I wasn't too depressed. The death of a friend tends to balance your perspective. The stud was important to me financially but otherwise, if it went under, I could live with it. I'd had my share of hardship in the past and always got through.

Martin would probably crack up, but he'd drained me dry of sympathy. Even if we came out okay in the end, I knew our partnership would never be the same. Idols with feet of clay, indeed.

I found some salad in the fridge and boiled a piece of fish. Less than 300 calories and it would keep me going till evening. I had to do ten stone at Uttoxeter tomorrow, which meant losing at least three pounds. A five-mile run this afternoon would help and a sauna tomorrow morning. The thought shook me, and I knew I wouldn't sit in a sauna again without thinking of Brian Kincaid through every sweating minute.

After lunch, I cleaned up around the flat then changed into my running gear, pulling on two extra sweaters. As I laced my shoes, the phone rang.

'Eddie, still want me to tell the police about Tranter?' It was McCarthy. He was notorious for trying to tease, for not coming to the point.

'What do you know, Mac?'

'I know Tranter left Stratford soon after racing finished on Friday.'

'Maybe he did but what was to stop him turning round and coming back.'

'Well, for one thing, he didn't have a car.'

I waited. Mac said, 'About five miles from the course, a Mercedes 600 ran into Tranter's Volkswagen at traffic lights. His car had to be towed away and the Merc driver took him home.'

'Who told you all this, Tranter?'

'No, one of the Stewards who was acting at Stratford, for 'twas he who was driving said Merc.'

'So how come we haven't heard this juicy piece of gossip on the grapevine?'

'Because our rather embarrassed Steward asked Tranter to keep it quiet, and Tranter, knowing which side his bread is low-calorie-spreaded, has done exactly that.'

'So who told you?'

'The crasher. The Steward.'

'Who is.?'

'Not for publication, Eddie.'

'Fine.' I was miffed and not yet convinced. Tranter could have hit Brian on the head before leaving, I supposed, but could he have wedged that door closed, confident nobody would have discovered it?

'Also,' Mac said, 'to put the proverbial tin lid on your theory, Tranter was in Ireland when the weighing room at Stratford burned down. If you still think Brian Kincaid was murdered, Eddie, you'd better find yourself another suspect.'

A blue haze hung over the vast parklands as I ran along an old cart track. The sweating had started before I'd broken into a jog and now, beneath the layers of clothing, under the tight-cuffed plastic body suit, I could feel and hear the sponginess under my arms as they pumped out a steady rhythm. I was thinking more clearly and had spent the first two miles wondering who could tell me more about Brian Kincaid. I was certain he hadn't lied about sending the samples to a lab. Before leaving the flat I'd even taken the chance of checking with the Equine Fertility Unit at Newmarket, the one I'd made Brian promise he wouldn't use. They had nothing.

That was the first piece of the puzzle. The second was that Brian had been murdered, I was sure of that. And the third was that Tranter no longer seemed a suspect.

So what had Brian Kincaid done to make somebody kill him?

It was pointless returning to his professional partners. Martin had blown any potential trust there. But who else had Brian associated with?

The best bet would be to speak to Judy again. I owed her a call anyway but visiting after bereavement was never easy, least of all when your motive was selfish.

I took a cool shower, fighting the temptation to lay my head back and drink from the gushing jets. Any intake of liquid would counteract the sweating. I gargled a strong mouthwash, dressed, and dialed Judy's number. Her sister Amanda answered and told me Judy was with the police in Worcester.

'Couldn't they have come to her?'

'They did, yesterday. She wants to know more so she's gone to Worcester Police Station to see the chap from Warwick.'

Brian died in the county of Warwickshire so the cops there would be in charge of the investigation. Her sister said Judy had found strength when she learned that Brian's death was being treated as suspicious. 'She badly needs someone to blame for taking him away. Now she's got the bit between her teeth, she's determined to do all she can to discover who was responsible.' I told Amanda I'd like to help if I could and she said Judy would be in that evening, and she was sure she'd appreciate a visit.

When I got there, Judy, in pressed tan slacks and a cream blouse, welcomed me. Slim, with cropped fair hair, she was tall, almost gangly, and wore no make-up. Her cheeks always carried a reddish bloom; a true country girl. Her blue eyes were defiant despite signs of weeping.

She led me through the house to a big garden where Amanda was rocking the baby in a shaded cradle. Amanda's husband Dave was barbecuing meat that sizzled temptingly and smelt delicious, making me regret I was wasting hard for Uttoxeter tomorrow.

I asked about plans for the funeral. Judy didn't flinch. She said, 'The police said that if evidence of suspicious circumstances might come to light, it would be better to delay the funeral until after the coroner's inquest.'

'When will the inquest be?' I asked.

She shrugged, 'They said, weeks, maybe months…but it's for the best…for justice for Brian.'

I nodded. I had no way of knowing if the police had simply been paying lip-service to Judy's concerns, but I was glad Brian wouldn't be buried until someone had investigated, even if that someone was me.

We sat until dusk, when marauding insects made things uncomfortable. What I'd expected to be an ordeal turned out to be enjoyable and uplifting. We talked about Brian, recounting stories, remembering funny episodes, laughing freely; even Judy, whose eyes sparkled at times with memories. If anyone had happened upon us, they'd have assumed we were discussing a dear friend long dead but it had been less than a week since his murder - a word, understandably, still forbidden.

I worked the conversation around to Brian's friends and associates, and by the time I left I had the names of three people who'd been fairly close to him. Judy told me he'd probably thought highly enough of them to confide, talk about any worries.

Judy said, 'I'd try Alex Dunn first. Brian loved Alex. He was Brian's mentor. "The best vet in the world", Brian called him. Used to call him it to his face, too, and Alex always blushed.' She smiled again then the smile disappeared and concern took its place. She said, 'God, I wonder if Alex knows. He and Brian had spoken half a dozen times in the week before, but Alex hasn't called since.'

I tried to show only a casual interest. 'Have they always stayed in close touch?'

Judy, distracted, shook her head slowly. 'I don't think so. It must have been Christmas when they last spoke. Until lately, that is.' She turned toward me. 'Brian said Alex was helping him out with what he called a "fascinating little problem."'

Chapter 23

Alex Dunn's practice was in Newmarket and although I'd heard his name, we'd never met. When I got home, I rang a friend down there on the pretext of looking for a good vet I could recommend to someone.

Without prompting, he mentioned Dunn. 'Got a reputation as a bit of a nutty professor, likes experimenting, does some homeopathic horse stuff if you can believe that, but he gets results. Works on his own in a little place at Six Mile Bottom. Lives alone, doesn't smoke or drink, but bets like a lunatic.'

He gave me a couple more names. We hung up, and I called Martin and told him I had an idea where the samples might be, though I didn't elaborate. He wanted more info, but the last thing I needed was him racing off to Newmarket to grab Alex Dunn by the lapels.

He said, 'So what are you going to do?'

'I'm going to try and see this guy as soon as possible but it'll have to be Thursday at the earliest. I'm riding at Uttoxeter tomorrow.'

'Give me his name, I'll go and see him.'

'No, Martin, leave it to me. I'll call you as soon as I know something.'

He argued his case, temper flaring again. He slammed the phone down on me.

I saw Tranter at Uttoxeter next day. He ignored me, even during the race we contested and which I won. My other two rides were unplaced, but with earnings for the evening of almost £700, I wasn't too unhappy, and drove home eagerly anticipating tomorrow's trip to Newmarket.

They were racing there, and I learned from the racecourse office that Alex Dunn was attending in an official capacity. There was no break in the weather and as I steered along the drive approaching the racecourse, heat haze distorted the images of cars and pedestrians ahead.

After the first race, I spotted McCarthy. He was walking toward the stables at right angles to me, his chubby face trying to sweat itself cool. I hadn't seen Mac for a while. Looked like he'd put most of his weight back on. His wife tried to keep him on a sensible diet, and when he'd been pitching for promotion last year he'd followed it, but when he was pipped for the big job he'd let himself slip again. Pushing seventeen stones now by the look of him.

He didn't see me till I was almost by his shoulder, and when he did his scowl deepened.

'Hi,' I said. 'Hot, eh?'

'What are you doing here?'

'Nice to be made welcome at the headquarters of racing.'

He stopped and turned, mopping his brow with a handkerchief. From the front, I could see a tinge of grey in the dark hair at his temples. He said, 'You don't like flat racing, Eddie, what are you up to?'

'Same as I was last time we spoke. I'm trying to find out who killed Brian Kincaid.'

'Leave it to the proper authorities.'

'What exactly are the proper authorities doing about it?'

Mac glanced around. At six foot two, his vision covered a wide sweep. He didn't care to be seen talking to me. We'd been in a few scrapes together, though he'd always come out of it well enough. He said, 'Look, I need to speak to one of the stable security staff. Can we meet somewhere quiet during the next race?'

The bars would be quiet while a race was on, but flat races seldom lasted longer than a few minutes. I suggested meeting at the stables. He agreed. I asked him where I'd find Alex Dunn.

'Why do you want him?'

'I'll tell you in ten minutes.'

Mac said if Dunn wasn't out on the course, he usually watched the racing from the owners and trainers stand. He told me I couldn't miss him - six foot six and very thin with white hair.

I recognized Dunn immediately from the description. He was in the stand. On the steps behind him was a noticeable gap; few would have a decent view over his head topped by a Panama hat. I watched him throughout the mile race that was in progress: a rolled up newspaper in his left fist, fixed like a pathfinder to the binoculars, which moved slowly as the commentary built, the crowd murmur grew to a rumble, the approaching hoofbeats drummed louder.

Then they were past the post.

The noise died. Dunn's binoculars came down but he stared gloomily into the distance, as though watching a large wager disappear over the horizon.

He gripped the crush barrier with both hands and almost slumped forward. My inclination was to let him compose himself, but my instinct told me to move in while his defenses were low. He stood like a skinny breakwater as the crowd moved around him and the stand emptied. Within a couple of minutes, he was alone.

I approached him head on up the steps, smiling. 'Mister Dunn?'

He nodded, wondering if he should know me, frowning as he searched for a name. 'Eddie Malloy.' I said, holding out my hand. 'I am a friend. I mean I was a friend of Brian Kincaid.'

There was an immediate change in his brown eyes. He swallowed dryly then held out his hand. He looked to be in his late-fifties, though the hat hid most of his hair, which was Aspirin white and would, I guessed, make him appear considerably older.

'You knew Brian?' I said.

He nodded, struggling for normality but showing no surprise at my change of tense. I decided to go for it, but the PA system drowned out my next words. I repeated them. 'The samples you were helping Brian with, they were from one of my horses.'

He was already quite pale but that spooked him, driving what remained of the colour from his bony face. At the same time, his whole body recoiled a few inches as though I'd raised a hand to hit him. A poker player he wasn't.

Taking off his hat, he ran skeletal fingers through his thin hair, put the hat back on and said, 'Which samples?'

He was trying.

I stared at him. 'The samples from my stallion. The semen, blood, biopsies.'

He checked his watch, hand shaking slightly, and said, 'I'm very sorry but I'm actually on duty today.'

'I can wait. We can meet after racing.'

'I have quite a few appointments.'

'We need to talk, Mister Dunn. I'm sure you know why.'

He looked at me as though I was a bailiff. I thought for a few seconds he was going to start crying. He said, 'Perhaps you could come and see me at home?'

'Fine. This evening? Six-thirty?'

He nodded slowly, watching me like I was the snake, he the rabbit. He gave me his address and phone number when I pressed him. I left and went to meet McCarthy.

He was still inside the racecourse stables. I waited, pacing the perimeter. I was pretty keyed up. Dunn had behaved as though he'd murdered Brian himself. Surely his demeanour couldn't simply be down to his involvement with the samples analysis? I smiled. Maybe there'd be a bonus in this yet. Maybe Dunn could crack Town Crier's problem. Maybe he'd already cracked it.

McCarthy waddled toward me and we walked into the shade of the stable buildings. He told me the autopsy on Brian had shown up a long thin bruise on the scalp above the right temple which could have been caused by a 'blow from a third party' or from a fall. The fire that destroyed the weighing room had started, they reckoned, as a grass fire outside after the weeks without rain. What they couldn't say was whether it had been arson.

'Come on, Mac, at three in the morning? It's hardly going to be spontaneous combustion.'

'They're still looking at it, Eddie. I'll keep you in touch. Now why did you want to see Alex Dunn?'

'Why do you ask? You interested in him too?'

'Should I be?'

'Are we going to spend the rest of the afternoon swapping questions?'

'Would you like to?'

We smiled. Mac said he wasn't particularly interested in Dunn, and since I was nervous about the Town Crier samples, I played it as cool as I could and told him that Brian and Alex Dunn had been close friends and I'd wondered if Dunn could give me a lead.

'And did he?'

I tried to look disappointed. 'Nah, nothing. He's still in shock too from Brian's death.'

'I didn't know they were good friends.'

'Well, old friends. Judy Kincaid told me they didn't see much of each other but they were in touch recently. Just a shot in the dark.' I was keen to move McCarthy off the subject in case he sent the police to talk to Dunn. The vet would probably drop dead at the sight of a warrant card.

Mac said, 'So, what next?'

I sighed. 'I don't know. Any suggestions?'

He put a hand on my shoulder. 'Yes, go home and hang up your pipe and deerstalker. Let the police handle it. You're getting too old for all this amateur sleuthing stuff.'

I smiled. 'And what does that make you?' Mac was at least ten years older than I was.

'I'm a professional sleuth.'

I raised a mischievous eyebrow but resisted saying, 'Oh, yeah?' He promised to keep me informed of police progress, and I wandered off trying to convey an air of resignation though it was important not to overplay it. Mac knew I wasn't a quitter.

I had a sandwich in a pub then rang Martin to tell him I'd set up a meeting and was hopeful of having something more solid soon. He grunted… moody bastard.

Alex Dunn's place wasn't easy to find. I asked directions of a garage attendant and got there at 6.25. An old bungalow with flaked cream masonry and mustard-coloured door and sills, it lay down a narrow road facing acres of deep woods. There was no car in the drive, and if Dunn was at home, he wasn't coming out. I went around the back along paths bordered by colourful but neglected plants and shrubs.

The house looked much bigger from this side. I tried the door of the long porch. It was open. I knocked on the half-glassed door inside. Silence. I returned to the car and waited. An hour later Dunn hadn't showed, and I was angry with myself for so easily accepting his suggestion of meeting here.

If he had no intention of keeping the date, I had little intention of breaking it. Starting the engine, I cruised along and found a track into the woods. I turned in and drove till I could no longer see the bungalow.

I got out, taking with me the waterproof I always carried, and headed through the woods for the house, stopping twenty yards in and settling on the ground where I could see without, I hoped, being seen.

Come darkness, no vehicles had passed. The only sounds were from nocturnal creatures on the prowl. I decided to do some prowling myself and just after eleven, I returned to Dunn's place and broke in.

Chapter 24

The biggest room had been converted into a lab, which, unlike the rest of the property, was clean and tidy to the point of obsession, to the point where I replaced each phial, each box, in its exact spot. I spent more than an hour checking cupboards and shelves, searching for anything marked with Brian Kincaid's name.

I tried a door in the corner of the lab. It was locked. I rooted in drawers for keys and found one that fitted. It was a big cupboard piled high with cardboard boxes marked with huge letters: Guterson's Gloves. Hauling the top box down, I eased aside the already open flaps. Nothing but blue arm-length gloves for use in veterinary examinations. Why lock up a stock of rubber gloves?

I went to the office and raked through filing cabinets, drawers, and a Rolodex telephone list where I found Brian's office number, and, in fresher ink, his mobile number.

Beneath the big wooden desk, I discovered a box file of copy invoices. Under the bright lamp, I worked through them until I saw a name I recognized, a name that halted my finger on the page and brought me to a breath-holding stop, as the man himself would have done had he appeared in front of me - Edward F. Malloy: my father.

I felt faint as his figure loomed huge in my mind. I'd spent years trying to erase his memory, succeeding only after psychiatric help, and now he was back, unintentionally, uninvited, but with almost the same shattering impact of the worst days of my life. I had to get out of the room.

I stood outside, leaning against the corner of the house, the dry old paint flaking under my hand. Staring at the full moon, I recalled the disciplines of old and made myself breathe deeply, hearing the breaths, focusing on them, using them to clean my mind again, to erase that picture before the well-remembered anxiety attack set in.

But I was out of practice, and the face of my father stayed stubbornly where it was. I resigned myself to the anxiety attack but it didn't come. And I stood there for God knows how long, wondering if finally, at the age of thirty, I was capable of coping with thoughts of the past.

I went inside, sat down and looked again at his name, which seemed to take up the whole page. I stayed there till the impact lessened, until the name diminished and took its proper place on the page above the address: a stud in Newmarket. Someone had told me years ago that they'd moved here. And then I thought of my mother too, and the dread drained from me and sadness seeped in.

I pulled myself together enough to start wondering how long my father had been a client of Alex Dunn's. The invoice was marked 'Quarterly as agreed' and was for £1,050. It was dated 30 March. I skipped through and found one other issued at the end of December. Both, unusually, were headed 'Professional Services'. Most invoices in Dunn's file carried details of the work, like scanning, cyst removal, etc.

What was Dunn doing for my father that had already taken six months and looked to be ongoing? Why were the details not shown? I noted the address and phone number of my father's stud then checked the remaining rooms and left.

I'd brought no overnight bag but I was confident I'd pin Dunn down next day at Newmarket races, so I drove into town and found a hotel.

Next morning, Saturday, I called the number Dunn had given me as his home telephone. No answer. I tried several times without success.

Faced with a few hours to kill before racing started, I asked the hotel porter for directions to my father's place. It was a short trip. I drove fifty yards beyond the entrance and parked. Turning in my seat, I watched the gate. Trees and bushes shielded the house from the road. I just kept staring at the gate, hoping for I don't know what. This was the home of my parents, a home I had never known.

We'd come to England from Ireland when I was seven and I'd spent the next nine years on a farm in Cumbria. My father kept horses and had dabbled in breeding. It had always been his ambition to own a proper stud farm. Now he did, though it looked to be a small operation. Now I watched, wondering what I would do if he suddenly appeared, or my mother. And my first thought was that I would duck out of sight. Would they recognize me now? I looked in the rear-view mirror. Had I changed much in the fourteen years since I'd left home?

In looks, maybe not; inside me, immense changes. Forty years was what it felt like in my head, not fourteen. I started the car again and pulled slowly away.

Dunn failed to turn up at Newmarket races. I drove to the bungalow. It was deserted, the broken glass still on the floor in the porch.

Where the hell had he gone and why had he panicked? I went in and spent more than an hour going through the copy invoices again, making notes of all his clients then getting their phone numbers from his Rolodex.

On the long drive home, I tried to figure out what it was I'd said that had scared Alex Dunn so badly. I'd only raised two issues: Brian's death and the samples from Town Crier. Which one had set him off? And what exactly was Dunn working on for my father?

A possible link came to mind. Tenuous but worth exploring.

At the flat, I skimmed through the stallion ads in the Directory of the Turf, checking the stud names below the glossy colour pictures. The Keelkerry Stud, named after my father's hometown, had a quarter-page ad dominated by the picture of a bay stallion called Heraklion whose career highlights, and those of his offspring, were listed in bold type.

I rang Martin and told him what had happened in the past twenty-four hours. Dunn's sudden disappearance cheered him immensely; he was convinced the vet must know something about the Town Crier samples and equally sure that we'd soon find Dunn. I asked Martin to call the Keelkerry Stud posing as a breeder who wanted to send a mare for a very late covering.

'Why don't you call?'

'We don't get on. I haven't spoken to my father in years.'

Martin said, 'They'll think I'm mad calling this late, the season's virtually over.'

'Act a bit eccentric then. Tell them you made a last-minute decision.'

I explained how I wanted him to go about it: to ask advice on which stallion to use then name two or three from the ad and see what the reaction was.

Ten minutes later Martin called, excitement in his voice. 'No Heraklion!'

'Who did you speak to?'

'I think it must have been your mother.'

'What did she say?'

'She didn't question me at first, seemed anxious to have the chance of some unexpected revenue. She did a bloody good selling job on every stallion but Heraklion. When I suggested him she said he'd been retired for the season and I said, "Oh, still hasn't recovered from his problem then?" which threw her. I told her some friends of mine had tried to book mares to him a couple of months ago and the horse had been on the easy list. She rallied then, I'll say that for her, said he'd been suffering from a complex fracture of the off hind after being kicked by a mare. "An accident," she said, "inherently sound, you know, and we're sure he'll be back to his best next season."'

So, two smallish studs who'd lost their best stallion. Perhaps Heraklion had been kicked, but the stud's link with Alex Dunn made it too much for coincidence. Martin told me my mother had almost desperately tried to sell him a covering from one of the other stallions. Business must be pretty bad. I felt a pang of remorse having deceived her.

Martin was set on finding Dunn, determined to stake out his place if necessary, and I knew by his tone he wouldn't be argued out of it this time. I could have used some help but Martin was too fiery. He promised to stay calm and be guided by me, so I gave in and told him Dunn's address, warning him that he mustn't pounce.

'If he turns up, try and follow him. We'll learn more that way.'

'Sure,' he said. 'Don't worry.'

'Stay in touch with me on my mobile. I'll probably be in Newmarket tomorrow anyway so let's meet.'

When Martin hung up, I resisted the urge to replace the handset because I knew I'd find it hard to pick it up again to call my mother. I dialed and tried to steel myself for the voice I'd last heard when little more than a child.

It rang seven times then, 'Keelkerry Stud.' It was my father. The voice had changed; less volume, weaker, as though the edges had worn away. I couldn't bring myself to speak. 'Hello!' he said. 'Hello!' And that impatience, that pent up anger I remembered so vividly, was still there. My top lip filmed with sweat. My mouth dried up. I replaced the receiver quietly, irrationally afraid he might be able to tell it was me and call me to account for it. I lowered myself slowly onto the chair by the window and sat gazing out, seeing nothing. My throat tightened and I swallowed repeatedly, pumping out silent tears.

Chapter 25

The following day I packed an overnight bag and headed to Newmarket, determined to speak to my parents. I was no longer a child and I wasn't going to let my father return me to that state. I was a grown man with a legitimate interest in his association with Alex Dunn, and I was damned well going to ask some questions.

That was the theory at least, but much as I disciplined my brain, my emotions mutinied. A few times I checked the speedo and found it registering way below my normal speed from subconscious dread of reaching my destination.

Martin called me at nine o'clock. He complained of being cold and stiff after sitting in the woods for half the night waiting fruitlessly for Dunn. I offered to meet him for lunch in town, but he told me to come to Dunn's place, said he wouldn't move till the vet appeared.

I was in Newmarket before ten and on the approach to the Keelkerry Stud, my stomach tightened, causing me to shift in my seat. I pulled into the verge about a hundred yards before the gate, steeling myself not to drive past this time. I'd get out here and walk across, go through the gate and straight to the front door. No hesitation. No stopping.

I checked my face in the mirror. As I reached for the door handle, a light blue Vauxhall Estate coming toward me slowed and indicated then turned and nosed up to the gate. The driver was so tall he had trouble getting out of the car. It was Alex Dunn. He opened the gate and drove through, then closed it behind him. The driveway was screened by a high hedge.

I ran across the road, making my way along the hedge line. The stud stood alone on open land. I heard Dunn switch off the engine. A car door slammed. I hoped my father might be there to meet him. Perhaps they'd start talking in the yard. No. Just faint footsteps on gravel then another door closing. No knock. No greeting. It sounded as if Dunn had simply walked right into the house.

I looked across at my car on the verge and the sunlight glinted on a side window, almost blinding me. I couldn't leave it there much longer. If anyone in the stud saw it, they might become suspicious.

I'd have to drive about half a mile round a long steady bend before the car could be parked out of sight. I hurried to the car, did a U-turn and sped down the road. On foot again, I came at the stud from a different angle, cutting across meadows to see how far back the trees and hedges ran. They seemed to border the rear and sides of the property in a looping semi-circle. A couple of furlongs down from the house and stables, they thinned enough for me to peer through at eight fenced-off paddocks with maybe a dozen horses grazing quietly in the sunshine. All were in view of the buildings. Once through the trees and onto the property there was no decent cover.

I'd hoped to get inside, close to whatever horse Dunn was visiting and eavesdrop on his conversation with my father or the groom or whoever. But unless I could get through the thick hedges beside the stables, then it would mean crossing open ground, which would leave me exposed. If I was to face my parents again, it wouldn't be as an intruder.

I circled the perimeter, but couldn't find a safe way in. I returned to the hedge close to where Dunn's car was parked. Perhaps I'd hear something as he left.

But he didn't leave. At dusk his car hadn't been moved. I'd had my phone switched off in case someone rang as Dunn came out. As darkness fell, I walked what I considered to be a safe distance away and called Martin. He was still outside Dunn's place, hungry and frustrated, and when I told him where I was and why, he said, 'Why the fuck didn't you call me? You knew Dunn was there, you could have saved me hanging around this shithole any longer!'

'I thought he'd leave at any time and maybe head your way.'

'Well, he didn't, did he?'

We were silent for a long moment then Martin said, 'Did you say he's been there since this morning?'

'Around ten he arrived.'

'Fuck me! That's one long consultation. I wouldn't like your old man's vet's bill.'

'I think he could be paying in kind.'

'Huh?'

'Dunn might be living there. He's been doing some unspecified work for my father for the past six months or so.' I told him about the invoices I'd found, mysteriously short on detail. Martin arrived within twenty minutes and we watched together until the last light went out in the house just after 11. So Dunn was a guest.

We were tired and hungry and I suspected I also looked as scruffy as Martin with his heavy stubble and soiled clothes. We returned to the hotel I'd stayed in the night before and persuaded a bored young girl to fix some sandwiches. We downed a large scotch each and trudged wearily to bed after arranging a 6 a.m. alarm call.

In the morning, Martin was going in to collar Alex Dunn.

Chapter 26

We were outside the Keelkerry Stud just after dawn. Alex Dunn's car was still in the drive. We'd travelled in separate cars and we met around the bend, half a mile from the stud. Martin joined me on watch, on foot in the chill of morning. We dissected what we'd learned, theorized, argued quietly then finally agreed a plan.

At 8.40, Martin pulled away toward the stud and parked outside the gate. From a distance, I watched him go in.

Twenty-five minutes later, he reappeared and drove off, as agreed, in the opposite direction from where I was stationed. I hurried to my car and cruised past the stud and out of sight again, where I turned quickly and came past once more. As I slowed to turn again, Dunn's blue estate overtook me at speed and I accelerated smoothly, following him.

I stayed well behind until approaching the edge of Newmarket town, where I had to close up for fear of losing him. He slowed going down the Bury Road as strings of racehorses crossed at regular points on their way to and from the gallops. Near the bottom close to the town centre, Dunn took a right, and as I turned off, I saw his tailgate disappear in another right turn through the gates of a famous racing yard.

I parked and phoned Martin. 'How did it go?' I asked.

'He's rattled all right! He knows something. I told him if he didn't come up with the samples and the results by this time tomorrow, I'd bring the police in.'

'Did you speak to him alone? Was my father there?'

'Just Dunn. He was coming down the drive as I was walking up. He kept trying to get away, said he had an important appointment, and tried the same thing with me that he did with you: "Come and see me at home this evening."' Martin put on a whingeing voice.

I said, 'Well, he's reached his important appointment. I'm outside one of the big yards in the town. Think it's worth keeping a tail on him?'

'No, no way. He's too scared to do anything now. He said he'll definitely meet us at his house tomorrow morning. Ten o'clock.'

'Do you believe him?'

'Eddie, he'll be there.'

He wasn't. Next day we were there before 9.30 and waited till 11. Dunn had been home. The broken pane had been replaced, the shards swept up. I broke the new one and we went inside. The house had been cleared, very effectively, not a thermometer left in the lab, a pen in the office or a sock in a bedroom drawer. Each empty room seemed to deal Martin a physical blow. By the time we'd finished the tour he looked stunned, defeated, and sounded that way too when he spoke. 'What do we do now, Eddie?'

'We find out where he's gone.'

'How?'

I looked at him, the tired eyes, the hangdog look, and I realized how much he was pissing me off. Martin was fine if things were going well; otherwise, he either blew his top or whined and moaned, expecting somebody else to solve his problems. 'We'll find him,' I said coldly, and walked out and along the path to the front gate.

Martin followed. 'But, Eddie, I can't spend any more time here. I've got stuff to do; we've got a business to run.'

'Go home and run it then.'

'Just for a few days, then I'll come back and help you.'

Yeah, when I've found Dunn, you'll ride in and play the tough guy.

'Fine,' I said.

I watched him drive off and wondered how he could so quickly become disheartened. My resolve had been strengthened by Dunn's disappearance. You didn't flee your home and workplace over a few stallion samples. Dunn was involved in something serious. And how close was he to the Keelkerry Stud? To my parents? Could they be implicated?

I headed for their stud, a cold determination in me suppressing the emotions of the past few days. I parked at the gate and marched up the drive. The house was of yellow stone, big deep windows, climbing plants around the door where my gaze was fixed. The white door, coming closer as though a movie camera lens was tightening on it. I was conscious of the sounds of gravel crunching, but seemed somehow removed from the notion that it could be my feet making the noise. All I was aware of was my unblinking focus on that door.

I reached it.

Pressed the bell.

Waited.

It opened slowly. My father stood there. Still taller than me but age showing: thinning grey hair, hollow cheeks, loose skin on his face, his throat. Shoulders drooping, hair growing from his ears, eyebrows getting bushy - and hatred in his eyes. No, not hatred, scorn. His jaw muscles clenched and he slammed the door shut so hard I felt a mild shockwave on my face.

I didn't move. Stayed there, chest out, head high, and was proud of myself for it. And I reached for the bell again and I pressed it and I held it and I could hear it inside hammering like a fire alarm. The ringing went on for more than a minute before the door opened again. My mother. Older, smaller, softer, kinder-looking, the way I remembered her from my infant days. Her hair shorter but shining rich auburn as I remembered it, a small vanity from a bottle which looked so out of place framing the pale skin, the pale, pale skin.

No hint of shame on her face as she looked at me. I'd never known her speak a word against my father for his treatment of me, but there had never been any hatred in her either. Sadness, yes. Despair, maybe, but at least she'd never hated me for what had happened.

'Eddie,' she said quietly, and stepped aside, pulling the door fully open. Not trusting myself to handle the emotion of saying the word 'Mum', I just accepted the silent invitation to go inside.

She led me along the hall, her slightly splayfooted walk exactly as I remembered it, to a small cluttered office with one swivel chair. No cozy sitting rooms; this was to be a short formal discussion as far as my mother was concerned. She said she'd bring another chair for herself and politely offered me tea. I declined, unwilling to accept the little gestures that moved me into the same bracket as any trade caller at the stud, that helped her forget she'd carried me inside her, nursed me, and loved me once, her first-born.

She returned with a light pine chair, closed the door and sat opposite me, open-faced, pleasant, receptive. And, setting my emotions aside for the first time when thinking of her, I wondered what kind of woman this was. How could she not be moved enough to show some feelings? How could she stand so rigidly by her man to the exclusion of everything else on the planet? Had she never questioned that loyalty? Still closely involved in racing, she must have known about my troubles over the past eight or nine years. Had there never been a twinge of regret, an ounce of longing to come and comfort me?

Here she sat waiting for me to state my business. No 'How have you been, son?' No 'Good to see you after all these years.'

She said, 'Edward's out in the yard.' A cue to start talking, reassurance we wouldn't be disturbed by the man she could no longer even bring herself to refer to as my father.

I said, 'How have you been, Mum?'

'We're all right.'

We. The Siamese marriage.

'My father looks very strained.'

She blinked at the word 'father'.

'Edward has... this has come as a bit of a shock to him.'

'It would after fourteen years.'

She nodded, blinked again. Some emotion there at last. I said, 'Aren't you going to ask how I've been?'

'You look fine.'

'I'm well practiced in looking fine, Mum, at making it look like I'm solid and sane.'

She looked at me, determined not to be drawn in. 'Why did you come here, Eddie?'

'After all this time, you mean? You forgot to tag that on to the end of your question, Mum.'

She stiffened slightly in her chair. 'If you've come to open old wounds.'

I leaned toward her, elbows on my knees, hands clasped in what I realized was close to anguish. I'd willed myself not to react like this but I couldn't help it. I said, 'Open old wounds? Mine never closed, Mum! They bleed and weep every day of my life. They keep people away from me! They fester. Don't talk to me about closing.'

Her pale face flushed. She wasn't coping any more, not with this adult, this son who was no longer a child.

I said, 'Was there no remorse? Ever? Even in the early days?'

She stood up, held on to the chairback, tears rising. 'Please go,' she said.

I shook my head. 'No, I'm not going.' And I felt filled with power, with knowledge that I could stay if I wanted, that neither of my parents was a threat any longer. I could stay and take revenge, dish out some torment.

Then just as suddenly, the notion seemed vile, abhorrent, shameful. I stood, calmed myself, and in a quiet voice said, 'I'm not going until I know what Alex Dunn's been doing for the Keelkerry Stud.'

Chapter 27

When I left, my mother saw me out and watched till I was through the gate. Driving into Newmarket town, I tried to come to terms with my feelings; a strange mixture of personal achievement, self-renewal, a growth in stature that felt almost physical, and a wish that I had come years ago and said my piece.

But there was also a feeling of being used. When she'd sussed that I could actually help my father, my mother had become quite enthusiastic. She'd admitted that Heraklion, their top stallion, had suffered a similar loss of fertility to Town Crier and at around the same time. Faced with a ruined investment, my father had asked Alex Dunn to do what he could. It seemed Dunn was an old friend and had offered his services for the comparatively small retainer of £350 a month.

She said Dunn had been sworn to secrecy and that was why he'd panicked when I had confronted him at the races. I told her it had to be more than that but she said she had no reason to doubt him. Yet Dunn had so far failed to find a cure for Heraklion.

If my father knew I was involved, he'd reject my help. My mother accepted it on his behalf on the condition that he mustn't be told. Whether or not the stud was saved, my father must never be allowed to believe I'd done anything for him. My mother's side of the bargain was that she would try to discover Dunn's whereabouts. He and my father were friends, and my mother thought she should be able to get information without arousing suspicion. She had my home and mobile numbers though I departed the house under no illusions. As soon as this was over, the phone numbers would be burned, and I would once again become the invisible member of the Malloy family.

That prospect bothered me little now. For a few days, I'd harboured a fantasy that I would appear on my white steed after fourteen years and save the Malloy business, drag my parents back from the brink, finally winning the approval I'd craved. But the last couple of hours had brought home to me that although there would always be an instinctive, emotional link to them, a vague longing, they were people in their own right - and as people rather than parents, I cared little for either of them.

Dunn's story of being rattled by my questions didn't stand up. Vacating his house overnight, lock, stock and stethoscope, smacked of abject fear. Was he linked to Brian Kincaid's death? How many other small studs were harbouring infertile stallions? How many of these cases had Dunn been working on? Well, I was in the best place to find out. Newmarket was nothing but a racing community and redolent with jealousy and bitchiness. A few days spent in the pubs and hotels should prove productive.

I couldn't afford to go on staying at the hotel I'd been using, so I found a bed and breakfast for two nights, got my phone out and booked a place on the gossip train, first stop Francis Loss, racing manager to Sheikh Ahmad Saad.

F. Loss was an old friend, known since his riding days as Candy. Sharp and well educated, he'd landed himself a top position with one of the most prominent Arab racehorse owners and breeders in the world. His job was to offer advice to the Sheikh on every aspect of his thoroughbred operation, from buying foals to setting fees at the two major studs he owned. If there was anything afoot with local stallions, Candy would know about it.

Candy agreed to meet me for half an hour. He was flying to the Middle East that night. We met at seven in a hotel in town and I felt distinctly underdressed as Candy approached in about a grand's worth of clothes and footwear. Five foot eight, late-thirties, Candy had kept the slim athletic shape he'd had when riding. He smiled as he shook my hand. Good teeth and tan, dark brown eyes and shiny chestnut hair, which, most of the time, successfully hid, his only physical blemish: a port wine stain below his right ear, the shape of Italy on a map.

I bought him a mineral water and we did the long-time-no-see routine for a few minutes. Candy had never got above himself. People always found him the same way, open and friendly, but I thought I detected an air of wariness. I knew I'd have to be careful. Gossip conduits are two-way and I needed to get what I could without Candy picking up any link with Brian Kincaid.

I said, 'Listen, you know I do a little bit of amateurish nosing around from time to time?'

He smiled. 'Not quite so amateurish over the last year or two from what I hear.'

I returned his smile. 'I've got a guy who's offered me a few quid to try and help him out. He owns a smallish stud which ain't gonna be a stud much longer unless he discovers what's gone wrong with his best stallion.'

I thought I saw a sudden spark in Candy's eyes but it lasted a millisecond. He sipped his drink and looked interested. I said, 'The horse completely lost its fertility at the start of the season. The vets have tested everything except its IQ but they're stumped. If it's not sorted out before next season he's finished.'

'Which stallion?'

'Sorry, Candy, I can't say. The guy's managed to keep it a secret from most breeders, or at least he thinks he has. I know you'll think I've got a cheek asking you for information and not offering much from my side, but I'm trying to do my best for him.'

'So what are you asking me, Eddie?'

I shrugged. 'Just if you've heard anything on the grapevine about anyone else who's got the same problem?' I was taking the chance Candy was unaware of my involvement in the Corish Stud, far from Newmarket, and a partnership I'd never publicized.

'Stallions have fluctuations in fertility.'

'We're talking more decimation than fluctuation here. From eighty-eight percent to zilch as quick as you could say, "No foal no fee".'

He fingered the port wine stain under his hair and looked thoughtful. 'So why did he bring you in? Does he think the horse has been got at?'

'As I said, he's desperate.'

'Do you think the horse was got at?'

'I don't know. What would the motive be? How would you do it so the vets couldn't detect it?'

He shook his head slowly, fingered his tanned chin. I said, 'So you haven't heard of any other stallions in the same boat?'

He continued thoughtful, staring at the tabletop, and said, 'No.'

I sighed and sipped some scotch. He said, 'Sorry, Eddie.'

'Not your fault.'

'What's your next move?'

I almost started shooting off about Alex Dunn disappearing but something in my brain slipped the safety catch on and I settled for saying I'd heard Dunn specialized in fertility and I was hoping to track him down. 'Any idea where I could find him?'

'Sorry, Eddie, I've heard the guy's name but I don't know much about him except that he's a bit of a quack. I wouldn't set too much store by this "specialist" stuff.' Candy seemed anxious to finish the conversation. He said, 'It's an interesting one. I'll sniff around a bit myself over the next week or so, see if I can find anything out.'

'Good. That'd be great, Candy.'

'No problem. Maybe you could keep me in touch with progress from your end?'

'Sure. Sure I will.'

'Fine. Give me a ring any time.'

I smiled. 'They've got phones in Lear jets now, have they?' He stood up, smiling, and finished his drink. 'It's not all a bowl of cherries, Eddie, as the saying goes.'

'Strawberries and cream, more like.'

He laughed. 'See you. Keep in touch on this.'

'Will do.'

He turned and left. I waited a few seconds then followed quietly and watched him cross the car park. He got into a Range Rover and immediately made a call. I had a hunch Candy knew more than he was saying.

I rang Martin, gave him some work to do to take his mind off things. 'I want you to ring round as many studs as you can and give them that story about a late booking. Make a list of who's willing and any stallions they try to steer you away from.'

'What about my phone bill?'

'Our phone bill,' I reminded him. 'Come on, Martin, twenty-four hours ago it was death or glory to get to the bottom of this. Now you can't even be bothered making a few calls?'

He grunted something and hung up. I called McCarthy.

'Mac, did you know Alex Dunn's moved out of his house?'

'It's not the sort of thing I get wildly curious about, Eddie.'

'I know, but if you could find me his new address you'd be doing me a favour.'

'Why? I thought you'd spoken to him and he said he didn't know anything about Brian Kincaid's death?'

'That's right, but as I said to you he was in pretty deep shock at the time and I just wondered if maybe, once he'd had time to think, something might have come to him.'

'Like what?'

'I don't know, Mac, but I want to speak to him again.'

'Eddie, tell me what this is really about?'

'I've told you, it's a quiet time for me. I'll be lucky to get ten rides in the next month and I don't mind filling my days in trying to make sense of Brian's death.'

'And I've told you, leave it to the coroner, let him try and make some sense of it!'

'Mac, come on! I don't like doing this but you owe me one. More than one.'

'You don't like doing it? You're always doing it! I should have kept notes! Traded bloody IOUs!'

I smiled. 'Your hysterics are coming on again, Mac, careful!'

'I'll ring you back.'

'When?'

'As soon as I know something.'

'Soon, Mac, please! On my mobile. I'm in Newmarket for a few days.' That brought him up short. 'Newmarket? What for?'

'I've just told you, I want to speak to Alex Dunn.'

'Eddie, you'd better not be working for Compton Breslin.' He sounded genuinely annoyed. Breslin was a rich bookmaker.

'What would I be doing for Breslin?'

'Don't be so bloody disingenuous.'

'Me? I don't know the meaning of the word!' Which was the truth but I didn't need to ask anything else. Dunn was obviously a serious gambler. I wondered how much he owed Breslin.

Mac said, 'I'll tell you this now, Eddie, if you're working for Breslin I want nothing more to do with you.'

'Mac, you've got my word on it. When did I ever break my word?'

'Okay. Fine. Goodnight.'

He hung up. The smile was still on my face. I loved these little jousts with McCarthy.

It wasn't yet 8.30 and I knew there were two evening racemeetings on. Breslin's credit office would be open. I'd never met the guy but I'd seen him on the racecourse. He was renowned as a proper bookie of the old school, one who'd back his own opinion and lay large bets. He paid promptly and expected the same from his clients. I rang his office. He answered the phone personally. I said that we might have a common interest in Alex Dunn and he agreed to meet me in a local Chinese restaurant at 9.45.

Chapter 28

Breslin was your stereotypical big fat bookmaker: jewellery, checked suit, torpedo cigar, slick hair, and Chaplin moustache. He looked like he'd just stepped off a Blackpool postcard. He was watching my face as he lumbered toward me, and sat down in a jingle of watch chains and bracelets. He smiled at me. 'Bet you thought this was my showman's gear, strictly for the racecourse?'

'Well, I did, actually.'

His smile grew wider, moustache spreading. 'You're always on show in my business,' he said, looking down at the checked waistcoat. 'The more prosperous you look, the more people want to take money off you. And the more they try, the more I get to keep.'

I nodded, smiling. He glanced around and beckoned a waiter. 'Anyway,' he said, 'that's my excuse for prancing about dressed like one of the Marx Brothers. At night, alone in my room, I slip on my Versace, which has seen nothing but lamplight and a long wardrobe mirror. Sad, isn't it?'

I smiled. I liked Breslin. He ordered the best wine and half a dozen courses as though listing runners in a race. The waiter didn't seem at all surprised, and I guessed this was a regular haunt. He said, 'Need to keep the waistline up to Industry Standards. Dirty work but some bugger's got to do it.'

We got talking about Dunn. 'You're looking for him?' Breslin asked.

'I'd quite like to speak to him.'

'Been a bad boy, has he?'

'Not that I know of. I just think he might be able to help me out.'

'Got a veterinary problem?'

'More of a personal one, really. Well, on behalf of a friend.' I mentioned Brian Kincaid and gave him the same spiel I'd given McCarthy.

'I can give you his address,' Breslin said.

'The bungalow out at Six Mile Bottom?'

'You know it?'

I nodded. 'But it's no good.' I told him about the moonlight flit. He laughed. 'Well, bugger me; I wonder if he'll welch this time?'

'Does he owe much?'

He shrugged his big shoulders. 'About seven grand. It's not the end of the world.'

He wasn't showing off. He didn't seem that concerned about it though he said sure, he'd like to know where Dunn turned up if I managed to find him. In exchange, he told me a few details about Dunn's gambling habits. One tidbit was to prove very useful.

Thankfully, Breslin brushed aside my offer to pay the bill and we parted on good terms. Always a better audience than a performer, I'd enjoyed his company. He gave me his card and we made mutual promises to stay in touch.

My first stop next morning was a newsagent's shop where I picked up a little tourist booklet about Newmarket, Headquarters of British Racing. Inside was a map listing the names of all the training yards, along with the trainers currently inhabiting them. Breslin had told me that a significant number of Alex Dunn's bets in the last eighteen months to two years had been on horses trained by William Capshaw, a highly successful Newmarket trainer.

I found Capshaw's yard location on the map, and just to double check, I walked down the Bury Road past the yard. It was the same one Dunn had gone to after Martin had confronted him. I thought it unwise to pass the yard gates again and took a different route to the High Street.

So Dunn was getting information from Capshaw's yard. In exchange for what? Veterinary services? I couldn't recall seeing Capshaw's name among Dunn's copy invoices, though that might be the deal, no cash.

In a small cafe, I ordered coffee and got out Dunn's client list: no sign of Capshaw's name.

Perhaps Dunn was holed up at Capshaw's place. If so, would he be careless and park his car close by? It was worth risking another walk past, more slowly this time. My mobile rang, shattering the peace in the sunny little cafe and bringing sour looks from three elderly ladies. It was Martin. I went outside. He'd phoned thirty-nine studs. Eight had given him reasons for suspicion.

I didn't want him with me and managed to persuade him to look more closely at the studs involved. I asked him to plot their locations on a map, find out their histories: who was running them, their background, if they'd had the same employee through their hands, etc. - enough work to keep him in Wiltshire for a few days and out of my hair.

On the off chance I'd been spotted around Capshaw's yard, it would be best to delay another stroll in that direction until this afternoon. If I watched the yard from a safe distance around lunchtime, maybe I'd see some of Capshaw's lads heading for the pub. It would be easy to strike up a conversation over a drink and try to find out if the vet was a temporary lodger, but some of the lads might recognize me and start spreading the wrong kind of stories.

I decided to stick to lone observation, at least until late afternoon, and found a car park close enough to Capshaw's place to let me watch the main exit road from the yard. I had no view of the yard itself, and if Dunn came out of it and turned right, I'd miss him completely, but better to cover half the options in relative safety than all of them in an exposed position.

In the car, with the windows rolled down, I settled back with a copy of The Sporting Life which would offer extra camouflage if necessary.

I wondered how Dunn was running his business. Would he be having his calls automatically transferred to wherever he now was? I called his number. Answerphone. That meant he would have to play it back, although he could do that remotely.

As the 11.30 radio news began, my phone rang. 'Alex Dunn is at his house at Six Mile Bottom.' The caller immediately hung up. I started the car and headed for Dunn's place, wondering who my informant was. Perhaps Breslin had put the word out. Quick work if he had.

I pulled up, blocking Dunn's driveway in case he made a run for it, but his car wasn't there. Either I'd been hoaxed or I'd just missed him. I went through the green iron gates to the rear of the bungalow. As I turned at the end of the wall, I stopped short. Two men were sitting on an old garden bench. They wore expensive summer suits and lounged lazily, faces, in very dark glasses, tilted to the sun.

The man closest to me stood up and came forward, smiling, welcoming. 'Mister Malloy, how kind of you to drop in.' Bewildered, I shook his hand, waiting for him to introduce himself. He didn't. His friend was standing now, smoothing out imaginary wrinkles on the front of his trousers. They were mid-twenties, fit and hard looking, tall as University oarsmen.

I said to the one who'd greeted me, 'You called me?'

'That's right. I understand you're seeking advice.'

'Information. I've got all the advice I need at the moment.'

He was still smiling. It annoyed me that his eyes were hidden, the high sun glinting off his gold framed dark glasses. He said, 'The wrong kind of advice, Mister Malloy. It's good reliable advice you want, and luckily that is our specialist business. Come and sit down.' He put a hand lightly on my elbow. I eased it away. 'No, thanks.'

'Fine. I give the same high-calibre advice standing up.'

'Which is?'

'Drop what you're involved in and go home. Stick to riding horses.'

'Who do you work for?'

'We're a charitable organization dedicated to keeping people out of hospitals.'

'You're threatening me?'

The smile faded. Stern-mouthed he said, 'I'm offering you genuine professional advice. You won't realize how valuable it is unless you don't take it, then you'll reflect on this conversation with a bit more circumspection.'

An educated hit man. He took off his sunglasses, exposing blue eyes, which looked very sincere. He said, 'It is very important to me that you leave Newmarket within the hour and that you stay away from the town and the people who live here. It is vitally important to me that you stop asking questions.'

He was serious. I didn't know what to say or how to take it. 'Do you understand how important it is to me?' he pressed.

'If you tell me why, it might just drive the message home.'

A flicker of anger in his cold eyes and what seemed a conscious effort to regain the calm expression, and that was when I knew how potentially dangerous he could be. I thought it best to call it quits for the time being.

They came out onto the road and watched me till my car was out of sight. Curiouser and curiouser. No heavy stuff but they'd looked the part all right, and I was in no doubt the gloves would be off next time. Where had Dunn got these two from? The guy spent all his money gambling, how was he paying them?

And why had things accelerated so quickly?

By the time I reached Newmarket, I'd decided to pack up and leave immediately. Dunn would have his spies out and would think I'd fled. Maybe he'd return home then, and it would be a nice surprise for him when I turned up there in a couple of days. At my digs, I made a show of throwing my things in my bag, leaving it unzipped as I hurried to the car and scooted along the High Street and out of town at a pace that would have drawn attention. Hamming it up, but if it helped tempt Dunn to the surface I could forgive myself.

I returned to my flat for a change of clothes. It was late afternoon. The yard was still as quiet as it had been since the end of May. It would be another month before the horses were back. A racing yard without thoroughbreds is a melancholy place.

I thought about Charles Tunney, the trainer. The man who'd buggered off to Alaska for a month after watching some TV series about a town there. Impulsive man, Charles. I smiled, thinking about him.

Charles and the stable lads were my only regular contacts, a big bantering family without emotional obligations. I missed them all.

I'd planned to avoid Newmarket for a few days in the hope Dunn would think I'd given up, but I couldn't face another day in the flat. I packed enough clothes for a week and headed east again, stopping only to fill up and buy groceries.

I pulled up in front of Dunn's bungalow, blocking the drive again. I went down the path, heels clicking loudly on the flagstones, and round the back.

Nobody on the garden bench. Nobody in the house. The second glass pane I'd broken hadn't been repaired nor the mess cleaned up. On the trip across, I'd decided on a plan of attack. Anxious to get started, I returned to the car and drove to the clearing in the woods I'd used last week. I took my kitbag and walked to Dunn's, where I unpacked the bag then cleared away the broken glass.

I listened to the messages on Dunn's answerphone; all were from customers and had been left that morning so he was emptying his machine regularly. Next time he did, I'd try Martin's trick of dialing the recall code to see where Dunn had called from. I used the phone to call McCarthy on his mobile. He didn't sound delighted when he heard my voice. 'Did you find Alex Dunn?' he asked.

'Nope, that's why I'm calling. I need to see you, Mac.'

'That means you want a favour.'

'Have any of the "favours" you've done me in the past worked against you? You've always come up smelling of roses.'

'Mostly because you dropped me in deep shit to begin with.'

'Ha! Where have you been sharpening your wit?'

'On the horns of all the dilemmas you've left me in.'

'Touché, Mac. First two rounds to you.'

I could almost feel his smug smile down the phone. I said, 'Where are you going today?'

'Got a meeting in London. A long one.'

'Want to come here afterwards for dinner?'

'Where's "here"?'

'Newmarket.'

'No, thanks. I promised Jean I'd take her out.'

'Where are you tomorrow?'

'Sandown.'

'Can you spare me half an hour there?'

'I suppose so.'

'I'll get there before racing. Want to meet by the parade ring?'

'No. Meet me in the car park an hour before the first. I get nervous talking to you on course.'

'Okay. I'll see you in the car park.'

'Eddie, I'll stay in my car. Come and find me.'

'Sure.'

I didn't want to leave Dunn's bungalow in case he came back, but I thought it was time to start building up a few alternatives. I'd have to tell Mac more than I'd originally planned to, but not enough to compromise his position in Jockey Club Security.

I rang Martin, who was barely halfway through the task of analyzing all the information on the suspect studs. The staff histories were proving the toughest, as I'd known they would. I left him to it.

I found three tea bags lying on an otherwise bare shelf in Dunn's kitchen and made a mug of strong black tea, which I sipped as I dialed Compton Breslin's office. A girl told me he was betting at Yarmouth. I called his mobile. His cheery voice brought an immediate picture of him in his loud suit. I asked him for a list of all Dunn's bets this season. He promised it would be ready for me to collect in twenty-four hours.

I sat by the silent phone for a while then paced the living room. Looking out of the front window I saw the glint of the sun reflected from deep in the woods and realized I hadn't driven the car far enough into the trees. I was reluctant to leave in case Dunn called to empty the answerphone then someone else called immediately after him, wiping out his recall number.

I'd need to be desperately unlucky for that to happen. Deciding to chance it, I hurried out into the woods and ran toward the car. I couldn't have been gone more than ten minutes, but when I returned the flashing light on the answerphone had stopped.

It had been emptied. I grabbed the handset from the cradle before another call could come through and dialed 1471. I jotted down the number given by the recorded voice, even said thank you to the lady. Dunn must still be in Newmarket; that was the STD code.

My impulse was to dial it immediately but that might prove counter-productive. If Dunn realized I'd tracked him down, he'd probably take off again, sending me rapidly back to square one. It would be much better if I could find out the address the number belonged to. Mac should be able to get that. I rang his mobile again: switched off. I tried him every fifteen minutes until six then gave up. Tomorrow would have to do.

Chapter 29

I wandered through Sandown's car park looking for Mac, and then I saw his silver Rover come in off the road. He bypassed the turn into the officials' entrance and backed into a space against the fence. I walked over and opened the passenger door to see Mac's belly touching the steering wheel.

He was red, flustered, and trying not to look it. 'Sorry I'm a bit late, Eddie. The traffic's deplorable.'

'No hurry. Not on my side anyway.'

'Well, I don't exactly have all day. What was it you wanted to talk about?'

'Alex Dunn.'

'Again?'

I told him about Dunn's disappearance, about the two hard men I'd run into at his house, about how anxious Dunn was to discourage me from finding him. I was still playing it around Brian Kincaid's death, not mentioning anything about the stallions.

Mac said, 'So you think Dunn's involved in Kincaid's death?'

'I don't know. But I do know that a simple question from me sent him into a panic that was bad enough for him to up stakes and leave his home and business.'

'What makes you so sure you were the catalyst?'

This was where things got tricky. I didn't want to bring Martin's name into it at all, let alone tell Mac it was the confrontation with him that had been the real cue for Dunn's vanishing act. I busked along, trying to convince Mac that the pure shock on Dunn's face when I'd first approached him at the races told me that he had to be deeply worried.

I chose my words carefully, but Mac assumed I was trying to implicate Dunn in Brian's death. He shifted heavily in his seat so he was looking straight at me. 'You'd best be very careful, Eddie. You can't make accusations on hunches.'

'Come on, Mac, it's more than a hunch, you've known me long enough to realize that.'

'The same as your first suspect in Kincaid's death was more than a hunch? Tranter, he of the cast-iron alibi?'

'Okay, fair enough. That was a mistake.'

He sighed. 'So what do you want me to do?'

I looked at him. 'Mac, don't make it sound like it's all for me. You guys should be investigating Dunn's disappearance.'

'What disappearance? He's told the racecourses that normally use him he's unavailable until further notice. If we "investigated" every vet, doctor or starter who decided to take a few weeks off work, we'd never get anything done.'

'It's more than that, Mac. He's up to something. I'm tipping you off, trying to make sure you're not left with large helpings of egg on your face.'

'Very philanthropic of you.'

A frown I knew well gathered on Mac's face. This was the poker hand where he had to decide whether to fold and leave me to it or draw some cards. He'd be worried about coming in too late if this blew up. Not much point in the Jockey Club Security Department having their finger on the pulse of a dead case. He said, 'Okay. Let me see what I can find out.'

'Maybe you could start with this?' I said, giving him the recall number used by Dunn to clear his answerphone. Mac promised to ring me when he had something then asked me to leave the car 'as unobtrusively as possible'.

I did and he drove away to take up his customary spot in the car park. I'd considered going into the racecourse for an hour to see if I could pick anything up, but decided against it. Until I'd nailed Dunn, it was important to make him believe I'd been scared off.

I'd just settled and turned the ignition key when I noticed a familiar figure step out of a black Mercedes parked about six rows in front of me. It was old Iron Fist in a Velvet Glove himself, the guy who'd warned me off at Dunn's bungalow. He set off toward the stands.

I let him get up the steps and through the main doors before I started to get out to follow him. As I did so, the driver's door of the black Merc opened and out stepped another man I knew, another man I'd seen recently: Sheik Ahmad Saad's racing manager, Mr. F. Loss. Candy.

I stayed in my car, waiting to see if anyone else would come out of the Merc, but Candy locked it and headed for the stands, striding out boldly in his perfectly cut pinstripe suit.

I relaxed in the seat, drumming on the steering wheel, trying like hell not to jump to conclusions. What was Candy's connection with the hit man? Were they associated 'professionally' or had Candy simply, and perfectly innocently, offered him a lift to the races? If so, why had they sat so long in the Merc? Why had they entered the racecourse separately?

What should I do next?

Before I could make any connection, I had to find out who this guy was. Maybe Mac would know him by sight. It was simply a matter of getting Mac within safe viewing distance of Iron Fist, which might not be too difficult. Today's crowd wouldn't be that big and it was still half an hour before the first race.

I locked the car and headed for the entrance.

Chapter 30

Wending my way through the parked cars, I came upon an old friend, Charlie Harris, a racecourse photographer. Charlie was unloading his gear. I had an idea and asked him to lend me one of his cameras with a zoom lens, promising to return it by first race time. He told me it was a spare and that I could keep it all day if I needed to.

I soon found Iron Fist. He was by the parade-ring rail with his equally tall friend from Dunn's place. Two for the price of one. I climbed the steps to the balcony. Three horses were being led round and as each of them approached the pair, who were deep in conversation, I raised the camera and took a few shots; more than I'd intended with the first burst as the rapid motordrive reacted to my heavy finger and fired off a salvo. I shot the whole film, then found Charlie Harris by the unsaddling enclosure and returned the camera.

Esher High Street is a short walk from Sandown Racecourse. I doubted I'd find a one-hour-development place but not only did I find one, the girl offered to produce standard size prints within ten minutes. My intention had been to order eight by sixes to give Mac a clearer picture, but I could get those done later.

My luck had been good and I didn't want to push it by going back into the racecourse. I couldn't be sure that the hard men, or maybe Candy if he was involved with them, hadn't already seen me. I sat in my car and dialed Mac's number.

'Mac, can you spare a few minutes to come to the car park?'
'When?'
'Now. It's important. I won't keep you long.' Shortly afterwards

I watched his grey-suited bulk amble toward me.

Mac, grunting as he stooped, settled into the passenger seat, his dark wavy hair brushing the roof. I showed him the pictures, told him I'd just taken them. 'Recognize them?'

He stared, brushed his finger over a slight flaw on one of the prints. 'No.'

He didn't convince me. 'You've never seen them before?' I asked.

'Can't be certain I've never seen them before but I definitely don't know them.'

'Think you could find anything out?'

He nodded thoughtfully. 'Maybe.'

I turned to face him. 'Mac,' he looked at me, 'can you still make the telephone number top priority? This was a bonus today, and I'm glad for it, but what I really need is the address that call was made from.'

'I'll do my best.'

'Good. Thanks. Can you call me when you get it?'

'Okay.'

He left. I was glad he hadn't drawn it all out with the usual whys and wherefores. I drove to Dunn's place, stopping off at Compton Breslin's office to pick up a Private & Confidential envelope and the last three seasons' formbooks as promised. Heavy skies hung over Six Mile Bottom, particularly dark and sombre above the woods opposite Dunn's bungalow.

No lights flashing on the answerphone. I dialed 1471 again to reassure myself and found it was the same number as this morning. In the dim kitchen, I shifted the table and a chair close to the window. I couldn't risk switching the light on. I plugged in the charger for my mobile and left the phone slotted into it. Armed with a cup of coffee, pens and a thick notepad, I settled down to try to find some strategy in Alex Dunn's betting habits.

The computer printout listed 2,418 bets in the space of 123 weeks with total stakes of £482,115. Almost half a million.

It worked out at an average of just under £200 per bet. Dunn's losses in the period were £98,777.

Breslin's customer monitoring was very efficient. He'd put a note in telling me that his profit margin on Dunn's bets, 20 percent, was slightly worse than average for Breslin since he normally expected a margin, on all business, of around 22 percent. Breslin also apologized for being unable to provide a more detailed analysis of Dunn's bets.

The printout showed every horse he had backed but there was no trainer or jockey information, something Breslin said was being built into his new computer programme.

Almost all the bets had been struck on course, which meant betting tax wouldn't be deducted. Comparatively few had been placed by phone. I stared at the list of horses' names feeling like a commentator studying for the Charge of the Light Brigade. I'd sat down to this with considerable optimism but now it looked as if it would take days.

I sighed, sipped tepid coffee and set up list headings on my pad: Owner, Trainer, Jockey, Date and Racecourse. Then, starting with Dunn's very first bet, I opened the relevant formbook.

By the time McCarthy rang, I was working by a flashlight lodged between books.

'Any news, Mac?'

'Yes, though I'm not sure it's what you want to hear. The telephone number you gave me is from a public callbox in Newmarket.'

'Public or in a pub or something?'

'In the street, the High Street.'

'Where exactly?'

'Well, I don't know exactly but there can't be many, it's hardly Sunset Boulevard down there.'

'Can you find out exactly where it is?'

He sighed. 'It'll have to be tomorrow.'

'Morning?'

'I'll do my best.'

'What about Butch Cassidy and the Sundance Kid?'

'Nothing, I'm afraid. I've showed the pictures to my own people. Nobody can put a name to either though some mentioned seeing them around recently.'

'How recently?'

'The last three or four months is the best guess.'

'Mac, could you put a man on one of them for a few days?' That sigh again, louder this time. 'Eddie, it's very difficult.'

'I know it is but I need a favour. I'm sure it'll be worth your while finding out who these guys are.'

'Leave it with me.'

'Till when?'

'Please don't push me, Eddie.'

'I'm in a pushy mood.'

'Are you ever any other way?'

I smiled. 'Where are you tomorrow?' I asked.

'Back at Sandown. Aren't you riding at Market Rasen?'

'Not unless there's a message on my answerphone, promising me a winner. I'll still be here in Newmarket. Will you call me in the morning?'

'I will.'

'And Mac, look out for those guys again tomorrow. I'll be interested to know if they turn up and more interested to know if either of them is seen in the company of Francis Loss.'

'Why?'

'I saw one of them getting out of Loss's car at Sandown today.'

'So?'

'Just a thought. No big deal but if either of them is seen with Loss again, I'd like to know.'

'Leave it with me.'

'Okay. Call me tomorrow.'

At 9 p.m., my mobile rang.

'Hello?'

'Mister Malloy, it's Alex Dunn.'

The last person I'd expected. Odd, too, to feel I was sitting in his house.

I stayed silent. He said, 'Do you still want information about your stallion?'

'I want to know what's wrong with him.'

'I can tell you that. Meet me tomorrow at noon at your father's place.'

'Are you there now?'

'No, but I'll be there at noon tomorrow, I promise.'

'You've promised before.'

'I know. I'm sorry.'

There was something wrong. Dunn's heart didn't quite seem to be in what he was saying.

'Why this time?' I asked. 'What's changed your mind?'

'Today I... look, I'll tell you tomorrow.'

I still had doubts but there was little to lose. 'Okay. I'll be there.'

'I'll see you then.'

I considered ringing my mother, hesitated, put down the receiver and picked it up again. Dialed. The answerphone at the stud clicked on, my mother sounding all proper. I hung up.

I decided it was best not to let Martin know I was meeting Dunn next day. He might go blundering in, scaring him. There was also a strong chance Dunn wouldn't turn up and I didn't want another scene with my partner if that happened.

Best if I went alone.

I was there at 11.45. Dunn's blue estate was in the drive. There was no sign of any other vehicle. I wondered where my father's car was. I went to the house first and rang the bell. No answer. I waited a minute then pushed through the creaky gate into the stable yard.

Something wasn't right.

A row of empty boxes. Last time I'd been here all six had been occupied. Now the doors stood open.

I resisted calling Dunn's name and moved forward slowly, quietly.

I thought I heard a groan coming from the box in the corner and something moving in the straw. I glanced behind me as a car passed on the road, the sound fading quickly into the distance. I walked toward the open box, stopped outside and listened. Silence.

I looked round again then took a step inside. The half-doors were unevenly opened, the gap throwing an oddly shaped wedge of sunlight against the wall of the box, highlighting the dust motes, tiny stars above the straw landscape.

A sudden noise made me turn, but someone pushed a wide hood over my head, light cloth, the sun still bright through the material as I was spun round, as a pad was clamped across my nose and mouth, sweet-smelling but sharp, recognizable even as consciousness left me. Ether.

Chapter 31

When I woke up the sun still shone. Blue sky. No clouds. I was staring at the sky without having to tilt my chin. Couldn't understand it. Blinking wildly, screwing my eyes up against it as consciousness returned, senses revived. And I could feel something familiar beneath me, feel it and smell it. A horse. Warm, reassuring.

But skittish. Whinnying lightly. Shuffling.

Couldn't see the horse. Wasn't astride it. But fixed there. Uncomfortably. Tied on spine to spine. Wrists bound under the neck, ankles roped underneath, as though girthed. Thought it must be a dream, an after effect of the ether. I tried to get up, almost wrenching my wrists out of their sockets. Tried my legs: the same. They'd been splayed across the animal's ribcage, fastened under her belly, fixing me like a hog on a spit except that nothing had been shoved in one end and out of the other. Not yet.

The sun was hot on my body. I raised my head. I was naked.

Nearly laughed.

Tied to a horse. Naked.

I'd heard of King Midas in reverse. Now Lady Godiva in reverse.

No blonde hair to cover my modesty. Nothing. Funny. I might have laughed if I hadn't been so uncomfortable.

What was happening? What the hell was Dunn doing to me?

As my mind began to clear of ether, there came a sound that blew away all my comical notions: the unmistakable snort of a stallion. Off to my left, not underneath me.

He neighed excitedly and tramped the ground and I realized that I was tied securely to a mare in season.

I turned as far as the bindings allowed, trying to see exactly where he was. The first pass reminded me of the shark in 'Jaws'. His head glided past, mouth open, big stained teeth, eyes wide, ears pricked. Black he was.

I swallowed, prayed for my brain to clear properly.

The mare moved nervously beneath me. I could hear her ears flick. I realized her spine was noticeably dipped. An old hand, her back curved with age and the strain of bearing foals. God only knew what was going through her mind.

The black stallion came alongside, rubbed himself against her, jamming my right leg. The mare shied. Somebody said, 'Whoah!' quietly and held her steady.

'Dunn!' I called out. 'Dunn! Is that you?'

No answer.

'You crazy bastard! Get me off this!'

The stallion came in again, nipped my bare calf, snorted, rubbed again. I could feel no bridle. I raised my head. No one was holding him.

I pulled with hands and feet but the rope bit tight and the mare whinnied and reared, giving me a brief rollercoaster view of the big black stallion as he prepared to mount her. They held her steady then suddenly he was up, his huge dark head and wild mane blotting out the sun. I yelped in fear as his front legs clasped mine hard to the side of the mare, and his big open brown-toothed mouth bore down on me.

But he slipped off.

Then he was up again, more anxious now, eyes wide and white, staring madly at this strange intruder, this naked helpless chaperone. Then he was in her and on me, grunting, slobbering and biting at her neck, catching my left arm, biting me. I wanted to cry out in pain and fear but didn't want to enrage him so I lay there, eyes closed in terror, feeling the rhythmical pump of his loins, thinking of the times I'd sat astride others of his breed beating just as rhythmically with my whip.

I curved my spine desperately downwards, trying to follow the line of the mare's, trying to get some of the weight of the stallion off me as his belly spread on my pelvis. Sweat lubricated our backbones, allowing me to slip that vital few inches lower as the stallion's sweat rubbed into a froth covering my genitals and thighs. His huge lolling tongue painted saliva on me as his head rose and fell, and I heard his teeth grate against the hair on her neck and I prayed he wouldn't take my arm in his mouth.

Suddenly the mare neighed and moved as voices urged her forward. The stallion raised his head and almost screamed as he tottered after her, struggling to keep his penis inside. I saw what I thought was a pitchfork arcing upwards, the tines hitting the stallion in the mouth. He squealed and backed off, and I lost sight of him as the mare trotted off, bouncing and bending my spine. She went in a straight line and I realized she was still being led. Raising my head again, I saw us approach the gate in the corner of the sandy quadrangle we'd been locked into. The gate was open. The escape route was there. I sighed long and loud.

But the mare was pulled up short and my bonds quickly cut. I was dragged to the ground, landing hard on a sharp stone that bit into my buttock.

Then the mare was away through the gate.

And the gate swung closed.

And I rolled over to find myself alone with a half a ton of dark wrathful thoroughbred. He stood foursquare by the gate staring after the departing mare, his neighing almost a roar, his huge penis pulsing and swinging, pushing through the bars of the gate as he reared.

I began moving sideways at a crouch, anxious to stay below his line of vision. All around me was a high paneled fence, sheer and unscalable. The stallion blocked the only exit route.

He reared again, pawing the air then catching the top bars of the wooden gate with his hooves as he plunged down. I'd crept into the far corner. The fading sound of the mare's hooves finally went out of human earshot, and a few seconds later, he turned and came toward me as if he'd known exactly where I was all the time.

Big black head down, thick neck stretched, eyes rolling wildly, ears laid flat, his shoulder muscles bunched and flexed as he came at me in a determined swinging trot. I sprang to my feet, painfully aware of my nakedness, blood running down my bitten forearm as my hands automatically covered my genitals. His open mouth twisted sideways, dripping red where the pitchfork had pierced him, and the sun caught silver strands of saliva spanning those teeth.

I looked around for a weapon: nothing. Nothing but loose dirt.

The dirt.

I bent and scooped a double handful as, teeth snapping, he came at me. I threw it at his eyes and saw most go in his mouth, but it slowed him long enough for me to race past him, deliberately brushing his shoulder so he would have to make a full turn to come after me.

I heard him splutter and cough as I sprinted for the gate about thirty yards away. Then his hooves grinding as he spun, and his angry snort. My bare feet pounded the small stones but I wasn't aware of any pain as the strongest surge of adrenalin I'd known for years carried me to that gate, hoping and praying that whoever had put me in here wasn't lurking, ready to cut off my escape.

I could hear the stallion's hoofbeats, swore I could feel his breath on my neck, but I was within springing distance of the gate and my outstretched hands caught the top bar with perfect timing, helping me vault over to land on my back and roll in the dirt, praying once again that the bastard wouldn't try to follow me.

He didn't. And I lay laughing with relief and saying, 'Jesus! Jesus!' giggling nervously and uncontrollably at the craziness of it all. I thought how ridiculous I must look.

Only his head was over the gate and he stared at me, snorting in rage and frustration. Smiling I said to him, 'It wasn't me that put her off. Maybe it's your technique.' I rose, very relieved, still smiling but feeling some sympathy for the stallion. 'You need to treat them better. Bottle of bubbly. Some nice flowers. Try that next time.'

Then the elation ebbed quickly as I realized my attacker was probably still around. I stood and listened but could hear only the stallion breathing loud and pawing.

Where were my clothes?

Moving stealthily outdoors on bare feet isn't easy, but I made a reasonable attempt at it, nursing my injured arm as I went in the direction the mare had been led. I found her, unperturbed and alone in a box. I rubbed her nose and she shied away, staring at me.

I said, 'I didn't mean to break up the party, honestly.'

I skirted the buildings, checking the other boxes, the feed room and the barn where I picked up a shining hand scythe.

Nobody. No more horses. Working my way to where I'd started, I returned to the open box where I'd been grabbed. I remembered thinking there'd been someone in there.

Holding the scythe loosely in my right hand, I pushed the bottom door of the box fully open and saw the straw behind it. Then I pushed the top door. It was gloomy inside, but I couldn't hear so much as a breath. Cautiously I went in.

My clothes were on the floor beside the thin white-headed corpse of Alex Dunn. His body held some warmth but no pulse. He lay on his side in the foetal position, his face frozen in a painful grimace.

There was nothing I could do for him, and I felt a powerful urge to get dressed and get my wound attended to. The last thing I reached for was my shirt. Lying on the straw beneath it was a large brown envelope.

My name was written on the front in broad black letters. Opening it carefully, I moved toward the light as I drew out a handful of typewritten notes. I stood in the sunshine but had never felt colder as I read those pages. They listed the most painful, shameful episode of my life, baring and freezing my soul in a few hundred words of harsh detail. I closed my eyes, raised my face to the sun, tried to find some hope, some miracle that would let me look again at the papers and find something different.

There was no accompanying note, no blackmail threat. None was needed. What I held were photocopies.

Someone somewhere had the originals.

Chapter 32

In four separate interviews with the police over the next forty-eight hours, it became obvious they were highly skeptical about my story, especially with regard to the stallion and mare. If it had happened, they said, then Dunn had been trying to take some crazy revenge on me before killing himself. The vet had left a typewritten suicide note claiming I'd been hounding him over gambling debts. Still unable to disclose the real reason, I insisted that all I'd been seeking from him had been information on Brian Kincaid.

When the news of Dunn's death broke, my parents reappeared to be grilled by the CID. Dunn had offered them a two-day break in a Welsh holiday cottage he owned. He'd volunteered to move in and look after the horses while they were away.

In the days after Dunn's death, I frequently found myself swamped by anger. Rage at my mother and father and the police and Dunn; anger at him more for dying than anything else, dying and removing my only solid lead to this whole bloody complicated mess. What the hell was going on? Who was behind all this? What was behind it? Much more than the gambling problems of a racecourse vet, I was certain.

Then there was the dire prospect of the blackmail call when it finally came, the task of convincing these people who held the originals of the photocopied documents that I'd do whatever they wanted to keep this quiet. And all the time the fury of old was building in me, bolstering the determination to find them and deal with them, pay them back. I thought I'd mellowed in the past couple of years, God knows I'd worked at it, but it must simply be part of my character to react badly to threats. Well, not badly; foolishly. My fear threshold is always overcome by cold anger and pig-headedness - a poor survival mechanism.

It had been three days since Dunn died, and I'd left the flat only briefly to buy fresh dressings for my bitten arm though the wound wasn't deep and would heal quickly. The papers I'd found in the stable were locked away in a small metal filing box. I'd expected a call from the blackmailers. None had come. They were making me sweat.

I'd like to have established a link between Dunn and Capshaw the trainer, but I simply hadn't had the time to cross-reference all Dunn's betting records with the formbook to check Breslin's suspicion that an unusually high percentage of bets had been on Capshaw-trained horses.

Now I had all the time it took for the blackmailers to get in touch. Hours, days, weeks. I'd best get to work on the printouts. I sat long into the night, stopping occasionally to look at the silent phone, never expecting there to be a cut-off point when they might not call.

They didn't. I woke, stiff and uncomfortable, to sunshine through my window, my head on one of the thick printouts, the heat from the desk lamp warm on my right cheek. I filled the kettle then dragged the phone as close to the bathroom door as possible, and stepped in the shower.

Wet-haired and chewing toast, I returned to the desk to review the previous evening's work. A high percentage of Dunn's bets had indeed been on Capshaw's horses. The first place Dunn had gone that morning when we'd given him a fright at my father's stud had been Capshaw's. There had to be a link.

One person who'd seemed close to Dunn was my father, and only he or my mother could have told the vet what had happened all those years ago. And Dunn had told the blackmailers and they had killed him. I'd yet to learn how he'd died. The cops refused to release the cause of death, pending further enquiries. I needed to talk to my father.

I called the stud. Mother answered, sounding very strained, still shocked.

'Mother, it's Eddie. Are you all right? You sound quite—'
'I'm fine.' Tension now too on hearing my voice.
'I need to see you both.'
'Edward is ill, he's not seeing anybody.'
'I think he'll be seeing me all right.'
'He's not at all well.'

'I'm afraid he'll feel even worse when he sees what I've got. Please prepare him for a shock - another shock, I suppose I should say. And you too.'

'Wait until things are better, Eddie.'

The first time since childhood that I'd heard her say my name. A strange feeling, like a drowning man staring hopelessly up at the deck of a liner only to see a hand stretching down toward him. I was silent for a moment. Then, more softly, I said, 'Things aren't going to get better, Mum, I'm sorry. Not until we sort this out.'

'Please.'

Her voice, cracking, almost brought me to tears. 'You'll understand when you see this, Mum, you will. I'll be there this evening. I'll try for around seven.'

I heard the shortest of sobs before she hung up.

When I arrived, my mother stood at the window, arms folded, eyes cast down, not looking at me as I came along the path. Then she moved away and I heard her footsteps in the hall. She opened the door, her weary, unsmiling face, tired and old but not yet defeated. That touch of iron in her eyes, a look she'd always had.

'Hello,' she said quietly and stepped aside to let me in.

'Hello, Mum.'

Still no smile.

This time she led me into a large drawing room, tastefully furnished but sadly unlived in. A lonely old table and two easy chairs, a cold empty fireplace, two horse and jockey paintings facing each other from opposite walls as though they'd been waiting centuries for this race that would never start.

I stood awkwardly in the middle of the room. My mother looked up at me. 'Would you like some tea?'

I smiled. 'No, thanks.'

She gestured toward a chair. 'Please sit down.'

I did and the fat cushion sank, leaving my arms on the rests almost at shoulder level. She moved silently in old blue shoes and perched on the hard edge of the chair opposite, waiting. Waiting to find out what was in the bulging brown envelope I'd brought. I placed it on my knee.

'Where's my father?'

'He's ill. He has to stay in bed.' She looked calm but determined. I said, 'He's got to see this, Mum.'

Mum. Again. I watched for her reaction to the word. None. She reached out, her bony arm emerging from the sleeve of her beige cardigan, her wrinkled work-worn hand. I placed the envelope gently between her fingers. She opened it and drew out the papers. I settled slowly and watched as she read, her hand steady as she turned the pages, eyes set hard, the only sign of emotion the occasional flex of jaw muscles.

She put the papers back in the envelope and offered it to me. 'Why did you do it?'

'What?'

'This. After all this time?'

'It wasn't me. I found these in one of your boxes the other day, close to Alex Dunn's body.'

'Who wrote it?' Anger rising.

'That's what I'm trying to find out. That's why Father's got to see it.'

'No. It will kill him.'

'It'll kill him even quicker if the press get hold of it.'

She sat rigid, staring straight ahead, defying the welling tears to rise any higher. Determination to protect him, something that had served her all her life, was no longer going to be enough and she knew it. I edged forward in the chair and said quietly, 'Did Father tell Alex Dunn this?'

She shook her head, not looking at me.

'Are you sure?'

No answer. Tears winning now, glistening in her eyes, softening them, slipping out, seeking the widest wrinkle in her cheek. And I knew he must have told Dunn, and I realized she knew. And Dunn had told whoever was behind all this, maybe not intentionally, but he'd done it, betrayed my father, and condemned himself.

'Where is he?' I asked softly.

'Upstairs. In bed.'

I rose. 'I'll go up.'

'No.' She got to her feet. 'I'll take it. You wait. Please. Wait.'

She took the envelope from my hands and left the room. I sat down again, hearing her climb the creaking stairs, a door opening then dull voices punctuated by silence. And my mind drifted to the dark evenings when I'd lie in bed and hear those same voices rise from around the kitchen range, making me smile with delicious anticipation as I listened to them discuss plans for all the years ahead.

All the years.

The horses, the children - me and my brother and sister - the stud farm we'd build, the biggest in Newmarket. The champions we'd breed. The fun we'd have. All the years. All the dreams.

Then the world caved in.

Sitting in this strange house, I wished I had tears left for it. But they'd been used up a long time ago. That part of my heart was shrivelled.

I became aware of my mother standing in the doorway. I hadn't heard her. 'He'll see you,' she said.

An audience bestowed by the mighty one, the withholder of happiness. I followed her up the stairs.

The room was gloomy, curtains drawn. The papers lay under a lamp on the bedside table. His gold-framed spectacles were on the top page, reflecting a coin of light onto an empty glass stained inside with a rim of white powder. The bed was high, wide. He had sunk into the middle of it, the horizontal position removing the superiority he'd always found in his height.

I went and stood by the bed, my mother behind me. He stared straight up at the dark ceiling, the gloom too deep to let me see the depth of his pallor, but his cheeks were hollow, his eyes dull. I tried to find some sorrow for him, but that had gone the same way as the tears.

'Hello, Father.'

His jaw clenched.

I waited. After a minute or more, he said to the ceiling, 'Who wrote that?'

I watched him. Demanding still. In a moment, it would be a command. 'Who wrote it?' There was grit enough in his voice. I didn't answer. He kept staring upwards. I heard my mother shuffle uncomfortably. I said to him, 'Look at me.'

He flinched noticeably though I'd spoken quietly. The jaw clenched again.

'Look at me,' I said.

All three of us waited. Just the sounds of our breathing. Gradually his jaw relaxed, and he turned his head on the pillow until our eyes met. A challenge from his strong son. It couldn't be declined. I hunkered down level with him and held his gaze. He never blinked. 'Who wrote that?' he repeated.

'You wrote it, Dad.'

Indignation flared in his face. I raised a finger to my lips to hush him. Surprise softened his features. 'You wrote it when you told Alex Dunn everything, just as surely as if you'd sat at the typewriter yourself.'

His head rolled back, breaking eye contact. 'He was the only person I ever told,' he said, voice shaky. 'It helped me…to tell.'

Look where it's got you now.

He closed his eyes, squeezed them tight shut. Mother moved forward and reached to take his hand, interlocking fingers with his. I looked up at her. She stared down at him, her eyes showing love and hurt, her jaw and mouth clamped with determination.

I stood and moved to the end of the bed where I could look at them both. I said, 'We might be able to stop this getting to the papers. I've got to find the person who wrote it and left it there. Whoever it was will call soon.'

My mother looked at me. I said, 'He'll call one of us.'

She said, 'What do you want me to do if he rings here?'

'Just listen to what he says. Write it down. Try to hear if there's anything in the background that might help us pinpoint where he's calling from. You know, like trains or heavy traffic.'

I watched her face as she accepted this new role, her brain making yet another adjustment in a lifetime of coping. 'Should I ask him anything?'

I half-smiled, trying to ease the tension. 'You can ask him who he is and why he's doing this, but I doubt you'll get an answer.'

She nodded thoughtfully and looked at my father whose eyes were closed again. I said, 'Dad, are you awake?'

At the sound of the word 'Dad', he seemed almost to stop breathing for a moment then, eyes closed, he nodded.

'You trusted Alex Dunn?'

Mother said, 'He was a very old friend.'

'So what would have made him betray you like that?'

She shook her head. My father frowned angrily. I said, 'Who did Dunn associate with? Somebody must have had a hold over him.'

Mother looked at Father, and he seemed to sense her gaze on him. He opened his eyes but looked at her as he answered. 'He did a lot of work for Capshaw, didn't he?'

Mother nodded as she reached again for his hand and squeezed it.

'Dad.' Slowly he brought his head round to look at me. 'What sort of work?'

'Just standard vet stuff as far as I know.'

'And what was he doing for you?'

Mother said, 'He was trying to find out what was wrong with Heraklion.'

'Did he say he knew of any other stallion suffering the same ailment?' I asked.

Father said, 'It baffled him. I'd never known him so annoyed or frustrated.'

I changed tack. 'Did he strike you as the type to commit suicide?' Looking at the ceiling again, he said, 'Alex could get pretty down when the horses weren't running for him. He gambled a bit.'

'So I've heard. But would he have killed himself?'

He shook his head quite vigorously. 'Not that way he wouldn't.'

'What way?' The police had been withholding the cause of death.

Father looked at me. 'One of the CID men told me he injected himself with prostaglandin.'

I flinched involuntarily. I knew prostaglandin was used regularly on mares to abort them, to clean out the uterus. God only knew what it would do to a human being.

The ridiculous scenario of a TV game show came to mind. 'We asked one hundred people their favourite method of committing suicide.' I'd bet injecting prostaglandin wouldn't be top choice. 'What sort of death would that have been?' I asked my father. He looked at Mother, probably wondering whether the conversation was getting too morbid. She responded by nodding encouragement. He stared upward again and said, 'It would have been agonizing, I'd have thought, but you'd be best asking an expert.' Mother said to me, 'Do you think Alex might have been killed?'

'It's a possibility.'

Father turned again to Mother, forlorn hope in his eyes. 'But maybe he did commit suicide. Maybe he wrote everything out, knowing we'd find it when we came back, before the police or anybody. That means nobody else would know about us.'

I felt a momentary anger as he excluded me from this potential get-out. But he was only following the habits of a lifetime. And anyway, I knew Dunn hadn't planted those papers, there were too many other things going on. My parents didn't know about all the peripheral stuff yet, it wasn't safe to tell them.

My father looked at me, animosity still in his eyes. 'You've brought this on us. Why couldn't you just have left Alex alone? What does it matter to you if he owed some bookie money?'

'It's nothing to do with that.'

'That's what the note said.'

My mother, too, was staring accusingly at me.

'I wasn't chasing Dunn for gambling debts,' I said. 'He was involved in something serious. Criminal.'

'Rubbish!' my father cried, then went into a coughing fit. Mother glared at me and fussed over him. I left quietly and waited downstairs. Ten minutes later, she came into the room. 'Is he all right?' I asked.

She nodded then sat down across from me, looking serious. She said, 'If Alex Dunn was involved with something criminal, is it possible those papers, that story, was meant to frighten you off?'

'It's probable.'

She clasped her fingers and moved uncomfortably. 'Well, couldn't you do what they want and not interfere anymore?'

I stared at her. She met my gaze. I said, 'Do you want these people, this person, to hold it over us for the rest of our lives?'

She shrugged, opened her palms. 'I just thought.'

'Mum, it won't work. We can't live that way.'

She lowered her eyes, stared at the floor.

I sat forward. 'The best I can do is promise that I'll keep a very low profile. I'll try and make them believe they've scared me off, try and convince them that it's worked.'

She looked at me again. 'But how will we know if they believe that?'

'I think that they won't call unless they decide I need another lesson. If the blackmail call doesn't come, it means they think I've dropped out.'

She knew from the look in my eyes I wouldn't change my mind. She said, 'Promise me you'll try hard?'

'To find them or to convince them I've given up?'

'Given up.'

'I'll try to convince them, but only to make it easier for me to find them. I'm not giving up.'

She watched me and I think I saw in her a hint of distorted pride, of realizing she had passed on to me much of her own iron will.

I stayed another half-hour or so, prodding gently for more information on Alex Dunn but learning little. He was an excellent vet and a terrible punter. He had never married and had no family that she knew of. But, said Mother, he was a nice man.

Well, he'd got in with the wrong people. The only link I had to

Dunn now was the trainer, Capshaw. It might take a while to find out all I needed to about him, so it would be best if I was based not too far from Newmarket though I wouldn't want to be in the town itself. All part of lying low for as long as I could.

Mother came to see me out. I explained that I needed to be nearby for the next couple of weeks. She tilted her head to look up into my eyes, knowing what I was really asking, knowing it was the first favour I had asked since those dreadful days when what I'd begged for hadn't been in her power to grant.

'I'll speak to your father tonight. Perhaps you could call me tomorrow.' I nodded, smiling. Her neck was still arched and I felt a strong urge to kiss her gently on her upturned cheek. We stood by the door. I noticed how quiet the yard was. 'Where are the horses?' I asked.

'Gone,' she said flatly. 'We just can't cope for the moment. We've sent them to various people we know.'

People we know. No use for the word 'friends'.

She stayed at the door, watching me cast a long shadow in the beam of the security light as I walked to the car. That night I slept in a small hotel, closing my eyes with a strange mixture of fear and hope in my heart.

Chapter 33

Next morning's Sporting Life told me William Capshaw had two runners at Ascot. Not all trainers appeared at the races when their horses ran, but Ascot was sufficiently prestigious for most to make an effort.

Even if Capshaw wasn't there, I'd get a chance to see Candy again. Sheikh Ahmad Saad had six entered at Ascot and his racing manager would be bound to be there. I wondered if Candy might just happen to bump into the same hard man I'd seen him with at Sandown.

If that had been coincidence and the tough guys were nothing to do with Candy, I couldn't risk talking to him. I didn't know who I could trust. The more I considered it, the more I convinced myself that the papers I'd found with Dunn had been meant as a silent warning. So long as I kept my nose out of things, no blackmail call would be needed. The day the call finally came would be the day I'd know I'd been rumbled.

It would be impossible for me to track Candy and Capshaw, so I arranged for Martin to meet me in the car park and to bring two cameras. Before getting heavily into booze, Caroline had been a photography buff, and Martin arrived with a couple of bags full of gear and began unloading them.

Bearing in mind my intention to keep a low profile, I was confident that few of the flat-racing community would recognize me, especially in 'civvies'. But I didn't want to bring attention to myself or to Martin.

I said, 'Martin, for God's sake! We're supposed to be moving around unobtrusively, taking a few discreet pictures. All we need is a camera each with a reasonable telephoto lens.'

'Okay, okay!' He spent a few minutes choosing and fitting lenses then gave me four rolls of film. 'If you need any more, give me a shout.'

'I won't. It's best if we don't speak to each other once we're through the gates.'

The plan was that we would take turns following Capshaw and Candy at what we hoped was a safe distance.

Capshaw had a runner in the first. I took up an early position by the parade-ring rails, watching the horses go round until owners and trainers filtered in. Capshaw was with two men and two women, smiling at them, fielding excited questions from all sides, stoking their enthusiasm and hope.

He was small and dapper in a well-tailored navy suit, white shirt and patterned tie. The tallest man in the party pointed to the ground and Capshaw smiled and bent over to fix his shoelace. As he straightened, he mouthed the words 'Good luck' and the party smiled and nodded, a slim dark-haired girl nervously patting his arm. I checked the racecard: the owner's name was K. Semple. I wondered which of them it was. I shot a few frames.

Their horse ran okay before fading to finish fourth. All seemed delighted. I tracked Capshaw as best I could, though he disappeared from time to time into places like the owners' and trainers' bar where I couldn't follow. The only sign all was not well with him came when he was alone. In company, he was animated and jolly. It was a good act. As soon as his companions turned away, Capshaw looked troubled.

Sheikh Ahmad Saad's horse won the fourth, and I moved toward the winner's enclosure to watch connections have their usual post-race discussion. Martin stood against the opposite rail and I saw him snap a few pictures then nodded to indicate that I'd take over.

The Sheikh's Racing Manager, Candy, tanned, fit and elegant, was among the entourage as usual. He too looked worried. The race they'd just won was hardly top class, but I'd have thought it would have produced a smile. Through the long lens, I scanned the rest of the party - mostly glum faces. The Sheikh himself had a smile of sorts, but grim and fixed, professional.

Here was an elite gathering on a fine afternoon at one of the world's biggest racecourses. Their horse had just won and their oil wells were pumping out more cash than they could spend - and all they could manage was an interesting variety of frowns.

I followed Candy for twenty minutes or so on the chance he'd run into the hard men who'd warned me off from Dunn's place. If Dunn had the clout to recruit those guys and he was as afraid of me as he'd claimed in the suicide note, why hadn't he sent them back to teach me a proper lesson? Or had they been the ones who'd doped me and tied me to the mare? The culprits must have known Dunn lay dead in that box. Could they also have killed him?

Even discounting the grim method of death, Dunn was an unlikely suicide candidate. Part of the nature of the compulsive gambler is the constant belief that something will turn up, that tomorrow will be the day fortunes change. Hopelessness tends to be a temporary condition.

Also, why kill himself at my father's place, and why with prostaglandin? I was certain Dunn would have had access to many more types of drugs that would have offered a more peaceful passing.

I recalled my first meeting with him and how shocked he'd looked when I'd mentioned Brian and the lab samples. He knew something crucial about one or both of those matters, and now he was dead. Did the burden of the knowledge make him kill himself, or was he murdered to keep him quiet?

All this was turning over in my mind while I followed Candy at what I hoped was a safe distance. He spoke to two of the trainers the Sheikh employed and various other dogsbodies, but the heavies didn't appear.

Martin and I swapped quarry again for the next race, then once again, for the last where Capshaw trained the winner. I went to the winner's enclosure to watch them coming in. Capshaw seemed relieved and I wondered if his owners had had a serious bet. They looked pleased enough. There were four of them around the sweating chestnut, patting and kissing the horse and posing for pictures while Capshaw spoke to the press.

I saw Martin in the corner, still snapping away.

Checking the racecard, I noticed that the winner was owned by Guterson's Gloves Ltd, and that the race had also been sponsored by them. It was always nice to win your own money. The company's name rang a bell with me, though it took me a few minutes to recall why: Guterson's had been the name on the boxes of rubber gloves stored in the locked cupboard in Dunn's bungalow.

The usual back scratching then; Guterson had a horse in training with Capshaw, Dunn is tied in with Capshaw, Dunn had to buy

Guterson's gloves. Neat.

I stayed for the trophy presentation, which was made by Mr. Bob Guterson to his own marketing manager at Guterson's Gloves. Guterson certainly had a grasp of monopolies.

When we met again in the car park, neither Martin nor I could claim to have photographed anything that looked crooked, but he said he'd get the films developed and I said I'd ask Mac to go through them to see if he could spot any dodgy characters.

I rang my mother. She said Father was no better but that I could stay in the spare room for a few weeks if I would try not to disturb him. I promised and hung up, unsure if this was a tiny repair in that long-shredded umbilical cord. I realized that the invitation was motivated by their terror of disclosure; it wasn't the way I'd have wanted it, but there was a bitter-sweetness I could almost taste.

I changed routes and headed north to pick up as much stuff as I could from the flat. If my stay in Newmarket turned out to be an extended one, I didn't want to be travelling back and forth.

I reached Shropshire just after eight. The yard was quiet. I hurried upstairs to empty my wardrobe and grab a few books and tapes. The light was flashing on my answerphone though, as always, I'd emptied it remotely that morning.

One message from a trainer, Ken McGilvary, offering me two rides at Exeter next day. I thought about it as I stuffed extra toiletries into a plastic bag. I hadn't ridden for a while and was missing it. I could do with a break from all the sneaking around and, more to the point, if I was seen to be riding again so soon, the people who wanted me out of the stallion case would be reassured that I'd given up and returned to normal life.

That decided it. I called Ken and accepted. He was confident about the chances of my first ride and advised me to have a bet. Jockeys aren't allowed to gamble, but many place bets through a third party. Personally, I avoid it. I find owners and trainers to be the worst tipsters in the land. They are optimists by nature and their default state is to favour their own horses.

I was at my parents' place for 10.30. My mother managed a strained smile as she led me along the hall toward the rear of the house, the sound of snoring from my father's room growing louder then fading as we passed. The big bed made the room seem small. Fresh flowers on a chest of drawers by the window scented the air. The patterned wallpaper was tobacco brown in the dim light, and this room gave the same impression as the others: that of steady decay.

But the sheets were clean, the quilt thick and the pillows deep. I laid my bags down by the bed. 'Thanks Mum.'

She nodded slightly, not convinced she'd done the right thing, but offered me tea and sandwiches. By the time I joined her in the long kitchen, they were on the table, though she couldn't quite bring herself to sit with me as I ate.

She asked if I had 'made any progress today'.

'A little. We certainly didn't take any steps backward.'

That short nod again. I was already becoming familiar with it. She excused herself then, saying that she must sit with my father a while. We said goodnight and I sat in silence, the sound of my chewing echoing in my head. I thought again of the old days when it was I who'd lain in bed while my parents sat in the kitchen. When it was I who'd relied on them. For everything.

They'd failed me.

Would I fail them now?

Chapter 34

Exeter Racecourse lies high on Haldon Hill where the weather was clear and sunny. I drove steadily down the main approach, weaving through the heavy pedestrian traffic, the usual herd of optimists moving confidently and excitedly toward the front lines to engage the bookies in battle.

When I entered the weighing room, I realized I hadn't smiled for weeks. It was so good to be among familiar faces, trusted people, friends. I had a strong desire right then never to leave these guys again. I wished we could all form some full-time travelling band of companions, going from course to course, sticking close together, never having to face the outside world.

But if I'd have told any of them how I felt, they'd have taken the piss for the rest of my life. I settled for talking to and laughing with as many of them as possible throughout the day. The horse McGilvary had said would win skated in by ten lengths. His other one fell when going well, dealing me a neat kick in the ribs as he scrambled up, but I was okay although I accepted a lift back in the ambulance.

I picked up a spare ride that finished third, and overall had a bloody good day until the cloud of gloom those papers had created settled on me again. I was sitting in the weighing room after the last, enjoying the banter as everyone packed up, thankful to be heading home still sound in the head, unbandaged and stitch-free. As I looked around, I wondered what they'd all think of me if this story got out.

A few of them were planning a drinking session at a local hotel. I'd been tempted but the creeping depression persuaded me to give it a miss despite plenty ribbing.

As I approached my car, I saw there was a bit of a party going on by the BMW parked beside mime. Two young men in light suits were wielding champagne bottles by the neck and singing tunelessly. I smiled. I hoped they had a sober driver stashed away somewhere.

They were sitting on the bonnet, backs to me as I opened my rear door and slung my kitbag inside. 'Beat the bookies?' I asked cheerfully. They both turned, smiling, holding their bottles toward me and moving in my direction remarkably quickly for drunks. They wore sunglasses. I recognized them too late. The darker one dropped his smile and his bottle and pushed me in through my half-open driver's door while the other guy climbed in the passenger side. I glanced desperately around the car park, but there was nobody nearby.

Dark Hair got in behind me. I heard my kitbag squeak on the upholstery as he pushed it across the seat. 'Drive,' he said.

I drove.

He gave simple directions till we were heading south. I'd planned to go north but I wasn't too despondent. At least this was something, a further step. Anything was better than blundering blindly looking for unfindable clues.

Anything, Eddie. Death?

Maybe not.

When we were travelling at speed, Dark Hair said, 'Should old acquaintance be forgot, Mister Malloy?'

'You've often been brought to mind,' I said.

'But not with sufficient nous on your part to want to avoid a resumption of that acquaintance.'

'You made such an impression on me,' I said, 'I just had to see you again.'

'Well, let's find out if we can consummate our relationship to your satisfaction this time. I'd hate to think you'd want to come back for more.'

At least that told me they didn't plan to kill me. I was scared, but wasn't for showing it. I said, 'I just can't get enough of such riveting company.'

'Riveting. Now there's a thought. We're not too far from a shipyard, actually.'

The thought of a hot rivet gun against my flesh was enough to silence me for a while. In less than an hour, we were on the North Devon coast. As the big orange sun began sinking, Dark Hair directed me through a series of winding single-track roads until I realized we were heading for the sea.

The further along the track I drove, the higher we climbed. The ocean lay far below as we drove across the grass, toward what could only be a cliff edge. I took heart from the fact that there were two other cars parked within sight of where we stopped. The people I assumed were their owners strolled in silhouette against the pinkish sky and sea, following their dogs.

I was told to switch off the engine. We sat in silence, watching the dog-walkers, my companions with growing impatience, me with the fervent wish the walkers would stay all night.

But they didn't. Within minutes of each other, they led their pets to the cars and drove away, the smell of their exhausts wafting through my half-opened window.

When the sound of the departing vehicles faded to silence the tension in the car increased. None of us spoke. After maybe fifteen minutes, the gulls broke from riding silently on the air currents over the cliffs and swept down on us crying for the show to begin.

Still the pair waited. The sun was huge, dropping gradually below the glassy horizon like an enormous orange coin into a wide slot. And I realized that what they'd been holding off for was dusk.

Dark Hair got out and opened my door while his friend sat next to me. With the door just halfway open, I'd already decided to kick out and slam it against Dark Hair's legs. Before I moved my foot an inch, the guy beside me hit me hard and fast on the point of my chin, and I felt my legs buckle and my eyes water as Dark Hair dragged me out.

They pulled me to my feet and half-dragged me to the cliff edge as I fought desperately to regain my senses. The blow had taken me by surprise. I'd been dazed often enough, concussed a few times, but somehow this was different. Falling from a horse at speed can be bone crunching, but that split second of warning is sufficient to prepare yourself mentally and physically for what's coming. Being hit in the face by a professional was another matter.

By the time we reached the edge, my brain had stopped rattling in my skull though my legs remained weak. Dark Hair gripped the back of my neck with his big left hand and pushed me forward.

The sea was calm. Low tide. Dusk and distance softened the rocks hundreds of feet below till they looked no more threatening than chocolates lying haphazardly in a box. The ozone-rich air rose in currents off the cliff face, sharpening my senses and my fear.

Dark Hair said, 'Ready? There'll be top points for artistic impression depending on the degree of difficulty.'

Smart answers didn't seem so clever any more. I thought of my mother and felt the strongest pang of regret that my plans to be a proper son again would never be realized.

Dark Hair said, 'Goodbye, Mister Malloy.' Then he pushed me over the edge.

I fought to keep my balance in what seemed an absurd slow-motion replay of those hundreds of cartoon characters windmilling wildly and pedalling furiously at fresh air, but there was no Hanna Barbera storyboard to keep me upright and I went over, head plunging downwards.

Then I stopped. I threw out my hands to prevent my nose hitting rock as I swung toward the cliff face. They had me by the ankles.

Suspended.

Suspended belief.

Renewed hope.

They lowered me slowly. My fingers scrabbled for a hold, a crack, in case they dropped me now. I felt damp vegetation, scratched it, releasing a rich smell. They held me there, panting. I saw the rocks way below. Nothing between them and my eyes. I closed them. Sweat prickled.

Then, very slowly, my tormentors hauled me up. They tried to make me stand but shock had triped my leg muscles. They laid me flat in the grass, and I went from staring at earth and sea to gazing lovingly at a darkening sky.

Dark Hair leaned over me, looked into my eyes. 'Stop following people. Stay out of this. Go back to riding horses for a living. Next time we'll drop you.'

Then they went away. I heard my car start up but didn't turn to watch them leave. I just lay there staring at the sky till it was black and sparkling with stars.

It was after midnight by the time I reached a garage. I called my mother and told her I'd been delayed with the lads, and she said she had been worried, which cheered me. My next call was to Johnny Westmead, a jock I'd spoken to that day at Exeter. He lived in Barnstaple, which, the kid in the garage assured me, was only half an hour away by car.

Sleepy as he was, Johnny agreed to come and pick me up and give me a bed for the night. I spun him a tale about picking up a girl at the races and bringing her to the cliff top, only to have her steal my car while I was dozing in the grass. He laughed; he'd get plenty of mileage out of it whenever my name came up.

Next morning I rang the police and reported my car stolen from Exeter races, that I'd left it there overnight when I'd gone for a drink. They told me it had been found abandoned on the slip road exit of Taunton Deane services on the M5, and that my keys and kitbag were in the possession of the Taunton police.

Johnny agreed to drive me there, and after completing a surprisingly small amount of paperwork, I was heading northeast for Newmarket. On the long journey, I had plenty to occupy my mind.

Whoever Dark Hair and his friend were working for was being extremely patient with me. Okay, last night had been scary, but that was all.

Was the cliffhanging episode really engineered by the same guy who'd had Brian Kincaid and Alex Dunn killed? If so, then why go easy on me?

More interestingly, why hadn't they used the much more potent threat of publication? Could it be that my father's hopeful guess had been right, and that Dunn had indeed kept the story to himself?

No, that didn't make sense, not if he'd been killed. In that case, the killer had laid the envelope out for me to find, knowing I was going to be there to meet Dunn. The killer must have known Dunn personally or he wouldn't have had that information.

Even if it had been suicide, Dunn knew I'd be the only one on the scene. If he'd never meant to expose the secret to anyone then why leave it for me, knowing I was already too well aware of everything in it?

Someone else had to know, and if it was the person controlling Dark Hair and partner, then why hadn't he simply used it? A phone call would have been all that was needed, rather than a trip to the Devon coast.

It made no sense.

Unless the person in charge specifically didn't want me hurt, in which case he or she must know me pretty well. The only lead I had on these guys, apart from my first meeting with them at Dunn's place, was seeing Dark Hair with Candy at Sandown. I'd like to have thought that Candy felt some bond with me, we'd been pretty good mates in his riding days. I knew him well and that was the trouble: I simply couldn't see him being involved in mayhem and murder.

As the noon radio news came on, I was ten miles along the M4. My mobile rang. It was Martin. 'Eddie! I need to see you! We're in bad trouble!'

He sounded panic-stricken. 'Martin, calm down. What's wrong?'

'Eddie! Eddie!' He broke down, sobbing.

'Martin! Listen, are you at home?'

Incoherent noises in reply.

'Hold on, Martin. I'll be with you soon.'

I had to assume he was at the stud. I reckoned I was less than an hour away.

I'd risked speeding on the motorway, which made it very frustrating having to slow down for the speed bumps on the driveway to the stud. But that caused me to roll quietly up to the cottage rather than arrive in a cloud of dust and burning rubber.

As I hurried toward the front step, I heard raised voices through the open door. Fiona first. 'It won't do you any good, you know that! You admitted it yourself!'

Then Martin. 'Look, fuck off and leave me alone!'

'They won't have to kill you, Martin, you're killing yourself!'

'Leave me alone, you bitch!'

Fiona began sobbing. 'Martin, please, for God's sake!' Her voice was softer, trying not to upset him further. She said, 'Tell Malloy. He'll help us. Tell him about Dunn. Let me tell him.'

'No. Tell him nothing. I'm out of this now. He can do it on his own. He can have the stud. And he can have you! And Caroline! He can have the whole fucking lot of you!'

I heard breaking glass, furniture moving, and then Martin came blundering out carrying a half-full bottle, almost knocking me over. He stank of whisky. He was clean-shaven for once, but a fresh bruise was rising on his right cheek and on his left jawbone was a crescent-shaped ridge of weeping blisters.

He stared at me, rage draining from his eyes as he realized I might have heard what he'd just said. Fiona appeared in the doorway, red-faced and sullen. When she saw us, she turned and went back in. Martin's hangdog expression drew the last of the anger from him and he sat on the step and swigged from the bottle.

I sat beside him. 'What's happened?'

He was washing the whisky around his mouth, staring at the sky. He swallowed it and said, 'Somebody took the pictures off me. And the cameras.'

'The pictures we shot at Ascot?'

He nodded.

'When?'

'Early this morning.' He drank again. 'He caught me as I went down to feed the horses.'

He swallowed a lump in his throat. A tear bulged at the corner of his left eye. I waited a few seconds before asking any more questions. Between swigs and tears and nervous swallows, Martin told me that a man with a gun had demanded the pictures and negatives he'd had developed yesterday. Then he'd taken Martin to the forge, made him fire it up, heated a horseshoe and branded him lightly on the jaw, threatening the full treatment if he continued 'following people around'. That was the same message I'd had from Dark Hair, but I bore no scars. Martin's description of the guy didn't match either of the heavies I'd chauffeured to the seaside.

Before leaving, the man had knocked him unconscious and locked him in the forge, which was in a small building well away from the main yard. Fiona only heard his shouts because she was out looking for him.

When he finished his story, he sat staring at the ground, his bottle two-thirds empty. 'Was that full when you started?' I asked.

He nodded. Still gazing at the ground, he said quietly, 'I'm finished, Eddie.'

I watched him.

'I'm scared,' he said, voice breaking.

I moved closer to him and put an arm around his shoulder, and he slumped against me and started crying, softly at first then the floodgates opened and Fiona came and helped me get him inside and into bed. He lay, eyes closed, gripping her hand as she dried his glistening cheeks. Gradually his breathing leveled out and I left them together and went to the kitchen.

Ten minutes later Fiona came in alone. She filled the kettle and washed two mugs. 'He's asleep,' she said calmly. I was revising my opinion of her. For all Martin's problems and booze now looked a serious one, she'd stood by him. He was nothing more than a child inside and here was she, twenty-five years younger, looking after him, carrying his baby.

She brought mugs of coffee to the table and, business-like, unfolded the Racing Post. There was a big colour photo of Alex Dunn above a story about the coroner's report whose verdict was suicide by self-administration of prostaglandin.

Fiona said, 'I'm sure Dunn came here about two weeks before Town Crier started firing blanks.'

'Go on.'

She smoothed the paper. 'He came here one day when Martin was out. I recognized him from this picture. He told me he was an RSPCA man come to check the horses.'

'And did he?'

She nodded.

'Did he say what he expected to find?'

'He said someone had reported that they weren't being fed properly.'

'And did he check them all?'

'Yes.'

She looked slightly doubtful. 'Did you go round with him?' I asked.

'Most of them.'

'What did he do?'

She shrugged. 'I don't know. Took a few tests, temperature, blood, that sort of thing.'

'Did he show you any ID?'

'He showed me a card or something, I think.'

'You certain it was him?' I indicated Dunn's picture.

'Almost. I think it was.'

'Apart from his looks, is there anything else you remember about him?'

'He was tall. Very tall and thin.'

'Did you tell Martin at the time?'

'I think I did but he was probably drunk. The man left saying everything was in order, so it didn't seem all that important.'

So, Dunn had been here and he'd had pretty much free access at my parents' place. Fiona found the list Martin had compiled of the other studs where we suspected one of their stallions was suffering from the same loss of fertility as Town Crier and my father's Heraklion. We had to try to find out if Dunn had visited those studs too. Fiona watched me pondering. I came close to asking her to help me further, but she had enough on her plate and it would only cause more friction with Martin, whose heart was no longer in it. I told her to look after him and not to worry. I said I'd make sure he was kept out of it in future and gave her my telephone numbers, making her promise to call me if she needed help.

She looked surprised when I kissed her goodbye.

Chapter 35

On my journey home, I wondered if my mother would agree to ring round the five studs posing as an RSPCA employee and saying something like, 'We've heard that a bogus vet is visiting studs, and wanted to warn you and to check with you in case he's actually been.'

It was worth a try.

Mother was in the kitchen mixing tuna and mayonnaise and chopping salad vegetables. A pungent mixture of smells filtered down the hall. She turned to look at me but couldn't quite manage a smile. 'You haven't shaved.'

'I know. Things were a bit hectic this morning.'

She sliced carrot lengthwise with smooth sweeps. 'When men reach a certain age they should never miss shaving. And they should always wear a tie.'

I smiled. 'And you think I've reached that age?'

'Yes, I do.'

'Okay.'

'Don't humour me.'

'I'm not. I mean it.'

We were quiet for a while, listening to the rhythm of the knife on the chopping board. 'How's Father?' I asked.

'Still unwell. Quite ill, I'm afraid.'

Sick of facing the world and his responsibilities, I thought. 'We need to talk later,' I said, 'all three of us.'

'We'll see.'

'It'll move us another step forward, Mum.'

She turned slowly to look at me. 'We'll see.'

I left her and lay for half an hour in a hot bath, noting the renewed colour in the old bruises on my ribs like a part-refilled artist's palette. Gazing at the steam-sheened brass taps, I turned over the new developments in my mind.

Our trailing of Candy and Capshaw at Ascot must have activated the visits from the heavy mob, but why had Martin been assaulted? Because he'd been the one with the pictures? How had they known that? Why hadn't Dark Hair mentioned pictures to me when dangling me over that cliff?

Whatever the answers, at least we knew we were on the right track. Pity Martin had taken it so badly. Terror could be tough to deal with. I couldn't condemn him for wanting out.

The news of Dunn's RSPCA venture also added a very strong flavour. Again, there came that frustrating feeling of just having to shake everything up the right way for things to fall into place. I knew it wasn't far off.

That evening I ate alone again. My parents took their meals in Father's bedroom, and I realized I was still just a stranger in their house.

Next morning, after much canvassing by my mother, Father agreed to grant me another audience. I told them both about Dunn's deception in posing as an RSPCA man. Mother checked the diary and found that Heraklion's fertility had started failing a fortnight after one of Dunn's visits.

Most mares stay on at a stud after being covered, and are scanned within a few days of the mating to see if an egg has been fertilized.

Mother sat by the bed, the book open in her lap, and glanced at my father, his face pale in the curtained gloom. He wheezed breathing out, but there was some brightness in his eyes as he turned to me. 'Do you think Alex was doing something to those stallions?'

'It seems possible.' I was wary of condemning Dunn immediately, my father's friendship with him making me cautious. 'I think he was being forced into it somehow, possibly blackmailed.'

Father looked puzzled. 'Why? Who profits from knocking half a dozen small studs out of business?'

I shrugged. 'I don't think that's the objective. If these people had a grudge against the studs in particular, then why not just burn the buggers down?'

At the word 'buggers', my mother glanced up sharply at me as though I were still seven. I smiled but her expression didn't soften.

Father said, 'Then why are they doing it, and who are they?'

'The sixty-four-thousand-dollar question,' I said. 'But if we can find the answer then we'll have the people who left those papers with Alex Dunn's body.' Father's mouth straightened to a thin line as he clenched his jaw. Mother reached for his hand again. All three of us spent the next twenty minutes discussing how Dunn could have 'got at' the stallions. If he'd been responsible for their fertility loss, how had he done it, why, and how could we cure them?

Father brooded throughout most of it, throwing in only the occasional remark, but Mother had been anxious to grasp the lifeline, to explore any option. But there were few and the room was soon silent again.

Father shifted uncomfortably and tried to clear his throat, which brought on a coughing fit. Mother propped him up on his pillows and he reached to squeeze her hand, the first time I'd noticed him initiate any affection. She knew he was going to speak. He looked at me and said, 'When I first met Alex Dunn, I remember he was very enthusiastic about chemical castration.'

Two words that came together like scissor blades cutting through all the supposition and speculation. My senses were suddenly sharp. He said, 'Alex was convinced that colts could be made much easier to handle when still in training by injecting chemicals on a regular basis.'

'Something temporary?' I asked.

He nodded. 'When they were finished racing and were ready for stud, the injections would be discontinued.'

I almost held my breath before asking, 'What was the chemical? Do you know?'

He shook his head slowly and I thought I saw just a trace of satisfaction in his eyes, a glimmer of spiteful pleasure that I was still going to have to work very hard to save this. But maybe it was the poor light.

We talked a while longer then Father glanced at Mother and closed his eyes, effectively dismissing me. She looked up and mouthed the words, 'He's tired.' I nodded. Before leaving, I said goodbye to him. He raised both eyebrows but didn't open his eyes nor speak.

I went to my room and found Martin's list of studs. When Mother came back, I explained what I needed, and she set to immediately, scanning the list as she picked up the phone. I felt like making a few calls too but was conscious of the risk of exposing myself, especially after the events of last night. How did they fit into the puzzle?

The more I thought about it, the more it bugged me. It made no sense. Why hadn't they simply threatened me with publishing the papers? I sat on the bed, Dunn's betting records spread out in front of me. I doodled lightly in pencil in the narrow margin of one of the printouts.

What had Dark Hair said to me? 'Stop following people. Stay out of this.' The message to Martin had been the same, albeit more forcefully delivered. Capshaw and Candy. Candy again cropping up with Dark Hair, his Sandown travelling companion.

Okay, assumption time. No hard evidence, so some speculation might prove worthwhile.

Candy sent the heavies after us. The first confrontation, at Dunn's place, had come with a friendly violence-free warning. The second was to scare the shit out of me but leave me unhurt. Martin hadn't had the protection of an old friendship to rely on, or maybe they had to frighten him more as they had no blackmail hold over him as they did me.

Could it be Candy was taking a similarly 'sympathetic' view with the papers, knowing what publication would do to my parents and me? Possibly, but that shouldn't have stopped him using them as a threat.

So did someone else have the papers? Were we up against two different groups? What was Candy's interest in Dunn's activities? Supposing he knew Dunn had been scuppering those stallions? Supposing he knew about Dunn dabbling in chemical castration? But what would that be to Candy? His boss had the top vets, the best of everything for his horses…something gnawed at my memory, something that hadn't rung true with me… Candy's party at Ascot the other day. How strained they'd all seemed, from the Sheikh downwards. Candy, in particular, had looked under pressure. The same Candy who'd reacted just slightly oddly, just a little out of character, when I'd met him in Newmarket and told him about the stallion fertility problem.

The Sheikh.

What makes a fabulously rich, high-powered businessman unhappy?

A poorly performing business?

The Sheikh's racing empire was huge, probably the biggest in the world. What had started ten years ago as a hobby had developed into an obsession, some said, a desire to dominate racing the world over. The building blocks for that, the very foundations, were the Sheikh's luxurious studs, the largest of which was in Newmarket. He had most of the top stallions and many of the best mares. Although that didn't guarantee success, it went a long way toward seriously reducing the odds against failure.

His worst nightmare would have to be losing his stallions. Or the stallions losing their fertility. Maybe Alex Dunn's stallion-sabotage programme hadn't been confined to small studs.

No wonder Candy didn't want me blowing it wide open. If Martin Corish was petrified of breeders getting to know about Town Crier's infertility, how must the Sheikh feel if some of his stallions were also infertile?

I put down the pencil and sat back, trying to focus again, trying to pull away from the global implications and figure out the hows and whys. It was the equivalent of industrial sabotage in a multi-billion pound business. Who was behind it and what was the motive? Why mess around with a few insignificant stallions in tiny studs as well as the cream?

Was someone else involved? Had Dunn concentrated on the small studs? Was an accomplice still operating in the Sheikh's studs? If so, how? Security there must be tighter than Fort Knox.

I sighed and got to my feet. I had to slow things down, remind myself that all this had stemmed from a couple of assumptions. I was going to have to speak to Candy.

The door opened. Mother came in, still wearing her reading glasses and carrying the list of studs. She seemed quietly pleased. Of the seven calls she'd made, four studs told her that they'd had a visit from the potentially bogus RSPCA man in the previous six months. One couldn't recall what he looked like. The other three gave a good description of Alex Dunn.

'Excellent,' I said. 'Have you told Father?'

'He's asleep. I'll tell him later.'

I watched her. Outward calm. Inner turmoil. 'Is there anything else I can do?' she asked.

I smiled. 'No, thanks, Mum. You've done well.'

That slightly surprised look again then a trace of a smile before she turned to leave. Quietly I moved to the open door and watched her walk wearily along the hall. Her straight shoulders drooped now that she thought no one was watching and her feet dragged as she took a break from constantly bearing up for the sake of others. She seemed old and broken, and when she stopped and almost slumped against the wall, I resisted the urge to hurry toward her.

That decided it. I would contact Candy.

Chapter 36

I phoned The Gulf Stud, where Candy had a house, which went with the job. He wasn't there. A secretary gave me his mobile number. It rang seven times then he answered and I concentrated acutely on his reaction as I said, 'Candy, Eddie Malloy.'

A moment's hesitation, then, 'Eddie, nice to hear from you! How are you?'

'Still full of health-giving ozone after yesterday's trip to the coast.'

Another moment's silence then his voice tightened noticeably. 'You, er, been taking a bit of a holiday?'

'You might say that. Just hanging around by the sea for a while.'

There was a long pause as we realized the stage we'd reached.

I said, 'Remember I told you I was working for that small stud on a stallion fertility problem?'

'Uhuh?'

'I think I found the answer.'

Another pause then he said, 'Have you told anyone else?'

'You're my first call.'

More silence. 'I think we should meet,' he said, 'but not in Newmarket.'

We met at a garage about fifteen miles from town. I followed Candy for a further three miles, speculating as I watched his head through the rear window whether Dark Hair and his friend were hiding in the back. He pulled off the road and down a slope into a long lay-by concealed by trees. I was relieved to see him get out of the car alone and walk toward me. He got in beside me and managed a grim smile.

I laid everything out.

'Well,' I asked, 'am I right?'

He stared at me, unsure if I was saviour or executioner, then nodded slowly and told me the story. All eight stallions which had retired to the Sheikh's Newmarket stud in the past eighteen months had completely lost fertility within weeks of taking up stud duties.

'Was Alex Dunn your vet at the time?'

Candy ran a hand through his thick chestnut hair. 'Alex Dunn's never set foot inside the place.'

'One of his deputies?'

Candy shook his head. 'We've checked every single person who's crossed the threshold in the past two years. All employees are thoroughly vetted as a matter of course. Every visitor has to go through a security point where a Polaroid is taken and logged on file. We've gone back on everyone right down to the newspaper delivery boys, put private investigators on to many of them. The budget for this just topped half a million and climbing.'

'How much are you paying to keep it out of the papers?'

'Nothing. That's one thing we've been terrified of. No more than half a dozen people know about the problem.'

'What about the private investigators?'

He shook his head again, shiny hair swinging. 'They were given a specific brief on each individual, that's all.'

'It was your boys who warned me off at Dunn's place and took me to the seaside yesterday?'

He made an apologetic face. ''Fraid so.'

'I wondered why they'd been so soft on me.'

'I told them not to hurt you.'

'You're too kind, considering I was on your side.'

He shrugged. 'Sorry, Eddie, we simply couldn't risk you stumbling on what had been happening at The Gulf.'

'Why the strong-arm stuff on Martin Corish, then? Was it just for the pictures?'

'What?' He looked baffled.

'You sent someone else to the Corish Stud yesterday to get those pictures we took at Ascot.'

'What pictures? I haven't a clue what you're talking about.'

I watched him closely, trying to figure out why he'd lie about it. I couldn't think of a reason. 'Do you know Martin Corish?'

'I know of him.'

I explained about our partnership. Candy said whoever called on

Martin wasn't sent by him. That narrowed the field. Capshaw was in a one-horse race. I didn't dwell on it with Candy. I wanted time to assemble my thoughts.

He said, 'Can you keep this quiet, Eddie? It'll be worth a lot of money to you.'

'I'd rather find out who killed Brian Kincaid. And Alex Dunn.'

'I'm sure we can do that, in time.'

'How much time?'

'As long as it takes to find a cure for these stallions and mares.'

I sat forward. 'Mares?'

Candy rubbed his handsome face again, nodding slowly as he did so. 'Of the mares we've managed to get in foal, seventy-three percent have aborted within days of the pregnancy being confirmed.'

'Seventy-three percent?'

That weary nod again. 'They're still losing them. It's gone on right through the season.'

'Jesus, no wonder you look like shit!'

He let out a huge sigh. 'I've never felt so under pressure in my life, Eddie. Picked exactly the wrong time to saddle myself with a mortgage that would choke a Clydesdale. Bought a holiday home in Barbados just after New Year. Now the boss is looking around at us and all I can see in his eyes is my P45.'

'Spelt in Arabic?'

He managed another smile and I admired him for it. I knew I needn't ask about the quality of the veterinary care in trying to nail this. The Sheikh could afford the best in the world and that was what he'd bought. The horses had been given false names and taken in small groups to expert vets to avoid raising suspicion in the mind of any individual vet. No reason for the infertility had been found, let alone a possible antidote.

If the Arab stallions were suffering the same affliction as Town Crier and the others, I believed the clue to any antidote lay among Dunn's papers and lab samples, which had to be somewhere. Whoever was behind this wouldn't want to stop at eight of the Sheikh's stallions.

We talked about Dunn who, until now, hadn't entered Candy's equation. He'd concentrated solely on people who'd had access to The Gulf Stud. He accepted that there had to be a very strong chance that Dunn or his secret serum had to be involved, but the lack of motive troubled him.

'He had close links with Capshaw, didn't he?' I said.

'So?'

'Didn't the Sheikh take all his horses away from Capshaw?'

'That was three years ago.'

'Revenge is a dish best savoured cold, as they say, Candy.'

'Nah, he's not the type…Capshaw's not the type. He knew there was no malice in the horses being taken away.'

'What was behind it?'

He shrugged. 'Simple, the Sheikh was experimenting in having some of his horses trained in the Middle East. We'd seen improvement in the best we'd taken there and the Sheikh wanted to see what would happen by taking a full batch of horses of mixed ability at exactly the same time and preferably from the same stable. The idea was that they should, theoretically, show the same level of improvement.'

'And did they?'

'A large percentage did, quite a few.'

'And you don't believe Capshaw would have held a grudge?'

'I know him quite well, Eddie, he was philosophical. We never ruled out sending some horses back to him.'

'And did you?'

'Not so far.'

I looked at him. 'Maybe he ran out of patience?'

Candy sighed. 'Even if we assume he did, do you really think he'd go to all this trouble to stick one up the Sheikh, for the sake of twenty lost training fees? Also, believe me, Alex Dunn has not been near those horses. Thirdly, what about the mares? Was Dunn giving them some sort of serum, too? And if he was, why are ours still aborting after his death?'

I didn't have any answers. Candy looked even more tired and depressed. His brown eyes duller, as if leaking hope.

'Do you want my help on this?' I asked.

'What I want, what I need more than anything else, Eddie, is for you to keep it quiet. I'm running out of options but I know that the only thing keeping me in a job is the fact that this hasn't got out yet.'

'You've got my word on it.'

He nodded, almost managed a tired smile.

I said, 'Come on, the show ain't over till the fat lady sings.'

He looked at me. 'I think she's doing her final warm-up in the dressing room.'

We talked some more and agreed that it would be unwise for me to be seen at The Gulf Stud. We arranged to meet again next morning, and Candy promised to have a full brief with him listing everything they'd done so far.

I expanded on my theory that Dunn hadn't killed himself then asked Candy, 'Can you find out exactly what effect a syringeful of prostaglandin would have on a man? I mean, chapter and verse: how it would actually kill him, how long he'd take to die, that sort of stuff.'

'Okay.' He noted it in a small leather-bound book. 'I'll speak to one of the vets and see you here at noon tomorrow.' I nodded. As he turned to get out, I asked about his two henchmen and how much they knew.

'Very little. They don't ask questions.' He grinned.

'What's so funny?'

'Their names are Phil and Don. I call them the Heavenly Brothers.'

'Most amusing. They were a big hit with me.'

'Sorry, Eddie.' But the grin grew wider, and when he left, I even managed a smile myself.

Chapter 37

I drove home at speed, boosted by renewed enthusiasm and relief at no longer having to face cracking this alone. All I needed was the link between Dunn and The Gulf Stud. I also felt considerably easier knowing Phil and Don wouldn't be paying me another visit.

Discovering Candy wasn't behind it all brought relief too, and a strong confidence boost. It had to be Capshaw or someone close to him. My only reservation now was Candy's insistence that Capshaw simply wasn't the type. Was the trainer being controlled in the same way Dunn had been?

One thing was certain: somebody connected to Capshaw had those blackmail papers. And they had to know I'd been doing the same as Martin at Ascot, so why no threat to publish? Maybe branding Martin was meant to scare me off too. And perhaps I'd be best pretending for the moment that I'd taken fright.

I called Charlie Harris, the racecourse photographer, who agreed to send me copies of all the pictures he'd taken at Ascot the day we'd been there. Then, still convinced that Dunn was a key figure, I spent the rest of the day and long into the night with his betting records. The bets were broken down between those placed 'live' on course by Dunn and those placed by phone. By the time I met Candy again next day, I had an extensive chart showing which courses Dunn had attended on which days over the past ten months.

Candy, informal for once in yellow polo shirt and cream trousers, stared at the hand-written columns covering a dozen pages. 'What's the point?' he asked.

'Those eight stallions. I need to see their racing records.'

'Why?'

'Because if you're convinced that security hasn't been breached at The Gulf by Dunn or an accomplice, then Dunn must have got at those stallions on the racecourse.'

'Impossible.'

'Why? Each of the stallions had to be in the racecourse stables. Dunn would have been one of the few people with legitimate access.'

'To do what? Every one of those stallions was tested for fertility before retirement and just afterwards. Every single one was satisfactory at the least. If anything was administered to them, it would have to have been after they'd finished racing.'

'But you've already said it was impossible for anyone to get at them once they'd entered the stud. You can't have it both ways, Candy. Now let me follow this hunch. Get me those racing records.'

He stared at me as though he wasn't sure he trusted my judgment.

I said, 'Come on, you've been negative for too long.'

His expression softened. 'Okay. Fair enough. You'll have them tomorrow.'

'Today. Ring me with them later.'

'No, it's not safe to talk on the phone.'

'Ring me from a call box.'

'I'll think about it. You'd better have a look at this first.' He opened his black briefcase and pulled out a grey laptop. He entered a password and sat the PC on my lap. 'When you're ready to start reading hit that button, but as soon as the text starts scrolling up you have to concentrate hard to take everything in. You can't return to anything you've missed because as each line moves up it's deleted. No copies can be printed and it's a real pain setting it up to run again. It's a complete record of what has happened and what steps we've taken.'

I nodded, bemused, then hit the start button and concentrated like a man with a DIY vasectomy kit.

Most of it was unabsorbable: dates, times and results of veterinary tests on horses with annoyingly similar Arab names, employee biographies including some fairly detailed sexual histories and one sudden death, monies paid out to various 'contractors', Phil and Don the most recent. And all the time, the words disappeared off the top of the screen as though some invisible harvester was scything them. After God knows how long I was left with a grey void.

Bug-eyed and brain fizzing, I asked Candy who was supposed to benefit from this blizzard of information.

'I told you, it's a complete record.'
'But what use is it?'
'It logs everything that's happened, everything we've done.'
'Oh, I must have missed that part, the bit about what you've done. If this is it, Candy, you've done nothing. You're no further forward. No wonder the old Sheikh's spitting sand. If you can't blind them with science, baffle them with bullshit. Is that the principle?'

He looked miffed. 'The principle is to keep the whole thing under wraps, and that's what we've achieved.'

I sighed and leaned back in my seat. 'My old mum found out more yesterday morning than you guys have in all the months this covers. You should have brought someone in ages ago, someone who knew what they were doing.'

'Eddie, it's too sensitive and you know it.'

He was getting huffy now, but I was angry that all this money had been spent on vets and tests and badly briefed private investigators. Angry that I was still pretty much where I'd been two days ago. I'd expected Candy to have some serious stuff offering good leads. He reached across and snapped the lid closed on the computer, then took it and stuffed it back into the case.

We sat in silence, giving each other time to cool off. Candy's window was open. I rolled mine down and the car sucked in a breeze that ruffled Candy's thick hair. He pushed it back into place and stared out at the trees.

One coldly reported fact that had scrolled past my eyes was the death of another vet. It stuck in my mind. I said, 'The vet who died, did they do a post mortem?'

'Heart attack so far as we know.'
'How old was he? What was his name again?'
'Simon Nish. He was thirty-four.'
'And he specialized in mares?'
'Uhuh. He was good.'
'But he didn't know what was making them abort?'
'No. It got him down badly.'
'Did he have a history of heart trouble?'
'Not that I know of. Why?'
'I don't know. It's young for a heart attack.'
'Not these days. I'm due about three myself.'

I looked across and smiled. Candy did too and that eased the tension. We talked some more about Simon Nish, who'd been found dead in bed at home just over two weeks ago. 'Definitely natural causes? No question of suicide?'

'Nope. Poor bugger probably died of exhaustion. He tested those mares to distraction, had his arm inside so many of them in was unusual to see him without a mare's arse attached to his shoulder.'

'And he had nothing to do with the stallions?'

'Nothing.'

'Never went near them?'

'What difference would it make if he did? He was trusted. He'd been with us for years.'

'I'm not slagging him off, Candy. I'm just trying to eliminate the possibility of him having been killed off as Dunn was.'

'He had absolutely no connection with Dunn.'

'Can you double check that?'

'I don't need to!'

'Candy, we're all on the same side here. Please just double-check it. Today if you can, and tell me tonight when you're confirming those stallion racing records.'

He bit his lip then nodded. Much more used to giving orders than obeying them, he was finding the adjustment tough. 'Did you get the details on the prostaglandin injection?' I asked.

He looked baffled.

'The thing that killed Dunn,' I said.

'Oh, yes. I spoke to one of our vets this morning.' He produced a black Dictaphone and pressed the rewind button then clicked to play, releasing the tinny voices. Candy first: 'How would an injection of five ccs of prostaglandin affect a human being?'

A slightly effeminate voice in which I could almost hear the flinch replied: 'Pretty grimly, I should think. Death would come from internal suffocation. First, you would feel sick, sweat heavily, the skin would turn very white as the shock effect hit the body. The chest, abdominal, and all other smooth muscle groups would contract, causing bronchial spasms then severe vomiting and diarrhea. As intense pressure built, the heart rate would increase rapidly and the system would quickly suffocate and cease functioning.'

'Painful.'

'Agonizing, I would guess.'

'How long before he'd die?'

'Three, maybe five, minutes.'

'Not the way you'd choose to go?'

'As the saying goes, I'll settle for being caught in bed with a young woman at

the age of eighty-seven, shot by her jealous husband.'

Candy clicked it off. I looked at him. 'Still think Dunn wasn't deeply involved in this?' I asked.

'I'm coming round. We just need something more solid.'

'Call me as soon as you can with those racing records. That's the next step.'

He rang from a call box just before seven that evening, and I noted the information on the racecourse appearances of the eight infertile stallions. 'What about the dead vet, Simon Nish? Definitely no links with Dunn?'

'Absolutely none.'

We agreed to meet in the lay-by next morning at 8.15.

Chapter 38

A thick mist rolled low over the flatlands. I drove through it, slowing automatically even though it reached only to the wheel-tops, making the car look like some air-cushioned vehicle in a sci-fi movie.

I was ten minutes early, but Candy was in the lay-by waiting. I got in his car and smiled. 'We can't keep meeting like this,' I said.

'You're cheery.'

'For good reason, my friend.'

He waited, anticipation in his eyes. I said, 'Your horses had a total of thirty-nine runs in the past eighteen months. Alex Dunn was at the course on every occasion.'

'In an official capacity?'

'I don't know, but he was definitely there.'

'But if he wasn't officiating, how would he have got access to the stables?'

'Come on, Candy, the security guys have known him for years. He'd walk into the stables without a question being asked.'

'Mmmm. I suppose that's possible. But I still think you're up against it statistically. The guy's job was on the racecourse, he must have been at the races more times than not. I'd have thought it would have been more unusual if he hadn't been there the thirty-nine times those horses ran.'

'But—'

'And, bear in mind that if we're now assuming those colts were got at before they were retired to stud, we're talking about investigating their different trainers, hundreds of stable staff, all the visitors to those yards including other vets. It's a fucking nightmare, Eddie!'

I was annoyed. I'd travelled here feeling very positive after working late and hard. I said, 'That doesn't mean you can ignore it. You can't just carry on building up reams of facts and figures, Candy. You need to take some action.'

'And how do we keep the damn thing out of the papers then?' He was almost shouting but it was end-of-the-tether stuff rather than anger at me. 'How do we work our way through, our detailed way through, all those people and not alert anybody?'

'That's why I'm saying, try it my way first. Believe me, Dunn is a very strong link, we've just got to build on it.'

'How?'

'We need to find out for sure if he visited the stables on each of those racedays. You know Peter McCarthy, Jockey Club Security. He'd be able to get the records checked. Every visitor should be logged.'

Candy looked nervous. He said, 'I can't risk making McCarthy suspicious.'

I thought for a minute then suggested he get one of the Sheikh's trainers to request the list. 'Tell him to tell Mac it's for an industrial tribunal hearing against a sacked lad or something. Ask for an additional few days outside those thirty-nine if you like, that'll help throw him off the scent if he does become suspicious.'

He looked at me as though I was crazy. 'Then the trainer would be suspicious!'

I sighed with frustration. 'Candy, this is the reason you've got nowhere on this so far. At some point you'll have to take a calculated risk.'

'It's not mine to take! How can I make you understand that?'

'Somebody has to bite the bullet. What about the Sheikh himself?'

'No way!'

'Why not? If nobody can make a proper decision without his approval then you're going to have to put it to him.'

He sat staring wide-eyed out of the window as the prospect sank home. 'Candy, if you don't, you'll be sitting here next year with maybe eighteen bloody stallions firing blanks and you no further forward. Believe me!'

He turned to me. 'Why don't you ask McCarthy? You know him. I'll make sure you get well paid if you can handle this side of things discreetly.'

'I told you before, I need to keep a low profile on this. I can't say why just now but I do. I'm willing to do anything you need behind the scenes, I'll direct the whole damned show if you want, but you're going to have to put a degree of trust in some people.'

He was shaking his head slowly. I said. 'Speak to the Sheikh. If you give him an honest summary of where you've got to, he will have to accept that something more needs to be done.'

Candy rested his elbow on the car window and chewed at his thumbnail. All that his expression told me was that he wanted the world to go away. I touched his arm. He turned slowly toward me, frowning, thumbnail still between his lips.

'Listen,' I said, 'you're fucked anyway, not to put too fine a point on it. Your boss won't tolerate this much longer, you admitted that yourself. The worst that can happen is that you bring things forward a month or two.'

I watched his eyes change. The frown faded and something of the old Candy came back with his smile. 'You're right, Eddie. What the hell? The job's not worth it anyway. I can do without it. I'll always work.'

'Of course you will, but don't admit defeat just yet. We can crack this if the Sheikh gives you a bit more of a free hand. When can you speak to him?'

'Tonight. I speak to him every night.'

'Good. Will you call me when you've talked?'

'Sure.'

I spent the rest of the day in my room trying to make a more detailed analysis of each horse's run, looking for a pattern. If my theory was right and Dunn was treating these horses in advance of their retirement to stud, then this chemical he was using had to be powerful stuff. I found one colt that went ten months between his last appearance on a racecourse and the announcement of his retirement. How the hell could Dunn's serum remain effective so long? And why were the horses showing up so positively in fertility tests well after Dunn must have got at them?

That night Candy rang. Sheikh Ahmad Saad had agreed to give him a much freer hand and had even volunteered to take a more active part himself. The Sheikh was a Jockey Club member and rather than having to ask McCarthy for that list of stable visitors, the Sheikh was going to request it himself via McCarthy's boss. No one would dream of asking the Sheikh for a reason, so confidentiality would be maintained.

Candy reckoned they'd have the list by tomorrow afternoon.

He had it before 11.30, and brought it with him for our daily meeting. I could tell by the satisfied look on his face as I sat beside him in the car that he'd come up with something. He handed me the list of stable visitors. On every one of the thirty-nine the name Alex Dunn appeared, gleaming in a broad yellow stroke of highlighting ink.

We smiled widely at each other and he reached over to shake my hand. 'Well done.'

'All in a day's work,' I said.

'What next?'

'That depends on your priorities. We need to find out what Dunn did to those colts, and we need to find out who was behind it.'

'How do you know he wasn't acting alone?'

'Well, what do you think? The guy couldn't even control his gambling habit. How's he supposed to plan something like this?'

I said. 'Capshaw has to be the next logical step. Dunn did a lot of work for him and as far as I know spent time at his place. He also spent plenty backing Capshaw's runners. That might have been part of the deal. Maybe Capshaw gave him information in exchange for damaging those horses.'

'You honestly think Dunn would try to destroy a multi-million pound business for the sake of a few tips from a trainer?'

'Maybe Capshaw put him up to it? I know you say he's not the vengeful type, but what else, who else might be involved on Capshaw's side?'

A big green van pulled into the lay-by and edged past to park fifty yards in front. We stopped talking and watched the driver's door. Nobody got out.

Candy said, 'If you don't think Dunn had the ability to organize this campaign then I'm telling you that Capshaw didn't either. I know him well. He's not up to it.'

I shrugged. 'Fine, so someone else is. But that still makes Capshaw the next link in the chain. It was after we followed him at Ascot that Martin was attacked and the pictures taken from him. Now, if Capshaw or some of his cronies didn't set that up, who did? We need to find out more about him, more about his personal life, his history.' I made a mental note to chase Charlie Harris for those pictures.

'Okay, I'll get a man onto it this morning. Anything else we should be doing?'

'What about Dunn? This chemical castration idea he first had years ago, he must have discussed it with other vets, surely?'

'Maybe.'

'If we could find out the basis of it, the particular chemical he had in mind, it might help us solve the second problem more quickly. Even if we never catch the people behind this, at least with an antidote the stallions would be back to normal.'

'If only.'

We sat in silence for a while then I said, 'Bear in mind that if this is guy hates the Sheikh enough, he probably hasn't finished yet. He could already have someone else out there. If not, he'll want to recruit a replacement for Dunn.'

Candy nodded, looking grim.

I said, 'Put a man on Dunn's past too if you can. And maybe somebody could check with removal companies to see if any of them picked up stuff from his place out at Six Mile Bottom. It would be nice to know where all his lab kit and papers are now. That would cut through a hell of a lot of the crap.'

'Leave it with me.' Candy noted it in his little leather book then said, 'What are you doing for the rest of the day?'

'I'm going to bed to try and give my brain a rest. I haven't had a decent sleep for weeks. Then I'm going to go for a long sweaty run in the hope that a few more pieces get jogged into place. Can you give me a call this evening if there's anything to report on Capshaw and Dunn?'

'This evening? You're hopeful.'

'Let me know anyway, even if it's something that seems insignificant.'

'Okay.'

Back at the stud, I rang Charlie Harris and asked him to send those Ascot shots as soon as possible.

Chapter 39

I put on my running gear. Leaving by the back door, I headed across the fields into the woods, building up a pace I knew I could maintain for miles.

And I started again to dissect the scraps of information in my mind. I had the niggling feeling that I'd overlooked something or misinterpreted it, so I mentally broke down the structure I'd built and tried to look again at each of the individual pieces. The steady rhythm of my feet on the forest floor seemed to help the process.

Most of my discussions with Candy had been centred on the conspiracy against the stallions and the commercial fallout. The deaths of Brian Kincaid and Alex Dunn had somehow faded into the background. My guess now was that Brian had simply been unlucky that I'd approached him about Town Crier.

Dunn had been his mentor to a large extent, and Brian would have been aware of Dunn's interest in chemical castration and sought his help to solve Town Crier's problem. Recalling Dunn's frightened reaction the day I confronted him at Newmarket, Brian's approach a few days before mine would have panicked him. If Dunn had blabbed about Brian to whoever was running this, the decision to kill him would have been taken quickly.

What effect would that have had on Dunn? I was assuming he had some affection for Brian and maybe at first believed the sauna death was an accident. What if he later came to a different conclusion? Would he have been horrified? Terrified? Would he have planned to go to the police? Was that why he disappeared so suddenly? Was he removed from the equation, kept alive for as long as he was useful then killed off like Brian?

Toward the southern edge of the forest, shafts of sunlight through the tall trees sliced my moving shadow into fragments.

Brian Kincaid. Whoever was running things hadn't killed him personally. He had hired someone to do it. I'd been so blinkered about Tranter, I'd never given the matter any objective thought. As I did so now I realized how stupid I'd been. The fact that Brian had died in a sauna in the weighing room narrowed down the potential murderers dramatically.

The killer must have been well known on the racecourse. At Stratford at the very least, but more probably around other courses too. Jockeys and valets, trainers and racecourse officials, were the only ones entitled to use the weighing room area. The changing room itself was restricted to jockeys and their valets.

So, if it wasn't Tranter then it was another jockey, or a trainer, valet or official. A simple check through the newspapers or racecard for that day would tell me almost every one of the above who'd been at Stratford. Valets would be difficult, but if pushed I could probably come up with most of their names from memory.

Such a modern contraption as a shower was unheard of in my parents' house, and I had to settle for a cool bath before changing into jeans and a white T-shirt. I called Candy but got his answerphone. I left a message then drove into town to find a betting shop.

The manager agreed to dig through his file copies of The Sporting Life till he found the one from Stratford. I took it to the local library, photocopied the section I needed then returned it. I had no inclination to do any more work in that small cell I slept in at the stud, so I set off for the library again where I settled in the reading room to study the Stratford card from that day.

Working through the list of trainers and jockeys, I tried the simple method of rejecting those I considered incapable of murder. It didn't take long to go through the card without ticking even one suspect. I then tried going through again and awarding points in a sort of Man Most Likely To Murder game, nobody notched up more than three.

Next, I did racecourse officials, but apart from the two who scored very highly on boring people to death, I came up empty again. Valets were about the only ones whose names weren't published so, using pen and pad, I worked up a list from memory: six valets, all of whom I'd known for years. I'd have bet my life none would have killed a cat, never mind Brian Kincaid.

And yet somebody among all those I'd just discounted had murdered him. A stranger might gain access to the weighing room for a few minutes before being rumbled, but no way would he get to the sauna and, indeed, spend some time inside, as he must have done with Brian.

But...Brian would have gone in there after the last race. People would be packing up and heading home, rushing around. Maybe a stranger would have got further than usual at that time. The valets would be the guys to talk to. Their duties meant they were usually last to leave the weighing room. I scribbled a few more names and resolved to get contact numbers for them.

That too would have to be done through Candy, as I still couldn't risk putting my head above the parapet. Outside the library, I called him: answerphone. I tried Candy ten times over the next two hours without success and after hearing the start of his answerphone message yet again, I shouted in rage and frustration.

This reliance on others was really beginning to piss me off. I was finding it very tough to handle the fact that I couldn't simply ring up someone I wanted to ask a question of or jump in the car and go to the races.

Candy finally contacted me that evening with nothing new to report. Still annoyed at him, I complained that I hadn't been able to reach him all day and he got spiky, saying he had a business to run and couldn't sit waiting for me. It developed into a childish argument fuelled by my frustration. In the end, I apologized and explained why I was so wound up.

Candy said, 'Don't worry, I can get one of my guys to speak to all the valets that were at Stratford, see what they remember.'

'Which guy?'

'One of the investigators who's been working for me.'

'Racing man?'

'Well, no, but he knows his stuff.'

'Come on, Candy, valets are hardly going to be falling over themselves to tell him what they know. And not just valets, everyone else. Shit, you know how secretive racing people can be!'

'Well, what else do you suggest? Why don't you go and do it?'

'I've told you, I can't fucking do it!' Bitter frustration again. I apologized immediately.

'Forget it, Eddie. I know you're under pressure.'

'I'm sorry, Candy. I'll tell you about it when this is all over.'

'Eddie, promise me it's nothing that will affect your confidentiality on this?'

'I promise. Don't worry, I promise.'

There was a long pause then Candy said quietly, 'You okay?'

'Yeah.' I didn't sound okay and I knew it. 'I'll call you tomorrow.'

I flipped the phone closed and laid it on the quilt, then sat rocking back and forth till I ended up elbows on knees, head in hands, almost crying with frustration in this big silent loveless house; feeling my life dry up, feeling this place and my parents sucking the life from my every pore, killing me slowly but just as surely as that terrible sauna had done to Brian Kincaid.

Unable to face the night here, I shoved a few things in an overnight bag and drove into Newmarket, booked a hotel, went on a pub-crawl, got as drunk as ten men and opened my eyes in the morning with a blank mind and a major headache.

Unable to stomach breakfast, I paid my bill and left to take a long walk up to the gallops to try to clear my head. It was one of those hangovers where your brain is two seconds behind everything else that's happening to you, and after an hour, I decided that the best place for me was bed.

Praying I wouldn't be stopped and breathalyzed, I drove to my parents' place. As I approached the stud, I became aware of a flashing blue light through the trees. When I was a hundred yards from the drive an ambulance pulled out from it and, light still flashing, accelerated away. I swung fast and hard into the drive, jumped out and ran, cursing my shaking hands as I tried to separate the front door key from the others.

I leaned on the bell with my shoulder as I fought to find the key. Finally inside, I bolted upstairs. My father's room was empty, the door open, bedcovers pulled back. If he was gone, Mother would be with him.

Within five minutes, I'd caught up with the ambulance. I trailed it to Cambridge Hospital.

Chapter 40

Almost certainly pneumonia, but they'd have to run a few tests before offering a prognosis. We settled in the waiting area. Mother looked as though she'd aged ten years. Distraught but silent she stared at the wall, deaf to words of comfort. After a while, I just sat in silence beside her, suffering an appalling thirst and a burning headache and a scorched conscience for not being there when I was needed. Ashamed too that I was sitting with my mother, at this time of the morning, unkempt and unshaven and stinking of booze.

But even at my lowest ebb, I couldn't find any real sorrow or sympathy for my father. It crossed my mind that he might die and that caused me no dismay, the opposite in fact, which did make me feel a twinge of coldness. But no guilt.

After more than two hours a doctor invited us into a small office and told us that Father would have to stay in hospital for a 'considerable period.'

'How long?' I asked.

'Six weeks, maybe more. He is very weak. His lungs are badly infected.'

'Will he die?' Mother asked. I looked at her to see if she was really prepared for the answer. She gazed at the young doctor with intense concentration.

'If he responds to treatment, he has an excellent chance of returning to full health.'

'Is there any reason he shouldn't respond to treatment?' she asked.

'Occasionally it happens.'

'When will we know?'

He smiled. 'Within a week or so.'

Mother straightened in her chair. 'I'd like to stay with him.'

'I'm afraid that would be difficult, certainly in the early stages. Your husband will be treated in ICU - sorry, the Intensive Care Unit. We simply don't have the staff to cope with twenty-four-hour visiting.'

I looked at Mother who was staring past him now, into the distance, the future, her eyes clouding with misery. I thanked the doctor and helped her out. Dazed, she leant heavily on me all the way to the car. I took her home, promising to bring her back as soon as she'd packed what she needed. I told her I'd find her a room in a hotel close to the hospital so that she could spend as much time with Father as they'd allow.

This financially rash promise brought to mind my last bank statement. Six or eight weeks of hotel bills. Whatever fee Candy was going to pay would have to be good.

My mother spoke little. She moved silently around the house looking at things, touching small ornaments, gazing through the window across the fields. It was as though she feared she'd never come home again. Eventually she wandered upstairs and I heard her go into my father's room. I knew then what I had to do.

After five minutes, I walked in to find her sitting in her usual chair, staring at the bed. I put my hand on her shoulder. She didn't acknowledge me. I said, 'Come on, Mum, I've made some tea. We have to talk.' I led her gently to the kitchen and sat her down at the big beech table.

I stirred sugar into her tea and pushed it across to her. She stared into the swirling liquid. 'Drink some,' I said. 'It'll help.'

She lifted the cup and sipped mechanically. After another silent minute, she looked at me and said, 'It's the pressure of this that's killing him.' We both knew what 'this' meant. And although she added nothing, it was implicit in her eyes that she thought I should somehow have done something to prevent it, to catch the people who might expose us, to make the future safe.

I said, 'I know, Mum. I have to find whoever's doing this.'

She nodded slowly, robotically, and sipped tea again. When we returned to the hospital, I'd ask that she be checked for shock. I drank some tea then said, 'Listen, the way we decided to do this, to lie low, make it look as if we'd pulled out - it's not going to work.'

She raised her tired eyes again to watch me almost like a disinterested observer.

I said, 'It's causing too many complications. It could drag on for months and months and I'm not sure Father can stand it that long. I think I'm going to have to go for these people, all out. That way we either stop them quickly or at least we get the painful part over with.' Her look changed to one I recognized, one that said, You don't understand, do you?

She spoke. 'It will never be over with, not if it gets out. People will never let it be over with. It would kill your father.'

I leaned toward her, wanting to take her hand, squeeze some reassurance into it. 'Mum, it's killing him now, slowly and painfully. The waiting's killing him. I'm sure I've got enough to go on now to crack this in a couple of weeks at the most.'

That was a lie but I could live with it. She said. 'Would we have to tell him?'

'If we didn't, and the news got out, could you live with it if he thought you'd…' deceived was the wrong word '…kept it from him?'

She gave the smallest of shrugs and her expression changed. She was trying to convey something with her eyes but I couldn't read it. She spelt it out. 'Maybe he would think you'd kept it from both of us.'

My heart sank. I said, 'Will there ever be a point in my life where you'll want him to see me in a fair light? Is it always going to be me that's to blame for everything that's gone wrong in this family?' She stared stony-faced at me, and I knew that so long as he was alive my father would be all that mattered to her. So I resolved then to do it with or without their approval, knowing that the whipping boy was on another hiding to nothing.

As I left, I saw that the Ascot pictures had come in the post. I picked up the thick envelope and took it with me.

I found a small hotel within a five-minute taxi ride of the hospital, booked my mother in, wrote the wide-eyed proprietor a cheque for a thousand pounds, and promised Mother I'd ring every night at the very least and try to make the visiting hours whenever I could.

I'd cleaned myself up before leaving the stud and although my hangover still simmered, the prospect of action started the adrenalin pumping again. I felt good. Nervous but good. I called Candy, got him first time.

'I'm coming out of the closet,' I said.

'Meaning?'

'You've got yourself another private dick.'

'No comment.'

I smiled. 'Candy, can you arrange an advance on my fee for this?'

'Sure. How much?'

'Five grand.'

'Is that the advance or the fee?'

'The advance.'

'You don't work cheap.'

'I don't think it'll make too much of a dent in the half a million you've already spent on this.'

'True. Very true.'

'Can you transfer it direct to my bank today? I'd like it to catch a cheque that's about to drop from a great height.'

'Give me your bank details.'

I called McCarthy next. 'Thought you'd died,' he said when he heard my voice.

'Felt like it when I woke up this morning.'

'Mister Booze?'

'That's the man.'

'Well, you should be sleeping it off so why are you calling me?'

'I'm back on the Brian Kincaid case.'

He sighed. 'Eddie, the case is that the police could find no evidence of suspicious circumstances.'

'On account of that evidence being reduced to a very fine grey ash.'

'Maybe, but what were they supposed to do next?'

'What I'm about to do, if you can give me a little help, Mac?'

'A little or a lot?'

'I need the names of all the valets working at Stratford that day, just by way of a double check.'

'Why?'

'Because I want to speak to them.'

'Why?'

'Because I think I might learn something,'

'You're in one of your determined moods again, aren't you?'

'Make a bulldog look meek.'

He promised to call me within a couple of hours. It took a bit longer, but by early evening I had eight names, six of whom I knew well. I reckoned at least four of the eight would be at Uttoxeter next day. I'd turn up at the track and see how they reacted to a few informal questions.

Chapter 41

I don't think I can remember going to Uttoxeter on a dry day. The rainclouds must see my car coming and hurry over to the course to guarantee the usual wet welcome. Today was no different, though trainers and owners travelling in the same direction would have little complaint about the weather. It had been a long dry summer of firm racing ground.

Most trainers preferred good or soft going before risking their horses. Galloping and jumping on jarring ground can damage a horse's legs.

As I pulled into the car park, I checked the back seat to make sure I'd brought my riding gear. I'd nothing booked but it paid to come prepared. There were still two hours before the first and most of the valets would be fairly relaxed. Their job is to look after a jockey's kit, make sure it's kept clean, that saddles, girths and stirrups are safe, that the correct amount of weight is loaded into the saddle 'cloths' if necessary.

They also act as friends, confessors, marriage guidance counselors, hairdressers, denture finders, bankers, and God knows what else. The camaraderie in the changing room can be as addictive as the most powerful drug. Many valets are ex-jockeys, hooked for life.

Half a dozen of them were already there making preparations. Two of them had been at Stratford. I filled three Styrofoam cups from the tea urn and went to join them in the corner.

We chatted for a while then I steered the conversation round to Brian Kincaid's death. They were happy to talk about that day at

Stratford and answered my questions openly, but neither had seen anything they'd have called suspicious; no strangers hanging around, no odd behaviour from any of the other jocks. And neither could remember any particular racecourse official showing his face.

While we were talking, two of the other valets who'd been at Stratford turned up, and I managed to grab five minutes with each of them. But I learned nothing new. Before leaving I spoke to all four again, asking who had been last to leave the racecourse that day. Pete Crilly, who was my valet, said the only person still in the weighing room when he'd left had been Ken Rossington, also known as Oz.

I didn't know Rossington as well as the others. He'd been a valet for just over a year after arriving in Britain from Australia. He was a bit of a practical joker, always looking to create a laugh at someone's expense, but he seemed a nice enough guy. Crilly said Rossington told him on Monday he was having a few days off but that he was fairly sure he'd be at Bangor tomorrow.

Something about Rossington came to me. That day at Stratford when Brian had moved aside to let Tranter past, he'd stood on Rossington's foot and the valet had made a considerable song and dance of it. If Rossington had been that close, there was every chance he would have heard Brian say he was planning to use the sauna after racing.

I picked up a spare in the fifth that finished nowhere but jumped well enough for me to enjoy the ride round. The riding fee more than paid my expenses for the day, and the rain stayed off during the race only to resume as I drove home, wipers swishing at double speed.

Ten minutes from the yard, my mobile rang. It was Candy. He had the reports on both Capshaw and Dunn. 'Anything interesting?' I asked.

'Not really, unless you can see something I haven't spotted.'

'Are the reports actually in written form?'

'All neatly typed. Six pages on each.'

'I'll be at the yard shortly. Can you fax them to me?'

'Is that safe?'

'If you make sure you dial the right number it will be.'

'Okay, what is it?'

I told him.

The reports were hanging from the fax machine when I got to my flat, and I read while the kettle boiled. Candy had been right. Nothing was of any real interest, just gossip, mostly about Capshaw. Dunn seemed to have led a solitary life. His father had also been a compulsive gambler who had achieved 'the impossible' by quitting for good after a major win. Dunn hadn't been so lucky.

I called Candy.

'Well?' he asked.

'Dross.'

'I thought so. What next?'

'Good old-fashioned legwork.' I told him about Rossington the valet and that I was hoping to see him at Bangor. Then I talked again about my gut feeling that Capshaw was the key to the way forward. I'd been putting a scheme together in my mind over the last twenty-four hours. I told Candy what it was, and advised him to begin preparing for it. He said, 'You know how to make a bloke nervous, Eddie.'

'All in a good cause. Start practicing. And listen, I need you to look through some pictures of the people Capshaw was with at Ascot, see if you can identify any of them.'

'Fine, whenever you're ready.'

Chapter 42

I was at Bangor by noon and found Rossington already in the weighing room, spit-polishing a boot slipped over his arm.

'Hi,' I said.

'Hi, Eddie, how are you?'

'I'm okay. You?'

'Good fettle.' He swiped a shine into the long black boot with the red-banded top. 'Don't know why they don't make these buggers all the one colour, you know, life would be a damn sight easier for us guys.' He stopped polishing, leaned forward, his sandy-coloured fringe dropping into his eyes as he winked at me. 'Not that I'm complaining, Eddie, know what I mean?'

I wasn't quite sure I did but I let it go. 'Did you have a good break?' I asked. He looked puzzled. 'Somebody mentioned you were taking a few days off.' For a microsecond, I thought anger sparked in his eyes, though I couldn't be certain. He polished harder. 'Just caught up on my kip,' he said. 'Too many late nights, early mornings and long trips. To racecourses, I mean.'

I hadn't thought he meant anything else. Rossington seemed nervous. It was the first time I'd said more than hello or goodbye to him, and I didn't know whether he was always like this when the lads weren't around to be entertained or if he was hiding something.

I asked him about Stratford and Brian Kincaid. He polished faster, his voice flat as though making a conscious effort to keep it steady. And he wouldn't meet my eyes.

After a minute talking about Brian, he seemed to settle again, become calmer.

'Did you see him go into the sauna?' I asked.
'Can't say I did, I'm afraid.'
'Were you around quite late that day?'
'Not that I can remember, no later than usual.'
'Weren't you the last to leave?'
'No, definitely not. Pete Crilly was still there when I left, I'm sure he was.'

That wasn't what Pete had said. Rossington still wouldn't look at me. He knew something. I thanked him, and left to call Candy but got his answerphone. I hung around the weighing room for a while, saw Pete Crilly and briefly considered checking with him if he was sure Rossington was the last man left at Stratford.

But he'd been certain on Thursday and I didn't want him asking Rossington to confirm it. The Australian seemed nervous enough already.

Candy rang. I told him about Rossington and asked him to find out what he could about the guy, not forgetting he'd spent most of his life in Australia. 'That might take a while.' Candy said.

'I ain't doing anything else in the meantime.' I said.
'Okay.'
'What about our other cunning little plan, have you spoken to the boss?'
'He's given the go ahead.'
'Good, I thought he might. When do we start?'
'Monday. Windsor. I'm not looking forward to it.'
'Into every life a little rain must fall.'
'Except that this time every other bastard's going to be under cover watching me get wet.'
'Pack your shampoo. You can wash that lovely hair of yours.'
'Very funny, Eddie. It's not you who's going to be humiliated.'
'That makes a change, believe me. Call me if you learn anything, especially about Rossington. I'll be back in Cambridge this evening to see my father.'
'How is he?'
'No change. A very long-standing diagnosis.'
'Pardon?'
'Nothing. Maybe we can meet for breakfast tomorrow.'
'Call me this evening when you reach Cambridge, and we'll arrange a time.'
'Fine.'

Only twenty minutes remained of the visiting period when I

reached the hospital, which didn't dismay me unduly. Father was sitting up, eyes closed but breathing on his own, albeit through lungs that sounded like decayed organ pipes. Mother was in her customary position by the bed, holding his thin jaundiced-looking hand. She looked more contented than when I'd last seen her. We nodded to each other and I gently placed the fruit I'd brought on the bedside cabinet.

I mouthed the words, 'How is he?' Mother nodded slowly and it was only when we got outside I learned there had been no change. She'd decided to treat this as positive news. I offered to take her to dinner but she said she'd rather go back to the hotel to be by the telephone. I took her there, and then returned to the stud to spend the night.

Candy thought it unwise for us to be seen having breakfast together. We met in our old reliable lay-by where he told me that the feelers were still out on Rossington, and that it might be midweek before he'd have any news on him.

It was a warm morning. We rolled the windows down and sat looking through the pictures Charlie Harris had sent me. Most of the shots had been taken either in the parade ring before each race or in the winner's enclosure afterwards. Capshaw's party in the last race featured in nineteen photos, a mixture from the same general pool in each.

Most of the pics were of the celebrations after the Guterson's Gloves-sponsored race that the company had won with its own horse, trained by Capshaw. Candy pointed to the smiling face of Bob Guterson. 'I've seen him around.'

'Bob Guterson. Owned the winner. Got three others in training with Capshaw.'

He nodded, scanned the others then stopped and held one up to the light. 'See the guy in the corner, grey hair, dark suit?'

The face was indistinct in the background, slightly out of focus. 'Uhuh?'

'I think that's Simeon Prior. What on earth would he be doing with that lot?'

'Who's Simeon Prior when he's at home?'

'He's the chairman of one of the biggest sales companies in Europe.'

'Sales?'

'Bloodstock sales. An outfit called Triplecrown.' He squinted closer. 'Could you get this one blown up?'

'Sure. Do you think there's any significance in Prior's being there?'

'They're simply not his type, Capshaw and this Guterson, a rubber-glove-maker.'

I looked again at the picture. 'Are you sure he is with them? He's standing well away from the main team.'

Candy shrugged. 'I don't know. It just seems odd. He seldom goes racing.'

'You know him well?'

'Not really, met him a couple of times, said hello.'

'I'll get an enlargement done.'

Candy flicked through three more and stopped at one in the parade ring. He smiled and pointed to an attractive blonde woman presenting what I assumed was the prize to the lad for the Best Turned Out Horse in the Guterson's Gloves race. 'Know who that is?' he asked.

She seemed vaguely familiar but I couldn't name her. 'Jean Kerman,' Candy said. 'Mean Jean.'

Kerman was the vicious gossip columnist who specialized in sports. She'd been the one Spindari had threatened us with. 'Is that her?' I asked in surprise.

'She's all right, isn't she?' Candy said. 'Doesn't look poisonous from here.'

'What the hell's she doing presenting the prize?'

'Maybe Mister Guterson had a giant Hooley to celebrate his sponsorship. They normally invite press and celebs, these corporate people.' Almost every race sponsor has a private box and makes a major day out of it, inviting business contacts and sometimes paying celebrities to mix with guests. The only reason for my suspicion was that Capshaw was in there somewhere. Everyone else in these pictures might well be completely innocent, but Capshaw was in deep.

It was getting hot in the car. We got out and walked to the end of the lay-by then back again. Candy wore an immaculate fawn suit, pale blue shirt and very expensive-looking shoes. Despite his year-round tan, he looked drawn.

'You're not looking forward to tomorrow, are you?' I asked.

'Not in the least.'

'It's for the best.'

'I know it is.'

'What's the plan?'

'Jidda runs in the first at Windsor. He cost us two point two million, bought on my advice. Wherever he finishes, the Sheikh is going to tell the press he feels he was badly advised, that he paid too much.'

'Even if he wins easily?'

'Yes. He'll do it another two or three times till they're in no doubt I'm not flavour of the month.'

'Then the word will spread that you're on your way out.'

He nodded.

'It'll be an interesting experiment in finding out who your friends are.'

'A very clinical summary, Eddie. I wonder if you'd be quite so nonchalant about it if you were the guinea pig?'

'Maybe not. I'm sorry, I didn't mean to make it sound like nothing at all, but everything will be put right once we catch these people. The Sheikh will tell the press then about the whole plot, won't he?'

'I don't know. I just hope he tells them enough to recover my reputation. What's left of it.'

'Don't worry.'

'One of the easiest used phrases in the English language, usually spoken by those who have no worries themselves.'

I looked across at him as we walked. His face was grim.

Chapter 43

By the end of the following week, everybody in racing knew Candy was for the chop. The racing media are too protective of their own to break a story like this, but one of the tabloids featured a paragraph about 'unrest', as they put it, between the Sheikh and his racing manager, confirming also that Candy had almost three years of a five-year contract to run.

Nothing happened that week to help us. Rossington, the Australian valet, came up cleaner than bones from an acid bath. Using Candy's private investigators to compile personal histories of suspects had quickly become a lazy habit. I gave Candy the names of all the racecourse officials and the other valets at Stratford that day, and asked for a report on each.

If they came through clean, I wondered how long I'd be able to resist setting Candy's investigators on my fellow jockeys. Brian's killer was seldom out of my mind now and unless I accepted that a stranger had somehow gained access to the weighing room, then it had to be someone who knew Brian.

I'd called Mac again and pressed him about Tranter's alibi with the Steward and the car crash. I wanted to be absolutely certain that he was out of the picture. Mac assured me he'd had word straight from the mouth of the Steward concerned. He could think of no reason why the man in question would simply have concocted that story.

I suggested Tranter might have had something on him. Mac said if he did then it hadn't affected the Steward's judgment three days ago when he'd stood Tranter down for what some had thought was a minor offence. Fair point.

That brought me full circle to the conclusion that someone in the weighing room that afternoon killed Brian Kincaid. My mind returned to how nervous Rossington had seemed when I first questioned him, and toward the end of what was probably the worst week of Candy's life I met him at the lay-by again and prodded him to get a double check done on the Australian. 'Why do you want another report? We've already done one?'

'A gut feeling. He was uncomfortable when I was questioning him.'

'Eddie, he didn't kill anybody. He has no history of crime or violence. He worked with sheep and horses in Australia. Came from Melbourne racetrack with good references.'

'Candy, he was nervous!'

'So maybe he's been smuggling fucking kangaroos or something! For Christ's sake, Eddie, gimme a break with these fucking personal profiles! They're costing more than the horses!'

I shut up for a while to let him cool down. Finally, he said, 'Sorry. I didn't mean to blow like that. It's been a bad week.'

'Yeah, my fault. I'm afraid I'm not the most sensitive guy in the world.'

'Leave Rossington with me, I'll ask them to have another look.'

'No, it's okay. Just get me the name and number of the guy who compiled that profile. Maybe he can tell me something or give me a few of his sources.'

'It would be best if I had him call you.'

'Fine, give him my mobile number.'

We walked in silence for a while. 'I'm going to see Capshaw tonight,' he said.

'Have you spoken to him?'

'Met him at Sandown yesterday.'

'Does he know what you have in mind?'

'I doubt it.'

We got back in the car. Candy sat rigid in the seat for a few seconds then leant forward, elbows on steering wheel, face in his hands.

I said, 'You'll be okay, Candy. You'll pull it off.'

He continued rubbing his eyes and temples, then his hands went down and he sat back, leaning against the headrest and triggering a long sigh. 'You think everybody finds this sort of stuff as easy as you do, Eddie. Why? Why do you think everybody sees things the same way as you, thinks the same way?'

'I don't.'

He turned to me. 'You do. You ought to listen to yourself sometime, watch yourself performing.'

Performing?

I smiled. 'You're performing pretty well yourself this morning, going all prima donna-ish on me. I'm not asking you to play King Lear. Just go to Capshaw's and be convincing, which means being nervous and hesitant and insecure, all the things you're feeling anyway. That's what he'll expect, not a command performance. 'Cos you look like a movie star it doesn't mean that's what everyone expects you to be.'

He sighed again. Then smiled.

'What time are you seeing him?' I asked.

'Seven-thirty.'

'I'll be in the royal box, cheering you on.'

The plan was for Candy to approach Capshaw and offer him a three-year contract to train ten of the Sheikh's horses. Candy would confess he'd fallen out of favour with the Sheikh and that he thought his employer was going to get rid of him soon, but that he still had the power to sign contracts that would have to be honoured or bought off for large amounts.

He'd say that, to take revenge on the Sheikh, he intended to approach five trainers offering this contract based on a fifty-fifty cut from the compensation money when the Sheikh subsequently cancelled. Capshaw was to be the first trainer on his list.

The purpose of the exercise was to flush out the lizards.

We reckoned that if they were still looking for a replacement for Alex Dunn, someone to carry on the sabotage at The Gulf Stud, then they would be sorely tempted to recruit Candy, an embittered member of staff with the power to do untold damage personally or else quietly put someone in place that could do it after he'd gone.

I wanted to see Candy as soon as I could after he left Capshaw's yard, but he was nervous about meeting twice in one day, especially if it meant coming to the lay-by again. He reluctantly agreed to drive to a derelict farm we both knew within two miles of my parents' stud. I reminded him to take his Dictaphone to Capshaw's.

I'd been waiting at the farm since 8.30, parked behind a half-ruined grey stone wall. I stood by the corner of it now, and as twilight fell on the empty fields, I watched the road junction half a mile away. By 9.45, I was getting worried about Candy. Maybe Capshaw had twigged the plan and called in the big guns. But how could he have known? There was no way.

The doubts niggled until I saw a car slow and turn down the track toward the farm, headlights bouncing wildly on the uneven ground. I waited until I was certain it was Candy before stepping out as he nosed along the weed-strewn drive and parked.

As Candy approached I noticed how much more relaxed he seemed. The stiffness and tension of this morning had gone from his limbs and he moved like the natural athlete he was. No frown either. He looked pretty pleased with himself.

I smiled. 'It went well, obviously.'

His white teeth flashed in the dusk. 'Hook and line. Sinker maybe tomorrow or the next day.'

'Brilliant.'

We leant on the bonnet of my car and he replayed the tape on his Dictaphone. At first Capshaw acted dumb about Candy's troubles with the Sheikh, though I got the impression his reaction was aimed at not embarrassing Candy. When he realized the whole subject was the reason for Candy's visit, he listened more and talked less. Until, of course, Candy offered him the horses; then he became very animated.

Capshaw cooled as the proposal was revealed. He seemed more interested in having the Sheikh's horses back than collecting a large compensation payment for breach of contract. I warmed to him for that.

But Candy played it smart and said that although the Sheikh might want out of some of the contracts, he did need to place horses with new trainers and there would be a chance, bearing in mind how well Capshaw had taken the Sheikh's previous clear-out of his stable, that the Sheikh would let him keep this batch for the full term.

Capshaw began asking about the horses Candy planned to give him, their breeding, cost at the sales, etc. Candy said he couldn't really give details at this stage but promised that, since Capshaw was the first he'd approached, he'd let him have his pick.

The trainer's enthusiasm increased a few notches then, and it was some time before he seemed to realize that maybe someone else might have an interest in this, at which point he started cooling off. He asked Candy if he could wait for an answer. It might be tomorrow or maybe in a couple of days. Candy said, of course, don't worry, no problem, and generally left Capshaw with the impression that there wasn't a high degree of urgency. But he did say he couldn't wait longer than a week. Capshaw promised him a call tomorrow.

Candy clicked the tape off and looked at me. 'What do you think?'

'I think that Mister William Capshaw is not the brightest guy in the world. He seemed far too open. I'd have thought he would have showed some suspicion at least. It only confirms to me that someone else is running things. I just wonder what hold they've got over him.'

'Me too.'

We never got to find out.

Chapter 44

The call from Capshaw didn't come. When we heard early on Wednesday morning of his death, the sense of dejection, almost despair, was palpable. I thought Candy was going to quit on the spot. Candy got hold of a copy of the police report, which said Capshaw had received a call just before 10 on Tuesday night, and immediately told his wife he had to go out. He gave no reason but said he'd be home by midnight.

A police patrol found him dead under his car in the early hours of Wednesday, on a straight stretch down by Six Mile Bottom. It seemed he'd been changing a wheel when he'd been hit by a passing vehicle that hadn't stopped. The impact had shattered his pelvis, severed his spine and driven the jack out of its support, causing the car to collapse and crush Capshaw's skull.

The police had taken the unusual step of sparing Mrs. Capshaw the ordeal of identifying the body, and had accepted the head lad's assurance that the corpse was indeed Capshaw's.

The police were seeking a dark blue vehicle that probably had bull bars fitted at the front, though they did not think it had been a jeep.

We'd gone through the report back at our derelict farm, standing in the sunshine leaning against Candy's car. He folded the papers and threw them in disgust through the open window onto the seat. He was angry too about Capshaw's death. He'd quite liked him.

'What now?' he asked.

'We find out who called Capshaw. Whoever it was must have arranged the rather convenient puncture and equally convenient hit and run.' Candy stared and I could see he was baffled by my certainty.

I said, 'Between you seeing Capshaw and him getting that call, something happened. Whether he took cold feet and wanted out or Mister Big decided Capshaw had made a big mistake talking to you, who knows, but Capshaw had obviously served his purpose. Whoever the guy is, Capshaw was scared of him, scared enough to go dashing out as soon as he received the call.'

'So how do we find out who made it?'

'Why don't you ask your contact to get hold of the phone records? I'm sure the cops will have requested them already.'

Candy nodded thoughtfully then said, 'The guy's hardly going to be stupid enough to call from his own base.'

'Probably not, but who knows?'

'What if this Mister Big, as you call him, approaches me direct?'

'All the better, but I doubt it.'

We stood in silence for a while then Candy said, 'What if we can't trace the call?'

I shrugged. 'Rulers and pencils out and back to the drawing board.'

'Oh, fine! I feel I've been pinned to the drawing board this last week or so, and half my fucking life's been erased!'

'No point in giving up now then, is there? Let's get you sketched in again. We'll see if we can make a better job of you second time around.'

To his credit, he managed a smile.

The phone records showed the call to Capshaw came from a public telephone in Cambridge. Candy became disheartened. I told him we must press on and try to find out who killed Brian Kincaid at Stratford. The candidates were relatively few and that offered us the best chance of success.

The guy who'd compiled the profile on Ken Rossington called me at Candy's request, and we talked about his sources and what he'd found out. Rossington's persona in Australia - reserved, industrious, a private man - sounded quite different from the one he'd adopted when he'd stepped off the plane over a year ago. Unless Qantas had started dishing out personality changes along with the in-flight meals, then Rossington had transformed himself virtually overnight into the ebullient practical joker who now inhabited the weighing room.

I wondered where Rossington had been the day Alex Dunn died. I called McCarthy who came back fairly promptly with the information that Rossington had not been racing that day, so he could have been at my parents' stud injecting prostaglandin into Alex Dunn and tying me on to that mare.

Maybe a quiet spot of tailing Mr. Rossington for a day or two might pay off. I pestered McCarthy again to find out where he would be next day. Mac was annoyed. 'What's this thing about Rossington, what are you up to now?'

'I'm trying to persuade the guy to admit he was the last man to see Brian Kincaid alive.'

Mac sighed. 'You know, Eddie, when you're an old man walking with a stick, you'll still be tottering around racecourses looking for the fictitious murderer of Kincaid.'

'I know. Tenacious, ain't I?'

'Tendentious, more like.'

'What does that mean?'

'It means partisan, biased, bloody stubborn.'

'I think I like tenacious better.'

Mac called me within five minutes with the news that Rossington would be at Worcester races next day. 'So will I, then,' I said. 'So will I.'

Chapter 45

There's a small public car park just off the main road as you enter Worcester Racecourse. Most drive through it and over the track crossing to park in the grassy centre of the course. But it could be a bitch getting out and I needed to be close to Rossington when he left, so I got there early and found a space in the small car park.

I saw him a few times throughout the afternoon but did no more than say hello. I never strayed far from the weighing room. If the Aussie came out, I wanted to see where he was going. Sod's law was in operation that day and I was offered a ride in the last, which I had to refuse, as none of Rossington's jocks were in the race and there was every chance he'd leave before or during it.

He didn't, and was among the last to go. The horse I could have ridden got beaten half a length and Rossington hung around so long that there was no way I could safely tail him to the official car park to see which car was his. I left before him and got to my car, where I watched through binoculars until I saw him come walking bow-legged toward his, a green Nissan Estate. He slung two obviously heavy bags in then seemed to have some trouble opening his driver's door.

Eventually he came trundling out and I had to let him get onto the main road before following. Rossington lived near Bristol. If that was where he was headed I wouldn't lose him, we were only ten minutes from the M5 and a straight run south.

When we reached the motorway I tucked in a few vehicles behind on the inside lane, but the Aussie made life difficult by staying below sixty - the only person in racing who didn't drive everywhere at full tilt.

After twenty miles or so, he began varying his speed and I wondered if he'd sussed me. I dropped further behind, but ten minutes later the bastard pulled in on the hard shoulder, hazard lights flashing. I passed him on the outside of a truck so he wouldn't see my face.

I took the next exit and waited on the bridge for Rossington to come by. When he did, I rejoined and tucked in again. Five minutes later, he pulled the same stunt on the hard shoulder, and I thought it safest to give up. He was onto me.

I drove home with some degree of satisfaction. If Rossington was nervous of me, he might make a mistake or force someone else to make one. When I reached the flat, I made coffee and a sandwich and called Candy.

'Anything more on Capshaw?' I asked.

'Nothing.'

'How's old Sheikhy taking the setback?'

'Calm as ever on the surface but I think his patience is running out.'

'I'm not surprised.'

'And we've got another vet badly ill.'

'Who?'

'John Snell, the guy who took over from Simon.'

'Simon's the one found dead in bed?'

'That's right, Snell took over his duties. Now he's poorly too.'

'He's doing the mares now?'

'Uhuh, been doing loads of tests on the ones who lost foals.'

'Any findings?'

'Not a jot so far.'

'And what exactly is wrong with Snell?'

'They don't know. They're still doing tests on him too. He thinks it might be exhaustion, which they say could have been a contributory factor in Simon Nish's heart attack.'

'Can't you tell these guys to slow down a bit?'

'The vets? Eddie, everyone's the same here! It's not just them. We're all under pressure, we want this sorted out.'

'Okay, okay, but they're only horses, for God's sake! It's only a job even if it does pay well. Are you going to kill yourself for it, too?'

'Listen to who's talking. The scrapes you've been in!'

'But I do it for the love of it, not the money.'

'Ha, bloody ha.'

'Keep laughing, Candy. I'm planning to up the stakes now and you'd better get yourself in gear too. I'm beginning to think that whoever's behind all this might have sussed what we were trying to do through Capshaw.'

'Plant me in there, you mean?'

'Exactly. And if they do suspect that then they know we're closing in. Okay, we might not have them surrounded, but they'll realize we're on their heels. Also, Rossington's rattled, and if he is involved, I think we can expect some action soon.'

'If you're right then I think Rossington will be more worried about his own health than doing us any damage.'

'Maybe, but they've got to stop killing their own guys at some point.'

'And start killing us?'

'Start trying.'

Candy's man got me the names of three people in Australia who knew Ken Rossington. None of them was available to talk when I called, though one, Clive Torpen, promised me a call back later if I could 'stay awake long enough'

I don't know what time I dozed off but the trill of the telephone woke me. In a daze, I reached out and scooped up the receiver, trying to remember the name of the Aussie I was expecting a call from, but all I heard was a dial tone.

A phone still ringing somewhere.

Then a click and the sound of my fax machine working.

I rolled off the bed and went to the machine whose digital clock read one minute past midnight. The paper spooled out. No first-page identification, just heavy dark print in a large typeface like a newspaper headline. The words below were laid out in newspaper-style columns and the content was a reproduction of the document I'd found beside Alex Dunn's corpse. The headline read 'Shameful Secret of Top Jockey'.

Chapter 46

I didn't think they'd given it to the press. That was their ace and they wouldn't play it this soon. Also, whoever got the story would do the usual and ring me for my comments 'in the interests of fairness', which really meant in the interests of possibly getting some more salacious information. Still, thinking about it kept me awake, the light of the single lamp glowing on my scribbled notes on which I'd drawn boxes and arrows in the hope that some pattern would emerge to pull together damaged stallions, aborting mares and dead men.

At 2.10, my contact in Australia rang. Five minutes later, I told him how much I appreciated the call and how grateful I was he'd taken the trouble to tell me about Ken Rossington.

'No trouble, mate, anytime.'

Come morning I'd had no more than three hours of troubled sleep, and promised myself I'd catch up by having an early night tonight. Then, over breakfast, Charles Tunney, the trainer I rode for, reminded me of a dinner date we both had in London.

'Shit, that's not tonight, is it?'

'Afraid so.'

'I thought that was next month.'

'Afraid not.' He was smiling, his chubby cheeks red from an hour out walking the gallops, checking and planning. Six of our horses were due back in tomorrow and Charles, as optimistic as most other racing folk, was looking forward to a good season.

I told him I'd have to call off from this charity dinner but he reminded me that it was a 'three-line-whip' from Broga Cates who owned the property, the horses, and paid me a retainer to ride for the stable. Broga had 'bought' a table for this high-profile event at a cost of three grand. Charles and I were to be two of his nine guests.

After breakfast, I called Candy and told him what I'd discovered about Rossington, asking him to cancel any pending enquiries about the Aussie for fear of alerting him. Then I contacted McCarthy. I couldn't afford to tell him everything about Rossington; he'd have gone all official on me. But I said enough to convince him he should carry on co-operating with me over Rossington's past movements. I also arranged to take advantage of my trip to London by having a meeting there with Mac next morning.

At Euston station, the taxi rank was empty of cabs and full of people. We took the tube then walked the remaining few hundred yards to the Dorchester, skirting the edge of Hyde Park and its dog-walkers, roller-bladers and tourists.

It was a fine sunny evening and we smiled and chatted as we entered the pedestrian underpass to walk beneath Park Lane, at which point our smiles faded as we saw the ragged rows of homeless people already settled for the night in makeshift cardboard beds while chauffeur-driven limousines glided above their heads, carrying the lucky ones to their clubs and casinos and three-hundred-pound-a-night rooms.

My three-hundred-pound-a-head-dinner took some forcing down, and I couldn't quite bring myself to join in the applause as egos fuelled by liquor paid crazy prices for sports memorabilia. It was for charity, which made it palatable, but I wondered what charity would help those poor bastards sleeping in the basement of the world. Especially when winter came.

By 11, the tables had been cleared, the lights were low, the orchestra played in the background and alcohol had draped its usual soft curtains around each party, making them think they were the only ones who really mattered. Nonsense was talked, boasts made, libidos stoked, promises sworn - until finally I decided to have a few more drinks and stop being so bloody judgmental.

Charles had been away from the seat beside me for about twenty minutes when it was quietly filled by a woman in a black dress, a string of pearls and a sweet haze of perfume. Early- forties, blonde shoulder-length hair, pale pink lipstick on narrow lips, grey-blue eyes wrinkled pleasantly by her smile, biggish nose but not unattractive given her strong bone structure. Her breasts were too heavy for whatever wire support was pushing them up, making little wrinkles either side of the tight line of cleavage.

She smiled at me as if I should know her and I did. I recognized her from that picture at Ascot. 'Eddie?' She held out her hand. 'Jean Kerman.'

The newspaper columnist. The gorgon of the gossip pages, destroyer of reputations, specializing in sports personalities the way a forensic pathologist specializes in bodies - the difference being the medic has the good grace to wait till you're dead.

I took her hand. 'Nice to meet you at last,' she said.

'Likewise,' I lied.

A stalking waiter, eager to help seal what he obviously saw as a potential liaison, appeared and offered champagne. Kerman, without acknowledging the man himself, took two glasses and placed one in front of me. She drank half the other at a gulp. I left mine untouched.

We small-talked, but I was finding it tough to hide my wariness of her. I was tempted to ask if she shouldn't be moving around looking for someone to write about, but I had the uncomfortable feeling that was exactly what she had been doing.

She inched her chair closer and lit a cigarette, thin lips closing to a pencil line as she drew on it, then tilted her head to blow a stream of smoke from the corner of her mouth. Chin raised and eyes half-closed, she thought she was posing sexily, but the most striking part of the view was up her wide nostrils.

The band was doing some nice slow forties stuff and the floor was pretty full. Kerman stood up and asked if I wanted to dance. I didn't but nor did I want to embarrass her, so I got up and she led me onto the floor, turned and moved in so close her breast wrinkles washed backward like a wave. Her high heels brought her to my height and she pulled my head forward, raising her shoulder to nudge me nearer her neck.

'I never inspect ears on a first date,' I said.

She laughed, pulling back to look at me. I managed what I hoped was a reasonably pleasant expression with a hint of warning attached that I wasn't quite so keen on having sex on the dance floor of the Dorchester as she appeared to be.

She settled a bit then and we moved in a slow but rhythmic circle. She tried to ease her pelvis closer to me but her stomach got there first. Her perfume seemed muskier close up, her body warm. As the music came to an end, I was still trying to figure her out when she raised her chin, putting her mouth close to my ear. She said, 'You dance well. Did your mum teach you when you were a boy?' She drew back like a cobra and looked at me, eyes much colder now. Then she said, 'Or were you too busy going out for walks in the bracing Cumbrian air? Walks by the river. Or climbing trees? Maybe that was your favourite, Eddie, eh?' And I wondered if, in the relative darkness, she could see the colour draining from me. A smile glinted hard and steely on her face as she turned and walked away.

Chapter 47

I went out into the brightly lit busy streets and found a newspaper seller. Kerman's paper was called The Examiner and tomorrow's early edition was already on the stands. I scanned through quickly, knowing that if she'd run the story it would probably be over two full pages.

It wasn't there.

I leant against a lamppost, trying to breathe deeply, tension pulsing in my throat, realizing that the sense of relief I was feeling was false. It would be followed by another bout of fear, another steady winding of the anxiety spring as I waited for Friday's edition then Saturday's and so on.

The evening suit suddenly felt tight, the wing collar choking. I reached up to loosen it. Sweat broke through on my forehead as I stared at the sky.

It was after midnight when I reached the hotel, too late to call Mother and warn her. And what good would it do anyway? I'd goaded these people, tempted them to come out, and they had. They'd given the story to Kerman and she'd teased and goaded me and I knew she would publish the story soon. She had to, that was her job.

I spent another sleepless night, which led into the longest day of my life. The next morning I met Mac at Jockey Club HQ, Portman Square.

He looked at my face as we sat down in his office. A rich smell of coffee permeated the whole floor we were on and Mac ordered a pot. He said, 'I can't tell whether it was a good night or a bloody bad one, but you look like you've been up for most of it.'

'I was. One way or another.'

He smiled. 'One of those, eh?'

'No, not one of those.'

He kept smiling stupidly until the coffee came. I hadn't planned to tell him about Rossington, but Kerman had increased the pressure so much I was determined to get these people. I was going to suffer the consequences anyway, and if I could bring them down too it would help ease the pain.

I drank, savouring the long aftertaste, then said to Mac, 'Ken Rossington's not who he says he is.'

'He says he's Ken Rossington. His passport says he's Ken Rossington. His racecourse ID from Melbourne says he's Ken Rossington.'

'He's not.'

Mac settled behind the big desk in that comfortable way I'd now become familiar with. Before he knew me properly or trusted my judgment, he used to stiffen, sit straighter when I started setting out my theories. But experience had deflated the mild pomposity and quelled the doubts. We'd been through a few things together, arguing and falling out along the way, but always building respect for each other.

Slowly he drank his coffee. Lifting my cup and holding his gaze, I mimicked his action. We both smiled. 'Go on,' he said.

'The Ken Rossington who worked at Melbourne was at least three inches shorter than our man and maybe twenty pounds lighter. He was quiet, reserved, industrious and private. Our guy behaves like CoCo the Clown half the time. His hair and eye colouring are the same and he has the same general facial shape but they are two different men.'

Mac shrugged. 'Maybe they are. Maybe it was us that got them confused.'

I shook my head. 'Rossington's CV lays claim to everything his Melbourne counterpart has done.'

'Okay, who is our man?'

'I don't know.'

'Why is he impersonating Rossington?'

'I don't know.'

'Where is the real Rossington?'

'You've just completed the hat-trick. I don't know. The real Ken

Rossington left Melbourne on March the twelfth last year, after the break-up of a long-term affair with a jockey.'

Mac sat forward. 'A jockey? A female jockey?'

'No, the type with the hanging genitalia.'

Mac looked shocked. 'A homosexual jockey?'

'I certainly hope so, or it must have been a touch unpleasant for him.'

He sat back again, slowly shaking his head.

'Why do you say "a homosexual jockey"?' I asked. 'Rossington was the other half, why don't you say, "a homosexual valet"?'

'I don't know. It just seems odd.'

'We're all human under those silks, you know.'

He nodded. 'Anyway, go on.'

'Rossington decided to make a new life for himself in England. He had dual nationality so didn't see a problem getting work in racing. The rumour is that an owner he knew out there, a guy who also had horses in England and France, promised to help him get started here.'

'Who was the owner?'

'I'm still waiting to find out. My man says he'll get back to me.'

'Well, when he does your problem is solved. If the owner knows Rossington well enough to offer him a job, then he'll be able to tell you if our man's an imposter.'

'Question is, how long can we afford to wait?'

Mac drummed on his thick blotting pad with a pen, finishing off with two pings on the edge of his coffee cup. 'Does this all lead to Kincaid?'

I nodded. 'And maybe Alex Dunn.'

He stared at me.

'And William Capshaw,' I said.

I watched him. When Mac felt matters had reached what he called a 'delicate' stage, he preferred to ask no more questions and hear no more theories. This was his boundary line. Beyond it lay formal obligations. His unblinking gaze told me we'd reached it.

'If you could just do me one favour?' I asked. 'I know you've got friends in Melbourne. Whoever Rossington really is, he does seem to know about horses and jockeys. Can you get hold of a photo of Rossington and send a few prints to Melbourne, see if anyone recognizes him?'

He made a note. 'Okay, I'll deal with it.' It looked like the potential implications were beginning to sink in. He agreed to do what he could on our usual understanding that if the shit hit the fan, he'd be free to claim he was nowhere in the room. I asked one more favour of him; to contact Ascot Racecourse and ask for a copy of Bob Guterson's guest list on the day he sponsored that race. He got me that by fax within minutes. It included the table plan for lunch. Kerman's name was there, seated between Guterson and Simeon Prior. There were nineteen more names on the list and Mac went through it with me, but of the few he knew none gave him any reason for suspicion though he raised the same point Candy had: that Simeon Prior, the chairman of Triplecrown Bloodstock, seemed out of place in that company.

Why then had Prior accepted Guterson's invitation?

I left and went straight home to wait by the phone. Kerman had to run the story next day, Friday. I sat waiting for her, waiting for the 'chance to comment'.

But the call never came, and the piece didn't appear on Friday or on Saturday. Sunday was their biggest circulation day; she had to print it then or risk losing it to a rival. Her informants wouldn't wait forever. She didn't, and I began to wonder what Jean Kerman's role was. Sitting on this must have been killing her.

Had she been invited to Ascot just so someone could plant the story about me in her mind? If so, how had they restrained her from running it? Had they fed her only the small part she'd teased me with? No, that wouldn't have been acceptable to her.

And why had she taken such a personal line with me? Why not simply ring me up and tell me she knew and that she would have to publish? I recalled that cold hard look in her eyes as she'd left me on the dance floor, that cruel glint almost of revenge.

Was she involved with them? Could Kerman be in on it somehow?

I rang Candy. Although I couldn't tell him why I wanted it, he agreed to put someone straight to work on finding every destructive racing piece Kerman worked on in the past five years.

'How many bodies can you spare?' I asked.

'How quickly do you want it?'

'Yesterday.'

'What's the big hurry?'

'I think the key to the next move might be in there among those stories.'

He sighed. 'Let me make some calls. I'll ring you back.'

'Candy…While you're at it, see what you can find out about Bob Guterson.'

Chapter 48

I travelled south and went to my parents' place to wait for Candy's call next day. I spent a miserable visiting hour at the hospital, my small talk ricocheting off the almost tangible barrier my father had erected round himself and my mother, resenting my presence, glorying in my discomfort, drawing every moment of my mother's attention toward himself.

I sat there, elbows on the edge of the bed, feeling like a trapped audience of one to a terrible soap opera that would never be turned off. And I took cold-hearted wicked comfort in the fact that when the Kerman story broke he would know some of the suffering I'd endured.

I dropped my mother at her hotel and drove away in a desolate mood. After re-establishing contact with her and moving into the house, I'd held such hopes for the future, such plans for repairing all the hurt. Now I wished earnestly that the pneumonia would kill him before all chance with her was gone.

My contact in Australia came through with the name of the owner who'd got Rossington the valet's job: Bob Guterson. Surprise, surprise.

Dunn, Capshaw, Rossington, Guterson…the links were steadily joining. Did Kerman fit in somewhere? Candy arrived with the cuttings and I told him about Guterson fixing up Rossington, or whoever he was, with the job. Candy already had some information on the guy. Guterson had sixteen horses in training in Europe and Australia; not a very big string to be so thinly spread, but understandable perhaps when Candy told me Guterson did business on both continents.

He'd been in racing as an owner less than three years, though his company had been supplying the veterinary industry with rubber gloves for quite a bit longer. Not a huge market, but one in which Guterson had a major share with large sales throughout Europe and Australia. The connection with Simeon Prior became clearer too: eighteen months ago, Guterson had bought a twenty percent share in Triplecrown Bloodstock, an investment that had seemed particularly poorly judged, as the company hadn't been performing well for some time. Nor had profits improved since Guterson bought in.

We kicked things around for a while without coming to any conclusions. I could see Candy was anxious to start going through the cuttings on Kerman's past victims. I made coffee, and we settled down at the big kitchen table and worked through the night sifting, sorting, discussing. Kerman had already laid bare most of the lives of her victims but we dissected them all at length, including our own memories of them, and Candy showed how sharp an eye for detail he had by recalling small facts and anecdotes.

We found three people of particular interest, all of them speared by Kerman within the last fourteen months. The first was Ben Campbell, who'd been the Sheikh's Racing Manager before Candy. Campbell had a heavy cocaine habit which was exposed by one of Kerman's 'reporters', who'd set the guy up.

The next to go was a man called James Summerville, a respected bloodstock journalist and agent who was heavily pro-Arab in his writing. Summerville supported Sheikh Ahmad's attempts to establish his own superior thoroughbred bloodlines, arguing that this was in essence the original intention behind thoroughbred breeding, which went back to the days of the Crusades.

Unfortunately, it was proved that while wearing his agent's hat he'd accepted bribes to help inflate the prices of horses he'd been entrusted to buy. Again, it looked like he'd been set up by a Kerman stooge.

The last one to go, and maybe the most significant to us, was a top vet who'd been based at the Equine Fertility Unit in Newmarket. His name was Stephen Spenser and he was the best man in his field. Kerman nailed him after discovering he'd conducted experiments on live ex-racehorses, two of which had died as a result of his research. Spenser had been struck off. Candy was certain he'd gone to America. He'd been one of the people Candy had considered trying to recruit when the stallion problem blew up. 'You think he could have cracked it?' I asked, sipping tepid coffee.

'He would have had a better chance than most,' Candy said, 'and I'd have used him if I could have traced him in the States.'

'And if he was that good, our friends might have known it and wanted him out of the picture before they started on those stallions.'

'Possibly,' Candy said absent-mindedly as he pulled the Ben Campbell page back under the lamp beam and stared at the picture, frowning. 'You know,' he said, 'I think Campbell was related somehow to Alex Dunn. Either related or his godson or something.'

'That would make sense. Dunn would probably have been very reluctant to damage Campbell's career. Whoever's behind this would realize that so he simply took Campbell out of the equation before involving Dunn.'

Candy sighed and shook his head. 'Shit, you could say all three of these affected our situation, directly or indirectly. You're talking about some pretty elaborate planning here.'

'Not to mention three killings. Somehow I think we're dealing with a slightly stronger motive than a simple dislike of the Sheikh and his empire.'

We still knew neither motive nor method, and were both getting too tired to think sensibly. We sat gazing at Campbell's smiling picture.

Candy sighed, and stretched and yawned, long and large as a hippo. Within seconds, I followed. We laughed gently then I stood up. 'You get the coffee. I'll get the fresh air.' And I went and opened the kitchen door to let in the cold night, to brace us. I stood on the step looking up at the black-blue sky and diamond-sharp stars.

Candy moved around behind me, fixing more coffee. 'We're close to something here, Eddie,' he said. I listened. 'Those three pieces point to Kerman doing more than her journalistic duty. She's working for somebody other than The Examiner.'

I smiled at the sky, knowing I couldn't tell him about her approach to me at the Dorchester, but feeling more and more certain she was in with these people. Because if she was, and we could bring her down with the rest of them, shame her, then there wouldn't be any Examiner story about the Malloy family. And maybe, just maybe, things would be all right again.

I turned to Candy as he poured hot water into a mug. 'I think it's time we got your personal profile man to work again. Let's see if the secrets of Jean Kerman's life can stand the test.'

Chapter 49

Next morning Candy rang The Gulf Stud to tell them he'd be there later in the afternoon. He came off the phone looking serious. 'What's up?'

'John Snell's back in hospital.'

'Who?'

'Snell, the vet who took over from Simon Nish, remember? He returned to work four days ago, now he's in hospital again, very ill, showing signs of heart failure.'

'You shouldn't have let him come back so soon. I thought they said it was exhaustion?'

'He wanted to. He seemed okay.' Candy slumped on a hard kitchen chair and rubbed his tired eyes. 'Jesus Christ! When are we going to get a break?'

Heart failure. That's what Dunn ultimately had died of, and so had Simon Nish. Now Snell.

I sat opposite Candy. 'Was he working on the mares?'

Candy nodded wearily.

I went to the phone and rang my mother at the hotel. She was surprised to hear from me so early in the day. 'Is anything wrong?' she asked.

'No, everything's all right. How's Father?'

She sighed quietly. 'Not much change.'

'Listen, Mum, did you have many mares abort this year in the early stages of pregnancy?'

She was quiet for a moment. 'Yes.'

'How many?'

'Quite a few.'

'More than usual?'

'Possibly three times as many. It was one of the reasons business was so bad.'

'Who treated all these mares?'

'Alex Dunn.'

I told her I'd call later and hung up. Candy watched me. 'What are you on to?' he asked.

'Your vets, Snell and the dead man, Simon Nish. Which brand of gloves did they use for examinations?'

He looked bewildered. 'Whatever we supplied them with at The Gulf, I suppose.'

I carried the phone to the table and handed him the receiver. 'Find out. Quickly.'

He dialed The Gulf Stud and asked the manager. Covering the mouthpiece, he said, 'Guterson's.'

'Tell him to stop using them immediately.'

He frowned at me.

'Go on!'

He told the manager to suspend all testing on mares, then slowly put down the phone and waited for an explanation.

'Just a hunch,' I said, 'a wild hunch. What makes mares abort?'

He shrugged. 'A number of factors.'

'What do vets use to clear out the uterus?'

'Prostaglandin.'

'What killed Alex Dunn?'

'Prostaglandin.'

'What would continued exposure of the skin surface to prostaglandin do to a man?'

'Kill him, I suppose, if he got enough of it. Or make him very ill.'

'Like John Snell and Simon Nish?'

He looked puzzled. 'I still don't get it.'

'Guterson's Gloves. What if they were impregnated with prostaglandin? It's a naturally occurring substance in mares, hence the reason that all the testing in the world wouldn't show up anything unusual. This way they get the mare and eventually the vet who's pulling on fifty gloves a day. What sort of prostaglandin dose does that add up to?'

He nodded silently, taking it in, then said, 'So why aren't mares aborting all over the country?'

'Because they're only impregnating selected batches. Dunn used

Guterson's Gloves and he worked on my father's mares, which also showed a high abortion rate. I saw boxes of the gloves at his place and couldn't figure out at the time why they were under lock and key. He must have been trying them out on Father's mares.'

'What about the risk to himself?'

'Insufficient numbers, or more likely he'd have worn skin protection when using them.'

Candy shook his head and a smile slowly warmed his face as he gave me an admiring look. I was chuffed. Candy hurried to The Gulf Stud to arrange analysis of Guterson's Gloves.

He rang me within the hour, triumphant but angry. 'We've checked more than fifty gloves. Every single one is saturated with prostaglandin. Let's get that bastard Guterson!'

If I'd learned anything since that day five years ago when I'd been forced into amateur detective work, it was that cat skinning could indeed be done in several ways. I persuaded Candy it was pointless to go waving glove samples at the cops, asking for Guterson to be arrested. Although it seemed likely he was behind everything, we needed more evidence, especially about what we were now convinced were the killings of Kincaid, Dunn, Capshaw and Nish.

Also, it would have been nice to try to establish a motive for this madness. I thought it was time to pull in Jockey Club Security officially, and tried to persuade Candy we were close enough to cracking it to justify involving them. Maybe all I really wanted was an increased sense of personal safety. At the moment, it was Candy and me, and as the killings mounted, it was getting to feel more and more like we were defending the Alamo.

Candy put the blocks on me asking McCarthy. He was fearful things would drag on and that word about the Sheikh's stallions would get out. One thing we did agree on was that the man calling himself Rossington was the weak link in the chain. Strong circumstantial evidence pointed to him as Kincaid's killer, and if that was so, there was reason enough to assume he'd been involved in the deaths of Dunn and Capshaw.

I thought of Rossington's behaviour on the motorway, and concluded he'd known I was following him. The faxed mock-up of the newspaper article and Kerman's poorly veiled threat had come shortly after that. Rossington must have gone running straight back to tell them I'd been on his tail. I wondered how wise that had been from his viewpoint. Once I'd latched on to Dunn and Capshaw, they'd been killed. If the same policy was in force, then Rossington must be sleeping uneasily in his bed.

But who would they get to hit the hit man?

I called Candy. 'Have you still got those two heavies working for you, the ones who were using me as a yo-yo at the seaside?'

'They're available.'

'We need to pick up Rossington.'

'What do you mean, pick up?'

'For his own protection.' I explained my thinking but Candy was nervous. I said, 'Look, until we can prove Guterson's involved, and maybe Kerman, we need to keep Rossington alive. The guy is scared. If he's got any brains, he might welcome the chance of protection.'

Candy finally agreed to try to have Rossington picked up, by which time I was sure we'd know more about his real identity. Before hanging up I said, 'And, Candy, ask your guys to have a good look around Rossington's property for a blue vehicle with bull bars.'

Chapter 50

There were still big gaps to be filled, like motive and Dunn's method.

The latter intrigued me. Whatever he'd done to the Sheikh's stallions, he'd done it in the racecourse stables, I was sure of that. It was the only time he'd had access to them. But whatever he'd treated them with had only been activated once they'd retired from racing. What the hell had he done, planted some sort of radio transmitter that could be switched on remotely?

I crossed my ankles, linked my hands behind my head and let everything I knew about Dunn run through my mind again. He'd been keen on experimenting with chemical castration, so we must assume he'd perfected something in that field that was undetectable. Then he'd had to test it, which he did on my father's stallion and on maybe half a dozen others, including Town Crier, in small studs around England.

But why? Why take that risk, the posing as an RSPCA man, the visits to different places? If the stuff needed road testing, he could easily have used it on my father's other three stallions. He'd buggered his business, so what difference would it have made to sterilize the other stallions? Whichever way I tilted it, I couldn't work it out.

I channeled my thoughts into filtering the hard facts. There were two definites: whatever he had used, he'd used it on Town Crier, and when he'd administered it, Fiona had been with him.

I rang the Corish Stud. Fiona answered. I asked how Martin was.
'Still drinking.'
'As much?'
'Almost, though he sleeps a lot now.' Her voice was flat, robotic.

'Are you all right?' I asked.

'Mmmm.'

I told her I wanted to come and see her to talk about Dunn's visit. She said she wasn't going anywhere.

By the time I reached the Corish Stud, the sun was low and insects buzzed among the trees. I stopped at the bungalow and watched the round figure of Fiona gathering washing from the line.

She told me Martin was asleep, passed out. She led the way to Town Crier's box. Standing in the gloom, the big horse seemed happy to see Fiona, but wary of my presence. I stood outside the box door. Fiona went in and rubbed his nose, clapped his neck, looking as if she was taking more comfort from it than the stallion was.

I said, 'Think hard about the day Alex Dunn came here, the tall guy posing as the RSPCA man. I need you to try and picture everything he did when he was checking Town Crier over.'

She looked vacantly at me for a while then shrugged. 'Just what you'd expect; he checked his coat and his teeth, his eyes, legs, feet, ears. He had me walk him round the box a couple of times. He took a blood sample.' She hesitated, frowned slightly. 'That did seem odd, seemed to take him longer than normal. Usually they whiz a syringe in under his neck and draw what they want. This seemed to take a few minutes and he worked on the other side of the horse, quite high up, for a sample.'

'What do you mean, the other side?'

'The side I couldn't see.'

'Were you holding him?'

'No. I suppose that was a bit strange too. He asked me to tie him up and stand by the door, saying he might get a bit fractious.'

'Quite high up, you said.'

She nodded, frowning again. Town Crier looked down at her as if to enquire what was wrong. She rubbed his nose. 'He seemed to be working under his mane.'

I moved into the box. 'Can you hold him, Fiona?' She gripped the halter. 'Which side?' I asked.

'Near side.'

I walked round, Town Crier's suspicious eyes following me, his muscles tensing. Fiona tightened her grip. I put both hands on his neck. He moved sideways. 'Whoah, boy. That's a good boy!' I said quietly, and kept up the horse talk as I ran my hands softly over every inch of his neck under his mane till, high up, just below the ridge where the hard hair starts growing, my middle finger came to rest on a small bump, a node the size of a pea.

I felt it, ran my index finger over it. It gave slightly, like a jelly capsule. We brought the horse out into what was left of the daylight and Fiona held the tuft of mane away. I could see no incision or damage to the hair around the bump, but that could easily have healed. I smiled and asked her to meet me back at the bungalow. By the time she returned, Candy was already on his way to check under the manes of the Sheikh's stallions.

I sat on the edge of the kitchen table, smiling stupidly. Fiona looked confused. I smiled wider, luxuriating in the feeling of having guessed correctly once again. It was a sensation I rarely experienced. Right on cue, at the height of my self-congratulation, the phone rang.

'Every fucking one of them! Exact same spot!'

'Yeehaaa!'

Fiona stared at me as though considering leaving quickly.

I said to Candy, 'Get them out and get them analyzed.'

'Already arranged! Results in under an hour!'

'You sound like an advert for Acme Pharmacies.'

'I feel like a glass of champagne.'

'Have one for me. I'll call you.'

Fiona stood open-mouthed. I smiled at her. 'You'd best close that before a fly gets in. Tomorrow I'm sending a vet to look at Town Crier. I'll let you know his name and I'll make sure he's carrying ID. If Martin sobers up sufficiently between now and then, tell him I think our problems are almost over.'

Chapter 51

I left Wiltshire in the dusk and reached my parents' stud in darkness. My heart sang for most of the trip. The thought that my luck was running out kept entering my mind. I'd long ago learned the folly of tempting fate. But I prayed all the same, prayed that it would hold long enough to nail Kerman, to silence her, to save the secret.

Save the secret.

I didn't care about Guterson any more, or Rossington or Dunn or Capshaw. Or, to my shame, Brian Kincaid. I was obsessed with my own ends. At my parents' place, the phone was ringing as I turned the key in the lock. I ran inside. It was Candy. 'Can I come down there now?' he asked.

'Sure.'

'See you soon.'

It was almost midnight when he arrived, but Candy was bright-eyed, elated. He smelled of aftershave. 'You haven't shaved, at this time of night?' I asked.

He smiled, strong teeth white against the tan. 'Second shave of the day. Got to keep up appearances.'

'God save me from vanity!'

'He will.'

We sat down with a full teapot and two mugs, neither of us really wanting to risk a premature celebratory drink. Candy pulled a notepad from the pocket of his yellow polo shirt, and then dug in again to produce a small green capsule, which he rolled toward me. I squeezed it between my fingers. It reminded me of a cod liver oil pill.

Candy said, 'Filled with a variant on methyl testosterone which

Dunn must have concocted himself. They're still working on it, but the early verdict is that the chemical would lie dormant until set off by a surge of sexual activity, during which the increased testosterone levels play a dual part: they neutralize all traces of the drug in the system and they rapidly sterilize the sperm.'

'Hence the reason Dunn could pre-plant them in horses that were still racing, knowing they wouldn't take effect until the horse became sexually active.'

'Correct.'

'So yours were done in the racecourse stables as per the old list of visits, matey.' I smiled.

Candy returned it. 'You're a right bloody clever dick, aren't you?'

'Now all we need is the motive.'

'And the perpetrators.'

I nodded.

'Speaking of which,' Candy said, 'our boys picked Rossington up.'

'Where is he?'

'They're holding him at Dunn's old place at Six Mile Bottom.'

'Has he said anything?'

'They haven't asked him anything. We were sort of waiting for you.'

'Sort of?'

'Well, we were. I'm getting a wee bit nervous about it, to be honest. I think it's time we brought in the authorities.'

'The police?'

'Yes.'

'Not yet, Candy.'

'Why? We're in the clear.'

'You're in the clear. Your stallions will be operational again. But all we've got is one of the mugs. We need to get Guterson and whoever else is involved.'

He waved the suggestion away. 'Nah, the cops can do that.'

'The cops might fuck it up and I can't afford that!'

He looked surprised. 'Don't worry, Eddie. I'll make sure you're well paid.'

'I know you will, but it's not the money. You know I've got another interest in this that I can't tell you about. You can't dump everything just because your problems are solved!'

He lowered his eyes. 'Okay. I'm sorry. I forgot. What do you want to do with Rossington?'

'I'll go and see him tomorrow. Will those profiles on Guterson and Jean Kerman be ready?'

'I'll chase them in the morning.'

'Okay.'

'Right.' He got up. 'Brilliant. Well done, Eddie.'

'Save it till the fat lady's done an encore, Candy, I'm due a turn of bad luck.'

I walked with him to the door and watched him go out into the darkness. I lay in bed, luxuriating a while longer in the afterglow before settling down for what I hoped would be a rare peaceful night's rest.

In the middle of the night, the phone rang. Groggy with sleep, I didn't recognize McCarthy's voice at first. He had to introduce himself. 'I thought I'd best ring you straightaway. I've just been wakened by a call from Melbourne about your man Rossington.'

'Uhuh.' I was struggling to get my brain in gear.

'Remember, you gave me those pictures of him?'

'Yes, I remember.'

Mac told me what he'd learned and I extended the chain of early morning alarm calls by ringing Candy, though I gave him more time to come to his senses than Mac had given me.

'According to McCarthy's contacts in Melbourne, our man Rossington is a ghost. His real name is Paul Cantrell and his body was found on a road near Melbourne Airport in March last year in a hit and run incident very similar to the one in which Capshaw was killed. I've asked Mac to try to find out how positive the identification of Cantrell's corpse was. What would you like to bet that his face was badly disfigured?'

'You think the real Rossington was the hit and run victim?'

'A very convenient way to exchange identities. Cantrell was wanted by the police when he "died".'

'What for?'

'Armed robbery.'

'Shit!'

'Are your guys contactable at Dunn's place?'

'On mobile.'

'I think you'd best warn them Cantrell's a lot more dangerous than we thought.'

Chapter 52

Exhaustion caught up with me and I slept late next morning, Candy's phone call rousing me at ten. 'Kerman and Guterson. We've got a connection by the look of things.'

'Uhuh?' I was still half-asleep.

'Should I bring the reports?'

'Sure, yeah, sure. I'll have a bath,' I said stupidly.

He arrived while I was still soaking and shouted through the letterbox. I wrapped a towel around me, let him in and told him to put the kettle on while I got dressed. He told me Rossington or Cantrell, whoever he was, was still securely locked up.

With my hair still wet, I sat at the table looking at the highlighted parts of the two reports Candy had brought.

Jean Kerman's maiden name was Prior. She was the daughter of Simeon Prior, the Triplecrown Chairman. Candy also had a breakdown on Triplecrown's business. They did everything from arranging matings to selling the subsequent foals, and in the past three years, turnover and profit had been on the slide.

When Bob Guterson acquired his 20 percent stake in Triplecrown, Simeon Prior had bought a 25 percent share in Guterson's Gloves.

I read it through again. 'Motive?' I said.

'Let me try this time,' Candy said, beaming. 'Triplecrown Bloodstock rose to prominence in the years when the Arabs were buying from them. They made millions. But now the Arabs are spending less and less as they build up their own breeding operation. Not only that, they're starting to do everything in-house and offer their facilities to other breeders. So Triplecrown hasn't lost only the Arabs' custom; all their other customers have the option of doing their business with the Arabs instead.'

I nodded, smiling. Candy went on, 'Simple solution for Triplecrown: smother the Arab operation at source by taking out the stallions.'

I applauded softly and Candy looked chuffed. 'Now prove it,' I said.

'Rossington will snitch to save his skin.'

'I doubt it. He's none to save. It's likely he's killed three men, at least. No plea-bargain there.'

Candy looked flustered. 'Okay, but he won't take the rap on his own. He'll take the others with him.'

I smiled. '"Take the rap?" You've been watching those old Edward G. Robinson films again, haven't you?'

'Well, you know what I mean.'

'I do, and you might be right, but we can't chance it and the police won't just take his word for it anyway. We'll need something more concrete, something that definitely incriminates Guterson and Prior.'

'Surely there's enough circumstantial evidence?'

'Where? All you've laid out is based on assumption, pure theory. There isn't a single piece of solid evidence linking Guterson, Prior or Kerman.' I said.

'It's obvious that Triplecrown would have the strongest of motives to—

'And what about Town Crier and Heraklion and the other half-dozen stallions at the smaller studs? Where's Triplecrown's interest there?'

He shrugged, confused. 'Red herrings. Decoys set up for exactly this type of situation, so they can use it in their defense. You know how well they've planned this, Eddie!'

'I know I'm only playing Devil's Advocate. You're probably right but how do we prove it?'

'We've got to get this guy Rossington, or whatever he's called, to talk.'

'But how?'

The phone rang. It was Martin. I was surprised. He sounded bright and sober. 'Fiona tells me we might be out of the woods,' he said.

'Not quite. We can see the edge of the trees.'

'How long do you reckon?'

'I don't know. Soon. A couple of days, maybe.'

'Anything I can do?'

The question provoked a sudden surge of anger in me. Martin had been unable to hack it when things got tough. Now here he was offering help because he thought it was almost over. I was tempted to concoct something dangerous and ask him to deal with it, but I resisted. 'If there's anything I can think of, I'll call you. It might be best if you stay off the booze for a day or two in case I do need you.'

He laughed. 'Sure. Keep me informed, eh?'

'Okay.' I returned to the table. Candy had been thinking. 'Maybe it is just Guterson. Maybe it was his stake in the company that made him set this up.'

'So how come Prior's daughter so effectively removes three of the possible stumbling blocks to the success of the whole thing in Campbell, Summerville and the EFU vet guy, what do you call him?'

'Spenser.'

'Yeah.'

Candy looked thoughtful. 'Good point.'

'I know, but having said that you can bet your boots Prior's kept his own hands lily white. Jean Kerman and Guterson will have done the high-level dirty work and Rossington the basics.' We sat around for an hour trying to figure some way to trap Guterson and the others. Martin's offer of help sparked an idea. I called him. He'd gone to the pub. I spoke to Fiona. 'Do you remember that guy Spindari, the one we had you make a phone call to when he was trying to blackmail us?'

'I remember.'

'Do you still have his phone number?'

'I'm not sure. I can probably find it.'

'Good, here's what I want you to do.'

Fiona called back within half an hour. 'He'll be here at two-thirty.'

'Fine. We'll see you then.'

Chapter 53

When Candy and I walked into the office at the Corish Stud, the tall, dark and handsome Simon Spindari seemed to lose some of his Latin colour, not to mention his composure. He turned on Fiona. 'You little bitch! You said you had a good story for me!' Smiling, I said, 'We have, Simon, we have. Sit yourself down.' Glowering, he sat on the chair by the desk and swept the thick hair away from his eyes. 'Thanks, Fiona,' I said, and she left without looking at Spindari.

I explained that we knew everything about his blackmail attempt way back at the beginning, and he agreed to cooperate if we promised not to tell the police what he'd been doing. He admitted having 'investigated' a couple of other cases for Jean Kerman and said she still contacted him from time to time.

I told him what he had to do and watched as he made the call to Kerman, telling her he had a brilliant story for her about a guy named Paul Cantrell who was impersonating a certain man on British racecourses, and that if Kerman wanted the details she should meet Spindari in a pub in Newmarket and he'd take her to Cantrell.

'Incidentally,' he said, acting it out well. 'The guy he's impersonating is probably dead! How's that for an exclusive?' As I'd expected, Kerman didn't ask too many questions. She agreed the time and place, a popular pub on a country road not far from Dunn's place at 7 o'clock. Spindari arranged to meet her in the beer garden.

By 6.30 McCarthy, Candy and I were concealed in the woods behind the beer garden. Spindari sat at a white table sipping lager in the evening sunshine and reading a newspaper. At 6.50, a big blue BMW with smoked glass windows purred into the car park of the pub. Jean Kerman, wearing a tight black two-piece, got out of the back and walked toward Spindari's table. He saw her coming, smiled and reached into the pocket of his jeans as though to go and buy her a drink. Kerman shook her head and spoke animatedly.

Spindari pointed to the half-full lager glass and sat down again. Kerman turned to look at the car. The passenger door opened and a fat man in a dark grey suit hauled himself out and hurried forward. He was completely bald. Mac whispered, 'Guterson.' Candy and I smiled.

We crept backward through the trees to where our car was parked, and then headed for Dunn's place.

Within ten minutes of our arrival, we watched from inside the bungalow as the BMW slowed and pulled into the driveway. Each of us moved into position. I stood by the edge of the curtains at the side window, hidden, I hoped, from view.

Car doors clunked closed. 'Two heavies,' I warned everyone. In the corner, Phil and Don grinned. I watched Spindari, still smiling and playing the fool a bit, chatting to them as he approached the porch door. He knocked loudly. McCarthy was behind it and opened it almost immediately.

We could hear his voice along the hall and I could see reactions on some of the faces: bafflement, shock. I heard Mac say, 'Mister Guterson, how nice to see you again.' And I watched Guterson offer a very tentative hand. Mac shook it and stepped aside. 'And Mrs. Kerman, always first on a hot story. Do come in.' Kerman turned and glared at Spindari.

The two heavies looked at each other, seeming unsure if they should be on red alert. All five filed in past Mac. 'This way,' he said, and led them right in among us in the living room. Kerman and Guterson looked around at me, Candy, Phil and Don, bewilderment giving way to anger then worry on both their faces.

Still smiling, Mac said, 'I think you both know Mister Malloy and Mister Loss. These other two gentlemen are from Cambridge CID.' Phil and Don smiled and nodded pleasantly. Kerman turned and looked at Guterson, whose face and head were reddening by the second. He reached up to loosen his gaudy tie.

Mac said, 'Now maybe your chaps and Mister Spindari could go into the kitchen and have a nice cup of tea. Would you both like one?' Kerman and Guterson shook their heads in unison.

'Coffee?' Mac offered pleasantly. He was better at this than I'd expected.

'No, thanks!' Kerman said bitterly.

Phil and Don walked forward. 'We'll show you where the kitchen is.' Guterson turned to his guys and nodded. They left. A smiling Spindari followed. They went to the kitchen and closed the door. A few moments later Phil and Don rejoined us. Mac said to Kerman and Guterson, 'There's one person you haven't met yet, if you'd like to come this way?' He moved along the hall toward the office, saying, 'Well, you have met him but not today.' Candy and I followed.

Mac turned the key and eased the door open. Kerman and Guterson moved into the doorway to look. I watched their faces go pale as Mac said, 'Mister Ken Rossington, alias Paul Cantrell.'

He closed and locked the door again before anyone could speak and we all returned to the living room. Kerman sat down on a chair, straight-backed, knees clamped, looking defiant, but Guterson slumped on the sofa, beaten and dejected.

Mac pulled some papers from his inside pocket. He looked at Guterson. 'Cantrell spent much of yesterday dictating this statement to our CID friends here.' Mac started reading everything Candy and I had put together, all the theories starting from Kerman's setting up of Ben Campbell, Summerville and Spenser through to the recruiting of Dunn and his methods of implanting the horses.

Every so often Kerman would splutter, 'Nonsense! Ridiculous!'

But when Mac started listing the dates that Dunn had visited the racecourse stables and implanted the Sheikh's horses, she seemed finally to give up, physically to deflate as though the weight of evidence had crushed the fight from her.

Shaking his head, Guterson said to no one in particular, 'Cantrell didn't know half of this. How the hell...?'

Kerman glared at him. 'He was obviously a damn sight smarter than you thought, you stupid bastard!'

Guterson was still shaking his head. 'But why? Why drop himself in it after what he's done?' He grunted then as he pushed himself to his feet, becoming more animated as the instinct for self-preservation took over. He went toward Phil and Don and said, 'Look, I don't know what else is in that statement but I was only acting as an agent for Simeon Prior. He's the main man. He thought the whole thing up.'

'Shut up!' Kerman yelled. 'Shut up, you silly bastard!' Guterson said, 'Ignore her, she's his daughter!'

Then began a long cursing argument, all of which was caught on tape along with everything else that had been said. Mac excused himself politely and went to call a police inspector he knew in Cambridge.

A proper one.

Chapter 54

The cops had to let Guterson's heavies go, as they'd done nothing. When Guterson, Kerman and Cantrell were being led out, Kerman turned to me, spite contorting her face. 'You'll regret this for the rest of your life, Malloy!'

I smiled. 'I don't think that even The Examiner will publish your stuff anymore, Mrs. Kerman.'

'There'll be someone else, don't worry.'

And there was.

The Examiner made no announcement about the departure of Jean Kerman. It simply trumpeted the arrival of the most 'exciting voice in investigative journalism: Cynthia Clarke. Look out for her debut story on Wednesday which will shock the racing world'.

Cynthia Clarke rang me on Monday evening just after I'd returned from visiting my father, who seemed coldly determined now to stay in hospital as long as he could. He'd been moved to a new ward and had effectively trained Mother into this routine where she was with him for more than half the day, coming and going at his bidding.

Clarke was quiet-voiced, polite but unshakeable. She told me there was a story on file which she planned to run on Wednesday and she wanted to make sure I was aware of the contents, and to give me 'a chance to comment'.

She read it through to me and though I knew it word for word, my heart dropped a step closer to hell with every line she spoke. I told her that I thought that The Examiner was the last paper to be moralizing, bearing in mind the charges its previous columnist now faced. But Clarke was unmoved. 'It's news, I'm afraid, Mister Malloy.

If we don't run it, someone else will. Now can I speak to your father?'

'He's very ill. If this story runs it could kill him.'

'Is he in hospital?'

My hopes rose for a moment. 'Yes.'

'Which one?'

'Will you put a hold on the story?'

'I can't, but I must give him the chance to comment.'

'He won't comment. Doesn't it make any difference to you that this might kill him?'

'I'm only doing a job, Mister Malloy.'

'I'd rather shovel shit!' I said, and banged the phone down, that familiar feeling of desolation engulfing me quickly. Filled with impotent rage, I drove at speed to the hospital to warn my mother.

We sat in the coffee lounge. She looked completely worn out. 'Is there anything we can do?' she asked weakly.

I shook my head. She bowed hers, accepting defeat for the first time in her life, then unexpectedly her hand reached across the tabletop for mine. Gently I clasped the warm, wrinkled skin, the fragile bones, and squeezed softly. Her head was down and a tear dripped silently into her lap.

I arranged to be with her at the hospital when the paper was due out on Wednesday. She warned Father about it, and suddenly he decided he'd discharge himself on Tuesday afternoon. He couldn't bear the thought of everyone at the hospital knowing.

First thing Wednesday I drove to a petrol station where nobody knew me and bought a copy of the newspaper. It was on the front page. I folded the paper and headed for the derelict farm Candy and I had used as a meeting place.

I got out of the car and went to lean against the ruined wall. The sun was beginning to warm the morning, but inside I was cold as I opened the paper. There was a smiling picture of me under a banner headline: Top Jockey 'Killed' His Brother.

"The father of top jump jockey Eddie Malloy believes Malloy killed his younger brother, Michael. When Malloy was just ten years old and living on a farm near Penrith, Cumbria, he was in charge of young Michael, six, when the child fell into a swollen river and was swept away.

Eddie Malloy, apparently unable to face his parents with the terrible news, returned home to tell them Michael had disappeared into the woods. It was two days before Malloy admitted to police and search parties what had happened.

Edward Malloy Snr. has always believed that had Eddie acted immediately to report his brother's fate, Michael could have been saved."

The story was continued on page three. Dry-mouthed and shaking, I turned to it with a picture in my mind of a million others doing the same thing.

"Malloy Snr.'s resentment of his eldest son led to the boy becoming an outcast. He was cruelly banished from his parents' house and sent to live with the horses in the stable block. For the next six years, the young Malloy's bed was among straw bales and his only companions were the horses he came to love and trust.

His mother, Constance, brought him meals three times a day in a regime that was almost prison-like. But there was to be no remission for the frightened ten-year-old. Malloy Snr. duped the local authorities into believing that his son was being educated at home.

But the only education Eddie found was in the racing books his mother smuggled out to him during the early period of his 'imprisonment', a privilege that stopped the moment his father found out about it.

The boy's misery ended on his sixteenth birthday when he was finally banished permanently from the farm and sent out to make his own way in the world.

But the years of living so close to horses served Malloy well, and maybe today he looks back with less resentment than some might expect. Within a week of being thrown out, he took a job with the late Peter Sample, a top trainer in Lambourn, and less than five years later he was champion National Hunt Jockey.

Eddie Malloy's parents now run a small stud in Newmarket where they've lived for..."

Clarke rambled on about my parents and how deep and damaging family rifts could be. Tell me about it, Cynthia. Tell the whole world about it. You just have.

I sat on the wall staring at the front-page headline, at the colour picture of me smiling and punching the air as I came in on Cragrock at Haydock, the first big race winner after my comeback.

There I was three years ago, jubilant, delirious.

Here I was now, ashamed, empty, desolate.

I stood staring into the distance. The sun was well up, drying the night's rain from the surrounding fields and raising a beautiful smell of freshness and newness. Away to my right, the road stretched straight and tempting toward the horizon, and I wished to God that I was in one of those old cowboy movies and could just get in the saddle and ride off to where nobody could ever find me.

Ride off to wherever our Michael was and tell him what I'd longed to tell him since that terrible day when I heard him shout and looked down through the thick branches of the tree I'd climbed, and sat there in horror, rooted as surely as the tree itself, unable to move as his fair head bobbed on the surface, as his little hands reached and scrabbled at the morning air. I could hear him crying in panic and confusion as he wondered what was happening to him and why his big brother wasn't there to help him, to save him, to pull him out.

Sometimes he'd come to me in dreams and tell me it was all right, tell me he'd died quickly and quietly after a few minutes in the water, tell me that he didn't blame me for what I'd done, tell me that heaven was a great place for kids, tell me that he loved me, tell me that someday he'd see me again.

And I'd tell him I was sorry.

'I'm sorry, Michael…'

An animal-like howl rose from my chest and burst from my throat, and my legs gave way as I slid slowly down the side of the wall to lie slumped and weeping uncontrollably by the front wheel of the car.

I don't know how long I lay there, but somehow I hauled myself up and drove, weak and shocked, to my parents' place, carrying the newspaper into the house as though it was the corpse of our Michael himself.

Chapter 55

The most heartening thing over the next week or so was the level of support everywhere from people I hardly knew. The warmth was unexpected and welcome. My parents didn't fare quite so well. There were a number of terrible phone calls and poisonous letters, and no matter how much they'd tried to prepare themselves, the shock was nightmarish.

My father never recovered from it. His health deteriorated steadily throughout the autumn. On the 2nd of December, he died in that prison-like room. My mother and I were there, and my sister Marie came back. She too had been scarred by what happened all those years ago. Her exile had been self-imposed.

Guterson, Simeon Prior and Cantrell are on remand, charged with the murders of Brian Kincaid, Alex Dunn and William Capshaw. Jean Kerman was released on substantial bail. Brian Kincaid's widow, Judy, made his funeral a true celebration of the life of a very good man. Afterwards, her concern for me showed in weekly telephone calls, and Judy has become as good a friend to me as Brian was.

Martin's been off the booze for over two months and tells me he can't wait for the birth of his baby. Candy's a changed man, too. Alive again, happy, looking forward to the new breeding season as I guess his stallions are.

Things are going well for me. Charles's horses are back to their best. I've ridden 67 winners for him so far.

My mother, at last, is showing signs of becoming her own person. Marie and I have stayed with her since Father died. On Christmas Eve, we travelled to Cumbria to visit our Michael's grave. In the early frost we stood in silence, facing the grey marble with my brother's name carved deep. My mother, standing between my sister and me, reached for our hands. A family again, what was left of us, but finally, I felt a sense of peace.

Thank you

We hope you enjoyed the omnibus.

All the Eddie Malloy books are available on Amazon as eBooks, paperbacks, and many as audiobooks through Audible

We send out very few emails, but would be pleased to have you on our list so that we can let you know about new titles in the series

Our website is pitmacbooks.com. Eddie also has his own Facebook page.

Best wishes
Joe and Richard

Printed in Great Britain
by Amazon

51417458R00418